HEAT

MW00803440

MIKE LUPICA

PUFFIN BOOKS

ACKNOWLEDGMENTS

I would like to first thank Lourdes LeBatard,
who so generously helped me with the beautiful words of Cuba.
Additional thanks go out to all the Little League baseball coaches
from whom I have learned along the way, from the great
Cliff McFeely to Kevin Rafalski. And to all the other coaches who
understand what Michael Arroyo does in the pages of this book:
The game belongs to the kids playing it.
Finally, Michael Green: Who always had a clear,
fine vision of what should be happening on both sides of
those blue barriers outside Yankee Stadium.

PUFFIN BOOKS
Published by the Penguin Group
Penguin Young Readers Group, 345 Hudson Street, New York, New York 10014, U.S.A.
Penguin Group (Canada), 90 Eglinton Avenue East, Suite 700, Toronto, Ontario, Canada M4P 2Y3
(a division of Pearson Penguin Canada Inc.)

Registered Offices: Penguin Books Ltd, 80 Strand, London WC2R 0RL, England

First published in the United States of America by Philomel Books,
a division of Penguin Young Readers Group, 2006
Published by Puffin Books, a division of Penguin Young Readers Group, 2007

9 10 8

THE LIBRARY OF CONGRESS HAS CATALOGED THE PHILOMEL EDITION AS FOLLOWS:

Lupica, Mike.
Heat / Mike Lupica.
p. cm.
Summary: Pitching prodigy Michael Arroyo is on the run from social services after being
banned from playing Little League baseball because rival coaches doubt that he is only
twelve years old and he has no parents to offer them proof.
[1. Brothers—Fiction. 2. Orphans—Fiction. 3. Illegal aliens—Fiction. 4. Cubans—Fiction.
5. Little League baseball—Fiction. 6. Baseball—Fiction. 7. Social services—Fiction.] I. Title.
PZ7.L97914Hea 2006 [Fic]—dc22 2005013521
ISBN 0-399-24301-1

Puffin Books ISBN 978-0-14-240757-8

Book design by Gina DiMassi
Text set in Charter.

Printed in the United States of America

THE PHONE RANG

Michael didn't even move to answer it, knowing the house rule—Rule Number One—about never answering the phone when Carlos wasn't here, just letting the ancient answering machine, the one with Papi's voice, pick up.

The voice on the other end belonged to Mr. Minaya, his coach with the Clippers.

"Mr. Arroyo," Mr. Minaya began, because he called all the parents Mr. or Mrs. "You don't have to get right back to me, but once we get to the play-offs, we're going to need parents to drive to the game and since, well, you are a professional driver, we were wondering if you might be able to help out. Please let me know."

Michael waited for the click that meant he had disconnected. But he wasn't finished.

"Unless of course Mr. Arroyo isn't back yet and I'm talking to Carlos and Michael . . . well, forget it. Just tell your dad to give me a call if he ever does get back."

Then came the click.

If he ever does get back.

Not when.

Does he suspect something?

Michael grabbed his glove off the kitchen table where he'd left it, stuffed the ball in the pocket, locked the apartment door behind him, headed for the field at Macombs Dam Park.

The field had always felt like his own safe place. But now Michael wondered if even baseball was safe.

OTHER BOOKS YOU MAY ENJOY

The Boy Who Saved Baseball	John H. Ritter
The Heart of a Chief	Joseph Bruchac
A Long Way from Chicago	Richard Peck
Over the Wall	John H. Ritter
The River Between Us	Richard Peck
Stand Tall	Joan Bauer
Sticks	Joan Bauer
Stormbreaker	Anthony Horowitz
Things Not Seen	Andrew Clements
Travel Team	Mike Lupica

This book is for Taylor Lupica.
She has always believed in me,
and that I should be writing books
children want to read.

It is also for our own amazing children:
Christopher, Alex, Zach, and Hannah.
They have not just made me a better person.
They have made me a better writer.

1

MRS. CORA WALKED SLOWLY UP RIVER AVENUE IN THE SUMMER HEAT, SECURE within the boundaries of her world. The great ballpark, Yankee Stadium, was on her right. The blue subway tracks were above her, the tracks colliding up there with the roar of the train as it pulled into the station across the street from the Stadium, at 161st Street and River.

The two constants in my life, Mrs. Cora thought: baseball and the thump thump thump of another train, like my own personal rap music.

She had her green purse over her arm, the one that was supposed to look more expensive than it really was, the one the boys upstairs had bought for her birthday. Inside the purse, in the bank envelope, was the one hundred dollars—Quik Cash, they called it—she had just gotten from a Bank of New York ATM. Her food money. But she was suddenly too tired to go back to the Imperial Market. Mrs. C, as the kids in her building called her, was preparing for what could feel like the toughest part of her whole day, the walk back up the hill to 825 Gerard from the Stadium.

Now she moved past all the stores selling Yankees merchandise—Stan's Sports World, Stan the Man's Kids and Ladies, Stan the Man's Baseball World—wondering as she did sometimes if there was some famous Yankee who had been named Stan.

He hit her from behind.

She was in front of Stan's Bar and Restaurant, suddenly falling to her right, onto the sidewalk in front of the window as she felt the

1

green purse being pulled from her arm, as if whoever it was didn't care if he took Mrs. Cora's arm with it.

Mrs. Cora hit the ground hard, rolled on her side, feeling dizzy, but turning herself to watch this . . . what? This boy not much bigger than some of the boys at 825 Gerard? Watched him sprint down River Avenue as if faster than the train that was right over her head this very minute, pulling into the elevated Yankee Stadium stop.

Mrs. Cora tried to make herself heard over the roar of the 4 train.

"Stop," Mrs. Cora said.

Then, as loud as she could manage: "Stop, thief!"

There were people reaching down to help her now, neighborhood people she was sure, voices asking if she was all right, if anything was broken.

All Mrs. Cora could do was point toward 161st Street.

"My food money," she said, her voice cracking.

Then a man's voice above her was yelling, "Police!"

Mrs. Cora looked past the crowd starting to form around her, saw a policeman come down the steps from the subway platform, saw him look right at her, and then the flash of the boy making a left around what she knew was the far outfield part of the Stadium.

The policeman started running, too.

The thief's name was Ramon.

He was not the smartest sixteen-year-old in the South Bronx. Not even close to being the smartest, mostly because he had always treated school like some sort of hobby. He was not the laziest, either, this he knew, because there were boys his age who spent much more time on the street corner and sitting on the stoop than he did. But he was lazy enough, and hated the idea of work even more than he hated the idea of school, which is why he preferred to occasionally get his spending money stealing purses and handbags like the Hulk-green one he had in his hand right now.

As far as Ramon could tell at this point in his life, the only real job skill he had was this:

He was fast.

He had been a young soccer star of the neighborhood in his early teens, just across the way on the fields of Joseph Yancy park, those fields a blur to him right now as he ran on the sidewalk at the back end of Yankee Stadium, on his way to the cobblestones of Ruppert Place, which ran down toward home plate.

"Stop! Police!" Ramon heard from behind him.

He looked around, saw the fat cop starting to chase him, wobbling like a car with a flat tire.

Fat chance, Ramon thought.

Ramon's plan was simple: He would cut across Ruppert Place and run down the hill to Macombs Dam Park, across the basketball courts there, then across the green expanse of outfield that the two ballfields shared there. Then he would hop the fence at the far end of Macombs Dam Park and run underneath the overpass for the exit from the Deegan Expressway, one of the Stadium exits.

And then Ramon would be gone, working his way back toward the neighborhoods to the north, with all their signs pointing toward the George Washington Bridge, finding a quiet place to count his profits and decide which girl he would spend them on tonight.

"Stop . . . I mean it!" the fat cop yelled.

Ramon looked over his shoulder, saw that the cop was already falling behind, trying to chase and yell and speak into the walkie-talkie he had in his right hand all at once. It made Ramon want to laugh his head off, even as he ran. No cop had ever caught him and no cop ever would, unless they had begun recruiting Olympic sprinters for the New York Police Department. He imagined himself as a sprinter now, felt his arms and legs pumping, thought of the old Cuban sprinter his father used to tell him about.

Juan something?

No, no.

Juantarena.

Alberto Juantarena.

His father said it was like watching a god run. And his father, the old fool, wasn't even Cuban, he was Dominican. The only Dominican who wanted to talk about track stars instead of baseball.

Whatever.

Ramon ran now, across the green grass of Macombs Dam Park, where boys played catch in the July morning, ran toward the fence underneath the overpass.

It wasn't even noon yet, Ramon thought, and I've already earned a whole day's pay.

He felt the sharp pain in the back of his head in that moment, like a rock hitting him back there.

Then Ramon went down like somebody had tackled him from behind.

What the . . . ?

Ramon, who wasn't much of a thinker, tried to think what had just happened to him, but his head hurt too much.

Then he went out.

When the thief opened his eyes, his hands were already cuffed in front of him.

The fat policeman stood with a skinny boy, a tall, skinny boy with long arms and long fingers attached to them, wearing a Yankees T-shirt, a baseball glove under his arm.

"What's your name, kid?"

The one on the ground said, "Ramon," thinking the policeman was talking to him.

The cop looked down, as if he'd forgotten Ramon was there. "Wasn't talking to you."

"Michael," the skinny boy said. "Michael Arroyo."

"And you're telling me you got him with this from home plate?"

The cop held up a baseball that looked older than the old Stadium that rose behind them to the sky.

"Got lucky, I guess," Michael said.

The cop smiled, rolling the ball around in his hand.

"You lefty or righty?"

Now Michael smiled and held up his left hand, like he was a boy with the right answer in class.

"Home plate to dead center?" the cop said.

Michael nodded, like now the cop had come up with the right answer.

"You got some arm, kid," the cop said.

"That's what they tell me," Michael said.

PAPI WAS THE FIRST TO TELL MICHAEL ARROYO HE HAD THE ARM.

Michael thought it was just something a father would say to a son. But he knew there was a look Papi would get when he said it, as though he were seeing things Michael couldn't, back when it was just the two of them playing catch on that poor excuse of a field behind their apartment building in Pinar del Rio, outside of Havana.

Back home—what Michael still thought of as home, he couldn't help himself—everybody knew his father as Victor Arroyo. But he was Papi to Michael and his brother, Carlos. Always had been, always would be.

"You cannot teach somebody to have an arm like yours," Papi would say, walking out from behind the plate and sticking the ball back inside Michael's glove. Like they were having a conference on the mound during a game. "It's something you are born with, a gift from the gods, like a singer's voice. Or a boxer's left hand. Or an artist's brush."

This was when Michael was seven years old, maybe eight, long before they got on the boat that night last year, the one that took them across the water to a place on the Florida map called Big Pine Key. . . .

"Someday," Papi would say, "you will make it to the World Series, like the brothers Hernandez did. But before that, my son, what comes first?"

Michael always knew what the answer was supposed to be.

"First, the Little League World Series," he would say to his father.

"On ESPN," Papi would say, grinning at him. "The worldwide leader in sports."

Papi always made it sound as if that was supposed to be Michael's first great dream in baseball, to make it to the Little League World Series in Williamsport, Pennsylvania—Papi always showing him Pennsylvania on the ancient spinning globe they kept in the living room—for the world's championship of eleven- and twelve-year-old baseball boys.

Michael knew better, even then.

Michael knew that it was more his father's dream than his own. Papi had grown up in a time when a star Cuban baseball player, which Michael knew Papi sure had been as a young man, could never think about escaping to America, the way others would later, the most prominent lately being the Yankee pitcher Ricardo Gonzalez. El Grande, as he was known. So Papi, a shortstop on the national team in his day, never made it out, never made the great stage of the major leagues.

He became a coach of Little League boys instead, in charge of grooming them even then to become stars later for Castro's national team.

And from the time he saw that Michael had the arm, he had talked about the two of them traveling to Williamsport together and having their games shown around the world.

Even now, Michael couldn't tell where Papi's dream ended and his own began.

The dream had moved, of course, from Pinar del Rio to the Bronx, New York. Papi was no longer his coach and Michael was no longer a little boy. He had grown into the tallest player on his team during the regular season, and now the tallest on his All-Star team.

It was the All-Star team from the Bronx that Michael's left

arm was supposed to take all the way to Williamsport in a few weeks.

As long as he didn't get found out first.

His brother Carlos had promised they could have a catch behind the building when he finished his day shift at the Imperial, the food market across 161st Street next to McDonald's, almost directly underneath the subway platform.

This was before Carlos went off to his night job, the one he said had him busing tables at Hector's Bronx Café, a few stops up on the 4 train. Carlos said he had lied about his age to get the job at Hector's, telling them he was eighteen already, and no one had bothered to ask him for a birth certificate. The main reason for that, Carlos had told Michael, was that he was being paid off the books. Making it sound like a secret mission almost.

"What does that mean, off the books?" Michael had asked.

Carlos said, "It means, little brother, that this is the perfect job for me, at least for the time being. In the eyes of Official Persons, I don't even exist."

Carlos was always talking about Official Persons as if they were the bad guys in some television show.

Now, cooking their Saturday morning breakfast of pancakes and *chorizo,* their Cuban sausage, Carlos smiled at his brother and said, "My little brother, Miguel, the hero of the South Bronx."

"Guataca," Michael said. Flatterer.

"Just eat your breakfast," Carlos said. "You're turning into a freaking scarecrow, Miguel. Even thinner than a *birijita.*"

It was a Cuban expression for a thin person.

In the small, rundown apartment, their conversation was always a combination of Spanish and English. Their old life and their new one. It was only here, when it was just the two of them, that

8

Carlos would ever call his little brother by his birth name—Miguel. To everyone else, it was always Michael.

Michael still thought of Havana as home, because he was born there. And he had been Miguel Arroyo there.

Here, he was Michael.

"You're not exactly a heavyweight boxer yourself," Michael said.

"I have an excuse," Carlos said, "running from one job to another."

"And then running from table to table, right?" Michael said.

Carlos smiled at him. "Right," he said. "Like I am passing plates in a relay race instead of the baton."

"Maybe I could get a job," Michael said.

Carlos laughed. "And maybe you're too busy fighting crime, somehow turning baseballs into guided missiles."

"I told you," Michael said, "it was a lucky throw. I saw him running, I heard the policeman . . ."

"Then you just managed to hit him in the back of his hard head from . . . how many feet away?"

Michael grinned. "The trick is leading him just right." He jumped up from his chair, his mouth full, made a throwing motion. "Like a quarterback leading his favorite wide receiver." Then he added, "If I'd known it was that purse you got for Mrs. C on her birthday, I would have run after him and hit him with a bat."

"Mrs. C is telling the whole building you were meant to be on the field, like you were an angel," Carlos said.

"The only Angels are in the American League West," Michael said, "with halos on their caps." He poured more Aunt Jemima syrup on his stack with a flourish, finishing as though dotting an *i*. "If there are real angels in the world," Michael said to his brother, "how come they're never around when we need them?"

"Don't talk like that." Putting some snap into his voice, like he was snapping a towel at Michael.

Michael looked over and saw him at the counter, opening an envelope, making a face, tossing it in a drawer.

"Why not? It's true," Michael said.

"Papi said if we had all the answers we wouldn't have anything to ask God later."

"I want to ask Him things now."

"Eat your pancakes," Carlos said, then changed the subject, asking if there was All-Star practice today. Michael said no, but a bunch of the guys were going to meet at Macombs Dam Park before the Yankee game.

"It must be a national TV game," Carlos said, "if it's at four o'clock. Who's pitching, by the way?"

"He is."

"El Grande? I thought he just pitched Wednesday in Cleveland."

"Tuesday," Michael said. "Today is his scheduled day."

"That means another sellout."

"The Yankees sell out every game now."

"It just seems like they squeeze more people in when El Grande pitches," Carlos said. "What's his record now since his family came? Five-and-oh?"

"Six-and-oh, with an earned run average of one point four five."

"Before the season is over, we'll get two tickets and watch him pitch in person," Carlos said. "I promise."

"You know we can't afford them."

"Don't tell me what we can and can't afford," Carlos said, slamming his palm down on the counter, not just snapping now.

Yelling.

It happened more and more these days, Carlos exploding this

way when he was on his way to one of his jobs, like a burst of thunder out of nowhere, one you didn't even know was coming.

"Sorry," Michael said, lowering his eyes.

Carlos came right over, put a hand on Michael's shoulder. "No, Miguel, I'm the one who's sorry. I'm a little tired today, is all."

"We're cool," Michael said.

"That's right," Carlos said. "Who's cooler than the Arroyo boys?"

He said he was going to get dressed for work, but had to pull out the stupid ironing board and iron his stupid Imperial Market shirt first. The one he said looked as if it should belong to a bowling team. When he was gone from the kitchen, Michael went over and quietly opened the drawer where Carlos had thrown the envelope.

It was their Con Ed bill. The same bill Carlos had been slamming in a drawer for the past three months.

We *do* need an angel, Michael thought.

Michael read the *Daily News* when his brother was gone, going over the box scores of last night's games as if studying for a math test. Then he listened to sports radio, to all the excited voices talking about how this would be a play-off atmosphere this afternoon, because the Yankees and Red Sox were tied for first place in the American League East.

At least this was a Yankee game Michael would be able to watch on his own television. When it was a cable game, on the Yankees' own network, he would occasionally ask Mrs. Cora if he could watch at her apartment, if there was nothing special on she wanted to watch. She would always say yes. Mostly, Michael knew, because she liked the company, even if she didn't really like baseball. Michael knew Mrs. Cora had a daughter who had run off young, but she didn't talk about her too often, so Michael didn't ask.

Sometimes, with Carlos's permission, he would go and watch the night games at his friend Manny's apartment, a few blocks up near the Bronx County Courthouse, as long as Manny's mother would walk him home afterward.

Carlos promised they would get cable the way he promised they would get to see El Grande pitch in person.

There were all kinds of dreams in this apartment, Michael thought.

Sometimes he didn't care whether the game was on television or not, even if his man was on the mound. Michael would take his transistor radio and go outside on the fire escape, the one that was on the side of the building facing 158th Street, and sit facing the Stadium and listen to the crowd as much as he did to the real Yankee announcers, hearing the cheers float out of the top of the place and race straight up the hill to where he sat.

From there, not even one hundred yards away, he could see the outside white wall of Yankee Stadium and the design at the top that reminded Michael of some kind of white picket fence. The opening there, he knew, was way up above right field, pennants for the Mariners and Angels and Oakland Athletics blowing in the baseball breezes.

Just down the street, and a world away.

Michael Arroyo would sit here and when the announcers would talk about El Grande Gonzalez going into his windup, the windup that Michael could imitate perfectly even though he was left-handed and El Grande was right-handed, he would be able to imagine everything.

Michael's teammates called him Little Grande sometimes, even though he was bigger than most of them.

The ones who spoke Spanish called him *El Grandecito*.

He didn't even try to understand why throwing a baseball came this easily to him, why he could throw it as hard as he did and put it where he wanted most of the time, whether he was pitching to a net or to the other twelve-year-old stars of the South Bronx Clippers, named in honor of the Yankees' top farm team, the Columbus Clippers.

Michael Arroyo just knew that when he was rolling a ball around in his left hand, before he would put it in his glove and then duck his head behind that glove the way El Grande did, everything felt right in his world.

He wasn't mad at anyone or worried about what might happen to him and his brother.

Or have the list of questions he wanted to ask God.

Papi would never stand for that, anyway. Papi always said, "If you only ask God 'why?' when bad things happen, how come you don't ask Him the same question about all the good?"

As always, Michael imagined Papi here with him now, using that soft old catcher's mitt of his, the Johnny Bench model, whipping the ball back to Michael, telling him, "Now you're pitching, my son," that big smile on his face under what Michael always thought of as his Zorro mustache.

And every few pitches he would take his hand out of the Johnny Bench mitt and give it a shake and say, "Did I just touch a hot stove?"

They would both laugh then.

Michael couldn't remember all of Papi's pet sayings, no matter how hard he tried. Mostly he remembered the way it felt when they were just having a game of catch, everything feeling as good and right to him as a baseball held lightly in his hand.

The way it did now, just sitting alone in the apartment, the way he was alone a lot these days, rolling the ball around in his hands, feeling the seams, trying different grips. Sometimes when he held

13

a ball like this on the mound, before he would go into his motion, Michael could trick himself into believing everything was right in his world. Sometimes.

The phone rang.

Michael didn't even move to answer it, knowing the house rule—Rule Number One—about never answering the phone when Carlos wasn't here, just letting the ancient answering machine, the one with Papi's voice, pick up.

Michael wanted to change the outgoing message, but Carlos said, no, it sounded better that way.

The voice on the other end belonged to Mr. Minaya, his coach with the Clippers.

"Mr. Arroyo," Mr. Minaya began, because he called all the parents Mr. or Mrs. "You don't have to get right back to me, but once we get to the play-offs, we're going to need parents to drive to the game and since, well, you are a professional driver, we were wondering if you might be able to help out. Please let me know."

Michael waited for the click that meant he had disconnected. But he wasn't finished.

"Unless of course Mr. Arroyo isn't back yet and I'm talking to Carlos and Michael . . . well, forget it. Just tell your dad to give me a call if he ever does get back."

Then came the click.

If he ever does get back.

Not when.

Does he suspect something?

Michael grabbed his glove off the kitchen table where he'd left it, stuffed the ball in the pocket, locked the apartment door behind him, headed for the field at Macombs Dam Park.

The field had always felt like his own safe place. But now Michael wondered if even baseball was safe.

3

THERE WERE TWO BALLFIELDS AT MACOMBS DAM PARK, A REAL GREEN-GRASS park in the Bronx.

The regulation diamond, one with big-league dimensions used by Babe Ruth teams and American Legion teams and even some high schools, was tucked in the corner of the park where 161st Street intersected with Ruppert Place. The Little League field was the one closer to the Major Deegan Expressway.

During the regular Little League season, Michael's first in America, his team was sponsored by the big New York sporting goods store, Modell's—they called themselves the Modell Monuments, after the monuments inside the Stadium—and played its home games here. Now, in the summer, the Clippers also played their home games at Macombs, when they weren't playing other Bronx All-Star teams, up in Riverdale and at Castle Hill Field and at Crotona Park, maybe a mile away by car from Gerard Avenue. Sometimes they would play games as far away as White Plains and New Rochelle, because there were even All-Star teams from south Westchester County in their district, District 22.

On summer days, the kind that seemed to have no clock on them except for the setting sun, the kind you never wanted to end, Michael and his friends usually had the Macombs Dam Park field to themselves, if they could get up enough guys for a pickup game. Even if they couldn't come up with two full teams, they would invent games, depending on how many players they had.

On days like this, baseball would make Michael as happy as it ever did. No umpires. No coaches. No rules except the ones you made up.

Just play, on what felt to Michael like his own personal playground.

Other times they would join the older kids on the regulation field, though Michael would never pitch in those games, from the mound sixty feet from home plate, because Carlos had forbidden that. So had Mr. Minaya.

"You can move back from home plate when you move up to the thirteen-year-olds next season," Mr. Minaya had said.

The only other player from the Monuments who had made the Clippers, the South Bronx All-Star team that would eventually try to qualify as the representative of the eastern states to go to Williamsport for the World Series, was his catcher, Manny. Manny was waiting now, along with two other guys from the Clippers, Kelvin Carter and Anthony Fierro, on the back field when Michael showed up.

It was still only two o'clock, two hours from when El Grande would pitch against the Red Sox, but already you could see more traffic getting off the Deegan above them, see the whole area around the Stadium coming to life, as it always did on game day.

Manny smiled when he saw Michael. Nothing unusual about that. Manny Cabrera always seemed to be smiling, except when he would strike out with the bases loaded, or when he would fail to throw out a runner trying to steal second base. He was almost a head shorter than Michael, twenty pounds heavier at least, and was the best catcher in all of District 22.

Some of the players on the other team would occasionally call him No Neck Cabrera, mostly because he didn't have one. Usually they did this when they thought he couldn't hear them. But even when he did, he still had that smile on his face, as if he and the world were in on the same joke.

"Here comes the superhero now," Manny said as Michael walked across the infield.

"Whoo whoo whoo," Kelvin said, pumping his fist.

"Which X-Man is he? I forget," Anthony Fierro said.

"Wish he was that fine X-Girl, Halle Berry," Kel said.

Then Kel whoo whoo whoo'd again, but it seemed to be more for Halle Berry this time than Michael.

"Do not start," Michael said.

"Oooh, listen to the starting pitcher, telling us not to start," Manny said, like a comedian playing to a crowd of three. "Maybe he's afraid we'll reveal his secret identity."

Kelvin Carter was the Clippers' shortstop. His father worked on the grounds crew at Yankee Stadium, which meant he was one of the guys who did the little dance routine to the song "YMCA" when it was time to rake the infield dirt in the fifth inning.

Kelvin said, "Dude catches criminals by day, does his bad Little League thing by night."

"Better not let Coach find out you threw it from home plate to dead center," Manny said.

"Who said I did?" Michael said.

"I think I heard it from Katie Couric," Manny said.

"No," Kel said, "it had to be Oprah!"

"I definitely heard about it from Dan Patrick on SportsCenter," Anthony said.

"Shut up," Michael said, unable to keep a smile down. "All of you."

"I can't believe it wasn't on the front page of the *Daily News*," Anthony said.

Michael knew there was no sense fighting them when they got going like this. The best thing to do was let them have their fun until they ran out of what they thought were hysterically funny lines.

"Okay, we'll stop," Manny said eventually. "But before we do, I have to ask you one question."

He got up from the bench, put his catcher's mitt on, which meant he was ready to start getting Michael warmed up.

"Knock yourself out," Michael said.

Manny looked at Kelvin and Anthony, both of whom were already giggling.

He said, "When you are fighting crime—what color cape do you wear?"

Howls.

Kelvin said, "Or do you wear those tights like Spider-Man and Daredevil and them?"

"Whoa, not Daredevil," Manny said, "the girl in that movie, the one from *Alias,* she took out more bad guys than Ben Affleck did."

Michael was throwing a ball high into the air, straight up, and catching it, sometimes behind his back, doing his best to ignore them.

"You know," he said finally, as if talking to the sky, "maybe the real Daredevil will be the guy who has to lead off against me today."

Everybody made a low whooooooo sound.

"In that case," Manny said, "it's a good thing Kel begged to hit first today."

"Did not," Kelvin said.

"Did, too."

"Did not infinity," Kel said, as if slam-dunking the word *infinity*. "That's the only time I'd ever ask to hit against Arroyo, by the way. On the twelfth of infinity."

"I promise I won't throw hard," Michael said, heading for the mound as Manny got into his squat behind home plate.

Kelvin was still shaking his head as he watched the guys going out into the field, deserting him. "Your half speed is faster than most guys' full speed, Arroyo. So don't be givin' me none of your 'I won't throw hard.' "

He reluctantly went over to the screen behind home plate where they'd all stacked their bats.

"Just don't be trying for the magic number today," he said.

"Eight-zero," Manny said.

The past couple of years, there had been more and more games from the Little League World Series on television, starting with the sectional qualifiers. Manny's family had cable, so he would invite Michael over to their apartment to watch the games on ESPN and ESPN2, and they would talk about this year, the year when they were sure they would make it far enough in the tournament to get on TV themselves. And in all the games they had watched—and Manny watched a lot more than Michael did—there had never been a time when one of the pitchers' fastballs had been measured at eighty miles an hour.

They had seen Danny Almonte, the star pitcher from another Bronx team, the kid who got even more famous when they found out he was fourteen instead of twelve the year he was pitching all his no-hitters, get to seventy-five miles an hour. Manny said he remembered someone he described as a big old boy from Kentucky putting up what he called a double-seven.

But no one had ever hit eighty.

Eighty was the magic number for Little League pitchers the way 100 was for radar guns in the big leagues. Except, Manny said, hitting 80 at their age was really the same as someone older hitting

110. That was his theory. Manny had theories about almost every-thing under the sun, Michael knew.

Here was another:

That Michael hit eighty all the time, even if they didn't have television cameras or radar guns covering the Modell Monuments, or the Clippers. Manny said that he didn't need no stinking gun for his Pudge Rodriguez mitt to know how fast Michael was throwing.

Kel had his bright red batting gloves on, but was still complain-ing about having to be the first to hit, making it sound as if they were sending him to detention. Or the principal's office. When he was finally done, he heard Manny call out to Michael, "Let me give you a sign." Manny put down one finger, which meant fastball.

Kel whipped his head around. "I saw that," he said. "You told him to throw his number one, didn't you?"

"Maybe I did, maybe I didn't," Manny said.

During the game sometimes, he would put down two fingers, or three, or even four, but that was just for fun, like a game he and Michael played with each other. Or if there was a runner on second base who had watched too much big-league baseball on television and thought it mattered if you stole a sign and knew what pitch was coming. But Michael and Manny knew that Michael's dad had told him he wasn't allowed to throw any kind of curve until he was in high school, it was bad for his arm. Not just his arm, but any arm, Papi had always said, attached to a Little Leaguer's body. So Michael didn't even fool around with curves when he was fooling around with his buddies like this.

Papi had drilled the dangers of breaking balls into him, from as far back as Michael could remember, the way he had drilled English into him.

Or the dangers of drugs.

So sometimes Michael would take something off his number

one, just as a way of setting a hitter up or getting him off balance, provided it was one of the handful of hitters he'd run into who could actually get around on his fastball.

Michael threw fastballs for six innings a week, which is all the innings Little League rules allowed him to pitch in one week. Mr. Minaya could break up those six innings any way he wanted. Michael could pitch six in one game, or three in two games. Or four one day and two a couple of days later.

Just no more than six a week in the regular season.

But this wasn't official pitching now, not against Manny and Kel and Anthony. This was just pure fun, from his first pitch, which he lobbed up there to Kel. Who looked shocked as he put his bat on the ball and hit one in the air to where Anthony was standing in short center field. Michael wanted Kel to hit a few balls to Anthony, just so Anthony would stop complaining about not having any balls to shag.

"I should have brought my homework," Anthony had said when he first got to the outfield, refusing to move more than ten yards back from second base.

"You don't do homework," Manny reminded him.

"Well, if I did," Anthony said, "this would be a perfect time to catch up on it."

After a few lob balls Kel said, "Okay, I don't want anymore of your pity, go ahead and gun it."

Michael made a show of rubbing up the old ball they were using. "First you don't want to hit because you say I throw too hard. Now you say I'm throwing too easy. You're giving me . . . Manny, what's he giving me here? You're the one with the words."

"A mixed message."

"Exactly," Michael said. "You're giving me a mixed message."

Kel, smiling out at him, made a show like he was about to give

Michael an upraised middle finger. "Like to give you something more than that," Kel said.

"Hey," Michael said, "there could be kids watching."

"I thought we were kids," Manny said.

"Nah," Kel said, "we're much cooler than that."

"We are soooooo cool," Manny said.

"Cooler than LL Cool J," Kel said.

Anthony, who had the deepest voice of all of them, had come into the infield. Now he made his voice even deeper, trying to make himself sound like a TV announcer. "Hey," he said, "all you South Bronx Clippers, where are you going as soon as you kick a little more butt?"

"Disney World?" Kel said.

Anthony made a sound like a game-show buzzer that meant, wrong answer.

"Where are we going?" he asked again.

In one voice, Anthony's included, they yelled, "Williamsport!"

Anthony ran back out to center. Manny got back into his squat. Then Michael threw a real number one to Kel that he missed by a mile, as if he were swinging at the sound of the ball going past him, not at anything he saw.

That wasn't the best part of the pitch.

The best part of the pitch was that Michael's best buddy Manny, who thought he was used to Michael's heat, who bragged on being the only guy in District 22 who could even think about handling Michael's heat, got knocked back so hard from the force of the pitch that he ended up sitting down.

Michael started in from the mound. "Are you okay?" he said.

"Fine," Manny said.

He just sat there as if nothing had happened, perfectly relaxed, staring at the ball in his glove. "Absolutely fine," he said.

Then he popped to his feet. Manny was agile for someone with a body shaped like a fire hydrant. Only Michael, of all his friends and teammates, knew about the dance classes he took, the ones he even admitted to Michael he liked, because they were a way for him to show off how light he was on his feet, not just some lump behind the plate. The guy who stayed in one place for so much of a baseball game loved to move, Michael knew.

He brought the ball out to the mound himself, handed it to Michael, said, "Eighty."

Michael looked around. "Did I miss the guy with the Jugs gun?" It was one of the first radar guns he'd ever heard them talking about on radio.

"I told you," Manny said. "I don't need no stinkin' gun."

He put his Pudge mitt between him and Michael. "I got this," he said. "And this never lies."

He yelled at Anthony Fierro to come in and hit if he wanted, then walked back to the plate.

"Eighty," Michael heard him say.

Some other ballplayers from the neighborhood, Babe Ruth League kids, showed up just as Michael and Manny and Anthony and Kel were about to pack it in and go to McDonald's. Then some older kids who'd been shooting baskets on one of the courts over near the Stadium asked if they could play. That made it thirteen players in all, enough to have a game. Three infielders, two outfielders, a pitcher. Manny had offered to be full-time catcher, saying he didn't need to hit, he'd already conquered hitting.

Michael played center field, saying he might throw a couple of pitches at the end, just for fun. But he loved playing center field, loved getting a chance to run across the outfield and pretend it was inside the Stadium.

Michael loved to move, basically.

So they played their pickup game, trash-talking each other, laughing, barely keeping track of the score, everybody trying their hardest to smoke balls past the two outfielders or, in the case of the bigger kids from the basketball court, trying to jack balls over their heads. When they were waiting to hit they could look past the batter's box, toward Yankee Stadium, and see the baseball afternoon coming to life now, gathering force like one of the late-afternoon storms you got in the summer. Occasionally they would hear the cheers from the fans lined up behind blue police barriers on both sides of the players' entrance to the Stadium as the players walked out of their parking lot on the Deegan side of Ruppert.

Michael was able to picture it in his head because of all the times he had come and stood behind those blue barriers himself, hoping to get a look at El Grande, even four hours before game time, knowing El Grande liked to get to the park early when it was his turn to pitch.

So Michael was fairly certain that El Grande Gonzalez was already inside the Yankee clubhouse by the time the Clippers and the rest of the kids on the far field at Macombs were playing their pickup game, one they had agreed at the start would be five innings. It turned out the four basketball guys had bleacher tickets to today's game, which they proudly showed off to Michael and Manny, bragging, pulling the tickets out of the pockets of their baggy gym shorts, shorts that went way past their knees, as if they were pulling out pieces of gold. But in the meantime, they had their own game to play.

It was in the top of the fourth inning that Michael noticed the beautiful girl watching them through the fence at the basketball court.

Michael was twelve, and a boy, and a ballplayer, and usually

24

showed no interest in girls because he knew his friends would act as if he had broken some kind of law. But even Michael Arroyo could see this was an uncommonly beautiful girl, with long dark hair and dark skin and big, dark eyes that somehow, even from a distance, looked sad to him.

The girl had a baseball glove under her arm.

Maybe she's sad, he thought to himself, because we haven't asked her to play.

The girl was still watching through the fence when it was Michael's turn to pitch in the top of the fifth.

For some reason, he looked over at her after his first pitch to the tallest of the basketball players, the one whose name was Eric Scopetta, whose nickname was E-Scope.

E-Scope was a banger. He'd already proved that when Kel had pitched to him, hitting a bomb to the place in dead center where there was a hole in the fence, the one the purse thief had been running toward before Michael took him down with a bomb of his own.

Now Michael went into his full windup, his El Grande windup, leg high, his ball and his head tucked briefly behind his glove, before he threw a fastball past E-Scope that made the older boy not only miss, but put very colorful swear words together, in a way Michael had never heard before, not even living in the Bronx, where you could walk past an open window in the summer and feel as if you'd discovered the capital of swearing.

Michael ignored him, looked back toward the fence, wanting to see if the pretty girl was still watching, if she'd seen him pour his fastball in that way.

She was watching. And no longer looked sad. She had her arms folded in front of her, the glove pressed against her chest, and Michael was sure she was laughing at him.

As if she had been waiting for him to look back over so he could see her laughing at him.

It was almost as if she knew—in that way that girls always seemed to know things that boys didn't—that he wouldn't be able to help himself, that he needed to see what her reaction would be.

But what the heck was so funny?

Michael struck out E-Scope on three pitches, struck out the next two guys not even throwing his hardest, jogged in to the bench, and put his glove down. He had made the last out the inning before, so it would be a while before he hit, if he hit at all, since this was his team's last ups.

He told Manny he'd be right back, and started walking toward the basketball courts. Not walking toward the girl at first. Walking with his hands in his pockets, head down, as if he were on his way to the small brick administration building for Macombs Dam Park, up at the corner of 161st and Ruppert.

But when he got about twenty yards away, he turned and started walking toward her, smiling at her now, calling out to her.

"Hey," he said. "What was so funny before?"

And that's when she ran.

She was wearing a white T-shirt and blue jeans and had legs almost as long as Michael's. Tall, pretty girl.

With those eyes.

She ran, fast for a girl, for *anybody,* up the hill toward Yankee Stadium, her glove under her arm, until she disappeared into the crowd of people coming around the corner from the subway station, all those who had their own tickets like gold in their pockets to watch El Grande high-kick his fastball into gear against the Red Sox.

Gone.

4

The following day, after Michael came home from church with Mrs. Cora, what had become a Sunday ritual with them, he read all about El Grande's shutout of the Red Sox in the *Daily News* and the *Post.* It was a way for him to experience that game all over again, even if he had seen every single pitch of the complete game in which El Grande gave the Red Sox just four singles, struck out ten, and walked just one batter.

The stories in the paper reminded everybody that El Grande, who had struggled in April, had not lost a game since his family had finally made it out of Cuba a month before, made it across the waters of the Florida Straits the way Papi and Carlos and Michael had two years before.

El Grande's wife and two children had made it despite the fact that the Coast Guard had picked them up twenty miles south of Key West in the middle of the night and chased them until dawn with three fast boats and a helicopter. All those Official Persons on the water in the night, Carlos said, smiling and shaking his head as he did, and they had still been unable to catch the spider boat with El Grande's people on it.

"That wasn't a high-speed chase on the high seas," Carlos had said when they watched the eleven o'clock news that night. "That was a police escort."

Michael had asked what he meant. It was the same with Carlos as it was with Manny Cabrera:

Sometimes it was as if they were speaking to Michael in code.

27

"They must have been tipped that they had the wife and kids of a star Yankee pitcher on board," Carlos had said. "I'm surprised they didn't let that boat go all the way to the Harlem River and drop everybody off a few blocks from the ballpark." Carlos was smiling that night, in a good mood, as he put his arm around his younger brother. "We should have told them the night we came that we had the famous pitcher Miguel Arroyo on board."

Carlos finally woke up around noon, took a shower, got dressed, and announced he was taking Michael out to lunch at McDonald's. While they were there, both of them having two double cheese-burgers with fries and chocolate shakes, Carlos asked when Michael's game was.

"Two o'clock," Michael said. "Against the best team from Westchester."

"I'm there," Carlos said.

Michael shook his head. "It's your one day off," he said. "You don't have to come and watch me pitch a dopey Little League game."

"Yes," Carlos said. "I do." He had already inhaled his first double cheese and was getting ready to start on his second. "How many innings for you today?" he asked Michael.

"The last four. We got rained out against Eastchester on Thursday, remember? And I only pitched two innings last Tuesday when we lost to Fordham Road."

"They must be good if they can beat you guys," Carlos said.

"They are," Michael said.

"Well, I will see you over there, little brother," Carlos said. "I haven't gotten to see you pitch four straight innings in a month."

When they were finished eating, Carlos cleaned up everything—plastic trays and garbage and cups. Maybe he thinks he's still on the job at Hector's, Michael thought. But lately Carlos tried to be very organized about everything. Always wanting to show Michael he was in charge. On top of everything. Even when it came to busing a table at what all of Michael's friends called Mickey D's.

Michael knew it was just his brother's way of acting older than he really was.

Like he was Papi Jr.

When he came back to the table, he told Michael to sit for one more minute, he had something he wanted to talk about.

"Sounds serious," Michael said. "Did I leave a towel on the floor of my room?"

Carlos said, "You did, slob face. But that's not what I want to talk to you about."

Michael waited.

Carlos leaned forward, made his fingers into a steeple, put them under his chin. Another grown-up pose of his. "I just want to remind you that as you and the other guys on the All-Stars continue to win games, there's going to be more attention drawn to you. Which means," Carlos said, "you're going to have to be more careful about what you say, who you say it to."

"I don't need reminding," Michael said.

"I know you don't," Carlos said. "You're smart, even if you are a slob. But you just have to keep it at the front of your brain that the bigger the games, the bigger the spotlight."

Carlos made the spotlight sound like one more thing for them to be afraid of.

His brother walked him back to the apartment, then told him he had some errands to run. Michael said it was Sunday, he should be resting instead of running errands, especially if he was coming to the game in an hour.

Carlos said for him to go rest himself for an hour or so, he'd see him later, in the top of the third.

• • •

Michael faced thirteen batters from Westchester South.

He struck out ten.

The Westchester team managed only one hit off him, on a little blooper that died in front of Kel at short, and then bounced away from him for an infield hit. The only other ball in play was a little roller their cleanup hitter, a blond kid almost as tall as Michael and looking a lot heavier, hit about halfway to the mound in the top of the third. Earlier in the game, the same kid had hit a three-run homer off Anthony Fierro, the ball just clearing the left-field fence. They were the last runs Westchester would get in the 4–3 loss.

The blond-haired kid didn't like looking foolish, and even tried to convince the home plate ump that the dribbler he'd hit back to Michael had ricocheted off his foot first.

"It was a foul ball," the kid kept saying in a loud voice until Manny took off his mask and said, "In your dreams maybe."

The blond kid said, "What's that supposed to mean?"

Manny just smiled, trying to let the kid know this wasn't something worth fighting about. "Hey, dude, you did good just getting your bat on the ball, don't be looking for a do-over."

The best comeback the blond kid, clearly the star of his team, could manage was: "I wasn't talking to you."

But Manny was talking to him, and once Manny got started it was hard—more like impossible—for him to stop. He walked out, dug the tip of his spike into the grass about where Michael had picked up the blond kid's roller. "The way my man is pitching today, this is the same as going deep on his butt."

"Maybe he is a man," the blond kid had said. "He throws like one."

It occurred to Michael that they were discussing him as if he weren't there.

The Westchester kid said, "How old is he, anyway?"

It was, Michael knew, like giving Manny a pitch he could drive.

Manny said, "Twelve years, two months, five days, and however many hours it was until you were a lucky boy to even touch the best fastball you're ever going to see."

The blond kid, dug in good now, said, "He doesn't throw it like any twelve-year-old I've ever seen."

Manny gave the big jerk a smile that seemed to stretch from the Deegan to the subway tracks over River Avenue. "No, he does not." Then he turned his head, spit, went back behind the plate and got into his crouch.

In the top of the sixth, trying to make sure the Clippers held on to their one-run lead, Michael had struck out the side on ten pitches. Of course the last hitter up turned out to be the blond kid, whose name, they had heard by then, was Justin.

"You can't get any more white-bread than bein' a Justin," Kel had said on the bench when they all heard the Westchester coach call the blond boy by name.

Manny would say later that the one called ball Michael had thrown old Justin, the one with two strikes on him, should have been a strike, too, but the ump had taken pity on the poor guy, not wanting to end the game on a punch-out.

The ump had come out to clean off home plate after he called the pitch a ball. While he did, according to Manny, he looked up at Justin and in a real quiet voice said, "You better be swinging on the next one, son."

Justin did swing. From his heels.

But Michael blew the ball right by him.

Ball game.

At that point, Justin threw his bat against the back screen. The ump hadn't wasted any time, calling out the Westchester coach and telling him that his star was suspended from the next game. The coach said that only happened if you got ejected, and that the ump couldn't eject somebody from a game that was already over.

"Watch me," the ump answered.

That was when Justin started yelling, as his coach tried to pull him away. The ump immediately pulled out his cell phone. The coach asked who he was calling. "The league commissioner," the ump said. "I want him to hear every word of this."

That was when Justin finally shut up.

At that point Michael got into line with the rest of the Clippers, shaking hands with the Westchester players, all except Justin, who somehow managed to veer off and head back to his bench just before he got next to Michael, staring hard at him from a distance, still acting more ticked off at Michael than he was at the umpire who'd just clipped him for a game.

"He can't be that mad just because I got him out," Michael said to Manny.

"He must think it's impossible for anybody his own age to make him look like that much of a girl."

"Hey," Michael said, "not so loud. We have a girl, remember? And she's *good*."

They did. Maria Cuellar, whose parents were Puerto Rican, was the second fastest player on their team, after Kel. She played second base, could play third or short if she had to, and could hit.

"I don't think of Maria as a girl," Manny said. "I think of her as one of us."

"Really?" Michael said. "I watch you sometimes watching her, and you don't seem to look at her the way you do our other infielders."

Manny turned to Michael, no expression on his face whatsoever, his voice completely calm, and said: "Shut up about Maria."

"I'm good with that."

Manny said, "Just so we're clear."

Mr. Minaya gathered them out in right field for a few minutes the way he always did after games, went over what he liked about what they'd done today, what he didn't like, told them what he told them after every game: That the object was to have fun, but to learn something every single time they went out there.

"You never know what thing you learn might make the difference between making it to Williamsport and watching the games from your sofa," he said.

It had already reached the point in the season, Michael and his teammates knew, where Mr. Minaya wasn't really interested in whether or not they were having fun, that was just his cover story. He wanted to make it to the World Series as much as any kid on his team. Maybe more.

Sometimes when Mr. Minaya got going about the World Series he sounded a lot like Papi, which meant he made Williamsport, Pennsylvania, that ballpark you'd see on television with happy parents in the stands and no highways in the distance, sound like baseball heaven. . . .

"Did you hear me, Michael? Or were you in Williamsport already?"

"I was, actually," Michael said. "Sorry, Coach."

"I was asking if anybody needed a ride over to Crotona Park on Tuesday night," Mr. Minaya said.

Michael looked down at his old baseball shoes, that hole in the toe of his left one, as he said, "I could use a ride."

There was a pause before Mr. Minaya said, "Can't your father bring you?"

Michael, trying not to look nervous, said, "No."

33

"He's still not back from Florida?"

Michael shook his head.

"I wondered why he hadn't called me back."

"It's still just Carlos and me," Michael said. "But Mrs. Cora looks out for us."

Mr. Minaya said he would swing by and pick Michael up at four-thirty. Michael said he'd be out front. Mr. Minaya said, "I hope your uncle gets better soon, it would be a shame if your father misses our first play-off games after missing the whole regular season."

Michael just nodded and told Mr. Minaya he would see him on Tuesday, told Manny he could call him later, picked up his glove and bat, and started walking fast in the direction of the Stadium. Then he was running, jogging at first, but then sprinting, just wanting to get home to the apartment, afraid to look back, afraid they might still be watching him.

He didn't want Mr. Minaya or his teammates to see him crying.

About the father that had been dead since May.

5

MICHAEL REMEMBERED HOW HIS FATHER USED TO LAUGH WHEN HE'D HEAR one of the sports announcers say something about how heart could only carry an athlete, or a team, so far.

"Little do they know," he'd say.

Then he'd give two little taps to his chest, the way the big-league ballplayers did sometimes just after they'd hit a home run.

Their grandfather, Papi's father, had died young of something to do with his heart, and so had their great-grandfather. Papi had never made a secret of that. And once, back in Havana when Michael was five or six, Papi had been in the hospital for a few days with what their mother described as a "mild attack to the heart."

Papi laughed off that one, too.

"Mild," he said, "usually means it attacked somebody else's heart."

Then he would tell them not to worry, he would not only die an old man, he would die in America.

It turned out he was half right.

Some of it Papi told Mrs. Cora himself, when he made it back to her apartment that day.

Some of it Carlos found out later on his own, because he said he had to know.

All of it became their secret.

Their father had been driving his gypsy cab on Kingsbridge Road, the middle of May, right before Memorial Day weekend. His fare was a woman. Papi let her off in front of her apartment building,

35

and she paid him. It was a beautiful day, and so he had the windows down, and just as he was pulling away, he heard shouting from behind him.

A man had been waiting for the woman.

An ex-boyfriend, Carlos would find out later.

Papi stopped his Crown Vic, the one with a hundred thousand miles on it, watching the argument now as well as listening to it.

He saw the man raise a hand to the woman, knock her to the ground.

"The rule is that once they are out of the car, they are no longer your responsibility," he said later to Mrs. Cora. "But that was not my rule."

Papi got out of the car, yelled at the man to stop. The man turned and yelled at him to mind his own business. The woman on the ground was crying. When Papi came up on them, the man took one swing before Papi put him down. A neighbor would tell Carlos this part. The man got up, tried to charge Papi like a bull.

But Papi put him down again.

That's when he felt something grab in his chest.

"He tells me this as he begins to fade," Mrs. C later told Michael and Carlos, "like an old photograph."

The woman later told Carlos when he went to visit her that she had thought something was wrong with the kind cabdriver then, but he had told her he was just too old to be engaging in schoolyard fights. At this point, the woman's ex-boyfriend had had enough and ran off. Papi told the woman to call the police and got into his car and drove away. Papi, even in America, had always warned his sons, you never want to spend too much time talking to the police.

He managed to drive home, getting back to their building just as Mrs. Cora was coming back from noon mass. Papi told her he felt as if a bomb had gone off inside his chest. She took him inside to her apartment.

"I am dying," he said.

The way he said it, a look he had, told Mrs. C he was telling her the truth.

"Let me call a doctor," she said.

"No," he said. "A priest. One who will keep my secret."

"What secret?" Mrs. Cora said.

"The secret," he said, "that I am gone."

It was already too late for the priest. Papi held on to Mrs. Cora's hand, telling her, "Keep my boys together." His last words.

Then he died.

Father Montoya came and gave him the last rites. Mrs. Cora told him that he was to tell no one, not even at the church, about Papi's death. He asked why. She said because those were the father's wishes, that if something he had called the Family Court found out the boys had no parents and no relatives, they would come for them.

Mrs. Cora said to the boys later, "The priest asked who would take care of you two. I told him you would take care of yourselves."

The super had a cousin who ran a funeral home over near Kennedy Airport in Queens. He handled the details of the burial, at a small cemetery near the Aqueduct Racetrack.

Father Montoya drove Carlos, Michael, and Mrs. C.

The boys used the emergency money they knew their father had kept in a box in the cupboard to buy a cheap casket. They made sure that the man from the funeral home put Papi's old catcher's mitt inside with him.

And the new ball he and Michael had played catch with the day before he died.

37

They came home and Carlos went looking for work. Mrs. Cora said she would adopt them as her foster children if she could. But her late husband had never bothered to get his papers. And besides, she barely had enough money of her own to live on. Papi had no brothers or sisters. Their mother, the one who had died so young of cancer Michael could not even remember her, had sisters still living in Cuba, but neither Carlos nor Michael had spoken to them in years, or had any idea how to get in touch with them. From the time their mother had died, it had just been the three of them, father and two sons.

The father who had always told them he was going to die old and die free, until his own great heart could only carry him so far.

"Maybe some family could adopt the two of us," Michael said one night, when Carlos was at the kitchen table, figuring out again how much money they would need to get by once the last of Papi's emergency money ran out.

"One teenaged boy and another about to be a teenager?" Carlos said. "Maybe there is that kind of family on a TV show, in the TV world. But not in the real world." He shook his head. "No, we just have to find a way to get by until I turn eighteen."

"That's not until next spring," Michael said.

"Little brother," Carlos said, "believe me, if I could change my birth certificate, I would."

"Will they really separate us if they find out?"

"I can only tell you what I read, mostly on the Internet," Carlos said. "There is something where they say they would try to keep siblings together. But they can't guarantee it. If someone finds out about Papi, then we go into Family Court. And after that, little brother? Then it's up to them. The Official Persons. If they can't place us in a foster home, then we could go into a group home. Maybe even back to Cuba."

"I want to stay here," Michael said. "This is our home."

Carlos got up from the table, came over, hugged him hard.

"And it's going to stay our home, Miguel. We are going to stay a family, and we are going to live in this apartment until you graduate from high school and the Yankees come and offer you a big bonus contract and then . . ."

"What?"

"Then we live happily ever after in America, the way Papi promised."

"You think we can keep everybody from finding out?"

"Do we have a choice?"

Michael said, "I'm afraid."

It was something he would never admit to Manny, or the other Clippers, or even Mrs. C.

"Let me worry," Carlos said. "You just pitch."

So they came up with the story, any time anybody would ask, that Papi had gone to visit a sick brother in Key West, Florida, and that Mrs. C was looking out for them. Whenever someone new would ask, Carlos would just tell them that Papi had only been gone a couple of days.

This had gone on for three months. Carlos worked, and worried. Michael pitched.

A family of three had become, in Michael Arroyo's young mind, an army of two.

6

THE GIRL SHOWED UP AGAIN.

It was two days after the Crotona game, which the Clippers had won, 3–2. Michael had pitched the first three innings, struck out eight of the nine batters he faced before handing the ball, and the game, over to Anthony Fierro and watching Anthony pitch his best three innings of his All-Star season from there.

There was no game or practice scheduled for the next day, but Manny told Michael he'd meet him at Macombs after his doctor's appointment for his stupid allergies, somewhere around three o'clock. Michael knew that could mean anywhere between three and four. He operated on Manny Standard Time, and there was no getting around it if you were Manny Cabrera's friend. He was loyal, funny, smarter than he let on, loved baseball as much as Michael. There were so many good points with Manny that Michael couldn't keep track of them all.

But none of Manny's good points, not a single one, involved him showing up on time for anything except a real game.

So instead of going straight down to the field, Michael decided to stop at the Stadium first. That night the Yankees were going to play the last game of an eleven-game home stand, El Grande on the mound. Michael had found a brand-new ball in the apartment, stuck it in the pocket of his glove, stuck a Magic Marker in his pocket, and walked around the Stadium to where the blue barriers had been set up near the Yankees' souvenir store, the one with so many of the players' jerseys in the front window.

El Grande's number 33 was front and center. Michael had heard the radio announcers saying the other day that it was currently outselling all the other Yankees jerseys combined.

As usual, most of the people waiting for the players to arrive were adults, carrying their own balls and programs and photographs and notebooks. Carlos had once said these were the people who only wanted autographs so they could turn around and sell them.

"But if you were lucky enough to get your favorite player to sign something," Michael had said, "why would you sell it?"

"Because baseball is a business to these people," Carlos answered. "Even a signature from one of their heroes."

"It's different with me," Michael said.

"And always will be," Carlos said.

Now, behind the blue barriers, Michael slithered to the front of the crowd as the people around him cheered and called out to Joe Johnson, the Yankee first baseman, and the rookie catcher, Tony DiVeronica, short and squat, built like an older version of Manny. Out of the parking lot after them came the new Japanese right fielder, Sazaki.

No El Grande.

Michael watched as a few more players arrived, a couple of the Yankee broadcasters. Finally he asked a boy about his age if El Grande had arrived yet.

"You missed him by like ten minutes," the boy said. "But it wouldn't have done you any good, the guy walked right past us like we weren't even here."

Michael said, "He's pitching tonight, he probably doesn't stop to sign on days when he's pitching."

"Dream on," the other boy said. "I've never seen the guy even look over here."

Dream on, Michael thought to himself, and made his way across

Ruppert Place and across the basketball courts to wait for Manny. Who actually showed up at three-thirty, almost on time if you were using Manny Standard Time.

"Before you say anything, my arm hurts from my shot," Manny said.

"Did the shot make you walk slower getting here?"

"It's not your fastball I'm going to remember someday," Manny said. "It's your compassion."

"I'm sorry about the shots," Michael said. "Really. Though if they'd give it to you in your butt, you probably wouldn't have felt anything."

"Ha ha," Manny said. "Ha ha ha."

He went and got behind the plate without being asked. Michael knew by now that it was the same with Manny the catcher as Manny his friend: He would do anything for Michael. On or off the field. It was never something the two of them discussed, or that required a thank-you from Michael. But if he announced right now that he wanted to throw pitches to Manny Cabrera for an hour straight, Manny would just nod. And in an hour, would still be snapping back throws to Michael out of his crouch as if Michael had just thrown his first pitch of the day. He'd still be yelling, "Now you're humming, bud."

He wouldn't even think about stopping until Michael did.

This was one of the moments when he wanted to thank Manny, or at least try, even if he knew he wouldn't get anywhere, because he never had in the past.

"You know," Michael said, "I don't think I could even think about pulling this thing off without you. . . ."

They both knew how much trouble Manny would be in if his mom ever found out the secret Manny was keeping, knew from Carlos that any adult who found out about two children living without an adult was supposed to report them, by law, to something called the Administration for Children's Services. Manny didn't want to hear about it.

"Shut up and pitch," he said.

Michael did, getting himself loose, keeping track of the number of warm-up pitches he'd thrown before starting to cut loose, throwing as hard as he could before long, somehow becoming more accurate as he did, hitting Manny's mitt wherever he had it set up. Inside corner, outside corner, high in the strike zone, low, it didn't matter. Michael hit the glove almost every time.

Manny finally stood up, soft-tossed the ball back to Michael.

"You might not need a break, Star," he said, "Star" being his personal nickname for Michael. "But I do. Let's get a drink."

Michael said he was cool with that and began walking in from the mound. Manny waited for him at home plate. When Michael got there, Manny was looking past him, toward the outfield. Grinning. "Check it out," he said.

"Check what out?"

"We have an audience," Manny said.

Michael turned around.

There she was, out behind the center-field fence.

Staring right at him.

He still had the ball in his left hand. And without thinking about it he planted himself, wound up, and chucked the ball all the way out there, an even longer throw than he made to get the purse stealer. Put it on one bounce over the fence to where she was standing.

He stood there now with his hands on his hips. Hoping she could see him smiling at her.

The girl, in her long-legged blue jeans, wearing a pink T-shirt today that had something written on the front, walked calmly around the fence, like she had all the time in the world. Or: Like she was waiting to decide just what she wanted to do.

When she got to the ball, she looked at him. Then put her hands on her hips, like she was mimicking him.

Then the pretty mystery girl with the long legs picked the ball up and threw it back to Michael.

On the fly.

Michael turned around and looked at Manny. Who was staring at the girl in the distance the way you stare at fireworks the first time you see them in the sky.

"I saw," Manny said.

Michael stepped back behind the plate now—to show her his arm was better?—and threw the ball back, really gunning it, putting everything he had into it, like he was trying to throw it into the river. Wanting to make sure he got this one over the fence without any bounces.

The ball tracked on the mystery girl all the way, like it was a fly ball in a video baseball game that you were carefully guiding into an outfielder's glove.

When it got to her, she reached up, casual, like a big-league outfielder making a routine out, and caught the ball in her glove, one he hadn't even noticed she had on.

From behind Michael, Manny said, "Can of corn."

Michael barely heard him, he was staring at the girl still, wondering where the two of them were going with the strangest game of catch he'd ever played.

"You ever seen an arm like that on somebody our age?" Michael said finally.

"Yeah," Manny said. "Yours."

"Who is she?" Michael said.

44

"Just a girl," Manny said, "with Superboy's arm."

"A girl I've seen twice now," Michael said. "I didn't mention it, just 'cause I didn't think it was important, but she was watching us on Saturday when we were messing around in that pickup game."

"With that guy E-Scope?"

"Yeah."

"You talk to her?"

"I was going to, because I swear, I thought she was laughing when I was pitching to him that day. Like she found it funny."

"Well, dude, maybe she just noticed how funny you looked, even from a distance," Manny said.

"Very funny," Michael said. "And don't call me dude."

They looked over. She was watching them, keeping her distance still, throwing the ball up in the air.

Catching it with her glove behind her back.

Michael held up his glove. Telling her, Throw it back.

She did.

On the fly, again.

She was right-handed. She had, Michael could see, a beautiful motion, graceful, as if it wasn't taking any effort at all to throw the ball as far as she was throwing it. Inside his own head, not wanting to give Manny any kind of opening, Michael thought:

She definitely does not throw like a girl.

"We gotta meet her," he said.

"Okay," Manny said, "but let me do the talking."

Michael said, "What's that supposed to mean?"

"It means that you do not possess the ability to talk to girls in any sort of coherent manner."

"Coherent manner?" Michael said. "Did you get that out of one of your books?"

Manny Cabrera, Michael knew, didn't just love baseball and

dancing and watching movies. And maybe Maria Cuellar. He loved to read, too, even if that was another secret he kept from their teammates. He loved to read books that weren't even assigned on their Summer Reading list. So he was always dropping what sounded like grown-up expressions on Michael.

Manny shook his head now. "Actually," he said, "Jim Kaat used that one with Michael Kay on the Yankee game the other day, saying that when there's a runner on second who could be stealing signs, Joe Johnson doesn't always put down his signs in what would be considered a coherent manner."

"Whatever," Michael said. "And I can too talk to girls. I talk to Maria more than you do."

"I'm talking about talking to girls you don't know," Manny said. "Which is when you turn into one of those guys in the scary movies who can't even get their screams out."

"Do not."

"Do," Manny said. "Infinity."

Michael looked back over at the mystery girl. She was still there.

"Let's go, before she disappears again," Michael said.

The two of them started walking toward her.

She didn't run this time.

7

Her T-shirt read:

> *Girls Rule.*
> *Boys Drool.*

She said her name was Ellie.

"Ellie Garcia," she said, and then gave them a look Michael couldn't read, as if she knew something they didn't. Or was just trying to act mysterious, which is something girls did all the time.

Manny said they couldn't help it, it was in their DNA.

After Manny handled the introductions for them, Michael said, "You didn't try to escape today."

"I didn't run away the other day. I was just late to be somewhere."

Up close, she was the most beautiful girl Michael had ever seen. This, he knew, was an observation coming from a boy who had no real interest in girls, other than his usual observation about them, which was how different they were from guys. "That will change, sooner than you think," Carlos always said when they'd have a conversation about girls. "I have no time for them," Michael would say back and Carlos would laugh and say, "Oh, you'll make time."

Michael wasn't so sure about that. All he knew with this girl right in front of him, not a hundred yards away now, was this:

Ellie Garcia was different from all the other girls.

"How old are you?" he said in a voice as loud as a door slamming.

Ellie jumped as if Michael had yelled directly into her ear.

Manny put a hand on Michael's shoulder. "Someday," he said, "my friend's dream is to host his own interview show on television. I would say like *Total Request Live,* except he doesn't watch MTV. No baseball highlights."

"Very funny," Michael said.

He felt himself coloring the way he knew he did when he was embarrassed. Manny liked to say it turned his coloring from baseball glove to New York Mets orange.

Ellie smiled. "I turned twelve last month."

Her accent, Michael noticed, was slightly heavier than his own. But pretty somehow. The way she was.

"Where are you from?" Michael said.

"The interview continues," Manny said.

"The Bronx," Ellie said.

At the same moment both Michael and Manny said, "Which part?"

All three of them laughed.

Ellie pointed to her left, at the cars going north on the Deegan. "Up there," she said. "But how come you two get to ask all the questions?"

"We don't," Manny said. "Your turn. And don't worry, I'm like Radio Shack, if you've got questions, I've got answers."

Ellie said, "I have no idea what you're talking about."

"Join the club," Michael said.

"Okay," Ellie said, "I'll keep it simple: Who are you guys?"

Manny then tried to tell her both his and Michael's life stories in the space of about five minutes. What his father did, where he lived, where they went to school. How Michael and Carlos and Papi had come over on the boat.

Everything except what had happened to Papi.

48

When he finally stopped, just to take a breath, Ellie said to Michael, "You're Cuban? Really?"

"Cuban American now," he said. "That's what I'm taught to say." He tilted his head at her. "Where are you from?"

The mystery look again. Same small smile.

"Oh, I'm from the Caribbean, too," she said.

"Ellie Garcia," Manny said. "From somewhere in the Bronx and somewhere in the Caribbean before that. The girl who shows up out of nowhere to throw like a boy."

"And you, Mr. Manny Cabrera, talk more than any of my girl-friends," she said.

Michael laughed too loudly at that one. Manny gave him his shut-up look.

Michael asked Ellie if she could hang around for a while.

"Does that mean you're asking me to play?" she said.

He said, yeah, he guessed he was.

Then Michael said, "I can't tell who's the cat here and who's the little mouse . . . "

"You're the cat," Ellie said. "Like one my father used to sing to me about when I was little. Misifuz the cat."

Michael couldn't believe his ears. "*My* father used to sing me the same song!" he said. " '*Misifuz dormido en su cama está.*' "

"Misifuz the cat is sleeping on the bed," she said.

Michael said, "I thought it was just a Cuban song."

"My father told me it was *our* song," she said.

They both knew about Misifuz.

Cool, he thought.

She reached into his glove, took the ball out, smiled at him one last time, again looking to Michael like there was some joke she wouldn't let him in on.

"I'll pitch," she said.

And Michael said he'd catch for a change.

"A left-handed catcher?" Ellie said.

"As much as it physically pains me to admit this, he's not just the best pitcher on our team, he's the best catcher, too," Manny said. "And the best center fielder and . . ."

"Enough," Michael said.

Ellie said to Manny, "But I thought you were the catcher."

"Only because he's the best pitcher and the best center fielder," Manny said.

"Please shut up and hit," Michael said.

They agreed that everybody would get ten hits, then they'd go pick up whatever balls were scattered around the field before somebody else took a turn at bat.

The problem for Manny was getting his bat on the ball ten times.

He hit a few of Ellie's pitches at the start, when she wasn't throwing her hardest. But when she turned up the heat, the way Michael did when he got loose, Manny started to miss. Badly.

Finally he dribbled one to where the second baseman would have been, which made nine hits for him.

"Okay," Michael said to his friend. "Two outs, bottom of the ninth, runners on second and third, our team down by a run. Base hit sends us to Williamsport."

"There's an open base," Manny said. "If she knows what's good for her, she'll walk me."

"Bases loaded then, smart guy. No place to put you."

"Does that mean I can pitch from a full windup?" Ellie said.

Manny whistled through his teeth, the way he did when he was impressed by something. "She's good," he said.

Michael said, "An ice cream says you don't put the ball in play."

"Make it both our dinners at McDonald's. We were going there, anyway. You okay with that?"

"I'm good," Michael said, "Carlos gave me money."

"It's on then."

Manny fixed his helmet, dug in the way he did with his back foot, the one closest to Michael, wiggled his bat back and forth.

Ellie threw one past him, down the middle, a blazer, for strike one.

As Michael threw the ball back, Manny said, "Good hitters swing and miss sometimes on a pitch they like, so the pitcher will throw it again."

"I never heard that one," Michael said.

Ellie threw strike two past him. Same place, maybe a little closer to the outside corner.

"That pitch you wanted her to throw again?" Michael said, trying not to grin. "I think she just threw it."

Manny kept his eyes on the girl. "Shut up," he said to Michael.

"But," Michael said, ignoring him, "if I'm following your thinking here, you've got her right where you want her."

Manny wiggled his bat harder, his face suddenly serious, as if this were a real game, real bottom of the ninth, the field full of players instead of just the three of them on an afternoon Michael suddenly wanted to last forever.

Now Michael watched as Ellie went into the same high-kick windup Michael used—was she trying to copy him?—and threw a total screamer, a smoke alarm, past Manny Cabrera for strike three.

When the ball was in Michael's glove, he looked out at her. She hadn't even changed expression. Or maybe she was just trying to keep a straight face. She didn't say anything and neither did he and neither did Manny. Michael hadn't even moved his glove yet.

Of course Manny spoke first.

He dropped his bat, turned to Michael, and in a little-boy voice said, "I could use a hug."

They all laughed again.

Ellie had a good laugh, Michael noticed. She wasn't shy when she laughed, or embarrassed. Just happy.

When they stopped, Ellie said to Michael, "I haven't had a chance to hit against you yet."

"I've already thrown enough today," he said. "And, besides, we've got a game tomorrow."

Ellie put a hand on her hip, tilted her head a little, gave him a suspicious look. "Afraid a girl might get a hit off you?" she said.

"No," he said. "I'm never afraid somebody might get a hit."

"Is that bragging?"

"No, no, no," Michael said. Blushing again, he knew. "I just mean that putting your best up against somebody else's, that's not something that should make you afraid. That's the fun of it all."

He wanted to explain to this girl he'd just met that there were plenty of things that made him afraid, just not baseball.

Baseball always made him happy.

Never happier than today, he thought.

"And if I did pitch to you, and let you get a hit, you'd know it," Michael said.

"How do you know that?" Ellie said.

"Because you're just like me," Michael said.

They were sitting in the grass, a few yards from home plate. Manny had gone to get his cell phone out of his bat bag, saying he had to call his mom. Ellie said she had to go soon. Michael asked, "Where?"

Ellie answered, "No more questions for today."

As she said it, Michael saw that her eyes were focused on the area behind home plate, on the other side of the screen. "Who's that with Manny?" she asked.

"Who's *who* with Manny?" Michael asked in return.

"The policeman and the other man," she said.

MICHAEL RECOGNIZED THE POLICEMAN WHO HAD HANDCUFFED THE PURSE stealer after Michael had hit him with the longest knockdown pitch ever, put the guy down not too far from where he and Ellie were sitting right now.

The other man wore a white shirt and a tie, even in the heat, carrying his jacket over his arm. He was smiling at Manny, then nodding, then laughing at something Manny said. Then lifting his chin and nodding in Michael's direction.

"Do you know them?" Ellie said.

"The policeman I do. Officer Crandall is his name. Officer Mark Crandall. I met him the other day."

"And who's that with him?" She was trying to angle her body to get a better look, because the policeman had moved now and was blocking her view.

"An Official Person," Michael said, knowing he was talking in capital letters.

"How can you tell?" Ellie grinned. "Officially, I mean."

"I just can."

Now he saw the Official Person giving Manny a friendly shove in their direction, the kind the coach gives you when he tells you to go get in the game. Manny jogged toward the outfield while Officer Crandall and his friend sat down on the home team's bench, on the first-base side of the field.

Michael got up now. So did Ellie.

When Manny was about twenty yards away, Michael couldn't wait any longer. "Who is that?" he said.

54

Ellie had moved a few steps closer to home plate, squinting into the sun at the two men. Before Manny could answer, she said, "He works for the Bronx borough president, Mr. Amorosa. I forget his exact job."

Manny said, "He works in public relations for Mr. Amorosa. He says his name is Mr. Lima." He stared at Ellie. "But how do you know him?"

Michael thought Ellie seemed nervous all of a sudden, even though he had no idea what she had to be nervous about. "I met him one time," she said. "With my dad."

"Anyway," Manny said to Michael, "he wants to meet you, is all. It turns out Officer Crandall said something to one of his superiors about what you did with Ramon—that was the thief's name, Ramon—and the superior said something, and it somehow ended up in Mr. Amorosa's office. Mr. Lima says they want you . . . and your parents . . . to come down and have your picture taken with Mr. Amorosa. People hear so much about crime in the South Bronx, he said, they want to play up their twelve-year-old crimestopper."

Michael felt himself looking all around Macombs Dam Park now, all corners of the green grass, everywhere except at the two men on the home team's bench.

He was never, under any conditions, supposed to talk to any Official Person without Carlos. The only reason that he had talked to Officer Crandall that day was because he had no choice. He had been afraid that if he ran off when he saw a policeman coming, he would look as guilty as that Ramon guy.

"What did you tell him?" Michael said. "Mr. Lima, I mean."

"You see him laughing before?" Manny said. "I tried to make a joke of it. I told them they were talking to your agent, and that I'd have to clear it with you first. That's when Mr. Lima told me to go clear it already."

Manny turned now, put on his biggest smile, waved at the two men, held up a finger. One more moment, please.

From behind them, Michael heard Ellie say, "I've got to go." He turned his head and saw her running toward Ruppert Place, the same as she had the first day.

"Wait!" he yelled at her back.

But she kept running, around the end of the basketball court, up the hill, toward the flow of people heading for the gates at Yankee Stadium.

She held up her hand in some kind of wave without breaking stride.

Michael looked at her, looked back at Officer Crandall and Mr. Lima, said to Manny, "Wait for me at McDonald's."

He ran after her.

"Michael, wait!" Manny said. "What the heck am I going to tell them?"

Over his shoulder, glove in his right hand, one ball still in the pocket, chasing after the baseball girl, one who seemed to have secrets of her own, Michael smiled, even as scared as he was.

"Tell them the truth," he shouted at Manny. "Tell them this is the first day of my whole life that I started chasing girls."

Only when he looked up the hill, she was gone.

Again.

There was another policeman right in front of Michael as he came racing up the hill, on this street where he always imagined his baseball world ended and the Yankees' began.

He wanted to ask the man if he had seen a pretty girl with a baseball glove under her arm.

Then he stopped to catch his breath, imagining how a scene like that would play itself out. What was he going to ask this policeman, had he seen a girl with a baseball glove outside the Stadium before a home game?

The man would probably look at him and say, "I've seen about fifty, would you care to narrow it down a little bit?"

Michael knew there was no point in even looking for Ellie up here. Or asking anybody for help. Or trying to explain why this friend of his, a girl friend, was running away from him in the first place.

So he slowed down now and walked right past the policeman, who seemed to be guarding the Stadium Club entrance to the Stadium. When he got to the corner of 161st and Ruppert, he stopped to look back on the field at Macombs Dam Park, saw Manny in the distance, walking away from the Little League field with Officer Crandall on one side of him and Mr. Lima on the other.

Michael could see Manny chattering away, talking with his mouth and his hands at the same time, in a way that always made Michael wonder if the hands were trying to keep up with the mouth, or if it was the other way around. He saw Manny look up at one man, then the other, then saw both men start to laugh.

Manny the Entertainer. Like that guy Cedric the Entertainer in the movies.

It had been such a perfect day, Michael thought to himself. Him and Manny and Ellie Garcia, laughing and playing ball and inventing games and being happy to be on the field, and with each other. A perfect summer day when it was as if Michael could hypnotize himself, make himself believe that everything was going to work out right, that the Clippers would make it to Williamsport, that he and Carlos wouldn't be found out before Carlos turned eighteen.

That he and his brother would always be together.

Except now an Official Person had come to his field, which in the summer was as much his home as 825 Gerard.

What was he going to do the next time this Mr. Lima came around?

Michael felt himself shiver, even though the heat of the day had carried over into early evening, to when the Yankee game was set to begin.

They knew where to find him now.

It was Carlos's regular night off from Hector's, so he and Michael and Manny were chowing down on all the food Manny and Michael had brought from McDonald's, listening to the Yankee game on the radio.

Actually, Michael was doing most of the listening while Manny caught Carlos up on what had happened at the field. As always, Manny made himself out to be the hero of everything. It was another part of their deal, except on the ballfield. Once they got to the ballfield, Manny was always content, or so it seemed to Michael, to play the part of sidekick.

"They definitely asked you for Michael's last name?" Carlos asked Manny.

"I thought about giving them a middle name or something, just to throw them off for now," Manny said, his mouth full of fries. "But if they found out later that I'd lied about something that easy to find out, I figured they'd be asking themselves why I lied about something that easy to find out."

"But they didn't ask you for an address?" Carlos said.

"Nah," Manny said.

He looked at Michael across the table. "You gonna finish your fries?" he said. Michael shook his head. Manny grabbed a handful, said, "I think they were probably about to ask me where, but it was right then that my boy here decided to run after his new sweetie."

"I was running away from them," Michael said. "And she is not my sweetie, dorkball."

Michael got up and walked over to where the radio sat on the coffee table, wanting to hear better, and not wanting to have Manny catch him blushing. Again.

Top of the third for the Orioles, runners on second and third against El Grande.

Two outs.

Manny wouldn't let up, of course. "You told me you were running after her, remember?" Manny said.

"Shhhhh," Michael said.

Then listened as John Sterling, the Yankee announcer, his voice excited, said "Heeeeeee struck out him out," and El Grande was out of the inning.

At least somebody was winning something today.

THE HAD DRIVEN UP TO NEW ROCHELLE TO PLAY WESTCHESTER SOUTH— the team they all thought of as the Justins now—in the old blue bus from the small bus company near the Third Avenue Bridge that Mr. Minaya managed, in what he called his day job.

Manny joked with Mr. Minaya that the shock absorbers from this particular bus seemed to have turned into shock producers, but the kids loved the old bus, anyway, loved the idea of any kind of road trip out of the Bronx, just because it made them feel big.

The field in New Rochelle turned out to be beautiful, the infield and outfield grass looking as if they were being cared for by big-league groundskeepers like Kel's dad. Even the infield dirt had been raked before they got there. There were colorful ads for local stores on outfield walls that looked pretty close to Michael— pitchers always noticed—and a concessions truck set up in the parking lot behind home plate, and even new-looking bleachers on both sides of the field, for the home team and the visitors, not that the Clippers ever had many parents who made road trips.

Michael even noticed what looked like a small green press box set up on the Westchester South side of the field, even though he couldn't imagine what kind of press would want to be covering their game. Maybe the public address announcer sat up there; they had heard somebody testing a microphone, a voice coming from unseen speakers, when they had filed out of the bus.

When he heard the voice coming from the speakers, Manny immediately turned himself into the Yankees' PA announcer, the one who sounded like the voice of God. "Now coming in to pitch for the

Clippers," Manny said, making his voice even deeper than Anthony's. "Michael Arroyo. Number thirty-three." Pause. "Arroyo."

Michael said, "I'm not sure that's exactly how he does it, the Yankee guy."

"Close enough," Manny said.

Michael said, "I still think it needs work."

"I sound exactly like him and you know it," Manny said. "Jealousy does not become you, Star. I'm just telling you that as a friend."

"I try to keep it under control," Michael said.

Justin the Jerk started for Westchester South.

As far as Michael and the guys could tell, he spent more time before the game staring Michael down than warming up.

After they had finished taking infield and outfield practice and were back at their bench, Anthony Fierro came up to Michael. Anthony could be just as funny as Manny, he just didn't try as hard.

Or as often.

"Blondie Boy seems to think this is the finals of the Olympic Staredown event," Anthony said.

Anthony was about the same shape as Justin. A little shorter than Michael, but heavier, and solid. One time in a game, there had been a grounder to Anthony at first, and Michael thought he had to get off the mound and cover first base. Only at the last second, Anthony decided to sprint for the base himself. They arrived at the same moment, Michael couldn't get out of the way, and the two of them collided.

Michael ended up about halfway to the home team's bench at Macombs. The star, Manny had said to him later, seeing stars.

Anthony, Michael knew, wasn't afraid of anybody or anything.

"That guy's a punk, you can just see it," he said.

61

"All I did was strike him out," Michael said.

Kel said, "Seems like the boy's still got some issues going for him on that there."

Justin was staring at them from the mound now, while his team took infield practice. Kel stepped forward, gave the kid what he called his "buggy look," eyes all wide. Giving a little shake to his head as he did.

"Kel," Michael said. "You've got to lead off tonight, and he's got the ball."

Manny said, "Yeah, but you've got it later."

They went and sat down next to Manny on the bench, giving him room, because he was doing what he did before every game, neatly laying out his equipment. Mask. Chest protector. Shin guards. Manny called them his instruments.

Anthony nodded at his instruments now. "You know what they really call a catcher's stuff?"

Manny was fiddling with the straps on his shin guards. "What?"

"The tools of ignorance," Anthony said, then put his hand up, as if inviting high fives from the group.

"I'm not even dignifying your ignorance with a comment," Manny said. "*You're* a tool of ignorance."

That got a laugh out of everybody.

From the mound, they heard old Justin say, "What's so funny?"

Manny, who couldn't keep a thought inside his head sometimes, said, "You are, Skippy."

The guy bit. "My name's not Skippy."

Kel stood up, stared out at him. "But you look exactly like a Skippy, no lie."

"Why don't you come out here and say that?" Justin said, gesturing with what looked like a pretty expensive glove.

Anthony stood up now, stepped in front of Kel. "Hey, dude, why don't you take a chill pill?"

Then Mr. Minaya appeared, as if out of nowhere, and shooed them all back on the bench, reminding them about the team rule: No trash talk.

Ever.

Under any circumstances.

No matter how much trash the other side was talking at them.

"Now quiet down," he said.

As usual, Manny thought "quiet down" applied to everybody on the team except him.

"Well, as my mom likes to say," he said, "this should certainly be a festive occasion."

Little did they know.

10

It was the top of the fourth inning.

Manny pointed to Justin.

"He may be as pretty as Brad Pitt," Manny said. "But the boy can pitch."

"Like, mad pitch," Kel said, Justin having struck him out twice now.

Michael was used to the way Kel talked by now, and how his cool way of talking seemed to influence the other guys on the team, and Maria, too. So "mad" with him was a way of amping up whatever word came next. Maria was mad good-looking. Michael had, like, a mad arm. Chris Rock, who Michael only got to see in the movies, never on television, was mad funny.

Like that.

"Before," Anthony Fierro said now, "we thought the guy was just mad, period."

"Dude," Kel said, using another one of his favorite words, one he could make into a question, an exclamation point, show surprise with, anger, anything. Sometimes, like now, he used it to end the conversation, as if saying, case closed on old Justin.

Michael didn't need to look at the scorebook to know that he was the only one on the Clippers Justin hadn't struck out yet. Michael was batting third today. Justin had come up and in on him his first time up, knocking Michael back off the plate and then glaring at him again afterward. But Michael had gotten back into the left-handers' side of the batter's box, dug back in, and promptly taken a low, outside pitch over the third baseman's head and into

64

the left-field corner of the cool ballpark, the ball rolling all the way to a Home Depot sign out there.

As Michael came flying around second, he saw their left fielder having trouble picking the ball up and just kept motoring into third, cap flying off his head.

Stand-up triple.

"Are you always this lucky?" Justin said when he got the ball back.

Michael ignored him. Thinking: I've never talked to a base runner in my life. Instead he turned to Mr. Minaya, who was coaching third. But Justin was still talking. Now Michael heard him say, "Great job out there!" Michael wondered what that meant until he turned back around and saw Justin pointing to his left fielder. Yelling at him in front of everybody for the crime of giving Michael an extra base.

The kid out there just got into his ready defensive position, like he was studying the grass at his feet for some kind of test later.

On the first pitch to Anthony, who was up next, Justin tried to throw the ball about two hundred miles per hour, and bounced the ball in front of his catcher, who had absolutely no chance to even block the ball. It rolled all the way to the backstop and Michael could have walked home—backward—with the Clippers' first run of the game.

This time when Justin the Jerk got the ball back he snapped at his catcher, "Get in front of the stupid ball."

To the catcher's credit, he said, "With what, the snack truck?"

Their coach stepped right out on that one and waggled his finger at the catcher. Not Justin. "Hey, Brendan," the coach said. "Just catch."

Manny said, "That's not just any coach. That's Justin's old man, I guarantee it."

Westchester South tied it off Anthony in the bottom of the fourth. Justin doubled with two outs, and later came around to score when Anthony walked the next three hitters. Then the same thing happened to Justin in the top of the fifth: He started walking guys all over the place. "He's lost the strike zone," Manny said on the bench, using one of Mr. Minaya's favorite expressions. Losing the strike zone. It made Michael smile, the way a lot of old-time baseball expressions did. Sometimes he imagined a whole team on their hands and knees, searching for the strike zone the way the Clippers did one time when Anthony lost one of his contact lenses.

It began when Justin walked Maria on four pitches even though she hadn't made contact with the ball the whole game. A girl. They were afraid on the bench it would make Justin's head explode. So it was no surprise when he walked the next hitter, Kel, on five pitches.

Then, with Justin's face getting redder and redder with each ball out of the strike zone, even whining to the umpire a couple of times on pitches that weren't even close, he walked Manny to load the bases.

Michael was up again.

The count went to three-and-oh, all three of the pitches high and wide. Brendan, the catcher, Michael could see out of the corner of his eye, twice had to make diving backhand catches to keep Maria at third base.

The coach, who they were sure now was Justin's dad, stood up in front of their bench.

"Just relax and throw strikes," he said.

Michael stepped out and smiled, he couldn't help himself. It was always the dumbest thing he heard from any coach in any game. Relax and throw strikes. Right. He'd look out and see some eleven- or twelve-year-old pitcher about to squeeze the seams off the ball, about to start crying because he couldn't throw a strike to save his life, and the coach would think the perfect thing to say was, Relax.

Throw strikes.

Justin thought Michael was laughing at him.

"You think this is funny?" Justin yelled in at him.

"Huh?" Michael said.

"Just pitch, son," the umpire said.

"He's laughing at me," Justin said.

"No I'm not," Michael said.

The ump said, "Play ball."

Justin went into his full windup and threw a fastball that hit Michael in the head.

The first thing Michael saw when he opened his eyes was the worried face of Manny Cabrera, close enough to Michael that he could smell the Orbit Bubblemint gum his friend was constantly chomping on.

"I know you think this is what heaven will look like," Manny said. "But you're not dead."

Mr. Minaya was crouched next to Manny. Standing behind them, Michael could see Kel, Maria, Anthony. Chris Nourse, their third baseman.

He sat up now. Mr. Minaya said, "Slowly."

Michael said, "I'm okay."

"Okay then," Mr. Minaya said.

Michael realized his helmet was gone. "Where'd it get me?" he said, because he honestly couldn't remember. He just remembered the ball coming for his eyeballs, turning away, hearing the ball on his helmet, hitting the deck.

Manny said, "Tip of the helmet."

"The bill," Mr. Minaya said.

"Check it out," Manny said.

He held up Michael's batting helmet for him to see. The bill was all crooked now, as if one of the wheels of their old bus had rolled over it.

Mr. Minaya said, "How's the head?"

Manny said, "Hard," obviously convinced that everything was going to be all right now that Michael was up and talking.

"It doesn't hurt, actually," Michael said.

"I can't believe they didn't throw that puss out of the game," Manny said.

Mr. Minaya said, "His dad pointed out that since he couldn't hit the catcher's glove when he wanted to, how could he hit Michael's head."

"But he thought Michael was laughing at him," Manny said.

"Hush," Mr. Minaya said.

Miraculously, Manny did.

Now Mr. Minaya said, "Mike, I'm gonna take you out."

"No!" Michael said.

It came out of him with more force than he intended.

Mr. Minaya put a hand on his shoulder. "I know what a gamer you are," he said. "But you just took the hardest fastball I've seen this season—next to yours—in the coconut."

"Helmet," Michael said.

The truth was, his head did hurt, but only around his forehead, where the helmet must have scraped him as Justin's high hard one had twisted it around. "Please let me stay in," Michael said.

"Hey guys," they all heard now.

Michael turned and saw the umpire standing over him. He didn't look much older than Carlos, but he had been doing a good job calling balls and strikes, and hustling down to first when there was a ground ball, since he was working alone. Some of the umps they ran into acted as if they didn't want to be there, as if they were just going through the motions until they got paid and got out of there.

This ump, Michael could see, cared about the game, doing things right. Michael always picked up on it right away, a passion for baseball, like they were wearing a sign.

The ump hunched down next to him. "You okay?"

"Yes sir."

"Is he staying in?" To Mr. Minaya.

Mr. Minaya looked at Michael, then at the umpire. "He is."

Manny helped Michael to his feet. The Westchester South parents clapped. Maria, who had scored on the play, handed Michael her batting helmet, since in Little League you had to wear a helmet on the bases.

Justin, soft-tossing with his third baseman to stay warm, didn't even turn around.

"Please, pretty please, tell me that punk is going down," Manny said, his voice low.

"Oh, he's going down," Michael said, and jogged down to first base.

He missed with his first two pitches of the bottom of the sixth, the Clippers still holding on to their 2–1 lead. Maybe I'm having a delayed reaction, he thought, going behind the mound to rub up a baseball they'd been using for three innings. He had been beaned. He could never understand that expression, either. Did that mean your head was a bean? Or the ball? Even now, following the twists and turns of English made him feel like he was trying to read one of those subway maps they had on the walls of the trains. . . .

Now all his teammates cared about was if he was going to bean Justin or not.

Manny had just come out to remind him Justin was up third in the inning.

"Go," Michael said. "Catch."

"Go, Manny," Manny said. "Sit, Manny. You ever notice you talk to me like a dog sometimes?"

When Manny got halfway back to the plate, Michael couldn't help it. "Good boy," he said. Then he threw three straight blazers. The guy swung and missed at all of them. One out.

Three more to the second guy. The kid, a black kid who seemed to be smiling the whole game, whether things were going good for his team or not, was walking back to the bench before the ump even called strike three.

Two outs.

Justin now.

Manny called time. Anthony came in from first, Kel from short, Chris Nourse from third. Maria stayed at second, saying to Michael, "You guys just do your guy thing, I'm fine here."

Manny said, "You owe the sucker one."

Kel said, "Check it out: You could hit the next three of those suckers and still win the game."

Anthony, who never came to the mound, mostly because he didn't need to when Michael was pitching, took off his cap, rubbed a hand over his new buzz cut, and grinned. "Buzz him," he said.

The ump, Michael saw, had come out in front of the plate to stand with his hands on his hips. "How's about we save the rest of this for instant-messaging later?"

They all left.

The ump turned and walked back to the plate. As he did, Michael saw Mr. Minaya get up off the bench and take a few steps toward the field, as if he knew what they had all been talking about on the mound. Michael looked over and Mr. Minaya gave him a look that said, Don't.

Michael got ready to pitch. Justin did his big-leaguer pose, fiddling with his two batting gloves, motioning with his right hand for the umpire to wait while he dug in. When he was ready, he finally looked out at Michael.

He's scared, Michael thought.

He would never say this out loud, but he knew exactly why Justin was scared.

Because as hard as he throws, I throw harder.

Michael went into his high-kick windup, ducked his head behind his glove, brought his arm forward as hard as he ever had.

And threw the only curveball he was going to throw all season.

And not just any curve. Michael threw the kind of big, slow hook that El Grande would throw sometimes, one that seemed to float out of the sky like a Frisbee, one that the radar gun would clock at fifty miles an hour sometimes.

Justin was a left-handed hitter, too. As easy as Michael threw the ball, all Justin saw was the ball coming for his fat head, which is why he fell away from it, bat flying out of his hands, as if Michael were trying to drill a hole through his helmet.

Except that as the ball started to lose altitude, it also started to break, breaking down, spinning right into Manny's mitt about belt high as the umpire held up his right hand and yelled, "Stee-rike!"

The Clippers did nothing. Not even Manny, who seemed speechless for the first time in his life. It was Justin's teammates who laughed at how silly Michael had made him look. When Justin got back up, Michael could see the back of his uniform full of dirt. He glared at his own bench now, quickly got back into the batter's box, looking as if he wanted to hit the next pitch into the parking lot. "Go ahead," he said to Michael, "throw that junk again, see what happens."

Michael shook his head, like he was shaking off Manny. "Nah," he said.

Manny put down one finger and Michael threw a fastball past Justin, who took a violent cut and missed. Then Michael did it again.

Strike three.

Game over.

After Michael had gotten high fives from his teammates in back of the mound, he turned around to see Justin still standing at home plate.

"How old are you, really?" he called out.

Michael just stared.

"Don't you understand English?" Justin said. "I asked you a question."

"I'm twelve," Michael said, knowing as he did he shouldn't have been talking to the guy.

Justin wouldn't let it go.

"What'd you do, drop a couple of years on the boat over, like you guys do?"

Manny stepped in now.

"Dude," he said, "you're lucky you didn't drop a little something there on strike one."

Justin walked away then, as if he wasn't paying any attention, waving them off, not looking back.

Michael watched him go.

Wondering how a kid from Westchester knew anything about his boat ride over.

And why he even stinking cared?

11

MR. LIMA, FROM THE BRONX BOROUGH PRESIDENT'S OFFICE, THE MAN FROM the park, in his white shirt and tie, was in front of 825 Gerard when Mr. Minaya dropped Michael off after the Westchester South game.

Mrs. C was with him.

She was sitting in the lawn chair she would set up on the sidewalk sometimes, on warm summer nights like this. Sometimes some of the older people in the building would be there with her, with chairs of their own or just sitting on the front steps, listening to music on a battery-powered radio one of them would bring with them. Or somebody would open one of the front windows, in one of the first-floor apartments facing the street, and they would listen to one of the Spanish-music stations. Unless the men would win out and there would be a Yankee game on. Sometimes, if the game was on, Michael would come down and sit with them, imagining that the residents of 825 Gerard were one big family, with Mrs. Cora the grandma of them all.

Mostly the old people would just talk, in English and Spanish, like they were making two languages into one, and watch the world go by.

Michael wanted it to go by 825 Gerard right now.

He felt his heart racing inside him as if he'd just gone from first to third on a single. Or as if he'd run all the way here from New Rochelle.

Maybe getting hit in the head wasn't going to be the worst thing that happened to him tonight.

Usually Mrs. C didn't get out of her lawn chair until she was ready to go to bed. She would joke that picking herself up was even harder at the end of the day than walking up the hill from River Avenue. But she got right up out of her chair now, no problem, popped up like one of those little pop-up messages he'd see at Manny's when Manny would make him watch a music video on MTV, greeted Michael like he really was her grandson.

Her long-lost grandson.

Mrs. C hugged him to her so fiercely, Michael had trouble breathing for a second, kissed the side of his head, and whispered, "Say as little as possible, little one."

Then she pulled back and plopped back down in her chair as Mr. Lima came over and put out his hand.

"Fred Lima, son," he said. "Press secretary for Mr. Amorosa, the borough president for these parts."

Making the Bronx sound a little bit like the Old West or something.

Michael shook the man's hand the way Papi had taught him, firmly, looking him right in the eye.

"Michael Arroyo," he said.

"Finally I get to meet the boy hero," Mr. Lima said.

Manny always said that the only player on the team who never got nervous was Michael.

Except now.

"I just got lucky, is all," he said.

He looked up Gerard, to where some kids were playing catch with a football, and imagined himself sprinting past them, away, the way he'd sprinted away from Mr. Lima the other night.

"Not what I hear," Mr. Lima said. "I hear that the only twelve-year-old who could have made that throw is the twelve-year-old who did."

Michael looked at Mrs. C. She said, "Just say thank you, little one."

"Thank you," he said, looking down.

Mr. Lima said, "Mrs. Cora here tells me that she's sort of been looking out for you and your brother while your dad's out of town."

Mrs. Cora jumped right in, not waiting for Michael to answer. "You should see the two of them eat my *paella,*" she said. She pointed at Michael. "But this one here," she said, "no matter how much he eats, he stays as skinny as one of my sewing needles."

Now no one said anything. From one of the high windows, Michael could hear the voices of the Yankee announcers. Where were they tonight? Detroit? Chicago?

Chicago. To play the White Sox.

Mr. Lima cleared his throat. "Well," he said, "I'm glad I finally tracked you down, Mr. Michael Arroyo. The other day I would have needed one of those little motor scooters the police use to ride around the Stadium to catch up with you."

Michael said, "I was running after my girlfriend."

Girlfriend? That came out a little too easily.

Mrs. Cora said, "My Michael has a new girlfriend?"

"She's a girl, and a friend, Mrs. C. Somebody I met in the park."

Then he yawned. It just came out of him, the way it did on the mound sometimes. Manny thought it just showed how super-relaxed he was, no matter how close the game. Michael knew better: The yawn meant he was feeling some nerves. He heard Tom Seaver on a Mets game one time say how he used to yawn in big spots and his teammates all thought he was crazy. It made him feel better, a little less crazy about his own yawning.

He covered it now by saying to Mr. Lima, "I'm kind of tired, sir. We had a tough game tonight, and I was going to head upstairs and listen to the Yankees–White Sox game until my brother comes home."

"Carlos," Mr. Lima said. "Going into his senior year of high school, right?"

Everybody knew everything all of a sudden.

Almost everything.

"Right," Michael said.

"Well," Mr. Lima said, "since I'd never want to keep a good Bronx boy from listening to his favorite team, let me tell you what I've been telling Mrs. Cora here, since she turns out to be the one whose purse you rescued: We'd like to have you and her and your brother and your father, if he gets back in the next couple of days, come down and have your picture taken with Mr. Amorosa. And Officer Crandall, of course."

Michael said, "Oh, you don't have to go to all that trouble."

"We want to, that's the thing," Mr. Lima said. "And it's no trouble, really. This is the kind of story, right from our neighborhoods, that people need to know about. A boy from the neighborhood coming to the aid of a woman like Mrs. Cora, one who turns out to be one of his best friends. In the process, the boy isn't just a friend to her, but to the police."

Mrs. C started to say something but Mr. Lima put up a hand, smiling. "Please, I promise this is the end of my speech," he said. "There's still too many people who only want to talk about crime in the Bronx, even though we're much safer now than we've ever been. We want to shine a spotlight on a crimestopper."

He handed Michael his business card. "Tell your dad about it when you talk to him," he said. "Will he be calling you tonight?"

"Probably not," Michael said, looking off.

He looked at the card. There was a business phone number,

a home phone number, a cell phone number, a fax number, an e-mail address.

"Or you can just have your dad call me directly," Mr. Lima said. "We'll set something up for next week maybe."

He leaned down, shook Mrs. Cora's hand, told her it was nice chatting with her, and not to get up.

"Don't worry," she said, "I won't."

Mr. Lima shook Michael's hand one more time, then said he was going to go jump on the next train and head home.

"Your father must be very proud of you," he said to Michael, and was gone.

For now.

"What are we going to do?" Michael said.

"Eat," Mrs. Cora said, extending her hand in a way that meant Michael needed to help her up this time. "I made pot roast."

"I meant . . . ," Michael said, folding up the lawn chair.

"I know what you meant, little one," she said. "And I said, let's go eat."

Mrs. C thought food could cure just about anything.

12 ⚾⚾⚾⚾⚾⚾⚾⚾⚾⚾⚾⚾⚾

MANNY SUGGESTED THEY HIRE SOMEBODY TO PLAY THE PART OF Michael's dad.

Have the guy show up in a nice suit, Manny said, smile for the camera, say how proud he was of his little boy, and then they could all be done with it.

"Don't take this the wrong way," Michael said to him. "But you're insane."

They were in Michael's apartment in the middle of the afternoon, hanging out until the Clippers–Grand Concourse game at Macombs Dam Park. Manny had been coming up with one crazy plan after another even though Carlos had decided that they weren't going to do anything about Mr. Lima's invitation, at least not for the time being. If Mr. Lima called again, or stopped by, Carlos would say they were going to wait a few more days for their father, and if he wasn't back by next week, then they'd just have to come down to the borough president's office without him. For now their story was that their uncle had suffered a setback.

"I'm sure you understand, sir," Carlos had said, rehearsing the scene, pretending Michael was Mr. Lima. "Family has to come first."

Manny said they were just putting off the inevitable, that they should do it now and get it over with. He imagined the whole thing as a movie now, one he was making up as he went along, the kind where the kids got together and put one over on the adults.

The kind, Michael thought, that always had a happy ending.

"Work with me on this, Star," Manny said. "We could use one of the men who live in the building."

"Yeah," Michael said. "We'll get Mr. Chu, that ought to fool them."

"It's a good thing I'm the only one who sees the snippy side of you," Manny said.

He was still lying on the floor in front of the pillows they'd set up as goals in sock hockey. On his back, hands laced behind his head, eyes full of fun. Michael knew his game: If he acted as if he wasn't taking any of this too seriously then maybe Michael wouldn't worry as much.

"What about your super, Mr. Ruiz?" Manny said.

"What about him?"

"He's about the right age, he's dark like us. And," Manny said, "you seem to be the only person in the whole world he actually likes."

"Until Carlos can't come up with the rent money."

"You know my parents would help out if it ever came to that."

"You know the deal," Michael said. "Carlos and me don't want your parents to get involved. Your dad's with the fire department. It makes him an Official Person, even if he doesn't act like one. If he finds out there's no parent here, he's supposed to tell."

"He'd never tell in a million years, officially or unofficially," Manny said. "I'm getting hungry again, by the way."

"Huge surprise."

"First, back to my brilliant plan."

"No."

"We could get Mr. Ruiz to shave that ugly beard of his and that mustache, nobody'd recognize him when he's standing there like a proud papa."

Michael said, "If I let you finish the Oreos, will you drop this?"

"You didn't tell me there was a backup bag of Oreos."

"You didn't ask."

"Where?"

"Fridge. In the drawer where Carlos keeps the lettuce."

Manny rolled up into a sitting position, gave Michael what was supposed to be a mean look, disappeared into the kitchen. From in there Michael heard, "Somebody puts Oreos in with vegetables, it means they're hiding them."

He came in with a fistful of the greatest cookies ever invented and tossed one to Michael. "Back to my plan," he said.

Michael said, "We lie enough already, Man the Man. And that is no lie. Every time an adult says something, like, your father must be soooo proud, I feel like all they have to do is take one look at my face to know something's wrong."

"We just need to get through the season, Star, we both know that."

"Carlos keeps saying we will, but he never tells me what his plan is."

"He's probably afraid you'll shoot the sucker down like you do my plans," Manny said. "We need something to wash these down with." Back up, back into the kitchen, back with two glasses of milk. Sometimes Michael found himself wondering how many visits to 825 Gerard per week Manny would have to make before Carlos had to think about taking on a third job.

"You sure you've had enough snacks?" Michael said. "I wouldn't want your stomach to start growling about the fourth inning."

"Is that a dig? Are you saying I eat too much?"

"Never," Michael said. He drank down all of his milk and said, "You ready to go play baseball?"

"I can't believe you even have to ask," Manny said.

Maybe Ellie would be there today, Michael thought. Even with everything else on his mind, he never went too long these days without thinking about the pretty girl, the mystery girl, with the long legs.

Sometimes he wondered what her secrets were.

Grand Concourse was their second-to-last game before the play-offs. The Clippers had played them the very first week of the season, but Grand Concourse—their team nickname was the Pinstripers, in honor of the Yankees—didn't have three of their best kids that day, because they'd come down with some kind of stomach virus. Michael had started that game, but it was 12–0 for the Clippers after two innings and 14–0 in the fourth, at which point the slaughter rule had gone into effect. Game over.

But the Pinstripers, they knew, had become a good team after that, and were now in fourth place in District 22.

"They're going to have a little something to prove," Mr. Minaya said during batting practice. "So we're going to need our 'A game' if we want to stay in first."

Mr. Minaya talked about their "A game" a lot. Another one of his favorite expressions.

Now Manny said to Mr. Minaya, "You sure you don't think B-plus will do the job tonight?"

Before Mr. Minaya could answer, Kel said, "This close to the play-offs, when we might have to play their sorry butts again, I'm not sure we should show them our 'A' game, or even our 'B' game."

Michael smiled. "I see what Kel means, Mr. M."

Manny said, "Coach, you think Michael's saying we only need our 'C' game? Wow, I hope he's not taking them lightly."

Anthony Fierro sang, "Now we've said our ABC's . . ."

Mr. Minaya walked away, shaking his head, saying, "We've all obviously spent too much time together."

"No worries, Coach," Manny called after him. "We always give you an 'A' for effort."

"Just play hard," their coach said. "And . . ."

Together, Michael and Kel and Manny and Anthony yelled, "Have fun!"

Michael struck out the side in the top of the first, three up, three down, eleven pitches. He also hit his first over-the-fence home run of the season, a two-run job in the bottom of the first. It looked like they might be on their way to another slaughter-rule win when they scored five more runs after that, to make it 7–0. At that point Mr. Minaya announced he was going to let Michael pitch one more inning, and then was going to let Maria pitch for the first time all season.

Michael saw Ellie after he struck out the first two Pinstripers in the top of the second.

She was sitting on the hill beyond the basketball courts, by herself, as usual. He'd heard somebody on the bench say it was five minutes to seven, which meant the Yankee game was about to start. They were back from their road trip, El Grande scheduled to start against the Minnesota Twins, a team he'd nearly no-hit the other time he'd faced them this season, back in June.

Michael got two fast strikes on what was going to be his last batter of the night, unless the guy got on. Which Michael knew he wasn't going to do, not the way he felt tonight, one of those nights when he felt as if he could pitch this way for all six innings without even breaking a sweat.

One strike to go now.

For Ellie's benefit, nobody else's, he kicked his right leg even higher than usual, El Grande high, really doing it up.

But he must have moved slightly on the rubber, to where the

Pinstripers' pitcher had been pushing off into the dirt, and his left toe got stuck in a small hole there. And because of his high kick, he lost his balance.

And proceeded to fall right on his butt.

The ball still in his left hand.

Even the batter knew it was all right to step out of the box and laugh, because all of Michael's teammates, and Mr. Minaya, were doing the exact same thing.

Sitting there next to the mound, Michael couldn't help it.

He laughed, too.

Manny called time and came walking out to the mound. Michael was still down. Manny looked down at him and said, "I'm not sure what the degree of difficulty was, but you sure as heck stuck the landing."

Michael stood up, cleaned himself off as best he could, got back on the mound, and immediately looked past the basketball courts. He wanted Ellie to still be there, because he planned to hustle over there as soon as the half inning was over. At the same time, though, he hoped she had missed his clown show.

She hadn't.

It was as if she had been waiting patiently for him to look over at her. As if she knew he would. As if they really did have some kind of mental telepathy going. Because as soon as he looked at her, she went into an exaggerated high-kick motion of her own, a perfect right-hander's impression of what he'd just tried to do.

Then she was the clown show, only on purpose, staggering into a fall, rolling down the hill.

When she got to the bottom, she stood up, put her hands above her head, and applauded him. Michael could see she was laughing, too.

He shook his head as if shaking off one of Manny's signs and got back on the mound. He went with a shorter kick this time, then burned one in for strike three. When he looked past the basketball courts to see if Ellie had seen that one, she was gone.

Or maybe just hiding.

Michael thought about going over to look for her, then decided he would stay on the bench for the rest of the game, be a good teammate and cheer his team on even if he wasn't playing. So he did. Every once in a while he would remember Ellie tumbling down the hill, and smile.

One of these nights, he thought, they were going to have a lot to talk about, if she'd ever hang around long enough.

The Clippers ended up winning, 10–6. Maria gave up some runs, and they hit a few balls hard off her, but she did pretty well, pitching better than some of the guys Mr. Minaya had thrown in there during the season in blowout games, just to give them a chance. They all went rushing out to the mound after the final out, as if she were the one who'd won a World Series game, then got into the line to shake hands with the Pinstripers.

"You guys are only acting this excited because I'm a girl," she said.

"No way," Manny said. "You pitched great."

"Said a girly boy," Kel said.

Manny said, "I heard that."

It was right after that when Mr. Gibbs, the Grand Concourse coach, came over to Mr. Minaya and asked if he could have a word with him. Michael watched the two men walk down the right-field line. They stayed out there a long time, Mr. Gibbs doing most of the talking. And whatever he was saying, Michael could see that Mr. M didn't like it very much, because he kept shaking his head, taking his cap off, and rubbing his forehead hard, the way he would when something went wrong for the Clippers during a game.

When he came back to the bench, Michael asked him if something had happened during the game to make Mr. Gibbs mad.

"I wish," Mr. M said. "But it's a little more serious than that."

Then he told Michael that there had been an official complaint made by the Westchester South team, demanding that the Clippers produce Michael's birth certificate.

"But I gave you the envelope my father gave me," Michael said, knowing he had given it to Mr. M only days before Papi had died.

"You did," Mr. M said. "Just not one with your birth certificate inside."

Mr. Gibbs found out when he had somebody at the league office pull Michael's file. And what they'd come up with was the baptism certificate that the commissioners would sometimes accept for foreign-born players.

"If they'd asked me, I could have saved them the trouble of checking," Mr. M said. "Your father told me he thought your birth certificate was with the rest of the papers he brought over with him, but he couldn't find it, just the baptism certificate. Which I've used plenty of times in the past."

Mr. Gibbs said that as far as he knew, nobody had ever questioned the authenticity of one of those baptism certificates until now. But that unfortunately, everything was different now in Little League baseball, especially in the Bronx, ever since Danny Almonte turned out to be older than he said he was.

"Gibbs said the bottom line was they had to take it to the District 22 board of directors," Mr. M said.

"And did they?" Michael said.

Mr. M said they'd just gotten off the conference call, and called Mr. Gibbs on his cell.

Michael could tell by the look on Mr. M's face that the news wasn't good.

"They decided that until a proper birth certificate is on file, you're not eligible to play," Mr. M said.

13

"I DON'T WANT YOU TO WORRY ABOUT THIS," MR. MINAYA TOLD MICHAEL.

Yeah, right.

"Why are they doing this now?" Michael said.

"You know why."

"Because they don't believe I'm twelve," he said.

Mr. Minaya nodded. It was just the two of them sitting on the bench. The other kids were in a raggedy circle on the infield grass in front of home plate, eating the ice cream sandwiches Manny's mom had brought as the snack.

"Does the Grand Concourse coach think I'm not twelve?"

"No, he's on our side. He knows this is basically just sour grapes from Westchester South," Mr. Minaya said. "But he's one of the league commissioners and he's got to do his job. So when coaches file a complaint, he has to go by the rules, which we sort of bent when we accepted the baptism certificate."

"You said coaches," Michael said. "I thought it was just the coach of Westchester South."

Mr. Minaya put an arm around Michael. "He wrote the letter," he said. "But quite a few other coaches signed it."

"They all think I'm lying about my age?"

"No," Mr. Minaya said. "Just a bunch of coaches who think they're good enough to get to Williamsport this year, and that their chances improve tremendously if you're not pitching against them."

Now Michael didn't know what to say. It wasn't just Justin's dad. It was a whole gang of dads. Ganging up on him all of a sudden.

Mr. Minaya said, "This all got going because you showed up the man's son. I know it's probably going to be a pain in the butt for your father, because somehow he'll have to get help from somebody back in Cuba. He told me he probably could if he ever really had to." Mr. Minaya shrugged. "Well, now he really has to. You want to give me his number in Florida?"

Michael said, "No, it's okay. I'll tell him."

More than anything, Michael wanted to be eating ice cream with everybody else.

Be like everybody else.

"Mr. Gibbs said he's not even worried about it," Mr. Minaya said. "He joked with me that where he works during the day, he's got a lot more important things to sweat than pain-in-the-butt Little League parents."

Michael grabbed his bat and glove. "Where does Mr. Gibbs work?" he said.

"ACS," Mr. Minaya said. "Administration for Children's Services. It's a city agency, in charge of—"

Michael cut him off, not even worried that he might have sounded rude doing it.

"I know what they're in charge of," he said.

The next morning at breakfast Michael said to Carlos, "You're telling me there's nobody we can call back home to get me a birth certificate?"

"Papi used to say that if he ever asked somebody back in Havana for a favor like that, they would have thought he was *loco*," Carlos said.

Crazy.

"But he had my baptism certificate instead?" Michael said. "You saw it?"

Carlos nodded. "Signed by Father Morales at San Antonia de

Padua. Papi held on to it like it was a ticket stub to heaven. And when he realized he didn't have the birth certificate, he went and got some kind of paper from Mr. Brown, way back at the start of the school year."

Mr. Brown was the principal at Michael's school, PS 31, the William Lloyd Garrison School on 156th Street.

Carlos said, "You'd think somebody would just stand up and tell this commissioner from the Pinstripers—"

"Mr. Gibbs," Michael said.

"—tell Mr. Gibbs that they're busting your chops for no good reason, and just make the whole thing go away," Carlos said. "I'd tell him myself, if he didn't turn out to be from the Administration for Children's Stinking Services."

"You'll figure something out," Michael said. "Just like you always do."

Carlos reached across the table, put out a closed fist for Michael to touch lightly with his own.

"My little *tipo*," his big brother said.

Little man.

"If I was little," Michael said. "Or just more little than I am, maybe people wouldn't be saying I'm older than I am."

"That's a lie," Carlos said. "And we shouldn't have to prove a lie, Miguel."

"Carlos, how are we going to come up with a birth certificate if Papi couldn't?"

"When I figure that out," Carlos said, "you'll be the first to know."

After Carlos left for work, Michael went downstairs and used the key Mr. Ruiz had given him to the storage closet in the basement, got out his pitchback net, brought it outside, and set it up in the alley behind 825 Gerard.

He set the net up in its usual place, walked back to the little mound Mr. Ruiz had built up for him, with help from some friends of his from the Department of Public Works, who had been fixing potholes on 158th Street one day. Before the macadam had dried, Michael had run down to Stan's Sports World and bought a pitching rubber that he stuck on the top of it.

"Don't tell people I was the one," Mr. Ruiz said, giving Michael a wink. "I don't want them to think I'm a nice guy."

Michael had told him, "Your secret is safe with me." Then he grinned and added, "Besides, no one would believe me."

Now that pitcher's mound was his sanctuary. He threw easily at first, making sure to warm up the way he always did. Honoring his instrument, as Papi had always instructed him. Gradually, though, as he felt the familiar warmth in his arm—the heat—he began to throw harder and harder, even knowing that he required perfect control on the pitchback, that if he missed his spot and hit the net the wrong way the ball would go flying over his head and into the street.

Before long, it was as if Michael was trying to throw eighty on every single pitch, as if somehow he could strike them all out with fastballs, Justin the Jerk from Westchester South and his father and Mr. Gibbs of the ACS.

It's because they think I'm too good, Michael thought. And fired another one at the net, hitting it dead center.

I'm too good and they're acting like that's bad.

14

MICHAEL THOUGHT BY NOW HE WAS USED TO BEING ALONE, THAT IF THEY gave out awards for knowing how to be alone, he would win all of them.

He was more alone than ever now, without a baseball game to look forward to, not knowing if he would get to play again this year.

Because if there was a secret he had that felt almost as big as the one about Papi, it was this:

Baseball was Michael's real best friend. Even more than Manny.

Baseball was a constant companion for him, no matter how many times he came into the quiet of the empty apartment, especially at night. There was the game he had just played or the game he was getting ready to play, or the Yankee game, on the radio or on television.

There was no mother to make him a snack when he came through the door in the afternoon. There was no father now to sit with at the dinner table, the way he used to sit with Papi when he got home early enough, and talk about his day, or just talk about any silly old thing that came into his head. Most nights when he got back from a game, Carlos had left him food to heat up in the microwave Papi had bought for them a few weeks before he died.

Michael thought he knew everything about being alone, but somehow this was different.

He wasn't sad all the time, going through life with some kind of sad face on him. Papi always used to tell him and Carlos that anybody could get knocked down, it was how you picked yourself up that was important. How you got on with things. He had gotten on with things when he was the new boy in school, the one off the boat. He was proud of the way he had gotten on with things after they had lost Papi. And he knew there were plenty of things in his life to make him happy. Carlos could do it, when he would give Michael another pep talk about how it was the two of them against the world. Manny made him happy. Ellie made him happy, even though she seemed to be running away from him half the time.

Michael knew that if he ever tried to fumble around finding the right words—as good as he had gotten with his English in the last year—and tried to explain what he was feeling right now to Manny, how alone he really felt, his friend would give him one of his wall-to-wall smiles and say, "But, Star, how can you be alone when you've got me?"

Even Manny wasn't enough, not right now.

Baseball made Michael feel normal. It made him feel as if he had turned back the clock, that things were the way they used to be, before Papi died. Before Carlos became the man of the house, before they both had to live in fear of all these Official Persons, whether they worked for the Bronx borough president or the Administration for Children's Services.

Before.

It was why Michael never complained along with the rest of the Clippers when one of their games ran long. A pitcher would start walking the whole world and the game would go past two hours, and everybody would act like they couldn't get off the field soon enough.

Michael never cared how long the games took.

Because when the game ended, he knew the next stop for him was the empty apartment at 825 Gerard.

Manny called him "Star" and Michael let him, because Michael treated it like a joke, one more joke between the two of them, part of why they were the kind of friends they were. So Manny got to call him something that Michael would never ever call himself.

But with all that, Michael knew how good he was at baseball. He didn't need Manny to tell him, he hadn't even needed Papi to tell him. He knew what he could do when he had a ball in his hand.

Now that ball had been taken away from him.

It turned out the only team in the league that could beat him was a team of coaches.

He talked himself into going to the next Clippers game, the last game of the regular season, the one that could clinch first place for them, telling himself that being around the team would make him feel a little better. A little less alone, just for one night.

It made him feel worse.

The game was at Castle Hill, against the Castle Hill Hilltoppers. Michael had originally been scheduled to pitch four innings, maybe more if his pitch count was as low as it usually was. Not only was first place on the line, and the top seed in the District 22 play-offs, but there was more than a week before the play-offs started, so Michael would have had plenty of time off.

He had gone back and forth all day about going to the game. Finally, about five o'clock, Manny had talked him into it. "You get to spend the night with me, or being a mope," Manny said. "I think your choice is clear." So Michael had put on his uniform and taken the ride in the old blue bus over to Castle Hill, sitting in the same backseat he always did, next to Manny.

"I'm going to show everybody I'm a team guy, even when I'm not on the team," he said to Manny.

"Right," Manny said. "It's been keeping me up nights, worrying whether you were a team guy or not."

"You know what I'm saying."

"Actually, I do."

Michael brought two gloves with him, his regular one and the left-handed catcher's mitt Papi had found for him in a sporting goods store up near Fordham Road, just in case Manny ever missed a game. When the starting players were out on the field for infield practice, Michael warmed up Anthony Fierro, who was starting in his place.

He told Mr. M he would coach first base once the game started, and did, taking the job seriously, watching for all of Mr. M's complicated signs, making sure the base runner was paying attention in case Mr. M was calling for a steal.

When he was on the bench, he was full of chatter, encouraging whoever was at the plate, trying to be the best baseball cheerleader in the Bronx on this night. Michael tried to smile through it all. Even though he felt like he was on the outside of everything, despite how close he was to the action, the way he always felt like he was on the outside of Yankee Stadium. Even with it standing right there in front of him, bigger than life.

The Clippers won, 5–4. Anthony pitched the best he had all year, even cleared the fence with a three-run homer. He went four innings and Kel, with all his slow stuff, this little dinky pitch he had that always seemed to find the outside corner, pitched the last two.

But the play of the game came from Maria, a game-saver with two outs in the bottom of the last inning, runners on second and third. There was a slow roller to her at second, a ball past the pitcher's mound that Kel just barely missed. Maria had stopped for a moment, thinking Kel was going to get it. Then she came hard. Too late, Michael thought from where he was standing in front of the Clippers' bench. The Hilltoppers were going to tie the game at least, and have the winning run on third.

But Maria Cuellar wasn't thinking that way. She was about to make the play of her life, barehanding the ball the way a big-league third baseman does with a bunt, dipping her body to the right, underhanding it in almost the same motion to Anthony, who was finishing the game at first base.

It all seemed to happen at once then, Maria falling to the infield grass, Anthony stretching for the throw, the umpire hustling up the line from home plate to throw up his arm and call "Out!" as Maria's throw got the Hilltopper batter by a step.

Even without Michael on the mound, the Clippers had still managed to hold on to first place. Now, for the first time all night, he felt like he was a part of things, felt happy for his teammates, beating everybody on the bench out to the crowd of Clippers jumping up and down near first base.

After Michael had congratulated Kel for closing the deal, he saw Manny standing on the mound, cap backward on his head, mask in one hand and mitt in the other.

"That was the greatest ending of the whole year!" he shouted at Michael.

Michael came over to him, grinning. "Only because it gave you a chance to hug Maria."

"Shut up," Manny said. Then the two of them gave each other five, first up high, then down low.

As they walked off the field, Manny said, "You sure you're all right?"

"We won," Michael said. "I don't know what it would've been like if we lost. But we didn't lose. I told you all year this team would be good enough to make it to Williamsport without me."

Manny put an arm around Michael's shoulder. "Star?"

"What?"

"Let's not get carried away."

"I'm cool," Michael said.

Just less cool, a lot less, when he looked up and saw the Grand Concourse coach, the man from the ACS, standing behind their bench, motioning to Michael that he wanted to talk to him.

"Remember me?" he asked, sticking out a hand that Michael thought was surprisingly small for a man. "My name's Tony Gibbs."

Michael shook it. "I know who you are," he said. "From the other night."

"I'm happy things worked out all right for you guys," Mr. Gibbs said. "But I'm sorry you couldn't play."

"Me, too," Michael said.

"Rules are rules," Mr. Gibbs said, "even when they're dumb rules that grown-ups came up with."

"Yeah."

"I left a message at your apartment," Mr. Gibbs said. "Then I tried the work number your father left on file. At the car service."

Michael couldn't catch his breath. Felt like he did one time when he wasn't looking and a hard throw from Anthony had hit him in the stomach. . . .

"They said he hadn't been there for a few months," Mr. Gibbs said.

Michael thought to himself: Is that all it's been? But he knew Mr. Gibbs was right. Papi had died in May. Now it was August.

It just seemed so much farther away sometimes.

Something that happened in the life he and Carlos and Papi used to have. Now Michael wanted Carlos here with him. Right here, right now, telling him the right things to say.

The right lies to tell.

"My uncle . . . ," he started to say.

"Yeah, I know, he's sick in Florida, that's why your dad has been away."

"But he'll be back soon," Michael said. "My father. Really."

Really?

Where the heck did that come from?

"How're you guys getting by, him being away this long?" Mr. Gibbs said.

"My brother has two jobs!" Michael said.

Too loud, too fast.

"Good for him," Mr. Gibbs said, smiling at Michael, as if neither one of them had a thing to worry about, he was just asking a few questions here, like a teacher going over a simple homework assignment.

Like they were on the same page.

Even though Michael knew they weren't even in the same book.

"Has he come back and forth at all?"

"Who?"

"Your dad. From Florida."

"One time," Michael said. "He drove all the way back a few weeks ago, when he thought my uncle was starting to get better."

A good lie, Michael decided. Good boy. Not too big a lie, that was the key. Carlos had been saying all along that the simpler the lie, the easier it was to remember.

Mr. Gibbs wore a gray Special Olympics sweatshirt and blue jeans and old running shoes and a black baseball cap that said Arthur Ashe Foundation over the bill. Behind him Michael could see his teammates packing up their gear, the ones who needed a ride getting ready to board the bus for the drive back across the Bronx to Macombs Dam Park, where they'd get picked up by the parents who hadn't made the game.

Mr. Gibbs sat down on the bench and patted the spot next to him, as if he and Michael had all night. When he took off his cap, Michael saw a lot of curly black hair.

He was young for an Official Person, Michael thought. He'd always thought of them as being older than churches.

"Well, you probably know why I'm here, kiddo. We gotta come up with that birth certificate, and fast."

"My brother has been trying to call some of my father's old friends in Havana," Michael said. "And my father, of course he's been doing the same from my uncle's."

"Understand, we told the coaches who made the complaint that we're comfortable with what we already have. But they've called the folks at the District Office. And the District Office says that because you're such a great pitcher, and because your team has such a great chance to make it to the World Series, they don't want there to be any controversy, the way there was a few years ago."

"When Danny Almonte lied about his age," Michael said.

"You know about him?"

"Everybody in the Bronx does."

Michael imagined a tennis ball bouncing back and forth across a net.

"I want to help," Mr. Gibbs said.

Michael wanted to say, Sure you do.

"Thank you," is what he did say.

"Tell you what," Mr. Gibbs said. "If your dad's not back next week, why don't I stop by the apartment and see if I can help your brother out? This is a pretty complicated job for a seventeen-year-old kid."

"Okay," Michael said.

"I know this probably doesn't make any sense to you," Mr. Gibbs said. "Sometimes it's the grown-ups who act like children."

Michael heard Mr. Minaya yelling at everybody that he could still see a lot of garbage, to get back there and police the area one last time.

"For what it's worth, Michael," Mr. Gibbs said, "I'm on your side. I work with a lot of kids around your age, and I think I know a fourteen-year-old when I see one. Or at least like to think I do."

"I'm twelve," Michael said.

Then he couldn't help it, this wasn't one of the times he could stop himself, he started to cry.

"Hey," Mr. Gibbs said, putting an arm around him. "Everything's going to be fine."

Michael nodded as if agreeing with him, rubbing his eyes as he did, feeling like the dope of all times, the dope of the whole stupid world, hoping that nobody on his team could see him acting like a baby.

"I know," Michael said.

"You know what they say, right?" Mr. Gibbs said, still wanting to be his friend.

Somehow Michael knew what was coming next.

"No crying in baseball," Mr. Gibbs said. "Not even Little League baseball."

Manny tried to pump Michael for information on the ride home. Michael told him they could talk about it on the phone later, he didn't want anybody else on the bus to hear.

"You're asking me to be patient?" Manny said. "You know I don't do patient."

"Just this once."

"Okay," Manny said. "But let's not make a habit of it."

Mr. M did what he'd been doing the whole All-Star season when the Clippers had an away game, dropping Michael in front of 825 Gerard and not pulling away with the old bus until Michael was inside the front door. Everybody on the team knew that Carlos worked most nights and had heard the story about the sick uncle in

Florida and thought Victor Arroyo was still away. So nobody thought this was star treatment for Michael.

Even if they did, Manny always pointed out, nobody would have given a rat's rear end. His words.

Michael told Manny to call when he got home, promising he'd tell him everything about his conversation with Mr. Gibbs. Then he got out of the bus, ran up the front steps, took the stairs up to the apartment, unlocked the door, made himself a humongous chocolate milk shake, remembered with a slap to his forehead that the Yankees were on Channel 9 tonight. Regular TV.

He could watch.

They were playing the Texas Rangers at home. The announcers were saying that tonight had been Family Night at the Stadium, and there had been a one-inning game before the start of the regular one that involved some of the Yankees and their children, that was why the Yankees-Rangers game had been a little late in starting.

Keith Wright, the Yankees' rookie left-hander, was pitching tonight, and had a 2–0 lead in the third inning.

Michael sat on the couch, happy as always to have the Yankees as company in the empty apartment.

On the screen, Keith Wright threw a big, slow, breaking curveball that seemed to come up to the plate as slowly as the one that El Grande liked to throw. When the batter missed it by a mile, the camera went into the Yankee dugout, and found El Grande sitting there with a couple of teammates, pointing at Keith Wright and laughing his head off.

Then the camera went to a box near the Yankee dugout, where Michael Kay, the Yankees' play-by-play man, said El Grande's family was sitting tonight. Saying that it was unusual for the children to be here, they usually only came when their father was the one throwing the big, slow, breaking curveballs.

A little girl's face filled the screen. Michael Kay said that was El Grande's three-year-old daughter, Adriana. While the camera was on her, she turned and tried to climb over her seat into the box behind her, her mother grabbing her from behind right before she went up and over.

"The older daughter," Michael Kay continued, "is named Elisa."

"That's right, Michael," Jim Kaat, the Yankees' other broadcaster, said. "Elisa Garcia Gonzalez. A name as pretty as she is."

Michael stared at the screen.

"She's beautiful," Michael Kay said.

"No," Michael Arroyo said. "She's Ellie."

15 ⚾⚾⚾⚾⚾⚾⚾⚾⚾⚾⚾⚾⚾

THE OFFICE OF THE BRONX BOROUGH PRESIDENT, MR. AMOROSA, WAS located on the Grand Concourse. And for all the worrying Michael had done about going there and having his picture taken with Mr. Amorosa and Officer Crandall and Mrs. C, the whole thing had been about as exciting as posing for some dopey class picture.

Carlos went along, too, getting the morning off from the Imperial, switching shifts with a friend. When Mr. Amorosa asked about their dad, Mrs. C stepped right up and said she was standing in for him, once again being their honorary grandma, and that her dear, dear friend Victor Arroyo sent his deepest regrets from his brother's bedside in Florida.

When Mr. Amorosa said he'd say a prayer for the uncle, Mrs. C made the sign of the cross.

Knowing Mrs. C's theories about sin, Michael figured she'd be on her way to confession as soon as they were done.

There were four photographers in front of Mr. Amorosa's building. Michael wore his white church-shirt with the stiff collar and the tie Carlos had given him, one that was way too long for him. When they were in place on the front steps, Mr. Amorosa stepped to the microphone that had been set up there, even though there was no crowd to watch them, just the photographers. He presented Michael with a baseball signed by the Yankee starting pitchers, including El Grande, and a Bronx Good Citizen plaque with Michael's name on it, and a brief description of how he had "felled"—that was the word they used—a robbery with courage and quick thinking.

Then Mr. Amorosa made a brief speech in which he said pretty much the same things that were written on the plaque.

"We hear all the time in baseball about pitchers mowing batters down," Mr. Amorosa said. "This time a fine young man from our borough mowed down a petty criminal who had preyed on this sweet old woman standing next to me."

The ceremony took ten minutes, tops. When they were done, Mr. Amorosa posed one more time, shaking Michael's hand as the photographers took their pictures. Then he wished him luck in the upcoming play-offs, even saying he might try to catch a game. Michael knew there was probably as much chance of that as Mr. Amorosa wading into the Harlem River and catching fish with his bare hands.

When they were finished, Michael noticed that the cameras disappeared almost as quickly as Mr. Amorosa did. Carlos asked Michael if he wanted to ride back home in the car Mr. Amorosa's office had provided. Michael said, no, he and Manny would walk.

Michael had asked Manny to tag along, knowing he would. This was a big event in Manny's eyes, even if it didn't include him. He lived for events of any kind. Big games. School field trips, even if they involved going to art museums. School plays. The opening of any new movie they really wanted to see, even if it meant getting permission to take the subway all the way to Times Square and pay their way into one of the massive theaters Manny called plexi-plexes.

As soon as they were back on the street in front of 851 Grand Concourse, Michael yanked off his tie as if it had been a noose around his neck, and stuffed it into the pocket of his Old Navy khakis.

"What did I tell you?" Manny said. "No problemo."

"Yeah, we had him all the way," Michael said. "I wish I could get Mr. ACS Man off my back that easy."

"We'll think of something," Manny said.

"You just keep thinking, Butch," Michael said to Manny, using one of his favorite lines from *Butch Cassidy and the Sundance Kid,* one of his favorite movies. "That's what you're good at."

"You should have gone along with my brilliant idea about a fake dad," Manny said.

"Why," Michael said, "so the fake dad can come up with a fake birth certificate?"

"You know what I'm saying."

"Not always," Michael said, poking Manny with an elbow.

They were in no hurry to get back to Gerard Avenue. No hurry to do anything, really. The sound of the day, of the city, was all around them, as loud and busy as ever. It was another reason, Michael thought, why he loved baseball so much, loved the idea that all the action didn't start until he started it by going into his motion. There he'd be, alone on the mound, the ball in his hand, the ball feeling as small sometimes in his palm as a marble, almost like he was alone in his own world, not even hearing the infield chatter from behind him.

Sometimes Michael thought the two most quiet places in his whole world were the pitcher's mound and the apartment at night before he put the Yankee game on.

Manny said, "Well, are we gonna talk about her ever?"

He poked Michael now, as if waking him up.

"How much more can we talk about her?" Michael said. "She's not just a girl. She's El Grande's daughter. That happens to mean she's living in a whole different world than we're living in."

"But she's been hanging around in our world 'cause she wants to," Manny said. "Nobody made her."

"Why couldn't she just have told us who she really was?"

"Because," Manny said, "she was probably afraid you'd get your panties in a wad exactly the way they are right now." He put both hands over his heart, put his head back, closed his eyes. "Oh," he said, "I am just a poor Cuban boy from the wrong side of the subway tracks, and am not worthy. . . ."

That was as far as he got before Michael stepped back and gave him a soccer-style kick to the seat of his pants.

"Hey!" Manny said. "That actually hurt."

"Good."

"She likes you," Manny said now.

"It doesn't change who she is."

"I know," Manny said. "She's the great man's daughter. And yet she keeps coming around."

"At least now we know why she only showed up on days he was pitching," Michael said. "She must come in with him instead of her mom, and then get a little bored just hanging around the ballpark."

"I told you: She likes you," Manny said. "Deal with it."

"She doesn't like me enough to tell me the truth."

"Hey, jerkwad," Manny said. "Maybe you've noticed, people sometimes have a good reason for holding stuff back."

As usual when it turned into a debate, Manny had him.

They had walked long enough now that the Stadium was in front of them.

Manny told Michael to hang on, ran into a convenience store, came out with a couple of Snapple iced teas, with lemon, and handed one to Michael.

"Where do you suppose she lives?" Manny said.

"Riverdale," Michael said.

"You know that?"

"I read it in the papers."

Riverdale, they both knew, was the most expensive part of the Bronx, like a whole different Bronx, up off the Henry Hudson

105

Parkway, with big old brick mansions looking like castles guarding the river below. Michael had seen those mansions once on a boat trip up the Hudson their sixth-grade class had taken.

"She could have told me," Michael said one more time, being stubborn the way he was with pitches sometimes, going for a particular corner of the plate, inside or outside, even when he was missing.

"Are you thick or what?" Manny said. "She probably only hangs around with kids who can't get over the fact that she's El Grande's daughter, look at her for herself. And then she finds us and it's completely different, we don't know anything, we just like her for her. You and your faithful companion."

"Which would be you."

"Friends to the end," Manny said. "And then five days after that."

They touched their Snapple bottles together.

"I want to see her again," Michael said. Even though the thought now scared him.

"Duh," Manny said.

"You think she'll come around when the Yankees are home next week?"

"Duh," Manny said again.

"But what if she thinks I saw her on TV and now I know who she is and she just doesn't want me to turn into another El Grande groupie?"

"Star?"

"What?"

"Will you listen to me for one second?"

"All I do is listen to you."

"I mean really listen," Manny said. "You've got enough crummy stuff going on in your life. They won't even let you play right now.

But Ellie isn't part of that. Ellie is a good thing. A good problem to have. Am I right?"

Michael mumbled his reply, on purpose.

"I didn't quite catch that," Manny said.

"I said, you're right."

Manny Cabrera, light on his feet as always, more graceful than all the people who called him No Neck knew, danced now on the Bronx street corner, Michael's catcher celebrating as if he'd just scored a touchdown.

16 ⚾⚾⚾⚾⚾⚾⚾⚾⚾⚾⚾⚾⚾⚾⚾

TONY GIBBS HAD SPENT MOST OF THE MORNING AT A GROUP HOME JUST UP the block from the basketball courts at Rosedale Park. It had been a good morning. No, a great morning, because of the news Gibbs had delivered there to a twelve-year-old orphan named Beliz Ortega.

Both of Beliz Ortega's parents had been killed on 9/11, the father a security man in the North Tower and the mother a receptionist at a bond-trading company on the 101st floor, the two of them thrilled because they could make the long train ride to work together every morning. Beliz was an only child. He had gone into the foster-care system and ended up at this group home.

Now Tony Gibbs told the boy that he had a foster home for him in Ridgewood, New Jersey.

Gibbs lived for these days.

Beliz Ortega had met the foster parents twice, first when they came to visit him in the group home, the second time an overnight visit, approved by the ACS, to the family's home in Ridgewood. After that, as always, came the worst part for these kids, the waiting period to find out whether or not they had made the cut. Sometimes this went on for weeks, before some family decided they didn't want some twelve-year-old Dominican or fourteen-year-old Puerto Rican. Then Gibbs had to sit them down and tell them they hadn't gotten into the only club that any of them cared about.

A real home.

But this time they said yes. The Kimballs were an older couple with kids already through college. They had decided they wanted

108

children in the house again, had talked about various modern-day options. China. Romania. Then it turned out they had a friend who had joined the board of New Yorkers for Children, the city's best foster-care charity. The friend had put them in touch with one of Gibbs's bosses at ACS. Finally there came the day when the Kimballs came across the George Washington Bridge to say yes.

Days like this didn't wipe out a hundred bad days for Tony Gibbs, just carried him to the next good one. So on this morning he helped Beliz Ortega, a kid with the face of an angel, to pack his cheap bag, then walked him out the front door with the Kimballs, all of them turning around when they heard the cheers from the other kids in the group home hanging out the window.

Gibbs cheered along with them.

He hugged the boy and told him to have a great life and watched the Kimballs' Toyota SUV with Jersey plates pull away.

He thought about going back to his office then, in the Bronx borough president's office on the Grand Concourse. Instead, because he hadn't gotten a chance to make his morning run along the East River today, he decided to make the long walk across the Bronx to Yankee Stadium, where he knew the Yankees were playing an afternoon game. He knew one of the cops who worked security outside the Stadium. When Gibbs would show up after the game had started, whether it was a sellout or not, the guy would wave him in and tell him to go find an empty seat.

Gibbs loved the Yankees almost as much as he loved helping these stray kids.

Now he walked for an hour, forgetting how far it was from Rosedale Park to the Stadium, hailed a cab, got out on 161st Street.

161st and Gerard.

It made him think of Michael Arroyo, just because the kid had been on his mind a lot lately.

Gibbs didn't walk up 161st toward the Stadium. He hung a left and started walking up Gerard instead, pulling out his wallet as he did, making sure he had the address right.

He had done this sort of work a long time, working even harder at it after his divorce, throwing himself into the job with a vengeance. By now he had a sixth sense about kids, whether they were in the system or not, whether they were on his Bronx Little League team or not.

Something wasn't right in Michael Arroyo's life, he was sure of it.

Tony Gibbs had a feeling, one of his famous gut instincts, that the kid's old man had run out on them.

He saw the boy before he got to the entrance to 825 Gerard, in an alley behind the building, throwing to one of those old-fashioned pitchbacks. Gibbs stood across the street, watched that beautiful motion he saw from the boy in games, the high kick, that perfect arm angle of his, the ball coming straight over the top.

Like Koufax, his all-time hero.

Not many people remembered Sandy Koufax anymore. Maybe it was because Gibbs's dad had been an old Brooklyn Dodger fan, one of the few who still rooted for them after they left for Los Angeles. They would watch Koufax when Tony was little and his father would always remind him that Koufax had started in Brooklyn as a kid.

Now he watched this Little League boy who he believed had some Koufax in him, the boy lost in what he was doing, taking it seriously, then throwing another one with all his might that hit the net in a place that sent the ball right back to him like it was on a string.

Gibbs thought: This is better than anything I'm going to watch today with the Yankees and Devil Rays.

This kid is the real deal.

A car horn finally distracted Michael Arroyo and he threw one too high, and the ball came flying back over his head, right through the entrance to the small alley and across the street to where Gibbs was standing.

When Michael turned around, there he was.

"Michael, I'd like to ask you a question," Tony Gibbs said, picking up the ball, tossing it back with a little zip on it. "Where's your father, really?"

For some reason, Michael tossed the ball back to the ACS man, who caught it easily with his right hand. Just doing that, feeling the baseball in his hand, then throwing it to him, made Michael feel better, as if he could somehow pitch his way out of this jam.

"What do you mean?" Michael said.

"No games, Michael. Where's your father?"

The two of them kept playing catch, Mr. Gibbs on his side of 158th Street, Michael at the entrance to the alley. Mr. Gibbs was wearing blue jeans again, a different sweatshirt this time, one that said New Yorkers for Children.

Michael wondered if he was one of those children.

"My father's in Florida," Michael said.

"Tell me the town again?" Mr. Gibbs said.

He made it sound casual. Like they'd had this conversation before. But Michael knew they had never talked about what town Victor Arroyo was supposed to be in, visiting the sick brother who did not exist. Michael knew and Mr. Gibbs knew. He remembered watching *Law & Order* one time with Carlos and Carlos saying,

"Lawyers never ask questions they don't already know the answers to."

What did Mr. Gibbs of the ACS really know, now that he'd come around asking where Michael's father really was?

"It's near Miami," Michael said. "Carlos knows. The only thing I know about Miami is that the Marlins play there, and beat the Yankees that time in the Series."

"When did he go down there?" Mr. Gibbs said. He didn't want to talk about the Yankees and Marlins. "I mean, exactly?" he said.

He came over now to where Michael was, sat down inside the alley, his back against the wire fence. Michael noticed his sneakers. He always noticed sneakers, maybe because his were always so worn-down, having to last him from the start of one school year to the start of the next. Mr. Gibbs's soft old Reeboks looked like they were almost as old as Mrs. C.

"It was right around when I got out of school," Michael said. "Or a little before, maybe."

Keep the lies simple.

"Yeah, that's what they said at that car service," Mr. Gibbs said. "But your dad only works there part-time, right?"

"He owns his car," Michael said. "He likes to be on his own, my father. But they would call him when they needed extra drivers."

"They said the eighteenth of May was the last time they heard from him," Mr. Gibbs said.

"Yes," Michael said.

Yes. He said it very clearly. Papi never allowed yeah. Speak American, he always said. You're American now. Yes, Michael was thinking, May 18 was the last time the car service had heard from his father because that was the day his father had died.

"So he's been gone awhile now," Mr. Gibbs said. "He must really trust you and your brother."

"Carlos says he's like the dad who had to come off the bench," Michael said.

"You're sure he didn't just take off?" Mr. Gibbs said. "Your father, I mean. It's a terrible thing to say, I know, but I see it in my job all the time."

"He's with my uncle," Michael said. "Why don't you believe me?"

He wanted Manny to come walking right around that corner now, Michael knowing that all he had to do was give Manny a look and his friend would know he needed help, as though Michael had sent an instant-message right into his brain.

Or he wanted Mrs. C to come walking up the hill from the Imperial.

Or Carlos.

Anybody.

"Hey, relax," Mr. Gibbs said. "It's my job to ask questions like this."

"To everybody?"

"When I think there's a problem."

"My uncle's the problem, is all," Michael said.

"What's his name, your uncle?"

Shoot.

"Luis," Michael said.

There had been an old Yankee pitcher he knew about, just because they had the same last name. Luis Arroyo. He had first read about him in a book about Yogi Berra he had taken out of the library.

Mr. Gibbs said, "Hey, that's funny, there was a relief pitcher once, had that same name, Luis Arroyo. But that was before your time."

"My father told me about him," Michael lied.

"Did Uncle Luis come over on the boat with you?"

"No, he came a few years before."

Lie after lie after lie.

"And he doesn't have family of his own, down there in Miami, to take care of him?"

Michael said, "They stayed behind when he left, and then they didn't want to come later."

The questions were coming faster now. Michael felt the way he did when he sat in the subway car and the train was outside, and everything was flying past him.

No one said anything now, for what felt like a long time, until Mr. Gibbs said, "There's no uncle, is there, Michael?"

Michael took the ball out of his glove, bounced it off the pavement as if it were a basketball, did that hard once, then twice.

"You're calling me a liar?" he said.

"I think the lie is that your dad is ever coming back."

"No!" Michael shouted. "You've got it all wrong, you'll see."

"Will I?" Mr. Gibbs said. "My line of work, Michael? My job? I see parents running out all the time, for a million different reasons. It's not your fault, or your brother's, if he did."

Michael didn't know what to say to that.

"I can help you," Mr. Gibbs said. "You don't have to be afraid of me."

He looked up at him, tipped an old Yankees cap back on his head.

"I'm one of the good guys," he said.

Michael blinked fast and hard a few times, determined not to start crying, because this was another time when he knew crying would be like some kind of confession on *Law & Order*.

"If he's gone, you gotta tell me."

Gone, Michael thought to himself. Like Papi had gone out for cigars and never come back.

"My brother and I are fine," Michael said. "We don't need your help."

"The two of you are too young to be living alone for this long."

"That's the thing," Michael said. "We aren't going to be living alone much longer."

The words were out of his mouth before Michael could stop them, like a cartoon genie blowing out of the bottle.

"So your father's finally coming home?" Mr. Gibbs said.

"Day after tomorrow," Michael said.

17

MICHAEL WATCHED AS MANNY ACTUALLY BEGAN TO TALK CARLOS INTO IT. IT being his big idea that his uncle Timo, who had gotten some small parts in off-Broadway plays and even in some of the television shows shot in New York, could play the part of Papi, just for one day.

They were in the living room. Michael had called Manny as soon as Mr. Gibbs had left, told Manny what he had told Mr. Gibbs about his father coming back the day after tomorrow. He had also told Manny to get his butt over to 825 Gerard before Carlos got home from the Imperial.

"Why do you need me?" Manny said.

"As moral support," Michael said.

"As a human shield," Manny said, and then told Michael he'd be right over.

Michael expected Carlos to yell when he told him about Mr. Gibbs. But he didn't yell, or walk out of the room. He just sat there on the couch, still in his Imperial white shirt and tie, and listened to Manny, as if Manny were now the one in charge here.

"This can work," Manny said.

"I told you," Carlos said, "I'm listening."

"We can make sure Uncle Timo's English is a lot worse than your father's really was," Manny said, "that way he can act confused if he has to. Then all he has to do is keep thanking Mr. Gibbs for being this interested in his boys, tell him he's working day and night to get that stinking birth certificate, and that hopefully he'll see us all at the Little League World Series."

116

Manny stood up, bowed at the waist, then said, "You've been a great audience, don't forget to tip your waiters."

Michael had no idea what that one meant. He just laughed along with Carlos, who did seem to understand. Michael did this a lot, laughed at something Manny said even if Manny seemed to be saying it in some kind of foreign language.

Carlos said, "You're good, Manuel. And I'm sure your uncle is. But what if he makes a slip?"

"Let me ask you a question," Manny said. "What have we got to lose? This Mr. Gibbs was sure your father had just deserted you guys. Which means he's going to keep coming around like the truant officer unless we do something."

"I'm not saying we're just going to sit around and do nothing," Carlos said. "I'm just asking what happens if I agree to go along with your crazy plan and Uncle Timo makes a slip."

"He won't."

"How do you know that?"

"Because I know my uncle," Manny said. "My mother says he could sell sand in the desert."

"He would do this? Your uncle?"

"He's my godfather," Manny said. "He knows I look up to him, even though he's not close to being a star, because I think maybe I'd like to be an actor someday. If I ask him, yeah, I think he'll do it."

Carlos went into the kitchen, came back with a Coke, and sat down now in Papi's old recliner, with the tape on one of the arms and the cushion.

"This is crazy," Carlos said.

"Our whole life is crazy," Michael said.

"I'm telling you, this'll work," Manny said. "You and Michael can tell him everything he needs to know, and he can memorize it!" Michael saw that look come over his friend's face again. His big-idea look. "We can even have one of those mock debates like we do in class before a real debate. And you can pretend you're Mr. Gibbs and fire questions at him."

Carlos looked at Michael, then Manny, then back to Michael.

"I can't believe I'm letting you two knotheads talk me into this," he said. "Working two jobs must be making me way too tired."

"I promise, this is gonna be great!" Manny said.

Michael thought: Manny Cabrera is the one who could sell sand in the desert.

"We just need to give him something so he stops coming around, until you figure out a way to get that stupid birth certificate, Carlos."

"I called Father Morales," Carlos said. "Our old pastor. He was on vacation, but the priest who answered said he'd give him the message as soon as he got back."

"So for now, we work on Uncle Timo," Manny said, clapping his hands. "We gotta keep you guys together."

Carlos smiled and said to Michael, *"Al pan pan y al vino vino."*

"Hey," Manny said, "no keeping secrets."

"You never heard that one?" Carlos said.

"All I got was the wine part," Manny said.

Michael said, "It's a Cuban expression, about bread and wine. But it's really about calling things as they are, no lies."

"Until the next lie," Carlos said.

"You guys call bread and wine whatever you want," Manny said. "I'm gonna call Uncle Timo."

"You're actually going to let us do this?" Michael said to Carlos before his brother went off to work at Hector's. As always, his brother was wearing his favorite baseball cap, the one with the *W* on the front, which Michael knew was for the old Washington Senators, even if the new Nationals team was using a *W* on its caps now.

Papi had loved the Senators when he was a boy, even though they were usually terrible, because their star pitcher was Camilo Pascual, a Cuban by birth.

"I am *thinking* about letting you do this," Carlos said, checking himself out in the mirror, making sure the cap was just so. "Just because a few minutes with this Uncle Timo guy might get Mr. Gibbs off our backs."

He pointed a finger at Michael, then Manny, then back at Michael. "But remember, you two, nothing happens with Uncle Timo until I get to meet him tomorrow."

Michael said, "I'm just going to tell him stuff about Papi's life. Tell him some baseball things about the two of us. And Manny thinks we should show him some pictures of all of us."

"And don't forget to show him some of the Cuban expressions I wrote up," Carlos said.

"Do you think Mr. Gibbs will know the difference?" Manny said.

"Aquí hay gato encerrado," Carlos said to Manny.

"Say what?"

"He's saying there's a caged cat here," Michael said. "And the cat is me."

"I just want to make sure the cat has nine lives," Carlos said.

It got a smile out of Michael, not easy these days. "How many lives do I have left?" he said to his brother.

"That's what we're trying to find out, Miguel," his brother said, and left for work.

Uncle Timo showed up about an hour later, wearing a short-sleeved shirt outside his jeans, sandals, no socks. He was still wearing his sunglasses, even though the sun was gone from the sky, and wearing the kind of backpack Michael and Manny took to school with them.

He looked old enough to be a dad to teenaged boys, Michael thought. He even had a beard that reminded Michael a little bit of the neat, trimmed beard Papi always had.

Uncle Timo was carrying a plastic bottle of water.

"Dude!" he said to Manny when he came through the door, giving Manny a big hug. "Now you think you've turned into my agent?"

Michael's heart fell now, hard, as if he'd dropped it from a high place.

Uncle Timo sounded more American than baseball announcers.

"And you," he said, rubbing Michael's head, "must be the famous Mike." He stepped back and put out his hand. "Gimme some," he said.

Michael gave him five, but without too much enthusiasm. Uncle Timo noticed it, because he dropped his head to the side and gave Michael a funny look. "Where's the love, dude?"

"Don't worry," Manny said, reading Michael's mind, as usual. "He grows on you."

Uncle Timo dropped his backpack on the floor and plopped himself down in Papi's old recliner chair. "My nephew here gave me the setup," he said. "And, by the way, dude, I'm sorry about your pop."

"Thank you," Michael said.

Thinking to himself: He's more of a teenager than Carlos is!

"Manny laid out the plot for me," Uncle Timo said. "I'm Dad, I've been down in Florida, I'm back for a day, just to check in on my boys, then I'm back down there with my illin' brother."

"Illin'?" Michael said.

"Sick," Manny said, then grinned and said, "dude."

"What if Mr. Gibbs asks where your brother is?"

"Got it covered," Uncle Timo said. "I got a girl down there, her own place in Homestead. Working a dinner theater down there. He calls that number, she's the maid, not so good *habla*ing the *Inglesia*."

Michael closed his eyes.

"Besides," Uncle Timo said, "Manny said all we've got to do is convince The Man"—he made little quotation marks with his fingers around the last two words—"that I'm the man of the house, and that I trust you guys to keep things under control till I get back."

Manny said, "Sounds like a plan."

"Manny says the guy thinks your dad turned deadbeat and ran out on you?"

Michael looked at Manny. "He knows the whole story," Manny said.

"You can't tell," Michael said to Uncle Timo.

"Dude," Uncle Timo said, sounding hurt.

Michael noticed that every time Uncle Timo said "dude," he sounded more like Manny. Or Kel.

Even more like a kid.

"Seriously," he said to Michael, "don't worry, I don't spill my guts unless I'm getting paid to do it on a cop show."

Michael said, "The one you have to fool? Mr. Gibbs? He's very smart. So you've got to be good."

"I am good," he said. "My agent tells me all the time."

Michael wasn't so sure. Uncle Timo was a goof. But at least he was trying.

"What do you want to know about my father?" Michael said.

"First I want to see him," Uncle Timo said. "Manny said you've got pictures."

"But I don't understand why you need them," Michael said.

"Because if I'm going to be him, I need to know what he looks like."

"But you don't look anything like him, except for maybe your beard."

"I don't look like him yet," Uncle Timo said.

"Yet?"

"That happens," he said, "when the magic happens, kid."

Michael went into his room, reached up to the shelf in his closet, got down the shoe box with some of Papi's stuff in it: the small stack of photographs that the nice woman, a stranger, had offered to take at the Bronx Zoo that time; Papi's cigar cutter; the old black-and-white team photograph of the Cuban National Team, with Papi standing next to a smiling, happy batboy at the end, one who didn't look much older than Michael was now. Papi said the boy had snuck into the clubhouse that morning, just wanting to see some of his heroes. The manager of the team wanted to throw him out. But Papi had liked the spunk it had taken to sneak in there. Then he had proclaimed the kid batboy for a day, he told Michael every time he retold the story, and had gotten him into the team picture.

There was the photo of Michael and Papi posing outside Yankee Stadium, next to the huge bat that rose like a skyscraper.

There was the picture of Papi standing proudly next to his Grand Prix. Finally there was the photograph that was Michael's favorite, from the spring, not so long before Papi had his heart attack:

Michael in his Modell Monuments uniform, Papi with his arm around him, both of them smiling. Michael remembered Papi telling him that day that now he really was an official American boy. He was in Little League.

Only now he wasn't in Little League. . . .

Michael brought the box into the living room, set it on the glass coffee table, took out the Little League picture and showed that one to Uncle Timo first. He carefully took the photograph out of Michael's hand, stared at it hard, walked over to the window that looked out on Gerard Avenue, still staring at the picture, as if frozen in that position.

Michael whispered to Manny, "It's like he's in a trance."

"He's starting to get into character," Manny said. "It's an actor thing."

"Oh."

"Remember that scene in *Caddyshack*?" Manny said, referring to another one of his favorite movies of all time. "It's like when the guy tells himself, 'Be the ball.'"

"So he's trying to be the photograph?" Michael said.

"Something like that," Manny said. "He's cool, isn't he?"

Michael didn't answer, because he was thinking, weird is more like it.

This was never going to work in a million years.

18

Carlos had his own lies, separate from his brother's.

Here was one:

He had not worked at Hector's Bronx Café for a few weeks now.

Here was another:

At night, when Michael thought he was busing tables at Hector's, Carlos was working outside Yankee Stadium, scalping tickets to Yankee games, as afraid of being spotted by his brother as by the police.

And finally the Whopper, with cheese:

His boss for this new job as ticket scalper, the one who actually dealt with the broker who somehow owned the tickets, was a young man his age named Ramon Crespo.

The same Ramon who had stolen Mrs. Cora's purse.

Carlos had met him a few nights after he got laid off at Hector's. He had done nothing wrong, the manager assured him, he had been one of their best workers since his first night on the job. But business was slower than they expected, even after Yankee games, and some of the waiters had agreed to take a cut in salary rather than be the ones laid off, and so the busboys had to go.

Carlos was out of a job, at a time when he had a secret drawer full of past-due bills in the apartment.

"But I need this job," he had said to the manager, a man named Jose Guzman.

"You told me you work at the Imperial," Mr. Guzman said. "How much can a boy your age need a second job?"

"We have bills to pay at home."

"I'm sure your father will find a way to provide," Mr. Guzman said. "And if things change around here, I will be sure to call you."

You don't understand, Carlos wanted to say. I am the father, even if I'd give anything to be just a son again.

To have somebody take care of me the way I take care of Michael.

For the next few nights, he got dressed as if he were going to Hector's, his Senators cap on his head, and walked down to 158th Street instead, hanging around with boys from the neighborhood who would stand in front of Stan's Sports World. Somebody would always have a transistor radio to listen to the Yankee games, even though they would first try to guess what was happening inside when they heard the noise of the crowd, before the announcers would tell them what had happened.

One night he was listening to one of the boys on the corner tell the story of how he had cried in front of the judge in Juvenile Court, boo hoo, getting a laugh now by touching his tongue to his cheek and leaving a wet mark there, and how the nice woman judge had actually let him off.

"I wouldn't have been there at all if that stupid kid hadn't clipped me with a lucky throw."

Carlos couldn't help himself.

"He isn't stupid," he said. "And it wasn't lucky."

Ramon gave him a little nod with his chin. "How would you know?"

"That kid is my kid brother," he said.

He shouldn't have said anything, but he was in a bad mood and this Ramon, with his slicked-back hair tied into a ponytail in back, reminded him of a weasel. He was wearing a 50 Cent T-shirt and basketball shorts that were almost long enough and baggy enough to be a skirt. The purse snatcher didn't look so tough to Carlos. If he wanted it to be on, Carlos was ready to throw down with him. He even felt his fists clenching behind his back.

Ramon looked Carlos up and down, like he were some kind of item in a store window he was thinking of buying, his face almost curious.

Suddenly he laughed.

"You're right!" he said. "It wasn't a lucky throw. That boy's arm is, like, crazy."

"You don't seem too mad about it," Carlos said.

Ramon shrugged. "Easy come, easy go," he said. "Besides, I don't have to steal old ladies' purses no more, I've got myself a real job now."

Then he told Carlos and the rest of the guys on the corner about the scalper he had met at Stan's the week before, what he called the "preem-o" tickets the man had access to, how on a good night his cut of those tickets could be as much as fifty dollars.

Later on, when it was just Carlos and Ramon walking up 158th Street, Carlos on the lookout for Michael even then, even knowing Michael was home listening to the Yankee game on the radio, Ramon said, "You know what fifty bucks is in this neighborhood? Two purses sometimes, that's what."

And more than I was making at Hector's, Carlos thought.

Then he heard himself saying to the purse thief who bragged about fooling a judge in Juvenile Court, who didn't seem to be afraid of Official Persons or anything else:

"How could I get a job like yours?"

Ramon smiled a smile that reminded Carlos not of a weasel, but a cartoon shark.

"When can you start?" Ramon said.

. . .

Mr. Minaya said he had a friend who had a friend at *El Diario,* the Spanish paper in New York, who was making some calls to Havana, trying to see if there was somebody down there who would be willing to help track down Michael's birth certificate. And Mr. Minaya said he had talked to Mr. Gibbs, the ACS man, about maybe contacting the Little League in Havana, finding someone sympathetic to what Mr. Minaya called Michael's "plight."

The ACS man, meanwhile, was supposed to come to the apartment tomorrow and meet Manny's crazy uncle Timo.

Tomorrow was also the day of the Clippers' first play-off game, against the Rosedale Park Robins, to be played at Macombs Dam Park. Anthony Fierro would start in Michael's place, trying to make sure the Clippers hung in there until they got Michael back.

If they got Michael back.

"You know what's going to happen?" Michael said to Manny. "Somebody's going to come up with that stupid birth certificate of mine, but it's not going to happen until after the season's over. Wait and see."

"Well, there's a pretty great example of what my mom calls the power of positive thinking," Manny said.

They were sitting on the home team's bench at Macombs, Mr. Minaya having insisted that Michael come to practice. "They may not let you play," Mr. M had said. "But you're still a part of this team."

Problem was, Michael didn't feel like a part of the team.

"Look at it this way," Manny said. "Once you get out on the field it'll only hurt for a little while."

"How do you know?" Michael said.

"I don't," Manny said. "It just sounded like something I thought I should say." He stood up. "Come on, let's go test out the old rocket launcher, see if it's still firing on all cylinders."

"I know I've told you this before," Michael said, "but you sure can talk."

Then they were out on the field, in the bright sun, Michael on the mound, ready to go into his windup, Manny in his crouch behind the plate, all the green grass around them, and Michael was throwing and Manny was catching and saying, Wow, or Oh Boy, on just about every pitch, the way they had so many other times. Better times than these, Michael thought. Before there seemed to be something bad happening just about every single day.

He went into his high kick, tried to put everything he had into his next pitch, and did something to Manny he just had to do from time to time, when they both knew he had thrown one eighty miles per hour:

Knocked the best friend he had in the whole world on his butt. Again.

Laid him right out as if he'd run over him.

Michael took a few steps in from the mound, knowing Manny was just lying there to make it more of a show. "You okay?"

Manny's head came up first, big smile on his face. "I swear, I must have blacked out after the ball hit the glove," he said. "It was like you tried to throw one through everybody who's been busting your chops."

Michael walked all the way in to the plate, reached down with his left hand to help Manny up. "I don't know what you're talking about," he said. "That was my changeup."

"Cute," Manny said.

From behind the screen they heard a girl's voice say, "Hey. Hey, you guys."

They turned around.

Ellie.

He couldn't even remember how many days it had been since

they'd actually seen her. And now, here she was, as if they all had an appointment to meet behind the plate on this day. Now here she was, saying "you guys," but looking right at Michael, who looked right back at her and knew in that moment how much he had missed her.

Not that he was going to admit that to her. Or Manny.

Michael would wonder later why he said what he said, why he would want to hurt her feelings. Why he didn't let Manny do the talking, the way he always let Manny do the talking.

Why he would want to sound like a whole different person.

"Hey, it's Miss Gonzalez," he said. "Come to slum it up with us ordinary guys?"

Right away, Manny stepped in front of him, like he was cutting in on Michael in line, and said, "Hey, Ellie." He only paused long enough to stick an elbow into Michael's side, and say, "That was sweet," before he started walking in Ellie's direction.

She was wearing a Nike T-shirt and white jeans. Her sneakers, with a pink Nike swoosh, looked brand-new. Michael saw she had brought her baseball glove with her.

"You got time to play a little?" Manny said.

But Ellie wasn't looking at Manny or acting as if she'd even heard him. She was looking at Michael.

"You know," she said.

"Yeah."

"How?"

"They showed you on television," he said. "The other night. With your sister."

Manny said, "Okay, then, so now everybody knows who everybody else is, we can stop wearing our name tags." Manny made a motion like he was wiping sweat off his forehead. "Whoo, there's a relief."

Ellie was still ignoring him. "You're mad that I didn't tell you myself."

Michael said, "Who, me? Why would I be mad about a little thing like you lying to me?"

He still sounded like somebody else. And still didn't care. He felt like he was in some silly schoolyard fight, just with words, and wanted to beat her to the punch.

Out of the side of his mouth, Manny said, "Aw man, don't go *there*."

"I didn't lie," Ellie said. "I just didn't tell you everything. Do you tell everybody all your secrets?"

"What does that mean?" Michael said.

"What does what mean?"

"About secrets?"

"I was just saying . . ."

"It's different," Michael said. "You're his daughter."

"That's exactly why I didn't tell you."

"Blah blah blah blah blah," Manny said.

"What, you didn't think we'd like you for yourself if we knew who you really were?"

They were still talking through the fence, Ellie making no move to walk around to where they were standing behind the plate.

Like we're strangers all over again, Michael thought.

"Something like that," Ellie said.

"We liked you because we liked you," Michael said.

Another thing he'd wonder later: Why he dug in like this, like he was digging a hole with those old spikes of his into the batter's box.

"Not everybody does," she said.

"We're not everybody," Michael said.

"Boy," Manny said, still trying to lighten everything up, "you can say that again."

130

"You don't understand how hard it is, being his daughter," she said.

"I wish that was the worst problem I had," Michael said.

"That's not what I meant. . . ."

"It was stupid to keep it from us," Michael said.

He knew he sounded like a jerk, that he didn't even sound like himself. Carlos liked to say that his little brother would walk around the block to avoid hurting someone's feelings.

Now he was doing that to Ellie. On purpose.

"So now I'm stupid," she said. "Anything else?"

"I don't think my jerkball friend meant to call you stupid," Manny said. "Did you, jerkball friend?"

"No, he's right," Ellie said. "I think mostly I was stupid to come here today."

She didn't run away this time.

She walked.

Manny gave Michael about the meanest look he'd ever seen, then said, "Ellie, wait."

All she did was wave an arm, like, leave me alone.

She kept walking, across the basketball courts and up the hill, never once looking back.

19 ⚾⚾⚾⚾⚾⚾⚾⚾⚾⚾⚾⚾⚾

No baseball.

Now, no Ellie.

The next thing to go wrong would be Uncle Timo with Mr. Gibbs tomorrow. Michael could see it now, every time he thought about it. Just because of the way things were going. Uncle Timo would slip up somehow or Mr. Gibbs would trip him up with some question he already knew the answer to, like one of Carlos's know-it-all television lawyers. And all of a sudden, Uncle Timo would be calling the ACS man "dude," and before the ACS man left the apartment he would figure out that Papi hadn't run out on Carlos and Michael. Even worse, that he had been dead for almost three whole months.

And then . . .

Michael squeezed his eyes shut, as hard as he could, taking the same walk up the hill that Ellie had just taken, Michael just having told Manny that he didn't feel like practicing today, he didn't feel like doing anything, he just wanted to go home.

When he got to 825 Gerard, he went upstairs to the empty apartment. The quiet apartment. Never had it seemed quite this empty to Michael, quite this quiet.

Never had he felt so alone.

"Hello, little one," Mrs. C said after Michael knocked on her door. "Come watch *Oprah* with me, I think she's going to give away more cars today."

Mrs. C had the same kind of recliner chair Papi had, one that

Michael sometimes had to help her out of if she'd been sitting too long. He wondered how she got up and out of it when he wasn't around to help her. Somehow, though, she managed, the way she managed to get herself up the hill to Gerard when she was on her way back from the Imperial Market, having worked out a system where she bought her supplies a little bit at a time.

On days when she saw Michael in the back alley, throwing against his pitchback, she would take him with her to the Imperial.

"It is a two-bag day, little one," she would say. "Today you must be my assistant carrier. And maybe, just maybe, there will be a little candy in it for you when we get to the checkout."

Michael knew it wasn't maybe at all, she would always let him pick out whatever kind of candy bar he wanted, Nutrageous usually.

He watched her now, moving slowly across her own living room, the room as neat and clean as always, smelling, as always, of flowers, even when Michael couldn't see new flowers anywhere.

Lately she was moving more slowly. He could see that her ankles, showing underneath her long summer dress, looked more thick and swollen than ever, as if they had been stung by bees.

Michael worried sometimes that Mrs. C would be the next person he loved to leave him, even if he could not imagine his world without her in it.

"We should write a letter to Oprah the way some of these people do," she said to Michael now. "She is always trying to take care of strangers, why can't she take care of my two boys?"

Her two boys. Michael smiled. She made him smile as easily as Manny did, almost.

"Carlos and I don't need a new car, Mrs. C," he said.

"Oprah would know what to do about all your problems," she said. "I believe she is an angel on earth."

"But not a Los Angeles Angel."

It was a small joke between them, because Mrs. C talked about angels a lot, and knew so little about baseball.

"No," she said, "I don't think your baseball Angels are much of a help to us."

Now hush, she said, *Oprah* was almost over. Michael asked if he could get a drink of water. Mrs. C said there was a pitcher of iced tea she'd just made fresh in the refrigerator, and peanut butter cookies just out of the oven on the counter. He could have a couple if he promised to eat all his supper. Michael said he didn't know what Carlos had left him for supper and Mrs. C said, forget what Carlos had left, she was going to cook him up some *paella* just the way he liked it.

Michael left her with Oprah and went into the kitchen, where the baking smells were as familiar to him as everything else in Mrs. C's world. He poured himself a glass of iced tea—orange peels swimming in it as usual—and grabbed two cookies and when he came back into the living room, she had muted her set for the beginning of the five o'clock news.

She said, "Now what's on your mind, little one? There's always something on your mind when you come here. Usually something making you sad."

He told her all about Ellie then, trying to get in all the important parts, all the way to what had just happened down at the field.

She raised an eyebrow. "So this is the girlfriend you were chasing?"

"She's not my girlfriend."

"Sounds like one to me," she said, showing him just the hint of a smile. "Or you wouldn't be so upset about this."

"She's just a girl who happens to be a friend."

It's what Manny said about Maria Cuellar all the time. What guys *had* to say.

"Whatever you say." She raised an eyebrow at him, to let him know she was playing.

"I'm just trying to figure out what I did that was so wrong," Michael said.

"You hurt her feelings for no reason, little one, that's what you did wrong. And you know it. Because you are too smart *not* to know it."

"I didn't mean to, it was the words that came out wrong."

"You called her a liar, Michael."

"I said she *told* a lie she didn't have to tell."

"Obviously she thought she did."

"She should have trusted me."

Mrs. C put out her hand now, a gesture they both knew meant she wanted Michael to help her out of the chair. He did, and she shuffled over in her summer sandals and sat down next to him on the couch. Still holding his hand.

"She is the daughter of your hero," Mrs. C said.

"But . . ."

"Hush," Mrs. C said, the same way she had said it at the end of *Oprah*. "She is the daughter of the great baseball pitcher, and that is the only way everyone here sees her, no matter where she goes or who she is with. At school. Up where you say she lives, in Riverdale was it? And at Yankee games, too. Only now she makes two friends, Michael and Manuel, who have no idea who she is, who like her for herself. And she doesn't want to give that up right away, because she likes being liked for herself. Likes feeling normal for a change. You, of all people, must be able to understand that."

Michael stared at her face, her dark eyes set in the dark, smooth skin, underneath her white hair with all the curls. They were close enough for him to smell the soap smell she gave off, as if she had just come out of one of the bubble baths she always talked about, where she would rest her weary bones at the end of the day. As old as she was, Michael could look at her sometimes and see what she must have looked like when she was young and, he was sure, beautiful.

"Okay," Michael said. "I messed up. Big time. The same way I've been messing up all over the place."

"No, you have not," she said. "It's everything that has gotten messed up *around* you, little one. But it's all going to work out, I promise you."

"Right," Michael said. "Things have been working out so great for me, no reason they should stop now."

"Don't sound so resentful, little one. You know what Grandmama Cora says about people who are resentful in this world."

Michael knew it by heart. "It's like they take poison and then hope for the other person to die."

She squeezed his hand. "For now, just take care of the things you can take care of. And this Ellie of yours is as good a place to start as any."

"I don't know how."

"Call her and apologize."

"I still don't have her number, and it's not like I can call information and ask for El Grande's house."

"Leave a note for her at the ballpark."

"They'll never give it to her."

"You don't know that until you try."

"She only shows up when her father is pitching," Michael said. "And he doesn't pitch for a few more days, and the Yankees will be out of town by then. . . ."

He started to feel himself filling up again. It was happening a lot lately, when he started to think about everything and feel like he was Chicken Little, in the bedtime story Papi used to read to him, about the sky falling.

Mrs. C knew. "Come here, little one," she said, pulling him close to her. "Let's play our game."

It was the one where he would close his eyes and see the happy endings he wanted. Where everything in his world worked out the way he wanted it to. She would make him go through his wish list, one item at a time.

"Just do the baseball parts today," she said.

"I don't feel like it today, Mrs. C."

"You can do it," she said. "I'll even start you off. We've found your birth certificate and all of a sudden you're running out to the mound at Yankee Stadium, waving to Carlos and me in our front-row seats, and we cheer along with the rest of the crowd. . . ."

Michael took it from there, holding on tight to Mrs. C, his eyes closed, the smell of her soap covering him like one of her soft blankets.

Sometimes he still felt safe.

CARLOS MET UNCLE TIMO FOR BREAKFAST, JUST THE TWO OF THEM AT OREM'S Diner, three doors up from the McDonald's on 161st. The two of them went back and forth about what questions the ACS man might ask, the things Carlos said Uncle Timo absolutely had to know.

Like the two of them were studying for a test.

Carlos told Michael all about it when he came back to the apartment to change into his work clothes for the Imperial. Telling Michael he wished he could get off early from work to be there, but they needed every dollar right now.

"You think Uncle Timo knows enough about us to get by now?" Michael said.

"Fingers crossed," Carlos said. "But I have to tell you, with that guy, he's serious one minute and then acting like a total nut job the next." Carlos tapped the side of his head. "He's a little crazy up here, this one."

"We're the crazy ones," Michael said. "To think we could pull something like this off with somebody as smart as Mr. Gibbs."

"You mean somebody who probably has kids trying to scam him all the time?"

"He's going to see right through this," Michael said.

"We still have to try, Miguel. We can't be looking over our shoulders for him every day from now until my eighteenth birthday. Once he's out of the way, we can try to get your birth certificate before it's too late for it to do us any good."

Michael said, "You know what Yogi Berra used to say, right?"

138

"Even I know Yogi used to say a lot of things," Carlos said.

"One of his best," Michael said, "was when he said it sure gets late early around here."

Uncle Timo was supposed to arrive at the apartment at twelve-thirty, a half hour before Mr. Gibbs. Manny, who had come over to spend the morning with Michael, promised his uncle would be on time.

"He knows how important this is," Manny said.

"You sure about that?"

"Would it help if I told you to relax again?"

"No!" Michael said.

At twelve forty-five Uncle Timo still wasn't there.

Manny used the phone in the kitchen to try his cell.

No answer.

"You're probably on your way," Manny said into the receiver. "But please call when you get this."

Michael went over and sat on the windowsill, looking one way and then the other, hoping he would see Uncle Timo walking up the street before Mr. Gibbs.

All he saw was a street-cleaning truck, and some little girls from across the street playing four-square on a chalk outline on the sidewalk.

"What time is it now?" he said to Manny.

"Five minutes since the last time you asked me," Manny said.

Michael sighed and wished Carlos was around.

As soon as he went back to his perch on the windowsill, he saw Mr. Gibbs come around the corner of 158th Street.

Still no Uncle Timo.

"He's here," Michael said to Manny.

"Great."

Michael said, "What do we tell him when he asks where my father is?"

"That he's out running an errand and he'll be right back," Manny said.

There was a knock on the door. As Michael went to answer it, Manny said, "One more thing?"

"We have enough things."

Manny said, "I think it would help if you didn't look like you just broke a window."

Michael gave him a face and opened the door. Mr. Gibbs was wearing a faded short-sleeved shirt with a tiny crocodile on the front, hanging out over his pants, and the same beat-up sneakers he'd been wearing the other times Michael had seen him.

"My dad will be back any second," Michael said, not even bothering to say hello. "He had to run an errand."

He didn't move, just stood there with his hand on the doorknob. Mr. Gibbs didn't move. Finally Mr. Gibbs said, "Do you mind if I come in and wait inside?"

"Sorry," Michael said, making a sweeping gesture with his hand like he was showing him in. "Did you ever meet my friend Manny?"

"The catcher," Mr. Gibbs said.

Manny smiled, obviously pleased that Mr. Gibbs had recognized him.

At least somebody was in a good mood.

Mr. Gibbs said to Michael, "Is Carlos coming?"

Michael explained that Carlos had to work. Mr. Gibbs said he understood, and sat down. Michael, trying to remember his manners, asked if he wanted something to drink. Mr. Gibbs said he was fine for now. Then nobody said anything for what seemed like an hour to Michael until Mr. Gibbs said, "It must be great having your dad home."

"I just wish he could stay longer," Michael said.

"When does he have to go back?"

"Today or tomorrow, he's not sure."

Would Uncle Timo say that?

Shoot.

"He probably wishes you were pitching tonight."

"Not as much as I do," Michael said.

"Correction," Manny said. "Not as much as *we* do."

"On that subject," Mr. Gibbs said, "if there's anything I can do . . ."

Michael said, "Carlos keeps calling people. In Havana, I mean. But the phone calls are expensive, and always it seems that the person he's talking to isn't the person he needs to be talking to."

"I hate to say it," Mr. Gibbs said, "but in that sense, Castro's government sounds a lot like ours."

"Sometimes I think we need a miracle," Michael said.

The door opened then, and Uncle Timo walked in.

Only he wasn't Uncle Timo, at least not today, Michael could see it without his having said a word.

He knew he was staring, but he couldn't help himself.

Uncle Timo had turned himself into Papi.

21 ⊙⊙⊙⊙⊙⊙⊙⊙⊙⊙⊙⊙⊙⊙⊙⊙⊙

EVEN MANNY WAS SPEECHLESS FOR A CHANGE.

Uncle Timo was wearing Papi's favorite old khaki slacks, the ones Carlos had sent home with Manny the night before, and the kind of black T-shirt their father had always seemed to be wearing when he wasn't driving. Papi's old pocket watch, the one that had belonged to their grandfather, was attached to a thick chain hanging from Uncle Timo's belt.

But it wasn't just the clothes.

In just one day Uncle Timo's beard looked as heavy as Papi's had been the day he died. And he had shaved his head into the dark crew cut Papi always wore in the summer.

Even from where he stood across the room, Michael could see the tattoo on Timo Morales's right forearm of a tocoroco, the national bird of Cuba, the feathers almost as big as the bird itself.

Just like Papi's tattoo, the one he used to joke was better than anything any NBA player had on his arm or his leg or even his neck.

Michael was wondering if it was real as Uncle Timo walked toward him with his arms stretched wide the way Papi always did when he came through the door, hugged him close, kissed the side of his face, Michael feeling a familiar scratch of beard that actually made him shiver.

I feel like I'm with a ghost, he thought.

"*El ratoncito, Miguel,*" he said.

It meant, Mike the little mouse.

"Father," was the best Michael could do.

He even *sounds* like him, Michael thought, the words coming out in a husky voice, like the low growl of a dog.

The accent was perfect.

Uncle Timo pulled back now, winking at Michael as he did, saying, *"Silencio, no hay que gritas, no se vaya a despectar."*

Carlos must have given him Cuban expressions to use whether they made sense or not. If Mr. Gibbs did speak Cuban somehow, he was probably wondering why Michael's father was telling him not to scream and wake up the cat.

Uncle Timo turned toward Mr. Gibbs then, right hand extended toward him, saying, "How do you do, sir, I am Victor Arroyo and am here to be thanking you so much for taking an interest in my *ratoncito.*"

Papi's English, Michael thought, was better. Had been better. But Mr. Gibbs didn't know that.

The two men shook hands. As they did Mr. Gibbs said, "I speak a little Spanish, but not enough to know what that means."

"From the time he was born and made these little squeaks in his crib, Michael has been my little mouse," Uncle Timo said. "Even as I watched him grow up and start to throw a baseball like a young Sandy Koufax." He pointed a finger now at the ACS man, said, "You are the right age to have seen the great Koufax, am I correct, sir?"

"You got me," Mr. Gibbs said. "He was my favorite pitcher of all time. I grew up in Brooklyn, but I was one of the kids who kept rooting for the Dodgers after they left for Los Angeles."

"The way we Cubanos always rooted for our baseball heroes after they started leaving us for America."

The two of them standing here and chatting like old friends after knowing each other for, what, two whole minutes?

"Please have a seat, Mr. Gibbs," Uncle Timo said, gesturing toward the couch. "I will take my favorite chair, the one I have not gotten to sit in too much as of lately, and which my sons say should be condemned."

He put a little extra accent into the last word, making it come out "condemn-ED."

Mr. Gibbs took a seat on the couch. Uncle Timo gave Michael a quick wink, as if the two of them were sharing a private joke. "And what about you two? Would you care to sit down and join us, Miguelito?" Another Papi expression. "Or are the two of you just going to stand there like statues in a church?"

"I'm fine," Michael said.

"I'm good," Manny said.

Uncle Timo got right to it with Mr. Gibbs.

"I am so sorry," he said, "for somehow making you worry that I had abandoned my two boys."

"I just feel that in my job," Mr. Gibbs said, "it's better to be safe than sorry. And, believe me, the last thing we want to do at the ACS is put two more boys in the care of the city."

"Of course."

"There was a time," Mr. Gibbs said, "when we had over fifty thousand children in the system. But over the past several years, that number has dropped to under twenty thousand."

Uncle Timo sighed. "It is still a big enough crowd to fill the Madison Square Garden."

"It's why I'd rather be too nosy than not nosy enough," Mr. Gibbs said. "If I even get a whiff that two young kids may be living without a parent, no matter how well they think they're doing, I wouldn't be doing my job if I didn't check it out."

Uncle Timo's eyes locked on Michael's, the smallest of smiles on his face as he said, "We are so grateful that an Official Person like yourself took such an interest in our family, even if it has not been so much of a family lately." He nodded, as if he'd convinced himself of something, then said, "This is how we hoped America would work, people caring for other people in such a way as this."

Even Michael thought he was starting to spread it on a little thick, but he could see there was no stopping him now.

"Would anybody like some lemonade?" Michael said. "Manny and I were just going to make some when Mr. Gibbs showed up, weren't we?"

Manny said, "Right! Lemonade. Boy, I'm thirsty enough to drink a whole pitcher!"

They walked through the kitchen doors as they heard Mr. Gibbs say, "So, Mr. Arroyo . . ."

"Call me Victor, please."

"So, Victor," Mr. Gibbs said, "tell me about your brother."

Michael and Manny were standing just inside the kitchen door. Manny said, "This is *so* on."

Michael pinched Manny's arm with one hand, put a finger to his lips with the other.

"Ouch!"

"Shhhh."

Manny said, "I was just saying."

"You're always just saying," Michael whispered. "I just would appreciate it if you didn't say anything right now."

Manny couldn't help himself. "All I was trying to say . . ."

"Manny," Michael said, "just this one time, I don't want you to do play-by-play on your life."

They both listened at the door to Uncle Timo, who Michael thought was a clown when he met him, like one of the clowns that used to make him laugh at the famous Havana circus, El Guinol

Nacional. Now he was telling Mr. Gibbs a story that even Michael found himself believing, about an uncle of Michael's that did not exist:

About his brother's terrible blood sickness that was so far gone, but somehow could not kill him. About the woman his brother had lived with for years in a place called Homestead, Florida—where was *that*? Michael wondered to himself—a sweet, beautiful woman that Luis had hoped to marry once, before he took ill.

He said that her name was Julia, then actually gave Mr. Gibbs her phone number, in case he ever again had concerns about Carlos and Michael and needed to contact him immediately.

Michael poked Manny. "Who is Julia?"

"Will you *please* stop hitting me."

"Is she real?"

"Oh, now I can talk?"

Michael just stared at him, the way he did in baseball when Manny would come walking out for a chat and Michael would stare him back behind the plate.

"Julia is the name of the old girlfriend Uncle Timo told us about," Manny said. "The one from the dinner theater down there."

In the living room, Uncle Timo was saying, "I make a promise to my brother that I will be there for him until the end."

"I understand," Mr. Gibbs said.

"When I am down there, I am constantly on the phone, trying to find someone in Havana who can find a copy of Michael's birth certificate, which somehow has disappeared." There was a pause and then Uncle Timo said, "Maybe because we disappeared on the boat that night."

"It's stupid that Michael even has to be put through this, if you want my opinion," Mr. Gibbs said.

Next to Michael Manny said, "Tell me about it."

Michael made a motion like he was going to pinch him again.

"Don't come any closer," Manny said.

He cracked the door open just slightly. Uncle Timo was saying to Mr. Gibbs, ". . . I am the big stupid for making sure I did not have it in my possession before we are saying good-bye to Cuba forever and for good."

"I told Michael before you got here, and now I'll tell you," Mr. Gibbs said. "If there's anything I can do, let me know."

"Maybe if an Official Person from here called an Official Person there."

"I can't make any promises," Mr. Gibbs said. "But I'll sure give it a shot."

Uncle Timo raised his voice now and said, "I thought you two knuckleballs said you had the lemonade made already."

"Coming, Papi," Manny said.

"Papi?" Michael said.

"I want to get into the act."

"Wow," Michael said, "that doesn't sound anything like you."

Michael carried the pitcher they had put in the refrigerator. Manny brought four glasses on the kind of plastic tray you got for your food at McDonald's. Uncle Timo poured, like it was some kind of party and he was pouring wine or champagne for his guests.

Then he raised his own glass.

"To my Miguelito," he said. "May the next time we are all together be on the day when he pitches himself—and his proud papi—to the Little League World Series in Williamsport, Pennsylvania."

They all clicked glasses and drank lemonade. Uncle Timo drank his in loud gulps, then made a big show of wiping his mustache with the back of his hand, just the way Papi used to. Then, as if overcome by the emotion of this great moment, he spread his arms wide again, motioning Michael to come into them.

"My son," he said.

He put his arms around Michael and hugged him even tighter than he had when he came in, and then in a whispery voice just barely loud enough for Michael Arroyo to hear, he said, "Top *that,* dude."

22

IN HIS HEART, MICHAEL KNEW HE WASN'T GOING TO PLAY ANY MORE BASEBALL this season.

But it was all right.

Really it was.

Even if this was his one and only chance to make it to the Little League World Series. Even if it turned out he missed out on that. He told himself he would get over it, as long as he and Carlos got to stay together. And, Michael had to admit, he felt a lot better about their chances now that Uncle Timo had put on such a good show for Mr. Gibbs.

So he kept telling himself to feel good about that, mostly because he needed to feel good about something today, the first day of the play-offs for the Clippers. After all the surprises in his life lately, just about every single one of them bad, Uncle Timo turning himself into Papi the way he had, that was most definitely a good thing.

Maybe that was the way you should go through life, if you really thought about it. Maybe if you didn't expect good things to happen to you, well, when something *did,* it would seem much bigger and better than it actually was.

A few weeks ago, the only victory that would have mattered today would have been the Clippers over the Rosedale Park Robins at Macombs. Not anymore. The biggest win of the day was Uncle Timo. By a lot. Everything after this was going to be the cherry on top of the ice cream sundae that Manny was always talking about.

In Manny's view of the world, there was always another sundae coming along that needed another cherry, just because Manny believed every single day was going to be the best of his whole life.

Michael tried to remember the last time he had felt that way about stuff.

But he couldn't.

The Rosedale Park Robins were *really* good, at least when they had all their players.

The problem for them was they had played most of the season without their best player, Corey Allen. Their Michael Arroyo, as Manny referred to him. Corey Allen had managed to slice open the bottom of his foot playing soccer barefoot just a couple of days into the District 22 season. He'd had to get twenty stitches, or so Manny had heard from a friend of his who played on the Robins, and hadn't returned to his team until there were two weeks to go in the regular season, pitching well enough to get them the last slot in the play-offs.

"If he'd been healthy," Anthony Fierro was saying after infield practice at Macombs, "they'd have been good enough to fight us for the number one seed."

Manny at that moment was trying to stuff a world's record amount of bubble gum into his mouth, his right cheek already looking as if he had a baseball in there.

"Yeah," he said, "and if my mom had wheels, she'd be a bicycle."

"I was just saying," Anthony said.

Mr. Minaya said, "The great football coach Bill Parcells has a saying."

Michael looked at Manny, who rolled his eyes, just because for about the one thousandth time, Mr. Minaya had a saying that applied to whatever they happened to be talking about. Michael figured that the great Bill Parcells probably ran out of sayings eventually, but Mr. M never did.

Mr. M said, "Coach Parcells likes to say that in sports, you are what your record says you are."

"I liked our record a lot better when we had Michael," Manny said.

"We will win tonight and get young Mr. Arroyo back somehow before we play again," Mr. M said.

In your dreams, Michael thought.

And mine.

"Win one for Michael!" Manny said.

"Win one for Mike!" Anthony said.

Then all the Clippers were gathered around Michael, and chanting, "Mike! Mike! Mike!"

Almost making him feel like a real part of the team.

Right before the start of the game, Mr. M came over to where Michael was sitting, at the end of the bench, near the big duffel bag filled with their practice balls.

"I want you to coach third base tonight," Mr. M said.

Michael put a hand to his ear, as if he hadn't heard him correctly.

"Excuse me?"

"I want you to coach third."

"No way."

Mr. M grinned, "Way," he said, sounding like one of the kids on the team.

"Mr. M," he said. "You always coach third, every single game. And this isn't every single game, it's a *play-off* game."

"I know."

"Corey Allen is pitching," Michael said. "Which means every run is going to count."

"Yes, I'm aware of that," Mr. M said.

Michael looked around, to make sure nobody else could hear. "*Please* don't make me."

"You should want to coach third," Mr. M said.

"Why is that?" Michael said.

"Because coaching third is as close as you can get to the action without actually playing," Mr. M said. "And in my opinion, getting you as close to the action as possible gives us our best possible chance to win the game."

Michael could see there was no way he was going to change his mind. Once Mr. M dug in, he dug in.

"I hope you're right," Michael said.

"I am."

He was wrong.

In the bottom of the fifth, with Anthony Fierro—in Manny's words—pitching his lungs off, the game was still scoreless. Kel was on first, nobody out. Manny put a great swing on a Corey Allen fastball and drilled it up the alley in left-center, between the center fielder and the left fielder.

It looked as if the ball was going to roll all the way to the wall.

Until it didn't.

The center fielder came over and cut the ball off. By then, Michael was sure that the ball was deep enough to score Kel whether it got cut off or not. So he was sending Kel all the way, from the time he rounded second, waving his arms like he was a windmill, even as the center fielder made a perfect cutoff throw to Corey Allen himself, standing near second base.

Michael sent Kel home even though he could have held him at

third and the Clippers would have had runners on second and third, still with nobody out.

Corey Allen caught the ball and turned and threw home all in one motion, threw home as if he were throwing one of his fastballs, threw a perfect strike to the Robins' catcher, who put the tag on Kel and kept the game at 0–0.

Manny didn't take third on the throw to the plate. He hesitated as he watched the play at the plate, then must have decided that he didn't want to run himself into a double play, run the Clippers right out of the inning. So he only got to third when Chris Nourse grounded out to the Robins' second baseman, the kid making a terrific sliding stop to keep the ball from going into right field, then getting Nourse by a step at first.

Then Anthony Fierro struck out to end the inning.

Michael thought: Even with my bonehead play, Manny should have been on third. With one out, this late in the game, the Robins would have had to bring the infield in for a possible play at the plate on a ground ball, and Chris Nourse's ball would have gone past the second baseman before he even moved on it, and Manny could have walked home. . . .

Stop it, you jerk.

Mr. M always said: Never assume how things *could* have played out in baseball, or how an inning *could* have played itself out.

The truth was that Manny should have been on second and Kel on third with nobody out, and from there it would have been practically impossible for the Clippers not to be ahead 1–0. Only they weren't ahead, they were still tied.

Because of me, Michael thought.

What had he been *thinking*?

He had always taken pride in knowing the right play at any

given moment in the game. Papi had schooled him on fundamentals from the first time he had played organized baseball in Havana, back when he was seven. When he was in the outfield, he always hit the right cutoff man. When he was pitching, he backed up first base on even the most routine plays in the infield. He never took a chance on the bases, *never*, if he wasn't sure he could take an extra base.

Even as close as the backstop behind home plate was at most of the fields where they played, Manny knew Michael would always have his back on plays at the plate. Three or four times this season, there had been a bad relay throw that skipped past Manny, but Michael had been there to scoop the ball up and throw out somebody on the other team being foolish enough to take an extra base on him.

Now he had been responsible for the bonehead play of the year. The District 22 play-offs were double elimination, so the season wasn't over if the Clippers lost to the Robins. Just as good as over. Because as soon as you lost a game in the play-offs, you went into the losers' bracket—for losers like me, Michael thought as he walked slowly behind the screen to get back to the bench—and had to play another losing team the next day just to keep playing. Extra games meant extra pitchers, and the Clippers without Michael didn't have enough pitching to begin with.

Forget about making it to Williamsport.

If they lost tonight, they'd be lucky to make it to the end of the stinking week.

"Forget it," Manny said after Michael had taken what felt like a five-mile walk back to the bench and sat down with him. "We'll get 'em next inning."

Michael pulled his cap down as tight as he could over his eyes. "What makes you think so?"

154

"Because we are not losing to the Robins, that's what makes me think so," Manny said, using Manny logic.

"Maybe we just did." Michael tried to pull the cap down even lower over his eyes, like he wanted to use it as a mask. "I am *such* a loser!"

"Hey!" Manny said.

He reached over and tried to pull Michael's cap off his eyes and pulled it right off his head instead.

"Look at me," Manny said in a mean voice Michael almost didn't recognize.

Michael turned around, staring at his cap in Manny's hand, like he was the magician who came to school once a year and had just pulled the rabbit out of the hat.

Manny said, "If you're going to talk like a loser, go sit somewhere else, because I don't want to listen to you anymore."

Maybe there was another time when his best friend had talked to him like this, but Michael sure couldn't remember it.

"All I meant was . . ."

"All you meant was that you're feeling sorry for yourself, and you want to tell me all about it," Manny said. "I'm just telling you to stop, okay? Because it's not doing us any good. Okay?"

"Okay."

"You want to make yourself useful?" Manny said. "Figure out something that will help us win the game." He handed Michael back his cap. "Okay?"

"Okay already," Michael said.

Manny finished putting his catcher's equipment back on while Mr. M warmed up Anthony. It seemed like about five minutes later the Robins had the bases loaded with two outs.

Mr. M asked Michael, who'd been charting Anthony's pitches, how many he had thrown.

"Sixty on the nose," Michael said.

"Well then he's done, isn't he?"

"Coach," Michael said, "Corey Allen's up. You know he's their best hitter on top of being their best pitcher. Anthony only gave him a single first time up, and then he got him to fly to Teddy. He's still our best chance, even if he is right up against the pitch limit."

"Nobody pitches past sixty, Michael. Not even you."

Sixty for Mr. M, who always said he was never going to put a twelve-year-old pitcher's arm in jeopardy, was as much a magic number for him as eighty—as in miles per hour—was for Michael and Manny.

"Well, who are you going to bring in?" Michael said.

Mr. M leaned back, closed his eyes for a second, then said, "Kel. Maybe after seeing Anthony throw nothing but fastballs all game, Kel can fool Corey with a couple of those Wiffle balls he throws up there."

Mr. M sat up straight, clapped his hands together one time, as if that settled it. "Kel it is. For one batter. If he gets out of it, I'll go with Nourse in extra innings."

Mr. M called time, walked out to the mound, called all the infielders in when he got there, put his arm around Anthony's shoulders, took the ball from him. Then Michael saw Mr. M talking to Kel. Saw Kel's eyes get wide as he looked at Corey Allen in the on-deck circle. Saw Kel turn back to Mr. M and mouth the words, *No way.*

Mr. M said something else. Kel said something back. Then suddenly Kel laughed. Mr. M put Anthony at third, moved Chris Nourse to short, walked back to the bench as Kel began taking his warm-ups.

Michael asked what had been so funny that it got a laugh out of Kel.

156

"Manny."

"What did he say?"

Mr. M laughed now.

"Well, he didn't actually say anything."

Michael knew.

"I asked if anybody had anything they wanted to add and Manny made his, ah, famous whoopee cushion noise. The one he seems to be able to produce at will."

Michael said, "His signature move."

Then he and Mr. M both watched, neither one of them saying anything, as Kel, throwing pitches that really did seem to float up to home plate like buds blowing in the wind, finally got Corey Allen to take a huge swing at a 2-2 pitch and pop the ball to Nourse for the third out.

Inning over.

Game still 0–0.

Michael nudged Mr. M and stuck out his palm so Mr. M could give him a low five.

"*Righteous* pitching move," he said.

Mr. M said, "See, that's the thing, Michael. They're all good moves in baseball when they work."

23 ⓞⓞⓞⓞⓞⓞⓞⓞⓞⓞⓞⓞⓞⓞ

MARIA CUELLAR WALKED TO START THE BOTTOM OF THE SIXTH INNING FOR the Clippers. Corey Allen was still in there pitching for the Robins, but this was it for him, even if the game kept going, six innings being all you could pitch in one game in the play-offs. If you did pitch six, you had to take one game and one day off before you could pitch again.

The Robins' coach, a loud little guy in a Yankees cap, was yelling as much now, Michael noticed, as he had when the game started, moving all his fielders around, infielders and outfielders both, as soon as Maria got down to first base.

Manny always joked that he wished you could use the kind of electric fence that people used for their dogs at Little League fields, so you could zap coaches if they went near the field for anything except making a pitching change.

The worst thing that could happen now was extra innings. But nobody on the Clips' bench, all of them with their caps turned sideways—rally cap time—was thinking about extra innings now that Maria was on base. They were thinking about ending the sucker right now.

Nate Collins, the Clippers' left fielder, bunted Maria to second. One out.

Tommy Growney, the right fielder, grounded to second, Maria taking third on the play.

Two outs.

Their last shot at Corey Allen.

Bobby Cameron, the weakest hitter they had, at the plate.

The Robins' third baseman moved in a little. When he did, Maria said to Michael, "Any strategy here I ought to know about?"

"Soon," he said.

"How soon?"

"Right before you score the winning run."

"With *Bobby* hitting?"

"With Bobby hitting," Michael said.

Bobby was only in center tonight because the regular center fielder, Zach Frazier, was sick with some kind of summer flu. Bobby Cameron had been a decent player during the regular season, playing for the Willis Avenue Mets. But he'd stopped hitting almost as soon as All-Stars started, and now was completely clueless at the plate. He'd been up twice against Corey Allen and struck out both times on three pitches, both times making strike three easy, swinging at pitches over his head, as if he just wanted to get the at bat over with, and get back to the bench.

Now Michael could see, just by the look on Bobby Cameron's face when he looked down toward third for a sign—wanting to know if he should take a strike—that he wanted to be just about anyplace on the planet Earth except facing Corey Allen with what might be the winning run on third.

Michael knew the look, because he saw it from guys having to face him all the time.

Back when he was a pitcher, not a third-base coach.

Figure out a way to win us this game, Manny had said.

Mr. M said, "Hey," from across the field. Gave Michael the take sign that Michael was supposed to give to Bobby.

But instead of doing that, Michael called time, started walking toward the plate, motioned for Bobby to come up the line and talk to him.

He could feel everybody on the field looking at him. He gave a quick look across to Mr. M in the first-base coaching box, Mr. M giving him a look of his own. Like: What's going on here?

Michael would have told him if he could.

He was getting into the game.

The umpire said, "Let's not turn this into a chat room, boys, especially if this baby's about to go extra innings."

Even the ump didn't think Bobby had a chance to do anything against Corey Allen.

"I just want to go through the signs with him real quick," Michael said.

Michael put his hands on Bobby's shoulders, as a way of focusing him, the way grown-up coaches did when they had a conference like this. Bobby was a head smaller than he was, small and fast, a much better soccer player than he was a baseball player.

In a quiet voice Michael said, "Corey's getting tired."

Bobby said, "He'd have to be *asleep* for me to get a hit off him." He looked up at Michael and said, "And how do you know he's getting tired, by the way? You haven't had to hit against the guy."

"Trust me," Michael said. "Two people here know how tired he is. Him and me. He's dropping his arm. When he's missing, like he did with Maria, he's not just missing his spots anymore. He's missing by a lot. You know how the announcers say a pitcher's going on fumes? The guy's going on fumes. You can put your bat on him, even if it's just for a bunt."

"I can't."

"Yes, you can," Michael said.

The ump said, "Wrap it up, boys."

Michael told Bobby, "Listen up, here's what we're going to do."

"Is this Mr. M's idea?" Bobby said.

"No," Michael said. "It's mine." Then he watched Bobby walk

back to the batter's box, shaking his head, like he was being sent to his room.

Michael leaned in, made sure the Robins' third baseman wasn't listening, and told Maria what the play was, then got back into the coach's box, clapped his hands, and said, "C'mon, Bobby, let's do it!"

Corey Allen checked Maria, then went into his windup. As he did, Bobby Cameron squared to bunt. Just about every member of the Robins—and what sounded like half the neighborhood—yelled, "He's bunting!"

Their first baseman charged. Their third baseman charged. Corey Allen charged from the mound.

He didn't need to.

Bobby bunted at the ball and missed it by about two feet.

Now Corey Allen was the one shaking his head as he walked back to the mound, like he couldn't figure out what Bobby was thinking, trying some kind of squeeze play on him with two outs.

Michael leaned toward Maria and said, "Same deal."

Bobby squared again. Nobody needed to yell this time, everybody just charged the way they did the pitch before, and then watched as Bobby missed again.

Oh-and-two count.

Michael looked across at Mr. M, standing there in the first-base coach's box, arms out, palms up. Not looking at Bobby. Looking at Michael again, clearly mouthing these words:

What . . . are . . . you . . . doing?

Ignoring him, Michael took two steps toward third base, said to Maria, "Be ready to run home when he puts this one in play."

Maria was watching Corey Allen. Out of the side of her mouth she said, "*When* he puts the ball in play?"

Michael told her what he'd told Bobby Cameron: "Trust me."

161

Bobby squared this time before Corey Allen even went into his windup. Corey almost looked bored as he made the little rocking motion just before throwing the ball.

It wasn't until Corey's right arm started to come forward that Bobby jumped back into his regular stance the way Michael had told him to, got his bat back.

The pitch had nothing on it because Corey didn't think he had to put anything on it, he didn't even care whether or not Bobby was dumb enough to be bunting with two strikes.

Except.

Except Bobby Cameron, seeing the easiest pitch to hit he was ever going to see in his life, especially from a pitcher this good, was hitting away, putting his bat on the ball the way Michael had told him he would, slapping the ball to the left of the Robins' third baseman.

Who was coming down toward the plate as hard as he had on the first two pitches, and couldn't stop himself in time, or get his glove out in time. As the ball went past him, he looked a little bit, Michael thought, like a hockey goalie failing to make a glove save.

The ball was past him then, barely making it to the infield dirt next to third base. Maria was already across home plate when the Robins' shortstop, racing for the ball, picked it up barehanded and threw so wildly across the diamond trying to get Bobby at first—Bobby running as fast as he ever had on his little soccer legs—that Michael thought for a moment the ball might end up one-hopping the Major Deegan Expressway.

Clippers 1, Robins 0.

Game over.

Michael felt happy for everybody on the team, he really did.

And for a few seconds there at the end, when he was halfway

between third and home, running right along with Maria as she tore for the plate, watching their third baseman roll himself over on the grass so he could watch the ball slowly roll away from him, Michael almost felt as if he was in the game.

Almost.

And he had to admit to himself that it didn't stink watching the Robins' coach start yelling at everybody at once, even if nobody on the Robins had done anything wrong.

They hadn't lost the game, the Clips had just won it.

"How many times have we worked on situations like this?" His face turned into one of the big fat tomatoes Mrs. C was always bringing back from the Imperial for one of her special sauces. "How many times?"

Right, Michael thought, the old two-strike, two-out, runner-on-third, fake-squeeze-and-swing-away play.

We work on that baby all the time.

Michael walked away from the Robins' bench, across the infield, stopped at the pitcher's mound, found himself going there like it was the most natural place in the world for him to be, watched the Clippers' celebration from there. Half the guys were still around Maria. Manny, Michael couldn't help noticing, looked more excited at having a good reason to hug Maria than he was about winning the game.

The rest of the Clips were in a pig-pile over behind first base, little Bobby Cameron finally crawling out from underneath them, looking happier in that moment than Michael had ever seen him on a baseball field.

Bobby looked at Michael standing there on the mound then, pointed at him and didn't say anything, just mouthed a single word: *You.*

Michael shook his head, pointed his finger back at Bobby, mouthed these words right back at him: *No, you.*

Then he felt a hand on his shoulder and turned to see Mr. M right behind him on the mound.

"I know you don't want to hear this," Mr. M said. "And I know it could never be enough for you, Michael. But you did as much as anybody to win this game."

"Players win the game, Coach," he said. "You tell us that all the time. You tell us that it doesn't matter whether it's Little League or the Yankees, it's a players' game. Don't you?"

Mr. M said, "I do."

"Anthony won the game for us tonight by pitching the way he did. Kel pitched out of that jam against Corey Allen. Maria worked him for a walk when we needed a base runner. Then Bobby finally did something he told me he couldn't do. That was the coolest part of all, as cool as them beating those guys."

Mr. M tried to correct him. "*Us* beating those guys."

Michael grinned then and did a Manny, made his two thumbs and two index fingers into the *w* that every single member of the Clippers knew meant one thing:

Whatever.

"Okay," Mr. M said, "you got me there. But I do have one piece of information that *is* guaranteed to make you feel better. That coach over there with the other team? Mr. Bender? The one pouting like a kid who just lost his video game privileges?"

Michael turned on the mound. The Robins must have cleared away from the bench as soon as he stopped yelling at them. Now he was sitting at the end of the bench all by himself, staring at the Clippers players still celebrating on the field as if they were already going to Williamsport.

"I thought it got quieter over there all of a sudden," Michael said.

Mr. M said, "He's one of the coaches who signed the complaint about you and your birth certificate, and has been telling everybody there's no way you can be twelve."

"But he doesn't even know me," Michael said.

"We know him, though, don't we?" Mr. M said. "Him and all coaches like him."

Michael stared at the Robins' coach. "He belongs in the losers' bracket."

"Yeah, he does," Mr. M said. "And you helped put him there. So smile a little."

Michael did.

But Mr. M was right.

It *wasn't* enough.

He went over and gave Bobby a high five. And Kel. And then Maria. Manny came running at him and Michael knew what was coming next, the kind of flying chest bump the NBA players now did when you saw them being introduced before the game.

"I *knew* you'd think of something," Manny said.

"Bobby's the one who got the run home."

"Yeah, but you got the assist, bud."

Manny's mom had brought homemade chocolate chip cookies and Gatorade boxes for the snack. When everybody started to rip into the cookies, Michael turned and started walking toward the Stadium, where the Yankee game had either just started, or was about to start. By the time he crossed the Macombs' basketball courts, he could hear the PA music from inside. And could see people who had gotten caught in traffic or had just come late to the ballpark running for the turnstiles. As usual, he could feel the excitement that seemed to be coming through the Stadium's old walls, crashing right through them, even though it was just an August game against the Seattle Mariners.

This was one of those nights when he wanted to be inside even more than he usually did.

He didn't want to listen on the radio tonight. What he really wanted to do was sprint right up the hill, sprint past the security people working the turnstile at the press gate, blow right past them before they could stop him and head for the nearest entrance to the field, go all the way down to those choice seats near the field where he had spotted Ellie on television that time.

Tonight he wanted to be on the inside. Just once in his life.

One more dream just out of his reach, to go along with all the rest.

Michael didn't run anywhere. Nobody runs home to an empty apartment, he thought. Nobody runs to be alone.

He went up the hill, crossed Ruppert Place, made his way through the crowd, moved along the outside of the Stadium the way he did sometimes, dragging his hand lightly against the wall. Close enough to touch. Everybody else was rushing past him in the other direction, trying to get to their seats in time for the first pitch.

From inside, Michael could hear a woman begin to sing the national anthem.

Michael kept going toward 161st.

It was there, the corner of 161st and Ruppert, that he looked up, like this was another bad dream, not wanting to believe his eyes, and saw the two policemen walking Ramon the purse stealer toward the white van with "NYPD" written in huge blue letters on the side.

And not just Ramon.

Carlos, too.

MICHAEL DIDN'T KNOW WHAT TO DO.

He stood there, like he was frozen in place, like he was back at school and they were playing "freeze" in the yard at recess.

He didn't know whether to just run the other way, or yell out to his brother, or just walk over there and explain to the policemen that there had to be some kind of mistake.

Was Carlos being arrested?

And if that was true, what had he done to *get* arrested?

And what in the world was he doing with Ramon?

Carlos had said he was going to work at Hector's, like he did five nights a week and sometimes more, because he had told them to always call if one of the other busboys didn't show up for work. Now the tall black policeman had his hand on Carlos's shoulder. He wasn't shoving him toward the van exactly. Marching him in that direction was more like it. A smaller policeman was doing the same with Ramon the purse stealer. Michael could see Ramon talking away, the way he had talked and talked to Officer Crandall the day Michael's throw had taken him down in the outfield.

Every few steps, Michael saw, Ramon would stop and turn his head and say something, and the smaller cop would give him a push and Ramon would keep going.

Carlos didn't seem to be saying anything. Just kept his head down, with what Michael knew was his Washington Senators cap on his head. Carlos who had never done anything wrong in his life, who had never gotten a single detention in school. Carlos who worked practically all the time so he and Michael could stay together.

Now Michael stood there and wondered if these policemen were taking his brother away in some sort of portable jail.

But why?

The van, the size of a small bus, was closer to the subway station than it was to Macombs. Michael followed them toward it, keeping what he thought was a safe distance, afraid that at any moment Carlos might turn around and see him.

And what do I do if Carlos does see me? Michael thought.

He wanted to do *something* to help, it's what he thought a brother should do. He just didn't know what.

Where was Manny when he really needed him?

Michael had never paid much attention to the white van before, just knew it was always there for Yankee games, sitting there at the curb, part of the scenery on game nights the way the outside vendors were. He had never seen it arrive, was never around late enough to see when it left.

He had no idea what was inside.

He thought about going home as fast as he could, telling Mrs. C what had happened, seeing if she would know what to do, then coming right back. But then he wouldn't know if Carlos was still inside, or if they'd taken him someplace else.

He had some change in his pocket, and even thought about going to the pay phone at the bottom of the subway steps and actually calling Manny, hoping that he *could* come up with some bright idea. . . . After all, wasn't it Manny who had come up with the idea of a fake dad?

Or maybe that's what I should do, Michael thought, call my fake dad, Uncle Timo, the way kids called their real dad when they were in trouble.

An hour ago, it seemed like the worst thing that could possibly happen to him tonight was running Kel into that out at home plate against the Robins. . . .

The smaller policeman walked Ramon up some stairs and into the van. Carlos and the tall policeman stayed outside, Carlos with his head still down, the policeman pointing a finger at him and doing all the talking, Carlos just nodding his head sometimes.

Ever since Papi died, Michael and Carlos had joked to each other that they had to stay one step ahead of the law.

Not anymore.

For the first time, Michael noticed what was written on the side of the white van, in small blue letters underneath a huge picture of a badge, and the huge letters that said **NYPD:**

Prisoner Transport Trailer.

Michael waited. He had decided that if Carlos didn't come out in the next few minutes, he was going to walk over to the van, knock on the door, and ask to see his brother.

Just then, the door opened and Carlos came out, followed by the policeman.

Carlos hesitated for a second and in that moment looked straight at Michael as if he knew Michael had been there all along. Michael started to wave to his brother.

Carlos shook his head.

Michael pulled his arm down, stayed right where he was. Carlos came down the steps. The policeman followed him. Then the policeman was talking very hard to Carlos again, wagging his finger in front of his face, like he was saying, Don't ever let me catch you here again.

Carlos just kept nodding right along with him.

Then an amazing thing happened. Amazing to Michael, anyway.

The policeman shook Carlos's hand, and pointed toward River Avenue, like he was telling Carlos to go home.

Like he was letting him go.

Still Michael didn't move.

Carlos waved back at the policeman and walked toward the subway station, crossed River without looking back as Michael heard a huge cheer, what sounded like a Yankee home run cheer, from inside the Stadium.

He didn't understand what he had just seen. He didn't know what had happened to Ramon the purse stealer, and didn't care. He didn't know what he was supposed to do now.

So he started walking home, hoping that was where Carlos was going.

No jail, Michael thought.

There was another cheer from inside, as big as before. Back-to-back home runs maybe?

Michael wanted to cheer, too.

No jail.

They were in Mrs. C's apartment. She had made them both fried-egg sandwiches with crispy bacon and some kind of jalapeño cheese that was a little spicy for Michael, not that he would ever admit that in front of Mrs. C or his brother.

She was even letting them have soft drinks, Coke in those small bottles that Papi always said made the soda taste much better than plastic bottles or cans.

Carlos had been doing all the talking.

Mrs. C said she had told him when he called from what she

thought was a real police station to come knock on her door whenever he got home, even if it was the middle of the night. She was the one Carlos had called when the tall policeman—his name, according to Carlos, was Officer McRae—had told him he had to contact an adult or guardian.

That was when Officer McRae was still playing the part of what Carlos called "bad cop," acting for all the world as if Carlos was going to be arraigned as an adult in the Night Court at the Bronx County Courthouse that would be in session in a few hours. Where, Officer McRae told him, he would be given a court date and released in his own "recognizance."

"You know what that means, Miguel?"

Michael said he did, from all the times watching *Law & Order* with his brother.

"I know what you're thinking," Carlos said. "I finally ended up in one of our favorite shows."

"It's not what I was thinking," Michael said. "I was just thinking I'm glad we're here together."

Carlos told them the whole story then:

Meeting Ramon on the street after he got laid off from Hector's. Ramon telling him how much money a person could make scalping tickets if you knew how to do it right. Ramon finally talking him into it. Carlos telling himself he was only going to do it until he could find a better job.

"But why?" Michael said.

"Because I couldn't pay the bills," Carlos said, his eyes getting all red again, the way they had when Michael had run into their own apartment when he got back to 825 Gerard, run right across the room and hugged Carlos the way he hardly ever did. "Because," Carlos said, "if I paid electricity one month then I had to wait until the next month to pay the phone. Because I felt like one of those jugglers with the painted faces we used to see at El Guinol Nacional, Miguel. I tried, hombre. I really tried."

"You should have told me," Michael said. "Maybe I could have helped out."

"You never said anything," Mrs. C said.

"The man of the house isn't supposed to," Carlos said.

"Only when he is too proud," she said, wagging her finger at him the way Officer McRae had in front of the Prisoner Transport Van.

"Papi never asked anybody for help," Carlos said.

"And one day it helped kill him."

Michael didn't even realize the words were inside his head until he heard himself saying them.

Carlos whipped his head around and Michael was afraid he was going to get yelled at for saying something like that.

But his brother smiled instead. "Sometimes I think you're the older brother," Carlos said.

"Maybe that's why they think I'm too old for Little League."

"No," Carlos said. "It is because of the old soul Papi always said you had."

Michael had never understood what that meant, an old soul, just knew Papi used to say it all the time, before he would lean down and give Michael one of those kisses with his scratchy beard.

Carlos pounded his fist on Mrs. C's kitchen table. "I could have ruined everything!" he said. "Going for easy money."

Ramon, he said, had showed him the moves, how to discreetly hold up two fingers, as though making an old-fashioned peace symbol, looking for the eye contact that meant somebody was interested.

Told him to always be suspicious of any fan walking into the Stadium by himself and still seemed interested in buying two tickets, because sometimes that meant you had run into an undercover cop from the Stadium Detail.

Ramon had told Carlos that if that happened, if he even thought he had been "made," to get ready to run. And to always have the escape route he wanted to use mapped out inside his head.

Tonight it wasn't just one fan, as things turned out. It was a young couple, a man and a woman, both in Yankee home jerseys, saying they were in the upper deck, and were hoping to move a little closer to the planet Earth, if that was at all possible.

They were both from the Yankee Stadium Detail, pulled out their badges before Carlos could run or do anything, showed their badges to him just as two other plainclothes cops were grabbing Ramon about a hundred yards away.

The man and the woman then handed him over to Officer McRae, who walked him to the van.

"What happened to Ramon?" Michael said.

"What Officer McRae said was going to happen to me. They took him to Night Court. Ramon must have forgotten to tell me he'd been caught once before, and given a warning, been told exactly what would happen to him if they ever caught him again."

"Fast runner, this Ramon," Mrs. C said. "Slow learner."

"Two strikes and you're out," Michael said.

Carlos said, "Something like that."

Ramon had been taken to one part of the van, Carlos to another. Carlos told Officer McRae as much truth as he could, that his father was away and that he had been holding down two jobs and had lost one of them, then been dumb enough to listen to somebody like Ramon.

Finally, after Officer McRae felt he had scared him enough, he told Carlos he was releasing him because of what he called "officer's discretion."

"When he got me outside," Carlos said, "he told me that if he ever saw me at Yankee Stadium again, I better be handing the ticket in my pocket over to somebody at one of the turnstiles."

Carlos looked at Michael. "I am so sorry, little brother."

Michael had never seen his big brother cry, not even over Papi, but he was afraid he might now.

Mrs. C spoke before Michael could.

"Sorry for what?" she said. "Scalping is against the law. Loving your brother is not."

25 ⚾⚾⚾⚾⚾⚾⚾⚾⚾⚾⚾⚾⚾⚾⚾

TWO NIGHTS LATER CHRIS NOURSE PITCHED THE BEST HE HAD ALL YEAR, REGular season or All-Stars, and the Clippers won again, beating the Grand Concourse Condors, 5–2.

Somehow, even without Michael, the Clippers seemed to be getting on a roll.

"Since you can't pitch, we shouldn't have enough pitching," Manny said. "But right now, we have enough pitching."

Michael looked at him. "You don't just play Yogi Berra's position," he said. "You're starting to sound like him."

Nourse went the first five innings, throwing nothing but fastballs. Kel pitched the sixth, throwing anything *but* fastballs. Anthony Fierro hit a home run over the fence in dead center, a three-run job, catching a fastball from the Condors' starter right on the sweet spot. Manny wound up scoring two of their five runs and talked Nourse through every single jam.

The worst was probably in the top of the fourth. The game was still 2–2 and the Condors had the bases loaded, but then Nourse pitched his way out of it with two strikeouts. Before Michael went to coach third in the bottom of the fourth, Manny sat down next to him on the bench as he started to take off his chest guard.

"It's nice to have a pitcher who doesn't act like he might break out in a rash if we have an occasional conversation on the mound," Manny said.

Michael said, "By conversation, does that mean Chris gets to talk, too? Because I don't recall seeing his lips moving when you were out there chattering away."

Manny made a snorting sound. "There are all sorts of ways people can communicate."

"Yeah," Michael said, "but there's only one you really like."

"Which is?"

"You talk, the rest of us listen."

Anthony hit his three-run shot in the bottom of that inning and that had done it. They'd won again.

Michael stayed around after the game. Carlos was back working at Hector's for the next few nights, they'd called him because two of the waiters who had been serving as busboys were out sick. Manny had gotten permission from his mom to spend the night with Michael.

While they were eating their snack after the game, Michael thought for a second he saw Ellie watching from the top of the hill, not right above the basketball courts, more toward the corner of 161st and Ruppert. But when he went to get Manny, to see if he thought it was her, whoever it was at the top of the hill was gone.

"The Yankees don't get back from Boston until tomorrow," Manny said. "She never shows up when they don't have a game."

"And her father isn't pitching."

"Maybe you're seeing things," Manny said. "Wishful thinking, dude."

"What's that supposed to mean?"

"You know exactly what it means," Manny said. "You know you want to see her."

Kel came by, his mouth full of ice cream sandwich. "See who?"

"Nobody," Michael said, giving Manny a squinty-eyed look.

Kel said, "Michael got a sweetie?"

Michael said to Manny, "Tell him I don't have a sweetie."

Manny grinned. "Okay, I don't have a sweetie."

Now Kel grinned. "What, Maria don't count?"

"Shut up," Manny said.

When he got a line that worked for him, he stayed with it, Michael had to give him that.

He did want to see Ellie. In the worst way. Even if he would never admit that to Manny or anybody else.

He wanted to tell her he was sorry for being mean to her that day. He wanted to tell her that if he ever got to pitch another big game, he wanted her to be there to see it.

In his head, it was always the game at Yankee Stadium, the one Manny wouldn't let him talk about for fear of jinxing the Clippers, the game that would get them to Williamsport. *That* was the game he wanted Ellie to see, Michael standing wherever they would put the mound for a Little League game, bringing his own heat in the same place her father brought his. . . .

Out of all of his dreams, this was the one he liked the best, even if it seemed to be the one most out of his reach.

The way Ellie was out of his reach.

How could he get to her?

Was she still coming to watch every time her father pitched? Or did she stay away from the Stadium the way she was staying away from Michael and Manny?

Did he want to wait outside the blue barriers and call her name when she walked into the ballpark with her father?

If he did that, would she stop to talk to him, or just keep walking?

Manny always said it was much easier to figure out slugging percentages than it was to figure out girls.

Maybe, Michael thought, he could he ask the guard at Yankee Stadium to give her a message if he got over to the ballpark early enough, before the crowds began to form behind the blue barriers in the late afternoon.

Oh, right. Just walk up and hand the man a note and tell him to make sure to give it to El Grande's daughter when the two of them arrived. *If* she was with El Grande when he arrived. Like that was ever going to happen on *this* planet.

Sometimes he pictured himself taking the train up to Riverdale, but he could never figure out the next part. Ask somebody at the station for directions to El Grande's house?

There was no game for the Clippers that night. No practice. Their next game wasn't until the end of the week, Friday probably, depending on what happened with a losers' bracket game. Manny wasn't around, he'd gone into the city with his mother to see Uncle Timo in the rehearsal for what Manny called an off-off-off-off Broadway play—"If it were any more off Broadway, they'd be putting it on inside the Lincoln Tunnel," Manny said—and wouldn't be back until tonight.

They'd invited Michael to join them. Manny said it was a comedy, but Michael didn't feel much like laughing today. And he didn't need Manny and his mom telling him that things were going to work out, just wait and see.

He needed to come up with a plan.

A plan to see Ellie again.

At two-thirty, a little before the first Yankee players began to show up for a night game, he sat down at the kitchen table and wrote out the note and stuffed it in his pocket and headed for Yankee Stadium.

He didn't have a real plan yet. It was like the ghost captain said in *Pirates of the Caribbean,* when he was explaining to Captain Jack that something wasn't actually a pirate *code.*

What Michael really had was more like *guidelines.*

Sometimes, even if the Yankees weren't playing one of the top teams or their hated rival, the Red Sox, the crowd still began to form early between the players' parking lot and the players' entrance. Today was one of those days. By the time Michael made his way to the blue barrier, the fans were already six or seven deep.

He figured that the way things were going for him in his life, El Grande would already be inside the Stadium, even though he only showed up this early when it was his turn to pitch. But when he asked a boy in a Yankees cap if he'd seen El Grande yet, the boy said, "No. And I got here at two o'clock, before the manager even showed up."

"You're sure?" Michael said.

"No," the boy said. "I decided to trick the first kid who asked me."

"Sorry," Michael said.

Joe Johnson was the first Yankee to arrive after Michael got there. He wore a colorful, Hawaiian-looking shirt and baggy shorts and sandals. And dark sunglasses so big Michael thought he was worried about death rays from outer space.

The people around Michael seemed to scream in one voice: "JOE!"

Then everybody was shouting something different.

"Joe . . . Over here, Joe . . . Sign this ball, Joe? . . . C'mon, Joe, I've been waiting all season . . . Please, Joe . . . For my son, Joe . . ."

Like these were the words to some crazy song, all the words running together. People yelling their heads off, like they were warming up for the game. Though Michael always wondered how many of the people out here had tickets to the game, and how many were like him, and never made it inside.

Michael noticed the boy next to him had disappeared. Maybe he was up at the front, reaching with the baseball and pen he'd had in his hands along with everybody else.

Michael wasn't watching Joe Johnson now. He was watching the parking lot. Lot 14. Darren Rogers, the team's rookie shortstop, an all-star already, was the next Yankee out of the lot. Then the Yankees' closer, Dave Wirth, looking like a tight end, or maybe a power forward in the NBA, six-six and at least two hundred and fifty pounds. Then the other Cuban-born player on this year's Yankees, Orlando Gaza, the little leadoff man and left fielder who was hitting .330 and leading the league in runs scored.

All his Yankee heroes.

Only today he wasn't interested in heroes. All he wanted today was a father. And not even his own—Ellie's. Maybe that was what finally changed his luck. Because five minutes later El Grande showed up.

Michael recognized the shiny black Mercedes-Benz from all the other times he had seen it pull into lot 14 in the afternoon.

El Grande had the windows of the front seat all the way down and even from where Michael stood in the middle of the blue-barrier crowd, he could hear the music from inside the car, the loud horns from what had to be the Cuban jazz the announcers said El Grande loved. Maybe it was the music of the Buena Vista Social Club. The announcers always said they were his favorite group.

"*Grande!*"

Somebody yelled it and then everybody turned in the direction of the Mercedes at once.

"*Grande Grande Grande!*"

Michael stepped back, out of the crowd, toward the Yankee souvenir store, trying to give himself some room. But room to do what? He had come here thinking he could get El Grande to give Ellie a

180

message for him. Only now that El Grande had arrived, he wasn't sure what he would do even if he were in the front of all these people shouting El Grande's name instead of behind them.

How many times have you seen him walk past you, and the rest of these people, without even glancing in this direction? Michael thought.

He saw the Mercedes ease into one of the spots in lot 14 closest to Ruppert Place, right next to where the Yankee manager had parked. He saw the dark-tinted windows to the car go up. Saw El Grande, wearing some sort of long white shirt out of his slacks, step out of the car, carrying only his car keys.

El Grande shook hands with the two security guards posted at both sides of the open gate to the lot, then walked slowly across Ruppert, which was barely wider than a sidewalk. The people in the crowd got louder now, almost sounding desperate to get his attention.

Michael began to weave his way through the people in front of him as El Grande stopped to chat with a policeman. The people were so fixed on El Grande that they didn't notice Michael sliding this way and that, like a running back in football finding a hole in the line. Somehow Michael barely touched them. Carlos used to joke that Michael was the one who should be carrying trays through a restaurant, that he was so graceful he could carry a full glass of water through a crowded subway train without spilling a drop.

Now or never, he told himself.

Michael reached into his pocket and felt the folded piece of paper, the note to Ellie with his phone number at the bottom.

Dear Ellie,
I am sorry I hurt your feelings.

I guess I was having a bad day and took it out on you.
Please call.
Your friend (I hope)
Michael Arroyo

He got to the blue barriers as El Grande shook hands with the policeman, whom Michael saw was Officer Jasper McRae, the one with Carlos that night.

El Grande was maybe twenty yards from the entrance to the Stadium. The people around him were still yelling his nickname.

"Mr. Gonzalez!" Michael yelled, as loud as he had ever yelled in his life, trying to make himself heard, trying something different, hoping he would catch his ear.

El Grande didn't turn.

Michael felt like a swimmer doing a jackknife dive, bent over the blue barrier like he was, bent almost in half, certain if anybody touched him from behind he would fall right over.

"Mr. Gonzalez, over here, it's important!"

Knowing even as he said it that his voice was being drowned out by all the other voices, all of them trying to get El Grande Gonzalez's attention.

All of them failing.

El Grande was nearly to the entrance.

Last chance.

"El gato Misifuz!" Michael yelled now, louder than ever, his throat feeling as if it were about to explode.

The cat Misifuz. From the children's song Papi used to sing to Michael. The same one Ellie said her father loved to sing to her when she couldn't sleep.

El Grande stopped, tilted his head slightly in their direction.

"Vamos a ver quien va a tocarle a Misifuz el corazón!" Michael yelled again.

Let's see who can get to Misifuz's heart.

"Say *what?*" a voice from behind Michael said.

"What *did* the boy say just now?" another voice asked.

And finally somebody said, "Corazon? Who's he play for?" And all around Michael people laughed.

He didn't care.

El Grande was walking toward the blue barrier now, staring into it, like he was curious about something.

All around him, they started calling out to him again. But El Grande hushed them by putting a finger to his lips.

Now only Michael spoke. *"Misifuz dormido en su cama está."*

Misifuz is sleeping on his bed.

"Who is talking to me about Misifuz the cat?" El Grande asked, his eyes scanning the crowd.

Only six feet away from Michael now, just up the line. Michael smiled as if he had uncovered a secret. El Grande never answered the reporters' questions in English, Michael knew from reading the papers. He always used a translator.

But now he was asking one in English.

Michael felt as tongue-tied now as the day when he had first met El Grande's daughter. But he slowly raised his hand. The good boy in class again.

"I did," he said, his voice sounding so weak it was as if it were coming from across the street.

El Grande walked over to where Michael was standing.

From both sides of Michael the people reached toward El Grande with baseballs and caps and T-shirts and autograph books and posters and old game programs and Magic Markers.

Most of them probably thinking what Michael was thinking in this moment, that this might be as close as they ever got to El Grande Gonzalez in their lives.

El Grande put a finger to his lips again. All went silent.

Michael was certain all those close to him, El Grande included, could hear the pounding of his heart.

"El ratón puede tener corazón, para reír, para cantar, para bailar," El Grande said in a soft voice, looking down at Michael.

It was the part in the song about the mouse. Michael the mouse. What Papi used to call Michael. The little mouse in the song who loved to laugh, to sing, to dance.

Michael said the next line from the song, somehow able to get the words out, maybe because they never felt as true as they did right now.

"Las cosas son realmente malas. . . ."

Things are really bad.

El Grande nodded, then put out his right hand for Michael to shake it.

Michael did, slipping the note to him as he did.

He was about to explain who he was, why he was giving him the note, but now the words wouldn't come. And then El Grande was turning away, walking back toward the players' entrance as the people all around Michael were shouting again, El Grande not even looking at what Michael had handed him, just sticking the piece of paper in the pocket of his pants before he disappeared inside Yankee Stadium.

26 ⚾⚾⚾⚾⚾⚾⚾⚾⚾⚾⚾⚾⚾⚾⚾

MANNY SAID THIS WAS THE WAY IT HAD TO WORK OUT, THE CLIPPERS AGAINST the Westchester South Giants in the semifinals, winner making it to the District 22 finals a week from Friday night.

The District 22 finals at *Yankee Stadium.*

Winner going from there to Williamsport for the World Series.

"Us against Justin the Jerk, basically," Manny said.

It had been four days since Michael had given his note to El Grande. Still no word from Ellie. The Yankees had played one three-game series at home, against the Royals, and then hit the road again. Two nights ago, the Clippers had made the semis by beating Harlem River Drive 8–7, Kel finally winning the game with an RBI single in the bottom of the sixth.

Now Michael and Manny were in Michael's apartment, killing time in the afternoon before the Westchester game, batting practice at Macombs not until five-thirty. They had the Yankees-Orioles game from Baltimore on the radio. The Yankees were losing again, the way they had the night before after El Grande had left the game with an ankle sprain, or something worse. Even now the announcers weren't sure. All they knew was that in the bottom of the first, after rain had delayed the start of the game for a couple of hours, he had landed awkwardly on his left leg, which collapsed underneath him. The original thought was that it was just a high sprain, but that morning, they had decided to send him back to New York to see the Yankee team doctors, and have an MRI, which would show whether he had done some ligament damage.

The bad news just never stopped, Michael thought.

Manny could always tell when Michael had stopped listening to him.

"Are you more interested in the Yankee game or our game?" he said.

"I can't be interested in both?"

"C'mon, you know you still want a piece of old Justin."

"Yeah, only I won't be playing," Michael said. "When you look at it that way, Justin and his dad have already beaten me."

Somebody on the Orioles must have belted one into the gap because John Sterling, the Yankees' radio announcer, was yelling about the ball rolling all the way to the wall. Manny reached over and turned down the sound.

"Hey!" Michael said.

Manny said, "I just want to say this one time today, and then I promise not to say it again. It should be you sticking it to Justin tonight."

There was no good answer to that, so Michael didn't say anything. There were a lot of differences between them, but this was the biggest: Manny always kept talking, whether he had something to say or not.

"I was sure they would've found it by now," Manny said.

"My birth certificate?"

"I thought that Mr. Gibbs guy was supposed to help."

"He said he'd try, and he did," Michael said. "He spoke to Carlos the other night. But all he could tell him was that he hadn't made any more progress in Havana than we had."

"Great," Manny said.

Manny asked if Michael wanted to watch *Little Big League,* one of their favorite baseball movies, saying there was just enough time before BP for them to watch it all the way to the end.

"Because if you didn't see the end, you wouldn't know if everything came out all right," Michael said. "Even if it has all the other nine thousand times we've watched it."

"It's why I love the movies, bud," Manny said. "Got to have those happy endings."

Manny pushed the tape into the VCR, came over, his face serious now, reached out and gave Michael a closed fist. Michael tapped it.

"You really are due for a happy ending one of these days," Manny said.

They heard the phone just as soon as they closed the apartment door behind them. Manny kept walking down the hall but Michael fumbled to get his key out of his pocket, thinking it might be Ellie.

He got back into the apartment on the fourth ring and picked up the receiver, out of breath, the thought of Ellie making him forget for a minute Carlos' rule about not answering the phone. Only to hear that it was Mrs. C on the other end, telling him that she'd have a plate of pasta for him and Carlos after the game if they wanted it.

Michael thanked her and hung up. When he caught up with Manny at the elevator, Manny just raised his eyebrows.

"Not her," Michael said.

Forget it, he told himself now, just do what you've always done and focus on the game. Even if it's a game you're not playing. Beat Justin the Jerk and his dad and get inside Yankee Stadium finally, even if it wasn't the way you planned.

Or dreamed.

During the regular season, some of the Clippers, and sometimes a lot of the Clippers, would show up late for batting practice. Not today. When Michael and Manny got there at five-fifteen, the whole team except for Manny was already on the field.

"Must be a big game or something," Manny said, and grabbed his catcher's mitt out of his bat bag and went to warm up Anthony Fierro, who was waiting for him over by the Clippers' bench. Anthony had pitched three innings of relief against Harlem River Drive, but had gotten three full days off now, which meant he could pretty much pitch tonight until his arm fell off, if they needed him to.

The players from Westchester South had gone to run some warm-up laps around the basketball courts. Mr. Minaya, who'd been pitching BP, had gone over to the fence and was talking on his cell phone. He put it down for a second, and yelled for the guys and Maria to get out there for infield practice as long as Westchester was still running.

"Michael, you hit them grounders," he said.

Michael took his own bat out, hit a nice one-hopper to Chris Nourse at third.

The second time around the infield he heard somebody yell, "Hey, Arroyo."

It was coming from the Westchester side. He turned and saw Justin, leaning against the small chain-link fence that protected the visiting team's bench.

Michael turned and pointed to himself.

"Yeah," Justin said.

"Hey," Michael said, not knowing what else to say to him.

"Shouldn't you be warming up by now?" Justin said. Then, in a sarcastic way he said, "Oh, my bad. I forgot you're too old to pitch in this league."

"You know I'm not," Michael said. Then added: "And so does your father."

"Prove it," Justin said. Then he smacked his forehead and said, "My bad again. You *can't* prove it, can you?"

At that point a baseball smacked into the fence, about a foot from Justin's head, the impact of it making him fall back and nearly fall down.

Michael whipped around to see where it had come from and saw Manny standing halfway between home and first.

"Oops," he said. Then he rubbed his fingers together, like a fly rubbing its wings. "Darn thing must have slipped when I was trying to throw it to third."

Justin started around the fence, like he was coming for Manny, but his father jumped up from the bench, where he'd been writing in his scorebook, and grabbed him from behind, putting him in a bear hug.

It didn't stop Justin's big mouth. "You want some of me?" he yelled across the field at Manny.

Manny turned his head and spit, then said, "You have no idea."

Justin acted like he was trying to get loose from his dad, but everybody could see he really wasn't. "What's that supposed to mean?" he yelled.

"There you have it," Manny said to Michael, ignoring Justin now. "The guy is totally clueless."

Justin's dad walked his son back to the bench, then came back and stood inside the fence, at the spot where he'd coached most of the last game his team had played against them. He pointed at Manny and said, "Why don't you worry about your own team, son? And we'll worry about ours."

Michael thought: The dad has no clue, either, if he thinks that's going to be the last word. He had a better chance of going across the street and managing the Yankees than he did getting the last word in on Manny Cabrera.

"It's like my mom says," Manny went on, for all to hear. "The rotten apple never falls far from the tree."

"All right, Manny, that's enough," Mr. Minaya said now, stuffing his cell phone into the pocket of his pants.

Manny tried to look innocent. "I was just saying."

Mr. M sighed. "Always."

Justin's dad said, "You should do a better job of controlling your players, Coach."

"I know." Mr. M smiled, but Michael knew it was like a clown smile somebody had painted on him. "Don't you just hate it when boys act like boys?"

He motioned the Clippers to come in so that Westchester could take the field. And even now, a half hour before the first pitch, you just had to breathe the air around the Clippers' bench to know how big this game was, how excited they all were, even as they all tried to act as if they were just getting ready for another game.

Papi used to say that was the best of sports, just the air around a game like this. The excitement and the nervousness in your stomach and the waiting for the umpire to say, "Play ball."

Mr. M gathered them around him now and told them what he told them before every play-off game.

"There won't be an adult here tonight who wouldn't trade places with you in a heartbeat," he said. "And that includes me."

Michael was in the back of the group. He looked across the field to the Westchester bench while their assistant coach hit ground balls to their infielders. On the other side of the fence, Justin warmed up, pitching to his dad. He was throwing hard now and every once in a while, his father would point with his mitt, the way Papi used to, as if to say, Now you're humming.

Michael couldn't take his eyes off Justin.

The guy's the biggest jerk in the world, Michael thought.

And tonight, I'd give anything to be him.

• • •

It was not the best of beginnings.

Westchester got three runs off Anthony in the top of the first.

Walk.

Single.

Home run by Justin.

It was three-zip just like that, before all the Westchester parents, and there were a lot of them, had even filled the bleachers on their side of the field.

"How many pitches did that take?" Mr. Minaya said.

He was doing what he always did when he got nervous during a game, taking off his cap and rubbing his forehead with both hands. Like he was rubbing up a baseball.

"Six," Michael said, looking down at his pitch chart.

"That many, huh?"

He put his cap back on, stood up, yelled, "Time!" He looked back at Michael and said, "Meaning, time for me to go out and lie to young Mr. Fierro a little bit."

Mr. M stayed out there until the home plate umpire came out. And whatever he said must have worked, because Anthony got the Giants out one-two-three after that.

But the damage was done.

Michael ran out to coach third base. When he got there, Justin was finishing his warm-up tosses. The catcher threw the ball down to second and the Giants whipped it around the infield. When Justin got the ball back, he rubbed it up a little, looking at Michael the whole time.

"Guess they don't have any age requirements about coaching third, though, huh?" he said.

He tried to smile, but looked more to Michael like a mean dog baring his teeth.

191

Michael didn't say a word. He didn't look away, stared right back at him, no change of expression. But he didn't say a word. You weren't supposed to when you weren't really in the game. And he wasn't in the game, no matter how many signs he gave, even if he had helped the Clippers win that one time.

He was just the closest spectator to the game, and both he and Justin knew it. If he said anything back to him, it was no better than somebody yelling at a player from the stands.

Kel was batting leadoff. He struck out on three pitches. Then Maria grounded weakly to second. Manny up now.

Justin's first pitch to him was right at his head, missing the bill of Manny's batting helmet by maybe an inch. Manny dove backward, out of the way. His bat somehow came flying down the third-base line toward Michael. He ended up flat on his back, helmet in the grass behind him, Manny's body half in the batter's box and half out.

Only one person on the field said anything.

"Oops," Justin said.

He rubbed his hand on the side of his pants.

"Darn thing must have slipped," he said.

The home plate umpire took off his mask and knelt down next to Manny, as Mr. M came running in from the first-base coach's box shouting, "That was on purpose!"

The umpire helped Manny sit up, then looked at Mr. M. "In retaliation for what, exactly?"

Mr. M said, "Their kid thought my kid threw a ball at him during warm-ups."

"Juan," the umpire said to Mr. M, "I can't starting warning both teams for something that happened when I was still stuck in traffic on the George Washington Bridge."

"But he threw at his *head*."

Justin's dad was with Justin on the mound. "The pitch just got away from my son, is all," he said.

"Sure it did," Mr. M said.

Justin's dad put his arms out, shrugged, and said, "Don't you just hate it when boys act like boys?" and then walked back to his bench.

Michael handed Manny his bat after he cleaned himself off. Manny stood between third and home and stared at Justin. Justin walked off the mound a couple of steps and stared right back at him.

"Enough," the umpire said. "I mean it."

Michael was worried that Manny might still say something, or even charge Justin, and get himself thrown out of the game. Instead, he was just Manny.

"Tell me," he said, leaning close to Michael so only he could hear, "what sort of score did the Russian judge give me for my tumbling move?"

Michael couldn't help himself, despite the tension all around him.

He laughed out loud.

Justin said, "What's so stinking funny?"

They ignored him. Manny dug back in at the plate. And struck out on three straight fastballs. Michael thought Justin might have hit eighty with either one of the last two. Trying to throw a hole through the catcher's mitt.

The Giants came right back at Anthony in the top of the second and got two more runs, making it 5–0. When Mr. M went out to the mound again, those two runs in and just one out, Michael looked past them, all the way to Yankee Stadium.

Which all of a sudden seemed as far away as Williamsport, Pennsylvania.

．　　．　　．

"We gotta get to this guy," Manny said when he came off the field after the top of the second.

Manny was with Michael on the bench. The Giants' catcher had been on base when Anthony got the third out, so there was a slight delay while he put his gear back on. Michael decided to stay on the bench rather than go out to his coaching box and have Justin dog him a little more.

What did I do to become this guy's enemy? Michael kept asking himself. Become a better pitcher than him? Wasn't anybody in his league allowed to do that?

"Helloooooo," Manny said. "Did we lose radio contact there?"

"I'm sorry," Michael said. "What were you saying?"

Michael would never admit it to Manny, but sometimes he was just like background noise, like a game you had on and weren't really listening to while you did something else.

"We gotta get to this guy, that's what I was saying."

"I heard that part."

"Well, then I said the same thing in a different way, how it was time to knock some of the stinking apples out of this guy's tree, just to emphasize my point."

"Another one of your signature moves," Michael said.

"Very funny," Manny said. "Do you have any suggestions about old Justin?"

Michael said, "Our hitters could start by being a little more patient."

"Right," Manny said. "We're already down five runs to a guy pitching like . . . you. We've got five ups left to make that up or Justin the complete jerk goes to the Stadium and we go home. And you want us to be patient?"

"Pretty much."

He ran out to his spot along the third-base line then. And stood there helpless as Chris Nourse struck out, Tommy Growney rolled one back to Justin for an easy second out, and Nate Collins struck out looking.

With one out, the Giants loaded the bases in the top of the third against Anthony. Mr. M had seen enough and replaced him with Chris Nourse. "All hands on deck now," he said.

"Except for one," Michael said, holding up his left hand.

"Yeah," Mr. M said. "Ain't that the truth?"

Nourse got a strikeout. Two outs. But Justin was at the plate. Michael almost couldn't watch. He did what he did sometimes during a big moment in a Yankee game, *almost* closed his eyes, keeping them open just enough to see, as if he were watching through a slit in some closed blinds.

On the first pitch Justin, going the other way with an outside pitch, hit a screamer toward first base, the ball off his bat sounding just as loud as when he'd hit his home run in the first.

Michael opened his eyes all the way now, so he could see the ball going into the right-field corner and clearing the bases and . . .

Anthony Fierro got it.

He'd just swapped positions with Nourse and hadn't even come over to get his first baseman's mitt. Didn't matter. From where he was, playing back and off the line because Justin was a right-handed hitter, he dove toward the line, somehow knocked the ball down. Ended up on his belly, part of him in fair territory, part of him in foul.

At first he couldn't find the ball. Michael was sure Justin, coming hard down the line, was going to get there before Anthony could get up. Except here came Chris Nourse, running even harder from the pitcher's mound, covering first base the way you were supposed to but the way most pitchers hardly ever did in Little League.

Anthony managed to get to his knees, underhanding the ball to Nourse in the same motion.

Nourse hit the bag as Justin tried one of those headfirst dives coaches told you never to try at first.

The field ump, running over from the middle of the infield, had a great look at the base.

"Out!" he said.

Justin, the front of his uniform covered with dirt, jumped straight up in the air, hands grabbing for his batting helmet, taking it off his head like he planned to slam-dunk the sucker.

Michael thought: Do it.

Because it would have meant an automatic ejection.

Do it.

"Don't do it!"

Justin's dad had come running from his spot in the third-base coach's box. His voice froze Justin in midmotion.

Then Justin's dad said what everybody watching the game was thinking in that moment:

"It's not worth it. We've already got them beat."

Like he was slapping everybody on the Clippers right across the face.

Michael looked at Justin, wondering if he even listened to his father.

Only Justin wasn't looking at his father now.

He was looking past him, more toward home plate, helmet still over his head, holding it like it was some kind of trophy.

The Clippers infielders, suddenly frozen themselves, were looking in the same direction.

Mr. M was standing to Michael's left, blocking his view. But across the field, Michael could see all the Westchester fans standing now, some of them pointing.

Michael got around Mr. M, moved out to the fence in front of the Clippers' bench, saw what everybody else saw: The parade of people coming around the screen behind home plate.

Led by a man on crutches, his ankle in one of those big, soft casts.

El Grande.

His daughter right beside him.

27 ⚾⚾⚾⚾⚾⚾⚾⚾⚾⚾⚾⚾⚾

It wasn't just El Grande and Ellie.

Carlos was a couple of steps behind, walking with Mr. Gibbs of ACS. And another man Michael didn't recognize, but one who had Official Person written all over him.

All of them walking straight for Michael.

Michael knew he couldn't have moved even if he'd tried. So he stayed right where he was, just inside the fence, about even with first base. El Grande—moving pretty well on his crutches, Michael thought, as graceful with them as he was on the mound—stopped a few feet in front of Michael, Michael feeling as if he were towering over him the way he had at the blue barrier outside Yankee Stadium.

"So," El Grande said, "you are the one who has been making my daughter so miserable lately."

He took his time with *miserable,* breaking the word up into four pieces.

Michael looked at Ellie and said, "I didn't mean to."

She smiled that smile at him. "I know," she said.

Then Michael looked at his brother. "Carlos . . . I don't understand. . . ."

Carlos smiled. "Let them tell you."

"Show you, he means," El Grande said.

"Give it to him," he said to his daughter.

From behind her back, she produced the envelope, handed it to Michael.

"I believe you have been looking for this," she said.

"Open it, Miguel," Carlos said.

Michael did. At the top of the thick piece of paper were these words in bold, black type: **Cuban Ministry of Foreign Affairs.**

Underneath was this:

Certificate of Birth.

And underneath *that* was his name, Michael Victor Arroyo, and the date of his birth, and at the bottom was the signature that he knew was his father's.

Michael looked at Ellie. "This . . . it's real?"

"It's real," she said.

The man Michael didn't recognize stepped forward now, put out his hand. Michael shook it. "Son," he said, "my name is Steve Kain. I'm the chief executive officer of Little League baseball, in Williamsport, Pennsylvania."

Michael said, "Nice to meet you, sir."

"I just want to tell you I'm sorry I didn't know about your predicament sooner," Mr. Kain said. "We want our best players on the field, not the sidelines." Mr. Kain gave a quick look over his shoulder, in the general direction of the Giants' bench. And Justin's dad. "Especially when they are the age they say they are."

Michael said, "I still don't understand. . . ."

Then: "How?"

The adults looked at one another, like each one was waiting for the other to say something.

It was Ellie who did the talking, for all of them.

"I don't have time to tell you the whole story now. But basically, my father gave me your note. That same day, I got a call from Manny. He told me everything."

"It was nothing, really," Manny said.

Michael turned around. Manny was right behind him. Of course. Had his back, just like always.

Michael said, "You got her number?"

"I'd tell you how," Manny said. "But I'd have to kill you."

Michael looked down at the birth certificate again. It was shaking in his hand, like a leaf in a strong wind. He looked up at El Grande.

"You did this, sir?"

"Let's just say I still know some people in Havana," he said.

"Who know some people," Mr. Kain said.

"Long story short?" Mr. Gibbs said. "Here we are."

"Now," El Grande said to Michael, "are you going to be standing here talking all night, or are you going to warm up?"

Michael didn't even have his spikes with him.

Carlos pulled them out of the bag he was holding. "Got 'em right here, little brother," he said.

He handed Michael the spikes. Michael handed him the birth certificate.

As Justin's dad came running over, saying, "Now just wait a second here."

Michael was sitting on the ground next to Manny, trying to get his hands to stop shaking long enough to tie the stupid laces on his spikes.

Justin's dad was on the other side of the fence, the field side, and seemed to be talking to them as a group: El Grande, Mr. Kain, Mr. Gibbs. Mr. Minaya, too.

"You can't just send that kid into the middle of the game," Justin's dad said.

Mr. Kain was the one smiling now. "Sure I can," he said.

He stared at Justin's dad for what felt like an hour and then said, "You're the one who did this to this boy?"

"It wasn't just me. . . ."

"You wrote the letter," Mr. Kain said. "Didn't you?"

"I was just trying to make sure the rules were enforced." His face was redder now than even a Little League baseball game seemed to make it. "I didn't want us to get into another Danny Almonte situation. . . ."

"Big of you," Mr. Kain said.

Michael thought the head of Little League was looking at Justin's dad like something he just noticed on the bottom of his shoe.

Michael said to Manny, "You could have at least told me you talked to her."

"I didn't want to spoil the movie," he said.

Manny stood up then, pulled Michael up with him.

"Now shut up and pitch," he said.

By the time Michael had warmed up, there were two outs in the bottom of the third, nobody on for the Clippers. Bobby Cameron was due up.

"Listen," Mr. M was saying to the players he'd gathered around him behind the bench, "somebody's gonna have to come out for Michael to go in. Any volunteers?"

Every member of the Clippers raised a hand.

Except for one.

Manny.

He shrugged at Michael. "You need me," he said.

"I need a batter here," the ump said.

Nobody on the Clippers moved. All those arms still in the air, willing to give up their spot for Michael.

"Well, that narrows it down," Mr. M said.

Bobby Cameron said, "Let him go in for me, Coach. Right here." He looked at Michael and said, "Mike already got me my swing."

He put out a fist and Michael tapped it with his own.

Mr. M said, "You bring your bat, Arroyo?"

"Always," Michael said.

He wanted to run to the plate to get his hacks off Justin. But he made himself walk instead, like he had all day.

Digging in, he remembered what Justin had done to Manny with two out and nobody on in the first, and reminded himself to stay loose. Don't forget you're facing a loose cannon, he thought.

Somehow Justin still had that smirk-face going for him. Like he was telling everybody that his attitude about this game wasn't going to change just because Michael was in it.

Michael took a fastball for strike one.

Then two balls, the second one inside and tight, backing Michael off the plate.

He's trying to set me up, Michael thought.

He was.

Justin tried to throw Michael his very best fastball now, his number one, daring Michael, just off the bench, to catch up with it.

But Michael was ready.

Michael was *on* it.

He made sure not to overswing. Like he was making Justin's power work for him. The pitch was a little bit toward the outside corner and Michael went with it all the way, lacing it up the alley between the center fielder and left fielder.

By the time the ball made its way back to the infield, Michael was on third with a stand-up triple.

When Kel singled cleanly to center, Michael could have walked home. Kel got thrown out stealing to end the inning.

202

No matter.

They were on the board.

Top of the fourth.

Michael stood on the mound, ball in his left hand again, rolling it around in his palm like it was his lucky charm, as the Giants' second baseman dug in to face him. Not feeling anything like the season might be over in a few innings.

Feeling like it was just getting started.

Manny put down one finger.

Michael went into his windup, his El Grande motion, burned in strike one, the Giants' second baseman taking all the way.

Yeah.

He overthrew the next two pitches, like he wanted to throw both of them a-*hundred*-and-eighty. One of them nearly went over Manny's head. But then he came back to strike the kid out. Struck out the side finally. As he sprinted off the mound, he saw Ellie jump up from her seat in the first row of the stands. Then he couldn't help himself, he looked at El Grande to see if he'd gotten any reaction out of him.

The great man was slowly nodding in approval.

Oh yeah.

Whether Justin was shaken now that Michael was in the game, or whether the Clippers had rediscovered their confidence, they got two more runs off Justin in the bottom of the fourth. He walked both Manny and Anthony with one out, and then Chris Nourse doubled them both home.

"I'm telling you, we're in his head now," Manny said after the inning, still out of breath. Then he grinned at Michael. "And, boy, is there a lot of room up there."

Michael, overthrowing again, too excited now that the Clips were back in the game, walked the leadoff man to start the Giants' fifth. The next guy, their right fielder, tried to sneak a bunt toward third that was half sacrifice bunt and half trying to bunt for a base hit. Manny didn't even think about yelling "First base," which would have been telling Michael to go for the sure out. Just watched as Michael barehanded the ball over by the line, planted, and threw a perfect strike to Kel covering second.

When Kel brought the ball back to him at the mound, he took his hand out of his glove, flexed it a couple of times, said, "Okay, that hurt."

"Sorry," Michael said.

"We're cool," Kel said. "We're gonna win this sucker, right?"

"Sounds like a plan," Michael said.

Two more strikeouts to end the inning. When they all got to the bench, Manny gathered everybody around him, the way Mr. M had when he asked for a volunteer to sit out when Michael went into the game.

"Let's win this right here," he said.

Kel said, "Sounds like a plan."

"Right here, right now," Maria said.

It started with a Nate Collins single to left. Now Zach Frazier, bunting on his own, tried to put one down the first-base line. Justin was all over it the way Michael had just been. Maybe that play was still in his head. Maybe he wanted to show he could get the guy at second the way Michael just had. Only he rushed the throw, and the ball sailed over the shortstop's head and into center field, and if the center fielder hadn't been backing the play up, the way you're supposed to, the Clippers would have gotten back to within 5–4 right there.

Justin paced around on the mound, talking to himself in a too-loud voice, like he was broadcasting himself over a PA system.

"You *jerk!*" he yelled.

Manny poked Michael, who was standing in the on-deck circle.

"Finally he gets it," Manny said.

Second and third, nobody out.

Michael coming to bat.

Justin's dad called time and came out to the mound. Justin finally lowered his voice, but Michael could see the two of them arguing, not able to decide who looked angrier.

Or whose head looked more likely to explode.

The only thing Michael heard before the umpire broke up the father-son chat was this:

"*I know how to pitch!*"

"*Really? Somebody else must have put those guys on base.*"

"*Whatever, Dad!*"

Michael stood there at the plate, taking it all in, waiting for them to finish.

Michael hated all the little rituals big-league batters had when they got ready to hit, ones that he saw guys in Little League imitating all the time. When Manny did it, he wanted to laugh, just because he knew it was for show, because so much of Manny was show. But Michael wanted to groan when he'd see guys playing with their batting gloves and putting out a hand to the umpire, like telling him to wait, while they dug in. Then adjusting their helmets one last time, like they were football running backs about to carry the ball into the line. For one thing, he didn't even wear batting gloves, he thought the coolest guys in the big leagues were the few who still didn't.

But he wanted to make Justin wait, see if he could rattle him just a minute more. So he bent down, picked up some dirt, rubbed it in his hands, then regripped his bat.

Then he took his stance, not looking at Justin until the last possible moment, at which point he felt like he was watching a cartoon and could actually see smoke coming out of his ears, Justin was that mad.

Ball one wasn't even close to being a strike. Way outside.

Ball two was up in Michael's eyes.

Michael took a deep breath.

Practice what you preach now, Michael told himself.

Patience.

Then it was completely quiet for him. That place he got to on the mound where he couldn't hear a thing.

Just him and the ball.

Justin rocked into his motion.

The next sound Michael or anybody else heard in Macombs Dam Park was the ping of his TPX bat making contact with the ball.

He pulled a line drive over the first baseman's head, the kid not even having time to get his glove up until the ball was past him and rolling toward the right-field corner.

By the time their right fielder picked it up, Nate had scored easily.

The right fielder made a good relay throw, and the second baseman made a nice throw to the plate, but they had no shot at getting Zach.

Clippers 5, Giants 5. Still nobody out.

Michael took third on the throw to the plate. When he got there, he looked over at Ellie. She gave him the kind of underhanded first pump Tiger Woods was famous for. Michael just nodded. Papi always said: Act like you've done it before.

Justin, his control still shaky, walked Kel on five pitches. But to his credit, he gathered himself then and struck out Maria, Kel stealing second on strike three.

Michael was still on third. The game was still tied.

Manny up.

Michael had to put a hand over his mouth, because he didn't want anybody to see him smiling at a time like this. But he couldn't help it as he watched his friend go through all his little routines. Tightening the Velcro on both his batting gloves. Taking his helmet off as he wiped what Michael was pretty sure was imaginary sweat off his forehead. Looking over to the Clippers' stands as he did. Then over at the Giants' bench. Finally at Justin the Jerk.

Michael watched all this and knew exactly what Manny was thinking. And what he was thinking was that he was in heaven.

It was all about him now, and he was playing the scene for all it was worth, like he was Uncle Timo.

He got his bat back and gave one quick look toward third. Not to Mr. M. Not looking for any kind of sign. At Michael.

Manny winked.

Then he lined the first pitch he saw from Justin up the middle so hard it nearly took Justin's head off.

Clippers 6, Giants 5.

"Three outs away," Manny said after Anthony lined out to short to end the inning, the game still at 6–5.

"Shut up and catch," Michael said as Manny finished putting his catcher's gear on. Bobby Cameron had offered to warm up Michael, but he said he'd wait. When Manny had to, he could get his shin guards, chest protector, and mask back on so fast, you felt like you were watching one of those Nascar pit stops.

Manny ignored Michael, nodding at the Stadium across the way instead.

"Three outs and we are *there*," he said.

"Manny," Michael said. "We've had a deal all summer about talking about . . . that. So when I say shut up, I mean shut up."

Manny said, "I was just saying . . ."

"Don't be saying anything," Michael said. "About how many outs. About anything. The baseball gods you're always telling me about? They're hanging on every word right now."

"You're always stifling me," Manny said, popping up off the bench, ready to go.

"I wish," Michael said.

Michael ran out to the mound, held up four fingers to Manny. Four pitches. All he would need to get warm. When he was finished Manny threw down to Kel at second.

Michael watched his teammates throw the ball around the infield and thought:

Three innings ago I was done for the season and now . . .

Nah, he wasn't even going to think about how close they were. Just pitch, he told himself. The Giants were at the bottom of their order, Mr. M had showed him in the scorebook, as if Michael required some kind of written proof. Number eight hitter, number nine, leadoff man. It meant they would have to get two guys on for Justin to even get another at bat.

The first batter was their right fielder, a short kid with long curly hair coming out of the back of his helmet. With two strikes, it was almost as if he closed his eyes on Michael's fastball, somehow getting a bat on it, a slow roller past the mound, right at Maria. She had more time than she thought to make a play, but tried to barehand the ball instead of gloving it. She dropped it on the first try, panicked when she finally picked it up, threw wildly past Anthony Fierro. The ball rolled to the fence behind him. Runner on second.

Ninth batter now. Their second baseman. Michael's height, which meant tall for a second baseman in Little League. Big swing, Michael remembered. They must have had him in the nine spot to give them some pop at the bottom of the order. He'd hit a shot earlier in the game off Anthony that Nate had made a great running catch on. It didn't stop Mr. M from yelling, "Number nine hitter," from the bench. Michael loved Mr. M but he always hated when coaches did that—and they did it all the time in Little League—because it was usually their way of saying, "This guy can't hit." Every time one of them did it, Michael couldn't help himself, he found himself looking at the batter's face, knowing how bad it made the kid feel.

Justin's dad had the big guy square to bunt, maybe figuring his best chance to tie the game was to get the runner on second over to third, even if he had to sacrifice an out to do it.

The kid bunted the first pitch, but much too hard, between Maria and Anthony. Maria started for it. So did Anthony. Then both of them stopped at the same moment, thinking the other was going to get it.

By the time Maria picked it up, it had died in the infield grass short of the dirt and everybody was safe.

First and third, nobody out.

Michael never showed anybody up on the field, ever, no matter how badly they'd messed up. But he was hot now, really hot. They were so close. He walked off the mound toward second base, trying to look calm, rubbed the ball up hard. Took a deep breath.

"*Corazón*," he said to himself in a soft voice.

Heart.

Then turned back around to see Manny walking toward the mound. Even though Manny knew how much Michael hated conferences on the mound. But it was too late to stop him now.

When Manny got to Michael he said, "I've got a plan, case you're interested."

"Shoot."

"Nah," he said. "We can't shoot Maria, she's too cute."

"Jokes?" Michael said. "Even *now*?"

"Strike one, strike two, strike three, that's my plan," he said to Michael, handing him the ball.

He threw strike one. High heat. The kid on first stole second, Manny not even risking a throw down. Michael didn't sweat it, though. He could see the leadoff man had no shot at his fastball. Strike three, he knew when he released it, was the hardest pitch he'd thrown all night. Manny stepped out in front of the plate, checked the runners, zipped the ball back to Michael, and said, "Eight-zero, case you're interested."

Michael didn't have to be told.

He threw three more pretty much like that one past the next hitter. Two outs now, Justin coming to the plate. Like Manny had told him in the apartment this morning, this was the way things were supposed to work out. Michael looked around. Everybody in the bleachers behind the Clippers' bench was standing. Ellie, the quiet girl, the shy girl, put two fingers in her mouth and let out a whistle that was louder than a crossing guard's.

It made him put his glove in front of his face and smile. He almost felt like laughing, that's how happy the sight of her made him feel, even knowing there was still work to be done, one more out to get.

Michael was where he was supposed to be finally.

It was him against Justin and maybe him against all the other people who didn't want him to be here, or across the street ever, or even in Williamsport.

Michael knew the game wasn't over yet. Knew enough about

sports to know that getting Justin out was no sure thing. He'd already seen how fast things could go wrong earlier in the inning. But he was fine with all of it. Because this was the way it was supposed to be, the way it was *always* supposed to be:

His best against the other guy's.

He checked the runners, even though he knew they weren't going anywhere. Then he blew strike one past Justin, who was so late with his swing Michael thought he was trying to get a head start on strike two.

Manny didn't come out of his crouch, just got it back to Michael fast, the way Michael liked when he was going good. And he was going good now.

He let it rip.

Strike two.

One strike away.

He thought for maybe one second about wasting the next one, getting Justin to chase it. But why wait? He'd waited long enough. All he'd been doing for a long time was waiting for things to happen *to* him. Only now the ball was back in his hand. He allowed himself a quick look over to the stands again. Looking at El Grande this time.

Michael saw him nod.

He took a deep breath, went into his windup, kicked his right leg toward the sky, and one last time let the ball fly.

Pure heat.

Ball game over.

They were going to the Stadium. But first here came Manny, running toward Michael, helmet gone, mask gone, as happy as Michael had ever seen him as he jumped into Michael's arms, nearly knocking him over.

Then the rest of the Clippers came running from all corners of

Macombs Dam Park, and Ellie was out there with them, and Carlos. And just for one moment, Michael closed his eyes, like he was taking a picture of it all.

This wasn't his whole dream.

But he had to admit:

It would sure do for now.

28 ⚾⚾⚾⚾⚾⚾⚾⚾⚾⚾⚾⚾⚾⚾⚾

HE STOOD OUTSIDE THE STADIUM AT FIVE IN THE AFTERNOON, THE WAY HE had so many other times. Only this wasn't all those other times.

Today Michael was going inside.

Manny and Ellie were with him. So was El Grande, who had stayed behind when the Yankees went on their West Coast trip so he could continue to rehab his ankle.

No blue barriers today, Michael noticed, because anybody who showed up could go inside for free and watch the Clippers play Fordham Road in the District 22 finals.

Carlos was on his way from Manhattan, with Mr. Gibbs. Mr. Gibbs: Who had turned out to be another one of their heroes. Who the day after the Westchester South game had come to the apartment at 825 Gerard with Mrs. Cora and told them he knew about Papi. Told them that Mrs. Cora had gotten his phone number the day after Carlos had been picked up for scalping, and how he had come to her apartment, and she had told him the whole story, told him she was worried for the first time that things might not work out all right for her boys. Mrs. C had begged Mr. Gibbs to give her temporary custody until Carlos turned eighteen in late September.

But Gibbs had a better idea. He said he would start the paperwork that would give *him* temporary custody, knowing that the way things worked in what he called Red Tape City, Carlos would turn eighteen by the time the paperwork ever made it out of ACS.

But there was one condition. Carlos had to become an intern in the ACS's Bronx office and work as Mr. Gibbs' assistant until he turned eighteen at the end of September. And, Mr. Gibbs said, if he wanted to stay on the job after that, he could.

That day in the apartment, Mr. Gibbs had said to them, "You boys have quite an angel in Mrs. Cora, I hope you know that."

She put out her arms then and took Michael and Carlos into them with room to spare and said, "I told you about angels."

Carlos and Mr. Gibbs said they would pick up Mrs. Cora on their way to the ballpark, since she had informed them that she had no intention of missing a night like this for her baseball boy.

And now that boy was about to enter the stuff of his dreams.

El Grande was off his crutches by now, but still in a soft cast. Just to be on the safe side, he said. He'd replaced the crutches with what Michael thought was a pretty fancy cane. Which he used now to tap Michael on his shoulder, like he was knighting him in one of the Knights-of-the-Round-Table stories Michael loved when he was little.

"It's much better inside," he said. "The Yankee Stadium."

He always called it that: The Yankee Stadium.

"Are you ready?" Ellie said.

Manny, of course, answered for both of them.

"Are you kidding?" he said. "We were *born* ready."

Ellie went through the turnstiles first, blowing a kiss at the man who worked the players' entrance for Yankee games. Michael went next, then Manny. Then El Grande, already telling his daughter to slow down, so that her injured daddy could keep up.

Ellie led them through a doorway on their right, down some stairs, taking the steps two at a time. Michael thinking: She looks as comfortable here as she would in her own house.

When they were all at the bottom of the stairs and through another doorway, Ellie pointed at the ground. "Check this out," she said.

On the cement floor was a blue line that shot out to their right, a red line going off in the opposite direction.

"The blue takes you to the Yankees," she said. "The red to the other team's clubhouse."

El Grande said to Michael and Manny, "Follow the blue. Tonight you dress where the Yankees dress."

Manny smiled, put his hands together, looked up. "Okay, Lord, you can take me now."

"Before you even play the game?" Ellie said.

"Well," Manny said, "you make a good point." Manny looked heavenward again and said, "Check you later."

They followed the blue. Followed Ellie in her white long-sleeved shirt and rose-colored jeans, Michael and Manny nearly having to run to keep up with her.

El Grande had given up trying to tell her to slow down.

Ellie led them down a long, narrow corridor, pointing out what she said was the media dining room on her left. All of them still following the bright blue line.

Manny whispered to Michael, "You think this is what Alice in Wonderland felt like?"

Michael said, "I was thinking over the rainbow myself."

They came into an open area. Ellie hooked a thumb at the door to her right. "Back entrance to the manager's office," she said.

"Right," Manny said. "I knew that."

They took another right. There was a door in front of them with a plaque on it that said, "Pete Sheehy Memorial Clubhouse."

Michael said, "Who is Pete Sheehy?"

From behind them, they could hear the click-click-click of El Grande's cane on the cement floor as he caught up with them.

"Mr. Pete Sheehy," he said, "is a clubhouse man who they say was going all the way back to the great Babe Ruth himself."

"I have read a lot about the Yankees," Michael said. "I guess I must have missed him."

El Grande said, "He is just one of many, many ghosts here." He smiled. "It is one of the first things they tell you about the Yankee Stadium. About its ghosts."

"You think they'll be here for a Little League game?" Manny said.

"Not just here," El Grande said, "but smiling."

Then he opened the door to the Yankee clubhouse.

He showed them his locker, right around the corner from the manager's office. His locker having some kind of plaster replica of the top of the Stadium on it the way they all did. El Grande walked them across the thickest rug Michael had ever seen in his life, or felt underneath his feet, and showed them the trainer's room, and opposite that, the players' lounge, with its huge television screen and soft-looking sofas and even a couple of recliner chairs that would have probably gotten Papi more excited than anything in the place.

This place.

The Yankee Stadium.

"Only players allowed in here," El Grande said.

"That mean us?" Manny said.

"Tonight it does," El Grande said.

They went back into the main clubhouse. Michael noticed some gear he knew belonged to some of the Clippers in front of lockers across from El Grande's. He recognized Maria's bag, and Anthony's. Kel's.

All Michael had with him was his bat bag and a small gym bag with his spikes in it. He said to El Grande, "Which locker should I use?"

"Mine," he was told.

When he'd put on his spikes—in record time—Ellie said, "You guys ready to see the field?"

"Oh yeah!" Manny said.

They walked back through the door to the Pete Sheehy Memorial Clubhouse. Across the way was the runway leading to the Yankee dugout, Ellie said. Above the entrance was a sign that read this way:

I want to thank the Good Lord for making me a Yankee.
Joe DiMaggio

El Grande put a hand on his daughter's shoulder and said in her ear, "Let Michael go first."

Michael took a deep breath. Like he did sometimes before he delivered the next pitch. Then he walked down the runway and up the dugout steps and the next thing he saw was all the blue of Yankee Stadium, and grass, an ocean of green grass, greener than anything he had ever seen in his life.

He saw the temporary fences they had put up in the outfield for tonight's game, and the way they'd moved up home plate, putting a Little League screen behind it; saw how they'd reshaped the field so that the Clippers and Fordham Road could use the regular infield, just putting the bases closer together; and how they'd cut down the regular pitcher's mound to make it conform to Little League standards.

Nobody cared. It was still Yankee Stadium. Like a field within the field.

"Don't worry about my mound," El Grande had said in the clubhouse, telling him about the changes in the field. "The groundskeepers will build it back tomorrow, as good as new."

Michael saw all the outfield signs he had only seen on television. Saw the retired numbers out behind the left-field wall and saw the place next to that, Monument Park, that he had only seen in pictures, where they had the monuments for people like Babe Ruth and Lou Gehrig and Joe DiMaggio and Mickey Mantle.

Maria and Anthony and Kel had stopped playing catch off to his right, and were watching Michael now as he looked around the Stadium.

"It's so . . . big," he said to El Grande.

Best he could do.

El Grande smiled and said, "I said the same thing the first time."

Suddenly Manny just flopped down on his back, started flapping his arms like he was trying to make a snow angel in the green grass of Yankee Stadium.

"*Oh* yeah!" he said, even louder, and with more feeling, than before.

Ellie said to Michael, "He's crazy, you know that, right?"

Michael dropped his bat bag and just pointed to left field, then center, then right.

"*This* is crazy," he said.

Pretty soon the rest of the Clippers had shown up. He saw people beginning to take their seats, filling up the ground-level seats behind home plate first, then spreading out all the way down the first- and third-base lines. When Michael began to loosen up with Manny, he saw Mr. Gibbs and Carlos helping Mrs. C down the stairs behind the plate.

She waved at Michael with her green purse.

He waved back.

Almost game time now. Michael heard them testing the public address system, the one he had only ever heard from outside. He heard the famous voice of the Yankees' PA announcer, welcoming everybody to the District 22 finals, then asking them to rise for the national anthem. When the anthem was over, the announcer introduced the players and coaches from both teams, Fordham Road first, lining up along the third-base line the way the players did on Opening Day, or before play-off games in the big leagues.

Then it was the Clippers' turn.

"Batting second for the Clippers and pitching," the famous voice said, "number thirty-three, Michael Arroyo."

Manny's name was called next. He ran out and stood next to Michael and said, "This is the kind of ending I like in the movies."

"This isn't the end of the movie," Michael said. "We've still got a game to play."

Manny said, "Oh, *baby!*"

Anthony was introduced then, then Chris Nourse, then Tommy Growney. After Tommy ran past them and slapped them both five, Michael tapped Manny on the shoulder. Manny turned around, still smiling, just because he hadn't stopped since they'd gotten inside.

"Hey, Man," Michael said, feeling his voice start to crack as he did.

"Yeah, dude?"

"Thanks for everything."

"Shut up," Manny said.

The Clippers were the home team, so they took the field first. The PA announcer introduced the Yankee owner, who Mr. M had told them was going to throw out the first pitch.

When the owner, bigger in person than Michael had imagined him, the way everything seemed to be bigger inside here, got to the temporary mound, Michael handed him the ball.

"El Grande told me about everything that's happened to you,

son," the owner said. He looked as stern to Michael as he did when he was being interviewed on TV. But then he smiled. "I just want you to know we expect to see a lot more of you from now on."

"Yes sir," Michael said.

Best he could do.

The owner threw a strike to Manny, waved to everybody, and jogged off the field. Michael took his warm-ups. When he was done, Manny threw down to Kel. The Clippers threw it around. Business as usual.

Yeah, right.

The umpire yelled, "Play ball!"

Michael turned his back to the plate, rubbing the brand-new game ball up. As he did so, he saw a subway train, a number 4 probably, rumble by, past the opening in right-center Michael had only ever seen from River Avenue.

The sound of the train was much quieter in here.

He thought of all the ghosts El Grande had talked about now, the ones who were supposed to be smiling tonight as they watched him, knowing those ghosts had been joined by one more tonight:

His father.

Heard his father saying, *Now* you're pitching.

Michael turned back around. The Fordham Road leadoff man was already in the batter's box, bat held high. Michael went into his windup and threw strike one. Now the cheer from inside Yankee Stadium was for him.

Turn the page for a preview of
Mike Lupica's next novel,

ON 49th STREET

CHAPTER 1

$\mathcal{M}$olly Parker wasn't here for some stupid autograph.

She wasn't even here for the open practice the Celtics had run today, their last practice before they would begin the regular season tomorrow night against the 76ers. Though she had to admit that it was pretty cool to sit with the other kids and their parents inside the Celtics' practice gym at the Sports Authority Training Center at HealthPoint, which didn't so much sound like the name of a basketball court but the answer to some kind of essay question.

The Celtics had scheduled their annual Kids Day practice at four o'clock so that the parents—moms mostly, Molly noticed that right off—could pick up their kids at school or at the bus and get them here on time. Molly, who'd gotten out here to Waltham early, had watched a lot of them pull up to the entrance to the big public parking lot on the side, feeling as if she were watching some kind of parade for SUVs.

Yuppie limos, her mom liked to call them.

Of course, then her mom would wonder if anybody in America even used the word *yuppie* anymore, or if there was

1

some kind of new description for all the moms driving Suburbans and Land Cruisers and Explorers.

"Pretty soon there'll be double-decker versions of these monsters," Jennifer Parker would say to Molly. "Like our red London buses."

When they had finally come back for good from London, the only place Molly had ever thought of as home, her mom had acted as if everything was new to her, as if the country she'd grown up in had now become foreign, just because she'd been away for over twelve years.

One day when they were driving on the Mass Pike, Jennifer Parker—Jen to her friends—had found herself in the middle lane, with big SUVs on both sides of their rented Taurus.

"Okay," her mom said, "that's it. I know we've only been back a few weeks, but they're going to need to build a bigger country."

"Mom," Molly said that day, "you're going to have to let go on the whole car thing."

Her mom grinned then, because she was the coolest and always got the joke.

"Did I ever by any chance mention the Volkswagen bug I used to drive around in college?"

And Molly had said, "Oh, no, Mom. Never. Not one single time. No kidding—you used to have a Volkswagen bug in college? It wasn't fire-engine red by any chance, was it?"

Then they'd both laughed. Because they both always got the joke, even if it was one as old as the one about her old college car.

In the players' parking lot now, behind the Sports Authority building, leaning against the wheel of *his* SUV, Molly closed her eyes, picturing her and her mother in the front seat of the rented car that day, waiting to see how that particular snapshot, from the album she carried around her head, was going to affect her.

Nothing today.

Progress, Molly thought.

Or maybe progress had not one stinking thing to do with it, maybe she was just too wired—a Mom word—to focus on anything except what was going to happen next.

Practice had been over for twenty minutes or so. The players had scattered to different points on the court to sign autographs. All the players except the one the kids in the house really wanted: Josh Cameron.

Not just the biggest star on the Celtics, but the biggest star in the NBA, and maybe any sport right now.

One of the young guys who worked for the Celtics had gotten on the microphone and said that because they knew it would be a mob scene if Josh tried to sign something for every boy and girl in the gym, he—Josh—had a surprise for them all. In the lobby waiting for them on the way out, the guy from the Celtics said, everyone in attendance today would be handed a special Josh Cameron goody bag. Inside was an autographed youth basketball, Celtics cap, and a T-shirt from Josh's summer basketball camp in Maine.

Then Josh Cameron himself, looking a little bigger to Molly than he did on television, maybe because he wasn't standing next to some seven-foot monster type, took the microphone and personally thanked everybody for coming, said he hoped they'd had a great time, and promised them a great Celtics season.

3

"Always remember," he said, "we can't do it without your support. And I mean you guys."

"You're my hero, Josh!" a girl yelled from somewhere in the stands.

He smiled and wagged a finger in her direction, like she'd somehow shouted out the wrong answer.

"No," he said. "You guys are *my* heroes."

He told them to enjoy their goody bags, told them to study real hard when they weren't rooting their hardest for the Celtics, then left the practice gym.

That was Molly's cue to beat it out of there, sneaking through a side door she'd scoped out as the other kids were making their way down to the court. She didn't even bother to go to the lobby and pick up the bag with all the cute stuff inside.

Instead she went straight for where she'd seen Josh Cameron's black Lincoln Navigator parked. Molly didn't know anything about cars, not really. But she knew what Josh was driving because he'd won it for being MVP of the NBA Finals five months ago.

Molly knew about the black Lincoln Navigator the way she knew everything there was to know about him by now. Sometimes her buddy Sam would quiz her, out of the blue, no matter what they were doing.

"What kind of watch does he wear?"

"Too easy," she'd say. "Omega. They use him now instead of the guy who used to play James Bond."

"Deodorant?"

"Red Zone from Old Spice. C'mon, these aren't even challenging."

"Okay, how about this? What's the name of his new Labrador puppy, the one he just got last week?"

"He got a new puppy last week?"

Sam made a sound like a buzzer going off on one of the game shows he made Molly watch sometimes on the Game Show Network.

"Nah," Sam said. "I made it up. But I had you going for a minute. You thought I knew something about him that you didn't."

"But you didn't. Know something I didn't, I mean."

"But I did. Have you going. Which is enough to make my day, frankly."

"You're crazy," Molly said.

"What does that say about you?" Sam said. "You could have picked anybody to be your friend and picked me."

"Good point," she said.

If Molly didn't know everything important there was to know about Josh Cameron, she was sure she knew more than anybody else. Her mom had called it the joy of Google.

"I'm not big on technology," her mom would say, and then Molly would slap her forehead and say, "You have got to be kidding, Mom! I never heard that one before, either."

"But," her mom would say, ignoring her, "I do feel that life got a lot better when *Google* became a verb."

By now Molly Parker had Googled Josh Cameron so many times that she knew his first two Google pages, starting with his own Web site, by heart.

Basically, he was the most famous and best Boston Celtics basketball player since Larry Bird. And the best and flashiest point guard they'd had since Bob Cousy. But most people, Molly had found out in her research, seemed to think Josh Cameron was the basketball equivalent of Tom Brady, the Patriots quarterback who won all the Super Bowls and looked like he should be playing Hilary Duff's boyfriend in the movies, even if he was waaaaay too old for her.

Basically, Josh Cameron, six feet two, out of the University of Connecticut, winner of four NBA titles in his first nine years in the league, was the biggest and most popular star in sports right now. American sports, anyway. Molly didn't even try to explain to Sam or any of the other kids she went to school with about the whole David Beckham thing.

He was thirty-one now, about the same age as her mom. It wasn't crypt-keeper old, which was her favorite expression from *Freaky Friday*. But he was getting up there, even if you couldn't tell it by the way he was playing. The Celtics had just won again, and he had won another MVP award.

"He's one of those guys," Jen Parker told her daughter. "He'll get old about the same time Peter Pan does."

Now, after the T rides she had taken to get to the buses and then the walk from the last bus station, which seemed like a lot more than the mile the bus driver had said, she was finally going to meet him.

She had decided it was time.

She knew it would make everybody mad that she had skipped out of school early again with a made-up story, at least when they figured out she hadn't gone to Sam's house after school like she'd said. Molly didn't care. She knew they'd try to act all worried about her when she got home, but it would just mean that she'd

6

inconvenienced everybody.

Again.

Molly the Incovenience.

She took out her cell phone as a way of reminding herself to turn it off when she saw him coming. She knew that any kid her age with her own cell phone was supposed to consider that a huge deal. Not Molly. The Nokia she carried in the front pocket of her jeans always seemed to her like the business end of some long leash, one that stretched all the way to the Sports Authority Training Center from the old brownstone in the part of Boston known as Beacon Hill.

She tried to look through the smoked windows of the Navigator, wanting to see if it was true that he really had a portable fax machine in there. Molly knew about that the way she knew that Cherry Garcia ice cream was his favorite and that he had every single Rolling Stones song ever on his iPod and that . . .

She didn't just *know*.

She *really* knew.

It was why Sam was always making fun of her, even though he always had a sense when to back off, because in the end this was what they both knew:

This wasn't funny.

She decided to check the phone for messages real fast, just to see if they'd called Sam's house yet looking for her. Checking up on her.

One text message.

From Sam.

Pretty much her only real friend.

Molly was no big fan of text messaging. It made her feel as if she was five years old all over again and trying to spell out words by picking them out of her alphabet soup.

But she knew that if she didn't answer Sam, he'd just keep messaging her until she did.

ANYTIMENOW. STA TUNED.

Molly saw Josh Cameron now.

Saw him come out the door you could barely tell was a door. It was like a piece of the brick wall that just opened by magic, underneath one of the giant glass windows.

Molly's head poked just over the hood of the car.

He was alone, the way she'd hoped he would be, wearing jeans with holes in the knees and untied high-top sneaks and carrying a green Celtics bag. And he was wearing the leather jacket she somehow knew he'd been wearing, his favorite single item of clothing going all the way back to the University of Connecticut. And the wraparound sunglasses she knew were Oakleys, because they were the exact same glasses he wore in a new television commercial.

Molly had read a story about him in which one of his teammates, Nick Tutts, had said that his buddy Josh Cameron went through life as he if he owned the place. The writer had asked, "What place?" And Nick Tutts said, "*Any*place."

That was how Josh looked to Molly now as he moved across

the parking lot, fifty yards away, then twenty, pointing with his car keys now and unlocking the doors to the Navigator. Not just unlocking it, but turning the engine on at the same time!

She found herself thinking how awesome Sam would think that was, Sam being a gadget guy.

That was for later. For now, she took a deep breath and stepped out from behind the car.

"Hey," she said.

He smiled. But it was one of those smiles like he was smiling right through her or past her.

Shaking his head at the same time.

"Sorry," he said. "No autographs. It wouldn't be fair to the others."

Molly said, "Don't want one."

Josh said, "You know, you really shouldn't be in the parking lot. Everybody was sort of supposed to stay in the gym when practice was over."

"I snuck out early," Molly said. "I needed to talk to you."

Be cool, fool, Sam had said. Don't get ahead of yourself.

Josh Cameron looked back over his shoulder, toward the gate, as if maybe the guard could help him out here.

"Listen, honey, I don't mean to blow you off."

"Molly," she said. "My name's Molly."

"Molly," he said. "Nice to meet you, Molly. But, listen, I'm running kind of late. We've got our Welcome Home dinner later, in town, and I've got to get ready for it."

"At the Westin," Molly said.

"Right. So I need to get back and change and do a few things."

He took the Oakleys off now, as if giving her a closer look. "Do I know you?"

Molly was the one shaking her head now. "No reason why you should." Then, "Nice jacket."

"This old thing? We go way back, the two of us."

"To UConn. I know."

"Yeah, the sportswriters seem to get a kick out of it, maybe because they always think this is the year when it's finally going to fall apart." He shrugged. "No kidding, I don't want to be rude, but I gotta bounce."

He opened the door on the driver's side, like this was the official beginning of him saying good-bye to her and driving away.

Blowing her off.

He tossed the Celtics bag on the passenger seat in the front, then said, "Hey!" Like he'd come up with a bright idea. "Hey, I've got something for you, after all." Winking at her. "Even though I said no autographs."

He opened up the back door then, pulled out a regulation size basketball, grabbed a Sharpie out of one of the pockets of the leather jacket. "To Molly—is that okay?"—not even waiting for an answer as he started writing.

When he was done, he handed her the ball. She looked at what he'd written. "To Molly, a great fan and a new friend. Josh Cameron, No. 3."

Molly turned the ball over in her hands.

Then she handed it back.

It actually got a laugh out of him. "Now, wait a second. Nobody *ever* passes up Josh Cameron stuff." He put his hands to his cheeks, trying to make himself look sad. "I must be losing it."

Get to it, she told herself, you're losing him.

"I didn't come here for stuff," she said.

"Why did you then?"

Here goes.

"I needed to talk to you about something important."

He looked at his Omega James Bond watch.

"You know what's important to me right now? Making sure I show up for that Welcome Home dinner on time. So how about you have your teacher or your parents call the PR department and, who knows, maybe I could come speak at your school sometime."

Then he slid in behind the wheel and reached for the door and said, "Nice meeting you, Molly."

"She bought that jacket for you."

He turned off the ignition now and said, "Excuse me?"

"She said she had left you crying in your dorm room when you got back that night from not making the Final Four, saying it was all your fault and you had let everybody down. And the next day she went and spent all the money she had in her checking account on that jacket and told you the next year you could wear it to the Final Four. And you did."

She said it word for word exactly right, the way she had all the times when she'd rehearsed it with Sam, Sam playing the part of Josh Cameron.

He got out of the car and closed the door and got down in a crouch, so they were eye to eye. "You're Jen's kid, aren't you?"

"Yes," she said.

"I've always told people that this old jacket is my good luck

11

charm," he said. "But I never told why. We promised we'd never tell anybody."

"Don't be mad," Molly said. "She only told me."

"I'm not mad."

"She told me she never broke promises. Even when she promised you she wasn't ever coming back."

Molly was wearing a red cap Sam had given her, a Red Sox cap with "Believe" on the front, from the year they won the World Series. Josh tipped it back slightly, to give himself a better look at her. "No wonder I thought I might know you," he said. Then he nodded and said, "So she finally did come back."

Molly tried to swallow but couldn't. "She came back."

"Well, tell your mom she didn't have to send you if she wanted to let me know she was back. She could've come herself."

Molly said, "No."

"Same old stubborn Jen. And she used to say I was the one who'd never change."

"My mom died," Molly said. "Right before school started."

She watched as Josh Cameron started to fall backward, before he caught himself at the last second. "No," he said. "Oh, God, no."

Then he said, "How?"

"It was cancer," Molly said. "They found out about it too late, that's what the doctors back in London told her. Then she came home, and the doctors here told her the exact same thing."

He took her hands. "I am so sorry, kid. Thank you for coming out here to tell me, or I never would've known. I mean, I didn't even know she got married over there."

Molly said, "She didn't, actually."

12

A Perfect Slam Dunk?

They took the ball out on the left side, near half-court. Danny started dribbling right, toward the stands. As soon as he did, the Celtics started setting their screens for him, one after another. First Will, then Tarik, then Alex, who set a monster one on Ollie Grey.

Danny came tearing around Alex like a streak, hit the baseline at full speed, seeing he had a clear path to the basket now.

He knew how long Ollie's legs were, how quick he was to the basket or the ball when he wanted to be. But Danny had him now, by ten feet easy, maybe more.

He thought about going to his left hand as he came down the right baseline, showing Coach Powers that he could bank in a left-hand layup, but decided against it. He wasn't taking any chances. He was just going to float up a soft little layup and get the heck out of here, go to supper having scored at least one basket today.

He kept his chin up, eyes on the basket like his dad had always taught him, in a lifetime of telling Danny to play the game with his head up, putting what he knew was the perfect spin on the ball as he released it.

Then Danny kept running underneath the basket, the way you ran through first base in baseball, angling his body as he moved into the left corner so he could watch his shot go through the basket.

What he saw instead was Ollie.

OTHER BOOKS YOU MAY ENJOY

The Boy Who Saved Baseball	John H. Ritter
Free Baseball	Sue Corbett
Heat	Mike Lupica
Miracle on 49th Street	Mike Lupica
Over the Wall	John H. Ritter
The River Between Us	Richard Peck
Samurai Shortstop	Alan M. Gratz
Stand Tall	Joan Bauer
Travel Team	Mike Lupica
The Devil and His Boy	Anthony Horowitz
Under the Baseball Moon	John H. Ritter

SUMMER BALL

MIKE LUPICA

SUMMER BALL

PUFFIN BOOKS

PUFFIN BOOKS
Published by the Penguin Group
Penguin Young Readers Group, 345 Hudson Street, New York, New York 10014, U.S.A.
Penguin Group (Canada), 90 Eglinton Avenue East, Suite 700, Toronto, Ontario, Canada M4P 2Y3
(a division of Pearson Penguin Canada Inc.)
Penguin Books Ltd, 80 Strand, London WC2R 0RL, England
Penguin Ireland, 25 St Stephen's Green, Dublin 2, Ireland (a division of Penguin Books Ltd)
Penguin Group (Australia), 250 Camberwell Road, Camberwell, Victoria 3124, Australia
(a division of Pearson Australia Group Pty Ltd)
Penguin Books India Pvt Ltd, 11 Community Centre, Panchsheel Park, New Delhi - 110 017, India
Penguin Group (NZ), 67 Apollo Drive, Rosedale, North Shore 0632, New Zealand
(a division of Pearson New Zealand Ltd)
Penguin Books (South Africa) (Pty) Ltd, 24 Sturdee Avenue,
Rosebank, Johannesburg 2196, South Africa

Registered Offices: Penguin Books Ltd, 80 Strand, London WC2R 0RL, England

First published in the United States of America by Philomel Books,
a division of Penguin Young Readers Group, 2007
Published by Puffin Books, a division of Penguin Young Readers Group, 2008

3 5 7 9 10 8 6 4 2

THE LIBRARY OF CONGRESS HAS CATALOGED THE PHILOMEL EDITION AS FOLLOWS:
Lupica, Mike.
Summer ball / Mike Lupica.
p. cm.
Summary: In this sequel to "Travel Team," thirteen-year-old Danny must prove himself
all over again for a disapproving coach and against new rivals at a summer basketball camp.
ISBN: 978-0-399-24487-2 (hc)
[1. Basketball—Fiction. 2. Camps—Fiction.] I. Title
PZ7.L97914Su 2007 [Fic]—dc22 2006021781

Puffin Books ISBN 978-0-14-241153-7

Design by Gina DiMassi.

Printed in the United States of America

This is another book for my wife, Taylor,
and for our children:
Christopher, Alex, Zach and Hannah Grace.
They have, all of them, made me believe
in happy endings.

ACKNOWLEDGMENTS:

My parents, Bene and Lee Lupica.
And my wife's parents, Cecily Stoddard Stranahan and
the late Charles McKelvy. Who have always given so much,
and asked so little in return.

DANNY WALKER SAID TO HIS PARENTS, "YOU KNOW THAT GROWTH spurt you guys have been promising me my whole life? When does that kick in, exactly?"

They were all sitting at the kitchen table having breakfast: Danny, his mom, his dad. Richie and Ali Walker were finally back together, after having been apart for way too much of Danny's life, for reasons he always said he understood but didn't.

None of that mattered to Danny now. The three of them having breakfast like this had become strictly regulation, instead of something that felt like it ought to be a family holiday.

Richie Walker put down his newspaper and said to his wife, "Which growth spurt do you think he's talking about?"

Ali Walker, chin in her hand, frowning at the question, a real Mom pose if there ever was one, said, "It can only be the big one."

"Oh," Richie said, "the *big* one."

"Not to be hurtful," Danny's mom said to his dad, "but it's the growth spurt you never really had, dear. Whatever the nice people listing your height in the programs always had to say about you."

"Came close," he said.

Ali grinned. "Missed it by *that* much."

Now Richie looked at his son. "And despite being the size that I am, I still managed to be All-State at Middletown High, get a scholarship out of here to Syracuse, get to be All-America there and become a lottery pick in the NBA."

"Blah, blah, blah," Danny said.

"Excuse me?" his dad said.

"Kidding."

There was no stopping his dad on this one. It was like he was driving to the basket. You just got out of the way.

"And," Richie Walker said, "though my memory gets pretty fuzzy sometimes, I believe before I did all that, I was the point guard on the Middletown team that won the nationals in travel ball when I was twelve. Like another twelve-year-old I know."

"I get it, Dad," Danny said. "Seriously. I get it, okay? I know this act you and Mom like to do the way I know my *Boy Meets World* reruns."

His best bud, Will Stoddard, had gotten Danny hooked on the show. Will knew more about television shows, old and new, than about any school subject he had ever taken in any grade with any teacher. Danny thought Will secretly wanted to be an actor someday; he might as well get paid for performing, since he'd been doing it his whole life.

Ali said, "I thought *Saved by the Bell* was your fave."

"I go back and forth." Now Danny was the one grinning. He didn't know if other kids liked just sitting around with their parents this way. But he never got tired of it.

"Hello?" Richie said. "I wasn't quite finished."

"Sorry, dear," Ali said.

"Missing my own big growth spurt and never actually growing to the five-ten they always listed me at in those programs also didn't prevent me from getting the girl."

Girls.

It was the absolute, total, last thing on earth he wanted to talk about today. Or think about. Today or ever again, maybe.

One girl in particular, anyway.

"I'm happy for both of you," Danny said. "But, Dad, I know you weren't the smallest kid in every game you ever played. And I am. Sometimes it gets kind of old."

"Yeah, like you're getting old. You just finished the eighth grade, after all. And will be fourteen years old before you know it."

"And just had a losing record for the first time in my life," he said to his dad.

"Horrors!" Ali Walker said. "Six wins and seven losses. Shouldn't we have grounded him for that?"

"Funny, Mom."

"I don't suppose it matters that you were an eighth grader basically playing on a ninth-grade team, and going up against teams that had *all* ninth graders," his dad said.

"You know what your man Coach Parcells always said," Danny said, loving it when he could turn one of his father's sayings around on him. "You are what your record says you are."

"You did fine."

"And we wouldn't have won as many games as we did if Ty hadn't transferred," Danny said.

Ty Ross was his other best bud. Meaning a *guy* bud. And Ty was a lot more than that. In Danny's opinion, he was the best basketball player in town. Of any age. There were a bunch of people who said Ty and Danny were co-best, even though Ty was already a foot taller, but Danny wasn't buying it. He also didn't care what people said—he was just happy to have Ty playing Karl (the Mailman) Malone to his John Stockton, all the way through high school.

Ty had switched from his own travel team to Danny's the year

3

before, mostly so he could play with Danny, and then their team, the Warriors, won the same travel championship Richie Walker's team had once won. At the time, Ty was still going to the Springs School, the public school in town. But he had talked his parents into letting him move over to St. Patrick's, just for one year, so he and Danny didn't have to wait until they got to ninth grade at Middletown High to start playing freshman ball together.

Or maybe they'd even skip freshman ball, now that the new varsity coach at Middletown High, starting next season, was going to be Richie Walker himself. Sometimes Richie hinted that he might have them both go straight to varsity, since most of this year's team had just graduated.

When his dad would drop those hints, Danny would just go along, try to act excited, even though he wondered how he would be able to go up against high school seniors in a few months after nearly getting swallowed whole by the taller ninth-graders this past season.

"Wait till you and Ty are playing for Coach Walker," Richie said now.

"Yeah, Dad," Danny said. "It'll be *sick*."

He knew he'd made a mistake the minute he said it. The way he knew when he'd thrown a dumb pass the *instant* the ball left his hands.

He knew because his mom immediately went into one of her fake coughing fits, saying in a weak voice, "So, so sick."

"Sorry, Mrs. Walker," Danny said in a whiny student's voice.

"You can talk MTV with your friends," she said. "But in here, we sort of try to keep a lid on *sick*, right?"

Danny sighed an I-get-it sigh.

"I gotta grow!" he shouted.

"You will!" his parents shouted back.

"When?" A voice so quiet it seemed to be at the bottom of his bowl.

His parents looked at each other, smiling, and shouted again. *"Soon!"*

"I'm gonna be smaller than ever when I get up to Maine for the stupid camp," Danny said. "Seriously, Dad. If I'm as small as I am around Middletown, what's going to happen up there?"

"What's happened your whole life," Richie Walker said. "Every single time you've been challenged or gotten knocked down or had to prove yourself all over again, you are *sick.*"

"I give up," Ali Walker said.

It was the second Saturday after school had let out. The breakfast plates and bowls had been cleared by the men in the family, a Saturday rule. Danny and his dad were outside now, on the small court at the end of the driveway at 422 Earl Avenue, Richie feeding him the ball as Danny moved around on the outside and shot what passed for his jump shot.

Every time Danny put the ball on his shoulder and launched it the way he had when he was even littler than now, when it was the only way for him to get the ball to the hoop, Richie would yell "stop!" and make him shoot with the proper motion from the same spot, hands in front of him.

"This is the perfect time for you to go to a big-time camp," Richie said. "We've gone over this."

Danny, quoting his dad, said, "You gotta keep taking it to the next level, or you never leave the one you're at."

"I'm not sure that's the way your mom would put it in a sentence," Richie said. "But you know it's true, guy."

"I didn't do so hot at the level I was just at," Danny said. "And we weren't even playing all the best schools around here."

"You're being too hard on yourself," Richie said, then threw him a perfect bounce pass. Danny caught it, did the little step-back move he'd been using since he first started playing, the one that created the space he needed between him and taller defenders, the one that kept him from getting a mouthful of rubber every time he tried to get a shot airborne.

This one he swished, then he kept his right hand in the air, holding the pose.

"In the driveway you can show off," his dad said. "Never on the court."

"Gee, I don't think I've ever heard that one before."

"Let's take a break for a second," Richie said.

All he'd been doing was standing there feeding the ball, yet he looked more tired than Danny. His dad never mentioned it, but he couldn't stand for long periods of time anymore. He'd had two real bad car accidents in his life—the first one ending his NBA career, the second one on an icy road during the travel season last year—and joked that his body now had more spare parts in it than some old pickup truck built from scratch at the junkyard.

His knees were completely shot, he said, swelling up with new sprains all the time. Ali had made him go get an X-ray the day before, wanting to see if there was something more serious going on.

Now his dad groaned and rubbed the side of his right knee and said, "X-ray perfect, knee horrible."

The two of them sat down on the folding chairs they kept on the side of the court, like it was the Walkers' team bench, for one coach and one player.

"Dave DeBusschere told me something once that explains why you need to go to this camp better than I ever could," Richie said. "You know who he was, right?"

"Old Knick," Danny said. "He played on that Knicks team you said played ball as right as any team ever."

"Smartest team ever, even though they're like ancient history now," he said. "Clyde Frazier, Earl (the Pearl) Monroe, Willis Reed, Senator Bill Bradley. They were smarter even than Bird's Celtics or Magic's Lakers. Best passing team ever. All the stuff we think is cool about basketball."

"Soooooo cool," Danny said.

"Anyway, he told me something before a game at Madison Square Garden one night I never forgot. He was running the Knicks then. He said that we all start out just wanting to be the best kid on our block, and some of us get to be that. But as soon as we do, almost like the minute we do, you know what happens, right?"

Somehow Danny just knew. "You find out about a kid on the next block."

He and his dad bumped fists.

"So you find out how you can handle yourself against him. Prove to yourself you can play with *him*. Only, as soon as you do that, you hear about this kid on the other side of town. Then in the next town, somebody hears about you and thinks he can absolutely kick your butt. Now you gotta go play him. Because you just gotta know."

"It sounds like it never ends."

Richie Walker smiled, put his arm around his son.

"Not if you're good enough, it doesn't," he said.

"The first day up there," Danny said, "they're gonna think I'm ten."

"Only until you start dribbling that ball."

His dad left, needing a rest now. Danny stayed out there. It didn't matter where he was or who he was playing with, he was always the last one on the court.

Out there alone, as he had been about a thousand other times in his life. Not shooting now, just keeping the ball on a low dribble, right hand, left hand, through his legs, behind his back, never looking at it, doing his double-crossover, imagining himself as some kind of basketball wizard.

Danny Walker, alone with a basketball, and a secret.

The secret being this:

He was scared.

He was scared even though he'd never come out and admit that to his parents, even though there was a time not very long ago when he and his teammates had felt like the most famous twelve-year-olds in America. Not just scared about going off to basketball camp. Scared that the seventh-grade travel championship that he and the Warriors had won might be the best it ever would be for him in basketball.

Oh, sure, they had gone up against the other best seventh-graders in the country. But even though Danny was the smallest one out there, they were all the same age. Pretty soon, basketball wouldn't work that way. Danny Walker—who wasn't just smart about basketball, who was smart, period—knew that.

Basketball at camp was going to be like *real* ball. His age group wouldn't just be thirteen-year-olds. It went from thirteen through fifteen. If he couldn't handle some of the ninth-grade guards he'd gone up against this year, what was going to happen when he went up against some guy who was getting ready to be a junior in high school?

That was part of Danny's secret.

Here was another:

He wasn't going because he couldn't wait to take on the kid from the next block over, couldn't wait to get to the next level, oh yeah, bring it on. That was the way his dad looked at things. No,

Danny was going because he had to find out for himself if he could cut it once he got in with the *real* big boys.

When he'd gotten cut from travel that time, he knew in his heart that it was because a bunch of adults thought he was too small. And then he'd shown them they were wrong.

Now Danny, as brave as he tried to act in front of his parents and his buds, wasn't sure he could keep showing everybody forever.

This wasn't just about size anymore. It was about his talent and, if he really thought about it, his dreams. Especially the big dream, the one about him someday doing more in basketball than even his dad.

Danny had to *know*.

It wasn't just any summer basketball camp they'd finally decided to go to, not by a long shot.

This was Josh Cameron's Right Way Camp, about an hour outside of Portland, Maine, in a town called Cedarville.

Josh Cameron, just two years younger than Richie Walker, was
the star point guard of the Boston Celtics, having won more cham-
pionships with the Celtics than Larry Bird had. He was Danny's
second favorite player, after Jason Kidd, and he was always talking
about playing basketball "the right way." Right before he'd go out
in the next game and show people exactly what he meant by that.

He was listed at 6-2 in the program, which probably made
him five inches taller than Danny's dad in real life, not that Richie
Walker would ever admit to something like that. What Richie would
say about Josh, though, every time the subject came up, was this:

His size had never held him back, either.

And every time he would say that, Danny would think, *Where
do I sign up, right now, to be 6-2 someday?*

*Where do I sign up to be whatever height, 5-9 or 5-10, that my
dad really is?*

According to Richie, Josh Cameron had started Right Way with
the help of one of his old college teammates about ten years ago.
Now it was supposedly on a level with the Five-Star camps that all
teenage basketball players had heard about. It had become such a

big deal that college scouts would come up to Maine every July and even start looking at seventh and eighth graders they might want to think about recruiting someday.

The "junior" part of the camp, the July part, was limited to kids between the ages of eleven and fifteen. The elevens and twelves went into one league, Danny knew from the brochure; the older kids into another. Later on in the summer, there was a separate camp for elite players about to enter their senior year in high school. But in either session, Right Way was all basketball, all the time—clinics and instruction in the mornings, games in the afternoon and at night. Because of who Josh Cameron was, he got top college coaches to come to Cedarville and every year would get some of the most famous college players in the country to come work as counselors.

Starting next week, Danny and Ty and Will would be going up against the best kids in the country. Until then, Will and Ty seemed to have made it their sworn duty to bust chops on Danny every time he'd even suggest that he'd just rather stay home this summer and hang out.

"I'm the one who should be looking to stay home," Will said now. "You both know I'm not good enough to be going to this camp."

"Sure you are," Danny said, halfway believing it by now. "You're a great shooter and you know it."

"But all I can *do* is shoot," Will said. "The only reason I got in is because your dad made them take me."

Danny grinned. "Maybe he did."

"I *knew* it!" Will said.

"If you don't think you belong, why don't you stay home, then?" Danny said.

"And mow lawns in our neighborhood like my parents want me to?" Will said. "I'd rather miss jump shots for a month."

"In the place known as Will World," Ty said, "I guess that's what passes for a shooter's mentality."

Will ignored Ty and said to Danny, "You're not hacked off because you have to go up to Maine and kick butt, by the way. Oh, no, no, no. You, my friend, are hacked off because you're having trouble with your main *squeeze*."

Meaning Tess Hewitt.

Will looked at Ty for approval, which is what he did when he wasn't looking to Danny for approval after he got off what he considered to be a good line. The three of them were lying in the grass after a couple of hours of made-up shooting drills on the outdoor court at McFeeley, the best in Middletown. "Get it?" Will said. "Maine? Main squeeze? Gimme some love."

Ty lazily raised his right arm, got it close enough to Will that they could give each other high fives.

"Tess is not my main squeeze," Danny said. "And on what planet, by the way, do they still even talk like that?"

"She is, and you know it. *Everybody* knows it."

Louder than he intended, Danny said, "She is not!"

"Which happens to be the problem," Will said, "even if you are too terminally dense to see that."

"If there is a problem," Danny said, "it's her problem, wanting to hang out with him rather than do what she's always done and hang around with us."

Him was Scott Welles. Will called him Scooter, even though nobody else did. He had moved to Middletown halfway through the school year from Tampa, where he'd been about half a tennis prodigy at the Harry Hopman Tennis Academy, a place a lot of famous tennis players had passed through on their way to the pros. But his father was a doctor and had gotten a big offer from the North Shore Medical Center, not too far from Middletown. So the family had moved north and his parents had enrolled Scott for second semester at St. Patrick's.

As soon as he joined the tennis team at St. Patrick's, he proceeded to win every singles and doubles match he played all year.

He also won the occasional mixed doubles match he played with Tess Hewitt, who had taken lessons all winter, really concentrated on tennis for the first time in her life, and turned out to have a better forehand than Maria Sharapova's.

In addition to being the tennis star of the whole county and probably all of Long Island, Scott Welles proved to be one of the smartest kids in their class and looked like he ought to be starring in one of those nighttime shows like *One Tree Hill*.

And he was tall.

Taller than Ty and Will, even.

When Danny walked next to Tess, something that was happening less and less, he still looked like her little brother. When Scott Welles walked next to her, or stood next to her on a tennis court, he looked like a guy in basketball who'd gotten a good mismatch for himself in the low post.

Now that it was summer, the two of them were the best players on the town tennis team at the Middletown Field Club. Danny asked Tess one time near the end of school what had happened to photography and the way she loved to take pictures, and she joked, "You worried that I might get as good at tennis as you are at basketball?"

Town tennis in summer was sort of like travel basketball had been. They had started right in as soon as school let out and had played three or four matches against other towns already. All of a sudden, if Tess wasn't playing a match somewhere, she was practicing.

Mostly with Scott Welles.

Danny hardly saw her at all anymore, unless he happened to ride his bike past the field club or the tennis courts at McFeeley near the back entrance to the park. Every once in a while, Danny would talk to Tess online, but it wasn't every night the way it used to be. And it wasn't as fun, or *funny,* as it used to be. Nothing was the way it used to be when it was just the four of them—Danny, Will, Ty, Tess—when they were the Four Musketeers.

Before Scott Welles had to move to town.

On the grass at McFeeley, the afternoon stretched out in front of them like an open court. It was the kind of afternoon that made Danny wonder sometimes why he wanted to go anywhere this summer. He said, "She'd just rather be with him than with us, is all."

Back to Tess. Whatever kind of conversation they were having lately, somehow it always came back to that.

"I actually think she'd rather be spending more time with *you,*" Ty said.

"Captain Cool on the court," Will said. "Captain Klutz off it."

"What's that mean?"

"It means," Ty said, "that you and Tess used to be able to read each other's minds, and now you can't even talk to each other."

Before Danny could say anything back, to either one of them, Will said, "Dude, can we get *real* serious for a minute?"

Will didn't want to get serious too often. But when he did, you had to pay attention. Danny knew how smart Will was once you got past all his jokes, like you were breaking a full-court press. In school, he got straight As even though he studied about half the time Danny did.

"Talk to me," Danny said.

"You know Tess is just hanging around with Scooter because of tennis," Will said. "When we get back from camp, and for sure by the time we're back in school, the two of you will be as tight as ever."

"You don't know that."

"Yeah, I do."

Nobody said anything. They each had their own ball, and there was a moment when all three balls were being spun toward the sky.

"Okay, now you answer me a serious question," Danny said.

"About Tess or camp, those're the only things we talk about these days. Especially now that you and Tess *aren't* talking."

"Camp," Danny said. "Are you really all that fired up for it?"

Will grinned. "Doesn't matter whether I am or not. You know the only reason I'm going is because you guys are going." He acted like he was talking to both of them now, but Danny really knew he was talking to him. Will had known Danny longer, and better, than he knew Ty, no matter how much they hung with each other now. "If you're there, I'm there," Will said. "I got your back, dude. In everything. Forever. That's the deal."

The only thing you could do when he said something to you like that was bump him some fist. Danny would never tell it to him this way, but the coolest thing about Will Stoddard wasn't the way he made him laugh. It was that Danny already knew he had the best friend he was ever going to have in his life.

"I'm happy you're going with me," Danny said. "And that Ty's going, especially since he could go to any camp he wanted. I just wish I was happier *I* was going."

"C'mon," Will said. "Basketball *always* makes you happy. It's who you are, dude. Your whole life, every single time you need to show somebody new that you have game, you show them. *Big*-time."

"You sound like my father."

"Okay," Will said. "That hurt."

"All I'm *trying* to say," Danny said, "is that it's been a while since I had to go through all that first-day-of-school crap. And

15

don't tell me it's not gonna happen, because you both know it is. We'll be there about ten minutes, and somebody's going to tell me I'm not supposed to be up with the older kids. I just don't need that anymore."

It wasn't the whole truth, the part about him being scared, but it would do for now.

Ty and Will looked at each other, like they didn't know who should go first. Ty said, "You take it."

Will said, "Yeah, nobody's going to have any idea who you are after you've won travel and did all the TV we did. You got to be the most famous twelve-year-old in America for a while."

"We were all famous," Danny said.

Will shook his head.

"They *liked* us," Will said. "They *loved* you." He grinned. "The way Tess does."

"You're a freak," Danny said.

Sometimes Will called the whole thing *Saved by the Ball Handler*— everything that had happened after Danny had gotten cut from the regular seventh-grade travel team in Middletown, the Vikings. Right after that, Richie Walker came back to town and started up another team, one made up mostly of other kids who'd gotten cut, and somehow got them into the Tri-Valley League after a team dropped out.

Things got crazy after that.

Danny became a twelve-year-old player/coach after his dad's car accident. Ty, who'd been playing for the Vikings—a team *his* dad coached—switched teams. The Warriors ended up beating the Vikings in the league championship game on a *sweet* feed from Danny to Ty at the buzzer.

Then they really got on a roll, winning the regionals at Hofstra University, playing their way to North Carolina—the Dean Dome!—for the semis and finals.

They showed the finals, against the travel team from Baltimore, on ESPN2. By then a lot of media from around the country, not just from the New York area, had gotten pretty fired up about the team from Middletown coached by Richie Walker's son, trying to win the same travel title that had put Richie on the map when he was Danny's age.

It didn't seem to hurt the story that Richie Walker's son looked little enough to be ten.

If that.

Middletown ended up beating Baltimore in the final game, 48–44. Baltimore was supposed to be better, *lots* better, mostly because of a miniature Allen Iverson playing for them—same hair as number 3 of the 76ers, even a couple of tattoos—named Rasheed Hill. But Danny finally came up with a cool box-and-one defense after Rasheed had torched everybody who tried to cover him for twenty of his team's twenty-four points in the first half.

Rasheed fouled out with three minutes to go, Danny drawing a charge on him. The Warriors were down six points at the time, but from there to the finish, it was the Danny Walker–Ty Ross show in the Dean Dome. Danny kept feeding Ty the ball, or sometimes just running isolation plays for him, and nobody could stop him.

And when it was all in, like they said on the poker shows, nobody could get in front of Danny Walker.

Danny was the one who finally put his team ahead for good with a steal and a layup. Then Ty sealed the deal with a bunch of free throws in the last minute, making them as easily as he did when he gave Danny and Will a good beatdown at McFeeley if the two of them were silly enough to challenge him to a free throw shooting contest.

After that, everything was in fast-forward mode. They did a satellite interview on Regis and Kelly. The whole team got to go to New York City and do a Top 10 list with David Letterman. They even visited the White House. The highlight of their visit, at least as far as Danny was concerned, was Will Stoddard asking the president if he had any game.

When the president had shaken Danny's hand, right before Danny presented him with a Warriors jersey that had the number 1 on the back, the president had said, "You sure are following in your dad's footsteps, aren't you, little guy?"

Danny thought that day, *Man, you can even get little-guyed by the president of the United States.*

It was the beginning of the best year of his life. His dad got back together with his mom. Now his dad had decided to take the coach's job at Middletown, in addition to the weekend college basketball show he was doing for SIRIUS Satellite Radio. And, like the whipped cream on top of a brownie sundae, Ty had done his transfer thing so he could come play with Danny and Will and a lot of the other Warriors who were already attending St. Patrick's.

Basically, Danny Walker had still felt like he was getting carried around on everybody's shoulders.

Then came his varsity season at St. Pat's: six wins, seven losses, too many games when Danny didn't just feel like he got little-guyed by the other team but felt like some ninth grader on that team had made him disappear completely.

On top of that, Scott Welles moved to town.

So more than a year after the biggest win of his life, it didn't take some kind of nuclear scientist to figure out why he was feeling smaller than ever these days.

Will got up, saying to Danny, "You want to go to Subway with Ty and me?"

"Not hungry."

"You pack yet for camp?" Ty said.

"Not yet."

"You want to go see the new Vince Vaughn movie tonight?" Will said. "It's actually PG-13."

"Not in the mood."

"Not, not, not," Will said. "You know you sound like a *knot*head lately, right?"

"Thank you."

"Wait," Will said, getting that look he got when he was sure he had come up with another brilliant idea. "Why don't I call Tess on her cell, tell her why you're moping around like the world-class mope of the universe, and ask her if she can do something to make you less jealous, just till we get to Maine?"

Will wasn't trying to be mean. He wasn't wired that way. There were just times when he knew, and Danny knew, that he just had to push Danny's buttons to get him to lighten up.

Do anything to get a smile out of him, no matter how challenging that seemed sometimes.

Like now.

"You know," Danny said, "one of these days I'm going to figure out a way to out-annoy you."

"It can't be done," Will said.

Then he said he and Ty were going to Subway, and right then, whether Danny wanted to come along or not.

Danny preferred to stay and work a little more on his shot, said he was going to start getting his head right for Right Way now, so he'd be ready for the big boys next week.

"Got to bring my A game," Danny said.

"On the worst day of your life," Ty said quietly, meaning it, "you're an A-minus."

Will said, "You sure you don't want me to talk to Tess?"

"Please go," Danny said, then said something he said to Will all the time: "I'll pay you."

"But you do plan to talk to her before we go, right?"

"Sure," Danny said. "I just don't happen to feel like it right now."

"Well," Will said, "start feeling like it, Sparky. Because here she comes."

SHE WAS WEARING A WHITE, COLLARED TENNIS SHIRT AND WHITE TENnis shorts, carrying her racket, hair tied back into a ponytail. There were hard courts and clay courts at McFeeley, but you could see the hard courts from the basketball court. Tess must have been playing on the clay courts, on the other side of the big baseball field.

Probably with Mr. Perfect.

Danny watched her come toward him, happy to see her despite everything that had been going on—or not going on—but still thinking, *Man, her legs are longer than I am.*

He heard Will and Ty yell "hey, Tess," as they walked in the other direction, toward town.

"Hey," she said when she got to Danny.

"Hey."

Maybe he was Captain Klutz when it came to girls. Even this girl, who could walk around and be better looking than any girl in Middletown and still hang with the guys like a champ.

She dropped her racket into the grass, next to his big bottle of blue Gatorade. Danny always liked it better if they were sitting when they were together, because it made him feel like they were the same size.

"So," she said, forcing a smile on him, "you guys ready to go?"

"Next Saturday," he said. "Good old JetBlue from JFK to Portland. Then a bus to camp."

"So you decided on the one in Maine."

He hadn't talked to her since they'd made it official, chosen Right Way over a couple others Richie Walker had considered for Danny and the guys.

"We did," he said.

"What town is it in?"

"Cedarville."

For some reason, the name made Tess laugh. Hard. "Cedarville, Maine?" she said.

Danny said, "What's so funny?"

Tess said, "Nothing."

"Something."

"I'll tell you later," she said, like this was just one more inside joke that girls were in on and boys weren't.

They sat there, Danny with his head back now, staring at the clouds moving slowly across a blue, blue sky.

"You must be excited," Tess said.

"I guess."

"You guess?" Tess said, sounding like the old Tess. "You'll be great up there. You haven't gotten to play a real game since the season ended. I know you, Walker. The way you look at things, there's basketball games, and there's killing time."

"That's not true."

"Totally true."

The next thing just came out of him, like a dumb, dumb shot you knew you shouldn't have taken the second you hoisted it up. "Where's Scott? I thought the two of you did everything together these days."

Tess didn't say anything right away, just stared at him until she finally said in this low voice, "Wow."

"I just meant—"

"Pretty clear to me what you meant."

"Maybe it came out wrong."

"You think?"

There was another silence between them then, one that felt as big as McFeeley Park. Ever since they had known each other, from the first grade on, it had been like they could finish each other's sentences. Sometimes, when they were IM-ing at night, they would type almost the exact same thing at the exact same time. But when they were IM-ing each other every night. Before something had come between them.

Or somebody.

Maybe Will was right.

Maybe he was just jealous.

"Danny," Tess said.

She hardly ever used his first name when they were talking, even on the computer. But when she did, she meant it was time for them to get serious.

Danny waited.

"Things shouldn't be this weird between us," she said. "I mean, it is *us,* right?"

Danny had always figured that girls were smarter than boys when it came to understanding most things, figured that the only place where boys had them beat was sports and video games.

But Tess Hewitt was smarter than all of them.

"I don't know what you mean," Danny said, even though he knew exactly what she meant, as usual.

"Yes, you do."

Busted.

He said, "I'm not the one who changed everything."

"You're saying I did?"

"Maybe I am."

"You think this is all because of Scott, don't you?"

"You mean Mr. Perfect."

It came out more sarcastic than he intended.

Another air ball.

"What, you're the only one who's supposed to be great at something?" she said. "I must have missed that chapter in *Danny Walker's Rules for Life*."

She looked down and said, "In a way, you're the one who stopped hanging around with me."

"What's that supposed to mean?"

"Once Ty started going to St. Patrick's, all of a sudden it had to be the four of us or none of us."

"That's bull."

"No, it isn't."

He spun the ball on his finger again, then slapped it away from him. "No," he said. "Uh-uh. Stuff changed when you started spending all your free time with Mr. Perfect."

Tess shook her head. "It wasn't like that."

"Looked that way from where I was."

He knew he had to get out of this. But it was too late.

"You know what I really think?" Danny said. "If it's this easy for you to stop hanging around with me and start hanging around with somebody else, then maybe we were never really that close friends in the first place."

Tess opened her mouth and closed it, her face redder than ever now.

"Maybe it just made you feel big, hanging around with the little guy," he said.

She kept staring at him, eyes starting to fill up now, these little pink dots suddenly appearing all over her face. Danny was afraid she was going to start crying.

And he had never seen Tess cry.

Not the time her sled hit that tree when they were sledding in the winter at Middletown Golf Club and she'd broken her wrist. Not when Prankster, her first cat, had died. Not when she'd taken that tennis ball in the face a few weeks ago in a school match Danny had forced himself to watch, even if he hadn't told Tess he was going to be there.

He wanted to stop this now, in the worst way. The first time she cried in front of him, he didn't want it to be because of him.

He just didn't know how.

Neither did Tess. Who didn't cry, as close as she'd come, who just kept staring at him as she bent over to pick up her racket, her hand shaking a little.

He sat where he was, really not wanting to stand next to her today.

She left without a word, just turned and walked straight across the court. Danny suddenly wanted to yell for her to come back, tell her he was sorry for acting like a jerk. But just as he got up to do that, he saw Scott Welles, Mr. Perfect in his own perfect tennis clothes, looking like he hadn't even played yet, not even sweating, coming from the direction of the clay courts.

Tess stopped halfway between them.

Right before Scott got to her, she quickly turned around, just for a second, the sad look still on her face. Then Scott Welles took her racket from her, and the two of them walked through the main arch at McFeeley Park, like they were walking right out of Danny's summer.

As soon as they were gone, Danny collected his basketball, went back out on the court. It was usually his favorite thing, having a court like this all to himself. Just not today. Today, he stood on the half-court line and bounced the ball so hard, with both hands, it was like he was trying to put a meteor-size hole in it.

Danny dribbled the ball then, like a madman, up and down the court, putting it between his legs, behind his back, using his old double-crossover move, dribbling as well—almost—with his left hand as with his right.

He did this all nonstop, going up and back like there was a coach out there yelling at him to do it, and finally pulled up at the pond end of the court and drained a twenty-footer.

Nothing but net.

Was he some kind of moron, acting like he didn't want to get to camp, get away from here?

Get away from her?

Man, all of a sudden he couldn't wait to get to Maine. Maybe this is what he needed, to get mad about something the way he had gotten mad when he first got cut from travel.

Behind him now, he heard Will say, "Just for the record, are you winning the game against the imaginary player, or losing it?"

They must have wolfed their sandwiches.

Ty said, "Maybe he's replaying the game against Baltimore. Possession by possession."

"Or *maybe*," Will said, "he's going one-on-one with Scooter Welles," before he quickly covered up and added, "Please don't hurt me."

Danny said something his dad liked to say to him. "You guys want to talk, or you want to play?"

They played. Two against one. If you scored, you got to keep the ball. The rule was—well, there really weren't any rules. The two guys could come up and trap, or play a little zone defense, one up and one back. But if one of the two of them fouled, it counted as a basket for the guy with the ball.

First guy to whatever won.

It was usually Ty.

Sometimes Will would win if he was having one of his unconscious days from outside, no matter how far Danny and Ty pushed him away from the basket. Will still wasn't all that much bigger than Danny, even if he was a lot stronger. But he had made himself into a better shooter than ever. A *great* spot-up shooter. He couldn't defend very well, move his feet fast enough to cover fast guys. He was built more like a point guard; he just didn't have point-guard skills.

But if Will was open, he was money.

"My outs," Danny said.

"Don't we even get to warm up after our delicious Southwestern Chicken subs?" Will said.

"No."

"Thought so."

Will stayed inside. Ty came outside and guarded Danny tight, maybe thinking about the shot Danny had drained as they were coming up the hill.

Danny started right, crossed over between his legs and went left.

Dusted him.

Will was waiting for him now in the paint.

He hung back, daring Danny to shoot.

No way.

Danny wasn't in any mood to pull up today. He was taking this sucker to the hoop.

Bring. It. On.

He stutter-stepped now, the little move he made when he was setting himself to shoot from the outside, shoot his little step-back fade.

Will bit and moved out on him.

All Danny needed was a step.

All he ever needed was a step.

He was past Will now, going hard to the right side of the basket, planting his left foot, getting ready to attempt the kind of shot he always did when he was in there with the tall trees, one that was half scoop, half hook.

He could feel Will on his side, but behind him just enough.

Too late, bud.

Danny let the ball go, putting just the right spin on it.

Will blocked the ball so hard and so far Danny was afraid it was going to roll all the way down to the ducks.

Will, who could never get one of Danny's shots.

"Woo hooo!" Will Stoddard yelled.

The ball hadn't stopped rolling yet. Danny watched it and thought, *Well, that's not a very good omen.*

He had no idea.

IN THE BOARDING AREA AT JOHN F. KENNEDY AIRPORT THEY'D MET another kid on his way to Right Way. By the time they finally got on the plane, about a half hour later than they were supposed to, all the Middletown guys felt as if they had a new friend.

Tarik Meminger, from the Bronx, seemed to be permanently smiling, had awesome cornrows, was wearing a Derek Jeter number 2 Yankees jersey. Tarik was about the same size as Will but looked to outweigh him by a lot.

Please don't say you're a guard, Danny thought.

So he asked Tarik what position he played. Will sometimes said Danny was more likely to ask that than somebody's full name.

"I may be wearing my man Derek's number 2," he said, "but I mostly play the three."

Meaning small forward.

"Wait a second," Tarik said to them. "You guys are the travel team from out there on Long Island, right?"

Will said, "Guilty."

Tarik said, "I was talking to the other two, actually." But before Will even had a chance to act hurt or say something back, Tarik quickly put his fist out for a bump and said, "I'm just playin'."

Tarik went over and changed his seat then, so they could all sit together. On the flight to Portland, it was as if he and Will were in the championship game of trying to outtalk each other.

The ride from the Portland airport, in an old miniature bus that Will said reminded him more of a stagecoach, took about an hour and a half. The driver, Nick Pinto, said he was one of the counselors at Right Way. When Danny asked where he played ball, Nick said he was a senior guard at Stonehill College in Massachusetts.

"D-2," Nick said.

"I thought that was the strongest of the *Mighty Ducks* movies, frankly," Will said.

"Oh, yeah," Tarik said. "The one where the Iceland coach looked like he belonged in *Terminator.* And then the cute girl went into the goal at the end."

"I still love her," Will said.

Tarik said, "Makes that Lindsay Lohan look like a boy."

Nick waited until they stopped. "Anyway," he said, "D-2 is Division II. I could have gone to a couple of Division-I schools, but I didn't want to spend four years of college sitting next to the team manager."

When he had picked them up at baggage claim, carrying a Right Way sign, Danny had noticed that Nick wasn't all that much bigger than Will and Ty. Now Danny just asked him how tall he was, flat out.

He always wanted to know.

"How tall do you think I am?" Nick said.

"Five-eight."

"Nailed it, dude," he said.

"It's a gift," Danny said.

It seemed like they were only on the highway for about ten minutes before they started taking back roads up to Cedarville, with everybody in the red bus getting airborne again, Nick included, every time they hit a bump. Danny imagined a fight between the bumps and their seat belts that the seat belts were losing.

"You guys are from that travel team, right?" Nick said.

"Them, not me," Tarik said. "The only travel games I play are ones you can get to on the 4 train."

"I think I saw some of the final game on TV," Nick said to Danny. "You were pretty awesome."

Danny said, "Guess so."

"Well, get ready to take it to the next level," Nick said.

Danny found himself wondering if he was going to run into anybody this summer who didn't want him to take things to the next level.

"Because the deal is, just about everybody is awesome at Right Way." Then Nick told them to sit back and enjoy the ride. Will asked if he really thought that was going to be possible without shock absorbers.

"Feel like I still *am* on the 4 train," Tarik said.

They'd occasionally pass through another small town, but mostly it seemed as if they were just taking a long ride deeper and deeper into the woods. Tarik said at one point, "Oh, this is where all the trees are."

Eventually the bus passed underneath a huge arch, like the one at the entrance to McFeeley, with RIGHT WAY BASKETBALL CAMP in white letters on the wooden beam across the top. Now they bumped more than ever up a narrow dirt road, the bus slowing to a crawl as the hill got steeper.

Finally the road leveled off, though, and they were inside Right Way. Danny immediately felt as if they were in some little village that somebody had carved out of a forest. There was a lake in the distance that looked as big and wide as the ocean.

And that wasn't the best part.

The best part was that there seemed to be basketball courts everywhere.

As if basketball had them completely surrounded.

"Okay," he said to the other guys when they'd climbed out of the bus. "This might work."

There was another bus, a full-size yellow bus, unloading kids in another part of the parking lot off to their right. Then another yellow bus came in right behind them. In a car lot way off to their left, Danny could see kids pulling duffel bags out of station wagons and SUVs. These must have been kids who lived close enough for their parents to drive them to Cedarville. He noticed license plates from Massachusetts and Connecticut and Maine, one Vermont, one New York.

Counselor types were everywhere, checking names off their lists, herding kids and parents into a grassy area in the middle of the courts. Beyond the courts, down near the lake, Danny could see a row of bunkhouses that reminded him of log cabins and what had to be the main gymnasium.

Nick said that some kids had come up a day early, on Friday, and that most of the other counselors had all been here for three or four days, getting the place ready. He said most of the college and high school coaches would be arriving the next day. They usually waited until the last minute to show up. It was different for all of them, Nick explained, depending on what kind of arrangement they had with the camp. He said some stayed for two weeks, some would be there the whole time.

"A few of the older college coaches are retired and don't have much to do anymore," Nick said. "So they treat this like a paid vacation in Maine where they can still do their favorite thing."

"What's that?" Danny said.

"Yell at basketball players," he said.

Nick said he might have time to give them a quick tour, but just then they heard someone with a bullhorn welcoming them to Right Way, introducing himself in a squawky voice as Jeff LeBow, the camp director.

"As you can all see," he said, walking through the crowd of people scattered on the grass, "I am *not* Josh Cameron. But he did pass me the ball occasionally when we were in the same backcourt at UConn."

He had a big bald head, and Danny could already see beads of sweat popping up on it in the afternoon sun.

"I had four years of feeling like the most popular player in college basketball," Jeff said. "Because no matter who we were playing, the other team's guards were always fighting over which one could get to guard me."

That got a pretty good laugh.

Tarik said, "Bald dude gets off a got-em."

"Got-em?" Will said.

"Somebody says something funny back home, we just look at each other and say 'got 'em.' "

"Got it," Will said.

"Now, Josh is going to show up before the end of this session," Jeff continued. "And by the time he does, I promise every single one of you will be a better basketball player than you are right now."

Then he said it was time to get everybody settled into the bunkhouse they'd be living in for the next month and that he was going to call out their names alphabetically. After each name he'd call out the name of an arena: Boston Garden, Madison Square Garden, Staples Center, Pauley Pavilion, Gampel Pavilion. Like that. Nick had informed them in the bus that the bunkhouses for the teenagers were named after NBA arenas. The ones with college names were for the younger kids.

Tarik was assigned to Boston Garden. So were Ty and Will, as expected. Danny and Will and Ty were all supposed to be rooming together—Richie Walker had said he'd worked it out with Josh Cameron's people beforehand.

"You want us to wait for you?" Ty said.

"Nah," Danny said, "you don't have to wait for the Ws to get called. Go start unpacking your stuff. I'll be down there in a few minutes."

By now he was used to being in the front of every line, front row of every team picture and one of the last names to be called.

So he waited in the grass while all the other names were called.

Waited until he was the last kid out there.

Waited until he realized his name wasn't going to be called.

When it was just the two of them left, Danny went over and introduced himself to Mr. LeBow, who immediately said, "Of course, you're Danny Walker! Richie's boy, right?"

"Guilty."

"Well, nice to meet you, man," he said. "I've heard a lot about you." Then he told Danny to walk with him to the main building and they'd find out where he was supposed to be living for the next month.

"I think I'm sort of supposed to be at Boston Garden," Danny said.

"Why's that?"

"My dad said he talked to somebody so that me and my friends could all room together."

"Oh."

Now that didn't sound good.

"See, the thing is, nobody talked to *me*," Jeff LeBow said. "We usually like to mix everybody up as a way of enhancing the whole camp experience."

Danny said, "But my friends are together."

"Luck of the draw, pal."

They walked into a tiny office, where Jeff tossed his walkie-talkie on the couch and sat down in front of his laptop. He started furiously punching away at the keys, getting one new screen after another, until he said, "Oh."

Still not sounding good.

"We've already got a Walker over at Boston Garden," he said. "A *Darren* Walker. From Philadelphia. Somehow the computer must have gotten confused, the way computers do sometimes, and bumped you right out of there." He picked up the phone on his desk, punched a couple of numbers, told whoever answered what the deal was.

Then he didn't say anything for what seemed like an hour to Danny. Finally, he said, "Okay, don't do anything. Leave everybody where they are for now, and I'll see what I can do at this end."

They were full up at Boston Garden, he said. Every bed. Like a sellout crowd, he said.

"Mr. LeBow," Danny said, "are you saying that I'm not going to be with my friends the whole time I'm here?"

"No, no, no," he said. "We've just got a thousand first-day things going on right now, is all. So just for the time being, we're going to have to stick you someplace else."

He dialed another number.

Staples Center was full up, too.

And Madison Square Garden.

The whole time they were sitting there, Danny heard voices crackling through on the walkie-talkie. People asking Jeff if he was there. Or saying "please come in, Jeff." One time Danny even heard "Jeff, can you read me?"

Jeff finally just pointed at the walkie-talkie, shook his head and said to Danny, "So it begins."

Then he said, "Do you by any chance have a name for the person your dad talked to? Because to be honest with you, Danny, we usually don't make those sorts of exceptions, even if the kid is the son of an NBA player."

"If my dad says he did something, he did it," Danny said.

Jeff smiled, but it was the kind of smile you got from adults when they didn't want to be having a particular conversation anymore.

Like, *Even if you're right, I win. I'm older.*

"I'm sure he did, and the request just got lost in the shuffle," he said. "Let me work on it, okay? My problem is that a lot of the kids, from all the bunkhouses, are scattered all over the grounds right now. And a lot of the kids in that particular house got in yesterday, which means they're probably unpacked and settled in."

He went back to his computer, punched away at the keyboard again. "Well, here's some good news at least."

I could use some right about now, Danny thought.

Jeff said, "We've got a couple of extra beds at Gampel. We'll put you there for tonight."

"Gampel?"

"Gampel Pavilion," Jeff LeBow said. "Named after the arena on the UConn campus."

"I know what it is," Danny said. "But the college bunks are for the eleven- and twelve-year-olds, right?"

"Right."

36

"But I'm thirteen."

"Like I said, we're just putting you there for the time being with the younger guys. That's okay for a night or two, right?"

Now it was a night or *two*.

"Sure," Danny said.

That's what he said, anyway, because he wasn't going to act like a baby over this. He'd only been at camp for about an hour.

But what he thought was this: *So it begins.*

It turned out that Nick Pinto was the counselor for Gampel. He was the only person still in there when Jeff LeBow brought Danny over, right before Jeff and his walkie-talkie left.

"I'm like what they call hall monitors in college dorms," Nick said. "Except, as you can see, there's no halls in here."

Inside, it looked like a log cabin that had been turned into a place they were using for a massive sleepover. Gampel was broken up into all these little sections, three bunks to each section, each one with a small dresser next to it. Nick showed him the drawers, like lockers, under each bed. There were still lots of duffel bags on top of most of the beds. Hardly any were unpacked all the way, and there were sneakers spilling out of them, basketball shorts, T-shirts. Some kids had already set up their CD players on the tops of the dressers or were charging their iPods.

Danny liked music fine and had his favorite singers like everybody else. He just wasn't an iPod guy yet. Will said it was practically un-American.

Nick checked out *his* list and took Danny to a far corner of Gampel, where a window faced out to Coffee Lake. Danny asked why it was called Coffee Lake.

"Not a clue," Nick said. "But this does happen to be the best view of it in the joint."

Of the two other beds back here, only one had a duffel bag on it.

When Danny tossed his duffel on his bed, Nick said, "Ask you something?"

"Sure."

"You ever been to camp before?"

"No," Danny said.

"Ever been away anywhere on your own before? I mean, without a team?"

"No," Danny said. "But when I've got Will and Ty, I kind of do feel like I've got my team with me."

Thinking for one quick second that Tess Hewitt used to be on the same team.

"I'm just saying," Nick said, "that even though things got messed up for you, you're gonna be fine. I've been going to sleepover camps since I was eight. This is the best one I've ever seen, by far." He gestured around Gampel and said, "And as cribs go, this is as good as it gets here. Even for the older guys."

"Cribs?" Danny said.

Nick gave him a friendly shove. "Man, you did need to get out of . . . where are you from, again?"

"Middletown."

"You swear you never heard *crib* before?"

Danny shrugged, shook his head.

"Crib is where you put your head down, my brother. Where you do the throwdown with your stuff."

"Got it," Danny said, and then Nick showed him where the showers and bathrooms were at the other end of Gampel, told him the rules about no cell phones—Danny told him no problem, his parents weren't getting him one until next year—and respecting everybody's property.

Lights-out was at eleven every night, no exceptions, because everybody was supposed to be in the mess hall by seven for breakfast, which Nick said didn't stink.

"The other two guys in my . . . crib?" Danny said. "Do you know who they're going to be?"

"For now, you lucked out," Nick said. "There's only one. Boy named Zach Fox, from somewhere in Connecticut—I forget the name of the town. He's really small, but I watched him play a bit yesterday, and the little sucker's fast. And good."

Gee, I'm happy for him, Danny thought.

Nick asked if he needed anything else. Danny said, nah, he was good. Then he unzipped his duffel bag, thought about unpacking, then figured, *What's the point? I'm not going to be here that long.* So he just got out his new sneaks, the old-school, all-white Barkleys his dad had bought for him at Foot Locker a few days ago, changed into his blue-and-gold Warriors shorts—the NBA Warriors, not his travel team Warriors—and went looking for Will and Ty.

He walked past the outdoor courts, painted Celtic green, all of them with lights, Danny noticed. Half-court games, five-on-five, were being played on just about all of them at the moment, and Danny could not believe the size of some of the players. He knew that the oldest kids at Right Way were supposed to be fifteen, so he hoped against hope that some of the guys out there playing right now were counselors.

Because the bigger ones were bigger than Ty, bigger than Tarik. They looked like men.

He saw that there was one full-court game going on up ahead of him, on the court closest to the larger bunkhouses, and stopped to watch it for a second.

That's when he saw Rasheed Hill.

Rasheed Hill from the Baltimore travel team and the travel finals.

He was a lot taller than the last time Danny had seen him, when they'd shaken hands after the championship game. He still had the cornrows, and had gotten a few more tattoos, one even on his neck, just like Iverson. On the court now at Right Way, Rasheed out-jumped everybody for a rebound, put the ball behind his back on the dribble to get himself out of traffic, immediately pulled away from the pack of players around him, both on offense and defense, like he had a gear the rest of them didn't have.

He ended up with a two-on-one, his teammate on his left.

The defender tried to come up on Rasheed at the free throw line, still trying to stay between Rasheed and the other guy on offense.

When he did, like the exact same moment, Rasheed made this ball fake that was so good, sold it so well, that Danny was as sure he was going to pass as the defender was, because the defender suddenly backed up like crazy.

Only he didn't pass.

He just put the ball out there and pulled it back in the same moment and used his last step off the dribble to beat the defender and lay the ball in—no backboard—left-handed.

Danny found himself wishing he could TiVo the whole play, on the spot, and watch it again.

As Rasheed ran back up the court, he saw Danny standing there.

He didn't act surprised to see him or even change expression.

Not knowing what to do, Danny just put his hand up and said, "Hey."

Rasheed took a few steps toward him, then spoke loud enough for only Danny to hear.

"Why don't you come out here and see if you can foul me out with one of your little flops?" he said.

Then he was back on defense, picking off the first pass he saw, taking it the other way.

Danny walked away thinking, *Well, are we having any fun yet?*

Welcome to Wrong Way.

DANNY FOUND WILL AND TY AND TARIK SHOOTING AROUND IN AS
cool a gym—outside of a Dean Dome–type gym or the real Madison Square Garden—as he had ever seen in his life.

He should have known as soon as he saw the sign outside, one
that simply read THE HOUSE.

It had a high, high ceiling, with all these wood beams up there
and huge windows everywhere. They didn't need to have the lights
on, even in the late afternoon, because the sun was hitting the
place exactly right, like there was a spotlight trained on it. The
floor looked brand new, like someone had come in and polished it
that morning.

There were no games going on, just a bunch of guys shooting
around at all the baskets, the ones at both ends of the court and
the ones on the sides, maybe thirty or forty kids in all. The sound in
here was something that had always been the kind of music Danny
really liked the best:

The squeak of sneakers, bounce of the balls, balls hitting rim
and backboard, shouts, laughter.

And the most awesome part of The House?

They could pull back the walls on one side, the side facing Coffee Lake, like they were sliding doors. It made a backdrop for all
this basketball like something you'd put up for a school play, like
somebody had painted a picture of trees and water underneath

blue sky that seemed to stretch all the way to Canada, which Danny knew came next after Maine.

Will spotted Danny first and came running over.

"You *believe* this place?" he said. "They should call it The Dream House."

"Where've you been, by the way?" Will continued. "We waited over at our bunk for as long as we could—"

"As long as *he* could," Ty said, "which means about two minutes."

"My room thing got all messed up," Danny said. "They've got me over with the eleven- and twelve-year-olds for now."

"So when are they going to move you over with us?" Ty said.

"Mr. LeBow made it sound like he was going to do it as soon as he could," Danny said.

"How 'bout you switch with me?" Tarik said. "That way you can be with your guys."

"Thanks," Danny said. "But you're not moving. And, besides, us guys includes you now."

"Word," Tarik said, nodding.

He seemed to have his own language, the way Will did. But already you could tell Will liked Tarik's better.

"Word," Will said.

It was getting close to dinner, so some of the other kids were starting to leave. It meant the four of them got a basket to themselves, the one at the far end of the court.

"Hey, I forgot to tell you guys," Danny said. "Guess who I saw playing on one of the outside courts?"

"Who?" Will said.

"Rasheed Hill."

"Rasheed from the Baltimore team? The one you flopped out of the game? No way!"

"Way," Danny said. "And I didn't flop because I don't flop."

"Whatever," Will said. "I can't believe the dude is here. Did he act like he misses me?"

"I didn't get that feeling," Danny said. "Let's just say he hasn't let go on losing the finals yet."

"Tell him to get over it," Will said.

"*You* tell him," Danny said.

Will reached in then, flicked the ball away from Danny, drove in for a reverse layup, did a kind of shimmy that made Danny think he'd come down with the chills or something.

"You know what I bet Rasheed wants from you before we leave here?" Will said. He looked at Danny, then at Ty.

"A rematch," Will said. "With you."

"Hold on," Danny said. "What do you mean a rematch with *me*?"

Will smiled and patted the back of his head, the way refs do when they call an offensive foul.

"Hey," he said, "Ty and I aren't the ones who flopped on the poor kid."

Jeff LeBow came into the mess hall after their spaghetti dinner and announced that they were going to make this an instant movie night as soon as the dinner stuff got cleared and they could push the picnic tables out of the way and bring in a bunch of folding chairs. He said the movie the counselors had picked was *National Treasure* and seemed shocked when the kids cheered as if he'd just made a game-winning shot.

A good sign, Danny thought.

He and Will and Ty practically had *National Treasure* memorized by now.

Jeff said that anybody who didn't want to stay for the movie could scatter, as long as they were back at their bunks by ten o'clock.

Will and Ty were up for the movie, even though the last time they'd watched it together was a couple of nights before they left for camp. Tarik wanted to stay, too. But Danny said it had been a long day no matter how you looked at it, that he was going back to Gampel to chill and would catch them at breakfast.

Gampel was pretty empty when he got there. Even Nick Pinto must have stayed for the movie. Danny heard some rap music coming from the end of the room near the showers, saw a couple of kids sitting next to each other on a bed, one of them working his PlayStation Portable hard, the other kid staring at the PSP as if it were the most fascinating thing he'd ever seen. One guy, he saw, had attached a small hoop over his bed and was shooting a small rubber ball into it, over and over again.

When Danny got to the back corner where his bed was, he saw a boy who had to be Zach Fox, sitting with his back to the room, just staring out at the lake.

"Hey," Danny said.

When Zach turned around, it was as if Danny was looking at a miniature version of himself. Same color hair. The kind of T-shirt with the sleeves cut off Danny liked to wear. Same Barkley sneaks, even. Unlaced, of course.

Danny thought his eyes looked a little red.

"Hey," Zach said back.

"You're Zach, right?"

The boy nodded. "And you're Danny Walker."

They shook hands.

"Didn't want to watch the movie, huh?" Danny said.

"I've seen it like a million times."

"How old are you?" Danny said. "I know Nick told me, but I forget."

"Eleven. In May. But people always think I'm even younger than that."

Danny smiled. "Tell me about it."

No response.

All of a sudden, it had become a challenge, at least getting some kind of smile out of this guy.

Danny said, "Man, I wasn't even thinking about going to sleep-away camp when I was your age."

"Guess what?" Zach said. "Neither was I."

"C'mon," Danny said, trying to make himself sound convincing, "this place looks like it could turn out to be pretty cool."

"It's not going to be cool!" Zach shouted at Danny, way too loud, like a radio was way too loud sometimes when you first turned it on. "I hate it here!"

"Hey, take it down a couple of notches," Danny said.

Zach did, but not nearly enough.

"I don't know anybody and I wanted to stay home and my parents made me come!"

"Seriously, take it easy, okay?" Danny said. Across the room he could see the two PSP kids giving them a funny look. "This is only your first real day, right?"

"You don't understand," Zach said, leaning toward Danny now, his volume switch finally under control. "They make me do stuff all the time because I'm so little. My parents, I mean. Last year they even made me go to acting classes."

Great, Danny thought, *now I'm going to hear his life story because I tried to be nice to him. I should've stayed for the movie.*

"Listen," Danny said, "you don't have to be some kind of rocket scientist to figure out that I know something about being the little guy, right?"

"Whatever."

"And to be honest with you," Danny said, "even though I'm a couple of years older than you, I wasn't all that hot on coming up here myself. But now that I'm here, I figure the only thing to do is give it my best shot."

"But it's going to stink," Zach said. "If I was going to go to sleep-away, I would rather have gone to the one not too far from here that my friends went to, where it's not all about basketball, where you don't get sent because your parents think you're better than you really are. . . ."

Danny saw Zach's lower lip start to shake a little. *More great news*, he thought. *He's going to start blubbering.*

But Zach saved him then, saved both of them, maybe because he wasn't going to lose it completely in front of some kid he just met. Instead of crying, he grabbed the basketball at the end of his bed and practically sprinted out the backdoor.

Danny wasn't sure how to handle this, but something made him follow the kid. Maybe the two of them had something in common other than being short for their age. Because no matter what was happening in Danny's life, no matter how lousy he felt about something—when his parents were having trouble, a bad grade, getting cut from the Vikings—he'd always felt that basketball could cure everything.

At least for a little while.

Zach was on the small, lighted court between Gampel and Staples, already dribbling up a storm, and Danny could see right away how amazing he was with the ball, even as small as his hands looked on what Danny's eyes knew was a regulation-size ball. He went to the far end and shot a layup, collected the ball, came back the other way, pulled up for about a twenty-footer, what looked to be a little outside his range.

Air ball.

It made Danny smile, not because Zach missed, just because of his form, launching the shot off his shoulder as if he were launching a shot put.

The way Danny had always launched it until his dad made him change.

"Yo," Danny called out. "You want some company?"

"Whatever," Zach said when he turned around to see Danny standing there.

"Hey, don't sound so excited."

"You want to play?"

"I do."

"Well, okay, if you feel like it," Zach said. "But you don't have to just because you're feeling sorry for me."

"I never *have* to play basketball," Danny said. "I always *want* to play." Then he made a sudden cut to the basket. As soon as he did, Zach hit him with a pass, right in stride, money. Then Zach broke toward the opposite basket, like he was trying to sneak away in a game, and Danny hit him with a football pass.

Zach caught it and, without even dribbling one time, laid the ball in left-handed.

And smiled for the first time.

Had to, Danny knew from his own experience.

If you were righty, a left-handed layup always made you smile.

Danny asked if he wanted to play some one-on-one. Zach, as if suddenly remembering he was supposed to be in a bad mood, went back to his punk voice, the one with the attitude. "Whatever."

"Oh, you are definitely going down, sucker," Danny said.

How did things possibly work out this way? Danny thought. *Me having to cheer up somebody else after the crappy first day I had at camp?*

He decided to stop worrying about it and just play.

He didn't play his hardest, just hard enough so that Zach wouldn't bust him for not playing his hardest. Danny basically wanted it to be a good, close game, so that Zach's own even crappier first day wouldn't become something for the summer camp record books.

They played until the horn sounded from the main building, the one that meant back to the bunkhouses for lights-out. Zach actually ended the game laughing when Danny made a fadeaway, hold-the-pose shot to beat him 10–9.

Zach laughed so hard that it made Danny laugh, until the two of them realized a couple of guys had been watching them.

One was Rasheed Hill.

The other was a kid Danny didn't recognize, taller than Rasheed. He was wearing a yellow Kobe number 8. His face and short hair even reminded Danny a little bit of Kobe.

"Check it out," the other kid said to Rasheed. "These two musta got lost looking for the jungle gym."

Then he laughed at his own joke and got Rasheed to give him five.

Rasheed said to Danny, "What is this, the JV area?"

Before Danny could say anything back, the two of them walked away.

"Who're those jerks?" Zach said.

"I don't know the one who was doing the talking," Danny said. "The other one is this guy I played against once. Don't worry about it."

"You can probably kick his butt," Zach said, like Danny was his hero all of a sudden.

"I did once," Danny said.

Thinking to himself, *Yeah, but can you still?*

Monday afternoon. First full day of real camp at the Right Way Basketball Camp.

They'd worked their butts off all morning in ninety-degree heat, occasionally getting short water breaks—but not nearly enough of them to suit Danny, and he *never* got thirsty or worn out playing ball. The older guys were separated strictly by age today, thirteens with thirteens, fourteens with fourteens, like that, and went from a shooting clinic to a passing clinic to a defensive clinic, even to one for full-court presses, both zone and man-to-man, with a different college coach handling each station. Some of the names Danny knew just from following college hoops; some he didn't, because not all of them were from big schools.

The first clinic was at eight in the morning, and each one lasted an hour. At noon they all dragged themselves to the mess hall for lunch.

Will said to his buds, "If the afternoon is like the morning, I'm busting out of here like it's *Prison Break*."

"C'mon," Danny said, "it's not so bad. It's still basketball."

Ty, who could go all day the way Danny could, said to Danny, "Tell me you're not whipped already, and that was only the morning session."

Danny grinned. "You're right. I want my mommy."

Jeff LeBow came into the mess hall then with his trusty bullhorn and said they were getting two hours at lunch today instead of the usual one, so they could all be assigned to teams. Mr. LeBow said they'd been evaluated off the morning workouts, and now the coaches and counselors were going to basically choose up sides, trying to make them as fair as possible in terms of size, position, talent.

"The elevens and twelves are in one league, the Final Four league," Mr. LeBow said. "Thirteens through fifteens are the NBA, two divisions, Eastern and Western. In that one, we want at least three boys from each age group on each team. Once the games start at the end of this week, if we see we've made one team too strong or too weak, we'll do a little horse trading. But the group you get with today, you can pretty much expect it to be the group you're going to be with for the month."

It was a different place today, Danny had to admit. Everybody in charge moved a lot faster than they had on Saturday and Sunday.

All ball, all the time.

In that way, Right Way was his kind of place.

He felt that way until their long lunch break was over, anyway. Then they all went to the big message board where the teams were posted and found out that he and Will and Tarik were on the same team with Rasheed Hill.

Ty had been assigned to a different team, one that had two Boston kids, Jack Arnold and Chris Lambert, on it, but Ty didn't care. As long as there was a game being played and he was in it, he was cool.

He went off to Court 4. Danny and Will and Tarik headed off in the opposite direction, toward Court 2, the one behind Gampel, closest to the lake.

When they got down there and met their coach, the day only got worse.

Coach Ed Powers, a tall, thin man whose gray hair matched the color of his face, said that if anybody didn't know who he was, he'd been the head basketball coach at Providence College for thirty-five years before the good fathers there—the way he said it didn't make it sound as if he thought the fathers were all that good—had decided it was time for him to retire and turn his job over to a younger man.

Even in the heat, Danny saw, Coach Powers wore long pants and had his blue Right Way shirt buttoned to the top button.

He spoke in a quiet voice, but somehow his words came out loud anyway, at least to Danny.

"Boys," Coach Powers said, "prepare yourselves over the next few weeks to unlearn everything you think you've learned watching what I like to think of as TV basketball. Because if you don't unlearn that junk, you're going to spend most of your time with me running laps."

He stopped now, smiled the kind of smile you got from teachers sometimes right before they piled on the homework and said, "With me so far?"

Will whispered, "No, Coach, you're going way too fast for us."

Danny couldn't help himself and laughed out loud.

"You think something is funny, son?" Coach Powers said.

To Danny.

The players were sitting to the side of the court. Coach Powers came over to Danny and said, "Stand up, son."

He did.

Will's hand shot straight up in the air. "Coach, wait a second. It wasn't his fault."

Coach Powers said to Will, "Was I talking to you?"

"But—"

"It's good that we get this straightened out our first day together." Still talking to Will. "The only time I want an answer from you on this court is when I ask you a question."

It looked as if it took all the willpower Will Stoddard had to keep his mouth shut.

To Danny, Coach Powers said, "What's your name again?"

"Danny Walker, sir."

"Walker?" he said. "Where are you from, Mr. Walker?"

"Middletown, New York."

Coach Powers nodded, started to walk away, then turned back around.

"Oh," he said, "Richie Walker's boy."

It wasn't in the form of a question, so Danny just stood there, waiting.

"Thought I had your dad recruited, back in the day," he said. "Thought he was going to be the one to put me in the Final Four, which I was never fortunate enough to make in my long career. But then Mr. Richie Walker changed his mind at the last minute—or someone changed it for him—and it was the Orangemen of Syracuse he took to the Final Four instead."

Somebody changed it for him? What did that mean? Danny had no clue.

"Your dad ever tell you that story?"

"No, sir."

"No reason why he'd want to, I suppose," Coach Powers said. "But here's what I'd like from you before we continue: a couple of laps around the court. And your friend there can join you."

Danny, feeling humiliated, feeling everybody else on the team watching him, ran twice around with Will, not running his fastest to make sure Will stayed with him.

When they finished, Danny knew the heat he was feeling on the back of his neck wasn't just the sun, it was being called out this way in front of the whole team.

As he stood there catching his breath, Coach Powers said, "When I say run, boys, I don't mean jog like people my age do in the park." He didn't even look at Danny and Will as he said, "Two more."

This time Danny ran like he was in the last leg of one of those Olympic relays, even if it meant getting to the finish line about ten yards ahead of Will.

"More like it," was all Coach Powers said when they finished, before he addressed the whole group again.

"Make no mistake," he said, "we will all be on the same page here, from the beginning of the book. Which is going to seem like the first book on basketball you've ever read in your lives."

He took a whistle out of his pocket, hung it around his neck.

"There's something all you boys need to know," he said. "My team has won the camp championship the last four years. Walked away with a little something they now call the Ed Powers Trophy here. And as unlikely as it seems to me right now, looking at this group in front of me, I plan to make it five in a row a few weeks from now."

He blew the whistle, making Danny jump, and said to them, "Now stand up."

They all did, as if it were a contest to see who could get up the fastest and stand the straightest. "Least we got some size to us," Coach Powers said. "With a few exceptions.

"Players who want to win in basketball get with the program," he continued. "The ones who don't will end up doing so much of the running Mr. Walker and his friend just did they'll think they ended up at soccer camp by mistake."

Danny thought he was already getting paranoid because of this guy, because he was sure the coach was looking right at him as he said, "And from the look of some of the fancy players I saw at this morning's clinics, soccer camp is where some of you belong."

He had been walking up and down in front of them, a basketball he'd picked up on his hip. Danny was almost positive he could hear him creak as he moved. Suddenly he stopped in front of Rasheed.

"Now, from what I saw this morning, I was lucky enough to end up with the most complete player in this whole camp, young Mr. Hill, here," he said.

What, Danny thought, *he's not a fancy player?*

Then he watched as Ed Powers handed Rasheed the ball and said, "This is your ball, son, until somebody shows me they can take it away from you."

Danny just stared at the two of them, feeling Will's eyes on him like they were laser dots.

Danny just knew Will wanted him to turn around in the worst way, but he wasn't doing it, mostly because he knew what his friend was thinking:

His ball.

Not Danny's.

Before they'd even scrimmaged.

Coach Powers put his arm around Rasheed now, as if they were already one team, and the rest of the guys standing in the line were another.

"I know they call this camp Right Way," Coach Powers said. "But let's be real clear about something from the start. From now on, you young men are going to play the game my way."

Each bunkhouse had a designated night to use the pay phone in the old-fashioned phone booth outside the main building. Jeff LeBow had informed everybody that they were here to play, not do play-by-play for their parents.

Gampel's phone night was Monday.

Danny thought there'd be more kids wanting to use the phone, but the line that Nick organized—he seemed to put the saddest looking kids at the front of it—wasn't as long as he expected it to be.

Zach Fox still looked sadder than anybody in the whole bunk, but he'd stayed behind.

"I'm not going to lie to them and tell them I'm having a good time when I'm not," he said.

"But you said you liked your coach and some of the guys on your team."

Nick said Zach had gotten the youngest coach in Division I, Bill Brennan from Fordham, who was just thirty years old.

"Just because he's a good guy doesn't mean I want to spend half my stupid summer with him," Zach said. He flopped back on his bed and started rifling through the pages of a *Hoop* magazine.

Ali Walker answered when Danny finally got the phone. And she immediately started asking a lot of Mom questions about the trip up there, his counselors, the food, if he was showering and brushing every day, how pretty the property was, even asking a joke question about where the nearest girls' camp was.

"I have no idea," Danny said.

Ali said, "I could MapQuest it for you."

"Mom," Danny said, "if there is a girls' camp nearby, I guarantee you, Will Stoddard'll find it."

"Excellent point."

The two of them kept making small talk like that, and as they did, it occurred to Danny that he was making everything sound better than it really was, which meant telling the kind of lies Zach Fox was refusing to tell to his parents.

He told her about being in the younger kids' bunk, tried telling her it was no biggie before quickly changing the subject, but his mom was all over him. "Are you *sure* it's no biggie?" she said.

"I practically feel like one of the counselors," Danny said. "It's kind of fun being the old guy for a change."

There was a pause. Mom radar at work, even long-distance.

"You say it's fun," she said. "But you don't sound that way."

"It's fine, Mom, really," he said. "Plus this guy I'm with, Zach, could use a friend."

"Well," Ali said, "he couldn't have a better one than you." Then she said she was going to put his dad on the phone, they probably had big basketball things to talk about.

"Oh, wait, I almost forgot," she said. "Tess called."

Danny stood there in the old phone booth and couldn't help feeling ridiculously excited. But he wasn't going to let his mom in on that, even if she had her good radar going tonight.

So all he said, making his voice as casual as he could, was, "How's she doing?"

"We didn't talk all that long. She just wanted the address up there," his mom said. "I hope it was all right that I gave it to her"— Danny heard the smile in her voice as she added—"even in a time of war."

"C'mon, you know it's not war," Danny said, trying to use the same tone of voice, like this was no biggie, either, the subject of Tess. "It's much more serious than that."

He heard her laugh, a sound that had always made him feel better about everything, and then she said, "Love you."

Knowing he was safe inside the phone booth and that no one outside could hear him, he said, "Love you, too, Mom."

"Here's your dad."

The next thing he heard was Richie Walker saying, "Hey,

champ." As soon as he did, Danny cut him right off. "Dad, promise you won't tell Mom any of what I'm going to tell you."

"Promise," Richie said.

Then Danny told him as much as he could, as fast as he could, about Coach Ed Powers. He was out of breath when he finished, like he'd just had to run more laps.

Richie told him to relax, they could talk freely, his mom had just gone out to the store.

"I can't believe you pulled *him* for a coach," Richie said.

"Dad, the guy hates me."

"He hates anybody who thinks basketball is a sport and not chess with live pieces. And minds of their own. I don't know how this guy got to be some kind of offensive guru, but he did."

"He acted like every single thing I did today other than go to the water fountain was dead wrong."

"That's him," Richie said. "But remember, it's still only the first day. He probably just wanted to scare you all half to death to get you with the program. Even he has to know this is summer camp and not boot camp."

"But Dad," Danny said, "it's not just me. It sounds like he hates you, too."

"Oh, God," Richie said. "Did he give you all that BS about how I changed my mind at the last second about going to Providence, back in the day when he still let his players actually play?"

"He made it sound like you changed your mind at the very last second."

"Don't even get into it with him," his dad said. "But just so you know, I turned them down way early in the process, and then turned them down again after one of their rich alums offered me some money under the old table. I'll tell you the whole crazy story when you get home."

Danny said, "It's like basketball by numbers, Dad. That's not me. That's not ever going to be me."

"You'll just have to win him over," Richie said. "'Cause the guy's probably going to be as obsessed with winning there as he was coaching college. And he'll see that you can help him win."

"No way," Danny said. "Remember that kid Rasheed from Baltimore we played in the travel finals? Coach already announced that it's his ball."

"Take it from him."

There was a knock on the door. Danny saw Nick out there, pointing at his watch.

"Coach Powers is gonna wreck my whole camp. I just know it," Danny said.

Now he really did sound like Zach.

Richie said, "Only if you let him."

"But, Dad—"

"Listen, I'm not gonna try and tell you that you didn't get a bad deal," Richie said. "You did. But you'll figure it out."

"I can't play for him."

"Guess what? You are playing for him."

Nick rapped on the door again. Danny made a sign, like just one more sec.

"If you're good enough," Richie continued, "you can play for anybody."

Danny fired one up from half court.

"Is there any way you could call Mr. LeBow?" Danny said. "Since he didn't get me in the right bunk, maybe he could do something to get me on the right team."

"No."

"No?"

"You're going to have to suck it up, pal," his dad said. "You've had one bad day. Get the most you can out of the drills with the other instructors and then just make sure you show this guy what you've got when the games start."

"You make it sound easy."

"If basketball was easy," Richie said, "everybody'd be a star."

Then he said he loved him and would talk to him next week, and the next thing Danny heard after that was a dial tone.

Danny Walker stood there looking at the receiver in his hand, and for one quick moment, there and gone, he wished there was a way he could make one more call tonight.

To Tess.

Way after lights-out, Danny was sure he could hear Zach crying in the bed next to his. He was trying to be quiet about it, face buried in his pillow. Danny was sure he was the only one hearing it.

But it was definitely crying.

When it had gone on for a while, Danny whispered, "Hey, you okay?"

Silence.

"C'mon, Zach. I know you can hear me."

There was a big moon lighting the lake outside, so Danny watched as Zach turned his head on his pillow to face him now. "Leave me alone," he said.

"Listen," Danny said, "it'll get better."

"It won't!"

He was trying to whisper now, but it reminded Danny more of a hissing sound from some old radiator.

"But you said yourself that having me as your roommate was a good thing," Danny said.

"Not good enough. Besides, I'm only with you at night."

Danny didn't say anything. He was sorry he'd said anything in the first place, because he could see Zach getting worked up all over again. "How many times do I have to tell you I don't want to be here?" Zach said. "Give me one good reason why I shouldn't be able to leave."

"Because you'd be quitting," Danny said to him, knowing it was something his dad would say, remembering the day at McFeeley when he told Will he sounded just like Richie Walker. "And you can't."

"Why not?" Zach said.

The words came out of Danny before he even knew he was going to say them: "Because I don't quit. And you're just like me."

DANNY WAS LEAVING HIS PASSING CLINIC THE NEXT DAY—AT LEAST
the coach running that, an assistant coach from Duke, thought
he could still pass—when Jeff LeBow came running up and said,
"Great news! I found a guy at Boston Garden who's willing to move
his stuff over to Staples Center, where his cousin is."

The move, Danny figured, was about fifty yards, but it sounded
like some kind of NBA road trip.

Jeff said, "I don't know if I can get you in the exact same
area as your friends, but at least you'll be in the same building
with them."

"Thanks," Danny said, "but I'm good where I am."

Jeff looked at Danny as if he'd just asked if it would be all right
if he could help out cleaning the bathrooms every morning once
everybody had gone off to breakfast.

"You want to stay with the young guys?" he said.

Danny tried to make a joke of it. "I'll pretend you held me back
a year in school."

"All kidding aside," Jeff said. "You sure you don't want to think
this over? Because if I tell the kid at the Garden he has to stay
where he is, that's it for everybody. Done deal. Which means I'm
done being a real estate agent."

"I'm sure," Danny said.

When he explained it to Will and Ty at lunch, Will said, "Let me see if I understand this. You're staying in a bunk you don't really want to be in and passing up a chance to move to the bunk you *do* want to be in so you can look out for a kid who doesn't even want to be here?"

"Pretty much."

Will turned to Tarik and said, "And he calls me weird."

"He's not weird, dog," Tarik said. "He just sticks."

"Sticks?" Will said.

"That's what you do when you're loyal," Tarik said. "You stick, even if it's to somebody you barely know."

"Word," Will said.

"Beyond word," Tarik said. "Walker here, he's wet."

"I'm never gonna know all your words, am I?" Will said.

"Probably not," Tarik said.

Ty just sat there doing what he did a lot, only opening his mouth for the purpose of smiling at his friends.

The second day with Coach Powers was worse than the first.

Danny never opened his mouth, avoided any kind of eye contact unless Coach Powers was talking directly to him, hustled his butt off even if that just involved chasing a ball that had bounced off the court, and tried his best to learn the offense they were being taught—Coach Powers's famous Providence College passing offense.

It didn't take Danny long to figure out why it was called that, by the way.

Because all Coach Powers seemed to want them to do was pass, at least until somebody finally got a layup off one of the backdoor picks that seemed to be the only thing in the world that made him genuinely happy.

"No outside shots until you get it down," he said. "First team, you guys just keep running it all the way through, and if it doesn't produce an easy two, then swing it back to the top and start all over again.

"You're going to know what to do and where everybody is on the court at all times, as if you've been running this offense since your first Biddy Basketball league."

"And running . . . and running . . . and running," Will said to Danny on the down-low. "They should call our team the Energizer Bunnies."

They were on the second team, along with Tarik, who'd turned out to be slow but was a ferocious rebounder. Rasheed was on the first team, of course. Danny was actually curious to see how Rasheed was going to handle an offense like this, one that did everything except puncture the ball they were using to take the air out of it. Danny was sure an offense like this wasn't nearly big enough to fit Rasheed's game, no matter how much Coach Powers said he loved him now, even if the coach had practically declared that it was as much Rasheed's team as his.

Danny thought about asking him, but Rasheed hadn't said a word to Danny after the first time they'd seen each other. It was as if they were on different teams, even playing on the same team. Different teams or maybe just different worlds.

The first hour of practice was spent going through the offense over and over, Rasheed's five getting a lot more time with the ball than Danny's five.

Coach Powers finally blew his whistle and told them to get some water, because after that they were going to scrimmage all the way to dinnertime.

At one of the water fountains, a safe enough distance away from the coach, Will said to Danny, "Can I say something without you getting that shut-up-or-die look on your face?"

"If you can say it quietly."

Will said, "I just wanted you to know I did notice one guy having fun while we went through ballet class."

"Who?"

Will nodded at Coach Powers.

"Him."

When they were all back on the court, Coach Powers told them to match up with the guys they'd had before. "Now you're all going to do some *real* scrimmaging," he said.

Danny had been guarding Cole Duncan, a redheaded kid with a million freckles from a town in Pennsylvania Danny had never heard of, and the player on the starting five closest to Danny in size, which meant close enough that it didn't look like some ridiculous mismatch. Cole was much more of a pure point guard than Rasheed. Danny had seen that right away, the first day they were all together. Coach Powers had Rasheed at the point, anyway, and didn't seem to mind that even in the big ball-sharing offense, Rasheed still had the ball more than anybody else out there.

He went over and stood next to Cole now.

"Walker?" Coach Powers said.

"Yes, Coach?"

"Why don't you guard Rasheed and have your friend . . . " He hesitated, like he'd lost his place, and finally just pointed in Will's direction.

"Will Stoddard," Danny said.

In two days, it had become clear that Coach Powers either couldn't remember Will's name or didn't want to.

"Have Mr. Stoddard guard Cole."

Danny didn't say anything, just nodded as he and Will shifted positions.

"Thought it might be kind of fun for you and Rasheed to get

yourselves reacquainted in a game," Powers said to Danny. "I didn't see that big travel final the two of you played down in North Carolina, but I heard it was some game until the refs decided it."

The refs decided it?

Danny bit down on his lip so hard he was afraid it might split wide open, not wanting to say something that would get him in even deeper with this coach than he already was, or get him punished into running around the court for the rest of the afternoon while the other guys played five-on-four without him.

That was the smart thing to do.

Just shut up and play. Start trying to win this coach over, like his dad said.

But he couldn't do it. Not when the guy was this wrong.

Not about that game.

"All due respect, sir," Danny said, knowing Will's theory that nothing good had ever come after "all due respect" in the history of the universe, "but you heard wrong."

He looked up at Coach Powers and said, "The refs didn't decide it because *we* did."

Behind him he heard Will say, "That's *exactly* what we did."

Danny turned his head long enough to see Will shrug. His wingman forever.

Now nobody said anything on Court 2 at Right Way. Nobody said anything. Nobody moved.

Finally Coach Powers came over, stood in front of Danny and said, "Is that so?"

As if Will hadn't said anything, as if he wasn't even there.

Danny knew there was no turning back. So he stood his ground.

"My dad says the only way the refs ever decide anything is if you let them," Danny said.

"Well, I'm the ref today," Coach said. "I'll try to stay out of your way, Mr. Walker, let you boys decide things for the next hour or so."

He did exactly that.

While Danny and his team got leveled like they were in one of those end-of-the-world movies.

Richie Walker, Danny knew, overpraised him sometimes. He said he didn't, wanted to believe he was tougher on his son than anybody, held him to a higher standard. Promised Danny that he'd always be straight with him about basketball when the two of them really got down to it, when the conversation was something his dad described as being "point guard to point guard."

"The way all those ex-soldiers say they're talking marine to marine," Richie told him one time.

And most of the time, he *would* be honest with Danny.

Problem was, there was one thing he couldn't overcome: He was a dad. And unless you had one of those psycho sports dads who never thought their kids did anything right—guys who really did act like marines—dads couldn't help themselves in the end.

They saw the player they wanted their kid to be. Or just plain-old thought their kids were better than they really were. They especially thought that way if, like Richie Walker, they couldn't look at their kids without seeing themselves.

So Danny always thought his dad was going a little bit overboard when he'd talk about Danny having "the eye."

Which, Richie said, was something you were either born with, or you weren't.

When the subject came up, Danny would say, "Yeah, I know I have pretty good court vision, or whatever. I know that even when

I turn my back to one side of the court and head in the other direction, I still remember where everybody is behind me."

Then Richie would say, "No, no, no, it's more than that, and you know it.

" 'The eye,' " Richie said, "means you see things happening on the court before they actually happen. It's the reason why the other kids are still holding on to the ball like it's their blankie instead of doing what you do, getting the open man the ball the split second he breaks open on account of the fact that you're already passing the ball the split second before he gets open."

Even when Danny thought his dad was blowing smoke at him, he still loved how excited Richie would get talking deep hoops like this. It would be another one of those role-reversal deals they had between them sometimes, with Richie Walker the one acting like a little kid.

Sometimes Danny would throw one of his dad's favorite expressions back at him. "Pop," he'd say, "you sure you're not overthinking this?"

Richie would give him a brush-off gesture with his hand and say, "Make fun if you want. But with the best thinkers out there, the beauty of the whole thing is that they're not thinking at all. They're just playing a different kind of game. 'Cause they see things and know things the other guys don't."

Except on this day, Richie Walker's son played as if he'd forgotten everything he ever knew.

As if all the doubts he had before he came here weren't just doubts, they were all true.

He couldn't play with the big boys.

He didn't measure up.

He was pressing, he sure knew that, which meant he was going against one of his most important rules about sports, even if the rule sounded like it made no sense: You had to relax to play your hardest, to have any chance at all to play your best.

Danny kept telling himself he'd play through his nerves, the way he always had in the past when he got off to a bad start.

Never happened.

It also didn't help that Rasheed was all over him like a bad rash, all over the court, playing a camp scrimmage as if somehow it were the fifth quarter of their game in North Carolina. And it didn't exactly hurt Rasheed that he had bigger and better ballplayers with him on the first team.

None of it would have mattered, Danny knew, if he were on his game. He wouldn't even be looking for excuses because he never looked for excuses when he was on his game, which was most of the time. He'd gone up against bigger and better teams plenty of times, refusing to quit, like a dog with a bone, until he did figure out a way to win.

Just not today.

Today he was playing like a dog in front of Coach Powers. All his life, Danny had been the one the guy guarding him couldn't get in front of, no matter how big the guy was. Only now he couldn't get in front of Rasheed Hill, who was schooling him all over the place.

The eye?

It was Rasheed who seemed to have eyes in the back of his head on Court 2 and Danny who played as if he had rocks in his head. The more he tried to make perfect passes in front of this coach, show him what a good passer he was, the more he threw the ball away. When he would occasionally get a step on Rasheed and get inside against the two tall fifteen-year-olds they had on the team— David Upshaw from Philadelphia, Ben Coltrane from outside Syracuse—he would get completely swallowed up. Then David or Ben

70

would swat another one of his passes away like they were swatting away the summer bugs that seemed to swarm Right Way at night.

It was why Coach Powers was blowing his whistle about every two minutes, or so it seemed to Danny, constantly stopping the action and pointing out another bad decision or bad pass.

Blowing the whistle and barking, "Time out, Walker."

It wasn't long before Danny thought his name had been legally changed to Time Out Walker.

He wasn't the only one being singled out. Will couldn't do anything to satisfy this coach either. It seemed that whenever Will got an open look, he kept throwing the ball in the lake.

"I thought from the scouting report you were a shooter, Mr. Stoddard," Coach Powers said, surprising them by getting Will's name right.

"Me, too," Will said.

But everybody on the court knew something. No matter how much Coach Powers picked on the other guys, Danny was the one getting picked on the most.

The more whistles he got, the worse he played.

Practice was supposed to end at five o'clock sharp. At a few minutes before five, Coach told them to huddle up, they were going to pretend that the game was tied, one minute left, Rasheed's team with the ball. "Maybe if we do it this way," he said, "the Walker team can get me a stop before we call it a day."

Now it was the Walker team.

Danny ignored him, motioned for his guys to get around him: Will, Bobby Lowell, Alex Westphal, the closest thing they had to a center on the second team. And Tarik.

"Ask you something, Walker?" Tarik said in the huddle. "You slash the coach's tires and he found out about it?"

Will said, "When you threw that behind-the-back pass a few minutes ago? I thought his head was going to explode."

"Forget all that and listen up," Danny said, keeping his voice low. "And just for your information, behind the back was the only angle I had to get you the ball on the wing."

"Still—" Will said.

"Listen up!" Danny snapped at him, getting his friend's attention in the process and everybody else's.

Will's reaction was to break out into a huge smile. "I've been waiting for Coach Walker to show up," he said. "Because I sure have missed him."

Danny said that Rasheed's team would do what they'd been doing all day: run through the offense one time, look like they were starting it again, then go right to a high pick-and-roll.

"Even though we've all been acting like these were the first pick-and-rolls we've ever seen," Danny said, "we're going to take it away from them now."

"We are?" Tarik said. He turned and looked at where Rasheed's team was standing, waiting for them. "Who chose up these sides, anyway?"

Danny nodded at Powers. "He did. Mr. Basketball. But now we're going to give him and those other guys something to think about for tomorrow."

Then he laid out what he expected them all to do. When he finished, Alex Westphal said, "Dude."

Rasheed brought the ball up, Danny on him. Rasheed passed it to Cole Duncan, who gave it right back to him, then ran through to the opposite corner.

Danny was thinking, *He might as well run all the way to Vermont. That's the last touch he's getting, even in a pretend game.*

Rasheed passed it to David Upshaw, now at the foul line, who passed it to Ben Coltrane on the right wing. Rasheed ran through, came back, got the ball back up top. Right on cue, here came David, all 6-3 of him, built like one of those tank-looking Hummers, to set the killer screen he'd been setting on Danny all day.

Except that before he got to Danny, Will Stoddard, coming from the weak side, cut him off.

A defensive guy setting a pick on an offensive guy.

"Hey," Danny heard David Upshaw say, "What the—?"

David's man, Alex Westphal, then ran around both of them, cutting Rasheed off on his left. Danny already had him cut off if he tried to go to his right. Will stayed home, right in front of Rasheed.

Danny watched Rasheed's eyes, knowing what he knew: There had to be a whole bunch of his teammates open somewhere.

As soon as he hesitated, Danny reached in and for the first time all day, flicked the ball away from him, got a real good slap on it, knocking it toward the other basket.

For a second, Danny had a clear path to the ball, and to a layup.

Until Will went for the ball, too, and the two of them collided.

Big scramble now for the loose ball, bodies flying, what felt like all ten players on the court going for it, into it now, like this wasn't a pretend game at all, it was the real thing.

Somehow, pure luck, the ball ended up back in Rasheed's hands on the far left swing, about thirty feet from the basket.

Danny gave a quick look behind him, saw there was nobody on his team defending their basket, started backing up as fast as he could.

Rasheed Hill smiled then, the first time Danny had seen him change expression since he'd gotten here.

Just the two of them.

Rasheed's smile saying, Me and you.

Not exactly the way it had ended up when Rasheed fouled out in Carolina, but close enough. All day long from this side of the court, Rasheed had started off dribbling with his left hand, like he was going left, then crossed over to his right, attacking the basket that way. But Danny had a feeling he'd try to cross him up this time, go left all the way.

And maybe Danny still had the eye after all, because Rasheed *did* come hard to the basket off a left-hand dribble.

Danny beat him to the spot.

Danny beat him there, set himself, ready to take the charge if he had to, or at least make Rasheed pull up for a jumper.

But he wasn't pulling up, he was going straight at Danny and straight at the basket, elevating now, exploding into the air the way he could, putting his right knee into Danny's chest as he did, knocking Danny back as easily as a bowling ball knocks over a pin. Danny flew backward, twisting out of control, feeling himself going down in slow motion, unable to break his fall, and landed hard on his right knee.

Before he hit the ground, before his head snapped back on the court, he had a perfect view of Rasheed continuing to fly toward the basket, laying the ball in, no backboard, all net.

The only thing Coach Powers said after what Danny knew was a textbook offensive foul against Rasheed was, "Ballgame."

"But, Coach!" Danny yelled, rolling up into a sitting position.

"Are you okay there, Mr. Walker?" Coach Powers said.

For the last time that day, Danny felt everybody on the whole team looking at him, knew that if he said anything more, he'd just lose again. He wasn't okay. His right knee was killing him. But he wasn't going to tell Coach Powers that, or act like he wanted any sympathy.

"Perfect," he said.

"Anything else on your mind?"

Danny put his head down, almost like he was talking to himself.

"No, sir."

"Didn't think so," Coach said. "Because I know you want the players to decide the game, not the ref. See you in the morning."

And walked away.

Danny, arms hanging over his knees, feeling as if his head was about to split wide open, didn't move. He was trying to decide whether his head hurt the most or his knee.

Tarik Meminger came over.

"Before I say anything, you really okay?"

"I'm okay."

Tarik reached down to help Danny up, then grinned and said, "Look at you, dog. 'Sheed turned you into a damn speed bump."

THEY WERE GIVEN THE OPTION ON WEDNESDAY NIGHT OF EITHER going into Cedarville and walking around town for a couple of hours, or going to Casco, the next town over, where the one theater was showing the new *Batman*. There was a lot more interest in the movie, so two of the yellow Right Way buses transported those guys. The other bus and the vans were used for the Cedarville run, the counselors doing the driving.

The van Nick had used to drive Danny and the guys from the airport the first day sat eight passengers if everybody squeezed. Now Nick drove this group into Cedarville: Danny, Will, Ty, Tarik, Alex Westphal, the two Boston kids from Ty's team, Jack Arnold and Chris Lambert.

And Zach Fox.

Danny had invited Zach to come along with them, even though most of the kids from Gampel had chosen the movie.

"Okay," Will said when Danny told him Zach was part of the plan. "You've officially locked up Camper of the Week. Congratulations."

"Just be nice," Danny said.

"Won't be necessary," Will said. "You're nice enough for all of us."

They saw a lot of other Right Way kids walking up and down

the streets of Cedarville's small downtown area, which seemed to extend for about four blocks. There was one general store—it was easy to find, since it said THE GENERAL STORE on the sign out front—that had candy and magazines and a whole wall covered with comic books, more comic books than Danny had ever seen in one place. He'd never been much of a comic book guy—hardly anybody their age was—but he could tell just by looking at some of the Supermans and Batmans and Fantastic Fours that they were real old.

Will bought a Spider-Man.

Ty said, "Hold on. You said you were done with old Spidey after Dr. Octopus looked so lame in the second movie."

"*Spidey 2* was lame," he said. Then he held up the comic book and said, "This, however, is a classic."

He had a way of drawing the word out so it sounded as if it had a lot more syllables than it really did.

Classic was the highest possible praise from Will, whether they were talking about sports or music or movies or which flavor of Ben and Jerry's was best. You might have another flavor you thought was better, but once he proclaimed Phish Food classic, he was pretty much saying the debate was over.

Now he and Tarik, still trying to outtalk each other, the way they had from the day they met, tried to figure out whether *classic* was even better than *wet*.

"It's like my mom says about stuff all the time," Danny said to Ty, nodding at Will and Tarik, "it must've been destiny that brought them together."

The ice cream parlor they found a few doors down from the general store was also classic, right down to its name: Pops.

Standing outside, Ty said, "This whole town reminds me of the

Back to the Future town they went to and nobody could figure out why Marty had a skateboard."

There was a lot of outdoor seating at Pops, and most of the tables were full because the weather was so nice. Indoors, though, was better, mostly because it reminded Danny and Will and Ty so much of their headquarters back in Middletown, the Candy Kitchen. There was a long counter with swivel seats, homemade ice cream being served, even an old-fashioned movie popcorn machine next to the cash register.

Danny was with Will, Zach and Tarik in one booth. Ty and the other guys had the next one. Everybody in the group had camp war stories to tell, even after just three days at Right Way, stories about coaches, counselors, bathrooms, showers, food, the kid in the next bed snoring or making a noise much worse than that in the night, body odor, dorko questions from parents relayed by kids who'd called home already, how this guy or that guy or the other guy was overrated. Or how some fifteen-year-old had blown them away and was just going to absolutely dominate everybody before he went off to Duke or Carolina or Kentucky or UConn.

You heard the word *dominate* a lot at Pops.

Almost as much as you heard about Jeff LeBow's nonstop peppiness and how he seemed to be everywhere at once.

"Lemme explain something to you all," Tarik said. "Nobody is that happy. *Nobody*."

Will said, "Take his bullhorn away, I guarantee you, it's like that deal with Samson's hair. The guy's got nothin'."

Pretty soon they were laughing about everything that had happened so far, filling up the inside of Pops with happy summer noise.

This was more like it, Danny thought, hanging this way, not

just with his Middletown friends. This was more what he imagined camp might be like, even if he had to get away from it for a couple of hours to feel this way.

Tarik was across the table from Danny, facing the door. All of a sudden his eyes got real wide and he said, "Uh-oh. Coach Powers."

Danny dropped the long spoon he'd been using to get the last ice cream out of the bottom of his root beer float. His head whipped around as if it was one of the swivel chairs at the counter.

No one there.

Everybody, both booths, laughed. Danny couldn't help it, he had to laugh with them. And at himself.

"Got you, dog," Tarik said. "Got you bad."

"Only one problem," Will said, head down.

"What?"

"You thought of it first."

"Knew from the first day I met you I had to elevate my comedy," Tarik said.

"Well, you certainly did that tonight with your hair," Will said.

Tarik had let out his cornrows and now had an Afro that seemed to add about five inches to his height.

Tarik said, "Don't be talking about *my* hair with that hat hair you go through life with."

They all finished up their ice cream and drinks, knowing they still had an hour before they were supposed to meet Nick where he'd parked the van. Jack said he'd spotted a video arcade at the miniature golf place at the end of town, down by the lake.

They started walking in that direction, Jack and Chris wanting to know about Coach Powers, Danny and Will and Tarik laying it all out for them.

"Why can't you just ask for a different team?" Zach said.

"Doesn't work that way," Danny said. "They don't have free agency here."

"Man talks about playing basketball his way," Tarik said. "Seems to be because he can only see basketball one way. Like it's supposed to be one of those connect-the-dots pictures we all had to draw when we were little."

"Except when Rasheed wants to bust a play," Will said. "Then Coach My Way tends to look the other way."

"I know you talk to Rasheed," Danny said to Tarik. "How can he stand this guy?"

Tarik smiled. "Doesn't work that way with 'Sheed. He doesn't stand, sit or care. He told me that he can get with any kind of program, 'cause he's seen his man Iverson do the same thing. And he says no coach is ever gonna hold him back, anyhow, any way."

"He told you all that at one time?" Will said.

"Well, *over* time," Tarik said. "The brother said he wasn't going to worry himself about the coach he was playing for, because there's too many college coaches here watchin'."

"There's going to be a lot more of him to see if he's out there for three quarters and some of us are only out for one," Danny said.

Jeff had announced the first day they were with their teams that this wasn't YMCA ball back home. You didn't automatically get to play half the game. You were only guaranteed one quarter in the league games, and whatever you got after that, you had to earn.

Ty said to Danny, "You'll figure it out. You always have before."

Danny said to Ty, "Now *you* sound like my dad."

Ty's response was to point off to their right. "Hey, check it out."

The town of Cedarville was on the north side of Coffee Lake, Nick had informed them on the ride over. The miniature golf place and video arcade were at the very end of the downtown area, in a tiny harbor. A couple hundred yards before you got there, on the lakeside, was a white wooden Congregational church with a steeple that seemed to be the highest point in Cedarville.

Behind the church, Ty had spotted a basketball court, nobody on it.

"You're kidding, right?" Will said, as if he'd already read Ty's mind.

"About what?" Ty said, trying to act innocent.

"Well, look at that," Danny said. "A basketball court. A full basketball court. With nets."

"Oh, don't tell me this," Will said. "Don't tell me that just when we've gotten away from ball, you guys now want to play ball."

Danny ignored him, said to the rest of them, "Okay, who's up for a game?"

Will said, "You've been telling me since you got run over that your knee is killing you."

"I iced it."

"I know you think ice cures everything except strep throat," Will said, "but it's still swollen. You can't possibly want to play when we're on, like, recess."

Danny grinned. "Do you think you're, like, talking to some other Danny Walker?"

They took a vote. Everybody else was up for a game, so Will reluctantly went along.

"One problem, however," Danny said. "No ball."

Alex said, "I think I might have seen a couple at the general store."

But Zach said, "We don't need to buy a ball. I brought mine, remember?"

Zach always seemed to be carrying a ball with him, or dribbling one. Everybody at camp had noticed by now. Even though he kept saying he didn't want to be at basketball camp, it was as if having a basketball with him was some kind of security blanket.

When it was time to leave for town, he had his ball with him, as usual, and didn't want to take time to run back down to Gampel and stash it.

"Zach," Danny said, "you are the man."

"And you," Will said to Danny, "are truly sick. And I don't mean the good sick." He pointed at Danny's knee.

Danny made a move like he was a soccer-style kicker. "Actually, I feel better all of a sudden."

Zach said he'd run back up the street to where the van was parked, be right back with his ball.

"Hurry up," Will said. "We're timing you." When Danny gave him another elbow, Will added, "Hey, I time my little brother on stuff all the time."

But Zach must have taken him seriously, because he was back with the ball in about a minute, face red, completely out of breath, looking totally pleased with himself.

That kind of night, Danny thought. *Even Zach Fox, camp-hater, is happy.*

And for an hour before they had to get back in the van, without any whistles blowing, without Coach Ed Powers busting his chops, he wasn't Time Out Walker anymore. Danny was happy, too. He had Zach with him and Ty and Alex. Shirts against the skins.

Like they were back at McFeeley Park in Middletown.

For an hour, behind the Congregational church down by the

lake in Cedarville, Maine, basketball was fun again, the way it was supposed to be.

The way it used to be.

The feeling lasted until the next afternoon, when Danny's team scrimmaged Ty's team at The House.

Of horrors.

LEAGUE GAMES TRADITIONALLY BEGAN THE SECOND WEEK AT RIGHT Way. Until then, the coaches were free to schedule scrimmages among themselves. There was a big sign-up board inside the front door to The House, and getting court time in there was pretty much first-come, first-served. Jeff announced at breakfast the next morning that each scrimmage was limited to one hour.

The college counselors reffed the scrimmages, same as the league games.

Ty's team was called the Cavaliers. They were coached by Tom Rossi. Danny knew Rossi had started out as a college coach, then took over the Hornets for a few years and was back in college now at Florida State. He was a short guy, slicked-back hair. Ty said he was funny, talking from the time practice started until he blew the whistle and announced it was over.

According to Ty, Coach Rossi had told them the first day of practice to pay close attention, he was going to explain his entire offensive philosophy all at once.

"Run," he'd said.

Then came his defensive philosophy: "Press."

"Great," Danny had said, "you get the fun coach."

Tarik had said, "And we get Dr. Evil."

"No," Will said. "Dr. Evil was funny."

The Cavaliers were tall enough that Coach Rossi had Ty playing small forward. Their center, a fifteen-year-old named Oliver Grey, who Tarik said was from the same neighborhood in Coney Island as Stephon Marbury and Sebastian Telfair, was already 6-6, even if he was almost as skinny as Ty.

Their backcourt was the two Boston kids, Jack Arnold and Chris Lambert.

As soon as the scrimmage started, just after four o'clock, Danny saw that they ran as much as the guys said they would, ran as though there were some kind of invisible ten-second shot clock right above the backboard. And even though Jack and Chris were supposed to be the guards, it seemed to Danny that Ty ended up in the middle of more fast breaks than the two of them combined.

Danny saw something else. Oliver Grey had already figured out that if he busted it every time he got a rebound and started another Cavs fast break, Ty would make sure he led the camp in dunks.

At one point, after he had caught a lob pass from Ty and dunked over Ben Coltrane, Tarik leaned over and said to Danny, "I think after this, Ollie's gonna take Ty for ice cream."

After about ten minutes, the Cavs already led 24–6, and Coach Powers signaled for a time-out. Danny expected him to light into the first team for a change. But he didn't.

"That pinball basketball their coach coaches always looks impressive early in camp," Coach Powers said. "But don't get caught up in it. Let them keep running till their tongues are hanging out. You boys just keep running our stuff. Okay?"

Everybody nodded.

Right before they broke the huddle, Rasheed said, "Hey."

It stopped all of them. He never spoke in the huddle unless Coach asked him a direct question. Now he acted as if he'd just been waiting for Coach to stop talking so he could start.

"But we run when we can, right?" he said.

It came out a question, but Danny knew it really wasn't.

"Absolutely," Coach Powers said.

Rasheed said one more thing, to their big guys, Ben and David Upshaw: "You gonna let that Ollie guy school you all day, or what?"

Now he walked out of the huddle.

The Celtics proceeded to cut into the Cavs lead, mostly because Rasheed got hot, and because of the charge he'd put into Ben and David, who finally started competing against Ollie at both ends of the court. It wasn't until there were about four minutes left in the half that Coach Powers called down to Danny and said, "Mr. Walker, give Rasheed a rest."

Talking to him the way you talked to a scrub.

Like he was only here to give the star of the team a chance to catch his breath.

Danny made a couple of good passes once he got in, one of them to Tarik on a backdoor cut. Ollie got over there a step late.

The other one was on the break. Danny fed Will on the left wing for what he thought would be a jumper. But when the defender went for him, Will—already in midair—passed the ball back to Danny, who slap-passed it to Ben for a reverse layup.

The Cavs had most of their second team in there, but Danny didn't care, his team was cutting into that lead, and he was finally hooping as if he still knew what he was doing.

With forty seconds left in the half and the Celtics only down by a basket, Coach Powers asked for another time-out. He called them over, told them to run a play they'd been working on for a couple of days, one he called "Carolina."

Coach Powers had said it was a variation of the four-corners offense his friend Dean Smith used to run with the Tar Heels in the old days, when they wanted to run out the clock. He had told them to use the four-corners to set themselves up for a three-point shot at the end of a half or a game. The point guard would eventually have the ball in the middle of the court, and the shooters would run to their designated spots behind the three-point line.

With the second team, Will and Tarik were the shooters.

The Celtics ran down the clock the way Coach wanted them to, passing the ball around near the half-court line, weaving in and out. With ten seconds left, as if on cue, Tarik and Will ran into opposite corners, Alex and Ben ran to set picks for them, and Tarik and Will came curling around those picks ready to shoot.

Danny dribbled toward Tarik, not even needing the clock now, counting the time off in his head.

Nine seconds.

Eight.

Tarik's man seemed to read the play perfectly, getting right around the pick and cutting him off.

But Tarik, knowing how little time was left the same way Danny did, gave the guy a head fake, like he was determined to get open for a three, then cut for the basket instead.

Wide open.

Four seconds on the clock.

Danny fired about a thirty-foot bounce pass that should have had steam coming off it, even on a hot day.

Best pass he'd thrown at camp.

Wet, as Tarik would say.

But Tarik must have taken his eye off it for a second. Maybe it was Ollie Grey, back in the game now, scrambling to get back in the play from the other corner. Maybe he slowed down to get his feet right.

The ball went off Tarik's hands and out of bounds.

He looked at Danny, shook his head, banged his chest hard as if to say "my bad."

Then they heard the whistle blow.

Not a whistle belonging to either of the guys reffing the game.

Coach Powers had his whistle in his mouth and didn't blow it once. He blew it again and again.

He pointed at Danny, then at Tarik, and said, "You two. Take a seat!"

Tarik, not really thinking things through, pointed to the clock in The House and said, "Coach, there's only a few seconds left in the half."

Coach Powers gave Tarik a look that Danny thought might actually set him on fire.

"Take a seat," Coach said, "or take the rest of the day off."

It was like they were being sent to the penalty box.

Where, as it turned out, they should have stayed.

Because it was late afternoon and practices were ending all over camp, a lot of kids were filling up the stands to watch the end of the Celtics versus Cavaliers.

Coach Powers had Danny sit next to him for the first ten minutes of the second half, having calmed down by now. He pointed out why this offensive set went wrong or that one did, saying this guy set a pick wrong or that guy was slow to switch, see what happens when a play starts to break down like that?

He finally gave Danny a pat on the shoulder and one of those smiles of his, the ones where his lips seemed to disappear completely, and said, "Now, go in there for Rasheed and run the offense I want to run, not the one *you* want to run."

The score was 46–40 for the Cavs when Danny went back out there, along with Tarik and Alex Westphal.

The Cavs immediately went on a 16–2 rip.

Coach Rossi had his guys start pressing all over the court again, and as soon as they did, Danny felt like he was trying to cross some kind of busy street in traffic.

They had done some work at practice, trying to beat a press.

Not *this* press.

Danny kept trying to tell his guys what to do, where to go. Didn't help. Wherever the ball ended up, there was an immediate double-team, or a triple-team, one that somehow always seemed to include the long arms of Ty or Ollie Grey.

The only help they were getting from Coach Powers was this: *"Think!"*

"You know what *I* think?" Will said to Danny, while Ty knocked down a couple more free throws. "I think this dweeb only gets to be our coach for about twenty-two more days."

"And seven hours," Danny said.

Tarik pointed at the real clock, not the game clock. "And thirty-four minutes."

Danny threw the ball away twice. Dribbled off his foot when he tried to beat one of the Cavaliers' traps and get down the sideline.

He'd had one of his outside shots blocked by Ty, which made everybody in the stands cheer.

"Sorry," Ty said quietly after the ball bounced out of bounds.

"Me, too," Danny said.

Danny didn't look at the scoreboard again until it was 75–50 with one minute left. He was wondering by then why somebody hadn't invoked the kind of slaughter rule they had in Little League baseball.

For some reason, Coach Powers called one last time-out. In the huddle he said to them, "Nobody thinks so right now, but this has been a great lesson. Would you boys like to know why?" Without waiting for anybody to answer, he said, "I'll tell you why. Because everybody on this team got a real nice wake-up call today." He was nodding his head. "You all learned a lesson that boys learn the first week of camp every single year—that only the strong survive here."

Will, behind Coach Powers, made a gag-me motion, quickly sticking his finger in his mouth.

"So as we go forward as a team after today, we'll find out who our survivors are going to be," he said.

Then he told them to run what he called the old picket-fence play, from *Hoosiers,* Danny's true all-time favorite movie. He had had the play memorized long before Coach Powers showed it to them, the way he had the movie memorized.

They took the ball out on the left side, near half-court. Danny started dribbling right, toward the stands. As soon as he did, the Celtics started setting their screens for him, one after another. First Will, then Tarik, then Alex, who set a monster one on Ollie Grey.

Danny came tearing around Alex like a streak, hit the baseline at full speed, seeing he had a clear path to the basket now.

He knew how long Ollie's legs were, how quick he was to the basket or the ball when he wanted to be. But Danny had him now, by ten feet easy, maybe more.

He thought about going to his left hand as he came down the right baseline, showing Coach Powers that he could bank in a left-hand layup, but decided against it. He wasn't taking any chances. He was just going to float up a soft little layup and get the heck out of here, go to supper having scored at least one basket today.

He kept his chin up, eyes on the basket like his dad had always taught him, in a lifetime of telling Danny to play the game with his head up, putting what he knew was the perfect spin on the ball as he released it.

Then Danny kept running underneath the basket, the way you ran through first base in baseball, angling his body as he moved into the left corner so he could watch his shot go through the basket.

What he saw instead was Ollie.

Catching his shot.

Not just blocking it, *catching* it with both hands and letting out this roar at the same time.

Catching it like it was a lob pass Danny had been throwing to him.

Ollie was so high, had so much time to kill up there, he actually faked like he might throw the ball down, even if this was the Celtics' basket. Then he smiled and cradled the ball, landing as the horn sounded.

But the horn wasn't the sound Danny would remember.

He would remember the laughter, from what sounded like everybody in The House.

All of them laughing at him.

IF HE HAD BEEN BACK IN MIDDLETOWN, HE WOULD HAVE GONE OUT-side to the basket at the end of his driveway.

Danny would have stayed out there all night if he had to, come up with a new move so that nobody would ever grab one of his shots like that ever again. He would have taught himself to stop when he got to the basket—"Stop on a dime, get nine cents change," his dad would say sometimes, quoting some old comedian whose name Danny couldn't remember—so that the defender would go flying past him.

Or he would have practiced reverse layups, going underneath the hoop and then going left-handed, spinning the ball off the board, repeating the move a hundred times until he got it right.

He would have figured something out, the way he always had with basketball things.

Figure it out.

Isn't that what his dad had said about camp?

Problem was, there was no basket at Right Way that belonged only to him, even at night. No place where Danny could be alone. It was something you learned pretty quickly at camp: You were hardly ever alone. There were always other guys around.

He'd only been here a week, and already he knew that camp was pretty much the opposite of being alone.

Oh, sure, there were courts and hoops everywhere you looked. But when you did get a hoop to yourself, that never lasted for long. As soon as somebody saw you, it would be like there was some big flashing sign at the top of the backboard: Please come shoot around with me.

He and Will and Ty had joked about being famous when they got here, because of the way everybody wanted to talk to them about their travel team. Now he was famous at Right Way for something else, for being the first kid at camp to get laughed right out of the gym.

Ollie came over to him after it happened and said, "Didn't mean to show you up that way, little dude."

Danny had always prided himself on being a good loser. His dad always told him that if you didn't know how to lose you'd never know how to win. But all he said to Ollie was, "No, nothing like that."

"Being straight with you, little dude."

"Hope you make *SportsCenter*," Danny said, and walked away.

Outside, Will said to forget it, no biggie, it was just one stupid play. Tarik said the same thing. Danny told them he'd see them at the mess hall for dinner, he was just going to chill for a while.

Telling your buds you needed to chill could get you out of almost anything, Danny knew by now.

So he headed off in the direction of Gampel, wanting to be alone. Or maybe just not wanting to be here, not wanting one more person in the whole stupid state of Maine to tell him that it really wasn't so bad, Ollie Grey giving him that kind of diss-down in front of what felt like half the camp.

He passed Gampel, passed the court there, a bunch of eleven- and twelve-year-olds playing a pickup game the way they usually did at this time of day. He didn't see Zach out there but didn't look too closely, either. If he kept moving, nobody would talk to him between now and dinner.

The next bunkhouse after his own was Staples. There was another court behind Staples, one Danny figured would be empty, because the league games, Danny's and everybody else's, had just ended.

But as he came around the corner he heard the bounce of a single ball, then saw that this court was the private property of Lamar Parrish.

Rasheed's friend. The Kobe look-alike in the Kobe jersey who'd made fun of Danny and Zach that time. Danny knew his name now because everybody in camp did, because the consensus among the rest of the campers, no matter what age they were, was that if Rasheed didn't have the most pure talent at Right Way, then Lamar did.

Some other things Danny knew about him, mostly from Tarik: Lamar was supposed to have been on the Baltimore team Middletown had played in the travel finals in North Carolina, but had left the team halfway through the season when his mom had gotten a job at some fancy private school in Alexandria, Virginia, one with a big-time basketball program.

"His mama was just part of the deal," Tarik had said. "The coach there saw Lamar play in some AAU game that fall and wasn't gonna take any chances. So he recruited Lamar *and* his mama."

"Wait a second," Danny had said. "You're saying that this coach recruited a seventh grader?"

"Duh," Tarik said. "These guys see somebody they even *sniff* might be the next LeBron, they show you a first step even quicker than LeBron's."

Danny wanted to know why that same coach hadn't gone for Rasheed, too.

"He did," Tarik said. " 'Sheed's mama wouldn't let him do it."

Lamar Parrish was loud, cocky and, from everything Danny had seen and heard, a bully. Not the kind of bully you'd run into at school sometimes, the kind who went around looking for fights, who acted like fighting was the only thing he was good at. No, Lamar was a basketball bully, one who knew he could get away with acting however he wanted, acting as mean as he wanted or as obnoxious as he wanted toward the other team or his own team, just because he was better than everybody else. Danny had watched his camp team—the Lakers, of course—scrimmage one day, heard how much talking Lamar did even though there was supposed to be a camp rule against trash talk, watched how Lamar's coach— Rick Higgins, from Cincinnati—acted as if he was the only one on the court who couldn't hear the abuse Lamar was heaping on any player who wandered into his space.

That wasn't what blew Danny away that day.

What blew him away was how much Lamar shot.

He didn't just look like Kobe, he thought he was Kobe, hoisting up shots every time he got an open look, even if somebody on his team was a lot more open than he was.

According to Tarik, who was like some kind of one-man Google when it came to answering camp questions, Rasheed was the only friend Lamar had here. Now here he was, alone on this court, totally focused on some kind of shooting drill he seemed to have made up for himself, shooting from one corner, rebounding the ball, sprinting to the other corner, shooting from there, a crazy version of Around the World, where he kept crisscrossing the court as he moved himself along an imaginary three-point arc.

It was when he banged one off the back rim and had to run to half-court to retrieve the ball that he saw Danny standing there.

As soon as he did, he burst out laughing, laughed so violently he started coughing.

"I'd ask you to shoot around with me," he said when he finally got himself under control, had even wiped tears out of his eyes. "But what's the point if you can't get the dang ball to the dang basket?"

So he'd seen.

Who hadn't?

"Wait, I got a better idea, midget," Lamar said. "Why don't you make yourself useful, come shag balls for me?"

"I'm busy right now," Danny said, and started walking again, sorry that he'd stopped.

"Busy with what?" Lamar said, his voice getting louder, like he was playing to a crowd, even though there wasn't one. Or maybe he was hoping to attract one. " 'Cause after what I just saw, you can't be busy with no hoopin'."

Danny didn't know why, but he stopped, turned and saw Lamar shaking his head, heard him say, "What I just saw over at The House wasn't basketball. Was more like that beach volleyball. Know what I'm sayin'? Where the little people throw it up there so the big people can slam?"

He started laughing again.

"I've got a question for you," Danny said. "Does anybody except you think you're this funny, Lamar?"

Lamar's smile disappeared. "You smart-mouthin' me, midget?"

Walking toward Danny now.

"Just asking a question."

Inside his head, Danny was asking himself a better question.

Where were counselors when you really needed them?

Lamar was up on Danny now. "You know who's funny?" he

said. "You are. You think everybody in this whole dang camp isn't wondering how many strings your daddy had to pull to get you in here?"

"If I stink so much," Danny said, "how'd we win travel?"

Danny wanted to step back. The number 8 from his Kobe jersey, the old-school one that Danny knew was supposed to be like the one the old Minneapolis Lakers used to wear, was right in his face. But some dumb part of him wouldn't allow him to take even one step back.

This is how fast it could happen. Danny'd seen it his whole life, a basketball court like this turning into the dumbest place on earth.

" 'Cause I didn't play, midget. That's why you won," Lamar said. "The boy with all the basketball smarts the television guys talked about ought to be able to figure that out for himself." Danny noticed Lamar was palming the ball in his right hand. "So don't be comin' 'round and talkin' no smack about travel with me, or the two of us are gonna have a real problem."

Like we don't already?

"I'm not talking smack," Danny said. "But I have as much a right to be at this camp as you do."

"Well, then, why don't the two of us play a game of one-on-one and see just how much you belong, midget man?"

Then, as if he was throwing some kind of undercut punch, he put the ball hard into Danny's chest, knocking all the air out of him, doubling him over.

Danny couldn't say anything back because he couldn't breathe.

"Didn't quite catch your answer," Lamar said.

Danny, having finally managed to straighten up, said in a whispery voice, "I told you, I'm busy."

"Yeah," Lamar Parrish said. "Busy bein' the camp mascot."

This time he bounced the ball off the top of Danny's head, as hard as he'd punched him with it in the chest. Catching the ball in his huge right hand, he walked away laughing.

Last laugh of the afternoon.

The only quiet place Danny could think of was the lake, so he ran down there, ran all the way to the end of the dock and sat down, feeling like he was still trying to catch his breath. Sat there for a long time until Zach showed up.

This was another time when he felt as if Zach was tracking him by radar.

"Want some company?" Zach said.

"If I wanted company," Danny said, "I would have gone back to the bunk."

It was as if he'd whipped a ball at Zach's head.

"I just thought you might want to hang," Zach said. "Maybe play one-on-one later, like we did that first night—"

Danny cut him off. "Maybe after dinner."

"Okay."

Still not leaving.

Danny looked up at him and said, "Run along now, okay, Zach?"

For a moment, Zach looked as hurt as Tess did that last day at McFeeley, another time this summer when Danny Walker had known he was acting like a total jerk and couldn't stop himself.

Then Zach was the one who sprinted on this dock, sprinted away from Danny. With his trusty basketball, Danny noticed now, under his arm.

From the dock you could walk along the rocky little beach to get to where the coaches lived at Right Way. Or you could take a shortcut through the woods on a dirt road just wide enough for the golf carts that people over there got to use when they wanted to go back and forth.

Danny took the path. On his way over, Tom Rossi passed him in a golf cart, and Danny asked which cabin belonged to Coach Powers. Rossi told him it was number 7.

He was hoping that Ed Powers hadn't gone into town for dinner or gone to the movies or was just somewhere else. His mom had told Danny his whole life how brave he was, as though it were some kind of automatic that you were brave if you were small. But he wasn't sure he could screw up his courage twice to do what he had to do tonight.

He knocked on the door. When it opened, Coach Powers acted surprised to see him.

Or maybe he was surprised to see anybody coming to visit him.

"Well, well, well," he said. "This is rather unexpected, Mr. Walker."

He was wearing the same Right Way shirt he'd worn at the scrimmage, buttoned to the top as usual. The only difference now that he was home was that he'd changed into shorts, which showed off the closest thing to chicken legs Danny had ever seen.

In his hand was a pad of long yellow paper. When he saw Danny looking at it he said, "Used to take notes every night on what I wanted to do at practice the next day. Old habits die hard, 'specially for an old man."

He motioned to a couple of wicker chairs on his front porch, saying, "It's such a nice night. Why don't we sit out here? Would you care for some iced tea? I was about to fix myself a glass before I heard the knock at the door."

"Sure, thanks," Danny said.

The coach went inside and came back with two tall glasses. He handed one to Danny and took a sip of his own. "It's the splash of lemonade that makes it just right." He handed Danny his glass and nearly smiled. "Iced tea, my way."

He angled the chairs so they could face each other, and when they'd both sat down, said, "What can I do you for, son?"

Danny thought, *I came here on my own, and I still feel like I got called to the principal's office.*

But he knew he better get to it right now before he really did wimp out.

He took a deep breath and said, "Is there any way you can put me on another team before the games start?"

Coach Powers drank some more of his iced tea and carefully put the glass down on the deck next to his chair, as if he wanted to make sure it wouldn't make a sound. Then he leaned back and folded his arms across his chest.

"And why would I want to do something like that?"

Danny had his answer ready. He'd been practicing it inside his head since he'd walked out of The House after the scrimmage, practicing it on the dock, practicing it as he walked through the woods to get here.

"We're just not a good fit, you and me, Coach," he said. "It's all my fault, for sure, nothing on you, everybody knows what a great coach you are, what a great system you have. I just can't get it down, is all, probably because I'm not your kind of ballplayer."

Coach Powers raised one of his eyebrows amazingly high.

"Well, there's quite a mouthful. Is that coming from you or your dad?"

"Me," Danny said. "Me, definitely. Absolutely. I haven't even talked to my dad about this."

"Because it sure sounds like something he said to me once, back in the day, not being my kind of ballplayer, like he was some kind

100

of square peg trying to go into a round hole." He shook his head slowly. "Only he was wrong, and so are you. There's no such thing as *my* kind of player. In my thinking, you're a basketball player, or you're not."

"I'm sure you're right about that," Danny said. "I still think we'd both be better off if I was playing for somebody else, and I was hoping you'd agree."

He felt as if he said the last part in about one second flat.

Coach Powers sipped more lemonade. "So you get off to a bad start, and now you want to quit, is that it?"

"I guess you could say I want to quit your team," Danny said. "But I was thinking of it more like a trade or something. You know, one of those trades that they say afterward helped both teams."

Coach Powers leaned forward, hands on his knobby knees, and said, "It's not happening."

"But—"

"Hush now and do something you should do a little more of if you want to improve or learn anything while you're here—which means *listen*."

Danny, both hands on his glass now, realized how hard he was squeezing it and put it down on the deck.

"The team isn't your problem," Coach Powers said. "And I think you're an intelligent enough young man to know that." Now he was talking in that soft voice of his that never meant good news. "Do you want me to be honest with you, or do you want me to be one of those modern coaches who'd rather hold your hand than teach you proper basketball?"

"Be honest," Danny said.

Wondering as soon as he said that just how much honesty he actually wanted from this guy.

"The real problem here," the coach said, "is that since you've been here, Danny, you've gotten a look into the future." He paused. "*Your* future."

It was the first time Coach Powers had used his first name.

"And what you've seen, with your own eyes," he said, "is that this sport is going to break your heart eventually."

Cabin 7 was on a hill overlooking the lake. In the distance, over the coach's shoulder, Danny could see a couple of rowboats. From the beach, he heard somebody laugh. A small plane flew overhead. When the plane disappeared, Danny heard the first crickets of the early evening.

Danny wasn't moving, wasn't saying anything, just waiting to see where the coach was going with this.

Coach Powers said, "I was never one of those coaches telling his players only what they wanted to hear, like coaching was some kind of popularity contest."

All I wanted to do was get off your stupid team, Danny thought. *Now I'm going to have to hear your life story.*

Or mine.

"My dad says that sports always tells you the truth," Danny said. "Whether you always want to hear it or not."

"Oh, is that what your dad says?"

"Yes."

"Well, we're not here to talk about your dad. We're here to talk about you," Ed Powers said. "I don't want you to quit my team any more than I want you to quit this camp. And I'm not telling you that you can't be a fine player in high school. But—"

He stopped now. Came to a dead stop. Coach Powers did it on the court sometimes, as if he'd lost his place or had forgotten what he wanted to say next. The kids would just stand there and wait until he remembered what he wanted to say.

Finally he said, "What I guess I'm trying to say, in a nice way, is that you're probably never going to grow enough to get to where you want to be in basketball."

"What about travel?" Danny said.

"That's the seventh-grade world, son. I'm talking about the real world."

Danny put his head down, almost talking to himself as he said, "I'm a good player."

"I'm not saying you're not," he said. "And if sports were fair, and you were even close to being the size of the other boys, I'm sure you could shine. But sports aren't fair. And the other boys aren't your size. They're not just bigger, they're a lot bigger. And you see what's happening because of that, before we even start playing real games. You saw what happened out there today."

Coach Powers said, "I'm only telling you this for your own good."

Danny wanted to say something back to him. Tell him how wrong he was, that the problem was what he came here to talk about, that he was just on the wrong team. But he didn't. And knew why.

Here was a famous basketball coach, one he didn't even like, putting Danny's worst fears into words.

Saying them out loud.

"Danny," Coach Powers said, "you can learn things here. I can teach you things if you'll let me. I just can't teach you to be as big as you need to be."

The coach stood up then, his way of saying, Danny knew, that the visit and the conversation were coming to an end.

Almost over, but not quite.

Coach Powers said, "Let me leave you with one more thought I had which might sound crazy to you at first, but could be something for you to think on."

"What?"

"Soccer."

The word seemed to float there like one of the first fireflies of the night.

Coach Powers said, "I was only kidding that first day when I told you boys I was going to run you like soccer players. But the more I've been thinking about it, watching the way you can run, well, soccer's full of fast little guys like you."

Danny stood now. He'd thought that Ollie Grey catching his shot that way, then the other guys laughing at him, was going to be the worst thing he heard today.

"You're telling me to . . . to find another sport?" he said.

Coach Powers put a hand on Danny's shoulder.

"I'm telling you to at least think about it," he said.

DANNY WALKED BACK ALONG THE BEACH, STOPPING EVERY TEN yards or so to skip another flat rock across the water. Pretending he was trying to skip a long bounce pass to somebody cutting for the basket.

Find another sport, Coach Powers had said.

Not saying it in a mean way, the way he could get so mean on the court sometimes when you messed up. *That would almost have been better,* Danny told himself.

No, this was much worse, definitely.

He meant this.

His idea of finally being nice was telling Danny in a nice way that he couldn't play.

Danny reached down, found a smooth, flat rock, a perfect skipping rock, the kind you could bounce across the smooth surface of the water five or six times. But he threw it too hard, way too hard, so it dove into Coffee Lake and disappeared like a gull diving into the ocean back in Middletown.

Back home.

This sport will break your heart eventually, Coach Powers had said.

Danny was back at the dock by now. It was starting to get dark, and he noticed the lights from what he was pretty sure was the girls' camp across the lake, the summer homes on both sides of it.

What if Coach Powers was right?

What if he was somebody telling him the truth, somebody not afraid to hurt little Danny Walker's feelings?

What if he was an adult who didn't think it was his job to make Danny go through life feeling special?

Okay, here was another what-if:

What if Ollie Grey wasn't even one of the best big guys in camp? What if there were guys a lot better than him? What was going to happen when Danny went up against them? Reach for the sky, his mom had always told him. Well, how had reaching for the sky worked out for him today, in front of what felt like the whole stupid camp?

When Danny had walked out of the gym, he'd briefly imagined himself as somebody who'd just been gotten good on *Punk'd*, imagined somebody running up and telling him it had been some kind of prank they'd pulled on him, that it was all just a big joke.

Only there were no television cameras, because the joke was on him.

He'd never quit anything in his life. He'd thought about it a couple of times. He'd never done it. He hadn't even quit piano that year his mom had made him take it.

But he was sure of something now.

He needed a ticket out of here.

He didn't have the whole plan worked out yet. Just the start of one. And the start of it was acting like he never wanted to leave Right Way, like he was a kid trying to make a team.

That's how hard he tried at every single clinic.

When a ball would bounce away from one of the coaches, Danny would sprint after it. When they'd ask for a volunteer to get back on defense for a three-on-two drill, his arm shot straight up in the air.

When they needed somebody to feed a shooter, he volunteered to do that, too.

At one point Tarik got with him on a water break.

"Yo," Tarik said. "What kind of energy drink you got going for you today, that gnarly Red Bull?"

This was halfway through the defensive clinic.

"It's definitely more than Cocoa Puffs," Will said. "Nobody gets that much of a chocolate buzz."

Danny said to both of them, "You know what the great coaches say, right? You can't coach effort."

Tarik staggered back then, looking to the sky, saying, "Kill me now, Lord. He's done turned into Coach Ed."

In the afternoon, at practice with the Celtics, Danny was the same way he'd been at the clinics. Back home his dad would call him Charlie Hustle sometimes, explaining that that had been Pete Rose's nickname when he was a great hitter, before he gambled himself out of baseball, back when he was the kind of ballplayer all little guys wanted to be. Danny was Charlie Hustle today at Coach Powers's practice, diving for loose balls, playing defense as if his life depended on it, calling out switches louder than anybody on the team, making sure everybody on the second team ran every play exactly the way Coach wanted them to, being the first to give a high-five or a bump-fist when Tarik or Will or Alex would make a shot.

Let Coach Powers figure out if this was the old Danny Walker or the new one.

• • •

It happened about halfway through the scrimmage, with Nick Pinto and a buddy of his from Georgetown reffing, first team against the second team.

Danny had been guarding Cole Duncan to start. Will was on Rasheed, even though that was the world's worst possible matchup for Will; he didn't have the foot speed to keep up with somebody as quick with the ball as Rasheed Hill was. It was why the only time Danny had let Will get near Rasheed in the travel finals was on a double-team.

Now Rasheed was torching Will, both ends of the court, acting almost bored as he did. It was almost as if Coach Powers wanted to make Rasheed look even better than he usually did, and Will to look even worse.

It made Danny determined to get Will some open looks. So when Coach Powers motioned for Danny to call something himself coming out of a time-out, Danny told his guys they were going to run "Louisville," a play that actually gave Danny some freedom with the ball. He was supposed to try to beat his man off the dribble, get to the middle, draw the defense to him, then turn and kick the ball out to Will beyond the three-point line.

It all worked to perfection. Except that Will Stoddard, who loved to shoot, who only played to shoot, whose only real basketball skill was shooting, decided to pass up the open shot and get closer, as if that would somehow make the shot more of a sure thing.

Bad idea.

Rasheed, who had switched over on Danny, switched back now and took the ball away like he was taking Will's lunch.

Took it and started the other way, with only Danny close enough to chase the play.

Ben Coltrane came flying out from under the basket on those long legs of his, filling the left lane, so Rasheed stayed on the right.

Two on one.

Danny was at their free throw line. Rasheed was about twenty-five feet from the basket now. Danny decided to force the action, maybe force a mistake.

Cover Rasheed or cover Ben.

He took a quick step toward Ben, and that made Rasheed slow up just slightly. As soon as Danny saw that, he moved back to his left, set himself to take the charge.

Taking a charge from Rasheed Hill, now there was something new and different.

Only this time it was different.

This time he wasn't just trying to draw a foul.

This time it wasn't one of those things that happened in the heat of the moment—you saw the guy coming, you reacted because that wasn't only the best way to stop him, it was the best way to get the ball back.

This time it was something Danny had been planning all day, just waiting for the right moment. One of the television guys had called him a magician when he and the Warriors finally made it to North Carolina for the semifinals that time. Called him the smallest basketball magician in America. Said it was the same with Danny Walker as it had been with his father, that sometimes he was so quick it was as if he made himself disappear along with the ball.

Yeah, that's me, Danny thought, right before he got it again from Rasheed. Master of illusion.

Trying to make himself really disappear this time.

From this camp.

There was no knee to the chest this time, just because there wasn't enough time for Rasheed to elevate that quickly, or enough room between them. What Rasheed really should have done was pass the ball to Ben as he avoided Danny. Ben was so open he could have headed the ball through the basket.

Danny braced himself and Rasheed hit him ten times harder than he had the other day. Both of them went down this time, Danny landing on the court and Rasheed landing on him.

"Come on, man," Rasheed said, rolling over and off Danny and then getting to his feet. "Is that flop all you got?"

Then Rasheed saw what everybody else on the court saw, Danny rolling around on the ground, holding his right knee.

Holding what he'd decided was his only ticket out of here.

"Stop wiggling around. You'll only make it worse," Rasheed said.

Coach Powers told him the same thing and went to get a towel for Danny to rest his head on. Then Tarik was there, kneeling next to him, saying, "Listen to the man," then getting close to his ear and whispering, "for once."

Danny lay back down. He saw Will standing next to Tarik, just staring at Danny, not saying anything. For once.

To both of them Danny said, "My knee's killing me."

"Maybe it's just one of those stingers," Tarik said. "Yeah, I'll bet that's exactly what it is."

"No," Danny said, wincing as he tried to bend his leg. "I did something bad to it."

Coach Powers was back, with the towel and a cold bottle of water from the ice bucket. "The doctor's on his way. Don't even try to bend that leg till he gets here."

Then he shooed the rest of the players away. "You boys go take a water break now," he said, like he'd forgotten to be tough for a couple of minutes. "It might be the last one I give you for the rest of the day."

Danny closed his eyes, still feeling sick. When he opened them, Rasheed Hill was hunched down next to him.

"Wasn't a dirty play," he said.

Danny said, "Wasn't even a charge. My feet were still moving when you ran into me."

Rasheed said, "Just so's we're straight," as if he wasn't leaving the area until they settled this. "The other day, when I knocked you down? In my mind? We were even after that, for the flop in the finals."

Danny put his hand out. Rasheed grabbed it and pulled him up into a sitting position. "I hear you," Danny said.

"This today was different," Rasheed said. "I thought you were going over to cover Train." It was their nickname for Ben Coltrane.

"We're good," Danny said. "It wasn't your fault, it was mine."

Rasheed walked away.

Longest conversation we've ever had, Danny thought.

Dr. Fred Bradley, who looked young enough to be a counselor, was one of the Celtics' team doctors. He gently probed around Danny's right knee, remarking on how it was swelled up already, asking if this hurt or that hurt. Danny cried out in pain when he touched the swollen place on the outside of the knee.

"Let's get you back to the infirmary so we can take a picture of this," Dr. Bradley said.

He helped Danny up, told him to see how much pressure he could put on the injured leg. Danny said it hurt a lot, but they didn't need a stretcher or anything.

Danny said to Will and Tarik, "I'll check you guys later."

Tarik said, "Word."

Will, standing next to Nick Pinto, didn't say anything.

With Dr. Bradley at his side, Danny limped away from the court. As he did, he heard the rest of the Celtics begin to applaud.

It only made Danny feel sicker.

Dr. Bradley said that just because the X-ray was clear didn't necessarily mean Danny was in the clear.

"I think it's probably just a bad sprain," he said. "But a sprain isn't going to show up on these pretty pictures."

Danny knew that from his dad. He knew a lot about knees from his dad. Richie Walker told war stories all the time about how much basketball had banged him around even before he had the car accident that ended his career. He told Danny that he finally gave up on hoping doctors would find reasons why his knees hurt the way they did—all that mattered in the end was that they hurt.

He sat there thinking about his dad, all the pain he'd gone through in his life, not just in his knees, and felt worse than ever.

"There is a little swelling," Dr. Bradley said, looking at Danny's knee, at the last of the swelling that had been there since Rasheed had speed-bumped him. "But it doesn't look too bad to me."

"I don't know about that," Danny said. "I just know it's killing me."

Dr. Bradley touched the side of the knee again, and Danny winced.

"You're sure?"

"I'm not making it up," Danny said.

I *did* hurt the knee, he thought. Just not today. . . .

"Take it easy, son, I didn't say you were," Dr. Bradley said. "If

113

it hurts the way you say it does, maybe what we should do is run you over to the hospital in Portland for an MRI. Just to be on the safe side."

Danny said, "I'm gonna need to talk to my parents about that."

"About the MRI, you mean? Sure, no problem."

"No," Danny said. He was sitting on the examining table. "About my knee. My dad's got his own ideas about stuff."

"I'm not sure I understand."

"No offense, Dr. Bradley, but I think he might want to have his own doctor look at it," Danny said.

Dr. Bradley shut off the computer screen he'd been using to show Danny the two angles of the X-rays he'd taken.

"How old are you?" he said.

"Thirteen. Almost fourteen."

Dr. Bradley smiled. "Even the thirteen-going-on-fourteens want a second opinion," he said.

"My dad thinks he knows more than doctors, is all. Maybe because he's known so many in his life."

"Are you sure you want to go to all the trouble of flying home, though?" Dr. Bradley said.

"I'm not saying I want to do that," Danny said. "I just think they might want me to."

"Why don't we talk about it after you call your dad?" Dr. Bradley asked. Danny said he was good with that.

"Let me know what he says," Dr. Bradley said. "And you stay off that leg as much as possible for the rest of the day. Keep as much ice on it as you can stand."

He helped Danny off the table and walked him over to the main office. When they got there, Dr. Bradley told Jeff LeBow's sister,

Sue, that it was all right for Danny to make a couple of phone calls, even if it wasn't the designated time for that. This was the guy who'd gotten hurt.

Danny was all set to make collect calls from the pay phone, but Sue said he could use hers, showed him how to get a long-distance line.

He got the answering machine at home, didn't leave a message, tried his mom's cell instead. He heard his mom's voice saying she wasn't going to have her cell with her the rest of the afternoon, she was out on a hike with Horizons kids—underprivileged kids from New York City who came out to live with families in Middletown for a couple of weeks every summer and attend a camp she helped run though St. Patrick's School. She said wouldn't be back until at least five o'clock.

Danny told Sue he'd come back later and that if he couldn't get his mom then, maybe he'd shoot her an e-mail if that was all right. Then he walked back to Gampel, ice pack in his hand, taking it slow, taking the long way down there, along the woods, so he didn't have to pass any of the courts.

So nobody would ask him how he was doing.

The only person in Gampel at four-thirty was Nick Pinto, lying on his bed, music playing from his speakers.

"Hey," Danny said, "shouldn't you be working?"

"Coach Ed's guys are at The House, scrimmaging the Bulls," Nick said. "They already had a couple of refs when we got over there, so I decided to come back here and chill."

He sat up, making room on the bed for Danny, who'd brought his ice pack back with him. Nick was wearing a Stonehill T-shirt with the sleeves cut off, a pair of Knicks shorts that went to his knees, high-top Nikes with no socks, at least no socks that Danny could see.

"How's it feeling?" Nick said, pointing to Danny's knee.

"Not great," Danny said. "Dr. Bradley said it's a bad sprain. He wants to take an MRI, but says he has to wait until the swelling goes down."

"Looks like it already has, actually."

He doesn't seem real concerned about me, Danny thought. "Well, it hasn't gone down enough," he said. "And it's still real sore. And stiff, too."

Danny moved the ice a little, covering the area where the swelling had been in the first place. "I guess it was my rotten luck, hitting it in almost the exact same spot. That ever happen to you?"

"No."

"I just thought—"

"I'm a fast healer," Nick said. "You know how it is with us little guys, worrying somebody might take our spot. I get knocked down, I bounce right back up."

"I'm usually the same way," Danny said. "Until today."

"Until today," Nick said. He gave Danny a look that Danny couldn't really read, like he knew something Danny didn't know. "Anything else you want to tell me about today?"

"About what?"

"Like I said. Anything at all. About camp. About this so-called injury."

"What's that mean, so-called?" Danny said. "Are you saying I'm not really hurt?"

"I'm saying I saw the play."

"So that's it," Danny said. "You think I'm faking."

"I didn't say that," Nick said. "You did."

"You don't know me," Danny said, shaking his head. "You think you do, because you're small, too. But you don't know me. And you don't know what my knee feels like. Rasheed landed right on me."

"And then you rolled like a champ," Nick said. "It's what little guys like us do. The big guys have to know how to sky. We have to know how to fall."

Who was this guy? Ed Powers Junior?

"I'm just wondering how you're gonna play it from here," Nick said. "You know, bail and somehow save face."

"I don't know what you're talking about."

"Seriously," Nick said. "Because nobody's gonna believe what happened today is enough for you to quit the whole rest of camp."

"I'm not looking to quit," Danny said. "I got hurt, is all."

"Right. I forgot."

"Anyway, what's the big deal if I go home for a couple of days and have my own doctor look at it?"

"Because if you do, you're never coming back," Nick said.

He leaned forward suddenly, his face close to Danny's, and said, "You cannot do this. Do you hear me? You cannot quit."

"I'm not quitting. How many times do I have to tell you?"

"Keep telling yourself that," Nick said, as if the conversation bored him all of a sudden. "Let me know what you decide. You want to get out of here that bad, I'll drive your sorry butt to the airport."

He hopped off his bed, starting to walk toward the front door.

Then he stopped and turned around.

"One more thing," Nick said. "You want to tell Zach what his hero's got planned, or should I?"

He left Danny sitting there.

The afternoon session, Danny knew, had to be ending any minute. He figured he had time to go back up the hill, give his mom another shout, maybe she was back on the cell a few minutes earlier than she said she'd be.

He brought some change with him this time, so he could have the privacy of the phone booth if his mom was back on the cell. She wasn't. Same greeting as before, his mom sounding as happy talking about being on a hike as she would have been if his dad had bought her a new car. This time he left a message, said he'd banged up his knee today, nothing serious, don't worry, but maybe she could give a call to the office when she got a chance, somebody would come find him.

Then he went into the office, asked Sue if it would be all right to get on one of the computers and back up the message with an e-mail. Sometimes his mom checked her e-mails when she got home before she even checked her phone messages.

Danny liked to joke with his mom, ask her if she had a secret buddy list for IM-ing that he didn't know about.

She'd smile at him, give him one of her Mom looks and say, "That's for me to know and for you to find out, buddy."

Danny went to the computer room—six Dells in there—and sat down at the first one inside the door.

He hadn't been online since he left Middletown and had seventy-eight new messages. He was about to go through them, see if there was anything worth reading, when he saw that somebody was trying to Instant Message him.

He clicked on the message flag, then the box came on the screen asking him if he wanted to accept an IM from ConTessa44.

Tess.

Danny felt himself smiling for the first time all day. Or maybe all week.

He answered the question about whether or not he wanted to accept her message out loud in the empty room.

"Heck, yeah."

ConTessa44: Hey stranger.

He wasn't usually the best typist in the world, or very fast.
But he was now.

Crossover2: Is that really you?

He waited, feeling like a dope being this excited, realizing he
was holding his breath.

ConTessa44: No my evil twin.
Crossover2: Ha ha

He started to type something else. As he did, the message came
up in red that his buddy was typing something, too. So it was like
the old days now, him and Tess Hewitt trying to beat each other to
the next funny comment.
Only she wasn't trying to be funny.
Just Tess.

ConTessa44: So how are you stranger? How's camp?
Crossover2: Great.

He waited, getting the "Your buddy is typing" message.

ConTessa44: Great as in offthecharts travel team great?
     That great?
Crossover2: Well getting there I guess.

This wait seemed to be longer.

ConTessa44: You guess? You never guess in bball fella. You always have the right answer. Before they even ask the question sometimes.
Crossover2: I used to.
ConTessa44: USED TO????? Past tense.
Crossover2: Maybe just tense.
ConTessa44: Hey you. Something wrong?

Truth or dare? Tell her the truth now, or not.
Danny decided on the truth.
He needed to tell somebody the truth today.

Crossover2: Hate it here. Got hurt today.

He didn't tell her he was leaving.
This time Danny waited for what seemed like an hour while his buddy was typing.

ConTessa44: Come on Walker. Only a week. How bad can it be? It'll get better. Then you'll win. Like always.
Crossover2: Not this time. No no no.
ConTessa44: Yes yes YES!

He wasn't in the mood for a pep talk, not even from her.
So he changed the subject.

Crossover2: How's Middletown?
ConTessa44: Have no idea.

He closed his eyes, searching what was left of his brain. Was there a trip she was taking somewhere? Danny tried to remember if she'd said anything about that the last time they talked.

Then he decided he really didn't care where she was.

All he cared about was that they were talking again, even like this.

CROSSOVER2: Okay I give. Where R U?

He didn't have to wait long.

CONTESSA44: Across the lake.

Will and Ty were playing Ping-Pong at the outdoor table be-hind Boston Garden when Danny found them.

Will gave Danny a sideways look and said, "Oh, you're still here?"

Danny said, "I'm here."

"Because we were wondering."

"You guys don't have to wonder about me."

"If you say so."

"I say so."

"Hello?" Ty said. "Are we still playing to twenty-one, or are we stopping now?"

Will was getting ready to serve when Danny said, "I've got some news I thought you might be interested in."

Will held the pose as if Danny had paused him. "About your knee?"

"No," Danny said, "nothing about my knee. I'm tired of talking about my knee today."

"The reason I ask," Will said, going right on, "is that we ran into Nick Pinto and he said you might be fixing to leave and I just thought that might be something you'd want to mention to your two best friends before you did. Is all."

"Because if you want to quit—" Ty said.

"I'm not quitting!" Danny said.

"Chill," Ty said, holding up his racket like a stop sign. "I was talking to Will about our game."

Will started his service motion again. Paused again. Danny heard Ty groan. "What's your news, then?"

"Tess is across the lake."

That got his attention.

"No way."

"Way," Danny said. He grinned and pointed toward the lake. "Thataway, actually."

"How?" Will said.

"Her uncle," Danny said. "When we were sitting at McFeeley one day, she laughed when I told her our camp was in Cedarville. It turned out she couldn't believe we were going to be right near where her uncle has a place."

Will said to Ty, "No wonder he seems to have recovered from his near-death experience."

"Tess to the rescue," Ty said.

"So when do we get to see her?" Will said.

"Tonight."

"How?"

Danny said to his buds, "We'll know that as soon as we come up with a plan."

Most of the guys bunking at Boston Garden were over at The House by now, watching the nightly counselors' game.

Danny and Will and Ty were sitting on some big rocks at the edge of the woods, overlooking the water.

Danny told them that according to Tess, her uncle's place was a couple of miles away if you went the long way, which meant by car. But she said it was actually a lot closer if you went across Coffee Lake, maybe halfway between Right Way and the girls' camp across the water.

"Too far to swim," Will said.

"Ya think?" Ty said.

"So we'll take a canoe," Will said, "definitely." Nodding his head quickly—Will was completely happy talking to himself—"Brilliant," he said.

"Oh, right," Danny said. "They're just going to let us take a canoe out at this time of night."

Will looked at him like he was the biggest loser on earth.

"We're not going out on the lake now," he said. "We're going to wait until it gets dark, and then we're going to steal one of these long, skinny boats, and *then* we're going to see our friend Tess Hewitt."

"We're stealing a boat," Danny said.

"Well, borrowing," Will said. "I don't intend to keep it. What am I going to do with a canoe?"

"We get it," Danny said.

Ty said, "Why don't we just wait until the counselors' game is over and then ask Nick or somebody to drive us?"

"First of all, nobody ever knows when the counselors' game is going to end," Will said. "Sometimes they play until ten o'clock."

Will Stoddard smiled then, looking at Danny, then Ty, then back at Danny, his eyes, as always, full of fun and trouble at the same time.

"Second, and most importantly," Will said, "if Nick or somebody just plain old drove us over to her in the van, what kind of adventure would that be?"

Danny and Ty told him they hated to admit it, but he made a good point.

• • •

Danny said there was still time before it got all the way dark, so he went back to call Tess, tell her the plan they'd come up with, figure out exactly which place was her uncle's and how they were going to find it in the dark.

When he got to the main office, Sue LeBow said, "Where have you been? I had people looking all over the camp for you. Your mom called and wants you to call her right away."

Danny said he'd been hanging with his friends. Sue said he was lucky he showed up when he did; she was about to close up the office for the night. He could go ahead and use her phone while she went over to the mess hall to get a cup of coffee.

Danny didn't have a whole lot of time to waste, he knew, but he also knew he better make the call.

She picked up on the first ring.

"Hey, Mom."

"How bad is it?"

Not his cool, funny mom tonight. This was the mom who got right to it on the big stuff, like she was calling one of her English classes to order.

If she had been home when Danny called before, he had planned to start scamming a trip home to see the family doctor. But now he didn't want to even think about that, he just wanted to go see Tess. So he told Ali Walker about the play, about Dr. Bradley, about how he'd taken it easy the rest of the day, tried to make it sound as if he'd been icing for the last four hours straight.

"I'll live, basically," he said. "The doctor says he might want to go for an MRI when the swelling goes down."

"Good Lord," Ali Walker said, "what is it about the men in this family and their knees?"

"Mom," he said, "one bruised knee doesn't mean I've turned into Dad."

There was a pause, and then his mom said, "Do you want me to call your dad? He's still in Oakland until tomorrow night."

Quickly, maybe too quickly with his mom on the other end of the line, the way she could hear things in his voice that no other living human could hear, Danny said, "Why don't you wait until he gets home? Let me see how it feels tomorrow, and I'll call you guys."

His mom said, "No basketball until it feels better. Do you hear me, Daniel Walker?"

"Loud and clear."

"You promise your old mom?"

"Yes," he said—never "yeah," not with an English teacher for a mother. "And you're not old."

"And you're sweet, even with a bum knee."

"Hey, Mom?" Danny said. "I love you a lot, but the guys are waiting for me to go do something."

"Well," she said. "The guys. Waiting to do *something*. I wouldn't want to stand in the way of all *that*."

"Did I mention that you're not old?" Danny said.

"I love you, good-bye," she said.

After he'd hung up, he realized he hadn't even told her about Tess. Maybe tomorrow. He called Tess then, got the exact directions, even drew himself a crude map from what she was telling him about her part of Coffee Lake.

On his way back to where Will and Ty were waiting, he saw Zach playing a three-on-three game on the lighted court at Gampel. Danny knew he shouldn't stop, but he did, still feeling bad about the way he'd treated Zach on the dock.

When one of the other kids made a driving shot to win the game, Danny motioned Zach over.

"What'd I do now?" Zach said.

"Nothing," Danny said. "I just wanted to talk to you about something."

"What?"

The night before, when Danny had gotten back to Gampel, Zach had pretended to be asleep, even though Danny knew better.

"I want to talk about an adventure," Danny said, then pulled him out of earshot of the other guys and told him what they planned on doing.

"You're asking me to come along?" Zach said.

"Unless you don't want to."

"Are you insane?" Zach said. "Just give me one sec to put my ball away." By now Danny knew that you could have gone into Zach's living space at Gampel and taken all his clothes and games and whatever money he had hidden and the only thing he'd be upset about would be his basketball.

On their way down to the water, Zach said, "Nick was talking about your knee before—"

Danny thought, *Who hasn't Nick spilled the beans to?* But he just said, "I'll tell you all about it tomorrow. Right now, it's time to hit the high seas."

Zach Fox looked at him. "Now *that*," he said, "really is wet."

The counselor in charge of sending you out in the canoes was long gone by the time it was all the way dark. Nobody had a watch, but they guessed it was past nine o'clock when they snuck back down to the dock.

There were six canoes tied up there, paddles inside. On the other side of the dock were two Jet Skis.

"We could get there a lot faster on these very cool-looking Jet Skis," Will said. "Plus, it would be like a chase scene in James Bond."

"Faster and much, much louder," Danny said.

"I'm not looking to change the plan," Will said. "I was just making what I thought was an interesting observation."

"There's something new and different," Ty said.

Zach wasn't saying anything. He was just smiling at all of them at once in the light of a pretty amazing full moon, looking as happy as Danny had seen him without a basketball in his hands.

They sent Zach up the hill one last time, to make sure nobody was coming. He came racing back like he was trying to set the camp record and said the coast was clear.

"Well, then," Danny said, "I guess it's time to ship out."

They untied the canoe closest to the dock as Will asked for about the tenth time if Danny was sure where they were going.

"Sort of."

"Well, let's sort of start heading over there," Will said, "so we at least have a chance to get back before somebody realizes none of us are in our beds."

"Have any of you guys ever ridden in one of these?" Zach said.

Danny shook his head and looked at Will and Ty.

"Don't look at me," Will said. "My mom swears she used to take me kayaking when I was little, but I told her I was gonna have to see pictures."

From his seat at the front of the boat, Ty said, "I can do it."

"Should have known," Will said to Zach. "He could fly a plane if he had to."

Ty explained then that these were what were known as "guide canoes," because they were a favorite of Maine tour guides, and were about sixteen feet long. Will wanted to know how Ty knew that, and Ty said, "When you're not one of those people who *already* know everything, you ask questions sometimes."

"Is that a shot?" Will said. "Because that sounded like a shot to me."

There were four life jackets in the bottom of the boat, two of which were small enough to fit Danny and Zach. Ty said that the most people he'd seen in one of these babies since he'd been at camp were three, but there was nothing to worry about, guide canoes like this could handle up to six hundred pounds.

Will made a motion like he was writing a score on a board and said to Ty, "Okay, I get it. You've got me beat bad on canoes."

"And just about everything else," Danny added.

"Another shot," Will said.

Ty stayed in front, Danny said he'd handle the paddling in back, maybe switch with Will if he got tired.

"I'm going to be pretty busy navigating," Will said.

They pushed away into Coffee Lake, the only real sound in the night the sound of their paddles hitting the water. Danny had already told Will to keep his voice down as much as possible, that out here on the water it would carry better than if he were using Jeff's bullhorn.

They angled to their left, past the rope line you weren't supposed to cross if you had permission to take one of the canoes out, went around a bend and the Right Way dock disappeared from sight. They were five minutes into the trip, if that.

Will said, "Are we there yet?"

Danny and Ty were already in perfect sync with their paddling, as if they were on some kind of two-man rowing team in the Olympics. Or maybe just running one of their little two-man games on a basketball court.

"Hey, you guys are good," Zach said. "Danny, you sure you've never done this before?"

"Suck-up," Will said into his hand, like he was stifling a cough.

They glided across the water in the night, moving faster than Danny thought they would, still just hearing the slap of the paddles when Will piped down. Danny switched the paddle from side to side, feeling strong as he did.

Realizing something at the same time:

It was like they were out here in their own little world, apart from camp. He wasn't worried about anything, he wasn't mad at anybody, he wasn't all jammed up about what he'd decided to do before Tess called.

He would never say this out loud, certainly not to Will or Ty, not to Zach in a million years, but out here on Coffee Lake, Danny suddenly felt like he was floating.

Just then, Ty said, "There she is."

Tess had told Danny she'd come out to the end of her uncle's dock and be carrying one of those supersize flashlights that you only used when you lost power.

He was maybe a hundred yards away from her.

Will asked if it was all right for him to give her a shout-out now. The only way somebody from Right Way would be able to hear was if they'd been followed.

"Knock yourself out," Danny told him.

Will waved now and yelled, "Hilary Duff, is that you? Is it really you?"

"Hey!" Tess yelled back. Danny could see her flashlight bouncing up and down now as she did. "Hey, you guys!"

Will said to Danny, "Jump in anytime."

Without either one of them saying anything about picking up the pace, Danny and Ty both started paddling faster.

"Just pull alongside the dock," Tess said, "and I'll toss you a rope."

Maybe thirty yards away now.

Now Danny couldn't help himself.

Or contain himself.

After all the bad parts, he'd come to the good parts, finally.

Tess.

He tapped Will on his shoulder, handed him his paddle, stood up in the back of the boat. Usually he was soooooo cool toward Tess when Will and Ty were around, never acting like he was too happy or excited to see her.

Not tonight.

He shouted "ConTessa44 Hewitt!" at the top of his voice, waving his arm like he was calling for somebody to pass him the ball.

Will was standing now, giving Danny room to take his seat. But Danny didn't want to sit in it, he wanted to stand on it, wanted to be the tallest one in the boat for just this one moment.

Wanted Tess to see him first.

There was just one small problem.

Just enough water from the splash of those paddles had gotten into the bottom of the boat on their way across the lake.

It meant that Danny's Barkley sneakers were just slick enough.

His right sneaker got up on the little benchlike seat, no problem. But his left one slipped like he'd hit a patch of ice. And since there was no rail for him to grab on to, nothing but the night air for him to grab on to, Danny felt himself falling.

Zach saw what was happening, tried to dive across and catch him, but it was too late.

Danny Walker went over the side of the guide canoe and into the cold water of Coffee Lake.

THE FIRST VOICE DANNY HEARD AS HIS HEAD POPPED BACK ABOVE the surface was Will Stoddard's. "No worries, Tess. Your hero has arrived."

Ty reached over and helped Danny back into the boat, saying, "You know, when Will said to jump in anytime, I don't think this is what he had in mind."

Everybody in the canoe laughed then. As foolish as Danny felt in front of Tess, like he was the entertainment at SeaWorld, he had to join in. They all kept laughing until they got the canoe to the side of Tess's dock and she tossed Ty the rope.

"You sure know how to make an entrance, Walker," Tess said as she reached out to give him a hand.

"I think I might've held my tuck a little too long," he said.

Tess waved her arms above her head like a crazy person, doing this spazzy puppet dance. "Is that what they call a tuck now in diving?" she said.

She was wearing the gray Warriors sweatshirt they'd given her as an honorary member of the team after they'd won the travel championship, jeans with holes in both knees and what looked to be new Puma sneakers. Danny could spot new sneakers even in the dark.

And he knew it didn't matter what she was wearing, here or anywhere, she always looked great to him.

He thought, she's the same old Tess.

And I'm a mess.

On the dock, Will told Danny he should look on the bright side, despite the way he'd been playing lately, especially for his new coach.

"See, you *can* hit the water if you fall out of a boat," Will said.

"Not funny," Danny said.

"Well, we both know *that's* a total lie," Will said.

Everybody was talking at once then, Danny introducing Zach to Tess, Will saying they called him Danny Junior, Tess saying she could see why, Tess wanting to know if she should try to find Danny some dry clothes and Danny saying, no, he was fine, which was a total lie.

Tess said her aunt and her two cousins had gone into town for ice cream, but that her uncle was inside watching the Red Sox–Yankees game if anybody wanted to join him. She was sure he'd love the company.

"Television," Will said, making it sound as if he were talking about heaven.

"Not just television," Tess said. "He's got Direct up here."

"Yesssssss!" Will said, pumping his fist. "What kind of snacks we talking about?"

Tess said that her two cousins were boys, one twelve and one fourteen, so there was more junk food in the kitchen than you could imagine. Her aunt had taken them grocery shopping the day before and let them go wild.

Will said, "I am so there with my new best friend, Uncle . . . ?"

"Sam."

Then because he was Will, because he still had Danny's back, he immediately shoved Ty and Zach in the direction of The House and said, "Let's leave these two guys alone for a few minutes. Walker probably wants to show Tess his backflip next."

Over his shoulder, Will said, "Call us if you need us."

"We won't," Danny said. "Call you or need you."

When they were gone, Tess sprinted down the dock on her long legs, disappeared through the backdoor, came right back out with two huge red beach towels.

"You must be freezing to death," she said.

"You see now why Will says I turn into Captain Klutz when you're around."

"Nah," Tess said. "I'm still just seeing the captain of the team."

"Not lately," Danny said.

"You want to talk about it?" she said.

Danny said she had no idea.

They sat on the back porch in old rickety, squeaky, wooden rocking chairs, Danny feeling like some kind of old man with the red towel over his shoulders. From the television room at the front of The House, the only voice he'd hear occasionally was Will's, no shocker. From somewhere in the woods, they could hear an owl making hoot noises, as if saying that all these people had crashed his night.

Danny said that before he told Tess about everything that was going on at camp, he needed to apologize for something. Tess started to say he didn't, but Danny kept right on going, saying he had been the kind of jerk that even real jerks thought was obnoxious the last time he'd seen her.

She smiled.

"Oh, come on now," she said. "You're being much too easy on yourself."

"Very funny," he said, smiling back. "I get Will the comedian all day and now you at night."

"You lucky dog."

"Only if you mean a wet, mangy-type dog."

They sat there rocking and squeaking.

"I mean it," Danny said. "About being sorry."

"I know."

"Scott bugs me, is all. But you probably know that, too."

"I do."

"I can't help it."

Tess said, "He's actually not a bad guy, if you don't mind complete perfection."

Danny wanted to say it had never bothered him with her but kept that particular thought inside his head. The way he kept a lot of thoughts like that, about this girl, inside his head.

"You also have to care a lot more about Roger Federer than I do," Tess said.

"So you don't want to be the queen of Middletown tennis anymore?"

"I guess I'll wait until next summer to win Wimbledon," Tess said, then quickly told him how bored she got after he and Will and Ty left, and how after about two days of her moping around the house, her mom said she needed some kind of outing. Which, Tess knew, meant some kind of road trip. That night she got on her computer, MapQuested how far away her uncle actually was from Right Way, discovered the distance was 1.8 miles and now here she was, surprise!

For once, he wasn't Captain Klutz.

"I'm glad you're here," he said.

"I also know that," Tess said. "Now tell me some stuff I don't know."

Danny talked for a long time. Told her all about it, all the gory details. Finally admitted to her that Nick Pinto had been right when he'd called him out, that Danny had tricked up his knee injury, knowing his knee was already swollen even if it wasn't bothering him anymore, figuring it was the easiest way for him to get the heck out of there without looking like a total wussball.

Tess never said a word the whole time he was talking, never interrupted him once. Never looked anywhere except right at him and right through him.

When he finished, she said, "So do you want to know what I really think?"

"It's why we hijacked that dopey boat," Danny said. "Course I want to know what you think."

"Well, I think . . ." She scratched her head, paused briefly, like she was confused. "I think . . . that if you ever think about doing something this stupid ever again, I will personally break *both* your knees."

She went inside, came back with two bottles of Snapple and handed him one. She'd also brought him two more dry towels, even though he'd said he was okay with what he had.

"It can't be as bad as you say," Tess said.

"Really?" he said. "Well, guess what. The only time I really felt like I wanted to be at this stupid camp was tonight. And tonight what we basically did was get away from camp. And come to see you."

"You just have to show this guy," she said. "This Coach Ed."

"What if he's right about me?"

"He's not."

Just like that. Like she was saying, Case closed, done deal, next question.

"You don't know that," Danny said.

"I know you, Walker. I know you better than anybody. I know you better than he ever will. Or any coach ever will, outside of your dad, when you start playing for him. But you're acting like this Coach Ed is suddenly the world's expert on Danny Walker, that he has all these big insights into you that the rest of us don't. Get real."

Danny said, "How about I just get out?" Knowing how weak that sounded.

Air ball.

"You can't quit," Tess said.

"So I beat my head against the wall for two more weeks, with a coach who acts like he only wants to put me into games as some kind of last resort," Danny said.

He heard a war whoop from Will inside, which meant the Red Sox had done something. Will and Zach were Red Sox fans, Ty was a huge Yankees fan. Danny didn't know where Uncle Sam weighed in.

Tess said, "You know what this really is? It's Ty's dad cutting you all over again. Another grown-up telling you you're not good enough. I thought you always used to tell me that the championship you guys really won in travel was the championship of any kid who got told by an adult they weren't good enough?"

Danny knew he was smiling. He couldn't help himself, even after the two crummiest days on record. She never forgot anything. She remembered Danny's life better than he did sometimes.

"It's my dad's line, actually."

"So now you have to do that again," Tess said. "You show him, you show the whole camp, if you have to. You show this guy Rasheed who keeps knocking you down. You're not quitting, and you're not believing something from this coach you know isn't true and I know isn't true."

Danny wanted a ball in his hands now. Wished he'd let Zach bring his ball with him, so he could hold it, roll it around in his hands, dribble it on the back porch, flick it straight up in the air. A ball in his hands had always made him feel smarter, even smart enough to keep up with Tess. A ball in Danny's hands had always made him feel that he could figure anything out, like it was just a simple basketball problem, finding the smartest way to get the ball from here to there and then through the hoop.

"You didn't hear them laughing at me in the gym," he said quietly.

"For one play," Tess said. "One stupid play. Ty broke his wrist once because of one stupid play that wasn't even your fault." Tess shrugged, smiled. "Get over it, Walker."

There was a rap on the window. They both turned around. There was Will, pressing his nose against the glass, mashing it. Anything, Danny knew, to get a laugh. Anything and everything. "We gotta bounce," Will said. "Or we're going to get even more busted than we already are."

Danny nodded.

"You make the whole thing sound simple," he said to Tess.

"No, sir," she said. "From what you told me about this coach and the other players, it's going to be even harder than when you got cut that time. It's not Middletown now, it's not your dad's team, it's not all your friends cheering you on. But you *can* do this."

"Because you say I can?"

Tess put her hand out for a low five. When he didn't slap skin hard enough, she kept it out there, giving him a look, so he did it again, with more feeling this time.

"Now you're talking," she said, "like my Danny Walker."

Her Danny Walker.

Now she pulled him up out of his rocking chair, like a player helping him up after he'd gotten knocked down on the court, leaned down and gave him a quick hug before he knew what was happening.

"This one's for the championship of you, big guy," Tess said.

IT WAS TEN-THIRTY WHEN THEY STARTED BACK. WILL OFFERED TO help with the paddling this time, saying he didn't want to get ragged on for the whole rest of camp. But Ty said no, they needed to get back before breakfast.

Danny said, "What's the camp version of getting grounded for life?"

"Wait, I know that one," Will said. "You get more time with Coach Ed."

For some reason the trip back seemed to take twice as long to Danny, even though he was working just as hard with his paddle, still watching the way Ty did it, using his shoulders, bringing it back through the water until it was even with his hip, then lifting it straight up and doing the whole thing again.

Maybe, he thought, the whole thing felt like it was taking longer because he was moving away from Tess now instead of toward her.

Right before he had gotten into the canoe, he had asked her how long she was staying in Maine.

"I'm liking it better here already," she said.

"So you're going to hang around for a while?"

"Just to see how this all comes out."

Danny smiled, thinking about that part. Will must have been looking at him from where he was sitting in the middle of the canoe

140

because he said, "Nobody should look as happy as you doing row, row, row your boat."

Danny told him to turn around and navigate. Will said they were doing fine on their own, but he'd keep his eyes peeled for icebergs so they didn't turn into Leo and what's-her-name in *Titanic*.

"Speaking of girls," Will said, "how'd it go with you and your conscience?"

"Tess is my friend, not my conscience," Danny said.

"*Girl*friend," Will said. "And conscience."

"She basically told me to stop acting like a total idiot," Danny said.

From the front of the canoe Ty said, "Sounds like a plan."

"She tells you to stop acting whack and you listen," Will said. "Is that basically it?"

"Basically."

Zach's head whipped back and forth as he tried to follow the conversation, like he was watching tennis. Beyond him, in the distance, Danny saw the lights from Right Way getting closer, started to wonder what the last part of their plan was going to be. It was, like, they'd busted out, now how did they bust back in without getting caught? His mom, the English teacher, always said the more books you read, the more you admired a good ending.

"Bottom line?" Will said to Zach. "He's always liked her better."

There was nobody waiting for them at the dock when they got there. Which meant that maybe nobody had come down there looking for them. Or, if they had, maybe they hadn't counted canoes. Or didn't know how many there were supposed to be in the first place.

Or, Danny thought, they knew one of the boats was gone and were just waiting for them back at their bunks.

He really didn't know what grounded for life meant at Right Way, just knew there was some kind of honor council made up of other campers. Mr. LeBow had told them about it the first day.

"If we do get busted—" Will said.

"*When* we get busted, you mean," Ty said, easing the canoe toward the side of the dock.

"—what are we going to tell them?" Will said.

"I'll handle it," Zach said.

They all looked at him. It was the first thing he'd said since they'd pulled away from Tess's dock.

"You'll handle it?" Danny said.

Zach was the one who smiled now. "If you're really staying," he said, "I got you."

With that, he stood up and, instead of jumping onto the dock, jumped into the water, just deep enough to be over his head. He swam ahead of them to the dock, hoisted himself up on the ladder at the end of it, stood there waiting for them in the moonlight, soaking wet.

"Like I told you," Zach said to Danny. "Wet."

It was when they came into the clearing between the woods and Gampel that they saw Nick Pinto and the counselor from Boston Garden, Bo Stanton, walking toward them with flashlights.

"Well, well, well, if it isn't the Lost Boys," Nick said.

Bo, who was about 6-6, had long black hair and a thin mustache. He was a senior forward at Boston College. "Or maybe just boys who think they're on *Lost,*" he said.

Nick, all business, said, "I assume you guys know the rules about leaving camp, day or night, without a permission slip, right?"

Before anybody else could say anything, Danny said, "It was my idea."

"And what idea was that, exactly?" Nick said. "You decide to leave by water?"

Danny couldn't decide whether Nick was mad about whatever he thought they'd done on the water, wherever they'd gone, or because of the whole deal with his knee the day before. "Listen, if you want to know the truth—"

"Then let me tell it," Zach said. "They didn't take the boat. I did."

They'd asked him on the dock why he'd jumped in the water. All Zach said was, "That's for me to know and for you guys to find out." Now here he was, taking a step forward, still soaking wet, looking like the biggest little stand-up dude at Right Way.

"Whoa, there, Danny Junior," Will said.

"Shut up for once and let somebody else talk," Zach said.

Danny said, "Zach, you don't have to do this."

"Yeah, I do."

Then he told Nick and Bo that some of the older kids had been picking on him earlier, threatening to stuff him in a locker. Nick asked which older kids, and Zach said he didn't want to squeal on them, he just wanted Nick to know how the whole thing started. "Anyway," Zach said, like this was something he'd been rehearsing inside his head, "I managed to get away from them—I may be small, but I'm fast—and hid down by the water. When it got dark, I snuck over to the canoes and took one out so I could be by myself."

"You took one of these out by yourself?" Nick said.

Zach grinned. "I'm a strong little sucker, too."

Tell me about it, Danny thought.

"Danny must have been worried about me," Zach said, "because he came down to the dock and saw me paddling away and he went and got these guys and they came after me."

Danny just waited now to see how Zach's version of a fish story would come out, like this was something he was telling around a campfire.

"How come only you and Walker are wet?" Nick said.

"I dropped my paddle," Zach said. "And when I dove in after it, Danny dove in after me, because he didn't know what kind of swimmer I was."

Zach looked up at Nick and Bo. "You can't punish them for trying to come after me," he said.

Nick said to the rest of them, "And you guys back him up on this?"

Nobody planned it, but they all stepped forward at the same time so they were even with Zach.

"Yeah," Danny said. "We've got his back."

At least that, he thought, *was the whole truth.*

And nothing but.

In the morning Nick said that he and Bo had talked it over after Danny and the guys had finally gone to bed and decided they weren't going to report them to Mr. LeBow.

"There's some holes in the little guy's story. You know that, right?" Nick said before leaving for breakfast.

Danny didn't say anything.

Nick smiled then. "I did the same thing one time, but there was a girl involved."

"She must have been worth it."

When Nick was gone, Danny waited for Zach to come out of the shower—he was one of the guys who actually did shower in the morning—and asked if he'd rather play basketball than eat.

Zach said, "You even have to ask?"

Zach grabbed his trusty ball, and Danny showed him the way

to a court set way off by itself, on the far side of the tennis courts, past the dirt parking lot they only used when parents came to visit the third weekend. Danny had found it the other day because he had heard a lot of noise coming from that direction on his way to the mess hall. The reason for the noise was that a bunch of counselors were using it for a street-style hockey game, tennis balls replacing pucks.

It was far and away the worst outdoor court at the camp, with a couple of holes near mid-court, and a net that was hanging by its last couple of strings.

But it was by itself, hardly any chance of anybody seeing them, unless a coach happened to come riding by in a golf cart.

"I'm skipping Froot Loops to play here?" Zach said. "And this is because . . . why?"

"You are a Froot Loop," Danny said, "coming up with a story like that in front of Pinto."

"It worked, didn't it?" Pride in his voice. A lot of pride. As if he'd earned some kind of merit badge last night. "I knew I had him when I gave him my sad face."

"I know the face," Danny said. "Remember?"

Zach was carrying his ball. Danny was carrying a broom he'd borrowed out of a storage closet at Gampel.

"Now that I see this court, I can see why you brought that," Zach said, pointing to the broom.

Danny took the ball from Zach, handed him the broom now.

"I've gotta sweep?" Zach said. "After I backed your play last night?"

"Backed my play?"

Zach looked embarrassed. "I always sound like a nerd when I try to talk like Tarik, don't I?"

"Don't worry, we all do," Danny said. He put his hand to his fist, like he was speaking into a walkie-talkie. "Calling all units," he said. "White boys trying to sound black."

"Yeah," Zach said.

"The broom's not for sweeping," Danny said. "It's for defense. I need you to be Ollie Grey."

"Ollie the shot catcher?"

"Him," Danny said. "Get over there and hold that sucker up, and I'll see how much space I need to shoot over it."

"My dad does this with me sometimes," Zach said.

"Mine, too." *He started doing this drill when he turned back into a dad,* Danny thought. *And when he started trying to turn me into him.*

"All dads do it for little guys," Danny said. "Or when they're trying to teach big guys to get more air under their shots."

He had Zach set up on the baseline, about ten feet from the basket to start. He told him to block any shot he could.

The first time Danny came dribbling hard from the right corner and pulled up, Zach swatted the shot into the grass. Like Will had that day at McFeeley.

"Sorry," Zach said.

"Don't be."

The next time, he came in, up-faked Zach while he still had his dribble, felt like he was shooting the ball as high as the backboard and watched it drop through the net.

"It's like one of Steve Nash's teardrop shots," Zach said.

"Yeah," Danny said, "except I want to use it to make big guys cry."

They stayed there an hour, switching off sometimes so that Danny had the broom—he told Zach that he might as well start putting this shot into his game now. No sad face on Zach now. Just determination.

Like looking in a mirror, Danny thought again.

"Were you really going to leave?" Zach said near the end, when they were taking their last break.

"Yeah," Danny said, "I was. I was going to do the same exact thing I told you not to do."

"And that girl changed your mind?" Zach said.

"No," he said, "she just made me see what a loser I'd be, and then I changed my own mind."

They went back one last time to the rim with the good net. Zach in the lane now, holding up the broom to Ollie height. Danny drove at him like he was driving to the basket, leaned in, stepped back, put up the teardrop again. The ball seemed to spend more time floating through the air than a kite.

And fell through.

Danny looked at Zach and made the sideways peace sign Tarik had shown them.

"He's baaack," Zach said.

"Not back," Danny said. "Just a little less whack."

THE REAL GAMES, THE LEAGUE GAMES, BEGAN LATER THAT DAY.

From now until the end of camp, they were scheduled to do only two clinics in the morning, have a one-hour practice with their teams after lunch, then play games all over the grounds starting at four o'clock.

According to the schedule posted outside The House, the Celtics' first game was at The House, against the Bulls.

"Aw, man, that's sick," Tarik said.

"Good sick or bad sick?" Will said.

"Bad," Tarik said. "They got two Brooklyn guys I played against in AAU last year."

Zach was with them, checking his own schedule. The younger kids played their league games at two-thirty.

"What's AAU?" he said.

"Amateur Athletic Union. Like travel basketball plus. In New York City, it's like the NBA of kids' ball. You make your chops in AAU. It means you're going places."

"Who are the Brooklyn guys?" Danny said.

"Kareem Dell is one," Tarik said. "TJ Tucker's the other. Both of them are fifteen, but they look like they're going on twenty. Both 6-3 already. Both got those long arms going for them. Both got ups."

"We talking ups like Ollie Grey the shot catcher?" Ty said.

148

"Dog," Tarik said, his voice sounding sadder than if his own dog had died. "Compared to them, Ollie jumps like Will here." He put his hand on Will's shoulder as he said the last part, before adding, "No offense, dude."

"My legs accept your apology," Will said.

"Well, that doesn't sound good," Danny said. "Not that it's going to matter much to me personally, if I'm not in the game."

"Hey," Zach said, "what about that new attitude you were telling me about?"

"That's right," Tarik said, raising his voice up to what he liked to call preacher level. "Don't be backslidin' on us now, baby. Don't be backslidin' now. Especially now that you got your lady across the lake."

Will, Ty and Zach had told Tarik the whole Tess story at lunch.

"My attitude's gonna be fine from now on," Danny said. "But it's like my dad always says, you gotta be realistic."

Kareem and TJ were as good as Tarik said they were. For the first half of the game, the Bulls coach, Tim Pedulla, from Hofstra— Danny knew him because Hofstra had nearly made the Final Four a few months before—seemed to run the same basic offense every time, the Bulls' guards pounding it inside on one side of the low post or the other, then watching as Kareem or TJ abused whatever big guys Coach Powers had guarding them, Ben Coltrane or David Upshaw or Alex Westphal.

Boys against men, Danny thought.

On the bench Tarik said to Danny, "First offense I ever saw with no weak side."

Just then, even with Rasheed dropping down and trying to help out, TJ Tucker faced up on David and got so high on his jump shot that Danny had this picture in his head that TJ had shrunk David to Zach Fox's size.

Danny and Will and Tarik didn't make much of a difference when they got out there in the middle of the first half. Danny thought he had played all right, a few assists, no turnovers, no shots attempted. But if it hadn't been for Rasheed getting hot right before halftime, the Bulls would have blown them right out of the gym already.

Bulls 40, Celtics 24 at the break.

They were playing sixteen-minute halves. Eight minutes into the second half, because Coach Pedulla went to his bench a little more, it was 52–42.

That's when Cole Duncan dove for a ball and went sliding into the bleachers like he was sliding into home.

Coach Pedulla got a butterfly bandage on the cut above Cole's eye, explaining that the skin on your forehead split pretty easily—it had happened to him a few times when he was playing.

Cole, who had started to cry when it happened—when a guy cried, especially in front of a bunch of other guys he didn't know, you knew he was hurt—was sitting up by then, holding an ice pack to his head, his eyes still red. He kept telling everybody he was fine, really he was. But they had already called for Dr. Bradley by then, who showed up and said he wanted to take Cole up to the infirmary. Just a precaution.

When Cole stood up, everybody on both teams started clapping. Then both coaches got their players back into the huddle. When the Celtics were around Coach Powers, he stared off into space for what felt like a long time, tilting his head to one side, then to the other, like he was having some kind of debate inside his head.

Finally, he turned and pointed at Tarik. "Get in there for Cole."

Danny, standing next to Tarik, saw him immediately bend one

leg behind him from the knee, then the other, a little stretching thing he did right before he went into the game.

"No," Coach Powers said now, "I meant Walker."

Danny was as surprised as any of them.

"Me?" he said.

"Is there another Walker on this team?"

"No sir."

"And let's mix it up a little once in a while," Coach Powers said. "Walker, you give Rasheed a break once in a while and play some point. Okay?"

Danny said he was good with that.

He didn't care how many plays he got to run. He was a point guard again, with the big boys this time.

Danny and Rasheed played as if they'd played together before, as if the game in North Carolina hadn't ended the way it did, as if Rasheed wasn't still hacked off about what he thought was Danny's flop, as if he hadn't leveled Danny just a couple of days before. It was as if he and Rasheed, for this one game, had thrown out everything except this:

Winning the game.

The Bulls were still bigger, but Kareem and TJ weren't making all their shots now, maybe because the guys up front for the Celtics—Ben, David, Alex—were playing bigger, fighting harder.

The rest of the time, Danny and Rasheed did their best, even in Coach Powers's offense, to turn it into a guards' game.

The way God intended, as Richie Walker liked to say.

With three minutes to go, it was 58 all. The Celtics weren't running every play the exact way Coach Powers wanted in practice, but they were moving the ball so well, passing it around so cleanly on just about every possession, that he didn't seem to mind.

Will came off the bench to make a three. Tarik was getting as many rebounds as anybody on their team. Danny lost count of how many jumpers Rasheed made to get them back into it. With half a minute left, the game was still tied, 64–64. Kareem Dell was at the line about to shoot the front end of a one-and-one.

Coach Powers called time-out.

"If he makes both, we run 'Carolina,' " he said. "If he misses the first, or makes the first and misses the second, run that variation of 'Carolina' where Rasheed comes down the baseline and curls around Tarik for a jumper."

Rasheed nodded, as if Coach Powers was really only running the play past him.

"Don't start it too late, Mr. Walker," Coach Powers said. "If they double or triple on Rasheed, he can throw it back to you. Put it on the floor like you're going to make a dribble drive, then get it back to him."

Danny clapped his hands together hard, answering him that way: Let's do this.

He wanted to show everybody how fired up he was, not even give them a hint at how tired he was. This wasn't clinic ball or scrimmage ball. This was real ball. The real thing. For the first time in a long time, being into every possession this way, every play, every pass, every shot. There were times when Danny was so into the game he was afraid to take a breath.

Until he was out of breath.

He saw Will looking at him in the huddle, like he knew. Just because he knew Danny could usually go all day in basketball without ever getting tired.

Wordlessly, Will handed Danny the plastic bottle of cold water he was about to drink himself.

Danny glanced at Rasheed now, who not only wasn't breathing

hard, he wasn't even sweating, as hot as it was in The House, even with the walls pulled back on the lakeside.

Kareem made the first free throw, missed the second, Tarik got the rebound, Danny came and got the ball. Bulls 65, Celtics 64.

Rasheed ran to the right corner, waited there. TJ Tucker was on that side and wasn't even watching his own man, Ben Coltrane. He was watching Rasheed. Danny was watching the clock. Twenty seconds now. Rasheed sprinted down the baseline, hand up, faking like he was waving for the ball. Tarik dropped down, set the pick where he was supposed to; Rasheed came around it.

Danny threw him the ball.

The guy guarding Rasheed was named Phil, Danny'd heard them call out his name a few times. He was Rasheed's size, blond and quick. Just not as quick as Rasheed. It was why Kareem Dell came over to help, TJ covering the lane behind him.

For the first time, Danny saw Rasheed Hill change expression.

He smiled.

Smiled like he was saying he still had the Bulls outnumbered, even if it was their two to his one.

He smiled and put the ball on the floor and did two lightning crossover dribbles—the double that made Danny's own double crossover look like something that belonged on training wheels. The move he used when he wanted to dust somebody and drive the ball to the basket.

Neither one of them bit.

Phil held his ground. So did Kareem.

Even Tarik's man came over.

Ten seconds now, and they had Rasheed surrounded.

He threw the ball back over to Danny, who'd been prepared to watch Rasheed win the game like everybody else.

He wasn't expecting to get the ball back, but managed to catch the pass at the top of the circle. Too far to even think about shooting it himself, if he was even thinking about it. But there was open space in front of him, the way Coach Powers imagined there would be if they sealed Rasheed.

Dribble drive, Coach had said.

Danny did, expecting TJ to come up. He didn't right away. Danny was a step inside the free throw line then.

Now TJ came up.

Out of the corner of his eye, he saw that everybody had stayed home on Rasheed, even as Rasheed was calling for the ball.

Pass or shoot?

Danny's only shot against TJ Tucker was the one he'd spent most of the morning practicing against Zach Fox.

The one over the broom.

Three seconds.

He planted his foot, stepped back just enough as TJ's right arm went straight up in the air, got the ball over him nice and high, making sure to keep his own right arm going straight at the basket to keep the shot on line.

A rainmaker of a shot if there ever was one.

Danny didn't hear anything, which meant that he'd gotten it off in plenty of time.

He watched it come down now.

About six inches short.

Air ball.

RASHEED DIDN'T MOVE WHEN THE HORN SOUNDED. HE JUST STOOD there on the left wing until Danny looked over at him. Then Rasheed said, "I'm still open," before he turned and walked out the doors facing the lake.

Danny was about to go after him, apologize for losing the game, when he saw Coach Powers walking toward him from the bench area, gesturing for Danny to stay where he was.

"You did hear me say that even if he gave it to you after the first screen, you were supposed to give it right back," Coach Powers said. "Right?"

Danny looked down at this beautiful basketball floor, imagining up a hole for himself to crawl into. Knowing he was right back where he started with this coach, which meant in jail. "I didn't think there was time," Danny said.

"Too long an answer, son," he said. "All you needed to say was 'I didn't think' and leave it at that."

Then Coach Powers walked out of the gym in the exact same direction as Rasheed, as though they planned to meet up and talk more about how they gave Danny a chance to prove himself and how he'd screwed everything up.

"Yo," he heard from behind him.

Will.

Tarik was there with him.

"Before you say anything, I'm gonna say something, and it's that you played good," Will said. "And you know it. And the reason you know it is because you know more about basketball, and have more basketball in you, than that mean old man ever will."

"Scoreboard," Danny said in a small voice. Small as he felt.

Usually guys said that when they won. But to Danny, "scoreboard" always meant that however the game came out, that was the way it was supposed to come out.

"Wouldn't even have had a chance to win the game if you didn't play the way you did down the stretch, dog," Tarik said.

"I should have given it back," Danny said, not wanting to talk about this anymore, not wanting to be here anymore. "I don't agree with Coach about much. But the way Rasheed was going today, he could have made that J with his eyes closed, whether he had to rush it or not."

Will said, "Then maybe Rasheed shouldn't have given the ball up in the first place."

Then Will said they should go try to find Ty, maybe his game wasn't over yet and they could catch the end of it. Danny said, yeah, let's do it. Then he noticed the game ball sitting under the basket where somebody had left it.

Danny walked over, picked the ball up, dribbled out to the spot where he'd tried to shoot over Kareem. Like the hoop gods—his dad was always talking about the hoop gods, as though they watched every single game—were giving him a do-over. He dribbled in and shot the ball higher this time—nobody in his face, no long arms up in the air—and watched the ball drop through the basket.

Nothing but stinking net.

Then he jogged to catch up with Will and Tarik, wondering if those few minutes with Rasheed, before the air ball, was as good as it was going to get for him at the Right Way basketball camp.

• • •

It was Gampel's night to use the phone, which meant it was Danny's first chance to talk to his dad about everything that had—and hadn't—happened in the last day or so.

As soon as Richie Walker got on the line, he wanted to know everything about the knee, whether the swelling was on the inside or the outside, if the doctor was sure it was just a sprain and not ligaments, if the doctor was sure there was nothing floating around in there. His dad still considered himself a medical expert, not just on knees, but everything else after all the broken parts he'd had fixed in his life.

"Dad," Danny said, "I'm fine."

"Well, you're not fine if they still want to do an MRI," his dad said. "That doesn't sound fine to me."

Danny was in the phone booth with the door open, because it was a hot, muggy night in Cedarville. Zach was waiting to use the phone next. Danny closed the door now, even if Zach knew most of the story about the fake knee injury. It was more Danny being so embarrassed about what he was going to say next that he didn't even want *himself* to hear.

Like he was telling somebody he was afraid of the dark.

"When I say fine, Dad, it means I was never really hurt," he said. "I wanted an excuse to get out of here."

Out with it, just like that. He felt bad enough about having lied to the doctor and his mom and maybe himself. He was done with that, for good. He wasn't going to lie to his dad. Before he'd even considered doing something this lame, he should have thought about what his dad looked like in the hospital after his last accident. He should have remembered how his dad's basketball life—and nearly his whole life—ended in that first car accident his rookie year.

He could hear Tarik's voice inside his head now.

True *that.*

On the other end of the phone line, Richie Walker didn't say anything at first. It was one of those killer silences parents gave you sometimes, in person or over the phone, when they were trying to make you keep talking.

Or maybe his dad couldn't believe what he'd just heard.

"I'm not sure I heard you right," Richie Walker said.

Danny said, "You heard right."

Finally, Richie said, "That's not you." There was another pause and then he said, "Man, that's never been you."

"Dad," Danny said, "I know that now. I would have figured it out on my own. But Tess—she's here—got in my face the other night and made me see how dumb I'd been." He paused before he said, "Dad, believe me, there's nothing you could say that would make me feel worse than I already do."

"I don't care how much this coach got to you," Richie said. "You never fake an injury in sports. Never." He spit out the last word. "You quit before you do that."

"I know that now," Danny said.

"Do you?"

"Dad, I made a mistake, and I'm owning up to it. Isn't that what you always tell me to do?"

"You want a trophy for that?"

There was a lot more Danny wanted to tell his dad, to make him understand, wanted to tell him about Coach Powers saying he should switch sports, that maybe soccer would be better for him. But he was afraid it would come out sounding like one more lame excuse for faking the injury.

So he kept what had happened at Coach Powers's cabin to himself, through a silence from his dad that felt longer than eighth grade.

"You want to come home, come home," Richie said. "You want to stay, then show this coach he was wrong about you. Other than that, I've got nothin' right now. Talk to you soon."

Didn't say he loved him. Didn't wait for Danny to say that to him.

Just hung up.

Danny stood there, the receiver still to his ear, listening to the dial tone.

Then he took a deep breath, leaned out and asked Zach if he could make one more quick call. He pumped some change into the phone, called the number at Tess's uncle's house. He was going to tell her about the conversation with his dad, but when she came on, telling him in this happy excited voice about a fish she'd caught that afternoon, he decided against it. He would have skipped talking about the game, too, but she asked him about it once she was finished with her fish tale.

"Aren't you the one who always says there's a lot more that goes into a game than the last play?" Tess said.

"Yeah, but—"

Tess cut him off. "Forget the ending and think about the good stuff as a beginning."

"Okay," Danny said.

"Promise?"

It was a big deal with her, getting him to promise something.

"I promise," he said.

Danny wanted to know when he was going to get to see her again.

"I have my camera with me," she said. "Maybe my uncle can call Mr. LeBow and he'll let me come over to take some pictures."

"I'd be good with that," Danny said.

Tess said, "Until then, you can keep worrying about the way the game ended or suck it up and treat the good stuff like some kind of start."

"Are you trying to sound like my dad?"

"Your mom, actually," Tess said.

But at practice the next day it was as if the good stuff from the day before hadn't happened, at least as far as Danny was concerned.

Cole Duncan was back with Rasheed and the first unit, even with a bandage over his eye and a pretty impressive black-and-blue bruise showing around the bandage. Danny was with Will, Tarik, Alex Westphal and another forward, Tony Ryder, who'd missed the Bulls' game because of what Tarik and Will described as a truly epic night of hurling the night before.

On their way from practice to their four o'clock game against Lamar Parrish and the Lakers, Will and Tarik were still ragging on Coach Powers for the way he'd talked to them about what had happened against the Bulls.

"You listen to Dead Head Ed," Will said, "and Rasheed was going one-on-five when we came back on those suckers."

"Next year it's going to be 'Sheed saving the world on *24* instead of my man Jack Bauer," Tarik said.

It turned out to be a great game against the Lakers, even if Danny only played a quarter of it. The Celtics got ahead early because Rasheed couldn't miss and because their bigs, meaning David Upshaw and Ben Coltrane, were pretty much schooling the Lakers' bigs. And also because Lamar Parrish seemed to be making only about one of every three shots he took in the first half.

By halftime the Celtics were ahead by fifteen. Danny was hoping for a blowout, not just because he might get some extra minutes, but because he wanted to see Lamar Parrish suffer a little.

Or a lot.

But from the time the second half started, it was Lamar who couldn't miss. Didn't matter if Rasheed was on him or Cole. Or both. Didn't matter when the Celtics went to a zone, first a 3–2, then a box-and-one with Cole chasing. As much as Danny knew Lamar was a bad guy, it was like watching a pro take over a game.

Like watching the real Kobe.

With just over a minute left, he finally tied the game with a three-pointer. Danny was in the game now, because Will and Cole had both fouled out. Rasheed got fouled at the other end, made two free throws. Thirty seconds left. Celtics back up by two.

Wasn't enough.

Lamar calmly ran the clock down, drained another three, immediately ran to the other end of the court, holding the front of his jersey out, yelling "Uh-huh . . . uh-huh . . . uh-huh."

Only the game wasn't over.

One second left.

As soon as the ball had gone through the net, Danny had turned to the nearest ref, calling one of the two time-outs he knew they had left, just because he always knew stuff like that. Then he ran over to Rasheed and said, "I know you don't like me, but you gotta listen to me, I've got a play that'll work. But you gotta tell Coach. He'll never take it from me."

As they walked toward their bench, he told him as fast as he could. When they got into the huddle, Rasheed laid out Danny's play for Coach Powers.

Coach Powers said, "You can make the pass?"

"Yeah," Danny said, "I can."

"What if they put somebody on the ball?"

"They haven't done that all day."

"You can make the pass?" Coach Powers said again.

"Yes."

Hoping he was right.

He took the ball at half-court. Alex screened Lamar the way he was supposed to. Danny fired the ball quarterback style, not at Lamar but directly at the backboard, as Rasheed came flying at the basket from the opposite side.

Danny's pass was right on the money, hitting the board right above the square, like a carom shot in pool, bouncing right into the hands of Rasheed Hill, who caught the ball and laid it in and won the game for the Celtics, 62–61.

As soon as the refs made the motion that it was a good basket, Lamar rushed the counselor working the clock. His coach and a couple of teammates saw what was happening, that Lamar was really going after the kid, and managed to cut him off. They finally got him calmed down enough to start moving him toward the door.

Before he was out the door he yelled over at Rasheed about winning the game with some tricked-up play.

Rasheed shrugged and actually smiled. "Not my play," he said. He nodded at Danny and said, "His."

Danny never showboated. His dad always said it wasn't in their blood. But he couldn't help himself, just this once. Now he smiled at Lamar, pulled his jersey out in front of himself, real fast, just once, and walked away.

"That's right, midget!" he heard from behind him. "Have your little fun now!"

"I think he's taking it well," Will said.

Danny had still felt like a spectator for most of the game. It was still Rasheed's team, the way the Lakers were Lamar's. The way the Warriors had been his team once. Here he was a role player, one who had come off the bench to help beat Lamar Parrish today. He was the kind of player who was going to get to shine like this once in a while, be expected to blend in the rest of the time.

He knew that was the way he had to approach things the rest of the way, do his best not to mess up, on or off the court, maybe even get another chance to make a hero play.

No such luck.

The very next day he was in Jeff LeBow's office. In the office and in trouble.

THE FIGHT STARTED WITH LAMAR TAKING ZACH'S BALL.

Danny had found Zach shooting by himself on a half-court nobody ever used on the woods side of Gampel. A lot of guys, as usual, were at the counselors' game, but Zach wasn't interested in watching the counselors play. If he could catch part of one of Danny's games, he would, just because it was Danny, because he'd use almost any excuse to hang around with Danny during the day, even though they were bunking together at night.

The rest of the time Zach Fox just wanted to go play.

The kid who'd showed up as the unhappiest camper at Right Way was happy as long as he had his ball and enough room to dribble and shoot it.

He was more interested in playing than he was in eating or sleeping or hanging with kids his own age. Danny still wasn't sure how much Zach loved camp. But as much as he still liked to complain about being here, he couldn't hide how much he loved basketball. Clinics, practices, games, it didn't matter. He was into it now. He had ended up on what sounded like the best team in the eleven- and twelve-year-old division. He liked his coach, an assistant from Northeastern University in Boston, a lot. Since that night when Danny had heard him crying himself to sleep, he had never said another word about leaving.

Zach was pretty much having the kind of camp Danny had been hoping to have, at least before Coach Powers came into his life.

On this night, he was working on his outside shot, something he'd turned into his summer job, shooting it correctly now, not launching it the way he had before he got to Right Way, the way Danny used to.

Danny was helping him, calling out pointers, mostly feeding him the ball, feeling like he owed Zach one for the day when Zach had stood there holding up that broom.

That's when Lamar came along.

Right away, Lamar started calling Zach Frodo, asking if he was practicing for the championship of Middle Earth, ignoring Danny at first, but clearly directing his insults at both of them.

Tarik would say later that he was surprised Lamar had even seen a *Lord of the Rings* movie. "Or understood it," Tarik said.

Zach tried to ignore Lamar, just kept shooting the ball.

But Lamar, being Lamar, wouldn't let up.

"How come you don't have those big Frodo feet?" he asked Zach. "Like you was wearin' Charlie Barkley's real sneakers, instead of those baby shoes you got on yourself?"

Now Danny said, "Leave him alone, Lamar."

Lamar looked at him. "What are you, his lucky charm? You do look a little like that leprechaun guy on the side of the box."

"Seriously, Lamar, you must have something better to do," Danny said.

"Listen to the boy beat me with his little tricked-up play. You still feelin' all puffed out about that?"

"I don't get puffed out," Danny said.

"I saw you after the game."

Danny couldn't help himself. "I was just trying to be more like you."

"You want to be more like me? *Grow,* little man."

"Let it go, Lamar."

Zach was still trying to pretend Lamar wasn't even there. So he took a couple of dribbles, shot the ball.

Big mistake.

Lamar went and got the rebound.

Looked at the ball and saw Zach's name written on it in Magic Marker.

"Your own little ball," Lamar said.

He bounced the ball a couple of times, then said, "Oh, looky here—it needs air."

Zach said it was fine the way it was, it had never needed air from the day he got it and could he have it back?

"No, midget," Lamar said. "I can always tell when a ball's flat, and this one is flat." Then he walked over to the little storage box that was at all the outdoor courts. Every box had pumps and needles inside, along with a bunch of indoor/outdoor balls.

"It's fine, really," Zach said.

"Can't a brother try to help?" Lamar said, a pump in his hands.

He stuck the needle into Zach's ball, pumped a couple of times, then smiled at Zach as he broke the needle off, knowing it was going to be stuck inside Zach's ball for good.

Every kid in the world knew what *that* meant.

The ball was ruined.

Forever.

Only then did Lamar Parrish give Zach his ball.

Zach stepped back and whipped it right at Lamar's head, the ball either catching Lamar on the side of his head or his shoulder, Danny couldn't tell for sure from the side. But wherever it hit, it made Lamar real mad, because he grabbed Zach by his shoulders and started shaking him, hard. Zach's head bounced around like he was a bobblehead doll.

Then Lamar lifted him up by his T-shirt, so the two of them were eye-to-eye for a moment.

Danny'd seen enough.

"Put him down, Lamar," he said, trying to sound calmer, more in control, than he really was.

Lamar, still holding Zach in midair even as Zach twisted and kicked his legs around, as if this took no effort on Lamar's part, laughed and said, "Right."

"I mean it," Danny said.

"He asked for it," Lamar said. "You doin' the same?"

"Guess so."

The last fight he'd gotten into, what he promised his mom and dad was the last fight he'd *ever* get into, was with a Middletown kid named Teddy (the Moron) Moran, who'd played for the other travel team in town, the Vikings, the team that had cut Danny. But Teddy was more mouth than anything else, more a threat to your ears than any other part of you.

Lamar Parrish was different. A whole lot different. A lot bigger than Teddy, a lot stronger.

A lot meaner.

"You want to pick on somebody, go back to picking on me," Danny said, not getting any closer. He didn't want it to look like he was trying to get up in Lamar's face, but he wasn't going anywhere, either. He felt his fists clench at his sides and hoped he wouldn't have to use them.

Because if he did, Lamar was going to use *his*.

Lamar put Zach down but kept a hand on him, the way you did on defense when you wanted to watch the ball and keep contact with the man you were guarding at the same time.

Zach said to Danny, "I can fight my own battles."

It made Lamar laugh. "Right," he said. "If you stand on the other Hobbit's shoulders, maybe." And then, in a move so fast Danny almost missed it, Lamar took his big right hand, the one he had on Zach, and flicked it into his stomach like a jab.

Zach Fox doubled over and sat down, gasping for breath, tears in his eyes.

Lamar looked down at him and said, "What are you, a girl?"

Without thinking, Danny charged Lamar then, lowering his shoulder and grabbing him around the waist, surprising him enough that they both went down.

Lamar rolled back up on his knees first, staring down at the dirt all over tonight's Kobe jersey, the purple road version, as though he couldn't believe what he was seeing. Then he looked down at the blood on the back of his right hand where he must have landed.

He looked at Danny, this crazed expression in his eyes and said, "This is *so* on, little man." Then: "Get up."

Danny did, not knowing what else to do under the circumstances.

He had no chance against this guy. He never should have gotten him madder than he already was, but he couldn't run away. Next to him he could hear Zach still choking for air, but he was afraid now to take his eyes off Lamar.

Who took a step now, like that quick first step he had in ball, drew back his bloody hand the way tennis players did when they were getting ready to hit a backhand.

Danny froze. Just stood there frozen and closed his eyes, waiting to get backhanded right across the court.

Only the blow never came.

"Get off me!"

When Danny opened his eyes, there was Rasheed Hill behind

Lamar, one arm around his waist, the other one with a pretty good choke hold around Lamar's neck.

"Get off me," he said again, weaker this time, because now he was the one who was having trouble getting enough air.

"Never cared for him much," Rasheed said to Danny. "Or his game."

" 'Sheed?" Lamar said in what voice he had.

"What?"

Lamar acted like he wanted to get loose, but Danny could see his heart wasn't really in it, not with the grip Rasheed had on his neck.

Lamar said, "You're takin' *his* side?"

"Yeah," Rasheed said, "I guess I am."

LAMAR HAD GONE INTO JEFF LEBOW'S OFFICE FIRST WHILE DANNY and Zach and Rasheed waited outside. When he was finished, Jeff walked him out, to make sure there were no further incidents. It didn't stop Lamar from walking past them and saying "this ain't over" under his breath.

Now the three of them were in folding chairs set up across from Jeff's desk.

Principal's office, summer-camp version.

"Before any of you guys say anything," Jeff said, "you might as well know Lamar's side of the story. Basically, he says that Zach started it by whipping the ball at him, Danny blindsided him with what he called a block below the waist, then Rasheed jumped him from behind before those two counselors broke it up. There you have it."

Zach started to jump out of his chair, but Danny stuck out his arm, turning himself into a seat belt.

"Let me do the talking," he said to Zach.

To Jeff: "You're joking, right?"

"Do I look like I'm joking?"

"Mr. LeBow," Danny said, "that is, like, a total screaming *Liar, Liar*–like lie."

Zach couldn't restrain himself any longer, even if he did manage to stay in his chair. "He took my favorite ball away from me, one I brought from home, broke the needle in it on purpose—"

"He says it was an accident," Jeff said.

"—then he punched me in the stomach," Zach said, face red. "That's when Danny charged him."

"Listen, I know that Lamar can be a pain in the butt sometimes," Jeff said. "But he's the one with the bruised hand, and he's the one who was in the choke hold when my guys came by."

Now Rasheed spoke. "One he had coming to him."

"Three of you, one of him," Jeff LeBow said. "Just doing the math makes you guys look bad."

"Mr. LeBow," Danny said. "Do you think Zach or I would go looking for a fight with somebody Lamar's size?"

"Happens like this all the time in games," Rasheed said. "Guy hits you with a cheap shot, only the ref doesn't see that one. All he sees is when you go back at him."

"Then they make the only call they can," Jeff said.

Rasheed stood up now, pointed casually at Danny. "What he said happened, did. Do what you gotta do. I already did."

Then he walked out of the office.

The regular season at Right Way lasted fourteen games. There were eight teams in their league, so you played the other seven twice. The play-offs started the middle of the last week, which is when other college coaches and prep coaches from around the country showed up to scout.

Danny, Zach and Rasheed were suspended for two games each. In a short season like this, they all knew it was a lot.

Lamar got nothing. In the end, it was their word against his. Rasheed didn't help matters by saying if he wasn't worried about breaking his hand, he wouldn't have just grabbed Lamar when he wound up to hit Danny, he would have dropped him.

In addition to getting the two games, Danny, Zach and Rasheed got two days of helping clean out the bathrooms in the bunkhouses while the afternoon games were going on.

"I don't even like going into those bathrooms when I *have* to," Zach said.

"It could've been worse," Danny said. "They could've kicked us out."

"Nothing's worse than cleaning toilets," Zach said. "Nothing."

It was the next morning before breakfast; they'd just been told their punishment in Jeff LeBow's office. He said they could participate in the morning clinics but weren't allowed to practice with their teams in the afternoon.

"That's when we'll be polishing toilets 'stead of our games," Rasheed said.

"I'm doing the showers," Zach said.

He went off to breakfast. Rasheed said he wasn't hungry, he was going to shoot around a little before clinics started. Danny asked if he wanted company, sure Rasheed would say no.

But to his surprise, Rasheed said, "Come along, if you want." Then he said he wanted to use the bad court by the parking lots. That way nobody would bother them.

Danny smiled, told him there was no such thing as a bad court as long as the rims had nets.

"Maybe in Middletown," Rasheed said. "Try coming to Baltimore sometime. Might change your mind."

The two of them cut around the main building, grabbed a ball somebody had left lying in the grass. Danny and the kid at camp he thought hated his guts the most.

When they got to the bad court they played some H-O-R-S-E, then a game of Around the World, then 21. When they got tired of games, they did something else Danny thought they'd never do.

Talked.

Rasheed said that most people never got past the way he looked, the hair and the tats. That's what he called them. Tats. Said that even though he was a kid, people looked at him and thought he was just like Allen Iverson. Or maybe some gangsta rapper who could play himself some ball.

"Do the tattoos hurt as much as guys say?" Danny said. "When you get them, I mean?"

Rasheed said you get used to it. He said his mom finally said he could get a few, but the deal was, he had to get As in school. Rasheed said he thought that was a fair trade. Danny pointed to one on his upper right arm that said "Artis" and asked who that was.

"My dad. He died when I was eight."

"Oh," Danny said, not knowing what else to say.

"He got shot."

Now Danny *really* didn't know what to say. He was afraid that if he asked how, he might find out something about Rasheed's dad he didn't want to know. Or be asking Rasheed to tell something he really didn't want to tell.

"Wasn't what you think," Rasheed said, as if he'd seen something on Danny's face. "He was in the wrong place at the wrong time, is all. Coming home from work one night when some guys from a couple blocks up decided to rob a liquor store and started shooting."

"I'm so sorry," Danny said, picturing it like some scene from a movie.

Rasheed said, "My mom says that's the big cause of death where we live, being in the wrong place at the wrong time."

They sat on a rock above the court, Rasheed telling Danny that basketball was going to be a way out of the neighborhood for him and his mom.

"Do people still call it the 'hood?" Danny said.

Rasheed almost smiled. "Only saltines from the suburbs."

"Saltines?"

"Little white guys from Middletown, USA."

"Hey," Danny said, "I didn't call it the 'hood, I was just sayin'."

Rasheed said he'd had chances to move, like to the school Lamar went off to, but that his mom had a good job working at a bakery, and she wanted him to go to Dunbar High, where his big brother had gone.

"That's where Sam Cassell went," Danny said.

"You know that?"

"Even saltines know stuff," Danny said.

Rasheed Hill turned and gave Danny some fist to bump.

"Your mom sounds cool," Danny said, thinking this was something else they had in common besides ball, cool moms.

"She's the one first told me that coming from a single-parent home wasn't some kind of death sentence," Rasheed said.

Danny wanted to say he'd been in a single-parent home for a long time when his dad was away but knew that he'd sound plain old stupid if he tried to compare his situation, his life, to Rasheed's. So he just fell back on the same thing he always did. "You want to shoot some more?"

"I'm good just chilling." Rasheed shook his head. "You believe we got two games and Lamar got nothin'?"

"You know," Danny said, "the first night I met you guys, I thought you and him were tight."

174

"That's what he wanted people to think, that me and him are boys. But we never were, even back in Baltimore. He just got with me that night walking back from dinner. I shouldn't have let him diss you down like that."

Now he really smiled. It caught Danny off balance, how happy it made him look.

"But I was still mad at you because you flopped," he said.

"Didn't flop," Danny said.

"You say."

"Because I didn't."

Rasheed put his thumbs together, stuck up his index fingers. The universal sign for "whatever."

"Now who's acting like a saltine?" Danny said. "But this isn't a whatever. If I say I didn't flop, I didn't." He stood up, fired up all of a sudden. "We gotta be clear on this if we're gonna be friends. If it's about basketball and I say something, you have to believe me. I got position, he made the call, I took the hit. If the ref had called it the other way, I would've had to accept it. Okay?"

Rasheed gave him that sleepy look and then said, "Okay."

They bumped fists again.

"Maybe," Rasheed said, "we're more alike than anybody'd ever think."

In the distance, they could hear the sound of Jeff LeBow talking into his bullhorn. At this time of the morning, it usually meant he was telling guys coming out of breakfast they had five minutes to get to their first clinic.

Danny got up, grabbed the ball from where it sat at Rasheed's feet, went out onto the bad court, bounced the ball between his legs, reached behind his back and caught it, bounced it through again without looking down.

Rasheed motioned for the ball. He spun it on his right index finger, rolled it down his arm, bent over so it rolled on his shoulders behind his head. The ball seemed to defy gravity as it went up his left arm until Rasheed was spinning it on the index finger of his left hand.

Danny felt like he was at the Globetrotters.

Finally Rasheed flipped the ball into the air, headed it into the air like a soccer player, watched along with Danny as it hit the backboard just right and went through the net, like he'd been practicing this shot his whole life.

"Let's get out of here," Rasheed said. "We're in enough trouble, we don't want to be late for clinics."

"I still owe you one for Lamar," Danny said as they cut back across the parking lot.

"Just play good when you get the chance," he said. "No way Lamar Parrish is gonna win the championship of this place."

"I don't play enough to make a difference."

"Not yet."

"Well, you must know something I don't."

"Not about basketball I don't," Rasheed said. He stopped and gave Danny the kind of shove guys gave each other sometimes. A good shove. "It comes to ball, you're just like me."

This time Danny knew what to say.

"Thank you."

"We're boys now," Rasheed said, and something about the way he said it let Danny know the conversation was over.

They walked across one parking lot, then another, Danny dribbling the ball for a while, then handing it to Rasheed, letting him dribble it, back and forth that way until they were back in the middle of the morning action at Right Way.

Him and Rasheed.

Boys now.

THE CELTICS LOST BOTH GAMES THEY PLAYED WHILE RASHEED AND Danny were in the penalty box, which is how Rasheed described the bathrooms they had to clean.

The two losses did nothing to improve their coach's already crabby disposition. So even when they returned to practice, Coach Powers was still fixed on what had happened with Lamar that night and how it had cost the whole team.

How Danny had cost the whole team.

Coach Powers: "Because Mr. Walker here dragged Rasheed into his little drama, we have now lost two games and fallen to the bottom of our division and are on our way to having a bad seeding when the play-offs start."

Rasheed stepped out of the line, saying, "But, Coach, I thought I explained to you—"

Danny got in front of him before he could say anything else.

He wasn't going to let Rasheed fight his fight every day.

"It's all my fault, definitely," Danny said. "You're right, if I hadn't interfered in the first place, Rasheed wouldn't have had to."

"You should have thought of that two days ago," Coach Powers said. "But there's no point beating a dead horse."

When they got on the court, Tarik whispered to Danny, "Usually the man don't stop beatin' the horse till it's already at the danged glue factory."

Their game later that afternoon was on one of the outside

courts, against the Nets. Rasheed dominated from start to finish, as if all the ball he'd kept inside of him for the last two days just exploded out of him. And Tarik had his best game by far, twelve points and twelve rebounds.

Danny played his usual one quarter, down to the second. But on this day he might as well have not played at all, because he was afraid to make any kind of mistake and get his coach any madder at him than he already was. He didn't take a single shot or make a single pass that anybody would have remembered. Was basically just out there, especially in the second half, when the Celtics were running off as much clock as possible by way of protecting the big lead they'd piled up in the first half.

On this day, he was back to being Mr. Spare Part.

It was after the game, when they were sitting on the grass while Coach Powers wore them out telling them what he'd liked in the game and what he hadn't, that Rasheed informed them all that he thought he might have tweaked his hamstring and might not be able to play tomorrow.

Coach Powers said for him to go ice it—it would probably feel a lot better in the morning.

Rasheed said he wasn't so sure and made a face as he stood up. Danny tried to remember when he might have hurt himself. But all he'd seen, all day long, was another game when Rasheed seemed to be playing at a different speed than everybody else, in a different league, even though the Nets had come into the game with the second-best record in the division.

"Don't want to take any chances, is all," he said to Coach Powers. "I try to force it tomorrow and make it worse, I could end up missing the play-offs."

Coach Powers said they sure wouldn't want that to happen,

then reminded him about the ice. By now everybody on the team knew that in Ed Powers's world, ice could cure everything except chicken pox.

Rasheed left the court with Danny, Tarik and Will. Like the four of them had been hanging all along. *Being friends with somebody can seem like the hardest thing going*, Danny thought, *until it feels like the easiest thing in the world.*

"When *did* your leg start acting up on you, dog?" Tarik said.

"Didn't."

"But you said—"

"Know what I *said*," Rasheed said. "It's just not exactly the same as what *is*."

"I'm confused," Will said.

Tarik grinned. "Tell me about it."

"I mean about Rasheed," Will said. To Rasheed he said, "Are you hurt or not?"

"I felt a little something pull when I lifted Lamar up off the ground," he said. "That much is the truth. But it's not so bad that I can't play."

"But you told Coach you're not playing," Tarik said.

"I'm not," Rasheed said, then nodded at Danny. "He is."

"You're not taking a day off because of me," Danny said. "Uh-uh. No way."

"Way," Rasheed said. "I'm not just doing it for you. I'm doing it for the team."

"Okay," Will said, "now I really don't get it."

"We're never gonna be as good as we're supposed to be if Walker doesn't play more," he said. "You'd think that man would have got past himself and figured that out by now. But he hasn't. So now I'm gonna help him out a little."

Tarik said, "The way you'd help some real old person cross the street. Along the lines of that."

"Yeah," Rasheed said. "Along the lines of that."

Danny was on his way to the game the next day when he saw Lamar Parrish talking to Tess. She'd said she was going to just show up one day and surprise them, take a few pictures. Danny had only thought it was a good idea because it meant he got to see her again before she left.

Now here she was.

With Lamar.

Surprise! Danny thought.

There was nobody else around. It was just the two of them, in the middle of the great lawn at Right Way, where Jeff had greeted everybody the first day of camp.

There was a big old tree outside Jeff's office, and Danny stepped back to let it hide him, trying to decide whether to go over there or not, find out for himself what was going on.

He had managed to stay out of Lamar's way since the fight. Actually, he and Zach and Rasheed had been ordered to steer clear of Lamar until the end of camp. But Danny didn't need to be told that by Mr. LeBow or anybody else. He knew that if something else happened he'd only get blamed all over again. Or get kicked out of here. And even though that was something he had wanted to happen a few days ago, when he'd tried to weasel his way home, things had changed.

He'd promised himself he was going to stick it out. Get something out of these three weeks. It was like when you set your mind on getting a good grade in a class you stunk at, or just plain hated. He was going to do it, no matter what. A promise was a promise, even if it was one you made to yourself.

Only now there Lamar was with Tess.

Tess.

She didn't look as if he was bothering her, but that didn't mean anything. Maybe he just hadn't bothered her yet.

Should he go over or not?

Danny saw Tess hand Lamar her camera.

That's what happened across the lawn, anyway. Inside Danny's head, he couldn't help it, he saw Lamar taking Zach Fox's basketball.

That's when he came out from behind the tree, walking over there as fast as he could without it looking like he was running, like this was Danny to the rescue all over again.

"Hey," he said, trying to make himself sound casual when he got to them. "What's doin'?"

"Hey, yourself," Tess said. She smiled at Danny, the way she always did when she saw him, at school or at a game or just walking down the street in Middletown.

As nervous as he was, he smiled back. Then gave a quick look at Lamar, who was smiling himself. Only not because he was as happy to see Danny as Tess Hewitt was.

To Tess he said, "You're the one."

"Excuse me?" she said.

Lamar was nodding now, saying, "The one we all heard about the night him and his boys took the boat. His girl from back home."

Danny wasn't going to get into it with Lamar Parrish, of all people, about whether Tess was "his" girl or not.

Tess poked Danny and said, "Thanks for making me famous."

Danny said, "So what're you guys doing?"

"Lamar wanted to take a look at my camera," Tess said. "He's interested in photography."

Danny wanted to say: Yeah, but only if somebody's taking a picture of *him*.

"Cool," Danny said, though feeling decidedly uncool at the moment, just wanting to get Tess away from this guy.

But Lamar seemed in no hurry to go anywhere.

He said to Tess, "Sure is a fine piece of equipment you got here."

Now he turned and smiled at Danny, winked at him as he held Tess's camera high in the air, as if wanting to study it from all angles. "Yeah, no doubt, a fine piece of picture-taking equipment. Probably takes pictures a lot better than my cell phone."

He was really playing with Danny now. They both knew it. Tess was too smart not to see it, too, hear it in his voice. Maybe that was why she put her hand out, like she wanted her camera back, and said, "Well, I've got to take off. I want to get some pictures of the other Middletown guys as long as I'm here."

"I hear that," Lamar said, and started to hand the camera back to her. "I gotta bounce, too. Almost game time."

But as he started to hand over the camera, he fumbled it, like you did when you were playing Hot Potato, fumbled it like he was about to drop it.

Danny lunged and got his hands underneath it, the way you did when you tried to keep a ball from hitting the ground.

Lamar was just teasing them.

"No worries, little man," he said. "I got it."

He handed the camera back to Tess, gave her a small bow, said "nice talkin' at you" to her, ignoring Danny again. Then he left, walked away from them in the slouchy way he had, bopping his head, swaying a little from side to side, as though he knew they were watching him, as though he was the most awesome person in this whole camp.

"Well," Tess said, "that certainly weirded me out."

"That," Danny said, "was just Lamar being Lamar. Wanting me to know that he knows about us."

Tess smiled. "Us?"

Danny could feel himself blushing, so he looked away, like he was still trying to track Lamar. "Us being friends," he said. "You know what I meant."

"Always," Tess said.

"You ought to stay away from that guy," Danny said. "Everything that just happened, probably even talking to you in the first place, was for my benefit. There's something about me that makes him want to push my buttons. And I have a feeling it's going to get worse now that he sees Rasheed hanging around with me."

"Don't worry, big fella. I can take care of myself," Tess said. She slung her camera bag over her shoulder and looked like a total pro to Danny as she did. Danny knew how much she loved that camera, a gift from her parents last Christmas, probably her prize possession. It was why he had lunged for it the way he had. "You just worry about playing ball."

Now, she said, she was going off to take some pictures, since this was her one afternoon to do that, and her uncle was picking her up at dinnertime. She asked Danny where his game was and he said Court 4, then asked where Ty was playing, and Danny told her that, too.

"If you see Lamar, head in the other direction," Danny said. "That's my new policy."

"If I see him again, I'll tell him not to mess with Tess," she said, and laughed at her rhyme. Then she headed off across the lawn on those long legs, looking as if she didn't have a care in the world.

All these hotshot players at this camp, so many of them as stuck on themselves as Lamar was, and for this one day a girl was the most awesome person here.

Maybe it was seeing Tess right before the game, Tess who wasn't afraid of anything or anybody, that gave him the right kind of attitude adjustment. Whatever it was, he played his best game yet.

By far.

Even though Rasheed had said that Coach Powers would start him, Danny didn't believe it until it happened, until he was told right before the game against the Nuggets that it was going to be him and Cole in the backcourt. "They've got a couple of guys in the backcourt almost as small as you," Coach Powers said. "You and Cole should be able to handle them."

He told Cole to handle the ball. But in the first five minutes, Coach Powers could see what everybody else could, that the little guy guarding Cole was giving him fits, picking him up full-court, making him struggle just to advance the ball past half-court, much less get them into their offense.

They were down twelve when Coach Ed called a time-out and told Danny to go to the point.

"Your ball," Rasheed whispered to Danny when they broke the huddle.

Danny knew Coach was only turning the team over to him this way as some kind of last resort. He didn't care. He wasn't going to overanalyze everything this time, especially if this was going to be the one start he got in Maine. He was just going to let it rip, the way he had when it had been him and Rasheed together in the backcourt.

That was exactly what he did.

He started breaking down the dark-haired kid guarding him off the dribble, getting into the lane, feeding Ben Coltrane and David

Upshaw for easy buckets, even though both Ben and David had bigger guys guarding them. The dark-haired kid tried to press him all over the court, and Danny made him pay, even after made baskets, making it seem as if the Celtics were constantly on the break. The Nuggets coach—Tarik said he was from Manhattan College—switched Cole's guy over on him and that didn't help, either. Danny would keep pounding it inside or kicking it out to Will, who on this day was making threes as if he were back at McFeeley Park.

Today Danny played ball as if he still had the eye.

He played as if it was travel team all over again.

The Celtics got the lead by halftime. But the Nuggets hung in there in the second half, mostly because of their size advantage. Before long, the game was going back and forth, one lead change after another. Nobody had more than a three-point lead in the second half. One of those games. For once, even Coach Powers got out of the way and let them play. He still called out plays, just not every time down the court.

Ben Coltrane fouled out. The Celtics hung in, even with Tarik playing center now. David Upshaw fouled out. Still they hung in. Then Alex Westphal, their last real big guy, fouled out. They were going with four guards now, plus Tarik.

They were down two points with twenty seconds left when Coach Powers called their last time-out.

"Quick two and a stop," he said.

Quick two and a stop, Danny knew, meant overtime. Tarik had four fouls. When he was gone, it would look like the Nuggets were playing Zach's team.

Their best chance was to win now.

"But Coach—"

That was as far as Danny got. Coach Powers glared away the rest of the thought.

"Cole, you set a back screen for Tarik," he said. "Then go to a zone at the other end, pack it in, make them take the last shot from the outside. When they miss—and notice I said *when*—we'll get 'em in overtime."

Danny nodded as if he agreed, as if this was the best idea anybody had ever had.

Only he didn't agree. Will was on fire, and Danny knew their best chance was to win the game right here.

The five in the game joined hands before breaking the huddle. As they did, Danny made eye contact with Rasheed, who was behind Coach Powers, shaking his head no, holding up three fingers, as if he'd channeled himself right into Danny's brain.

Now Danny was sure he was right. This was Will's day, too, his chance to show Coach he was wrong about him, same as it was Danny's. Will's chance to do something he hardly ever got to do in basketball:

Make the hero shot and win the game.

But he had to make the shot. If he didn't, if Danny busted the play, and then Will missed, and the Celtics lost their third in a row, Coach Powers would banish Danny to the end of the bench once and for all.

On the way out of the huddle, he said to Tarik, "Do me a favor?"

"Whatever you need," Tarik said. "You've been makin' me look like a star today."

"Don't get open," Danny said. "Even if it means you don't get to take the last shot."

Tarik smiled. "We gonna roll the dice with the funny man, right?"

"You got it," Danny said. Then quickly told him the play they were going to run after they didn't run Coach Powers's play, right before he went over and told Will.

Cole set the back screen the way he'd been told, and it was a good one. Only Tarik cut the wrong way coming around it, giving his man a chance to pick him up.

Everybody was still covered.

There were still fifteen seconds left. All day. Danny looked over at Will and nodded. Telling him to make his move. The play was "Ohio." A play they used to run all the time with the Warriors in travel. Will would run from the left corner to the right corner, Tarik screening for him right under the basket as Will blew past him.

It worked the way it always had, and Danny, still with his dribble, saw Will break into the clear.

He threw the pass before Will even got to his spot behind the three-point line, fired this high pass over the top of the defense that must have looked like it was headed for the next court over.

Threw it to the spot the way quarterbacks did before the receiver even made his cut.

The kind of pass you threw if you still had the eye.

Will had to jump to catch the ball. But he caught it cleanly, came down with it as his man, this stocky kid with a buzz cut, came tearing at him. The buzz-cut kid was a step late as Will squared his shoulders and let the ball go, and the only reason he didn't see that it was money all the way was because the buzz-cut kid was blocking his view.

Celtics 51, Nuggets 50.

"I am so wet," Will said when Danny got to him, "my name should be Free Willie Stoddard."

All around them, the whole team was happy, like they were finally one team, even on a day when their best player had been sitting next to the coach. Rasheed, forgetting he was supposed to have a sore leg, hugged Will and lifted him off the ground the way he had Lamar that night, only in a good way this time. They were all high-fiving each other and then a few of them were in this pig pile on the court. Danny thought about diving on top, but then he just walked up to Tarik, jumped as high as he could, and chest-bumped him.

"Needs work, dog," Tarik said.

It was then that Danny noticed Coach Powers sitting in the same folding chair he'd sat in during the game, calmly motioning for Danny to come over.

Danny jogged to him.

"You ran your own play, didn't you?" Coach Powers said.

Danny looked off, to where the happy part of the team still was. "Yes."

No more lies.

Coach Powers didn't say anything right away, just got slowly up out of his chair, stood there towering over Danny until he said in his quiet voice, "Next year tell your father to send you to a camp where the boys get to coach the teams."

Even when I win here, Danny thought, *I lose.*

21

THEY WERE ALL AT THE END OF ONE OF THE LONG PICNIC-BENCH TA-
bles, about two minutes into dinner, when Tess showed up.

Danny, Will, Ty, Tarik, Rasheed, Zach Fox: They were all there,
ready to consume a record amount of camp pizza, planning the
game of Texas Hold 'Em they were going to play later using poker
chips Will had brought.

Then Tess was there, camera bag over her shoulder. She barely
got out the words.

"Someone broke my camera!"

The girl who could handle herself in any situation was crying.

Will jumped up right away, sensing everybody in the mess hall
was watching them and probably wondering what a girl was doing
there. "Let's take this outside," he said, and started walking Tess
toward the door.

The rest of them followed her, not worrying about pizza night
anymore, just wanting to get Tess outside as fast as they could.
Keeping her in the middle of them as they walked out the door and
around the corner, past the main building and out onto the lawn,
not too far from where Danny had seen Tess with Lamar.

Lamar: Talking about what a fine piece of equipment Tess's
camera was, then giving Danny that look.

"It was all my fault," Tess said.

"Somehow I doubt that," Will said.

Danny just kept staring at Tess, wanting to say or do something that would make her feel better. Her eyes were red, and there were those pink dots she got when she was upset, not just making her look sad, making her look younger. Tess Hewitt, who always looked, and acted, older than everybody else, certainly any guys she was hanging around with.

Who never cried in front of Danny or anybody else.

He stared at her and thought back now to how close she'd come that day at McFeeley. He felt more sure than ever that he was never going to be mean to her ever again if he could help it.

"What happened?" Danny said to her. "From the beginning."

She took her bag off her shoulder and removed what was left of her prized camera, which looked as if it had been dropped out of a high window.

Or run over.

"This happened," she said.

"We know," Danny said. "What we want to know is how."

She said that she'd shot some pictures of Danny's game, then decided to wander around for a little while, taking random shots for fun, finally stopping at a pickup game some older kids were playing at the court in front of Staples.

Her uncle had left her a text message on her cell phone saying he was going to be a little late picking her up in his boat, so when she heard the dinner horn sound, she figured she'd come find them and say good-bye before she walked down to the dock. So she headed up toward the mess hall. On her way, she ran into Mr. LeBow, who was going to dinner himself. She asked if there was a ladies' room she could use. He showed her the one next to Sue's office, on the other side of the main building, near the back door.

"I dropped my bag outside," Tess said. "You know, the way you drop your backpack at school."

She said she was in there for five minutes, tops, just washing up at the end of a day when she'd felt as sweaty as the players.

When she came back out, the camera was out of the bag, lying on the ground, looking the way it did now.

"Who'd do something like this?" she said, eyes big again, starting to fill up.

"Lamar, that's who," Danny said.

"True that," Will said. "Danny told us he was messing with the camera before."

Ty said, "Was he in that pickup game you talked about?"

"No," Tess said. "He was at the next court over, shooting around by himself."

"Figures," Tarik said.

"I need to go ask him something," Danny said, and took one step before Will and Ty blocked his way. Both of them had their arms crossed.

Shaking their heads no.

"Bad idea," Will said.

"The worst," Ty said.

"But he did this. He's got it in for me now, and you guys know it."

"We got no proof," Rasheed said.

"We only got what we think we got," Tarik said.

"You know," Will said, "if this were TV, we could have them dust Tess's camera for fingerprints."

"Dog," Tarik said, "you watch way too much of that dang *CSI*."

Danny asked Tess if there was anyone else around when she discovered what had happened to her camera. She said no. Did she report it to anybody? No again. "I did the only thing I could think of," she said. "I came looking for you guys."

"We gotta find Lamar and at least put it to him!" Danny said now. "Ask him why he'd do something to somebody who has nothing to do with any of this."

"Well, nothing 'cept you," Tarik said.

When Danny finally calmed down, it was decided they would go tell Mr. LeBow what happened. Only, when they got over to his office, it was locked up, probably for the night. So they got some paper out of the computer room, and Danny wrote a short note, trying to make his handwriting readable for once, telling Mr. LeBow what had happened, not putting anything in there about Lamar, just saying they'd tell him the rest of the story in the morning. Saying in the note that Tess was at camp for just this one day taking pictures and that whoever did this to her shouldn't be allowed to get away with it.

Then Tess asked Danny if she'd walk him to the dock.

He reached up without saying anything and took the camera bag off her shoulder, surprised at how heavy it was.

There was nobody on the beach, maybe because it had gotten cold all of a sudden, like the total opposite of the day. It was darker than it should have been at eight o'clock in the summer, probably because of the storm predicted for later that night.

"I loved that stupid camera," she said.

"I know."

"When I called my uncle, he said he'd drive me to Portland tomorrow. There's a great camera store there," Tess said.

"So you'll get a new one."

"It just won't be this one."

He saw the pink dots reappear on her face, saw her eyes getting big again. But then Tess gave a quick shake of her head, like she was telling herself that she was done crying, at least for tonight.

"You're sure it was Lamar," she said.

"I'm sure."

"It's got to be more than him just wanting to get at you through me," she said. "Doesn't it?"

She really wanted to figure this out, understand it. By now, Danny knew Tess was curious about everything, even Incredibly Dumb Guy Stuff.

"He's a bully," was the best Danny could do. "Bullies do stuff like this because they can. They do it even if they're as good at something as Lamar is at basketball. Heck, you see it all the time in pro sports." Smiling now as he heard himself say that to her. "Well, *you* don't, but I do. Guys like Lamar get away with everything until teams finally decide they're not worth the trouble. And even after that," Danny said, "they usually get a few last chances."

"That doesn't make it right."

"It's not right," Danny said. "It's just sports."

"But that's not the way it is with you in sports," she said. "Or Will or Ty or Tarik or even Rasheed."

"Nope," he said, "you're right about that. Maybe most right about Rasheed, even if he's the one of us you know the least. He told me that people can't get past his looks, and maybe I couldn't either, at least at the start. But it turns out he's more old school than I am."

"Impossible," she said. "Whatever the oldest school in the world is, you're older than that."

They heard two sounds, one after another. First, thunder in the distance, then the sound of the boat. Danny swiveled his head around and saw the floating water bed heading their way, Tess's uncle behind the wheel.

Danny handed Tess her camera bag and as he did, like it was all one motion, he got up on his tiptoes and gave her a hug. It didn't last long. But it was definitely a hug.

When he pulled back he said, "You okay for real?"

"I will be tomorrow," she said, then pointed a finger at him. "And remember. No going looking for Lamar tonight. No payback. No more trouble. Promise?"

He nodded.

"Say it, mister."

"I promise."

She told him he didn't have to walk her the rest of the way, ran down toward the boat and tossed her bag to her uncle, no longer having to worry about damaging what was inside. Her uncle reached up to take her hand. As he did, Tess turned around and shouted to Danny at the other end of the dock.

"Do not even think about losing to that guy," she said.

They both knew who she meant.

"Got it," he said.

I just hope we get the chance in the play-offs, he thought.

And if we do, I just hope I get my *chance.*

The rain started as the boat pulled away from the dock, and within about a minute was coming down hard. Danny ran up the hill, wondering if the guys might still be playing cards. But he didn't feel like cards tonight. He decided to go back to Gampel instead, read one of the actual books he'd brought with him to camp, an old-time book his dad had given him called *Championship Ball,* about a guy his dad always referred to as Chip Hilton, All-America. "When it comes to basketball," Richie Walker said, "Chip Hilton, All-America, is just like you, only taller."

Danny came out of the woods and took a hard right toward Gampel, walking now. There was no point in running—he was already soaking wet, the rain had become a storm that fast.

He was about fifty yards from Gampel when he saw Lamar standing alone in the rain between Danny and the front door, not wearing a Kobe jersey on this night, wearing a purple Lakers hoody instead, smiling at Danny like he'd been waiting for him.

Great.

Danny just put his head down and kept walking, remembering what he'd just said to Tess about no trouble. Even if trouble was standing right there in front of him.

Lamar, in a voice loud enough to be heard over the wind and rain, said, "Too bad there about your girl's camera."

Danny didn't think Lamar would try anything. There were other kids all around, coming from different directions, running for shelter. So he just kept moving, thinking as he did about an expression his mom liked to use in class when one kid would say he'd only gotten into a beef because another kid was bothering him or her.

Next time, she'd say, do not engage.

"The things people do to other people's property," Lamar said. "It's just a dang shame."

Danny was past him now, not wanting to run, almost to the door.

"What?" Lamar said from behind him. "You don't want to talk to me tonight?"

Do not engage.

Danny was at the door now, starting to turn the handle. He was that close to being inside and out of the rain and away from the sound of Lamar Parrish, who wanted to trash talk you even in the middle of a rainstorm.

Danny turned around, not even sure why, looked right at Lamar, smiled at him now.

"Hey, Lamar," he said.

"S'up, midget?"

Danny dribbled an imaginary ball, made a motion like he was shooting his new jump shot, showing him that perfect form he was working on, like he was putting one up over Lamar from the outside. When he was done, he held the pose in a way he never would in a game, right arm still high, the way Michael Jordan held the pose the night he made the shot in the Finals to beat the Utah Jazz that time.

As if the imaginary shot Danny'd just taken was money all the way.

Now he walked into Gampel, not waiting to hear what else Lamar had to say, not caring, closing the door behind him, thinking to himself, *That's the way I want camp to end.*

At least in my dreams.

LAMAR GOT AWAY WITH IT, OF COURSE.

"No nothin' for a know-nothin'," is the way Tarik described it.

When Jeff LeBow asked about Tess's camera, Lamar just said he shot baskets right up until he went to dinner with some of the guys from the Lakers and that if Mr. LeBow didn't believe him, he should go right ahead and ask them. Then he acted hurt that Mr. LeBow would even think to ask him about something like that, saying, "If I'm gonna be a suspect for every little thing that happens from now to the end of camp, maybe I should make a call to Hoop Stars right now, see if they still want me."

Hoop Stars was an equally famous, competing camp in western Pennsylvania, Danny knew by now, fighting Right Way for the best players every summer, even though Hoop Stars started a couple of weeks later.

"Fortunately, I got him calmed down," Jeff said.

Wow, Danny thought, *what a relief*.

This was after lunch the next day. Danny was in his office, and Jeff was describing his meeting with Lamar, actually trying to tell them how much Lamar liked meeting Tess, how he was hoping to get what he called some Kodak-taking tips from her if she showed up again, just so he could have his own pictures to take home to his mom.

Knowing he was wasting his time, Danny said, "He did it."

"If you don't stop saying things like that," Jeff said, "I'm going to end up breaking up a fight a day between you guys."

"I'm not looking to fight him," Danny said. "I can see now that he's going to win any kind of fight between us." Then he paused just slightly before saying, "except maybe on the court."

"What do you want?"

"For you to see him for what he really is, I guess."

"And what's that?"

"Another guy in sports who's a great player and a bad guy."

"I'm just a guy running a basketball camp," Jeff said. "Josh Cameron's camp. A camp Mr. Cameron is going to be showing up at any day now. And when he does, I'd prefer that he doesn't think the whole thing has turned into *Meatballs* or one of those other dumb camp movies. You say you want to beat him on the court, so wait and beat him on the court."

Danny said he'd try and left.

He was trying. His dad called it grinding. That morning he and Ty had gotten up early and worked out on the bad court, just the two of them, for an hour. Danny had worked more on defense than offense, knowing that one of the ways to get more minutes from Coach Powers in the games he had left was to show he could handle bigger guys, that when other teams tried to use his size against him—gee, that had never happened before—he wasn't going to give up easy baskets.

So they played one-on-one, and Danny told Ty to post up on him as much as he wanted, kept stopping the game to ask what he was trying to do on every play, what worked against that particular move and what didn't.

Ty said that what he concentrated on the hardest when he had a mismatch was to *not* bring the ball down. "Like coaches always say," Ty said. "Bring the ball down, and you turn a big guy into a little guy."

Danny said, "I wish it were that simple."

Eight in the morning and it was so hot already they were sweating buckets. "Coach Rossi talks about it every day," Ty said. "He says, anytime that ball comes down, it's ours."

So they worked on that. Your natural reaction on defense was to put your hands up when a guy was getting ready to shoot. But the key was making your move right before that, reading the guy, keeping your hands out in front of you, ready to flick at the ball or snatch at it as the guy went from his dribble into his shot.

Even against somebody as smart and good and long as Ty, Danny started to get the hang of it, getting his hands on the ball a surprising amount of the time. Every time he did, Danny told Ty not to make it easy for him. And every time he said that, Ty said he wasn't making it easy, Danny was actually starting to annoy him.

It was a good thing, they both decided, even if the long-range plan was annoying another guy Ty's size.

One who liked to go around in a Kobe jersey.

The Celtics were 6–6 with two games to play.

Danny was up to playing two quarters, without knowing if it was because Coach Powers thought he was improving or just because Rasheed was working on the coach every chance he got. But Danny was getting more of a chance, even when games were close in the fourth quarter.

The Celtics weren't the best team here, and Danny had seen them all by now. The two best teams were Ty's team, the Cavaliers, and Lamar's Lakers. That didn't mean the Celtics couldn't beat them in a one-game season. But in his heart—that old thing—he knew that could only happen if it was him and Rasheed in the back-court, and not just for a handful of minutes a game.

Nothing against Cole. Danny liked him as a kid and as a player, and he especially understood why Coach Powers liked him. He played hard, ran the offense the way Coach wanted it run and hardly ever deviated. Even on fast breaks, he did something Coach Powers was always preaching: stopped at the foul line every time, passed to one cutter or the other, only shot the ball himself as a last resort.

He was just the wrong partner for Rasheed.

Danny never said it out loud, even to the other guys, mostly because he knew he wasn't playing well enough himself to be talking about anybody else. But Cole had no feel for the game. He had no imagination. Cole had tunnel vision. He could only see the offense or the defense they were supposed to be running. Like he was some kind of RoboGuard. He didn't know when it was time to forget about the play, just give the ball to Rasheed no matter what they were trying to run.

Danny did.

Danny and Rasheed were both point guards, but that never seemed to matter. When they got the chance, they worked together the way Danny and Ty had with the Warriors.

If you looked at them, you might think they couldn't be more different, and they couldn't have come from more different backgrounds.

But Rasheed had been right: They played the same game.

And in a camp full of big guys, Danny was convinced that the Celtics were at their best when they went small. That meant either Ben Coltrane or David Upshaw at center, Danny and Rasheed at guard, Tarik at power forward and Will at small forward. If Danny were the coach here the way he had been in travel—yeah, right, another in-your-dreams, Walker—those would be the five guys on the court when they were trying to win the game. Make the other team match up with their speed and shooting and ability to push the ball.

Which is what they were doing now against Ty's team, the Cavs, at the end of the first half.

The game was originally scheduled on one of the outside courts, but the refs for their game had ended up someplace else. So it was being played in The House after the regular four o'clock game in there, and there were a ton of kids in the stands, even though it was getting close to dinnertime.

Danny thought, *It's the same with everybody*. If there was a game going on, you stopped to watch it. You couldn't help yourself.

Jack Arnold and Ty had scored most of the points for their team. Rasheed was carrying the Celtics, doing it today by scoring and rebounding. The Celtics were up four points with the ball, holding it for the last shot of the half. Danny had been in the backcourt with Rasheed for the past five minutes or so, playing at the Indy 500 speed that Coach Rossi and the Cavs always liked to play.

They had been in a time-out when Coach Powers told Danny to go into the game. He looked at Danny and Rasheed, pointed one of those bony fingers at them and said, "I want you to find a way to slow this game down."

Rasheed just shook his head.

"Coach, we can try," he said. "But it would be like trying to ride a bike in the fast lane. We can beat these guys at their own game."

"You're sure?"

"Yeah," Rasheed said, in that confident way he had. "I'm sure."

Now they were down to the last play of the half. The play Coach

Powers had called from the sideline was simple enough: "Spread." It was one you saw the real Cavaliers use all the time for LeBron James, at the end of a quarter or half or game.

Give him the ball, give him some room, tell him to make something happen.

On their team it meant giving the ball to Rasheed a few feet inside the half-court line and giving him so much room it looked like he and his man were playing one-on-one.

Jack Arnold, the Boston kid, was guarding him. But Danny could see Ty hanging off Tarik, his man, ready to cut Rasheed off if he tried to go all the way to the basket when he finally made his move. Danny was on the right wing, knowing he was nothing more than a place for Rasheed to dump the ball off if he got jammed up on his drive.

Will, who'd made a couple of threes earlier, was on the other wing, just to give the defense something else to think about.

With fifteen seconds to go, Rasheed took the ball off his hip. He was always saying that it drove him crazy watching the NBA, he always thought guys waited too long to make their move. He started his now. Left-hand dribble, then right. Then left and right again. Two lightning crossovers that did exactly what they were supposed to: staple-gun Jack's feet to the floor.

He was past Jack then.

Ty came up on his right, the Cavs' center took away any room he had on his left. When the center moved up, Will's man dropped down to guard Ben Coltrane.

Nowhere for Rasheed to go. He gave a quick look at the clock and then, to the surprise of everybody in the place, Danny included, he wheeled and put the ball over his head and fired a screaming two-hand pass to Danny.

Kicking it over to him the way he had that first time they'd really played together in the backcourt, the day Danny had shot the air ball instead of passing it back to him.

He was wide open, about twenty feet from the basket, having pinched in. Ty ran right at him, waving his arms, thinking Danny had to be shooting.

But Danny wasn't shooting, and not just because he couldn't even see the basket over Ty's long skinny arms.

He wasn't shooting because of this:

He wasn't making the same mistake twice on a last shot.

This time he was getting the ball back to Rasheed.

The clock above the basket said five seconds.

There was no way to get the ball over Ty, and way too much traffic on either side of Ty to try a bounce pass around him.

Only one opening Danny could see:

Between Ty's legs.

Danny put the ball on the floor and rolled it along the floor, rolled it through his legs as hard as he could, before Ty had a chance to react.

All Rasheed, wide open himself now, had to do was lean over and grab it, and he had a layup.

But he took his eye off the ball for a split second, like a baseball infielder taking his eyes off a routine ground ball—Rasheed was probably as shocked as everyone in the gym that a pass was coming to him this way.

The ball went through his hands as easily as it had gone through Ty and rolled out of bounds as the horn for the half sounded.

Rasheed banged an open palm against the side of his head in frustration, then looked at Danny and pointed to himself. Like, My bad. Danny just smiled. It would have been one heck of an assist.

When he turned from Rasheed, Coach Powers was already on him.

"What was that?" he said.

Not talking in his mean-quiet voice now, talking loud enough for people already in the mess hall to hear him.

He pointed the finger of death at Danny and said, "Did you think you were bowling? Are you ever going to learn?"

He's acting like I lost the game, Danny thought, *because of one stupid pass.*

Except it hadn't been stupid, that was the thing.

Nothing else was happening in The House. He could feel everybody just watching him and Coach.

"Are you *ever* going to learn?" Coach Powers repeated.

Danny just stood there with his head down, taking it again, good at taking it by now, when he heard the sound of the applause.

The guys in the stands were clapping because he was getting yelled at by his coach?

But then Danny heard something else, something much more amazing than applause, heard a calm grown-up voice saying, "Hey, take it easy there, Ed." Heard the voice saying, "That looked like something I'd try, to tell you the truth."

Danny turned around, feeling himself smile as he did, somehow knowing who the voice belonged to before he even put a face with it.

Josh Cameron.

Josh Cameron himself: in a Rolling Stones T-shirt and cut-off jeans and unlaced green Nikes, a baseball cap turned backward on his head, shaking Danny's hand and saying, "Cool pass, kid."

23

THE PLAY-OFFS IN DANNY'S AGE GROUP STARTED THE WEDNESDAY OF the last week at Right Way. If you won your first two games, the final was scheduled for Saturday night in The House, in front of the whole camp, plus any parents who had showed up that day to pack their kids up and take them home. So it was a little like having championship weekend and parents' weekend all wrapped up into one huge deal.

Now all the Celtics had to do was make it to Saturday night.

They were talking about that at dinner the night before the play-offs. It was a weird feeling, the Middletown guys had decided, knowing that if the Celtics won, it meant Ty lost. If Ty's team, the Cavs, won the championship, it meant that Danny and Will lost.

"Or we could all lose," Tarik said. "Any of you bracketologists ever think of that?"

"Shut up," Will said. "That would mean Lamar wins."

"Not happenin'," Rasheed said.

Danny said to Ty and Will, "When was the last time we all weren't on the same side for a big game?"

"Biddy," Will said. "When we were all eight. Ty made that layup at the buzzer, remember?"

"Over me," Danny said. "Like I wasn't there."

"Shoulda done your flop thing," Rasheed said.

"Thing" came out "thang" with him sometimes.

"I don't flop," Danny said.

Tarik groaned. "Oh, sweet Lord, here we go again," he said.

"Nah," Rasheed said. "Now we're on the same side."

"Except for Ty," Will said.

"Remember, it's only summer ball," Ty said.

"I know," Danny said. "It just feels like more now."

He had played a lot the last two games of the regular season, after they'd finally beaten the Cavs the day of his famous bowling-ball pass. Ever since then, Coach Powers had coached as if Josh Cameron were looking over his shoulder, especially in the second half of the Cavs game, when Danny had gotten to play the point as much as Rasheed, dished out a bunch of assists, played pretty much his best all-around game in Maine, maybe even fooled Josh Cameron into thinking this was the way he always played for Coach Powers.

When the game had ended, Danny actually felt good about things for a change, felt some of his old confidence coming back. Josh had come back over to him and said, "You're Richie Walker's boy, right?"

Danny said, yes sir, that was him, all right.

"I should've figured that out the minute you made that pass," Josh said. Then he clapped Danny on the back and yelled over to Coach Powers, "Hey, Ed, I've got my eye on this guy."

Coach Powers pointed at Josh and nodded, like the two of them were in perfect agreement.

When they were outside that day, Tarik had said to Danny, "Well, looky there. Coach Ed seems to have swallowed up his own bad self all of a sudden."

"For now."

"Know what that old man's problem is?" Tarik said. "He just plain forgot what he loved about this game in the first place."

Maybe it was a coincidence, maybe not, but their last two games, Danny had played as much with the first unit as Cole had. Sometimes more. A week ago, he couldn't wait to get out of here. Now he couldn't wait for the play-offs to start.

Summer ball.

Only more.

Danny talked to his mom that night on the telephone. He was hoping to talk to both his parents, mostly because he hadn't talked to his dad one time since the night he'd told him about faking the injury. But his mom informed him that his dad was out taking his nightly walk.

"My dad?" Danny said. "Walking for, like, *exercise*?"

"He says that if he's going to coach next season, he's not doing it from a folding chair."

"Mom," Danny said, "you sure he's not there and just doesn't want to talk to me?"

"He's calmed down about the whole knee thing," she said, then quickly added, "Somewhat, anyway. You know your dad. He just needs longer to work through things than most people."

Danny said, "Is he coming with you when you come to pick me up?"

When she didn't answer right away, Danny knew.

"It's a long time for him to sit in the car," his mom said.

"The finals are on Saturday night if we make it."

There was a pause and then his mom said, "I know. And now let's change the subject, shall we?"

"Fine with me."

Ali Walker said, "So, how goes the battle?"

"Still a battle," Danny said, then filled her in on his fight with Lamar, his suspension, Tess's camera. How he and Rasheed were boys now. Josh Cameron giving him a shout-out after he made the funky pass. When Danny was done, he felt like he'd just made some kind of presentation in front of her class: "How I Spent My Summer Vacation," by Danny Walker.

"I'm sorry about the fight, Mom," he said. "But he was picking on Zach."

His mom surprised him then. The way she surprised him a lot. "Don't beat yourself up because a big guy was about to beat up a little guy."

"I told you I wouldn't fight."

"And I told you," she said, "that one of the secrets to life is *picking* your fights."

"Play-offs start tomorrow," he said.

"How's the old coach?"

"Same old. But he's been letting me play more."

"*Hel*-lo," his mom said. "He wants to win, right?"

Danny smiled. "Thanks, Mom."

"You don't need more of a pep talk?" she said. "I've got a lot more material."

"I'm good."

"Yes, you are," she said. "You are the goodest."

Danny said, "And you're an English teacher?"

"See you Saturday night for the big game," she said.

"If we make it that far."

"You will."

"You're sure of that?"

"It's who you are, kiddo," she said.

"Do me a favor?"

"Anything."

"Remind Dad of that if you get a chance."

The Celtics, as the number 6 team, drew the Bulls, number 3, in the first round. If they beat the Bulls, that meant they were probably going to play the Cavs, Ty's team, in the semis.

Then, if everything worked out the way it was supposed to, they'd play the Lakers, the top seed, in the finals.

Them against Lamar.

Sometimes you didn't get to pick your fights.

Sometimes, Danny thought, *they picked you.*

"Winning the championship, that's what you came here for," Coach Powers said in their pregame huddle.

Danny wanted to say, No, that's what *you* came here for.

They had split their two games with the Bulls, basically a two-man team with the two Brooklyn AAU guys, Kareem Dell and TJ Tucker. The Celtics had lost the first one when Danny shot the air ball at the end, then won the last regular-season game, one Rasheed said didn't count because the Bulls' coach, Coach Pedulla, had barely played Kareem or TJ in the second half.

"Understand," Rasheed had said to Danny in the layup line. "They didn't *want* to win yesterday. They wanted the seedings the way they already were, them at three and us at six. You hear what I'm tellin' you? These guys wanted us."

"My mom always says, be careful what you wish for," Danny said, grinning at him.

"Mine, too."

Cole started with Rasheed in the backcourt. Danny figured the way Coach Powers had been using him, he'd get in at the end of the first quarter or maybe start the second. But when the Celtics got behind by ten points after the first three minutes, in a blink, Coach Powers said, "Walker."

Danny was a few seats down from him. "Yes, Coach?"

Coach Powers turned and said, "I was wondering if you might be interested in going into the game?"

Now Danny jumped up. "Yes, Coach!"

"Play the point for a little bit," he said, "and cover that pesky boy with the crew cut. See if we can get him to do the same with you at the other end."

The pesky boy with the crew cut, and more freckles than Danny had ever seen on one face, was Ricky Hartmann. By now, having gone through the regular season and seen a bunch of games, Danny knew Ricky was pretty much the one guy at Right Way you didn't want guarding you, under any circumstances. Will and Tarik, who had made it their mission to know as much as possible about as many campers as possible, said Ricky was a defensive back in football at home in Philadelphia. Before he would foul out of a game, and he fouled out of almost every game, he came after you like he was blitzing a quarterback, sometimes from the quarterback's blind side.

He took Danny now, the way Coach Powers wanted.

"Oh, man, is this ever taking one for the team," Danny said to Rasheed a couple minutes later, while Tarik took two foul shots. Ricky Hartmann had already fouled Danny once, sending him sliding into the first row of bleachers when the two of them dove for a loose ball.

"You're *part* of this team now," Rasheed said. "That's the main thing."

It wasn't as if Danny came into the game and started running rings around Ricky Hartmann. Ricky aggressively bodied up on him every chance he got, held him when the ref wasn't looking, even hip-checked Danny right off the court one time when Danny tried to get out on a fast break Rasheed was leading. Somehow, though, Danny held his own. More importantly, Rasheed, even with Kareem guarding *him* now, was getting some room to maneuver, starting to get his points in bunches.

The Celtics cut the lead to four by halftime.

It felt like a real game now.

Right before the second half started, Coach Powers said, "Same group we opened the game with." Then he paused. "Except for Cole. Walker, you take his place for now."

When they started to break the huddle, Danny felt somebody grab his arm, hard, from behind.

He turned around and saw that it was Cole.

"This should've been your spot all along," he said. "Now, go kick their butts."

There were no surprises from the Bulls, not in a play-off game. They were just going to ride Kareem and TJ as far as they could. With seven minutes left, the two of them had stretched the Bulls' lead to twelve points, their biggest lead of the game. The Bulls had gone to a zone, and Rasheed, playing with four fouls, wasn't just missing, he'd gotten frustrated trying to get open looks at the basket.

Finally Coach Powers, more out of desperation than anything else, called a time-out and put Will Stoddard in the game, said he was giving Will a chance to be what he called his designated zone-buster.

Even now, facing elimination in the first round, Will was incapable of being anybody except himself.

"You know what they say, Coach?" Will said.

"What do they say, Mr. Stoddard?"

Will hit him with one of his favorite lines then. "There's no greater tragedy in basketball than being hot and not knowing it."

"You think this is funny, son?" Coach Powers said.

"No, sir," Will said. "Just fun."

Will hit his first two threes. Then another shot with his foot on the three-point line. And all those baskets did was change everything for the Celtics, just like that. Danny had seen it before, a couple of baskets changing everything. Now it had happened here, against the Bulls. It was one of the things Danny loved about sports, how fast things changed. His dad always said that it was something that had always fascinated him about all sports, not just basketball—how fragile games could be, how they could turn on the smallest moment or play, and how you better be ready when they did.

Will had done exactly what he was supposed to do, which meant he had shot the Bulls right out of their zone. Ricky Hartmann was still on Danny when the Bulls went back to man-to-man, Kareem was still on Rasheed. With two minutes left, Rasheed beat Kareem off the dribble and seemed to have a clear path right down the middle. But Ricky Hartmann switched off Danny and got in his way just as Rasheed dropped his shoulder for his drive.

Rasheed went down, Ricky went down.

Ball went in.

Nick Pinto, reffing the game, didn't hesitate, signaling offensive foul.

Rasheed had fouled out.

Anybody else, Danny knew, including Danny himself, would have jumped up and protested the call, because it was that close. And usually a call like this, this late in the game, this late in an *important* game, went to star players.

Rasheed just sat there. Nick, answering a question Rasheed hadn't even asked, said, "He beat you to the spot."

Rasheed just shook his head, stayed where he was, arms folded across his knees. Chillin'. Even now.

Danny put a hand down to pull him up. Before Rasheed reached up to take it, he looked at Danny and said, "World's full of danged floppers, you know?"

"I thought it was on him this time," Danny said and pulled him up.

"Yo," Rasheed said. "Now you all got to pick me up in more ways than one."

Danny grinned at him. "Don't worry, dog," he said. "I got you."

Kareem chased down a loose ball with forty seconds left, turned around and made a truly outrageous three-pointer to put the Bulls ahead by one. Will missed a wide-open three at the other end, first shot he'd missed since Coach Powers put him in. As soon as TJ got the rebound, David Upshaw fouled him.

Twenty-two seconds left.

Coach Powers called their last time-out.

He said they were going small: Danny, Tarik, Will, Cole, plus David. Coach said that if TJ made both free throws, putting the Bulls up three, to look for Will at the other end, out beyond the arc.

If they only needed a two to tie or win the game, Coach Powers said for them to spread it once they got over half-court.

"Spread it for who?" Danny said.

"You," Coach Ed Powers said.

"Got it," he said, like he always ended up with the rock with the game on the line.

TJ, who could do everything on a court except shoot free throws, missed them both. David Upshaw got the rebound, Danny pushed the ball hard over half-court then put the brakes on, passed it to Will and got it right back.

He put the ball on his hip and checked the clock.

Ricky Hartmann was eyeballing him, in a defensive crouch, looking as if he really might try to tackle Danny as soon as he made a move.

Danny started his dribble with ten seconds left. Ricky got right up on him. Danny dusted him with a crossover that was up there with Rasheed's best. Then he broke into the clear at the top of the circle.

TJ Tucker came over from the corner, covering about twenty feet with about two long strides.

It had come down to Danny against TJ again, the way it had when Danny shot the air ball.

TJ Tucker, whose arms were even longer than broom handles.

Danny slowed up just slightly at the free throw line, pulled the ball in, went into his shooting motion, hands in perfect position.

TJ, with those amazing ups of his, went *way* up, like he wasn't just trying to block the shot, like he wanted to be another guy catching one of Danny's shots.

Small problem.

Danny didn't shoot it.

He sold his fake, though, sold it as well as he'd ever sold a fake in his life.

Then he waited for gravity.

What goes up, he thought, must come down.

When TJ did come down, like he was falling out of the sky, Danny leaned in and waited for the contact he knew was coming, then right before TJ landed on top of him, he fired the ball at the basket.

He landed hard.

But rolled like a champ.

The way Nick Pinto said little guys had to.

Then Danny got up, tucked his jersey back into his shorts, went to the line, knocked down the two free throws that put the Celtics into the second round, the whole thing becoming official once Kareem missed a wild heave at the very end.

Danny was at half-court when the horn sounded. He felt a tap on his shoulder and turned around.

"Glad you hung around this place?" Nick Pinto said.

THEY WENT INTO CEDARVILLE AFTER THE GAME, NICK PINTO DRIV-
ing. Even after everything that had happened at Right Way, it still
seemed to Danny as if it were just the other day that Nick had
driven them to camp from the Portland airport.

"Sure am going to miss that hooptie bus," Tarik said. "The
4 train doesn't shake like this when it comes into the Yankee
Stadium stop."

Nick dropped them in front of Pops and they went right for
their favorite booth, where everybody ordered milk shakes, except
for Rasheed, who said the only way to celebrate was with a root
beer float.

"Hooptie," Will said, shaking his head. "Another cool word."

"Maybe you should have been keeping a diary on stuff Tarik
says," Danny said. "In case you forget some of them when you
get home."

"Get home and deal with your general heartbreak on not being
black," Tarik said.

Will had ripped through his milk shake, now made a loud sucking sound as he finished it. "You have to keep throwing that in my
face," he said.

Ty wasn't with them—his coach had scheduled a nighttime

practice to get the Cavs ready to play the Celtics in the semis tomorrow night.

Will said, "We should have T-shirts made when we get home, saying, 'I Survived Basketball Camp.'"

"On the back you can put 'Barely,'" Danny said.

Tarik and Rasheed said they were going to walk down to the dock and buy some taffy. Will and Danny said they'd wait for them in front of Pops, on one of the benches near the front door.

Just the two of them for a change, not surrounded by the other campers at Right Way. *Now, this felt right,* Danny thought, felt like all the other times when it was just him and Will Stoddard.

"What?" Will said.

"I didn't say anything."

"But you want to," Will said. "You forget sometimes that I know you as well as Tess does."

There was a piece of paper near his sneakers, some kind of flyer somebody had dropped. Danny picked it up, crumpled it into a ball, tossed it into the wire basket near the curb without it even touching the sides.

"Money," he said.

"I'm good with that," Will said, grinning. "Because I am willing to pay you to find out what's bothering you all of a sudden."

"I've been thinking about something since the game ended," he said. "If we win, which means I win, that means Coach Powers wins, too."

"Only you want him to lose," Will said.

"Yeah," Danny said. "I want there to be some secret formula where we win and he loses."

"Because if we win the camp championship, he gets the only thing that matters to him," Will said, "even though he did everything possible to drag us down. Basically, it's like dealing with our parents. There are times when they know they're wrong about something and we know they're wrong, but they'd never admit that in a million trillion years."

"I want him to admit he was wrong about me," Danny said.

"First we win the game," Will said, "and then we worry about the rest of it."

"You do sound like Tess sometimes."

"I'm going to take that as a compliment," Will said, then gave him a sideways look. "She definitely can't hang around for the finals if we make it?"

"She's out of here tomorrow on JetBlue," Danny said. "Her mom wants her back."

"So we call her after the game and tell her all about it," Will said.

Danny looked at Will Stoddard, the best friend of his life, and said, "You think we're gonna win this game?"

Will reached out so Danny could bump him some fist.

"We always have," he said.

They beat the Cavs the next day, beat them by six points finally, beat them because of what became a one-on-one game between Rasheed and Ty, and Rasheed was better on this day. Maybe it would have been different the next day. But today is the only one that ever matters in sports.

It wasn't that either one of them was hogging the ball or being selfish, because neither was that kind of player. They hadn't suddenly morphed into being Lamar. It was just that Rasheed finally took over for the Celtics, and Ty took over for the Cavs, and the two of them guarding each other and getting after each other was the way this game was supposed to end. It was like an old-time play-off game that Richie Walker had taped for Danny off ESPN Classic once: Larry Bird and the Celtics went up against Dominique Wilkens and the Atlanta Hawks, matching each other basket for basket, until Wilkens started missing at the end and the Celtics won.

Even the coaches seemed to get what was happening. Maybe that was why Coach Powers finally let Rasheed guard Ty and Coach Tom Rossi put Ty on Rasheed at the other end and then both coaches pretty much stayed out of the way after that.

Rasheed scored the last ten points for the Celtics. Ty was on his way to doing pretty much the same thing until he missed a couple of open jumpers. Danny knew why, even if nobody else in the gym did, knew what happened to Ty's shot when his legs got tired. He stopped elevating enough, started firing line drives at the basket.

Ty even missed the front end of a one-and-one with forty seconds to go. After that, Rasheed made six straight free throws and the Celtics were in the finals against the Lakers, who had blown out the Knicks, biggest blowout of the whole camp, somebody said, in the first semifinal game.

When the Celtics–Cavs game was over, Rasheed went and found Ty at half-court, gave him what Tarik called the "brother snap." They shook hands by locking their thumbs, pulled close together and bumped shoulders, backed away, shook hands again with the tips of their fingers, snapped their hands away to finish.

Then Danny heard Ty say, "You were better."

Rasheed said, "Nah, I just had more legs than you at the end."

"You're the best I've ever played against," Ty said.

"Today," Rasheed said. He knew. It was always about today. "Next time it would probably be you."

"Hope there is one," Ty said. "A next time, I mean."

They all heard Lamar then.

"Don't come to me looking for a big hug when we whup y'all's butts in the finals," he said in a loud voice. Everybody in the gym looked at him now.

Which, Danny knew, was the point.

Rasheed just calmly stared at him, without saying a word. Stared for what felt to Danny like five minutes. You could see how uncomfortable it made Lamar.

"Got nothin' to say, 'Sheed?" Lamar said.

Rasheed just shrugged.

Lamar stood there, nervous now, cracking his knuckles, the scene not playing out the way he intended. "Well, we'll see what you got to say Saturday night. You and your little boy there."

Now Rasheed smiled.

And Lamar gave up.

"That's right, give me that big spit-eating grin now," he said. "Till I wipe it right off your face on Saturday."

He walked out of The House.

Danny said to Rasheed, "That was the coolest trash talk of all time."

"I didn't say anything," Rasheed said.

"That's why," Danny said.

On Friday night they watched Zach's team win the eleven- and twelve-year-old championship, win it so easily Zach didn't even have to play the last five minutes of the game.

He was the smallest kid on either team, and it didn't matter. If you knew anything about basketball—and maybe even if you didn't—he was the only player on either team you were interested in watching. Mostly because he was playing a different game than the rest of the kids, even the ones who were a lot bigger than he was.

It was as if he knew something the rest of them, even his own teammates, didn't.

When the game was over, before the trophy presentation, Danny saw an ending to this kind of game he had seen before, watched a couple of the bigger kids put Zach up on their shoulders and carry him around like he was the trophy.

Danny waited until the celebration was over before he went over to Zach, carrying the bag with the gift inside.

He handed it to Zach now, and Zach opened it up to find the same indoor/outdoor ball Lamar had wrecked on him. Danny had spotted it in the window at Bob's Sports in Cedarville.

"You didn't have to get me anything," Zach said. "I'm the one who should be getting you something."

"You were great tonight," Danny said. "Awesome, dude. I mean it."

Zach looked down. "I wouldn't have made it without you," he said.

"Yeah," Danny said, "you would have. My father always tells me something about sports." It was amazing how many times he quoted his dad. Even now, when his dad wasn't speaking to him. "He says that the guys who aren't any good, they're the ones who always find excuses. But the guys who *are* good enough, they always find a way. It just took you a little time to find your way here."

Then Danny said he'd see Zach back at Gampel later, there was something he needed to do right now.

Go someplace and play.

Danny cut across the lawn and made his way to the bad court. The lighting on it was as bad as the playing surface—the best light actually came from the end nearest the parking lot, where there were a couple of old-fashioned-type streetlamps.

Danny had picked up a ball along the way, one lying near the court outside Staples. And had stopped in the mess hall to get a folding chair. Something to use as a target for his passes, just like in his driveway.

So he had a ball and a chair and a court all to himself. When it was like that, there really was no such thing as a bad court.

He went through all his stuff now. Dribbled the length of the court with his right hand, came back with his left, then up and down again, this time switching hands as he went.

Free throws, outside shots, driving layups with both hands.

Hitting the chair with two-hand chest passes, then bounce passes, even a couple of no-looks, knocking the chair over and picking it up and then hitting it again.

Then he started moving the chair around. Drive and pass to one corner, then the other. Move it out to the wing and hit it there.

Getting ready for the game the only way he knew how.

He started driving hard to the basket, pulling up, shooting his high-arc shot over an imaginary tall guy, Danny imagining arms that stretched to the stars. He kept taking that shot until he could make it three times in a row.

It was late now, and he should have been tired, but he wasn't, even working himself like this. Mostly because this wasn't work, not to him.

He didn't know how much he'd get to play against the Lakers. Coach Powers had talked a lot at practice today about how big the Lakers were, even in the backcourt. But Danny knew this: He was going to be ready, no matter how little his name got called. His mom was going to be there tomorrow. He was *not* going to stink up the joint in front of her.

Or Josh Cameron.

When he finally stopped, out of breath, sweating, he felt like he'd just finished playing a game.

It was then that he turned and saw Coach Powers standing over near the woods, at the start of the path that took you back to the coaches' cabins.

Standing there like some kind of ghost.

Danny wanted to say something, call out to him. But there was nothing left to say. Nothing he could say at this point that was going to change anything between them.

So Danny just stood there, in what felt like the most natural pose in the world to him, ball on his right hip. Coach Powers stayed where he was, hands in his pockets. There was just the night between them.

Then he turned and walked into the woods. If Danny hadn't heard his slow steps on the gravel path he would have wondered if he really had seen a ghost, would have wondered if the coach had even been there at all.

THERE WAS SOMEONE WITH ALI WALKER WHEN DANNY FINALLY SPOT-
ted her Saturday morning in the crowd of parents walking up from
the parking lots.

It wasn't his dad.

Just the next best thing on this particular day.

Tess.

Camera bag slung over her shoulder.

After Danny had broken loose from his mom, after a Mom hug
that tried to squeeze all the oxygen out of his body, Danny said to
Tess, "You're supposed to be home."

"Change of plans," she said. "It turns out that I'm hitching a
ride back with you guys."

It had been arranged when they'd gone off to camp that Ali
Walker was the designated parent from Middletown and would
drive Danny, Will and Ty home. Ali had brought her Suburban, so
there was plenty of room for Tess.

"So you get to see the big game," Danny said.

"I guess," Tess said, smiling at him. "I mean, as long as I'm
here."

Ali didn't want to talk about the big game, she wanted to tell
him that he needed a haircut as soon as he got home and was he
packed and if he was packed, was he sure he had everything?

224

Danny said yes, to all of the above. She said, prove it, so he and his mom and Tess walked down to Gampel.

Zach was sitting on his bunk when they got there, his parents having left a message that they were stuck in traffic somewhere on the highway between Boston and here.

Ali said, "Is this the budding superstar I've been hearing about?"

Zach stood, looked up, shook her hand and said, "Nice to meet you, Mrs. Walker."

They all stayed in Gampel while Danny proved to his mom that he hadn't forgotten anything major, and then they all went outside so Tess could take some pictures before lunch.

The game wasn't until seven-thirty, which meant there were still almost eight hours to wait. But Danny was fine with that. It was a great feeling, the sense of anticipation and the nervousness you got before a big game, as long as the day of the big game had finally arrived.

The only thing better was actually playing the game.

That never changed, no matter where the game was, no matter who it was against.

Even at camp.

There was a barbecue for the campers and parents that began a little after four o'clock. Things were set up that way so the players from both the Celtics and Lakers would have time to not only get something in their stomachs but actually digest it before the opening tip. It was at the barbecue, after Ali Walker and Danny and Tess had taken a quick trip into town so she could see Cedarville, that she finally got to meet Tarik and Rasheed.

"My son tells me you're even better than he thought you were in North Carolina," Ali said.

Rasheed grinned. "He means how good he thought I was until he flopped on me."

"I didn't flop," Danny said.

Ali said to Rasheed, "You're both probably talking to the wrong parent on this."

Danny looked at her. "How's Dad doing?" It was the first time they'd talked about him all day.

"I'm under strict orders to call him the minute the game is over."

When they sat down to eat, his mom was between Will and Tarik, which meant she spent the whole barbecue laughing her head off. It was funny, Danny thought now, watching her, seeing her as comfortable as she'd always been with his friends. Sometimes you didn't even know what you were missing when you were away from somebody until you were back with them. And one of the things he had missed most being up here at camp was the loud, happy sound of his mother's laughter.

He still wished his dad were here, for a lot of reasons, one of them being that this reminded him of all the other games his father had missed when his parents had been apart all those years, all those years when Danny had pretty much convinced himself that his dad was never coming back.

It also brought him back to the start of camp when he felt lower than dirt.

He looked up then, all the way across the mess hall, like this was some kind of weird cue, and saw Lamar Parrish, already dressed for the game in his Lakers jersey, glaring at him.

Lamar pointed to himself first, mouthed the word *Me,* then pointed at Danny.

You.

Danny turned and said to Will and Tarik and Rasheed, "You guys wanna go shoot?"

His mom said, "You hardly ate anything, not that a person would consider that any kind of breaking news."

"Mom," Danny said, "I can't sit here anymore, I gotta move."

She smiled at him and said, "Like a streak of light."

All Danny heard from Tess was the click of her camera.

Danny thought there was an outside shot that he might start, but Coach Powers went with their normal starting five, which meant Cole was with Rasheed.

Before they went inside The House to warm up, a few minutes after seven o'clock, Coach Powers took them all over to the lake side of the building, and sat them down in the grass. There were no locker rooms at The House, just bathrooms, so all pregame meetings like this always took place out here. It was a perfect night, not too hot, not too muggy.

The Celtics were stretched out in one long line. Coach Powers got down on one knee, so he was facing all of them.

"You get only so many games in your life when you play for a championship," he began. "I read in a book one time, I forget where, the writer asked, If there were only three or four sunsets you were going to see in your whole life, how valuable would they be? So if I told you that tonight was only one of the three or four times in your life when you might play for the title of something, how dear would you hold this one game of basketball?"

There was something in his eyes now Danny hadn't seen before, a light in them, some kind of spark.

Without looking around at his teammates, Danny knew the coach had their attention.

"It doesn't matter where the game is, or who it's against," he said. "But you know the feeling inside you is different today. You know because that feeling has been inside you since you got up this morning." He paused. "Because today *is* different, that's why. Today is different because you're playing for something today. Not a trophy. Or to prove something to me or the parents who are here or the counselors or the other coaches, or even Mr. Josh Cameron himself. You're here to prove something to yourselves tonight—that you're the best of the best."

He paused again and said, "People who don't play sports will never have this feeling for one day in their lives."

He's right, Danny thought. He hated to admit it, especially about a guy he'd hated from the first day. But Coach Powers was right. For the first time, Danny at least could see why he might have been a great coach in the first place.

"Every pass, every shot," he said, once more in that voice of his that made you strain to hear, pointing his finger at them. "Play every play as if the whole game is riding on it. From the time you step on that court in a few minutes, you keep one picture in your heads: You picture what the faces of the other team will look like if they beat you. *And then you do whatever it takes to make sure they don't.*"

Now Coach Powers was standing up, raising his voice at the same time, like he was giving a sermon in church.

"Are you going to let them beat you?"

"No!" they yelled back at him.

"Are we going to win the game?"

"Yes!"

"Then let's do this!"

They ran back inside.

They got back into layup lines for a couple of minutes, then shot around until the horn sounded. Will always waited until everybody else on the team was finished shooting and then stayed out until he made one more three. Danny always waited with him, and did now. So they were the last two back to the Celtics' huddle, Will a few feet ahead of him.

Before they got there, Danny got popped from his blind side like you did when somebody on your team didn't call out a pick in time.

He should have known who it was.

"Sorry," Lamar Parrish said to him. "You're so little I didn't see you."

For the whole first quarter, neither team was more than a basket ahead. Lamar was taking most of the shots for his team, Rasheed was doing the thing he did best for the Celtics, letting the game come to him, doing everything he could to get everybody else on his team involved. They had come out in a man-to-man, Coach Powers putting Rasheed on Lamar. The Lakers were in a zone because they were always in a zone, because as talented as Lamar was, there was no place you could hide him in a man-to-man—he was that lazy when the other team had the ball.

He didn't care about defense the way he didn't care about anything except shooting.

And himself.

The Lakers scored three quick baskets to start the second quarter, extending their lead to eight. That was when Danny got into the game. It did more to hurt the Celtics than help them. The other Laker guard, a redheaded kid named Tommy Main, was as tall as Lamar and impossible for Danny to guard. With Lamar taking a rest—because nobody at Right Way, not even him, was allowed to play all four quarters, not even in the play-offs—Tommy Main started posting Danny up almost every time the Lakers had the ball.

By the time Coach Powers realized what he was watching and put the Celtics into a zone, the Lakers were ahead by fourteen points.

With two minutes to go before the half, Coach Powers got Danny out of there. As Danny went past him to take a seat at the end of the bench, Coach snapped, "In a championship game, defense wins."

The Laker lead was still fourteen at the half. Coach Powers hustled them back outside, sat them down and immediately laced into the whole team, his voice a raspy whisper somebody even twenty feet away wouldn't have been able to hear.

This was *his* kind of trash talk, that voice you had to strain to hear, those blue-looking veins trying to pop right out of his forehead.

"I thought you wanted this as much as I do," he said. "I thought winning a championship still mattered in sports, as long as it was the championship of something. But apparently I was wrong. You're all playing like a bunch of quitters."

They all just sat there, some of them with their heads down, just taking it from him. He didn't allow for one second that the Lakers might just be playing better, that the Lakers might want to win the game, too. As usual, Coach Powers was putting it all on them, calling them the worst thing in the world:

Quitters.

What Richie had called Danny.

All Danny could think of was getting back inside, doing whatever he could do to help his team win, and then leaving this one gym knowing that this guy was never going to be his coach ever again.

He would try to win the game for himself and for his teammates, and then he was gone. In the language of Tarik Meminger, he was taillights.

"Am I making myself clear, Mr. Walker?"

Danny knew he'd missed something. He just didn't know *what* he had missed, the way it was in class when your mind wandered and then you realized the teacher was talking to you. So he just said, "Yes sir."

Coach Powers said, "For the rest of this game, if you don't guard, you don't play."

He was standing over Danny now.

"But between you and I," Coach Powers said, "you haven't guarded anybody yet, have you?"

Danny heard his mom before he saw her.

"Between you and me," Ali Walker said.

Coach Powers turned around. Danny's mom was standing right there, a bottle of water in her hand, Tess at her side. .

"I beg your pardon," Coach Powers said.

"It's not between you and I," Ali said. "It's between you and me." She was smiling pleasantly, but Danny knew the look, it was the same as if she was hitting him right in the teeth.

"And you are?"

"Ali Walker."

"Oh," Coach Ed Powers said. "Mr. Walker's mother."

"Danny's mom," she said. "Richie's wife. I'm sure you remember my husband."

There was something about her body language, the way she was looking at him, that smile fixed in place, that let Coach Powers know he shouldn't tangle with her, not here. "I'm not too good with words sometimes," he said.

She said, "So I'm told," and walked away.

Coach Powers took a couple of steps away from his players,

as if he wanted to say one more thing to her, but didn't. Tarik took the opportunity to whisper in Danny's ear, "Oh, baby. Your mom . . . from *downtown!*"

Coach Powers came back to them now, trying to act as if nothing had happened. He talked about what they were going to do on defense and offense to start the second half. All the while Danny kept thinking, *However much I thought I was buried before with this coach, this time they're going to need heavy equipment to dig me out.*

As they started back toward the gym, Coach Powers caught up with Danny, stopped him with a tap on his shoulder.

"Between you and *me?*" he said. "I meant what I said before."

"I know you did, Coach."

"You don't guard, you don't play, whether your mother likes me or not."

Danny stopped at the outdoor fountain for a drink of water, splashed some water on his face, trying to get himself fired back up after everything that had just happened.

He didn't need to worry about that.

When he walked back inside, the first person he saw, just inside the door, was his dad.

26

His dad looked the same as always: plain gray t-shirt, jeans, unlaced Reebok high-tops. He needed a haircut. From a distance, anybody who didn't know him could have confused him with one of the counselors.

But there wasn't much distance between Danny and his dad for long. He ran right for Richie Walker and hugged him, not caring whether his teammates were watching or not.

"You came," he said.

"I would've been here for the start of the game, but JetBlue picked this day to have equipment problems at JFK," his dad said.

"You're here now. That's all I care about."

His dad pushed back, looked down at him. "I'm always telling you that you gotta let stuff go eventually. So I followed my own advice for a change. I was sitting there at the breakfast table this morning, thinking about you and your mom being here and me being there by myself . . ." He grinned at Danny and shrugged, looking even more like a kid.

Danny pointed to the scoreboard. "You haven't missed much."

"Can you beat these guys?"

"I honestly don't know."

"Wrong answer," Richie Walker said, but he wasn't looking at Danny now. He was looking over him and past him, in the direction of the court.

"Hello, Ed," he said.

Danny turned. There was Coach Powers, standing a few feet away from them with his arms crossed.

"Richie," the coach said. "Long time no see."

Neither one of them made any kind of move to get closer, maybe shake hands. Danny just stood there, feeling as if he were between them now in more ways than one.

Finally Coach Powers said, "I'm sorry to break up this re-union, but we've got a game we're trying to win here," and started walking in that slow, straight-backed walk of his toward the Celtics' bench.

Richie Walker squeezed his son's shoulder.

"So go do that," he said. "Go win the game."

"He might only play me for, like, a couple more minutes."

"If he does," his dad said, "then make them the best couple minutes of your life."

Rasheed kept them in the game in the third quarter, getting inside the Lakers' zone just enough, drawing the guys on the Lakers to him who actually wanted to play defense before he'd get another shot or feed David or Ben or Alex. And Tarik was doing a decent job on Lamar, bumping him every chance he got, whether Lamar had the ball or not, even getting Lamar to retaliate a couple of times and get called for fouls.

Still, the best the Celtics could do was trade baskets, and it was getting too late in the game for that. They were still too far behind.

Coach Ed wouldn't change his defense, though, wouldn't double Lamar or go to a zone. His way, to the end. The Coach Ed Powers My-Way-or-the-Highway Basketball Camp. Every once in a while, he would allow the Celtics to press for a couple of posses-sions. But as soon as Lamar or somebody got an easy bucket, he'd take the press off.

And through it all, Danny Walker was dying. Because he was just sitting there, feeling more like a cheerleader again than part of the team, trying to remember a time in his life when he couldn't get off the bench in the second half of a game like this.

Only he couldn't.

Maybe Coach Powers planned on sticking it to the whole family this time.

At the end of the third quarter, the Celtics were still down nine points, 47–38.

In the huddle Coach Powers said, "Now, listen up."

Rasheed Hill said, "No. *You* listen up."

Not raising his voice even a little bit. Just talking to Ed Powers the way he had always talked to them.

Rasheed pointed to Danny and said, "Put him in the game. Or take me out."

The only change of expression from the old man, Danny saw, was that big vein on his forehead.

"You're a great player, son," he said to Rasheed. "And I need you. But this is still my team."

"Play both of us or neither one of us," Rasheed said, standing his ground. "You got to declare now whether you want to win as much as you say." Rasheed looked at Danny. "How would you play these guys?"

Danny looked at Rasheed so he didn't have to look at Coach Powers, swallowed hard, then did something he'd wanted to do since the first day of practice:

Pretended Ed Powers wasn't even there.

Behind them he heard the buzzer from the scorer's table that meant the quarter break was over.

"Box-and-one," Danny said. "Me on Lamar, just to make him mad. Extend the help I get, and I'll need a lot, all the way to the three-point line. And press every chance we get, our zone press, except with me still on Lamar."

Nick Pinto, reffing the final, tapped Powers on his shoulder. "Coach, I need your guys to get out there."

Coach Powers nodded. He looked older than ever, sad and old. His eyes were on Rasheed when he said, "Walker, get in for Tarik." Then he went and sat down.

"Yesssss!" Will hissed in Danny's ear.

It was Celtics' ball to start the fourth. Danny and Rasheed went to take it out. Danny allowed himself one quick look at his dad, who put his right hand down next to his knee and made it into a fist.

Danny said to Rasheed, "What just happened back there?"

Rasheed, his face as much a blank wall as ever, said, "I thought I told you I didn't come here to lose."

He took the ball out, Danny brought it up, head-faked Lamar at the top of their zone, got past him as easily as if he were walking through his own front door, no-looked a bullet pass to Rasheed on the right wing.

Rasheed for three.

Game on.

Lamar reacted to Danny guarding him pretty much the way Danny expected him to.

"Shoo, fly," he said.

But right away you could see how much it annoyed him. When Lamar didn't have the ball, Danny shadowed him wherever he went, getting in his space, bumping him the way Tarik had.

Turning the tables, finally.

Getting under *his* skin now.

Every chance Danny got, he would put a hand on him, the way

guys did all the time on defense, trying to keep their man located. As soon as he would, Lamar would say, "Get offa me!"

Danny didn't say a word back to him, didn't react even when Lamar would wait until he thought the refs weren't watching and slap his hand away. Or just give him a shove. It was like tetherball. Danny just kept coming back.

With five minutes left to play and the ball on the other side of the court, Danny was the one who gave Lamar a little shove. This time Lamar slapped his hand away so hard you could hear it all over the House.

Nick Pinto, who happened to be looking right at them, immediately whistled him for a technical.

"He hit me first, man, are you blind?" Lamar said.

Nick, already walking with Rasheed toward the free throw line, stopped. "I didn't quite catch that?"

"Yo," Lamar said. "He's got his hand on me all the time and doesn't get a whistle on that, is all I'm sayin'."

"You play, Lamar. I'll ref. Let's see if we can make that work for both of us."

Rasheed made two free throws on the technical. Celtics ball, side out. Danny threw a bounce pass to a cutting Rasheed for an easy layup.

And just like that, the Lakers' lead was down to two.

Lamar, steaming now, came out of the time-out their coach called and made a three. "See that right there, midget?" he said to Danny as he held his pose. "That right there is a man shot."

With a minute and a half left, the Celtics were still down a basket. Tarik got another rebound and Danny did a run-out, trying to beat the Lakers down the court, Tarik threw him a perfect pass at halfcourt.

Danny was flying to the basket, ahead of the pack, when the lights went out.

Lamar had actually made a play on defense.

He had come from the other side of the court, come flying himself, blocked Danny's shot, knocked him right off the court and into one of the closed doors that opened into the front hall.

The lights hadn't actually gone all the way out.

It was like somebody had put them on dimmer.

Somehow Danny hit his head and his knee at the same time. Right away he took the kind of inventory you did when you got hurt and knew his right knee—the one he'd tried to use to get himself out of here—hurt much worse than his head.

He didn't even think about rubbing it.

Just rolled over and sat up, like the whole thing was no big deal.

The first people he saw over him, no big surprise, were his parents. Behind them, he saw Coach Powers, not over to see how Danny was doing but in Nick Pinto's face, yelling at him about a foul.

Ali Walker said, "You okay?"

"I'm good."

Richie Walker made a face and knelt down next to Danny. He had only spent his whole life taking hits like this. "You hit that knee hard."

"I'm good, Dad, really." Danny made himself pop right up like he was shooting out of a toaster, somehow fixing a smile on his face as he did, remembering a Will line as he did:

Nobody fakes sincerity better than I do.

He heard himself get a big ovation.

"You don't have to prove anything," his dad said.

"Yeah, Dad, I do," Danny said. "More than I ever have in my life."

Coach Powers was arguing for a flagrant foul, as it turned out. But Nick said, "Coach, I know he drilled him pretty good, but he was playing the ball. Two shots, that's it."

Now Coach Powers came over to Danny. "Are you okay to take these free throws? Because if you aren't, the other team can pick anybody off our bench to shoot them."

"I'm okay."

"We need these."

No kidding, Danny wanted to say.

"If you're hurting, I can take you out after you shoot them," Coach Powers said.

"You're not taking me out of this game." Danny walked away from him, went over to the line and took the ball from Nick.

Made both.

Celtics 60, Lakers 60.

They were tied for the first time since 2 all.

One minute left now. Lakers' ball. Lamar took a pass out on the wing, but rushed his shot, the ball banging off the back of the rim. The rebound came out to Tarik. He took a couple of dribbles, then spotted Rasheed at the other end cutting to the basket, hit him with a long pass. Layup.

Celtics by two.

Lamar took the inbounds pass, dribbled up the court, took a three over Danny right away. Didn't run any clock, didn't look to pass. Kobe to the end.

Drained a three.

Lakers by one.

Before Tarik inbounded the ball, he gave a quick look to Coach Powers, knowing they had two time-outs left. But the old man just made a sweeping motion with his hand like he was throwing a ball underhanded.

Push it, he was saying.

Tarik gave it to Danny. Danny pushed it. On his first dribble, he felt his knee buckle underneath him and nearly went down. But he stayed up, got past half-court, wanting them to clear out for Rasheed.

Rasheed looked him off with his eyes.

Somehow Danny knew what he wanted.

Rasheed was out at the three-point line, on Lamar's side of the court, open. Lamar started to cheat out there, probably thinking everybody was like him, that Rasheed was going to hoist up a three.

Rasheed yelled at Danny to pass him the ball.

Danny made a two-hand chest pass.

Or what would have been a two-hand chest pass if he'd released the ball.

Only he didn't.

Lamar bit on the fake, came running out at Rasheed just as Rasheed passed him going the other way. Now Danny threw it to Rasheed. Who pulled up and took the kind of midrange jumper the announcers always said was becoming a lost art in basketball, in the world of the three-point shot.

Wet.

The Celtics were ahead by one, twenty seconds left. Time-out Lakers.

As they walked toward the bench, Rasheed said, "I like it better, the end of these games, when we're on the same side." Then he slapped Danny such a vicious high-five Danny thought his shoulder was going to come loose.

"As opposed to you flopping and whatnot," Rasheed said.

"Didn't flop," Danny said.

In the huddle, Coach Powers spoke directly to the five in the game for the Celtics: Danny, Rasheed, Tarik, Will, Ben. He said, "There's a million theories about this game. Lord knows, by now I've heard 'em all. But as far as I'm concerned, they always start at the same place: by getting one stop."

When they were back on the court Rasheed said to Danny, "Our game to win."

"Ours, period."

When Danny got with Lamar, Lamar made sure the refs weren't looking and patted Danny on the top of the head. "Still sending out a boy to do a man's job," Lamar said.

Danny looked up at him, trying to do his best impression of Rasheed's stare.

The Lakers pushed the ball, got it to Lamar right away, who pulled up outside the three-point line, one more hero shot fired.

And missed.

This one caromed off the back rim even harder than the one before. There were all these bodies fighting for position under the basket. Danny saw the long arm of Ben Coltrane, their tallest guy, rise up above the pack. Ben, not able to get both hands on the ball, was just trying to swat it away, get it away from the basket somehow. Get it out of there.

It went right to Lamar.

Danny was the only one near him.

He looked down the court, at the clock over their basket. Ten seconds left now.

He remembered Lamar pointing to him in the mess hall.

You and me, he'd said.

Here they were.

Danny saw Lamar's eyes flash up to the clock above his own

basket. Lamar on his dribble now, right-hand dribble, no surprise there, he went right most of the time, only went left as a last resort.

But he crossed over on Danny, trying to cross him up, and went left now. Danny stayed with him. Had to be five seconds now. Danny was counting the time off in his head, keeping his eye on the ball, hands out in front of him, chest high, just like Ty had showed him that day on the bad court.

Lamar put on the brakes.

Now! Danny thought.

As Lamar stopped his dribble and started to transfer the ball to his right hand to go into his shot, Danny flicked his own right hand out.

In that moment, the ball out there in front of Lamar, they were finally the same size.

Danny slapped the ball away.

Slapped it away and grabbed it and dribbled away from Lamar Parrish. Then he heard the horn sound ending the championship game.

Celtics 64, Lakers 63.

His guys got to him first, Will and Tarik and Rasheed. And Ty Ross, out of the stands. They started to lift him up, but Danny pulled back, smiling and shaking his head. "Nah," he said, "that's for little guys."

"Boy plays too big for that," Rasheed said.

"He sure does," Josh Cameron said.

Josh Cameron was there with Ali and Richie Walker, looking as if *he* were the proud parent all of a sudden. "I thought it was a mismatch on that last play," he said. "It just turned out to be a mismatch the other way."

Usually it was Danny's mom who got to him first, but this time it was his dad, cutting in front of her on knees that suddenly seemed twenty years younger than they were, putting his arms around him, leaning down and saying, "It's always about how you get up," he said.

Then his mom put a Mom hug on him.

When she pulled back, Danny saw Zach Fox standing behind her.

"He took the ball from me, you took it from him," Zach said.

Danny asked Zach if he knew where Tess was, and Zach smiled and pointed to the other end of the court. There she was, over near the Lakers' bench, at the end of the bench where Lamar Parrish sat with his head in his hands. For a second, Danny thought she was going to take the last shot of the day.

She had her new camera out and started to point it at Lamar. Then she stopped herself, as if she somehow knew Danny was watching her.

As if he was in her head for once.

She turned then and smiled like she was the brightest light in the place and pointed the camera at Danny instead.

By now the Celtics were in a big, loud, happy circle at mid-court, waiting for the trophy presentation to begin, arms around each other, weaving back and forth the way NBA players did sometimes during player introductions, chanting "Whoo whoo whoo."

Danny started walking across the court toward them.

Coach Powers was in his way.

Danny didn't even try to read the look on his face, or figure out whether basketball had finally made him happy or not. He didn't wait for him to say anything, the buttoned-up coach in his buttoned-up Right Way shirt.

There was something Danny wanted to say to him, though.

But first he took the game ball off his hip, put it down in front of him and executed a *killer* soccer kick, catching the ball just right, sending it flying out the open doors, trying to kick it all the way to Coffee Lake.

Or maybe Canada.

"I could play soccer if I wanted," Danny said. "But I'm a basketball player."

Then he walked past the coach to be with his team.

Turn the page for a preview of
Mike Lupica's next novel,

The Big Field

IF YOU WERE A SHORTSTOP, YOU ALWAYS WANTED THE BALL HIT AT YOU.

Whether the game was on the line or not.

Keith Hutchinson, known to his friends as Hutch, had always thought of himself as the captain of any infield he'd ever been a part of, all the way back to his first year of Little League. Even back then, he could see that other kids were scared to have the ball hit at them in a big spot. Not Hutch. It was the shortstop in him. If the ball was in play, he always wanted it to be *his* play.

Especially now.

Because the game was on the line now.

And it wasn't just any old game; it was the biggest of the summer so far.

Hutch's American Legion team, the Boynton Beach Post 226 Cardinals, still had the lead against the Palm Beach Post 12 Braves in the finals of their 17-and-under league, even though this year's Cardinals didn't have a single 17–year-old on the team. But their lead was down to a single run now, 7–6. They were in the bottom of the ninth at the Santaluces Athletic Complex in Lantana, bases loaded for the Braves. One out to go.

1

If the Cardinals got the out and won the game, they moved on to the South Florida regionals next weekend, one round closer to the state finals.

If they lost, they went home.

Hutch walked over and stood behind second base, almost on the outfield grass, and waited there while their coach, Mr. Cullen, talked things over on the mound with Paul Garner, whom Mr. Cullen had just brought in to pitch.

Hutch knew what everybody on their team knew, that Paul was going to be the last Cardinals pitcher of the night, win or lose. He was going to get an out here and their season would continue, or the Braves' cleanup hitter, Billy Ray Manning, known as Man-Up Manning, was going to hit one hard someplace and it would be the Braves who'd be playing the next round.

Hutch and his teammates would be done for the summer. Done like dinner.

No more baseball, just like that.

He didn't even want to think about it.

Paul was one of his favorite guys on the team, normally their starting left fielder, but he was only the fourth best pitcher they had. Yet Mr. Cullen had been forced to pull their closer, Pedro Mota, after Pedro had suddenly forgotten how to pitch with two outs and nobody on and the Cardinals still ahead, 7–4. First he'd given up three straight hits to load the bases. He'd wild-pitched one run home after that, before walking the next hitter to reload the bases. Finally, he hit the next batter and just like that, it was 7–6, and Mr. Cullen had seen enough.

Now the one guy in the world they didn't want to see at the plate, Man-Up Manning—a seventeen-year-old lefty who actually did look like a man to Hutch—was standing next to the plate, waiting to get his swings.

No place to put him. No way to pitch around him.

Paul didn't throw hard, but he threw strikes, kept the ball down, got a lot of ground balls when he was pitching at his best.

One stinking ground ball now and they were in the regionals.

More important, they got to keep playing.

Hit it to me, he thought.

Mr. Cullen patted Paul on the shoulder, left him to throw his warm-up pitches. Hutch thought about going over to talk to Darryl Williams while he did. But they never talked much during the game, not even during pitching changes. When they did, it was usually only about which one of them would cover second if they thought a guy might be stealing.

Nobody was stealing now. Hutch wasn't paying much attention to the guy on first. Nobody was. He was a lot more worried about the runners on second and third, the potential tying and winning runs. Darryl? As usual, he didn't look worried about anything. He was staring off, lost in his own thoughts or lost in space. Darryl never seemed to look tense or worried or anxious. He knew he was the best hitter on their team—the best player, period. And yet . . .

And yet baseball seemed to bore him sometimes.

Paul threw his last warm-up pitch. Brett Connors, their

catcher, came out to have one quick word with him. As he ran back, the neighborhood people sitting on the other side of the screen behind home plate began to applaud, understanding the importance of the moment, as if they were all suddenly sensing the magic of what baseball could do to a summer's night.

Hutch watched them and thought: If we lose, some of these same people will be here tomorrow night watching the older kids play the 19-and-under game. Their season wouldn't end. Mine would.

Hit it to me.

He walked away from the bag, got into his ready position, watched Brett go through a bunch of signals behind the plate, all of which Hutch knew were totally bogus. Paul had one pitch: A dinky fastball with a late break to it that guys usually couldn't lay off of, even on balls that were about to end up in the dirt.

Paul threw one in the dirt now, but Man-Up Manning didn't bite.

Ball one.

"Be patient!" the Braves coach yelled from their bench. "He's trying to make you chase."

Paul threw a strike that Man-Up was taking all the way, then missed just outside.

Two-and-one.

"Still a hitter's count," the Braves coach said.

Is it ever, Hutch thought.

He could feel his heart in his chest, feeling the thump-

thump-thump of it the way you could feel the thump of rap music from the car next to you at a stoplight sometimes.

Knowing that this was when he loved playing baseball so much, he thought his heart might actually *explode.* He loved it all the time, Hutch knew, loved it more than anybody he knew, on this team or any team he'd ever played on, loved the history of it, loved the stats and the numbers and the way they connected the old days to right now.

Most of all Hutch loved it when you were playing to keep playing, when you were at the plate the way Man-Up was, or standing in the middle of a diamond like this and hoping—begging—for the ground ball that would get you and your teammates the heck out of here with a win.

Paul Garner took a deep breath to settle himself, let it out, shook his pitching hand before he got back on the rubber. Because of the way Paul snapped his wrist, his ball broke more like a screwball, which meant *away* from lefties.

He threw his very best pitch now, on the outside corner, at the knees, right where Brett Connors had set his glove.

And as mighty a swing as Man-Up tried to put on the ball, swinging for the fences all the way, going for the grand slam hero swing, the best he could do was get the end of his bat on it. It would have been a weak grounder for anybody else. But Man-Up truly was a beast, even when he got beat on a pitch this way.

He hit it hard the other way, toward the shortstop hole, between second and third.

Instinctively, as soon as he saw the ball come off the end of the bat, Hutch was moving to his right, knowing that the only chance they were going to have, if the ball didn't end up in left field, was a force at second.

The shortstop in Hutch processed all that in an instant.

Only he wasn't the shortstop.

Darryl was.

HUTCH WAS PLAYING SECOND, MOVING TO HIS RIGHT TO COVER the base, watching from there as Darryl was in the hole in a blink, moving faster than anybody else on the field when he had to, backhanding the ball, already starting to turn his body as he did, gloving the ball cleanly and transferring it to his right hand, snapping off a throw from his hip without even looking to see where it was going.

Do-or-die.

Make the play and the Cardinals win.

Throw it away and the other guys do.

The throw was on the money, as Hutch knew it would be.

The break they got, one they sure needed, was that it was the Braves catcher running from first. Slowest guy on their team. So he did matter after all. Maybe if the Braves coach had known how much it was going to matter, he would have sent in a pinch runner. But he hadn't. He was only worried about the tying and winning runs the way everybody else was under the lights at Santaluces.

Hutch stretched like a first baseman now, stretched as far as he could while still keeping his foot on the bag, his left arm out as far as it could go. . . .

Willing Darryl's throw to get there in time.

The shortstop in him still wanting the ball as much as he ever had.

Then it was in the pocket of his glove, the worn-in pocket of his Derek Jeter model, a split second before he felt the Braves catcher hit second base, heard that sweet pop in his mitt right before he heard an even sweeter sound from the field ump behind him:

"*Out!*"

Game over.

Cardinals 7, Braves 6.

They were going to the regionals.

Even if somebody else had gone into the hole.

• • •

"The golden boy makes one play," Cody Hester was saying, "and people act like he won the game all by himself."

Cody was the Cardinals right fielder, and Hutch's best friend in the world.

"The play *was* kind of golden," Hutch said. "Even you have to admit that."

Cody grinned. "Yeah, it was." He was finished with his milk shake, but made one last slurpy sound with his straw, just for Hutch's benefit. "I'm still not sure he's the greatest teammate in the world."

"When you're a great player, there's no rule that says you have to be," Hutch said.

Cody said, "Seriously, though. You don't think the guy's

a little too full of himself? He acts like he's better than everybody else."

"Only because he is better than everybody else." Now he grinned. "And I don't think he goes around big-timing anybody. He's just cool is all."

They were sitting on the steps in front of Hutch's house in East Boynton, finishing the milk shakes they'd stopped for on the way home from the game. Cody's dad, who worked for the phone company, had dropped them at the Dairy Queen on Seacrest and told them they could walk the rest of the way if they promised to go straight to Hutch's, which they had.

Hutch and his mom and dad lived here on Gateway, in a house faded to the color of lemon-lime Gatorade that his parents talked about painting every year and yet never did. Cody's house was right around the corner on Seacrest, not even a five-minute walk away. His family had moved down to Palm Beach County from Pensacola when Cody was five, and he and Hutch had been more like brothers than friends ever since. They didn't just have a lot in common, they pretty much had everything in common, starting with baseball. They didn't go through life worrying about how neither one of their families had a lot of money. Or that they lived in the neighborhood that they did. Or that Cody's house—a shade of pink that Cody liked to say even flamingos would find gross—was an even uglier color than Hutch's.

As long as they had each other, and a game to play, they thought things were pretty solid.

Now they had more games to play. First the regionals. If they got through that, they played for the state championship on the big field at Roger Dean Stadium in Jupiter, where the real Cardinals and the Marlins played their spring training games. Not only did they play at Roger Dean, they got to play on television, since this was the first year that the Sun Sports Network would be broadcasting the Legion finals, in all age groups, the way ESPN televised the Little League World Series.

Hutch knew it would be a cool thing to make it up the road to Roger Dean, maybe get the chance to play on television for the first time in his life.

Yet what mattered most to Hutch was that they were still playing, that they'd gotten out of the bottom of the ninth tonight with their season still intact.

Out of the blue, Cody said, "This is going to be the greatest summer ever!"

"You say that every summer."

"This time I really mean it," Cody said. "And you know I mean it because it isn't the summer we were *supposed* to have."

Hutch knew what he meant. That was the best thing about having a best friend—having a conversation and being able to leave stuff out.

What Cody had meant was this:

When they used to talk about winning the state championship of Legion ball, even before they were old enough to play Legion ball, it was supposed to happen with Hutch playing short and Cody playing second. The way things had always been.

Then Darryl Williams had come along. Now he was at

short and Hutch had moved over to second, forcing Cody to move to right.

Darryl Williams was already treated like he was the LeBron James of baseball, a kid who was supposed to be the best shortstop—no, the best *player*—to come out of the state since Alex Rodriguez came out of Miami.

He was the same age as Hutch and Cody, fourteen, eighth grade going into ninth. He lived in Lantana, and had played on a Lantana Babe Ruth team during the school year. But summers were for Legion ball and the best Lantana kids played for Post 226, same as the best Boynton Beach kids did. There had been some talk that Darryl, even at fourteen, was good enough to play up to the 19-and-under team from Post 226. But once Darryl showed up for tryouts, making it official that he'd decided to play for the Cardinals—maybe putting off facing nineteen-year-old pitchers for one more year—Hutch knew he would have to switch positions. It was just a question of whether it would be to another infield position or to the outfield.

This wasn't like when A-Rod got traded to the Yankees, and he knew before he even got there that shortstop belonged to Jeter. Hutch was new to the Cardinals the way the rest of the kids were, so it wasn't like this was his team the way the Yankees were Jeter's team. Hutch was moving and there wasn't anything he could say or do to change that. Once Mr. Cullen picked the whole team, he decided to move Hutch to second and put Hank Harding, an ex-catcher, at third.

So Hutch moved over from short, Cody moved from

second to right, and that was their team, the youngest ever trying to win the state championship at this age level. No 17-year-olds—just two 16-year-olds, Paul Garner and their ace, Tripp Lyons. And more 14-year-olds than 15-year-olds.

Now "Cullen's Kids," as Hutch's mom called them some-times, were one step closer to the title, having made it to the second round.

"You know what the real bottom line is with Darryl?" Hutch said. "He's the best player we've ever played with or against, and if you love baseball the way we do, you gotta love watching him play ball."

"I'd tell you I agree with you," Cody said, "but then I'd have to kill you."

"Darryl's the reason it doesn't kill *me* that I'm not playing short," Hutch said. "It'd be like a golfer getting bent out of shape that he has to play number two behind Tiger."

Cody stood up now, walked up the sidewalk and opened the gate to the chain-link fence in front of the Hutchinsons' house, one of the few two-story houses in the whole neigh-borhood, even if it looked like one of the oldest. Hutch had never given much thought to that fence, just because it had always been there, and was like a lot of the other front-yard fences in their neighborhood. It was Cody who made a big deal of it, saying that some people grew up in white-picket-fence neighborhoods, and other people grew up with fences like theirs.

"I'm gonna say it one last time," Cody said. "You won the game tonight, not him."

"Yeah, yeah," Hutch said.

Hutch watched him until he disappeared around the corner, thinking about what Cody had said about the game.

Yeah, he told himself. I did get those three hits tonight. I did drive in four runs. I *did* make a play in the fourth, going into short right, that saved a couple of runs.

But anybody who watched the game was going to remember the play Darryl had made in the ninth.

On *my* ball, Hutch thought.

He was never going to admit that out loud, not even to his best friend, but there it was. In his heart Hutch knew he would get over not playing short on a date Cody liked to call the twelfth of never.

• • •

He went up to his room and turned on the small fan he had on his desk. The heat was always brutal in Florida in the summer, but the past few days had been even hotter and muggier than usual, and even the thunderstorm that had blown through the area about an hour before the game tonight hadn't done anything to cool things off. There were only two rooms in their house that had air-conditioning: the living room and his parents' bedroom. But his parents were down in the living room watching a movie they'd rented from Blockbuster, and so Hutch had come up here to listen to the Marlins-Mets game on the radio.

He stripped down to his shorts, trained the fan at the head of his bed, lay down on sheets that wouldn't feel cool for long, and tried to concentrate on the Marlins.

Problem was, there were shortstops all around him. The poster of his hero, Jeter, over his bed and the one of Cal Ripken Jr. over his desk. On the ceiling was Ozzie Smith, "the Wizard of Oz," doing that backflip he used to do when he ran out to play short for the Cardinals.

Not to mention the best shortstop in the house, the one downstairs watching the movie:

His dad.

He had been the first Hutch Hutchinson, even if he no longer went by that nickname. He was just back to being plain old Carl Hutchinson. He'd told Hutch he was going to try to make the game tonight, but he never showed. Again. This time, he said, it was because one of the other drivers hadn't shown up at the driving service he worked for, and he'd had to make an airport run to Miami.

His dad always seemed to have a good reason when he missed a game.

Sometimes Hutch thought it was because he just didn't love baseball anymore, because baseball had broken his heart, because he was supposed to be on his way to the big leagues once and never made it out of East Boynton.

It's not going to happen that way with me, Hutch told himself now.

Even if I am playing second base—more like second fiddle, actually—to Darryl.

It's only for a couple of months, he kept telling himself. Cody liked to say that none of this was going to matter when they got to Boynton Beach High and Darryl was playing for

Santaluces Community and Hutch was back at his normal position.

But Cody didn't know something, even though he thought he knew *everything* about Hutch. Cody Hester didn't know, at least not yet, about Hutch's dream of getting out of East Boynton, getting out of Florida and playing his high school baseball a long way from here, on a baseball scholarship at one of the fancy boarding schools up north in New Jersey he'd been reading about. One of the schools with famous baseball programs to go along with their basketball programs.

Baseball was going to be his ticket out of here even if it hadn't been his dad's.

And Hutch believed in his heart that his best chance to do that was at short. If you followed baseball the way he did, and nobody he knew followed baseball the way he did, you knew that a great shortstop was worth his weight in gold.

Just look around: The Yankees had Jeter and the Rangers had Michael Young and the Mets had José Reyes, whom Hutch just liked watching *run* more than anybody else in baseball, playing any position. The Marlins had Manny Ramírez's brother Hanley, and even the little guy who played short for the St. Louis Cardinals, David Eckstein, had ended up the MVP of the World Series a couple of years ago.

On the radio now, above the noise from the fan, he heard one of the Marlins' announcers, Dave Van Horne, his voice excited, the words jumping across the room, talking about Hanley Ramírez moving to his left and snapping off a throw to first to beat the runner by a step.

"What can I tell you, folks," Van Horne yelled, "the kid's a star!"

Why not? Hutch thought. Hanley's playing a star position. You had to know that whether you were a team guy or not.

The scouts didn't come to see second basemen.

TRAVEL TEAM

MIKE LUPICA

PUFFIN BOOKS

PUFFIN BOOKS
Published by the Penguin Group
Penguin Young Readers Group, 345 Hudson Street, New York, New York 10014, U.S.A.
Penguin Group (Canada), 90 Eglinton Avenue East, Suite 700, Toronto, Ontario, Canada M4P 2Y3
(a division of Pearson Penguin Canada Inc.)
Penguin Books Ltd, 80 Strand, London WC2R 0RL, England
Penguin Ireland, 25 St Stephen's Green, Dublin 2, Ireland (a division of Penguin Books Ltd)
Penguin Group (Australia), 250 Camberwell Road, Camberwell, Victoria 3124, Australia
(a division of Pearson Australia Group Pty Ltd)
Penguin Books India Pvt Ltd, 11 Community Centre, Panchsheel Park, New Delhi - 110 017, India
Penguin Group (NZ), Cnr Airborne and Rosedale Roads, Albany,
Auckland 1310, New Zealand (a division of Pearson New Zealand Ltd)
Penguin Books (South Africa) (Pty) Ltd, 24 Sturdee Avenue,
Rosebank, Johannesburg 2196, South Africa

Registered Offices: Penguin Books Ltd, 80 Strand, London WC2R 0RL, England

First published in the United States of America by Philomel Books,
a division of Penguin Young Readers Group, 2004
Published by Puffin Books, a division of Penguin Young Readers Group, 2006
20 19 18 17 16

THE LIBRARY OF CONGRESS HAS CATALOGED THE PHILOMEL EDITION AS FOLLOWS:
Lupica, Mike.
Travel team / Mike Lupica. p. cm.
Summary: After he is cut from his travel basketball team—the very same team
that his father once led to national prominence—twelve-year-old Danny Walker
forms his own team of cast-offs that might have a shot at victory.
[1. Basketball—Fiction. 2. Fathers and sons—Fiction. 3. Schools—Fiction.] I. Title.
PZ7.L97914Tr 2004   [Fic]—dc22   2003025072
ISBN 0-399-24150-7

Puffin Books ISBN 978-0-14-240462-1

Book design by Gina DiMassi
The text is set in Charter Regular

Printed in the United States of America

For my sons,
Christopher and Alex and Zach,
who always play bigger.

This book is for them,
and any kid in any sport ever told he,
or she, wasn't big enough.
Or good enough.

And, as always, for Taylor.

ACKNOWLEDGMENTS

One last time,
my thanks and gratitude go to
my pal Jerry Hartnett,
to Coach Keith Wright,
and to one travel team I will never forget:
The 2002–03 Rebels.

HE KNEW HE WAS SMALL.

He just didn't *think* he was small.

Big difference.

Danny had known his whole life how small he was compared to everybody in his grade, from the first grade on. How he had been put in the front row, front and center, of every class picture taken. Been in the front of every line marching into every school assembly, first one through the door. Sat in the front of every classroom. Hey, little man. Hey, little guy. He was used to it by now. They'd been studying DNA in science lately; being small was in his DNA. He'd show up for soccer, or Little League baseball tryouts, or basketball, when he'd first started going to basketball tryouts at the Y, and there'd always be one of those clipboard dads who didn't know him, or his mom. Or his dad.

Asking him: "Are you sure you're with the right group, little guy?"

Meaning the right *age* group.

It happened the first time when he was eight, back when he still had to put the ball up on his shoulder and give it a heave just to get it up to a ten-foot rim. When he'd already taught himself how to lean into the bigger kid guarding him, just because there was always a bigger kid guarding him, and then step back so he could get his dopey shot off.

This was way back before he'd even tried any fancy stuff, including the crossover.

He just told the clipboard dad that he was eight, that he was little, that this was his right group, and could he have his number, please? When he told his mom about it later, she just smiled and said, "You know what you should hear when people start talking about your size? Blah blah blah."

He smiled back at her and said that he was pretty sure he would be able to remember that.

"How did you play?" she said that day, when she couldn't wait any longer for him to tell.

"I did okay."

"I have a feeling you did more than that," she said, hugging him to her. "My streak of light."

Sometimes she'd tell him how small his dad had been when he was Danny's age.

Sometimes not.

But here was the deal, when he added it all up: His height had always been much more of a stinking issue for other people, including his mom, than it was for him.

He tried not to sweat the small stuff, basically, the way grownups always told you.

He knew he was faster than everybody else at St. Patrick's School. And at Springs School, for that matter. Nobody on either side of town could get in front of him. He was the best passer his age, even better than Ty Ross, who was better at everything in sports than just about anybody. He knew that when it was just kids—which is the way kids always liked it in sports—and the parents were out of the gym or off the playground and you got to just play without a whistle blowing every ten seconds or somebody yelling out more instructions, he was always one of the first picked, because the other guys on his team, the shooters especially, knew he'd get them the ball.

Most kids, his dad told him one time, know something about basketball that even most grown-ups never figure out.

One good passer changes everything.

Danny could pass, which is why he'd always made the team.

Almost always.

But no matter what was happening with any team he'd ever played on, no matter how tired he would be after practice, no matter how much homework he still had left, this driveway was still his special place. Like a special club with a membership of one, the place where he could come out at this time of night and imagine it up good, imagine it big and bright, even with just the one floodlight over the backboard and the other light, smaller, over the back door. His mother had done everything she could to make the driveway wider back here, even cutting into what little backyard they had the summer before last. "I told them you needed more room in the corners," she said. "The men from the paving company. They just nodded at me, like corners were some sort of crucial guy thing."

"Right up there with the remote control switcher for the TV," Danny said. "And leaving wet towels on the bathroom floor."

"How are the corners now?"

"Perfect," he said. "Like at the Garden."

He had just enough room in the corners now, mostly for shooting. He didn't feel as if he was trying to make a drive to the basket in his closet. Or an elevator car. He had room to *maneuver*, pretend he really *was* at the real Garden, that he was one of the small fast guys who'd made it all the way there. Like Muggsy Bogues, somebody he'd read up on when one of his coaches told him to, who was only 5-3 and made it to the NBA. Like Tiny Archibald and Bobby Hurley and Earl Boykins, a 5-5 guy who came out of the basketball minor leagues, another streak of light who showed everybody that more than size mattered, even in hoops.

And, of course, Richie Walker.

Middletown's own.

Danny would put chairs out there and dribble through them like he was dribbling out the clock at the end of the game. Some nights he would borrow a pair of his mother's old sunglasses and tape the bottom part of the lens so he couldn't see the ball unless he looked straight down at it. This was back when he was first trying to perfect the double crossover, before he even had a chance to do it right, his hands being too little and his arms not being nearly long enough.

Sometimes he'd be so dog tired when he finished—though he would never cop to that with his mom—he'd fall into bed with his clothes on and nearly fall asleep that way.

"You done?" she'd say when she came in to say good night.

"I finally got bored," he'd say, and she'd say with a smile, "I always worry about that, you getting bored by basketball."

Everybody he'd ever read up on, short or tall, had talked about how they outworked everybody else. Magic Johnson, he knew, won the championship his rookie season with the Lakers, scored forty-two points in the final game of the championship series when he had to play center because Kareem Abdul-Jabbar was hurt, then went back to East Lansing, Michigan, where he was from, in the summer and worked on his outside shooting because he'd decided it wasn't good enough.

Tonight, Danny had worked past the time when his mom usually called him in, not even noticing how cold it had gotten for October. Worked underneath the new backboard she'd gotten for him at the end of the summer. Not the only kid in his class with divorced parents now. Not the smallest kid on the court now. Just

4

the only one. He'd drive to the basket and then hit one of the chairs with one of his lookaway passes. Or he'd step back and make a shot from the outside. Sometimes, breathing hard, like it was a real game, he'd step to the free throw line he'd drawn with chalk and make two free throws for the championship of something.

Just him and the ball and the feel of it in his hands and the whoosh of it going through the net and the sound one of the old wooden school chairs would make when he tipped it over with another bounce pass. He knew he was wearing out another pair of sneakers his mom called "old school," which to Danny always meant "on sale." Or that she had found his size at either the Nike store or the Reebok store at the factory outlet mall about forty-five minutes from Middletown, both of them knowing she couldn't afford what Athlete's Foot or Foot Locker was charging for the new Kobe sneakers from Nike, or Iverson's, or McGrady's. Or the cool new LeBron James kicks that so many of the Springs School kids were wearing this year.

He finished the way he always did, trying to cleanly execute the crossover-and-back five times in a row, low enough to the ground to be like a rock he was skipping across Taylor Lake. Five times usually making it an official good night out here.

Except.

Except this was as far from a good night as he'd ever known.

Basically, this was the worst night of his whole life.

Danny's mother, Ali, watched him from his bedroom window on the second floor, standing to the side of the window in the dark room, trying not to let him see her up here, even though she could see him sneaking a look occasionally, especially when he'd do something fine down on the court, sink a long one or make a left-handed layup or execute that tricky dribble he was always working on.

5

Sometimes he'd do it right and come right out of it and be on his way to the basket, so fast she thought he should leave a puff of smoke like one of those old Road Runner cartoons.

God, you're getting old, she thought. Did kids even know who the Road Runner was anymore?

"Nice work with that double dribble," she'd tell him sometimes when he finally came in the house, tired even if he'd never admit that to her.

"Mom, you *know* it's not a double dribble. *This*"—showing her on the kitchen floor with the ball that was on its way up to his room with him—"is a double *crossover*."

"Whatever it is," she'd say, "don't do it in the kitchen."

That would get a smile out of her boy sometimes.

The boy who had cried when he told her his news tonight.

He was twelve now. And never let her see him cry unless he took a bad spill in a game or in the driveway, or got himself all tied up because he was afraid he was going to fail some test, even though he never did.

But tonight her son cried in the living room and let her hug him as she told him she hoped this was the worst thing that ever happened to him.

"If it is," she said, "you're going to have an even happier life than I imagined for you."

She pushed back a little and smoothed out some of his blond hair, spikey now because he'd been wearing one of his four thousand baseball caps while he played.

"What do I always tell you?" she said.

Without looking up at her, reciting it like she was helping him learn his part in a school play, Danny said, "Nobody imagines up things better than you do."

"There you go."

Another one of their games.

Except on this night he suddenly said, "So how come you can't imagine a happier life for us *now*?"

Then got up from the couch and ran out of the room and the next thing she heard was the bounce of the ball in the driveway. Like the real beat of his heart.

Or their lives.

She waited a while, cleaned up their dinner dishes, even though that never took long with just the two of them, finished correcting some test papers. Then she went up to his room and watched him try to play through this, the twelve-year-old who went through life being asked if he was ten, or nine, or eight.

Ali saw what she always saw, even tonight, when he was out here with the fierce expression on his face, hardly ever smiling, even as he dreamed his dreams, imagining for himself now, imagining up a happy life for himself, one where he wasn't always the smallest. One where all people saw was the size of his talent, all that speed, all the magic things he could do with a basketball in either hand.

No matter how much she tried not to, she saw all his father in him.

He was all the way past the house, on his way to making the right on Cleveland Avenue, when he saw the light at the end of the driveway, and saw the little boy back there.

He stopped the car.

Or maybe it stopped itself.

He was good at blaming, why not blame the car?

What was that old movie where Jack Nicholson played the retired astronaut? He couldn't remember the name, just that Shirley MacLaine was in it, too, and she was going around with Jack, and then her daughter got sick and the whole thing turned into a major chick flick.

There was this scene where Nicholson was trying to leave town, but the daughter was sick, and even though he didn't care about too much other than having fun, he couldn't leave because Shirley MacLaine needed him.

You think old Jack is out of there, adios, and then he shows up at the door, that smile on his face, and says, "Almost a clean getaway."

He used to think his life was a movie. Enough people used to tell him that it was.

He parked near the corner of Cleveland and Earl, then walked halfway back up the block, across the street from 422 Earl, still wondering what he was doing on this street tonight, cruising this neighborhood, in this stupid small small-minded town.

Watching this kid play ball.

Mesmerized, watching the way this kid, about as tall as his bad hip, could handle a basketball.

Watching him shoot his funny shot, pushing the ball off his shoulder like he was pushing a buddy over a fence. He seemed to miss as many shots as he made. But he *never* missed the folding chairs he was obviously using as imaginary teammates, whether he was looking at them when he fired one of his passes. Or not.

Watching the kid stop after a while, rearrange the chairs now, turning them into defenders, dribbling through them, controlling the ball better with his right hand than his left, keeping the ball low, only struggling when he tried to get tricky and double up on a crossover move.

The kid stopping sometimes, breathing hard, going through his little routine before making a couple of free throws. Like it was all some complicated game being played inside the kid's head.

He hadn't heard anybody coming, so he nearly jumped out of his skin when she tapped him on the shoulder, jumping back a little until he saw who it was.

"Why don't you go over?" Ali said.

"You shouldn't sneak up on people that way."

"No," she said, "*you* shouldn't sneak up on people that way."

"I was going to call tomorrow," he said.

"Boy," she said, "I don't think I've ever heard that one before."

Ali said, "You can catch me up later on the fascinating comings and goings of your life. Right now, this is one of those nights in his life when he needs his father, Rich. To go with about a thousand others."

Richie Walker noticed she wasn't looking at him, she was facing across the street the way he was, watching Danny.

"Why tonight in particular?"

"He didn't make travel team," she said now on the quiet, dark street. "*Your* travel team."

"Look at him play. How could he not make travel?"

"They told him he was too small."

JUST LIKE THAT—LIKE ALWAYS, REALLY—IT WAS AS IF HIS DAD HAD APPEARED out of nowhere.

Danny sometimes thought he should come with one of those popping noises that came with the pop-ups on the videos.

Pop-Up Richie Walker.

"Hey," his dad said.

"Hey."

This was one of those times Danny always carried around inside his head, where his dad would get down into a crouch, like one of those TV dads coming home from work, and put his arms out, and Danny would run into them.

Only it never seemed to happen that way. It happened like this: Both of them keeping their distance and neither one of them knowing exactly what to say.

Or how to act.

Richie Walker had never been a hugger. It was actually a joke with them, Richie having taught Danny when he was five or six what he called the "guy hug" from sports, one without any actual physical contact, one where you leaned in one way and the other guy leaned in the other way and then you both backed off almost immediately and did a lot of head nodding.

"In the perfect guy hug," his dad had said, "you sort of look like you're trying to guard somebody, just not too close."

Like them: Close, but not too close.

Neither one of them said anything now. At least that way, Danny thought, they were picking right up where they left off.

His dad said, "How you doing?"

"I'm okay." Danny put the ball on his hip. "What're you doing here?"

All his dad could do with that one was to give a little shrug.

"You see Mom?"

"Just now."

"You want to go inside?"

"I always liked it out here better."

Danny thought about passing him the ball, knowing they'd always been able to at least talk basketball with each other. Instead, he turned and shot it.

Missed.

"You call that a *jump* shot?" his dad said. "Looks more like a *sling* shot to me."

His dad, Danny knew, had always been more comfortable giving him a little dig than having a real conversation with him. His mom once said that the only time Richie Walker had ever been happy was when he was one of the boys. So all he knew how to do was treat Danny like one of the boys.

Except sometimes Danny didn't know whether he was being sarcastic when he picked at him. Or just mean.

"No," Danny said, retrieving the ball. "On account of, I can't jump."

Richie Walker said, "You need to work on your release. Or you're gonna get stuffed every time."

Danny thinking: *Tell* me about getting stuffed.

Danny dribbled back to the outside now, desperate to make one in front of him, like this was some test he needed to pass right away, barely looked at the basket before he turned and swished one.

11

"That better?"

"Not better form," Richie said. "Better on account of, it went in."

His dad moved out of the shadows from the back door then. Danny thought his dad could still pass for an older kid himself, with his white T-shirt hanging out of his jeans, low-cut white Iverson sneakers, untied. And, Danny could see he still had those sad, sad eyes going for him, as if he weren't watching the world with them, just some sad old movie.

Same old, same old, Danny thought.

Richie was limping slightly, just because he'd limped slightly for Danny's whole life. Moving like an old man, not just because of his knees, but because of the plate in his shoulder, and his rebuilt hip, the one he used to tell Danny the doctors made for him out of Legos, and all the rest of it.

"Anything new with you?" his dad said.

And just by the way he said it, trying to make it sound casual, like he was making an effort to start a conversation, Danny knew his mom must have told him about travel.

Danny stood there, twirling the ball, wanting to hug the non-hugger, and then he couldn't help himself.

He started crying all over again.

The tears seemed to throw his dad off, like Danny had thrown a pass he wasn't expecting.

Even then, Richie Walker wanted to talk about basketball.

They sat in two of the folding chairs.

His dad said, "You still do the one I showed you?"

"The one where I tape the bottom of my sunglasses and try to dribble through everything without looking down?"

"Yeah."

"I raised the bar a little," Danny said. "Sometimes I put a do-rag over my eyes and try to do it completely blindfolded."

He actually saw his dad smiling then. Though Richie Walker could manage to do that without anything different happening with his eyes.

"So did I," Richie said. "Except we didn't call them do-rags, we called them bandanas."

He picked up the ball in his big hands. Danny was always fascinated by his father's hands, just because they didn't seem to go with the rest of him. Like somebody with a tiny head and Dumbo's ears.

Big hands. Huge hands. And those long arms that the writers used to say Richie Walker had borrowed from somebody 6-6 or 6-7; in one of the old stories he'd read, Danny couldn't remember where, one of his dad's old teammates with the Warriors had said, "Richie Walker is the only little 5-10 white man had to reach *up* to zipper his pants."

He had been listed at 5-10 in his playing days, anyway.

But his dad had said that was only if you counted the lifts in his sneakers.

Danny watched as his dad—without even trying, almost not aware he was doing it, like somebody not knowing they were cracking their knuckles—dribbled the ball on the right side of his chair, took the ball behind him, keeping the low dribble, picking it up with his left hand on the other side, finishing the routine by spinning the ball on his left index finger before putting it back in his lap.

"Your mom already told me what happened," he said.

Danny said, "I figured."

"They still do the tryouts the way they did in the old days—two nights?"

Danny nodded. "The dads running the twelves can't have one of their own sons trying out. There were, like, six of them doing the evaluation. Mr. Ross didn't get to do any evaluating because of Ty, but he was in the gym the whole time."

"Just in case they needed somebody to explain basketball," Richie said.

Jeffrey Ross was the president of the Middletown Savings Bank. President of the Middletown Chamber of Commerce. President of Middletown Basketball. Danny had always wondered if his son, Ty—the best twelve-year-old basketball player in their town, or any town nearby—was required to call his father Mr. President, or if he could get by with Dad.

"He still act as if somebody should stop and give him the game ball if he actually remembers your first name?" Richie said.

"Some of the other kids were saying that you don't have to worry about him blowing his whistle, because somebody already stuck it up his you-know-what."

Richie Walker said, "It was the same way when he was your age." He gave Danny a long look now and said, "He say anything to you?"

"Not until tonight, really, when he called to tell me how sorry he was that I didn't make it. He said he didn't want me to find out in a letter."

"Right," Richie said.

"The only other time I actually heard him say anything was when he welcomed us all the first night."

"He thinks he's the mayor."

"Mom says that in his mind, it would be a step down, from his current position as king."

"That's all you ever got out of him? That he was sorry?"

Danny said, "There was the one other thing, as we were break-

14

ing up into groups the first night. He was talking to a couple of the evaluators—you know, the clipboard guys?—and he told them, 'Remember, I want us to get bigger this year, last year we were too small and we couldn't even get out of the sectionals.'"

"He said that he wanted the twelve-year-old travel team from Middletown to get *bigger*?"

Danny nodded.

"What," Richie said, "so we can match up better with the Lakers?"

Danny told him the rest of it.

How the travel teams in town still went from fifth grade through eighth, but that seventh grade was still the glamour team in Middletown, in any sport.

Richie: "So that hasn't changed."

Danny: "You guys were the ones who changed it, remember?"

Richie: "Nobody ever lets me forget."

This year there were thirty kids trying out for twelve spots. The first night, Danny heard one of the moms in the parking lot saying that none of the other age groups had even close to that many boys trying out. Last year, Danny told his dad, they'd only had to cut seven kids when he'd made the sixth-grade team.

"This is all about the chance to get to the nationals," Richie said, "and be on television. Parents probably think it's the peewee basketball version of one of those *Idol* shows. Or one of those talented-kid deals. Think Dick Vitale or somebody is going to discover their little Bobby as a future all-America."

"That's what happened with you guys," Danny said.

"Yeah, and the town never got over it."

His dad didn't usually like to talk about what he called back-in-the-day things. Or talk about anything else, really. Tonight was different, and Danny didn't know why. He just knew it was the two of them, sitting here.

The way Danny had always thought things were *supposed* to be.

"Back to you," Richie Walker said.

Like passing him the ball.

Okay, Danny said, first night they all did some basic drills, shooting and dribbling and fast breaks and passing and one-on-one defending; they broke up the big guys and little guys as evenly as they could and scrimmaged for the second hour, while the evaluators sat in the gym at Middletown High School, carrying those clipboards.

Evaluating their butts off.

Richie said, "How'd you do?"

"I thought I was flying," Danny said. "I mean, I knew I was going to look better because I had Ty Ross on my team. But when I got home, I told Mom that I didn't want to get ahead of myself or anything, but I thought I'd made the team."

"He's that good? The Ross boy?"

"Better than good. He's someone for me to pass the ball to."

The second night, the one that killed him, they scrimmaged the whole night. When Mr. Ross called to give him the bad news, he said that what they'd tried to do, in the interest of fairness, was have the kids on the bubble spend the most time on the court.

Richie said, "He actually used those words? On the bubble?"

"His exact words."

"The whole goddamn world is watching too much sports on television, and don't rat me out to your mother for swearing."

"The second night," Danny said, "I didn't have anybody big who could catch, or shoot."

"Out of all those bubble boys."

16

Danny said, "They had this new kid from Colorado guarding me."

"How big?"

Danny looked down at his old white Air Force Ones, high-tops, noticed a new hole near his right toe. "Big enough."

He didn't know anything that night about being on some stupid bubble, he told Richie Walker now. He could just tell that everything got real serious toward the end; that he would look up sometimes when he made a good play, when he made a good pass or got past the Colorado kid—Andy Mayne—and got to the basket, hoping to see some reaction from the clipboard dads.

"Guys like that," Richie said, "they're too busy getting ready to agree with each other."

"Anyway," Danny said, "the last fifteen minutes or so I played like crap, I didn't need anybody to tell me that afterward. I was just hoping then that they hadn't forgotten how good I thought I looked the night before."

"They tell you they'd send out letters telling you whether you'd made it or not?"

Danny nodded. "We'd all filled out the envelopes with our addresses on them when we checked in."

"But Jeff Ross called you personally."

"Because you and Mom and him are old friends."

"What a guy."

They sat there in the cool night, listening to the sounds of Earl Avenue, up and down the block, an occasional car passing, the Malones' cocker spaniel yapping away, rap music coming from somebody's bedroom window, Danny content to sit here like this until morning.

Danny finally said, "You haven't told me yet what you're doing here."

Richie Walker grinned at his son, and did what he'd do sometimes, put a little street in his voice.

"Doing the same thing I have my whole life, dog," he said. "You know, chillin' and lookin' for a game."

He took the ball out of his lap and handed it to Danny. "Shoot for it."

"Winners out."

"You feeling any better?"

Danny had already decided something: He wasn't going to cry about this ever again. Not in front of his parents, not in front of him*self*.

No more crying in basketball.

"I'll feel better when I beat the great Richie Walker in a game of one-on-one."

He dribbled to the foul line, getting fancy, crossing over with his right hand to his left, wanting to come right back with the ball and go straight into his shot.

"Don't take this the wrong way, junior," his dad said. "But that move needs work."

Danny said to his dad, "Yeah, yeah, yeah, you want to talk or you want to play?"

SOMETIMES DANNY WOULD GOOGLE UP HIS DAD'S NAME WHEN HE WAS ON-line, Google being the Internet version of going through the scrapbooks that his mom still kept down in the basement.

Even if you practically needed a treasure map to find the scrapbooks.

He did it now with the two of them downstairs in the kitchen, drinking the coffee his mom had made, telling him they were going to catch up a little, his dad saying he'd come upstairs to say good night before he left.

Good *night*, Danny noticed.

Not good-bye.

His parents were acting friendly with each other when they left the room, smiling at him, at each other, as if nobody in the room had a care in the world. Danny loved it when adults tried to put a smiley face on something, thinking they were putting something over on you.

It made Danny want to yell "Busted!" sometimes.

Oh, sure. There was a definite kind of smile you'd get from your parents, your teachers, your coaches. Danny thought it should come with some kind of warning siren. Most of the time it meant they were pissed, but still getting to it. Pissed at you, about something you did, or something you said.

Or in this case, pissed at each other.

He couldn't remember a time when his mom wasn't mad at his dad for leaving them.

It was more complicated with his dad, who had been mad at everything and everybody for as long as Danny could remember.

Now they were downstairs, catching up on all that, probably trying to see who could say the meanest things without either one of them ever raising their voice. His mom, he knew, would do most of the talking, wanting to know what he was doing in town and how come he hadn't been sending enough money from Las Vegas, where he'd been working for the Amazing Grace casino the past few years, how long he was going to be in Middletown before he left and—her version of things—broke his son's heart all over again.

Only it didn't break his heart, that was the thing he could never get her to understand.

There were plenty of things that bothered him, sure. His father hardly ever called, start there. Never wrote. Are you joking? And wouldn't learn how to use a computer, which meant e-mail was out of the question. Maybe that was why tonight felt like the longest conversation they'd had in a long time. Or maybe the longest they'd ever had.

You want to know what came closest to breaking his heart? That Danny had to look up all the things about Richie Walker's basketball career, from Middletown on, that Richie Walker could have told him himself.

Basically, though, Danny had just decided his dad was who he was. Like some sort of broken and put-back-together version of who he used to be. He was who he was and their relationship was what it was, and Danny couldn't see that changing anytime soon. And maybe not ever. He'd never describe it to his mom this way, but he'd worked it out for himself. It went all the way back to something she'd told him once about heart, and how you could divide it up any way you wanted to.

So, cool, he'd set aside this place in his heart for his dad, and what his dad could give him. Wanting more but not expecting more, happy when his dad would show up, even unexpected, the way he did tonight, sad when he left.

You got used to stuff, that's the way he looked at it.

Even divorce.

He would never say this to his mom, but he always thought he'd gotten used to divorce a lot better than Ali Walker ever had. Or ever would.

He just didn't go out of his way trying to put a fake smiley face on it the way they did, at least when he was still in the room.

So now he was in front of the Compaq his mom had gotten him from CompUSA for Christmas, Googling away. He had typed in "Richie Walker," knowing the first page of what the search engine would spit back at him, the list of Web sites, knowing that the one he wanted was at the top of the second page.

ChildSportsStars.Com.

He clicked on *W*, knowing his dad's was there at the top of the list, Tiger Woods's down a bit lower. And Kerry Wood, the Cubs pitcher, even though Danny didn't exactly think you were a child because you made the big leagues when you were nineteen or twenty.

Then he clicked on his dad.

"The biggest little kid from the biggest little town in the world," the headline read.

And proceeded to tell you all about Richie Walker, the dazzling point guard from the tiny town in Eastern Long Island who took his twelve-year-old travel team all the way to the finals of the nationals—what was now known as the Little League Basketball World Series—and about the Middletown Vikings' last upset victory in their amazing upset run to the title over a heavily favored team from Los Angeles.

On national television.

Danny felt as if all of it had been tattooed to his memory, the way you wished you could tattoo homework to your memory sometimes.

He knew almost all of it by heart, including the stuff in the little box on the side that told you about how ESPN was just starting out in those days and was putting just about anything on the air; how they decided to give the full treatment to the twelve-year-old nationals once they realized what kind of story they had with Richie Walker and his team.

The bio in ChildSportsStars.Com said:

". . . and so Richie Walker and his teammates became a Disney movie even before Disney owned ESPN, the travel-team version of *The Bad News Bears.* There would even be the suggestion later that it was the story of the Middletown Vikings that had at least partially inspired the *Mighty Ducks* movies that would come later, the one about a ragtag hockey team from nowhere always finding a way. . . .

"But every movie like this needs the right star. The right kid. And Middletown had one in Richie Walker, the sandy-haired point guard with what the commentators and sportswriters of the day described as all the Harlem Globetrotters in his suburban game. . . ."

By the time Middletown had pulled off its first huge upset, over a heavily favored team from Toledo, Ohio, ESPN had fallen in love with Richie Walker and the Vikings. By the second week of the tournament, the whole thing had picked up enough momentum in the middle of February, the dead time in sports between the Super

Bowl and the start of the NCAA basketball tournament, that ABC came in and made a deal to put the finals on *Wide World of Sports*, just because ESPN wasn't getting into enough households in those days, cable television not being nearly the force it is now.

Or so it said on ChildSportsStars.Com, and anywhere else they gave you a detailed account of the life and times of Richie Walker.

Middletown's own.

He had heard so many people say it that way, his whole life, that he sometimes felt as if the last part, Middletown's own, was part of his dad's name.

The son an expert on the town's favorite son.

Before it was all over, there would be a small picture of his dad's face on the cover of *Sports Illustrated,* not the main part of the cover, but up in a corner. His dad would end up on *The Today Show,* too.

Even people who didn't watch the Middletown–L.A. final on a Saturday afternoon had managed to see the highlights of the last minute of the one-point game.

Most of which involved Middletown's little point guard, Richie Walker, dribbling out the clock all by himself.

Going between his legs a couple of times.

Crossing over in the last ten seconds and even pushing the ball through one of the defender's legs when it looked as if L.A. had finally trapped him in a double-team, while their coach kept waving his arms in the background and telling them to foul him.

Problem was, they couldn't foul what they couldn't catch.

You could watch the last minute by clicking on the video at ChildSportsStars.Com.

Danny had watched it what felt like a thousand times. Watched his dad and felt like he was watching himself, that's how much alike they looked (and how many times had people in town told him *that,* like it was breaking news?). Watched him with that old blue-and-white jersey hanging out of his shorts, dribbling. Finally being carried around the court at Market Square Arena in Indianapolis when it was all over and Middletown had won, 40–39.

They had that picture on the Web site, too.

The rest of it told how Richie Walker went on to become a high school all-America at Middletown High. A second-team all-America at Syracuse University and one of the first real stars who helped make the Big East a major draw on ESPN. First-round draft choice of the Golden State Warriors.

Finally a member of the NBA's All-Rookie Team, even though his rookie season was cut short by the famous car accident on the San Francisco side of the Bay Bridge after a Warriors-Spurs game.

Pictures of that, too: What was left of the Jeep Cherokee Richie Walker had bought before the season with some of his bonus money, the one they had to use the Jaws of Life to get him out of that night.

Danny knew the pictures the way he knew everything else about his dad's basketball career. . . .

"Hey sport," Richie Walker said now from behind Danny. "What you looking at there?"

Danny executed the essential kid laptop move, clicking off and folding down the screen, as slick as anything he could do on the court.

He gave his standard answer, no matter which parent was the one who'd suddenly appeared in the doorway.

"Nothing," he said.

He and his mom were in the kitchen having breakfast, both of them already dressed for school, him for the seventh grade at

St. Patrick's, his mom for her eighth-grade teaching schedule there. He went there because she taught there. They could afford Danny going there because she taught there, and his tuition was free.

His mom used to joke that it was usually private-school people that were supposed to be snobs, but that somehow they'd tipped that on its head in Middletown, and it was the parochial school kids, the ones who *didn't* go to Springs, that were supposed to be from the wrong side of the tracks.

"Even though we don't really have any tracks," she'd say.

He had *SportsCenter* on the small counter television set, sound muted. It was part of their morning deal, just understood. Sound on until she came into the room, then sound off.

If there was some important news story going on, they watched *Today*.

Danny said, "Did he tell you why he's here?"

"He says he's not sure, exactly."

Ali Walker stuffed one last folder into an already-stuffed leather shoulder bag, one that looked older to Danny than she did.

She turned and looked at him, hand on hip.

Giving him her smiley-face, even with his dad nowhere to be found.

"Sometimes he can't figure out why he's here until he's not here anymore," she said. "Part of your father's charm."

"I didn't mean to make you mad."

"Look at me," she said. "Do I look mad?"

Danny knew enough to know there was nothing for him with an honest answer to that. "No," he said.

"I'm not mad," Ali said, "I'm just making an observation."

"Right."

Aw, man, he thought. Where did that come from?

Rookie mistake, Walker.

"What does that mean?" she said. *"Right?"*

Danny took a deep breath, let it out nice and slow, trying to be careful now. Trying to make his way across a patch of ice. "It just seems to me, sometimes, no big deal, that he seems to make you as mad when he is around as when he's not around. Is all."

She started to say something right back, stopped herself with a wave of her hand.

"You're pretty smart for a guy who's really only interested in perfecting the double dribble."

"Crossover dribble."

"What*ever,"* she said, as if impersonating one of the girls in his class.

"Hey," he said, "that's a code violation."

Another one of their deals. There were strict rules of conversation at 422 Earl Avenue. No cursing of any kind, not even in the privacy of his own driveway. No *"duh."* And, under penalty of loss of video privileges for the night, no "what*ever."*

Ever.

Ali Walker taught English. And was constantly telling her son that in at least one classroom—hers—and one home—theirs—the English language was not going to sound as if they were communicating by instant-message.

"I was just making a joke," she said. "Trying to sound like one of the dear, ditzhead girls in one of my classes."

"Well," he said, imitating her now, "I'm going to let it go just this one time."

She laughed and came over with her coffee and sat across from him at the table, close enough that he could smell the smell of her, which was always like soap. She looked pretty great for somebody's mom, the way she always did, even before she started fussing with her hair and doing some fast makeup deal and getting ready for the day. Danny knowing that his mom was the prettiest woman in their school and probably in Middletown. Occasionally even described as "hot" by the high school boys at St. Pat's, something he wasn't sure should bother him or not. He just decided it was the ultimate guy compliment and left it at that.

This morning his mom wore the new blue dress she'd bought for herself last week at the Miller's fall sale.

Because Ali Walker was, in her own words, the "queen of sales."

As moms went, from his own limited experience with them, Danny believed you couldn't be much cooler than his was, even considering all the things she didn't know about guys.

Despite all she *thought* she knew.

"Straight talk?" she said.

He knew what was coming, just because sometimes he did, sometimes he got into her brain the way she got into his. Maybe because it was just the two of them.

"You have to be strong today, you know that, right?" she said.

Danny said, "I'd have to be strong at Springs. I don't even think anybody from St. Patrick's made the team."

"Are you sure? Did Jeff Ross tell you that?"

Danny pushed Waffle Crisp cereal around in his bowl. "I'm the best at St. Pat's," he said.

"Your friends are still going to ask you about it. And they're going to want to talk about it. Because that's what kids do, they talk dramas like this to death."

He was still staring down at what was left of his cereal, as if there were a clue in there somewhere.

Or a code he was trying to crack.

"Them asking me can't be worse than him telling me," he said in a quiet voice.

"Hey," she said, "is that true? The whole team is going to be from Springs this year?"

"Last year we only had three from St. Pat's. Me. Matt Fitzgerald. And Bren. Bren didn't even try out this year, he said he heard they thought he was too small to have made it last year."

Bren Darcy had been an inch taller than Danny since first grade, an inch Danny kept thinking he could make up on him but never did.

"But what about Matt?" his mom said. "He's the tallest seventh grader in this town. God, his sneakers look like life rafts. If the mission statement is to get quote *bigger* unquote, how does he not make the team?"

"The only reason he made it last year was because he is so big. But he really doesn't know how to play basketball yet, and I don't think anybody's ever really taught him. His dad's a hockey guy, and I still think he's pis . . . mad that Matt didn't want to be the world's tallest defenseman."

"Your father always said you can't teach tall."

"Matt had just made up his mind that he was lucky to make it last year and wasn't going to make it this year. Like the opposite of Bren. And that's pretty much the way he played in tryouts."

"A self-fulfilling prophecy."

Danny looked up at her. "Like you telling me how hard today is going to be at school."

"I'm just being realistic," she said. "You know some of your friends are going to know, I'm sure the news has been instant-messaged through just about every neighborhood in Middletown, USA, who made the team and who didn't."

"Mr. Ross said the letters won't arrive until today's mail."

"Right. And everybody in this town is soooooo good at keeping secrets."

28

"Mom," he said. "I'm okay. Okay?"

"Look out for the ones who bring it up first, like they want to commiserate."

He was pretty sure what she meant, just by the way she said it. The rule was, if he didn't know what a word meant, he was supposed to ask.

She said, "You know what I'm saying here?"

"They'll act like they feel bad, but they really won't?"

"They'll be the ones who are happiest that you didn't make it."

"I get it."

"And you'll get through this, kiddo," she said. "It's like I always tell you: Everything's always better in the light of day. Especially for my streak of light."

"Yeah."

"Danny?"

"Yes, I'll get through it. And everything *is* better in the light of day."

Ali Walker said, "I don't have to tell you about Michael Jordan again, do I?"

"Every time I go out for anything, you tell me about how he got cut from his junior high school team."

"There'll be other teams," she said. "There were for Michael Jordan and there will be for you."

He thought: Just not this team.

Not the one that'll probably be the first one to make the World Series since his dad's.

"Are you ready to rock and roll?" she said.

Danny took his bowl over to the sink—good boy, Walker—and rinsed it and placed it on the bottom rack of the dishwasher.

"'Rock and roll' is so incredibly lame," he said. "You need to know that."

"Rock and roll is here to stay," his mom said. "And will *never* die."

"You tell me that about as often as you tell me about Jordan getting cut."

She shut off the television, and the kitchen lights, made sure the back door would lock behind them when they left.

"I get with a good thing," she said, "I stay with it."

"I forgot to ask before," Danny said. "Is *he* staying?"

Ali Walker went out the door first, saying, "He actually mentioned that he might hang around for a while."

Danny made one of those looping undercuts like Tiger Woods made after sinking a long putt.

Without turning around, his mom said, "I saw that."

As soon as he walked in the side door at St. Patrick's, the side facing the baseball and soccer fields, Danny knew that everybody knew.

As if somehow his classmates had all Googled up "Danny Walker" and there was a place you could go to read all about how he hadn't made seventh-grade travel. How being a small, flashy point guard in Middletown wasn't nearly as big a deal as it used to be.

How Richie Walker's kid hadn't made the team.

He walked down the long hall to his locker, eyes straight ahead, imagining they were all watching him and they all knew.

Even the girls.

Tess Hewitt, who he really liked—though he was quick to point out to Will that didn't necessarily mean *liked* liked, and to please shut up—was standing next to his locker when he got there about ten after eight, five minutes before first period. So was the red-haired witch, Emma Carson.

Danny believed that Emma got to St. Patrick's every morning by taking the bus from hell.

Emma had started liking Danny in fifth grade, and had continued liking him right up until it was clear that not only did he not feel the same way about her, he was never going to feel the same way, he didn't even want her on his e-mail buddy list. That was when she apparently made a decision to torture him any chance she got.

Which meant today was going to be the closest thing for her to a school holiday.

Or a national holiday.

"Any word yet on travel?" she said.

Tess gave her a look and poked her with an elbow at the same time. Tess was taller than Emma, taller than Danny, too, by a head, with long blond hair that stretched past her shoulders, and long legs, and blue eyes.

Next to her, Emma Carson looked like a fire hydrant.

She wasn't as pretty as Tess, as nice, as smart. As skinny. Even at the age of twelve, Danny Walker knew that Emma going through middle school and maybe even high school standing next to someone who looked like Tess Hewitt wasn't the most brilliant idea in the whole world.

Danny tossed his backpack, the one his mom said was heavier than he was, into his locker, grabbed his algebra book; he'd done his homework in study hall the day before, knowing he wasn't going to be much interested in cracking any school books later if he happened to find out early that he hadn't made the team.

"I didn't make it," Danny said, his words landing harder in his locker than the backpack had.

He turned to face Emma. "But you knew that already, didn't you, M and M?"

Danny knew she hated that nickname, whether the other kids were talking about the rapper Eminem or the candy. Probably the candy more, since it was generally acknowledged by the male population at St. Patrick's School that Emma Carson could stand to lose a few.

"I didn't do anything, Daniel Walker," she said. "You're the one who didn't make travel."

"Well, you got me there," he said.

Tess said, "I'm sorry, Danny."

He wasn't sure whether this was technically commiserating from Tess or not, since Emma was the one who'd originally brought up the subject of travel, and him not making it. He was sure of this, though: He wanted to talk to Tess about this in the worst way; he'd even thought about going online last night to see if she had her own computer up and running and open for business.

It was a lot easier to talk about stuff like this online. To talk about almost anything, actually.

It's why he wished his dad would get a computer. Maybe then they could have a real conversation.

Maybe then they could talk.

"Whatever," he said.

Emma said, "I heard the whole team is from Springs."

Danny said, "Boy, you have all the sports news of the day, don't you? Tell me, Emma, have you ever considered a career in broadcasting?" And then before she could say some smart-mouth thing back to him, Danny said, "Wait a second, considering how you spread news around this place, you've started your career in broadcasting already, haven't you?"

"C'mon, Tess," she said. "I guess it must be *our* fault he won't be playing travel basketball this season."

Tess looked as if she wanted to stay, but knew that would be violating some code of girl friendship. So the two of them walked away from him down the hall.

Before they turned the corner, Tess quickly wheeled around, made a typing motion with her fingers without Emma seeing, and mouthed the word "Later."

Danny nodded at her, and then she was gone.

If yesterday was the worst day of his whole life, you had to say that today was at least going to be in the picture.

His best friend at St. Pat's was Will Stoddard, whose main claim to sports fame in Middletown was that his uncle was the old baseball pitcher Charlie Stoddard, who'd been a phenom with the Mets once and then made this amazing comeback a few years ago with the Red Sox, pitching on the same team with his son, Tom, Will's cousin.

Will's other claim to fame, much more meaningful to all those who knew and loved him—or just knew him—was this:

He could talk the way fish could swim.

He talked from the moment he woke up in the morning—this Danny knew from sleepovers—until he went to bed, and then he talked in his sleep after that. He talked in class, in the halls, in study halls, on the practice field, in the car when Ali Walker would drive him to St. Pat's, on the computer. When Danny would go to Will's house, he would watch in amazement as Will would carry on one conversation with him, another on the phone, and have four instant-message boxes going on his computer screen at the same time.

Knowing that he was going to have to listen to Will go on about travel basketball for the entire school day wasn't the most exciting prospect for Danny, but he'd caught a break when Will didn't show up at the locker next to his before the bell for first period; didn't, in fact, show up for algebra until about two minutes after Mr. Moriarty had everybody in their seats and pulling out their homework assignments.

When Will came bursting through the door, red-faced as always, his thick dark curly hair looking as if it had been piled on top of his head in scoops, Mr. Moriarty looked over the top of his reading glasses and said, "So nice of you to join us, Mr. Stoddard."

At which point Will stopped in front of the class and theatrically produced a note from the pocket of his St. Pat's–required khaki pants, like it was a "Get Out of Jail Free" card he'd saved from Monopoly.

"From my mother, sir," he said. "Car trouble. We had to drop the Suburban off at Tully Chevrolet this morning, and pick up a loaner, which turned out to be a piece of cra . . . junk, which meant we had to turn around and go back and get another one when we were halfway here. Plus, my father is out of town, and the car conked out at the end of the driveway. . . ."

"If it's just the same with you, Mr. Stoddard, I'll wait for the movie to find out the rest of it."

As he walked past Danny's desk at the front of the classroom, Will said, "Does this suck, or what?"

Danny knowing he meant travel, not being late for class.

Will had tried out for travel even though he knew he wasn't going to make it the way he hadn't made it last year or the year before. He had more heart than anybody Danny knew, more heart than Danny himself, he had always tried out, had always spent more time diving for loose balls than anybody in the gym.

But knowing the whole time he wasn't good enough.

Sometimes Danny thought that the only reason Will was even there was to cheer him on, to watch his back.

That kind of friend.

Now he was the friend saying "suck" too loud in Mr. Moriarty's classroom.

Mr. Moriarty said, "I don't believe I quite caught that, Mr. Stoddard."

Will stopped where he was, turned to face the music.

"I *said*," Will said, "that being late for a great class like yours, sir, really *stinks*."

There were some stifled laughs from behind Danny. When they

35

subsided, Mr. Moriarty said, "Why don't we just say it now, and get it over with."

To the rest of the class, Will Stoddard said, "You've been a great audience, don't forget to tip your waitresses."

It was his favorite line from some old *Saved by the Bell* rerun.

As always, there was a brief round of applause. Mr. Moriarty was older than water and liked to carry himself like a bit of a stiff, but he was a good guy. One who seemed to get it.

Or most of it, anyway.

Will was definitely right about one thing, though:

This did suck.

Even for a streak of light, even in the light of stinking day.

Even when the week should have been over, at the end of school on Friday, it wasn't over.

Because the Middletown Vikings were going to have their first practice, at five-thirty sharp, in the gym at St. Pat's.

Danny's mom had told him at lunch. The new basketball floor they'd put down in the Springs gym had suddenly turned lumpier than a bowl of Quaker oatmeal, and they were talking about tearing it up and starting all over again. And the high school gym was booked and there was an art fair at the Y.

And St. Pat's was always looking for any new ways to raise money and now they had this exciting moneymaking opportunity from the Middletown Basketball Travel Team.

Starting today.

"Figured you ought to hear it from me, sport," she said.

"They're coming to *my* school?" he said. "*My* gym? What's the next thing I'm going to find out, they expect me to ball boy for them?"

"Why don't you go with Will after school today instead of playing ball?" she said. "Or take the bus and I'll meet you at home?"

His mom usually had teacher conferences after school on Friday, and Danny would get the gym to himself.

He shook his head no, closing his eyes good and tight.

No crying in basketball.

"I'm staying until they come," he said.

37

"But I'm going to be late today."

Danny said, "I'm staying."

Will tried to get Danny to take the town bus with him after school. Or take the bus he took to the Flats, on the north side of town where he lived, a few blocks from Danny, and play his new *NCAA Football 2005* video game.

"My dad *played* college football," Will said. "He says *NCAA 2005* is better."

Will Stoddard basically said Danny should do anything except be anywhere near the St. Pat's gym when the "Springers"—it's what he called Springs School kids, in honor of *The Jerry Springer Show*—showed up for their first practice.

But Danny kept shaking his head every time Will came at him with a new alternative plan, even after they'd started playing one-on-one in the gym, and all the St. Pat's buses, including Tess's, were long gone.

Occasionally Will would whip out his cell phone, which he kept in his baggy white North Carolina shorts even when playing basketball. There was a part of Will, Danny knew, that believed that cell phones could even make sick people better.

"I'll call my brother," he said. "He got his license yesterday. He's *looking* for reasons to ride around. He *wants* to come get us, and he usually doesn't want anything to do with either one of us."

Danny shook his head from side to side, more slowly than before, trying to get through to him. "This is my day to have the gym to myself," he said. "I'm not going to go hide in my locker."

They had finished their first game of one-on-one, Danny winning, 10–7. The game was only that close because Danny had given Will his usual spot of five baskets. Sometimes he'd given him seven baskets in a game of ten and still beat him.

38

Will always took the points and always acted as if he was the one doing Danny the favor.

But then Danny would watch with great admiration sometimes as Will would borrow money off one of their other classmates and make the other kid feel as if this was his lucky day, that handing over five bucks to Will Stoddard was somehow exactly the same as the other kid winning the lottery.

Danny had just scored the winning basket by pushing the ball between Will's legs, flashing around him to collect it, and banking a combination hook-layup high off the backboard.

"Where'd you get that one?" Will said.

"My dad showed me."

"I've been meaning to ask you all day—is he still in town?"

They had finished playing now, were sitting on the stage, still sweaty, legs dangling over the side. Danny bounced the ball on St. Pat's floor. "Unless he left while I was in school today."

"You haven't seen him since . . . ?"

"No," Danny said. "But no biggie. You know how my dad is." He turned to look at Will and shrugged. "Sometimes he's as hard to cover as ever."

"Yeah," Will said. "I know what you mean."

Danny thinking: But how could you know, really? Danny knew how most people in Middletown were still obsessed with Richie Walker's comings and goings, how the Town Biddies still loved to gossip up a storm about the biggest star to ever come out of here, the kid who put Middletown on the map because of travel basketball, the kid who finally made it to the NBA, then left his wife and child not too long after the car accident that ended his career.

They didn't really know anything about his dad, any more than people who'd only ever seen him play on television or read about him in the newspapers knew about his dad.

Of course Danny felt the exact same way sometimes, not that he was going to put an ad in the *Middletown Dispatch* about that.

Danny said, "You don't have to stay until they come."

Will, whose hair looked even more like steel wool when he'd start to sweat, the Bob Marley T-shirt his parents had brought him back from Jamaica looking as wet as if he'd just gone swimming in it off Main Beach, said, "Correction: *You* don't have to stay."

"They're going to be practicing here for a couple of months," Danny said. "I'm going to have to see them around here eventually. I might as well get it out of the way today."

He hopped off the stage. "Like I said, I'm not running away, dude."

Will sighed, the sound like air coming out of a balloon. "No, why do something like that when you can get your butt run *over* by the Springers instead?"

"Don't take this the wrong way," Danny said. "But I don't remember asking for your opinion about any of this."

"Let me ask *you* something," Will said. "When have I ever cared whether you asked for my opinion or not?"

"You want me to spot you seven this time?"

Will said, "I don't want your pity. Make it six."

They were finishing that game when Ty Ross showed up. The first of the Middletown Vikings.

Ty Ross had gotten both taller and skinnier during the summer, which Danny knew from the tryouts.

He also knew Ty was still great.

Could still dribble with either hand, shoot with either hand when he got close in to the basket, see the whole court as if he had two sets of eyes going for him. He would pass the ball if somebody else even remotely had a better shot than he did *every single time*. Sometimes he would just give it up because in addition to all his other qualities as a ballplayer, Ty Ross was completely unselfish, sometimes to a fault. He wasn't the fastest kid in town, wasn't nearly as fast as Danny was, but he knew when to drive to the basket, when to step back and make one from the outside, from as far away as the three-point arc in the gym at Middletown High, when to pull the ball down and just set the offense all over again.

As far as Danny was concerned, Ty knew as much about the way the game should be played as he did. The two of them just seemed to know stuff that other kids their age didn't. Ty had been that way when they played fifth-grade travel together, and when they'd played sixth-grade travel together. He didn't just know more about basketball than the rest of the players, he knew more than the coaches, too.

He sure knew more than any parent yelling at them to do this or that from the stands.

All in the name of being good sports parents, of course.

That even went for Ty's dad, who, according to *Danny's* dad, acted as if he'd invented basketball, not Dr. James Naismith.

"You know those peach baskets Dr. Naismith used for the first basketball games?" Richie Walker had said one time. "Jeff Ross thinks he invented those, too."

On top of everything else, Ty Ross was such a nice kid that Will Stoddard said it made him physically ill.

He had dark hair, like his father, almost black, cut short this school year, his summer buzz still not having grown all the way out. He was wearing his own baggy basketball shorts, looking even baggier on him because his legs were so skinny they looked like stick-figure legs somebody had drawn on him. He was wearing a maroon Williams College T-shirt that looked to be about three sizes too big. Williams, Danny knew, was where Mr. Ross had gone to school.

Ali Walker had told Danny once that Ty was the player his father had always wanted to be. That he'd been the second-best player on the Vikings team that had won the World Series, behind Richie Walker, and that it had been pretty much the same way in high school. Danny's dad had then selected Syracuse—and the chance to play in front of thirty or forty thousand people every night in the Carrier Dome—after passing on most of the big ACC schools and even schools as far away as UCLA.

Mr. Ross, who had the grades, thought he'd have a better chance to play at a small school like Williams. Only he didn't, his mom said, never getting off the bench there before quitting the team his senior year.

"You know how your father says that the town never got over their team winning the travel-team World Series?" his mom said. "I'm not sure Tyler's dad ever got over being number two to your father during all their growing-up years."

"So," Danny remembered saying to her that night, "Mr. Ross was a real number two guard."

"That's basketball talk, right?"

"Mom," he said. "You know the point guard is called a one, the shooting guard is called a two, the center—"

"Stop," she said, and not for the first time when the subject was basketball, "I'll pay the ransom."

Ty and Danny had been teammates, starters both of them, on the fifth-grade team. Same thing the next year. Just not teammates this year. And maybe not ever again.

Now Danny watched as Ty came walking toward him with that pigeon-toed walk of his, walking straight down the middle of the gym, Danny knowing as he watched him what every kid in town knew already, that for as long as Ty Ross lived in Middletown, he was going to be the best kid walking into *every* gym.

All this time later, Danny thought to himself, it had worked out that a Walker was finally jealous of a Ross when it came to playing basketball.

Ty saw them over by the stage and came over, dribbling his own ball as he did.

"Hey, dude," Danny said to him.

Ty got right to it, not messing around, not even bothering with a greeting of his own.

"You should have made it," he said. "I should have called you as soon as I found out. You can ask my mom, I told her that night that you should have made it ahead of a lot of the guys who did."

It was the closest thing to a speech for him, coming out almost as if he'd rehearsed it.

"Thanks," Danny said, not knowing what else to say.

Wondering if Ty had expressed that same opinion to his dad, even though Ty was probably as intimidated by Mr. Ross as everybody else in town was.

Ty wouldn't let it go, as if this had been bothering him all week as much as it had bothered Danny himself. "You can play rings around some of the guards they picked ahead of you. And you know *how* to play better than *everybody* they picked ahead of you, that's for sure. And the whole thing is stupid and I wanted you to know it."

"Quick heads-up?" Will said. "I wouldn't let any of those other nose pickers who got picked ahead of our boy hear you saying that."

"Will," Danny said in a sharp voice, "I will pay you to shut up."

Will said, "I hate to reduce our relationship to money—but how much?" Then he said he was going to beat the soft drink machine out of a Coke, and did they want anything? Danny and Ty both said no.

Now it was just Danny and Ty in the gym.

Ty said, "You want to shoot around a little?"

"Nah," Danny said. "Will and me have got to be someplace. Maybe next week when you guys are here or something."

You lied enough, it got easier—that had been his experience, though pretty limited.

"Later," he said.

"Later," Ty Ross said.

Danny found Will at the soda machine and told him he was meeting his mom soon, which was technically true, as long as you had a pretty loose definition of the word *soon*.

"I'll call you later," Danny said, "or check you out on the computer."

"Either way," Will said. "You know my motto: We never close."

Then he whipped out his cell phone again to call his brother. The last thing Danny heard as Will walked down the hall was him saying, "Great news, you need to come get me at school." Then Danny saw him nod his head before saying, "You can thank me later."

Danny wasn't meeting his mother anytime soon. She was going to be later than usual on this Friday because she had promised to handle Drama Club rehearsals for Sister Marlene, the drama teacher at St. Pat's who had been out sick for a couple of days. The big first-semester production this year was *Guys and Dolls*, with Bren Darcy playing one of the lead roles, a gambler named Nathan Detroit.

"Just remember Nate Archibald, one of our all-time faves out of ancient history," Bren had said. "And the Detroit Pistons."

44

They both loved Nate Archibald because his nickname as a player had been "Tiny."

Ali Walker had said that rehearsal went from four-thirty to six-thirty, which had been just fine with Danny at the time, it meant more gym time for him. It wouldn't have been that way a few years ago, when this auditorium had served as both a gym and a theater at St. Pat's. But since then, the Annual Fund drive had raised enough money and the kids had chipped in with money of their own and now Drama Club kids held both rehearsals and the plays themselves in the brand-new theater that had been built next to the lower school.

Only now he couldn't make himself leave the gym.

He knew he was better off going over and sneaking into the theater, up in the top row, watching Bren try to sing so he could bust his chops to the high heavens on Monday.

Except.

Except here he was, like he was nailed to the spot on the old stage at St. Pat's. Here he was in what used to be the wings, stage right, peering through the sliding panel some St. Pat's kids had fashioned in the old days, like a sliding door, so on the night of the school play the kids could look out when they weren't on the stage trying to remember their lines, watching the audience while the audience watched them.

That was where Danny was watching the Middletown Vikings as they began their first practice.

In the past, the Middletown Basketball Association had hired outside coaches, usually young, to coach the various travel teams in town, boys' and girls', from fifth grade until the travel program ended in eighth. Danny had loved his coach of the last two years, a cool black guy in his twenties named Kelvin Norris, who'd thought nothing of making the two-hour car ride out from Queens twice a week, sometimes three times a week, for travel practices and games. Sometimes during the season, when there had been a Friday night game followed by a Saturday morning game, Coach Kel would stay over at the Walkers' house, or the Darcys', to the point where most of the travel-team parents considered him part of the family.

After coaching fifth grade his first year and sixth grade the next, moving up with them to the next level, everybody had just assumed that Coach Kel would move up again this season and work with the seventh graders. But then over the summer, Mr. Ross had called up Coach Kel at the summer camp he ran in the Catskills and told him that he, Mr. Ross, planned to coach the seventh graders himself this season.

Coach Kel had called Danny when it happened, wanting him to know, saying, "I think Mr. Ross's first choice to coach Ty all the way into the national spotlight was Phil Jackson. Obviously his second choice was himself."

"But everybody wants to play for you," Danny said. "Including Ty. *Especially Ty.* I don't think he's crazy about having his dad as his *dad.* Having him as a coach will probably just make him crazy."

That was when it still mattered to Danny who was going to coach the Vikings this season.

"Before I get too much older," Coach Kel said, "I've got to get as good at kissing butt as I am with those *X*'s and *O*'s and that passion-for-the-game stuff."

Mr. Ross said Middletown Basketball loved Coach Kel's enthusiasm so much that he wanted him to drop back and work with the fifth graders. Coach Kel turned him down, saying he wanted to work with older kids, not younger kids.

Danny didn't know what Coach Kel was doing now, whether

he was coaching somewhere or just teaching phys ed at Christ the King High School. Danny just knew that kneeling at the middle of the court with all the players around him, speaking in such a low voice that Danny couldn't hear what he was saying from his hiding place, was Mr. Ross.

Coach Mr. Ross, that's what he'd probably have them call him.

Danny could see all of the usual suspects out there, trying to act as if they were fascinated by whatever pep talk—or sermon—Ty's dad was giving them:

There was Ty's best friend, Teddy Moran, who was going to be one of the point guards on the team, along with the kid from Colorado, Andy Mayne. Danny noticed that Andy, who'd had long hair almost down to his shoulders for the tryouts, now looked as if he'd gotten his hair buzzed to look like Ty's. He was also wearing the same McGrady sneakers as Ty. Top of the line, a hundred bucks, maybe more. Andy's hair and sneakers at least made Danny smile. A lot of kids who grew up in Middletown tried to copy Ty Ross. Now the new kid from Colorado was the latest to run with the crowd.

Danny saw the two black kids on the team, two of the coolest kids in the whole town, Alex Aaron and Daryll Mullins, both of them as long and skinny as Ty.

Towering above everybody was Jack Harty, star tight end on Middletown's twelve-year-old travel football team. Jack, with his dark complexion, looking big and wide like some dark-colored Hummer H2, was a born rebounder, stronger than everybody else his age, one who had a way of finding the ball once the people around him stopped flying off in different directions, like characters he'd just terminated in a blood-gore video game.

Jack Harty was also famous in Middletown for being the only seventh grader who had already started shaving.

Huge deal.

So there they all were. Ty and Teddy. Alex and Daryll and Jack and the rest of them, Mr. Ross reaching into the big bag he had next to him and passing out *practice* jerseys, the guys trying those on before Mr. Ross went into the bag and came out with more goodies: long-sleeved navy-blue shooting shirts you could wear over your jersey while you were warming up.

Great, Danny thought. What did Tess and her friends call it when they went girlie-girl shopping?

Accessorizing?

Now they were even doing that with travel basketball.

"First class for you guys all the way," Mr. Ross said when he was done passing everything out. He was walking toward the stage now, where he'd left his bag of basketballs, walking straight at Danny as if he'd noticed the narrow hole in the wall. "First class all the way for a team that's going all the way this season."

He was a little taller than Danny's dad. Danny was always struck first by how tall somebody was, was always playing off this adult's height against somebody else's. He did the same with kids, like he was comparison shopping, never really knowing how tall other kids were in feet and inches, even if he knew exactly what he was on a daily basis, exactly fifty-five inches—no sneakers—by his last check in the door frame of his room.

Fifty-five.

The speed limit.

He kept looking through the narrow space, feeling as if he were on the wrong side of a fence.

"One ball," Mr. Ross said, taking a single ball, brand-new, out of the bag. "Three lines at the other end. Big guys—and there's more size on this team than ever, and not by accident—in the middle. I want you to bounce the ball off the backboard, grab it like it's a rebound, make an outlet pass to the guard on your right. Then guards, you pass it to the guy cutting to the middle from the other wing. Cut behind your passes. And make sure to get the lead out of those Hefty-bag shorts you all like to wear."

He threw the ball to the other end of the court and blew the whistle he was wearing around his neck.

Some of these guys love their whistles as much as they do their clipboards, Danny thought.

"I don't want to see that ball touching the floor," Mr. Ross said from underneath the basket closest to the stage, giving another quick blast to his whistle, as if he were using it like punctuation marks. "This is going to be a team that *passes* the ball, not a team that *dribbles* the ball."

The first three-man fast break came right at Danny.

Jack Harty started the play at the other end, wheeling around after he came down with his fake rebound, throwing a hard two-hand chest pass to Teddy, who got it to Ty, cutting toward the middle of the court from the other wing.

Ty gave it back to Jack Harty with so little effort, so quickly, it was as if the ball had never passed through his hands at all.

Jack passed it back to Teddy, who waited a couple of beats too long, hesitated just enough when he fed Ty near the basket—Ty needs *me* passing him the ball, Danny told himself, even in a boring drill like this—that Ty had to go underneath the rim and then twist his body around in the air to make a neat reverse layup.

As soon as those three got out of the way, here came the next three players on the break, Alex and Daryll so fast filling their lanes that they left fat Eric Buford behind, Eric's face already the color of one of the fat tomatoes Ali Walker grew in her backyard garden.

Danny Walker, his hands pressing against the wall above him, watching like he had a hidden camera, felt his knees buckle suddenly, without warning, the way they'd buckle when one of your buddies snuck up behind you and gave them a little karate chop.

Felt his heart sink at the same time.

He slid the board back in place, placed his forehead against it, stayed like that for a minute, listening to the basketball sounds from the other side of the wall, seeing it all with his hole closed up, with his eyes closed.

His gym.

Their team.

Hey little guy, he thought to himself, using the refrain he'd heard his whole life.

You're right back where you started, little guy.

You're with the wrong group again.

Danny Walker didn't pick up a basketball for a week, Friday to Friday, a personal best.

Or worst.

He didn't play the weekend after that first Vikings practice at St. Pat's. Or after dinner the first couple of nights of the next week. When his mom finally asked him about it on Tuesday, he shrugged and said, "My knee's been bothering me a little bit, is all."

"An injury?" she said, giving him that raised-eyebrow deal that Danny figured girls must master at, like, the age of ten and then always have in their bag of tricks after that. "To my six-million-dollar bionic boy?"

"Excuse me?"

"Never mind," she said, looking a little embarrassed. "I don't need other people to remind me I'm getting older, I do it to myself. Constantly."

"You're still young," he said, as a mild form of protest.

"Well, not if I'm coming at you with old TV shows like *The Six Million Dollar Man*. It was about this hunky guy who was half-hunky guy and half-superhuman robot."

Danny said, "How big did they make him?"

She acted as if she hadn't heard him.

"Is your knee really hurting you?" she asked. "Should I call Dr. Jim?"

He had muted the Knicks-Timberwolves preseason game he'd been watching when she'd come into the room. Now he pointed the remote at the set and let the voices of Marv Albert and Walt Frazier rejoin them.

"I think I'll just rest it a couple more days," Danny said.

"By the way," she said, "when are the tryouts for Y basketball?"

"Coming up pretty soon," he said, trying to be as vague as possible. "Will mentioned something about that the other day, I think."

"It would be fun if the two of you ended up on the same team."

On television, Frazier was talking about somebody whooping and swooping, then swishing and dishing, but Danny had missed the play.

"*Really* fun," he said. "Fun, fun, fun."

"Is that sarcasm, Daniel Walker?"

"Just kidding," he said.

Always the last line of defense, whether you were kidding or not.

He muted the set again. "Have you seen Dad?"

"At the Candy Kitchen the other day when I ran in to grab a sandwich. He was at the same seat at the counter he's been sitting at since high school. I'm going to petition the town to give it landmark status."

"By himself?" Danny said. "Not doing anything?"

"Yes," his mom said in a voice so soft it surprised him, just because of who they were talking about. "That's exactly what he was doing. Sitting alone. Not talking to anybody. Not doing anything except drinking a cup of coffee."

She came off the couch and knelt next to the easy chair. "Is there something you want to talk about that we're not talking about here? Like this knee of yours, maybe, and how maybe that's not the thing that's keeping you off the court?"

He looked past her to the Knicks game—you had to be careful about eye contact sometimes, eye contact could get you every time—and said, "What would you think if I didn't, like, play basketball this year?"

Danny had to give his mom credit. She didn't start yelling about it on the spot, though that didn't actually surprise him, she'd never been one of those parents who felt like she had to pump up the volume every time there was a disagreement in the house, or you stepped out of line.

Even when she got really mad at you about something, she didn't act as if you'd suddenly gone deaf.

Even when you were talking about quitting basketball, at least for the time being.

"You've always played, from the time you were big enough," she said.

Meaning, old enough.

"Maybe I need a break, is all."

"At the age of twelve?"

What she'd do in moments like this was, she'd start straightening up the room. Moving magazines about an inch, one way or the other, on the coffee table. Fluffing up pillows on the couch that didn't need fluffing.

Waiting him out a little bit.

Danny said, "Mr. Fleming has baseball workouts all winter, at the tennis bubble. Just about every weekend."

Danny Walker played second base in baseball, always batted leadoff because of his size. And he was good. Just not as good as he was in basketball. At least as good as he used to think he was in basketball.

"You could do both," she said.

53

Straightening a picture of her parents on the wall now.

"Like I said, I'm just thinking that maybe I need a little break."

Ali Walker said, "And what other essentials do you plan to take a break from now that travel basketball didn't work out for you—eating and sleeping and bathing regularly?"

Danny tried to lighten the mood in the room a little bit. Fluff things up a little himself.

"Is that sarcasm, Alison Walker?"

She didn't want to play.

"Have you decided that Y ball is some kind of step down?"

"Only on account of, it *is* a step down."

"Not every single good basketball-playing boy in this town is on travel," she said. "And don't say, on account of."

"Sorry," he said. "And, yes, all the good kids in town are on travel, unless they're playing hockey or something."

"You need basketball," she said. Again with the soft voice.

"Well, it sure doesn't need me."

Standoff. They had them sometimes.

"So you're telling me you're quitting."

"Not quitting permanently, Mom. Just for one season."

She had run out of things to move around. So she stood in the middle of the room, between him and the Knicks game, hands on hips. Danny saw that one long piece of hair had somehow gotten loose and had fallen over one eye. She blew it out of the way now, which sounded more like she was blowing off steam.

"I think you need to talk to your father on this one."

They both knew she never called him in.

On anything.

Sometimes, when he was in the house, when they were in the kitchen and Danny was upstairs eavesdropping, he would hear her say, "When I want your advice on parenting, I'll send up a flare."

54

In those moments, Danny wouldn't even recognize his mom's voice, as if it were another person doing the talking down there.

"I was planning to call Dad, actually. So's I could tell him myself."

She walked past him, probably on her way to straighten up the whole kitchen, do the dinner dishes all over again or mop the floor, saying to herself as much as him, "His two specialties, playing ball and quitting things."

Danny had forgotten to shut his computer off, so it was still on when he went up to his room, the screen giving off its spooky glow in the otherwise dark room, like a blue night-light.

He'd also forgotten to go offline.

He went over, sat down at his desk, was about to shut the whole thing down for the night, not even giving one last check to the sports news at ESPN.com, when he heard the goofy instant-message sound—"the old doodlely-doo," his mom called it, "the music of our lives"—come out of it, at the same time a message box appeared in the upper left-hand corner of the screen.

He closed his eyes, knowing he was worn out from talking to Will in real life, and he certainly wasn't in the mood to talk to him electronically, especially at this time of night.

But when he looked closer he saw it wasn't from WillStud, his screen name.

The sender was ConTessa44.

Tess, sitting at her own computer in her second-floor bedroom at 44 Butter Lane.

CONTESSA44: Hey. You there? Hello? Calling Mr. Crossover.

Crossover2 was his screen name. For obvious reasons.

CROSSOVER2: I'm here.

By now Tess knew that Danny wasn't any more chatty in their personal chat room than he was in person. She liked to joke that he had completely mastered the language of instant-messaging, which she called "instant shorthand." She also knew to be patient with him, even when he was only tapping out a couple of words, because he couldn't type nearly as fast as she could. He'd been with her at her computer once while she talked online to Emma, who Tess said was slower than boiling water, and saw how Tess bopped her head from side to side while she waited for Emma to hold up her end of the conversation, occasionally moved from side to side in her chair, like it was sitting-down dancing.

> **CONTESSA44: What's up?**
> **CROSSOVER2: Just chillin. You know.**
> **CONTESSA44: Oh, I get it. The big hip-hopper.**
> **CROSSOVER2: JK.**

More instant shorthand. For "just kidding."

> **CONTESSA44: I know. You were acting weird today. You OK?**

He waited a second. And imagined her waiting for him, doing the head bop, the side-to-side sway.

He hit the two letters. Then "send."

> **CROSSOVER2: No**
> **CONTESSA44: What up, dawg?**
> **CROSSOVER2: Now who's the hip-hopper?**
> **CONTESSA44: Seriously.**

56

Danny took a deep breath, as a way of taking his time, telling himself he didn't need to get into this with her now.

But knowing he wanted to in the worst way.

CROSSOVER2: I'm thinking about skipping b-ball this year.

It took so little time for the doodlely-doo to come right back at him he imagined their words colliding somewhere over Route 37, the road that divided Middletown in half.

CONTESSA44: NO NO NO NO . . . NO!
CROSSOVER2: Why not?

Now he was the one who waited.

CONTESSA44: Because basketball is who you are. Like taking pictures is for me. It's your gift, DW, no matter what the dumb Basketball Dads say. You can't quit. If you quit, they WIN.
CROSSOVER2: I'm just thinking about it, is all.
CONTESSA44: Stop thinking about it. Right now. That's an order.
CROSSOVER2: You sound like a second mom.
CONTESSA44: Wrong. I'm just your first biggest fan. Talk more tomorrow . . . Love, Tess.
CROSSOVER2: Back at you. With the last part, I mean.

He was reaching for the power button when he heard the goofy sound one more time.

CONTESSA44: I know.

· · ·

Danny always imagined there was some all-seeing, all-knowing Computer God somewhere, up there in microchip hard-drive heaven, monitoring all the computer monitors, checking out all conversations like this. Keeping a Permanent Record like they did at school. Knowing that Tess Hewitt always managed to get the word *love* into the conversation with Danny Walker.

And how he never stopped her, or made a joke about it.

He washed up, brushed his teeth, got into bed, hooked his hands behind his head, stared up at the poster of John Stockton on his ceiling, feeling tired all of a sudden, knowing his eyes weren't going to stay open for long. Still thinking about Tess, though. The tall girl. He didn't know exactly how to describe the feelings he had for her, just knowing that outside of his parents—and ball—he couldn't think of anything or anybody he cared about more.

He smiled to himself, the first time he'd felt like smiling all night, or all week.

Thinking at the same time:

If it wasn't love, for the Twelve-and-Under Division, it was certainly in the picture.

But he was still quitting.

THE BIGGEST PUBLIC PARK IN MIDDLETOWN, MCFEELEY PARK, WAS ABOUT three blocks from the middle of downtown, and included one regulation baseball diamond, two Little League fields, all the ballfields with lights. There were four lighted tennis courts, a playground for kids, and taking up the whole northeast corner of McFeeley, the part closest to town, was what all the kids called Duck Poop Pond, the kids finding it somewhat less charming than the adults who brought small children there to feed the butt-ugly ducks and little ducklings who resided there.

Up on a hill, past the tennis courts, was Middletown's best outdoor public basketball court, with lights of its own.

In many ways, the downtown area wasn't really the main plaza in Middletown, McFeeley Park was.

Danny sometimes thought that Middletown, even as small as it was, should be broken up into different divisions, the way sports leagues were. There were the Springs School kids, and their parents, and the St. Pat's people. There were the people who lived in the Springs, the nicer section of town, south of Route 37, and the ones who lived on the north side, where Danny and his mom lived, known as the Flats.

"We call it the Flats, anyway," Will Stoddard liked to say. "People in the Springs call it the Pits."

But there was always one day in the fall when the whole town came together, for the McFeeley Fair. It was organized by the Chamber of Commerce to raise money for the upkeep of the pond, the fields, the courts, the playground, all the land donated by the McFeeley family, which had originally owned about half of Middletown.

On the last Saturday in October, McFeeley Park was turned into a combination of amusement park and county fair, with rides and games and booths where you could dunk teachers and coaches, even a local garage band, picked every year in a big Battle of the Bands, providing the music.

Other than maybe an important Middletown High football game, it was the one day of the year when the town actually felt like one town.

"Look," Tess said as she kept training her camera on the people in the crowds, "Middletown being nice to Middletown."

Tess loved taking pictures the way Danny loved basketball. She'd even had a few of them published in the *Dispatch*. Color, black-and-white, it didn't matter. The ones she'd allow Danny to see, when she'd allow him to see her work, were always great. She liked to tell him that the way he liked to play in the dark, she liked to play in a darkroom.

"I think I even saw Mr. Ross looking happy enough to qualify as an actual human being," she said.

"It's some kind of trick," Danny said. "Like you big-time photographers do with lighting and stuff."

Somehow she had been able to ditch Emma. Even more amazingly, Will had decided to *work*, his dad having offered to pay him to handle one of the dunking booths. Will said he needed the money and that you could never go wrong watching a science teacher do what he called the *Finding Nemo* thing.

So it was just Danny and Tess. She had gone through two rolls of film already. He'd won her a stuffed animal by throwing a softball into the top of an old-fashioned milk bucket. After she'd picked out the huge character she instantly named Mr. Bear, she asked the St. Pat's mom running the softball game, Mrs. Damiecki, to take a picture of the two of them.

"C'mon," Tess said when Danny started grumping about it, "it'll take one second."

She was smiling as she said it, Danny could see by looking up at her. It killed him sometimes, having to look up at her.

When Mrs. Damiecki told them to smile, he gave Tess and Mr. Bear a poke and got her laughing so she wouldn't notice him getting up on the balls of his feet and making himself taller.

Now Tess said, "Let's go up to the basketball court, I want to take some shots of the game, in case I want to be a photographer for *Sports Illustrated* someday."

She made it sound casual, but he knew what she was doing. They'd both seen some of the seventh-grade Springers shooting around. There'd be pickup games going on all day at the McFeeley Fair if the weather was nice enough, and it was beautiful today. The crowd around the court had been growing for the last hour, as if people were looking for a diversion from the dunking and Ferris wheel and junky food and garage-band music that sounded like broken electric guitars and overamped speakers.

"Let's go back over to the dunking pool," Danny said. "I'll even give up my body and let you take a picture of me doing my imitation of Leonardo going down for the count in *Titanic*."

"Oh, come up the hill with me," Tess said. In her red plaid shirt and jeans that made her legs look longer than Danny's whole body. In her cute pigtails.

The tall girl, looking like a million bucks.

"You don't have to play," she said. "We'll just watch."

61

"You want me to play."

"Wherever would you get an idea like that?"

Danny said, "I don't have the right sneaks."

They both looked down at his Air Force Ones, with the hole in the right toe, as if on cue.

"They sure look like basketball shoes to me," Tess said. "Or were something very, very close to basketball shoes at one time."

"Well, they've been bothering me."

"Somehow," she said, "I don't think it's your Nikes bothering you."

"What's that supposed to mean?"

"It means that unless you've come down with some sort of weird virus, you would play ball barefoot if you knew there was a game anywhere near you."

"I thought we were having a good time," he said.

God, he thought, now *you* sound like a girl.

"It's time you started playing ball again," she said.

She had been maneuvering him up the hill as they talked, pushing him along, Danny in front of her. When he turned around, they were nearly eye-to-eye for once.

"Who told you I haven't been playing ball?" he said.

She gave a toss to her hair even though Danny noticed there wasn't any hair in her eyes. Then gave him one of her know-everything looks with that raised eyebrow.

One of those looks that seemed to say:

I know what you had for breakfast, whether or not you remembered to brush your teeth today. And if you're wearing clean underwear.

Danny said, "You talked to my mom."

Tess made a typing motion in the air in front of her.

"Doodlely-doo," she said.

There was a mix of St. Pat's kids and Springs kids laughing and pushing each other at half-court, as Ty and Bren Darcy tried to organize the teams.

They weren't doing it by school, or going from tallest to smallest, Danny saw, just trying to make the best and fairest sides. Jack Harty went with Bren, Daryll Mullins went with Ty, Alex Aaron, wearing an oversized Julius Erving replica jersey from the old New York Nets, went with Bren.

Danny stood next to Tess, who was casually snapping her pictures, and thought to himself: Kids always did the best job making the best game, especially when they took the old Dad Factor out of the equation.

It was Ty Ross who spotted Danny first.

Tess saw, and gave Danny a little nudge with her elbow. "Uh-oh," she said. "You've been made, as they say in the cop shows."

"You don't watch cop shows."

"I try to keep up."

Without even hesitating, Ty said, "I've got Danny."

They all turned to where Danny and Tess were standing.

"Wait a second," Bren said, trying to sound indignant. "I didn't know he was in the available talent pool."

Daryll Mullins said, "It's the McFeeley Fair, Darcy, not draft day on ESPN."

Ty said, "You in, Walker?"

They were still all looking at him.

Danny looked at Tess, then back at Ty. And smiled. "I'm in."

"These aren't fair sides now," Teddy Moran said. He'd already been picked by Ty and was standing with the rest of his team.

"I'll make them fair," Ty said. "Teddy, you and Andy go with Bren now. We'll take Danny and Matt."

Teddy Moran, career complainer, said, "I don't care about the squirt, but Matt gives you guys too much height."

Daryll Mullins, in that laid-back way he had, said, "But you give them more lip, Moran."

Teddy reluctantly moved over with Bren's guys, trying to give Danny the playground staredown with his small pig eyes as he did. Teddy Moran, every kid in Middletown knew, thought there was something in the Town Charter that said he was always supposed to be on Ty Ross's team.

Ty and Bren sorted out the rest of the sides. It wasn't quite warm enough for them to play shirts-against-skins; they all just agreed they'd have to know what everybody on their team was wearing.

Right before Ty and Andy shot to see who got the ball, Danny gave a little wave to Tess.

She looked at him without changing expression and snapped his picture, barely focusing it, using one hand, looking like a pro already.

What Richie Walker saw, wearing an old blue Middletown baseball cap, slouched against a tree on the pond side of McFeeley:

He saw his kid and the Ross kid play as if they were Stockton and Malone. Except the Ross kid had more imagination already than Malone ever had with his catch-and-shoot game. Had more of a feel for everything.

Was more interesting to watch.

That's what he saw.

And this: Nobody on the court could guard the Ross kid straight-up and nobody, not even the tiny kid with the freckles who'd helped pick the teams, the one who was like this crazed Mini-Me, could get in front of Danny.

With all the joking around and what he was sure was small-fry trash-talking, all the fake beefs about fouls and who had really knocked the ball out of bounds, with the way the kids in the game kept playing to the kids in the crowd, Richie couldn't take his eyes off Danny and Ty Ross.

They were doing what good, smart players could always do.

Make the game nice.

The word—*nice*—actually made him smile, the way some old song could make you smile if you just heard one lick of it. He'd had a teammate on the Warriors, Raiford Tipton, a forward out of the University of Miami, a dude with the hair rows and the tattoos and the strut. When Richie would hit Raiford Tipton just right on the break, Raiford would run past him when they were getting back on defense and say, "Richie Walker, that was niiiiiccccce."

Making the word sound like it had three or four syllables in it, making it sound as if what Richie had just done with the ball was practically illegal.

Danny and Ty Ross were *nice*.

They worked the pick-and-roll. When they had a chance to get out and run on the fast break, Ty would get the ball off the boards and throw a blind pass nearly to half-court, knowing Danny would already be there.

Or: Ty would draw two of three defenders to him in the low blocks and then kick it out to Danny, who kept launching that funny shot of his—though he was getting it more out in front, like Richie had showed him—and scoring with ease from the outside.

Then Richie would wait to see a smile or a fist-pump from his kid, or any kind of change of expression.

Only Danny never would.

Like this was the way it was all supposed to be.

There was a taller guard with a skinhead haircut who Danny couldn't guard sometimes, at least when Danny would let the skinhead get to his spot in close to the basket. But *only* if he could get to his spot.

Danny's team won the first game of eleven baskets easy, Richie keeping score to himself, into it now, and they were about to do it again. It was 9–4 and here was Danny dribbling through a double-team—the skinhead and the freckled kid who was just a little taller than Danny—beating them at the top of the key and stopping at the foul line and no-looking Ty with a perfect bounce pass for a layup.

Richie felt himself give a little fist-pump.

As he did, he heard: "Rich."

The voice made him jump the way Ali had that night outside the house. Like he was wearing some kind of sign these days that said, Please sneak up on me.

Or maybe he was just so used to living deep inside his own head, blocking out everything: Noise. People. The world.

He turned around to see Jeff Ross.

"Hey," Richie said.

"Hey yourself."

Ross put his hand out. Richie shook it, studying him as he did: The little polo pony on the shirt, expensive sunglasses, what still looked to be a summer tan on him, hair a little grayer and a little thinner than Richie remembered from the last time he'd seen him a couple of years ago, but the hair still hanging in there.

You still look like money, Richie wanted to say, you always did. But you're no kid anymore.

Of course, how old do I look to him?

Ross nodded at the court. "Kind of fun watching the next generation have at it," he said.

Danny and Ty came up the court on a two-on-one break, passing the ball back and forth between them at warp speed, neither one of them taking a single dribble, Ty finally blowing past the long skinny black kid trying to defend them and Danny lofting a little pass that Ty caught and shot in one smooth motion.

The crowd around the court, adults and kids, cheered like it was a real game.

"Ball didn't touch the floor," Ross said. "Just like I teach them."

Richie turned so he was looking right at him. "Speaking of that, how did my kid not make your team, if you don't mind me asking?"

Getting right to it. Knowing he sounded like every father of every kid who hadn't made the team, and not giving a rat's ass.

"Well, first of all, it's not *my* team," Ross said. "And secondly, I didn't pick the team. My son was trying out, too, and I'm the president of Middletown Basketball as well. So I took myself out of the process."

Richie let it go, like a bad shot that wasn't even worth contesting. They both knew it was bull.

"Let me put it to you another way: What kind of process do you guys have going here if a kid that good doesn't make your team?"

Ross took off his sunglasses, folded them, stuck them in the front of his polo-pony shirt, like it was all part of a rich-guy pose, buying time. He even cleared his throat.

"My understanding with Danny—whom we all love, by the way—is that it just turned out to be close with him and a group of other guards and he unfortunately had a bad second night of tryouts."

"Who gives a sh . . . " Richie put his hands out in front of him, trying not to get hot. "Who cares?" he said. "Have you been watching what I've been watching here? Anybody who knows anything about basketball can see how good he is. And he was on travel the last two years. Now you guys take him off because he has a bad night? Because he's too small? No kidding, Jeff, what's up with *that*?"

It was clear that the only thing Jeff Ross had heard was the part about Danny being small. "Who said he didn't make the team because he was too small?"

"Didn't you tell those crackerjack, basketball-savvy talent scouts of yours that you wanted the team to get bigger this year?"

"No, Rich, I most certainly did not. Did Danny tell you that?"

Richie ignored him. "In sports, the best kids are supposed to make the team."

"The evaluators were as fair as they could be. . . ."

"Maybe they were fair," Richie said. "But if they don't know what they're watching, they shouldn't be picking the stinking team."

"I'm sorry you feel that way," Ross said. He put the sunglasses back on, like he was putting a mask back on. "But sports isn't always fair. I guess you know that better than anybody."

Now they were getting to it, and Richie knew they weren't just talking about the kids on the court.

Ross said, "Here's something else you know: Sometimes the little guys have to play a little bigger when it counts."

"You turned away the wrong little guy and you know it."

"For somebody who's not around very often," Ross said, "you've certainly taken a passionate interest in Danny's career all of a sudden."

"I'm taking an interest in my kid, who just happens to be a hell of a player. That okay with you?"

Ross said, "Not all the players in town get the chance to be you. Even when they're related to you."

They were both watching the court now. As if on cue, Danny went behind his back with his own long arms—but those small hands—and dusted a fat kid who had just entered the game.

"There used to be a rule, back in our day, where you could add a kid after the tryouts," Richie said. "Put him on the team, Jeff."

"And what do I tell the other kids who didn't make it? No, he can try out next year. That's the system."

"Then the system stinks worse than the town dump."

Jeff Ross didn't say anything, so Richie kept going. "So that's the way it's gonna be? You're gonna get back at me through my kid?"

"This has nothing to do with you and me, Walker. But since you're such a concerned parent now, why not have your own damn system?"

Dropping all pretense that they were going to be any more polite to each other now than they had been twenty years ago.

"Maybe you should start your own team," Ross said, trying to be sarcastic. "The Richie Walker All-Stars."

Richie was silent. Staring at the court. Ross started walking toward the pond, away from the game, saying, "You were always a big movie guy, Rich. But life isn't always a movie. The little guy doesn't always win the day. I'll see you around."

"Yeah."

Ross left him standing there. Alone again, watching the kids playing ball.

Watching his kid.

Richie Walker's all-star.

He had to be leaving.

When his dad came over for dinner, when it was an official visit to the house, scheduled in advance and not a drop-by, it almost always meant he was leaving the next day.

At least he had stayed a whole week this time. Longer, if you counted that first night in the driveway.

"Hold on there, Mr. Gloom and Doom," Ali Walker said when Danny ran his theory past her. "He didn't say anything about his travel plans."

"He never does, until the last possible minute."

"He just asked if it would be all right if the three of us had dinner. Even offered to take us out, sport. I told him to save his money, I'd whip up my famous Wasp Girl Lasagna."

"At least he got to see me play at the fair," Danny said.

She was setting the table. Resetting it, actually. That meant she was putting the forks on the outside of the napkins, knives on the inside, after Danny had once again managed to do it the other way around.

She looked up. "You didn't tell me you saw him at the fair."

"I don't even know if he saw me see him. He was in the distance, kind of, just watching the game."

"Anyway," his mom said, "if he is leaving, he'll tell you."

"You don't mind, by the way? Him coming over?"

She was back in the kitchen, opening the oven door, checking out the famous lasagna, which was better than you got at Fierro's in town. "He's your father. I have never tried to keep you two apart, you know that. I told him tonight that if you guys wanted to have a boys' night out, go for it. He said, no, I was included."

"He's never not leaving when it's one of these."

"Double negative," his mom, the English teacher, said.

"Just negative," Danny said.

His dad showed up at six-thirty sharp, wearing a blue buttoned-down shirt, khaki slacks, the kind of nubuck shoes kids wore with their school clothes, his hair slicked back and still wet from his shower. He was carrying a bottle of wine.

Danny had been up in his room playing last year's NBA game on PlayStation when he heard the doorbell. When he came down the stairs he noticed that his mom had found time to change out of her school clothes, into a green, silky-looking blouse with some kind of print on it you didn't notice at first, and khaki-colored pants of her own, her slacks looking a lot nicer than what his dad had on.

The kind of dress-up clothes she'd wear when she went out to dinner with a friend. Male or female. Though, Danny had to say, there weren't a lot of males in Middletown she would give the time of day to.

It was Danny's impression that his mom was about as interested in dating as she was in video games.

But she'd dressed up tonight for his dad, whatever that meant. Maybe he'd ask Tess online later how much he should read into something like that.

Danny Walker, even at twelve, was smart enough to know this about girls: They were smarter than boys already. They were smarter about all the important stuff in life that didn't include sports, and would stay smarter from now on, which meant that he and the rest of the boys would be playing catch-up, trying to come from behind, the rest of the way.

"You look nice," his dad said.

"You still clean up pretty well yourself," his mom said.

It was Will Stoddard's theory that adults, even cool adults, behaved like space aliens about half the time, and now here it was right in front of Danny's eyes: With all the rotten things his mom could say to his dad when they were alone, she still wanted to look her best when he came over.

The three of them sat in the living room before dinner, eating cheese and crackers. His mom drank some of the wine he'd brought. His dad drank beer out of a bottle. Danny got to have a Coke. On account of, he figured, this being a special occasion.

Whatever the occasion was.

His mom tried to find out how things were going for his dad in that casual way she had, asking questions you were supposed to believe had just popped into her head, all the time getting to the one she hoped would make you spill your guts.

He was still living in Oakland, he said, even though his lease was about to be up. Said the Warriors had talked about him doing some work for them in community relations, but he hadn't decided yet. He had done some scouting for them in the past, but had quit that, saying he was tired of watching people he didn't know or care about play games he couldn't play.

He had thought assistant coaching might be different, taking a job at the University of San Francisco last season.

But he had quit that, too.

He had quit a lot of things since the accident, Danny knew.

"So it's back to the card shows," Ali Walker said. "Which you love so dearly."

The most money he'd made the past several years was from making appearances at card and memorabilia shows.

"It's not so bad if you limit the conversation."

"Your specialty." His mom smiling when she said it.

"Most people are all right. Step right up and see the guy who used to be Richie Walker."

He drank down about half his beer in one gulp, like he was incredibly thirsty all of a sudden.

"You're right," he said. "I hate it."

Now came one of those record-breaking, world-class silences that made you wonder if any member of the Walker family would say anything ever again.

Until Danny said: "When are you leaving?"

"It's actually what I wanted to talk to you both about."

She clapped her hands together. "Well, let's do it at the dinner table, before the lasagna turns into leftovers."

They passed the rolls and salad around. His dad remarked that her lasagna was as good as ever. She said, thank you, sir. She asked how things were at the place known in Middletown as the Inn. He said, hey, they even had cable there now.

Finally he put down his fork and said, "Listen, I'm thinking about hanging around for a while."

His mom had her wineglass nearly to her lips, stopped it right there. "In Middletown?"

"Yeah."

Danny thinking: *Yeah!*

His mom said, "What about the fabulous card-show appearances?"

"There's enough of them around here," he said. "Even though the money's not that great for somebody like me anywhere." He gave her a look and said, "As you know better than anybody else."

"We're all right, Rich."

Danny couldn't wait.

"What are you going to *do* here?" he said.

Richie Walker said, "I was thinking about coaching."

Danny's mom said, "You're going to coach a team in Middletown?"

"Yeah, an opportunity just presented itself in the past couple of days."

Danny and his mom waited. Sometimes you could try to wait his dad out on something and he'd be out the door and gone and you'd still be waiting. But this time was different, Danny'd had this feeling there was something he'd been waiting to tell them since he walked in the front door.

"To tell you the truth," he said, "it's an opportunity I sort of created for myself."

"*Dad!*" Danny didn't mean it to come out as loud as it did, but there it was. "*Who are you going to coach?*"

"You," he said.

"Me."

His mom said, "In the Y league?"

Richie Walker was smiling now.

Even with his eyes.

"You know what this town needs even more than cable TV at the Inn?"

Danny grabbed his arm. "*What?*"

"Another seventh-grade travel team," his dad said.

RICHIE CAME BACK FROM THE KITCHEN WITH A BRAND-NEW BEER, DRINKING IT out of the bottle this time. When he sat back down, Danny started asking questions immediately.

Like: "How are we going to get games?"

His dad said, "I'll call the Tri-Valley League and see if they've got room for one more team. If not, I'll get phone numbers for coaches and call them on my own. It's seventh-grade ball, after all. We're not trying to join the Big East."

They were all sitting around the coffee table, Danny and his dad on the floor, his mom on the couch, his dad showing them the to-do list he'd been scribbling on Runyon's napkins.

Ali said, "But won't they have their schedules set?"

"There's still a month to go before the season starts. I'm hoping they'll try to work something out, on account of . . ."

"On account of," she said, "you're Richie Walker."

"Yeah," he said. "What's left of him, anyway."

Danny said, "Even if we come up with enough players, where are we going to practice? Everybody was saying at the fair that because of what happened to the Springs gym, there's not enough practice time for anybody."

His mom said, "I can help at St. Pat's. But you may have to practice at some weird hours. Maybe after homework instead of before, as long as all the parents are willing."

Richie said, "What do they charge?"

"I don't honestly know. But I'll ask."

Danny said, "You think we can really get into the league?"

Richie said, "If we don't, we'll be one of those independent teams, like they have in minor-league baseball. You know, where all the bad boys go when they come out of drug rehab and nobody will give them a job."

His dad held up a couple of his napkins and said, "Hey, I don't have all the answers here, least not yet."

Danny said, "But if we don't get into the league, how do we get into the tournament?"

Richie said he might have one more beer. Ali said, "Why don't I go make up a quick pot of coffee instead," not even asking if he wanted coffee.

She came back five minutes later with two mugs, handing Richie one, saying, "Milk, two sugars," as she did. They all sat down on the living-room floor, like they were unwrapping some kind of Christmas present.

On the kind of Christmas morning, Danny thought, they'd never had.

"Listen," his dad said, "all we are right now is the Middletown Cocktail Napkins and you're already worried about making the tournament?" Giving Danny a shove to let him know he was playing. "If we pull this thing off," Richie said, "maybe it'll be enough for us to win the championship of all the kids who got told they weren't good enough."

Danny said, "But all the good players are taken."

"No," Richie Walker said, "they're not."

Danny looked up at the standing grandfather clock that belonged to some grandparent and saw that it was past ten o'clock now. Past bedtime. His mom hadn't said anything about that, at least not yet.

Maybe because she was getting into it about the Middletown Cocktail Napkins the way the boys were.

It had turned into another night Danny didn't want to end.

Now she was the one who said, "I know there are still good players out there, present company certainly included. But Danny's right: Are there enough so it doesn't turn out to be Danny and the Bad News Bears?"

Danny started ticking off names on his fingers: "There's me. Bren. Will."

Richie: "Can Will play?"

Danny: "He can make an open shot. And he can defend almost as well as he can talk."

Richie: "Could he start with you in the backcourt?"

Danny: "Bren's better."

He saw his mother's head going back and forth like she was watching a tennis match. A grin on her face, even though it was basketball talk, which she said usually was about as riveting for her as interest rates at the bank.

Just not tonight.

Danny said, "The only really big guy left is Matt Fitzgerald. He's already wearing size thirteen kicks. But he needs to be coached."

His dad said, "You know what I say."

The three of them at once, as if they'd rehearsed it, said, "You can't teach tall."

When they stopped laughing, Danny said, "That's only four guys."

"We don't need to come up with a whole list of possibles tonight," his dad said. "Over the next day or so, try to think of all those fabulous bubble guys Jeff Ross talked about. Or maybe some kids who didn't try out. All we need is ten, tops. And we could play with eight."

"I'll ask around," Danny said.

Ali said, "I don't want to throw cold water on this. But leagues cost money, Rich. Teams like this cost money, and not just for the gym."

He shrugged, held up a napkin. "I've got some thoughts on that. Hell, everybody's got a salary cap these days. Ours might just have to be a little lower than everybody else's."

He started to get up. And for a moment, it was as if he had forgotten how many busted parts he still had. He got halfway up before making a face, then started the whole process again, this time putting a hand on the coffee table to steady himself, then taking it much more slowly from there.

Danny wanted to help him, just wasn't sure how.

"Sweet dreams, kiddo," he said to Danny.

Danny thinking: You can say that again.

The two of them were still outside, standing next to his car.

Danny had snuck down the stairs once they were outside, gone out the back door, got behind where the garbage cans were, and eavesdropped on his parents like he was on a stakeout.

His mom was saying, "You can't start this and not follow through."

"You mean like my jobs."

"I mean with everything."

"I can do this."

"No," she said. "Now you *have* to do this."

"Okay," he said. "I can do this, I have to do this. I *will* do this."

"Because if you don't, you really will break this boy's heart this time."

Small silence.

"Hell, Ali, this is *about* his heart."

"You know you're not going to get any help from the Association. Thinking outside the box in this town can get you arrested."

"Screw 'em if they can't take a good joke."

"There's the old Rich."

"Listen," he said. "I know I'm not much of a parent. Not a parent at all, most times. But the more I listened to Jeff Ross, the more it occurred to me that my ass is just worn out having guys who can't find their own jockstraps running sports. At any freaking level."

"I'll help any way I can."

"Figured."

"You can pull this off?" she said.

It came out a question.

"We're sure as hell gonna find out," his dad said.

"Well, okay," Will Stoddard said, looking around the basketball court at St. Pat's, eight o'clock the next Saturday morning. "We're looking to assemble the first all-guard basketball team in history."

"Plus Matt," Bren Darcy said, correcting him.

"Plus Matt," Danny said. "Just so's people won't get the idea we're a sixth-grade team."

"I've seen sixth-grade teams bigger than us," Will said.

Danny and Will had written up fliers and left them around both Springs and St. Pat's, announcing tryouts for a new seventh-grade travel team this Saturday. Will, who said he knew more about computers than Bill Gates, had even figured out a way to set up a temporary Web site, though the Web site basically had the same information as the fliers.

The largest type on the page announced that this was all at the invitation of Coach Richie Walker, Middletown's most illustrious basketball alumnus.

Will had thrown in the last part.

They had left fliers at the Candy Kitchen and Jackson's stationery store and Fierro's and on the bulletin board they still kept in the lobby of the Middletown movie theater.

After all that, eight kids showed up.

Danny. Bren. Will. Matt Fitzgerald, who didn't just look tall, he was also as wide as one of those double-wide trailers at the trailer park outside of town when he stood next to the rest of them. Michael Harden, another decent St. Pat's kid. He was another fifty-five incher who'd given up on trying out for the real travel team the year before.

There was one Springs kid, Oliver Towne, a round black kid known to his classmates as the Round Mound of Towne, a play on words that came from Charles Barkley's old college nickname, the Round Mound of Rebound. Oliver was a little taller than Danny, but not by much.

Danny actually thought Oliver took up about the same space horizontally as he did vertically, as if every inch taller he got also became an inch wider.

Will used to call him Roker, because he was as fat as the weatherman on *The Today Show* used to be, but that was before the *Today* guy did that deal where he had his stomach stapled shut.

Will always seemed to know stuff like that, believing that most useful information in his life came from *People* magazine.

Whatever Oliver Towne weighed, he was the closest thing to an actual forward in the gym.

Finally, there were the only twins at St. Patrick's School, Robert and Steven O'Brien, who announced to the other kids they were only there because their mom had made them.

"She told us that if we weren't going to play hockey this year because we were tired of getting up at five in the stupid morning, we were going to do *something*," Robert said.

Or it could have been Steven. Danny was never completely sure which was which. The only ones who seemed to be able to tell the O'Brien kids apart *were* the O'Brien twins.

The other twin said, "She said our winter sports schedule

wasn't going to consist of us sitting on our skinny butts and playing video games."

Danny took a quick survey of his teammates and in his head heard one of those NBA-arena announcers shouting, "Give a big Middletown welcome to *your . . . Middletown . . . Cocktail Napkins!*"

Now, if they could scare up a couple of more players, maybe they could even scrimmage.

Danny's dad hadn't made much of a speech when he realized the eight players in the gym were the only ones coming. He addressed the kids, and a few of the parents who'd hung around to listen. Michael Harden's dad, Jerry, had played with Richie Walker on the championship seventh-grade team, even if he looked a lot older now, having gone bald and put on a few since his playing days. He was a lawyer in Middletown, and after he gave Richie a hug, he asked if he needed any help.

"All I can get," Richie said.

"I can help coach, I can make calls, I can organize a phone list, you name it," he said.

"All of the above," Richie said.

Then he told the kids that if they were here today, it meant they had a passion for playing ball, and he'd always had a soft spot for guys like that.

And told them that maybe, if he managed not to screw them up, they could all have a basketball season that was a lot more than a consolation prize.

His dad said, "Danny knows I'm the last guy who ever wants to give a speech. But bottom line here? Maybe, just maybe, we can turn out to be the kind of team nobody wants to play."

One of the O'Briens raised a hand.

"Mr. Walker? How do we do that if we don't even have enough players to play each other?"

"What's your name, son?"

"Steven O'Brien."

He was in the red T-shirt. It meant Robert was in black.

He motioned the other twin over. "And your name, son?"

"Robert."

Richie looked hard at one face, then the other, stood back. To the red-shirted Steven he said, "I think you've got a few more freckles than your twin brother there, Steven, though that's not going to help me a whole lot when you're out on the court, so we're going to have to ask you to color code each other at every practice."

They both nodded. "We switch T-shirts sometimes when our mother leaves the room."

"Zany," Will said.

"Anyway," Richie said, "I'll tell Robert and Steven and the rest of you that by the time we're ready to get serious here, hopefully we'll have found a couple of more players. If not, Mr. Harden and I will play when we want to go five-on-five."

Danny stared at his dad.

Because as far as he knew, the last time Richie Walker had played in any kind of basketball game was with the Golden State Warriors.

"One last thing before we start," his dad said. "There's only going to be three basic rules on this team, and I'm going to expect you all to follow them. One, if you're open, shoot. Two, if somebody has a better shot than you, pass the ball, let him shoot. Three? Have fun." He looked from face to face. "Did I go too fast for anybody?"

Will had to get the last word, of course.

"What if we're missing our shots?"

Richie said, "Keep shooting. That will be rule number four. Now get in two lines and let's see what we got here."

. . .

Nothing, Danny decided after the first hour.

They had nothing.

They were either hopeless or helpless, he could go either way.

He kept thinking that if the Vikings could see them, they'd think they were trying to get on one of those *Funniest Home Video* television shows.

Even the guys who could play couldn't play dead today.

Danny knew that Will and Bren—Bren especially—knew how to run a three-man weave fast break drill the way they knew their own screen names; they'd all had to run the weave for any team they'd ever played for in their lives.

Just not today.

Not to save their lives.

And when they'd mess it up again, his dad would just look at them calmly, no problem, and say, "Same group, let's try it again."

One time Matt was the last guy to get the ball, which meant he was supposed to shoot the layup. Only the pass from Michael Harden was too low and Matt had about as much chance of reaching down and catching it, and then shooting it, as he did of getting a good grade in Spanish.

But he did manage to drop-kick the ball off the court and up onto the stage.

Will immediately imitated one of those Spanish soccer announcers you heard during the World Cup.

"Goooooooooaaaaaallllllll!"

Even Richie Walker, whom Danny knew wasn't exactly the life of the party in the best of times, laughed at that one.

To keep from crying, most likely.

When Richie said they were going to try four-on-four, full-court, push the ball every chance you got, Danny thought things might get better, even though nobody had the height to guard Matt.

Instead, they got worse.

Even I stink today, Danny thought.

He kept checking out the old clock above the stage, knowing his dad had said they would only go to ten o'clock today.

Danny praying that none of the play-practice kids would come early and see a team that he was now thinking of more as the Middletown Rugrats. One that had scrimmaged for more than half an hour and managed to produce exactly five baskets, three for his team, two for Bren's.

Danny had all the baskets for his team, Bren had the two for his. He might have been slightly off with his math, but there had also been about six thousand turnovers.

Richie Walker finally put two fingers to his mouth and gave a sharp whistle, told them all they were done for the day and to come to the middle of the court.

"We suck," Danny said under his breath to Will.

Will said, "You're being much too easy on us."

Danny told Will his Rugrats line and Will said, "If you remember the show, I'm pretty sure Phil and Lil are bigger."

Richie Walker knelt down in the middle of them. When he did, he had to put his right hand out to keep himself steady, or from falling over on his side.

Maybe those weren't sad eyes on his dad as much as they were hurt eyes.

Richie said, "Before anybody starts to get down on himself, remember: This was our first practice. Wasn't even a practice, really, as much as it was, like, orientation. So hang in there, okay?"

Then he said, "Hey, the team I played on? The one that won?

Our coach threw us out of the gym three times the first month we were together."

Jerry Harden nodded. "Think it was four, actually."

One of the O'Brien twins raised a hand. "Are we going to practice this week? We need to know because we've got piano."

Will, whispering into Danny's ear, said, "Maybe they can *play* piano."

Richie Walker's response was a sigh.

Then he turned and looked at the clock.

They sat in front of 422 Earl for a few minutes after his dad drove him home from practice.

"You could come in," Danny said, "if you want."

"I've got some calls to make when I get back to the Inn. It's a big job—two jobs, actually—being both general manager *and* coach in travel basketball."

Danny could see his mom's blue Taurus in the driveway. Somehow he could feel her watching them from somewhere inside the house. Maybe even hearing what they were saying. He liked to tell her that she had the kind of mutant hearing that could have landed her a spot fighting crime with the X-Men.

There was just nothing much to hear right now in the front seat of the rental car.

Until: "Dad, why are you doing this?"

Richie turned in the front seat so he could face him, forgetting that the shoulder harness from his seat belt was still attached. He caught himself when he felt the pull of it, but even a sudden stop like that made him wince in pain.

"Why're you asking, bud?"

"Because you don't even *like* basketball anymore. And you

didn't like coaching, even though you're trying to make this sound like something you couldn't live with yourself if you passed up. That's why."

Deep breath.

Keep going.

Danny said, "The only reason you play with me in the driveway when you show up is because it's a way for us to have some kind of common language that doesn't involve us talking."

He shot him a look to see how that one went over. His dad was actually smiling, like Danny had gotten off a good shot. Swish.

"You're pretty smart for twelve," his dad said. "Smarter than I was, that's for sure."

"Whatever."

Richie said, "Can I talk *now*?"

"'Course you can."

"I don't hate basketball," Richie said. "Do I hate what happened to me? Yeah. Do I spend most of my life feeling sorry for myself? Yeah, I do, though I'm trying to cut down. I really hate what happened to me, that I never got the chance to find out how I stacked up against the big boys. And I did hate coaching the first time around. College boys with their attitudes who I could have run circles around when I was their age." His dad was the one who took a deep breath now, letting it go.

"Dad, I didn't mean . . ."

Richie carefully turned himself back around, so he was facing forward, those big hands on the steering wheel. "I hate that I don't have the game in my hands anymore. Or ever again. But I don't hate the game, bud, and I never will."

His dad never talked about the car accident that nearly killed him. Never, never, never. This was as close as he ever got, what losing control of his car on the wet road had done to him, how it made him feel. The whole thing feeling as if it were right next door to them.

"But why do you want to coach us?" Danny said. "We're gonna stink."

"You don't know that. And I have to say, if you act like you're giving up after just one practice, the other guys are gonna do the exact same thing, and we're all wasting our time here."

"I'm not giving up."

"I watched you today, Dan. You're the only one who acted like he hated basketball, every time you or somebody else would screw up."

"Yeah," Danny said, knowing he sounded just like his father.

"Yeah," Richie said. "And you can't let it happen again, because I need you. Because I'm gonna put this team in *your* hands. Give you more responsibility than you've ever had in your life."

Out of the corner of his eye, Danny saw his mom standing on the front porch, waving at them.

"What if I'm not good enough?" he said.

Richie said, "No, it was the other guys who told you you're not good enough."

Danny sat there. "It was a bad day."

"Let me tell you something I learned the hard way," Richie said. "There's no such thing as a bad day if you're playing. On a team you weren't supposed to be on. In a season you weren't even supposed to have."

"*We* weren't supposed to have."

"There you go. Go take a shower and tell your mom I'll give her a call later and talk about the availability of the gym."

Danny was going to tell him he loved him, the words were right there, ready to spill all over the dashboard.

But he didn't.

Because he never did.

He just got out and ran for the front door, trying to bluff his mom by looking happy.

It wouldn't occur to him until later that his dad still hadn't really explained why he was doing it.

THEY PRACTICED TWICE MORE DURING THE WEEK, EACH ONE A LITTLE LESS awful than the first one.

But not by much.

It was the Saturday of Veterans Day weekend, most of the town at the parade. They had to practice in the morning today, insanely early in the morning, seven o'clock, because the theater had been taken over by the Science Fair and the Drama Club kids needed the gym at nine. Mr. Harden was playing on the skins team with Will and Bren and Matt. Danny's dad was moving stiffly around for Danny's team, the shirts, pretending he was playing center, just as a way of putting a bigger body on Matt in the scrimmage and making the sides look even.

Matt Fitzgerald moved about as fast as a traffic jam on the Long Island Expressway, so even though the best Richie Walker could do was limp-jog up and down the court himself, they could sort of keep up with each other.

They were about forty-five minutes into what was half game and half practice, Danny's dad stopping them every few minutes to give them one more variation on the offense he wanted them to use against a man-to-man.

It was then that Danny spotted Ty Ross standing just inside the double doors, at the opposite end from the stage. He was in his baggy white shorts, down to his knees, new McGrady blue-and-white sneakers you could spot from a mile away, a Middletown High T-shirt with the sleeves cut off, Ty apparently wanting to show off arms as skinny as his legs.

Danny gave him the chin-up nod, Ty did the same back.

When Richie Walker spotted Ty, he told everybody to take a water break and relax for a minute.

Danny and his dad walked over to Ty, Danny saying, "You must be in the wrong gym, dude."

"Hey, Ty," Richie said.

"Mr. Walker." Ty ducked his head. "My mom was on her way over to Springs, she has to help them set up for some auction or something tonight. I was supposed to help her, but then I remembered that you guys practice early on Saturday." He grinned. "She sort of gave me a reprieve."

They all stood there for a moment, nobody knowing what to say about that. Then Richie said, "You want to play some?"

"Would that be okay?" Ty said.

Richie said, "If it's okay with your mom."

"She's cool."

Danny said, "What about your dad?"

Ty looked down at the McGradys, the left one untied. He was wearing those socks that barely made it above the top of your high-tops.

"He's playing tennis right now."

Richie put a hand on his shoulder. "It's just basketball, son. But I don't want you to get into trouble with your father."

"My mom said that as long as it was okay with you, it was okay with her, we—the Vikings—don't practice again until next Tuesday."

"Well, then, thank you for coming, Ty, because you may have saved a broken-down old man's life. You play with Danny. And I am going to sit my worn-out butt down."

Then he changed the teams around a little, stacking the other guys, making it Will, Bren, Matt, Michael Harden and his dad. He put Oliver Towne and the O'Brien twins with Danny and Ty.

"Let's play some damn ball," Richie Walker said.

They started over, jumping it at center court, Ty against Matt. Ty back-tipped the ball to Danny and as soon as he did, Danny gave him the eye, Ty breaking toward their basket, Danny feeding him perfectly, Ty catching the long pass on one bounce and laying the ball in off the backboard.

As they ran back to set up on defense, Ty changed lanes so he could give Danny a quick low five. He was smiling over the play, as if they'd drawn it up beforehand.

Danny wasn't.

He's not the one in the wrong gym, Danny thought.

I am.

When practice was over, Ty used Will's ever-present cell to call his mother and ask if he could go with Will over to Danny's house.

Most of the other kids had beat it out of the gym when Richie had said they were done for the day. A bad sign, Danny knew, for a bunch of guys who were supposed to be there because of their burning love of the game.

Of course the only reason Danny'd had any fun was because he'd had Ty to pass to.

Ty said he was getting a busy signal on his mom's phone, but she was probably on her way, since her shift at Springs ended at nine, and there was a better chance of her robbing the King Kullen supermarket than there was of her being late for anything.

So they were all standing outside in front of the gym—Danny, his dad, Ty, Will—waiting for Mrs. Ross when Mr. Ross pulled up in his black Mercedes, left the car in the fire lane that was really just a drop-off spot in front of the gym, came up the stairs fast at them, taking the last steps two at a time.

"What's *he* doing here?"

He was talking to Richie about Ty, as if Ty weren't even there.

Richie said, "You should probably ask Ty that."

"I'm asking you," he said, pointing a finger at Richie, not quite touching him, but getting it up there near his face.

"Ty showed up and it was lucky he did, because we're short players. I asked if it was all right and he said that his mom said it was, she's the one who dropped him off."

"My *wife*," Mr. Ross said, "doesn't make our son's basketball decisions for him."

Danny wasn't as interested in Ty's dad as he was in his own, wanting to see how he was going to play this, Mr. Ross bossing him now the way he liked to boss everybody else in town.

"You're making a big deal out of nothing," Richie said, standing his ground, not backing up, keeping his voice calm. Putting his eyes on Mr. Ross and calmly keeping them there.

"He doesn't belong here."

"He's twelve," Richie said. "If he can find a game on a Saturday morning, he ought to be allowed to play in it, you ask me."

Mr. Ross said, "You think I can't see what you're doing here?"

"You mean other than getting up to ten kids so we could scrimmage."

"Dad," Ty said.

"Stay out of this."

Richie said, "C'mon, Jeff. He didn't do anything wrong. I didn't do anything wrong. I told him that if he doesn't have a conflict with your team, he can practice with our team anytime he wants to."

Then Richie said, "And backing up a second? What *do* you think I'm doing here?"

"You've made it abundantly clear by putting this team of yours together that you think some grave injustice was done to the kids who didn't make the cut. Well, I don't. And I don't want the other kids on the Vikings to even get the idea, from my son, that they have some sort of alternative if they don't like the way things are going."

Richie Walker barked out a laugh. "You think I'm, like, *recruiting* your kid?"

Danny stood there, not moving, barely breathing, curious to see when Mr. Ross, the most important guy in Middletown, was going to figure out what a jackass he was making of himself, in front of them, in front of his son.

"You just coach your little team and I'll coach mine," he said. He took Ty by the arm now and said, "Let's go."

Danny was afraid that Ty was the one about to cry over basketball.

But he didn't.

Richie said, "Why don't you go easy on the boy?"

Mr. Ross stopped, turned around, nodding, a phony smile on his face. "You know," he said, "there's nothing I like better than getting parenting advice from the experts."

He and Ty went down the stairs to the car. When they got there, Mr. Ross stood on the passenger side and opened the door, waiting there until Ty was inside.

When the car was gone, Danny said to his dad, "He was pretty angry."

And his dad said, "Only for the last twenty years or so."

Danny imagined the scene at the Ross house afterward being something out of one of those *SmackDown!* wrestling shows, but Ty called
the next morning and asked if Danny wanted to do something.

"I thought you'd be under house arrest until Thanksgiving or
something," Danny said. "Now you get to do something with me?"

"It was a mom deal," he said.

Then they put both their moms on the phone and told them to
work it out.

"Hey, Lily," Ali Walker said when Danny handed her the
portable, then chatted with Lily Ross for a few minutes before she
put her hand over the phone and said, "Do you want Ty to come
here or do you want to go to his house?"

Danny waved his arms in front of him as if he'd been attacked
by bees. "It's like going to the *big* house. No way, Mom. Here.
Definitely."

Mrs. Ross, who seemed way too nice to be married to who she
was married to, brought Ty over after lunch. The two moms went
into the kitchen for coffee and gossip, while Danny and Ty went upstairs and began putting together their own superteams on *NBA
'05*, where the object was to have a final score of about 188–186.

Danny said, "How *did* you get to come over?"

He was on the bed with his controller, Ty slouched in a beanbag
chair on the floor with his.

95

Ty said, "They had a big fight about it that lasted into the night. She said I could play with who I wanted to play with. He asked whose side was she on, his or your dad's. She said she wasn't aware there were different sides on everybody's children being happy. One of those."

"My parents fight like that sometimes," Danny said. "But that's because they're only together sometimes."

Ty said, "Your team has my dad pissed, that's for sure, dude."

Danny paused the game. "You've seen us. You think *your* team has anything to worry about?"

"He thinks your dad is trying to show him up."

"I don't think it's like that. I think my dad, like, thinks this is something he had to do for me, even though he didn't."

Ty said, "You guys just need a couple more players, you'll be pretty good."

Danny said, "I know who the players are, too. Shaq and Duncan."

"Really. You just need one guy to catch and shoot, and one guy to rebound."

"Like I said. Shaq and Duncan."

Danny unpaused the game.

In a soft voice, one you could barely hear over the PlayStation crowd noises in the bedroom, Ty said, "Dude? I'd rather play on your team."

Danny didn't even look up from the game.

"I know."

Then they went back to fantasy basketball, which was almost always a lot simpler than real life.

The next practice was Tuesday night.

Danny and the rest of the Rugrats—he couldn't get the name

out of his head now, like they were a rock group—were waiting to get on the floor while the seventh-grade girls' travel team finished their own practice.

Will and Bren were on the stage, quietly dogging the girls as a way of entertaining each other, Will doing most of the talking, of course. Danny was up there with them for a few minutes, but then left, knowing that if they actually started bothering the girls, or were overheard by the girls' coach, Ms. Perry, one of the phys ed teachers from the high school, he'd be going down with them.

He went and sat with the other guys on the floor.

Richie Walker sat in a folding chair on the other side from them, legs stretched out in front of him, watching the girls.

Danny walked over there when the girls went past eight o'clock. Ms. Perry had shouted over and asked if it was all right if they went a few extra minutes, and Richie Walker said, go ahead, he was in no rush.

Danny said, "Even they're better than us."

"Who is she?" Richie said.

Danny didn't have to ask who "she" meant.

"That's Colby."

Colby Danes was out there doing what she always did in girls basketball, which meant scoring all the points, getting all the rebounds, passing like she was ready at twelve to go play for the women's team at UConn or Tennessee or one of those other colleges where the women's team was better and more famous than the men's. Danny had always thought of her as the girl player that Ty would have been, almost as tall as Ty, with her red hair in a ponytail, smiling her way through practice even when she'd occasionally do something wrong.

Another tall St. Pat's girl.

Richie said, "What do you think of her?"

"I think she's great," Danny said. "For a girl."

"She's great, period," Richie said. "Those two knotheads making fun of her up on the stage ought to be paying attention to the way she plays. On account of, they might learn something."

With that, Richie spun around suddenly and stared straight at Bren and Will, as if training a searchlight on them. They both froze, Will with his mouth still open.

Richie went back to staring at Colby Danes.

Really staring.

"Dad?"

"Huh?"

"You seem pretty interested in Colby."

"I just like watching people who know how to play. Girls or boys. That's all."

Ms. Perry announced next basket and they were done for the night.

"You think your friend Colby—"

"—I wouldn't really call her a friend—"

"—would like to practice with the boys sometime?"

On the court, Colby got the ball near the basket and turned and made a baby hook over the girl guarding her, a Chinese girl from Springs. Emily Ming.

"Dad?" Danny said. "What are you doing?"

"Doing what your mom said people should do more of in this town. Thinking outside the box."

"But she's a *girl*," Danny said.

"Yeah," Richie said, "a girl who knows what to do when you pass her the ball. A girl who can catch it and shoot it and go get it. And can run the court on her long legs almost as fast as you can, Dan the man."

On the court, Ms. Perry blew her whistle and told the girls to bring it in. Danny's dad pulled himself out of his chair, picked up the bag of balls that had been sitting next to him.

"You know what she is, if we're strictly talking basketball here?"

"What?" Danny said.

"The girl of your dreams."

Richie talked to Ms. Perry first. Ms. Perry told him to ask Colby's dad, Dr. Danes, who was standing with the rest of the girls' parents at the other end of the gym. Then Richie was standing with Colby and Dr. Danes and everybody was doing a lot of smiling and nodding and before you knew it, Colby was in the layup line with Danny and the guys.

Will whispered to Danny, "I knew nothing good was gonna come out of Annika playing golf with the boys."

Behind them Bren said, "This is just for practice, right?"

Then Danny heard himself saying, "Let me ask you basketball geniuses a question: Could Colby make us any worse?"

"Okay," Will said, "Walker has officially turned into the coach's son."

In the first five minutes of the scrimmage, she set a great pick on Will, rolled off it perfectly, and took a smooth bounce pass from Danny for a layup. Like Stockton and Malone. The pick-and-roll.

Then she went down to the other end of the court, stole the ball from Michael Harden, passed it to Danny, who passed it right back to her, then watched as she beat everybody down the court for another easy layup.

Danny looked over at his dad, still standing with Dr. Danes.

Richie Walker, no expression on his face, shrugged.

It went like that for half an hour and then Dr. Danes yelled out to Colby that she had homework to do. Even that made Colby smile. "One more basket?" she said. "Please, Dad?"

"One more. But then that's it."

Danny brought the ball up. He passed it on the wing to Colby. As she came up, Bren came from the other side and set a back-pick on Oliver Towne, who was guarding her now. Colby left-hand dribbled into the open, near the foul line, and had a wide-open shot.

When she went up for the shot, with everybody watching her, Danny cut for the basket from the other wing. Colby never stopped her shooting motion or seemed to even alter it as she went into the air, passing the ball off to Danny instead.

He caught it and, in the same motion, showing off a little—for a girl?—made a little scoop shot from the left side.

He looked over to see what Colby thought but she was already walking over to her dad.

When practice was over, Danny said to his dad, "Colby coming back?"

"Thursday," he said.

"Who *is* going to pay for this great team of ours?" Danny said to his mom when he got home.

He'd asked his dad if he wanted to come in after practice, but he said he had to be somewhere. At ten o'clock, Danny just assumed the somewhere had to be Runyon's bar.

"Your father wrote a check to the school for the gym time," his mom said, "I know that. Beyond that, if this thing keeps going forward, I assume he'll pass a hat with the parents for team uniforms, warm-ups, referees and whatnot. I forget all the costs, it's been a couple of years since I was a travel basketball mom."

Ali Walker was sitting at the kitchen table, grading compositions. Danny had finished his homework and had been watching a show in the living room where the contestants tried to see how long they could keep live grasshoppers and crickets in their mouths.

"Don't worry about money," she said. "Parents do that. You worry about school and sports. In that order, I might add."

She looked up at him over her reading glasses, which always made her look more like Mrs. Walker the teacher than his mom.

"Is there something else on your mind?"

"I was just wondering if Dad's going to stay at the Inn the whole season, now that he's staying," Danny said.

"He mentioned the other night that he might look into getting a small apartment somewhere if it was cheaper than the Inn."

"'Cause I was thinking, he could stay—"

"No," she said. "He could not stay here."

She put down her reading glasses as she said it, for emphasis, a judge banging her gavel, case closed.

"So he's okay for money right now?"

"He says he is, that he'd had a few good months doing those shows of his before he got here."

"You believe him?"

His mom said, "You don't?"

It was somewhere between a question and an observation.

"I just don't know what this whole deal is about sometimes," he said.

"Well, I thought it was about putting together a team for a bunch of boys—"

"—and girls. I think Dad's fixing to put Colby on the team."

That stopped her.

"*Your* father is going to put a *girl* on *his* basketball team?"

"He didn't come right out and say it. But he let Colby practice tonight and he says she's coming back on Thursday."

Ali Walker said, "Will wonders never cease."

"What's that mean?"

"It means your father, in his youth, was not exactly the biggest fan of girls' basketball."

"She's pretty good, you know."

"I know. For a girl."

Danny said, "You were about to tell me something before I told you about Colby."

"I was just going to say that I thought this was a team for a bunch of kids who'd been told by a bunch of adults they weren't good enough." She gave him a long look, then said, "Or big enough."

"He wants *us* to prove a point then?"

"Would you mind telling me what you're getting at here, Daniel Walker?"

"Sometimes I just think Dad's the one trying to prove some kind of point to somebody."

"Maybe it's to you," she said. "Ever think of that?"

Danny's thinking was more along these lines:

He wondered if the someone Richie Walker was trying to prove something to was himself.

. . .

CROSSOVER2: Hey, picture girl. You there?

CONTESSA44: We're here 24/7.

CROSSOVER2: Like those hotlines.

CONTESSA44: For troubled teens.

CROSSOVER2: I've only got b-ball troubles.

CONTESSA44: But I hear there's a new girl in your basketball life.

It was true, Danny thought.

News did travel faster than ever in the Internet age.

CROSSOVER2: **Who told?**

CONTESSA44: **I cannot reveal my source . . . Yes, I can, it was Will.**

CROSSOVER2: **He's got a big mouth even on a Mac . . . And she's not in my life, she's on my dopey team.**

CONTESSA44: **Dopey? Uh-oh. Somebody's Grumpy tonight.**

Tess Hewitt wasn't just a fast typist. She was fast, period.

CROSSOVER2: **She won't change anything. We suck.**

CONTESSA44: **You haven't even played a game yet.**

CROSSOVER2: **The only time I like playing ball is when I play with Ty.**

He waited longer than usual for her reply. Which meant trouble, because the longer she took usually, the longer the reply.

But he was wrong.

CONTESSA44: **Get over it.**

CROSSOVER2: **What?**

CONTESSA44: **Repeat: Get over it. As in, all of it. Stop feeling so sorry for yourself.**

CROSSOVER2: **Now you're my coach?**

CONTESSA44: **Just your IM cheerleader. But on to more important stuff . . . Do you think Colby's cute?**

Danny felt himself smiling.

Just not about the tall girl on his basketball team.

He was smiling through all the magic of computers, all the mojo, his screen to her screen, all the way across Middletown, at this girl.

CROSSOVER2: No.
CONTESSA44: You're cute.
CROSSOVER2: Gross.
CONTESSA44: Things will get better.

They were actually about to get worse.

He and Will had gone to the new Jackie Chan movie at the Middletown Theater, the one with the old-fashioned marquee out front, somehow hanging in there against all the multiplexes in the area, including the new one outside Twin Forks, in the factory-outlet mall that was roughly the same size as Texas.

Danny's mom had brought him and Will, and Will's mom was supposed to pick them up at the Candy Kitchen afterward.

That's where they ran into Teddy Moran and Jack Harty and fat Eric Buford.

Will saw them come in, scoping out the room with his back to the wall in their back booth. He always sat facing the room, afraid he was going to miss something, even if it was only who'd just come through the door.

"Check it out," Will said. "Terrible Teddy actually found *two* people who wanted to go to the movies with him."

He said it in his boom-box voice, as if everybody in the Candy Kitchen had suddenly gone deaf.

"You better repeat that," Danny said, "I think a couple of guys in the kitchen might have missed it."

"C'mon," Will said, "you're the one who always says that calling Moran a snake is insulting to a lot of innocent water moccasins."

There may have been less popular twelve-year-olds in Middletown than Teddy Moran, whose father hosted his own show on the town's AM radio station. But if there were, Teddy was trying his hardest to take the crown.

Somehow Teddy thought his father's celebrity made him one, too. He went through life with even more mouth than Will, as if doing the play-by-play for himself and everybody else. He liked to think he had a lot of friends, but really didn't. In fact, if there was one enduring mystery in Middletown, at least among guys their age, it was this: Why Ty Ross had anything to do with him.

Danny just wrote it off to the fact that Ty would find good qualities in a guard dog.

He even managed to do it with a punk-face like Teddy, with those pig eyes, with a mouth set in a smirky way that made it look as if he were always on the verge of getting a flu shot. Teddy Moran: Who always got a lot braver when he had somebody as big as Jack Harty with him, even though Jack usually seemed to be embarrassed to be in the same area code.

Danny was hoping that if he and Will ignored them, they'd go away. No such luck. Will hadn't just talked too loudly, he'd made the fatal mistake of eye contact.

So the three of them came over and stood near the booth, Teddy in front of the other two. Danny thinking: Yeah, Moran, you're a born leader.

"Hey, Walker," Teddy said, "is it true you're playing with girls now?"

Looking over one shoulder, then the other, at Jack and fat Buford, like he'd gotten off a good one.

Will said, "It's easier for us with girls than it is for you, just because they don't run the other way when they see us coming. Or, in your case, smell us coming."

Teddy ignored him, saying to Danny, "What color are your uniforms going to be—pink?"

Will said, "Did somebody say punk?"

Danny leaned forward and sipped his root beer float, then looked up at Teddy. "Is there some point you're getting to, dude? Or are you planning to go from booth to booth busting chops, and just happened to start with us?"

Jack and fat Buford turned and went to the counter to order, somehow bored by the sparkling conversation.

Teddy stayed. "Hear you're spending a lot of time with Ross," he said.

"Jealous?" Will said.

Teddy shot him a sideways glance. "Nice hair," he said. "Come home with me later, you can scrub some of our dinner pots with your head."

"Holy crap, that's a good one," Will said. "I've got to get a pencil from one of the waitresses and write that one down."

To Danny, Teddy said, "One of these days, you and your pals have to get over not making the grade."

"You're absolutely right, Moran," Danny said, feeling himself starting to get hot now. "The other thing I've got to do is get my dad to sponsor the team next year, just to guarantee me a spot."

Garland Moran's station, WMID, *was* the Vikings' sponsor this season.

"Your dad?" Teddy said. "Sponsor a team? With what, his bar tips?"

Will got up first. "Shut up," he said. "*Now.*"

Teddy Moran started to turn away from them, on his way to the counter, but decided to say one more thing.

"Loser coach," he said, "for a loser team."

Danny, in a quiet voice, said, "Hey, Moran," to get his attention. So he'd turn.

So Danny wasn't technically blindsiding him with what Will

107

would describe later as a blinding first step, coming out of the booth and up into Teddy Moran, grabbing two fists' worth of Teddy's stupid F.U.B.U. sweatshirt as he did, Teddy thinking F.U.B.U. made him a cool-black white kid, driving him back into the swivel chairs at the counter.

Teddy was bigger and heavier than Danny the way everybody was bigger and heavier, but his lack of guts made it a fair fight.

The two of them went down in the opening at the counter where the waitresses brought out the food, Teddy hitting the floor hard as Danny heard people start to yell all around them, heard Teddy himself yelling, "Get *off* me."

Danny was on top of him now, had him by the front of the sweatshirt, had his face close enough to smell movie popcorn on Teddy's breath.

He could feel people trying to pull him off, but he wasn't ready to let go.

Still wasn't sure whether he was going to bust him in the face and knock the smirk off it.

"Take it back," he said.

He knew how lame it sounded as soon as he said it, but it was the best he could do, he could barely breathe, much less think clearly.

Even now, Teddy was still all mouth.

"About him being a drunk, or a loser?"

Now Danny pulled back his right hand, ready to pop him, see if that would finally shut his fat mouth. But Gus, the owner of the Candy Kitchen, the guy that kids considered the real mayor of Middletown, caught his hand like he was wearing a catcher's mitt and said, "How's about we don't make this worse than it already is?"

Will finished the job of pulling Danny off Teddy Moran.

Teddy was already on his feet, safely behind Jack and fat Buford, a complete phony to the end, trying to make it look as if he were trying to get around them and back at Danny, and they were holding him back.

"Truth hurts, huh, Walker?" he said.

Will was moving Danny slowly toward the door.

"You're the one who's going to get hurt," Danny said. "When it's just you and me, next time."

"You talk tough for a midget," Teddy said. "Everybody in town knows the *real* truth about your old man except you."

Danny tried to turn around, but Will had him in a bear hug, saying, "You're probably only grounded right now. Let's not shoot for life without parole."

They stood on the corner, Danny breathing like crazy now, gulping in air like he'd just run a hundred-yard dash, Will saying they ought to get out of there, he'd call his mom and tell her to pick them up at Fierro's.

"I should have kicked his ass," Danny said.

"Everybody in there thinks you already did."

They walked down the street. When they passed Runyon's, they saw Richie Walker at his usual corner stool, his face fixed on the television set. Danny didn't know what he was watching, but he recognized the look on his dad's face, the one where it looked as if he was staring hard at nothing, all the way into outer space.

Danny staring hard at him.

What had Teddy meant?

The real truth?

Danny was grounded for the next week, not even allowed to attend practices. He pleaded his case to his mom as soon as Mrs.

Stoddard dropped him off at home that night, telling her what Teddy Moran had said, explaining that Teddy had lied when he told *his* mom that Danny had jumped him from behind.

He knew it wasn't going to help his case even a little bit, but he finished by telling her that if anybody in town deserved to catch a good beating, it was Teddy Moran.

"Are you finished now?" Ali Walker said.

"Pretty much. Yeah."

"You're right. He *is* a jerk. He happens to come from a long line of jerks, the biggest being his father. And having told you that? You're still busted, kiddo. You know my position on fighting."

He did, reciting it to her now the way he would have the Pledge of Allegiance. "The only thing fighting ever proves is who's the better fighter," he said. "And you usually know that before you start."

No phone privileges after dinner for a week. No after-homework television.

No computer of any kind unless it involved homework, which meant no instant-messaging.

"No IM!" Will said at school on Monday. Mock horror. "No tube? She's turned you into the Count of Monte Cristo."

What felt like one of the longest school weeks ever—no computer privileges always made him feel like he was stranded at night on some kind of desert island—finally came to an end. His dad stopped by Friday afternoon, telling him that he'd scheduled six games so far, the first one on the first weekend in December, the last of the six the Sunday before the Christmas holidays began. He also said that despite a lot of bitching and moaning—his dad's words—from Middletown Basketball, Colby Danes was leaving the seventh-grade girls' team and joining them.

He was at the front door when he turned and said, "Oh, by the way, one other thing? We're scrimmaging the Vikings tomorrow afternoon at St. Pat's."

"We'll get killed!" Danny said.

"I figure."

"You don't care?"

"Listen," he said. "I know *they'll* care, even though I'm not letting them use the scoreboard. They're not even supposed to keep score in a scorebook, though I figure they'll find a way. They're going to rub your faces in it. I just want to see what we've got, and who I should be scheduling, especially if it turns out we don't get into the league."

"The league hasn't told you yet?"

"They say they're still quote, considering my request, unquote."

"While they do, the Vikings get to use us as tackling dummies."

"It's just a scrimmage, not the Final Four."

Danny said, "More like a car wreck, if you ask me."

He felt like a jerk, talking about car accidents in front of his dad, as soon as the words were out of his mouth.

The stupid jerk of all jerks.

Inside his stupid head, he pictured himself using both hands trying to grab the words out of the air and stuff them back inside his mouth.

"What I meant . . ."

"Relax," Richie said. "I know you didn't mean anything. But it's not a car wreck, kiddo. It's just basketball. I used to think it was a matter of life and death, too. I found out the hard way that it wasn't."

It turned out to be a *train* wreck.

Mr. Ross hired a couple of refs Danny recognized from sixth-grade travel. Mr. Harden worked the clock. The Vikings wore black practice jerseys Danny didn't even know they had, with their own numbers on the backs and everything. Danny's team wore white T-shirts.

No spectators, not even parents. Just the players, the two coaches, the two refs.

In the huddle, Will said, "The refs want to know what our team is called."

They all looked at each other.

Will said, "I never really thought Rugrats was all that catchy, to tell you the truth."

Danny said, "How about the Warriors?" He looked up at his dad. "As in the Golden State Warriors."

For a moment, a blink of an eye, it was as if it were just the two of them, getting ready to play one-on-one in the driveway. His dad looked back at him, and winked. "Works for me," he said. "Warriors okay with the rest of you guys?"

"Why not?" Will said. "We'll be like the real Warriors. Just much, much smaller."

Richie had them put their hands in the middle, told them not to worry about who was winning or by how much, to play hard, have fun, work on their stuff.

When they broke the huddle and lined up to start, Danny looked around at the five starters for the Vikings, seeing how much bigger they were, knowing how much *better* they were. Then he leaned next to Will's ear and said, "Holy crap. Who *picked* these teams?"

The Vikings went with Ty, Jack Harty, Andy Mayne, Daryll Mullins, Teddy Moran.

Against: Danny, Bren, Matt, Oliver. And Colby Danes.

The only place where the Warriors had a height advantage of

any kind was Matt against Jack, but that didn't mean squat, Jack Harty was a better player in just about every way.

Richie had Bren guard Teddy Moran. Danny took Andy Mayne, Colorado boy. As they all took their positions before the older ref, Tony, threw the ball up, Teddy walked close enough to Danny to say, "I was wrong. This team needs *more* girls."

Somehow Matt got the opening tip from Jack, back-tapping it to Danny, who immediately put one finger in the air and yelled "Syracuse."

It wasn't just the number one play in their offense, it was pretty much the only play, even if Richie had given them some options they could run, depending on how the defense reacted to it.

Danny passed to Bren, then cut away from the ball and set a pick for Colby on the right wing. She was supposed to cut toward the free throw line if the pick worked, and Bren was supposed to pass it to her if she was open. If she wasn't open, Danny was Bren's second option, cutting right behind Colby.

The Vikings switched on her, so Danny got the ball back. He was supposed to look for Matt underneath the way Colby would have. Because while they were doing their pick thing out top, Oliver Towne was supposed to be flashing across the baseline and picking Matt's man—Jack—and seeing if they could free Matt up for an easy layup.

It happened just that way, exactly the way Richie Walker had drawn it up for them, the way it happened when he had walked them through it the first time they'd practiced together.

Jack turned his head to see where Colby was after the first pick, even though Colby was covered. Oliver set a perfect screen, and Danny whipped the ball to Matt who, amazingly, did two things that qualified him for his own personal Book of World Records:

1. Caught the ball cleanly.

2. Made the layup.

One more time, Danny thought: Holy crap.

We're winning.

Even without a scoreboard, Danny had always been pretty good at keeping score in his head. Not just keeping score, but knowing how many points every player on the court had. He didn't know how he could do that, but he could, almost from the first time he started playing organized ball.

Just another part of having a head for the game.

But even he lost track now, as the Vikings scored either the next thirty, or thirty-two, points of the scrimmage.

That meant between Matt's basket and the two free throws Danny made with four seconds left in the first half.

Ty scored at least half of them, maybe more. The Vikings were doing fine just using their regular man-to-man, but then Mr. Ross had them put on their full-court press halfway through the first quarter, at which point they seemed to score ten baskets in the next twenty seconds.

The Vikings started double-teaming Danny in the backcourt as soon as he touched the ball. Instead of coming to help him out, the rest of the Warriors, with the exception of Colby, kept running away from the ball. When Danny would find somebody to pass it to, they hurried so much trying to get it right back to him, they usually threw it away, which usually meant another layup for the Vikings.

When by some miracle the Warriors did manage to get the ball over half-court, the Vikings would double-team Danny there, daring anybody else on his team to make a stinking basket.

While all this was going on, Teddy Moran was holding a nonstop, trash-talking festival, as if he were winning the game single-handedly. It was all Danny could do to keep his cool. But he did, knowing that you couldn't pick a fight when you were getting your doors blown off this way.

His dad tried calling a couple of time-outs.

They didn't help.

It was basically like trying to call a time-out right after somebody had yelled "Fire!" at a school assembly.

At halftime, Richie told them for what felt like the hundredth time to relax, telling them they knew how to play a lot better than this.

Will raised a hand and said, "You absolutely sure about that, Coach?"

"Mr. Harden talked to Mr. Ross," Richie said. "They're gonna take the press off for the whole second half. And that one's on me, we didn't work enough on breaking the press. For now, try to stay with your man, and do the best you can running the offense."

Danny said, "What offense?"

Richie gave him a look. "Hey." That's all it took, Danny felt like he'd gotten a good swat.

"Sorry."

"You knew these guys were better. And bigger. They've had a lot more practice time than we've had and most of them have been playing together a long time. Like I said: Don't worry about what they're doing, let's just work on our sh . . . stuff."

He almost used another s-word, didn't.

The real s-word happened with about five minutes left in the game, as it turned out.

There was 5:25 showing on the clock. Danny would remember the exact time when Mr. Ross called a time-out and put Ty and Teddy back into the game, after he'd sat the two of them for most of the second half. Danny had been out of the game since the middle of the third quarter, and had started to wonder if his dad was going to put him back in, or if he might be done for the day.

But now his dad poked him and said, "Why don't you go guard your buddy."

"Ty?"

"I was being sarcastic," Richie said. "Take the mouth."

"You heard what he's been saying the whole game?"

"I don't need to hear it, I can tell just by looking at his face," Richie said. "I've been playing against guys like that my whole life. The only way to shut them up is to shut them down. So go do that."

After the substitutions, the Vikings took the ball out. Danny picked up Teddy as soon as he got the ball in the backcourt.

Teddy put the ball on his hip and said, "Look, it's Stuart Little."

But as soon as he put the ball on the floor, Danny took it from him, picking him clean off the dribble, and taking it to the basket for a layup. Teddy didn't even try to catch him, whining to the second ref, DeWayne, the one who looked like a dead ringer for Snoop Dogg, that Danny had fouled him.

Teddy let Ty bring the ball up next time. Ty started the Viking offense on the left side, while Teddy ran to the right. He waited until Ty passed to Daryll Mullins in the left corner, figuring everybody was following the ball. Including Danny, who was between his man and the ball the way he'd been taught.

As soon as he turned his head, Teddy stepped up and hit him in the neck with an elbow.

It felt like Teddy had hit him with a bat.

He couldn't catch his breath for a second, dropping to his knees and holding both hands to his throat while everybody else ran up the court after Daryll Mullins made his jumper.

"Hey!" Richie yelled to Tony, the ref closest to the play. "What was *that*?"

Tony saw Danny on his knees then, but made a quick gesture with his hands over his eyes; it was his way of telling Richie he hadn't seen what had happened. Then he blew his whistle, stopping play.

Richie knelt down next to Danny.

"You okay?"

He swallowed hard, the inside of his throat feeling as if he were swallowing tacks. "I'm okay."

"I'm taking you out."

"*No.*"

"You sure?"

"Yeah."

"Hey," Richie said, putting both hands on his shoulders, looking him straight in the eye. "Just play, okay? No payback, at least for now."

Danny nodded.

Two minutes to go. Vikings' ball. Everybody on their team except Ty was goofing around now, doing whatever they wanted on offense, shooting from wherever they wanted to, making showboat passes, even though Mr. Ross kept making a show out of being pissed and telling them to run *their* stuff.

Danny noticed Ty giving warning looks to Teddy a couple of times. Like he was saying, Cut the crap. But Teddy ignored him.

Jack Harty, who hardly ever took a long outside shot, decided to fire one up from twenty feet. Danny and Teddy ended up underneath, each trying to get position to get the rebound. Ty was there, too, already having the inside position on Will.

While everybody was looking up for the ball, Teddy gave Danny another elbow, this one in the side.

117

Enough, Danny decided.

More than enough.

The ball had hit the back of the rim and bounced straight up in the air, as high as the top of the backboard.

As it did, Danny got a leg in front of Teddy Moran, planted it good and solid, and, as he did, used perfect rebounding position, elbows out, to shove Teddy hard to the side, his left elbow like a roundhouse punch into Teddy's rib cage.

It knocked Teddy off balance, made him stumble to his left, just as Ty Ross, who had gone high up in the air when the ball had finally stopped bouncing around on the rim, was coming down with the rebound.

Danny saw it all happening like it was super slo-mo on television.

Or in a video game.

Only this wasn't fantasy ball.

This was Ty landing on Teddy instead of the basketball floor at St. Pat's.

This was Ty Ross, not just the best twelve-year-old player in town but the most graceful, the one who never made a false move on the court, rolling over Teddy's back, the ball flying out of his hands, nothing to break his fall as he landed hard on his right wrist—his shooting wrist—with a crack on the floor that sounded like a firecracker going off.

Then Ty was rolling on the floor at St. Pat's, cradling his right arm to his stomach, screaming in pain.

THERE WAS A SECRET PLACE IN HIS ROOM, NEXT TO HIS CLOSET, THE WALL hidden behind the poster of Jason Kidd.

It was where Danny had been measuring himself for a long time. Where he could check the progression he had made, say, between February 26 of fourth grade to October 16 of fifth grade.

He would use a pen, afraid pencil marks would fade over time or disappear, writing the date and the year, hoping there'd be one year where he'd see the growth spurt Dr. Korval kept promising him.

Only the growth spurt never came.

The lines just kept crawling their way up the wall.

Danny Walker was fast everywhere except here.

He would carefully untape the poster when it was time to make another entry, lay it flat on his bed, take his place next to the door frame, reach back, put the pen flat on his head and point it toward the wall, make another line. He never cheated. Not even on September 17 of this year, a couple of weeks after he started school, when he was desperate to break the fifty-five inch mark he'd hit back in July.

Except he didn't break the speed limit that day.

Or on October 2.

Or October 14.

His mom called him a streak of light and he even thought of himself as a streak of light sometimes when he was flying up the court, but he kept moving his way up the wall like an inchworm.

Now he took the Kidd poster down when he got back from the Vikings scrimmage, stared at all the lines and all the dates—the only progress he could see was that his penmanship was improving as he got older—and thought about measuring himself for the first time since October.

Instead he just sat in the beanbag chair Ty had been sitting in the other day.

Feeling smaller than ever.

Trying to squeeze his eyes shut so that he would stop seeing Ty lying there on the floor, rocking from side to side on his back, his injured hand not leaving his stomach.

Only closing his eyes didn't help. He kept seeing Ty. And hearing the voice of Teddy Moran.

"You happy now?" Teddy had said in the gym after it happened.

This was after Mr. Ross had decided not to wait for an ambulance and to take Ty to Valley General Hospital, just outside of town on Route 37, himself. The two of them had walked slowly out of the gym, Mr. Ross with his arm around Ty's shoulder, Ty holding his right hand in front of him with his left, the left hand shaking so bad you wondered why he even bothered.

"You couldn't have a real season for yourself so you had to wreck ours?" Teddy yelled at Danny when the Rosses were gone.

In a voice the size of a penny Danny said, "It was an accident."

Not even sure why he was saying anything back to him.

"He shoved me into him," Teddy said, addressing the rest of the Vikings now, not dropping the sound of his own voice one bit. Most of the Vikings were still there, along with some of the parents who'd shown up a few minutes early for pickups. Teddy pointed right at Danny and said, "*He* did this to Ty."

"It was an accident, you moron," Will finally said.

"It was," Danny said again.

"You keep telling yourself that, little man," Teddy said to Danny. "You tried to get me and you got Ty instead. Does *that* make you feel big?"

"I didn't mean to," Danny said.

He was going to say something else then, something that would explain what had happened, to the Vikings, to their parents, to the Warriors.

Maybe to himself.

Except his throat closed up suddenly, the way it had when Teddy got him in the neck with his elbow, and he started to feel his eyes fill up, and no words would come out.

He felt his dad's hand on his elbow.

"I'll run you home," he said.

"Nice team," Teddy said now, to both of them.

"Shut up, kid," Richie said.

Teddy's father, Garland, was standing next to him. Garland Moran had the same pinched face as his son, same pig eyes, just an adult version. "Hey," he said, "you can't talk to my son like that."

"You ought to try it once in a while," Richie said. "It might teach him some manners."

Then father and son began walking out of the gym, but not before Teddy hit Danny with one more sucker punch.

"He actually told me you were his *friend*, Walker."

Danny didn't turn around, kept walking toward the front doors. Wanting to run.

Now he felt as if Teddy's words had chased him all the way to his room. He got out of the beanbag chair, that move taking as much effort as his dad usually showed getting out of a chair, took a pen off his desk, put a mark about an inch above the floorboard, and the date.

You're as big as you think you are, his mom always told him.

You're as big as you feel.

He was in his room the next afternoon, lying there on his bed and listening to the Jets game on the radio instead of watching it downstairs, content to stay here by himself until it was time to go to high school.

"Hey there," his mom said, standing in the doorway. "It's my solitary man."

"Huh?"

"Another old song."

Danny turned down the volume on the radio when it was clear she was staying. That she was there for a Mom Talk.

"I just got off the phone with Lily Ross," she said.

He waited.

"It turns out he only broke one bone in the wrist," she said. "So that's pretty good news, right?"

"Wow," he said, "a broken arm. That's *great* news, Mom!"

"You know what I mean," she said. "Your father thought it could have been much worse just because of the way he landed and the pain you guys said he was in. The doctor told Lily that some Jets quarterback had a wrist injury in about the same spot a few years ago—"

"—not some quarterback. Chad Pennington—"

"—and broke four bones and had some ligament damage."

"They operated on him that time. Did they operate on Ty?"

Ali Walker nodded. "To put a pin in there. He'll be in a cast for a while."

Danny sat up on the bed. "How long?"

"They'd only be guessing."

"Okay, what was Mrs. Ross's best guess?"

"She didn't talk about how long he'd be in the cast, just that the whole healing process was going to take at least three months, probably closer to four."

November. December. January.

Back in February.

Maybe.

The official Tri-Valley League season, Danny knew, started the first week of January and lasted until the middle of February. The tournament was the last week of February.

So if Ty was lucky, he could get a game or two in before the tournament.

"So he'll be able to play again this season?" Danny said.

His mom said, "She didn't say that. The doctor reminded her that they just needed to keep their fingers crossed. And that if everything went well, he *might* be able to play again this season, as long as he is convinced—this is Dr. Marshall, the orthopedic surgeon, talking—that there is no chance of Ty reinjuring himself."

Danny let himself dead-fall back on his pillow, staring up at the Stockton poster.

"He *might* be able to play."

"If not, he'll be ready for baseball."

"Yippee."

"Might be able to play is better than won't be able to play."

Danny said, "You think I could maybe call him?"

Ali Walker didn't say anything.

Danny raised his head back up off the pillow, repeated himself as if she hadn't heard him the first time. "Mom? You think I could call Ty?"

"Maybe you ought to wait a couple of days. Lily said he doesn't want to talk to anybody right now. Including his own parents."

"You think it would be all right to e-mail him?"

There was another pause, not as long as the one before, and she said, "Why don't you just wait on that, too."

Danny said, "He blames me, doesn't he?"

"Honey, I think he's just hurting in general." She came over and sat on the end of the bed. "And you're hurting."

"I'm fine."

"You want to talk about this?"

"No," he said. "But I can see you do."

"I thought it might be better if you just talked it out a little instead of sitting up here and brooding about it."

"Actually, I've been partying."

"It was an accident," she said.

"How much did that help Dad?" Danny said.

"He learned the hard way," she said. "Accidents happen in life. Sometimes they just happen, and nobody's to blame."

"Somebody was to blame this time," Danny said.

THE WEEK AFTER THANKSGIVING, RICHIE WALKER STOPPED BY THE HOUSE, saying that the Port Madison Pacers had dropped out of the Tri-Valley at the last second. It turned out only seven kids showed up for their original tryouts, and then three of them decided they wanted to play hockey instead. When they had a second tryout, only two more seventh graders showed up, at which point the Port Madison Basketball Association surrendered.

Richie Walker said he'd just gotten a call from the league telling him that, and also telling him the Warriors could take Port Madison's place as the Tri-Valley's eighth team.

"I had the check ready, the paperwork, the insurance forms," he said, sounding pretty proud of himself. "I had already scheduled some games I hadn't told you about yet, against some other Tri-Valley teams. They said I could pick up the rest I needed from Port Madison, use as much of their league schedule as I wanted. And a few nonleague games before Christmas if I wanted them."

"Do we play the Vikings?" Danny said.

"No," his dad said. "We just needed twelve official league games. We can play the six teams besides them twice, and that's enough." He looked at Danny and said, "I didn't see any point."

"But we could see them in the play-offs, right? Doesn't everybody make the play-offs?"

"Eight teams, three rounds, like you're starting with the quarterfinals. Yeah, if it falls right, we could play 'em in the play-offs. Depending on what our record is. And theirs. They'll be pretty good even without Ty, I figure."

"I can figure what our record's gonna be."

Richie grabbed him by the arm, turning him slightly. The grip on his arm wasn't enough to hurt. Just enough to let Danny know his dad meant business.

He said, "I want you to stop feeling so sorry for yourself. I mean it. Grow up, for Chrissakes."

"I wasn't—"

"—Yeah, you were. You're feeling sorry for yourself today, you've been feeling sorry for yourself at practice, you've been feeling sorry for yourself since you got cut from the Vikings. And I want you to snap out of it. Or."

It was like he'd come to a stop sign.

"Or what?" Danny said, feeling some anger of his own now. "You're gonna quit? And leave?"

Richie looked down, and realized he still had Danny by the arm, let him go.

"I'm not quitting on you this time," his dad said. "All I'm asking is that you don't quit on me."

"I'm just being honest about the team," Danny said. "Aren't you the one who always says you are what your record says you are in sports?"

"It's an old Bill Parcells line," his dad said. "But we don't have a record yet."

"Right."

"You gotta trust me on something," Richie said. "We're gonna get better as we go. Swear to God."

"Oh, like you've got a master plan."

"I gave up on plans a long time ago," he said. The sad look came

126

back then. "It's like your mom says. You want to make God laugh? Tell Him about your plans."

They both had calmed down now. Sat there talking their common language, basketball, Richie telling him he was going to press more, and feature Colby more, and that he'd even told Matt's dad that he was willing to work with him alone a couple of times a week.

"I was on a team once they said made magic around here," Richie Walker said. "It's time to make some again."

In the two weeks after the Warriors-Vikings scrimmage, Danny had left one message on the Rosses' answering machine, using Will's cell during recess one day even though it was against the rules at St. Pat's; he wanted to do it during school because he knew Mr. Ross would be at the bank and Mrs. Ross would probably be doing her volunteer work at the hospital.

Ty hadn't called back.

A couple of nights later, Danny tried e-mail.

And instant-messaging, when he saw that Ty was online.

He got zip in response.

On Thursday after school, he and Will had gone into town just to goof around. When they had gone past Runyon's, Danny had seen his dad at the end of the bar, a glass of beer in front of him, staring up at what must have been a rerun of a college basketball game played the night before, since it was only five-thirty in the afternoon.

Ty was back at school, Danny knew that. But he hadn't seen him at the Candy Kitchen on weekends. Hadn't run into him at the Middletown-Morrisville football game the weekend after Thanksgiving, even though he was hoping he would.

The next Friday, while waiting for his mom, Danny had even used his old hiding place on the stage while the Vikings practiced, just to see if Ty might be hanging around with them, fooling around with his left hand maybe.

He never showed up.

The next day at Twin Forks, they lost 47–22 and didn't score a point in the fourth quarter.

On Sunday, they lost 50–20 at Morrisville.

They never had a chance in either game, no matter how much switching Richie did with the defenses, no matter how many different lineups he tried, even though he had them pressing all over the court until the end.

At one point against Morrisville, Danny said to his dad coming out of a huddle, "Uh, why are we still pressing?"

"Because it's the kind of team we have to be."

"Even though we're not even close to being that team yet?"

"'Fraid so."

"Does that make *any* sense?"

"To me it does."

Then his dad gave him a push. Like: Just get out there and play. He played hard until the end, doing what he was always doing, which meant looking for Colby Danes every chance he got; the girl on the team being the only one he could pass it to and not be more scared than he was of spiders.

Danny and Will Stoddard were at the water fountain together when the Morrisville game was over. For once, Will talked in a voice only Danny could hear.

"Remember how your pop said we were going to be the team nobody wanted to play?" Will said.

Danny said, yeah, he remembered.

"Well, he was slightly off," Will said. "We're going to be the team *everybody* wants to play."

THEIR NEXT PRACTICE WASN'T UNTIL TUESDAY NIGHT AT NINE.

Richie Walker, who was never late when basketball was involved, didn't show up until ten minutes after nine. Danny had gotten them into layup lines by then, using his own official NBA ball, his Spalding, last year's Christmas present—by mail—from his dad.

When they saw his dad come walking through the double doors, dragging his bag of balls, Will said, "Hey, Coach, we figured you finally deserted."

Richie said, "How about we have a new policy tonight? More playing and less talking."

Will, stung, said, "Hey, Coach, I was just saying . . ."

"Know something, Will? You're *always* just saying."

Danny, careful not to let his dad see him staring at him, watched him go to half-court and sit in the folding chair Ms. Perry, from the girls' team, had left there.

Danny had seen him mad before, usually because of something that happened between him and Danny's mom. Danny'd get sent to his room and then the yelling would start. When he was younger, before he wanted to know exactly what was making them that mad, before he would eavesdrop at the top of the stairs, before he even had music to play or headphones to wear, he would just get on his bed and put pillows over his head until it stopped.

Until it was over.

It was part of it all. Being their son. Being the son of their divorce. The part he didn't like to dwell on very much.

Adults got mad sometimes, that was the deal. They yelled sometimes. And kids figured out pretty early that there wasn't one blinking thing they could do about it.

There was really no point in trying, the way there was no point in trying to figure it. The way there was no point in Danny trying to figure what had pissed off his dad before he got to the gym tonight.

A few minutes after Richie arrived, he yelled from the chair that they weren't going to start scrimmaging until they could make five straight layups with their off hands. It meant left hand for everybody on the team except Oliver Towne, who *was* left-handed. When they couldn't manage that after a couple of trips through the line he said, fine, they could run some suicides, maybe that would improve their layup shooting.

Suicides: Get on the baseline. Run and touch the floor at the free throw line extended. Back to the baseline. Then run and touch the half-court line. Come back. Then to the *other* free throw line. And back. Finally the whole length of the court and back.

Every kid who'd ever played basketball would rather sing in the chorus or go to the dentist than run suicides.

Matt and Oliver Towne finished last.

Richie made them run another one.

While they did, Will made the mistake of saying something to Bren and Bren made the even bigger mistake of laughing.

Richie made them run another suicide, since they thought suicides were so funny.

When they were finished, Richie got out of the chair, slowly and carefully, as always. Tin Man in *The Wizard of Oz*.

"You know why this team looked like a joke this weekend?" he said. "Because you guys treat it like a joke, that's why."

The Warriors were stretched out in a line in front of him. Will and Bren still had their hands on their knees from running. Richie said, "Will and Bren, look at me when I'm talking to you!" Like he'd snapped them both with a towel.

They jerked their heads up.

"The worst crime in sports isn't losing," Richie said. "It's not competing. In my whole life I've never been associated with a team that didn't want to compete and I'm sure not going to start now. Now go out and let me see a real team."

Danny wanted to say, Make sure you tell us if you see it first.

There was only a half hour left for them to scrimmage, because they had to be out of the gym by ten.

Richie spent most of it yelling. Yelled, Danny thought, like every bad kid's coach he'd ever heard, in travel or rec leagues or at summer camp. Apparently yelled so much he had to keep going to the water fountain.

One time when he did, Will whispered to Danny, "Did he, like, forget we're twelve?"

Right before they finished, just a few minutes left, Matt Fitzgerald cut one way when Colby thought he was going to cut the other, and she threw a pass out of bounds.

"Come *on,* Colby!" Richie said. It was the first time he'd ever even come close to saying something in a mean voice to her. "Get your head out of . . . get your head in the game."

Colby took it better than he would have. Maybe better than any of the boys in the gym would have. She didn't look down, she didn't look away, she didn't try to make excuses. All she said was, "Sorry, Coach."

"No you're not," he said.

Everybody else on the court had stopped now, and was looking at Richie.

So was Ali Walker, standing with her arms crossed, just inside the double doors to the gym.

Richie saw her, too.

"That's it for tonight," he said. "Shoot around until your parents come."

Danny looked at his mom, still staring holes through his dad. She stayed where she was, nodding to the other parents who seemed to have showed up all at once for pickup, while Danny kept shooting free throws at one of the side baskets.

Richie made a big show of collecting the balls, as he tried to keep his distance from her. Finally, though, it was just the Walker family in the gym.

Richie said, "I didn't know you were picking him up tonight."

"I was on my way home from book club."

"Well, then, see you Thursday," he said to Danny, and slung the ball bag over his shoulder and started moving slowly, shuffling the way he did when he was tired, toward the door.

She still hadn't moved. "Rich?" she said. "I'd like a word with you. Danny? Go wait in the car. And I mean, *in the car.*"

He walked out to the parking lot, carrying his ball, knowing his mom was watching him through the doors. When he got to the car, he turned around, waved, saw her close the door.

He waited two minutes and then snuck back. He carefully closed the front door, walked through the foyer, got on his toes, peeked through one of the windows in the double doors.

They were standing close to each other in front of the stage.

Danny cracked open one of the doors just slightly, praying that it wouldn't make some creaking noise that would be like a smoke alarm going off.

Now he could tell how pissed off his mom was.

Because she *wasn't* yelling.

Danny knew from experience it was the absolute worst kind of yelling there was.

Because she was speaking in such a low voice, he could only pick up bits and pieces of what she was saying.

". . . don't lie to me, Richard. Sally saw you last night."

His dad had his head down.

". . . can't be invisible, not in this town," she said.

His dad taking it all, the way they'd taken all his yelling in practice.

". . . not the children's fault that you're still hungover the next night."

He said something back now, but must have mumbled it, because Danny couldn't hear a single word he was saying.

Her voice came up a little. "Yes, you *can*," she said. "We went over this already. You have to."

Danny could see him shaking his head, the head still down, acting as if he were the kid who'd done something wrong now, he were the one trying to act sorry.

Finally his mom said, "Quit drinking. Now. Or leave. No good-byes, no travel team. No Danny. Just leave. It'll be better that way than letting your son be the last one to find out what a drunk you are."

She left him standing there, the ball bag still over his shoulder, and walked straight down the middle of the court.

While her streak of light streaked for the car.

Thinking as he ran about the magic they were supposed to make this season.

Wondering just when the magic was supposed to happen, exactly.

EVERYTHING HIS MOM HAD SAID TO HIS DAD MUST HAVE GOTTEN THROUGH TO him, because he was back to being the dad Danny always thought of as the Good Richie by the time they played their next game, against Hanesboro.

It's what you were always looking for from your parents, Danny had decided a long time ago, that they would show up with their good selves most of the time, in a good mood, not tired or pissed off about something at work. Or hungover. Just happy with you and the whole world.

The rest of the time, when their evil twin showed up, you just had to ride it out.

His mom drove him to Hanesboro, which was about an hour away, as far as they had to go in the Tri-Valley League. Danny couldn't tell whether it was because she wanted to see a whole Warriors game from start to finish, or because she thought she still had to police his dad.

"You didn't have to come," Danny said.

"I love sports," she said, and he couldn't tell whether she was the one being sarcastic, or not.

When they got to Hanesboro Middle School, his dad was on the court, moving around in his Tin Man way, shooting around with the O'Brien twins, and Oliver Towne, and Will.

He was even joking around with Will again.

"You been in the weight room?" Richie said to him. As he did he nodded at Danny, and winked.

"You want to touch these guns, Coach?" Will said, flexing his biceps in a bodybuilder pose.

Will was just making fun of his own skinny self, he knew everybody was in on it, that his arms, from wrist to shoulder, were about as thick as the lead in pencils.

Richie said, "They look more like cap pistols to me."

Will tried to look fierce as he kept staring at his right bicep. "You do *not* want any of this," he said. "Trust me."

When Colby showed up with Dr. Danes, Richie made a point of working with her in the corner, defending her with his arms up in the air, showing her how to get her shot against taller players.

Even Colby Danes, tall girl, was being asked to guard players taller than her, every single game. It was funny, Danny thought. Just not laugh-out-loud funny. Not funny the way Will Stoddard was. Because Colby had always been tall to Danny, from first grade on, the way Tess was taller. She was tall even when you put her up against most of the boys, she was tall when they'd have fool-around games in basketball or dodgeball or capture the flag at recess.

She still looked tall to him when the Warriors scrimmaged against each other.

Then they'd show up for a travel game and she'd go match up with the forward she was supposed to guard, or who was guarding her, and Danny would watch her shrink in front of his eyes.

Against Hanesboro, they didn't even have a size advantage at center, their guy was even bigger than Matt Fitzgerald.

It didn't matter over the first three quarters.

This time they were actually in the game.

It looked like another blowout when they got behind by ten points in the first quarter. But Richie told them they were "going small" in the second quarter, which meant starting Danny, Bren, Will, and Steven O'Brien, the better of the two twins.

And Colby at center.

He said they were going to play kamikaze ball, and they did, pressing after every Hanesboro basket, even pressing after a Warrior miss and a Hanesboro rebound, if they could match up quickly enough. Colby was smaller than their center, by a lot, but she was a lot quicker, and started beating him to rebounds; a girl doing that made the kid look as if he wanted to take up another sport. Every time Colby would get a rebound, the Warriors would run, and keep running, and Danny was dishing on the break, and by halftime the game was tied.

Richie stayed with the same group to start the third quarter, even though he got Oliver and Matt in there for a few minutes later.

It was still tied going into the fourth quarter.

Middletown 28, Hanesboro 28.

When the third quarter ended, the Warriors raced to the sideline, slapping each other five, pounding each other on the back. Feeling like a real team, maybe for the first time.

Danny, playing his best game, having assisted on just about every single basket they'd scored, was breathing hard in the huddle, like he'd just run a race, and gulped the red Gatorade that Richie handed him. As he took the bottle, the two of them locked eyes.

His dad made a small fist.

"Settle down now," Richie said. "It's not enough to just be in it. We're here to win it."

He looked around, talking to them in his quiet voice again. The one that had gotten their attention from the start.

Who knows, maybe he was the latest grown-up to crack the code on that.

"Don't change anything you're doing 'cause it's the fourth quarter," he said. "Get back as fast as you can, push it up as fast as you can. Okay?"

They all nodded.

"Same group that ended the quarter," he said. "Now bring it in."

He put his big hand out and then all these small hands were on top of it, and each other.

"One, two, three . . . *defense*," he said.

The Warriors yelled that out now, they were the ones doing the yelling, and came firing out of the huddle.

Danny scored the first basket of the fourth quarter, on a two-on-one break with Will. He was on the left with the ball, Will to his right. All game long, Danny had given the ball up on plays like this. The Hanesboro kid between him and Will expected Danny to do that again, especially coming at the basket on the left side.

The Hanesboro kid, a forward, all arms and legs—Danny was only worried about the arms right now—backed off at the last second, going with Will.

Danny slowed up just slightly, as if getting ready to make his pass.

Then he put it into another gear about ten feet from the basket, imagining himself exploding to the basket the way big guys did when they were going to throw down a dunk.

Pictured himself doing that, and flying.

Laid the ball up with his left hand.

Definitely not his strong suit.

But he put it in the exact right spot on the backboard, in the middle of the square behind the rim, got what one of the ESPN announcers always called the Kiss.

The ball dropped through and the Warriors were ahead for the first time in the game.

Hot dog.

Danny turned around as soon as the ball was through, looking over to his dad, pointed out of bounds, his face asking the question: Keep pressing?

Richie waved his arm hard, like a traffic cop. His face saying: Damn right.

The Warriors stayed right in their faces. Hanesboro hung in there. With two minutes to go, Danny dusted the blond kid guarding him, the one with the long mullet haircut, crossed over on him at half-court—the single crossover, not the double—and fed Will for an open fifteen-footer. Which he drained.

They were ahead by two again, 38–36.

Mullet Head got loose when Bren didn't switch and threw in a long one from his butt. They were tied again. Colby missed from the corner, Mullet Head missed, Will missed. Still tied. With thirty seconds left, their big guy got away with shoving Colby on a rebound, got the ball, had a wide-open layup until Colby grabbed him from behind.

Two shots.

He made the first, missed the second.

Hanesboro 39, Middletown 38.

Richie called time.

"You do not have to rush," he said. "Thirty seconds in basketball is longer than church. Forget trying to run the play. Will, Bren, and Matt—you guys go over and stand on the left wing. We're gonna give the ball to Danny and let him and Colby run a little two-man . . ." He grinned, then said, "Two-*person* game over there on the right. Colby, do whatever you can do to get open. Step back from your guy like you want to shoot, and if he bites, and takes even one step toward you, bust it to the hoop. Okay?"

Still talking to them in the quiet voice.

But as excited as Danny had ever seen him.

"Dan? Just read the play. If she's open, get it to her. If the kid guarding you—the one with the Barbie hair?—turns his head, *you* blow by *him*. Will, after Danny and Colby make their moves, you be a bail-out guy in the left corner. Bren? You come behind Danny after he does whatever he's gonna do."

"What about me?" Matt said.

"As soon as somebody shoots, you crash for the rebound. Just don't foul anybody."

As they broke the huddle, Richie put a hand on Danny's shoulder. "You can do this," he said.

"Is this the fun?" Danny said.

"I'm pretty sure."

The guy guarding Colby didn't bite when she stepped out on him. When she ran for the basket, he ran right with her, step for step. Nothing there.

But she called for the ball the way she was supposed to, and Mullet Head turned his head for one second and, as he did, Danny crossed over to his left hand and broke by him and into the clear in the lane.

At first he thought he was going to have a clear path to the basket. But Will had run to the corner too soon, and not deep enough into the corner, which brought his guy, a Hawaiian-looking guy, into the play. The Hawaiian-looking guy left Will and came over on Danny.

Danny could hear Mullet Head yelling "Switch! Switch!" even though Will's guy had already done that.

Eight seconds left.

Seven.

Six.

Danny wanted to dish one more time, to Colby, who *was* wide open now in the left corner, just because his first instinct was always to give it up.

But he was worried that there might not be enough time.

He was going to have to shoot it before the Hawaiian guy was in front of him and before Mullet Head got back in the play: The passer having to put it up.

He was two steps inside the free throw line when he released the ball over the Hawaiian guy's long left arm, which suddenly seemed be made of elastic; which seemed to keep growing like he was a comic-book guy.

Danny released the ball in front of him, the way his dad had been teaching him, not off the shoulder, and felt like he'd put perfect rotation on the ball.

Saw the last of the time disappear from the clock behind the basket as the ball came floating down toward that basket.

Saw the ball catch a piece of the front rim, but softly, bouncing just slightly as it settled on the back of the rim, hanging there for what only felt like three or four hours, as if making up its mind about how this one was supposed to come out.

Then it fell off like it had rolled off the end of the kitchen table.

Hanesboro 39, Middletown 38.

Final.

His mom kept trying to cheer him up on the ride back to Middletown, he had to give her that.

Somehow he felt like he was with some smiley-faced nurse trying to make him feel better about being at the doctor's.

"C'mon, it was a great game," she said, "even if it didn't come out the way you wanted."

"Ya think?"

She had let him sit in the front seat. Technically, they both knew he didn't weigh enough, wasn't big enough, to get out of the backseat yet, even though he was twelve and just about everybody his age was sitting in the front seat with their parents. But she had said, ride with me today, I want the company. As if she knew making him sit by himself in the back today would make him feel worse than he did already.

"You guys looked really good in the second half," she said.

Danny, sitting there with his ball in his lap, said, "Great."

"I would think," she said, "that a game like this would have you excited about the rest of the season."

"That might be the only chance we have all season to win a game," he said.

"Get 'em next time. Right?"

Danny turned to face her. "Mom?"

"You want me to stop trying to cheer you up now."

"I'll clear the dinner dishes for a week and load the dishwasher if you'll stop trying to cheer me up."

"And take out the trash?"

"*Mom.*"

"Okay, okay, I'll stop."

He went straight up to his room when they got home. Noticed when he got there that he'd left his computer on. Again.

The IM box was up there and waiting for him, along with a message from Tess.

ConTessa44: Hey? You there? I heard about the game.

Danny thought: God Bless America. It was one of his mom's expressions when she wanted to swear. God Bless America, the air traffic control guys couldn't track airplanes the way kids his age tracked travel basketball in Middletown.

He heard the doodlely-doo now.

A new message.

Maybe she had radar tracking him, knowing he was back in his room.

CONTESSA44: C'mon, you must be back by now from HanesUnderwearBoro.

He walked over and shut off his computer and cranked up PlayStation2, then proceeded to stack one of his teams on *NBA '05* with all the best guys: Duncan, Iverson, Shaq, McGrady, Kidd, LeBron.

The guys on the other team were all scrubs.

He was going to get a sure thing somewhere today.

God Bless America, why hadn't that stupid shot fallen?

He had let everybody on his team down. And he knew it was his team more than anybody else's, there wouldn't even be a stupid team, his dad wouldn't even have invented the Warriors, if he hadn't gotten cut from real travel.

Real travel, he thought.

As Will liked to say, Ain't that the truth?

I need you, his dad kept saying. Don't you quit on me, his dad had said. Then, when he had a chance to make one stupid shot to win one stupid game, he couldn't measure up.

He got up suddenly, shut off his game, cranked up his computer, ignored another IM from Tess—he'd explain to her tomorrow why he hadn't felt like talking—and Googled up the place where he could watch his dad dribble out the clock against L.A. in that championship game.

Watched again as young Richie Walker was in complete control of everything: The clock, the game, himself, his team, the other team. The moment. Like he was the one alone in a driveway.

He didn't choke.

Maybe you only got one nonchoking point guard per family, maybe that was it.

Then he shut down the computer for the night, hearing one more IM jingle before he did. Tess, for sure. But he didn't want her trying to cheer him up any more than he did his mom.

It was definitely a girl deal, wanting to put a Band-Aid on the whole thing.

He didn't want to feel better tonight. He *wanted* to feel like crap. He *wanted* to remember what this felt like so that maybe—maybe, maybe, maybe—he wouldn't let everybody down the next time.

Danny remembered listening to his mom on the phone once, talking to one of her friends, saying that the best thing about youth sports was that an hour after the game ended, most kids couldn't even remember the final score.

Not this kid.

Not this score.

Hanesboro 39, Middletown 38.

Final.

God Bless America.

His mom was meeting Will's mom for a girls' brunch after church on Sunday. She asked if Danny wanted to be dropped at the Stoddards' so he could hang with Will while she and Molly Stoddard went into town. He said, no, he wanted to meet up with Tess at McFeeley Park.

He changed after church into jeans and sneaks and last year's shooting shirt from sixth-grade travel, then grabbed his ball, knowing he'd get time to shoot around because Tess was always late.

"Why don't you show up a few minutes late, then you don't have to wait for her?"

Danny said, "Me waiting for her, that's part of our whole deal."

"Oh," his mom said. "Sometimes I forget I was a twelve-year-old girl once."

"Duh."

"But if you and Tess go into town, you'll have to carry your ball with you."

"So?"

"You don't mind?"

"I like carrying my ball with me."

She sighed. "And I know *nothing* of significance about twelve-year-old boys," she said.

When they drove through the high arch that was the entrance to McFeeley, she said, "You seem to be feeling better today."

145

"Only 'cause I couldn't feel any worse."

"I know we've gone over this before," she said, "but basketball isn't a matter of life and death."

He smiled, to let her know he was playing, and said, "No, it's much more serious than that."

She said she'd pick him up in front of the Candy Kitchen at four. Then she called out the window that she loved him. He waved good-bye as if he hadn't heard.

You never knew who might catch you telling your mom you loved her back.

He heard the bounce of a single basketball as he came up the hill toward the big court at McFeeley. He couldn't see who was up there right away—he was too short, the hill was way too steep—but as he got near the top he gave a little jump and saw that it was Ty Ross.

Danny had told Tess he'd meet her by the tennis courts. He turned one last time and saw she wasn't there yet, kept going toward the basketball court. Ty didn't look up until he heard Danny bouncing the ball at the other end of the court.

Having just come from church, he wasn't sure whether he should be praying for stuff like this, but he was praying hard now that Ty Ross didn't really hate his guts.

Maybe there was a way they could talk basketball with each other the way he talked basketball with his dad when neither one of them knew what else to say.

Danny thought: What would guys do if they couldn't speak sports?

"Hey," Ty said.

"Hey."

Danny could see his fingers sticking out of the top of what looked to be a pretty light cast, one that had more writing and graffiti-looking squiggles on it than some of the subway cars he'd see going past Shea Stadium when he'd go to a ball game there.

It was pretty cold out, down to the high forties, his mom had said, but Ty was wearing a Knicks' orange sweatshirt with the sleeves cut up to his shoulders, black sweats, and brand-new sneaks that Danny would have been able to spot a mile away.

The new LeBrons from Nike.

Ty turned away from Danny and pushed a simple layup toward the basket with his left hand, making it look like shooting with that hand was the most natural thing in the world.

Holy crap, Danny thought, he looks better shooting with his weak hand than I do with my good one.

Danny stood at half-court, holding his favorite ball, as Ty stepped back with his—same model, an Infusion—and made the same shot Danny had gagged on against Hanesboro.

He's better than me at basketball with a broken wrist.

"Yo," Danny said.

Changing the conversation up a little.

Ty turned.

Then Danny just came out with it, knowing he'd better do it now before he lost his nerve.

"I'm sorry," Danny said. "I am *so* sorry about what happened, I've been trying to tell you—"

Ty raised his right hand, his way of telling him to stop, forgetting that it was the hand with the cast on it.

"I know," he said.

Danny kept going anyway.

"Teddy had cheap-shotted me right before with an elbow, then he did it again under the basket, and I just reacted and gave him one back. But I never meant—"

"I know all that," Ty said.

You had to drag things out of him the way you did with Richie Walker sometimes; Danny had been reminded of that just hanging around with Ty in his room that day.

Ty Ross was really good at a lot of things—*excellent* at a lot of things—but conversation wasn't one of them.

"How do you know?" Danny said. "Teddy's been telling everybody I did it on purpose."

Ty said, "His name should really be Teddy Moron."

"Thought you guys were buds."

"Not anymore."

"Because?" Danny dragged the word out the way Tess did sometimes.

"Because once I stopped feeling sorry for myself I knew you weren't the guy he wanted me to think you were." Ty smiled. *"He's* the guy he wanted me to think you were."

Danny bounced his ball in front of him, left hand to right hand to left hand. Feeling better for the first time since he'd missed the shot against Hanesboro.

Maybe it was seeing Ty with the cast on his wrist, and realizing things weren't so bad, after all, that missing a game-ender wasn't an epic tragedy.

Danny said, "Who told you about what happened before you fell?"

"Tess," Ty said.

"You guys talk?"

Ty laughed. "Now we do. My mom thought I should try something new while my wrist was getting better. Something *not* sports. We decided on that photography course at the Y. On Wednesdays?"

Danny nodded. "The one Tess is in."

"The first one was last Wednesday. She grabbed me as soon as it was over, said I was gonna listen to something she had to say." Ty made a whoosh sound. "Man, she's got this way of getting you to do what she wants you to do."

"Ya think?"

"Anyway, she told me what happened. And that I couldn't blame you, because she wasn't gonna allow it."

"She's the best-looking girl our age in this whole town," Danny said. "But she's already got some mom in her."

Ty said, "Ya think?" He flipped another left-handed shot toward the basket, missed. The ball bounced away from him. "I got it," Danny said, passing Ty his ball while he retrieved the other.

"I'm supposed to be meeting her here," Danny said.

"I know."

Danny smiled. Imagining a cartoon lightbulb going on over his head. "She told you to be here."

Ty shrugged. "She said you'd expect her to be late."

Tess Hewitt. Secret Agent Girl.

"She said she told you twelve, but wouldn't be here until twelve-thirty," Ty said. "You want to play H-O-R-S-E?"

"I can't shoot well enough left-handed," Danny said. "'Course after yesterday, I'm not even positive I'm *right-handed* anymore."

He told Ty all about Hanesboro 39, Middletown 38.

"You'll make the next one," Ty said. "That's the way I always look at it." He nodded at the basket. "I'll shoot lefty, you shoot righty."

Danny said that if he lost, he was definitely quitting basketball. Ty said, fine, they could both take up photography.

They played H-O-R-S-E and talked. Ty said he didn't really know how fast his wrist would heal. Said he hoped he'd be able to get in a couple of games before the play-offs. In the Tri-Valley, he said, you didn't have to set your official roster until the week the play-offs began. So even if he hadn't played at all, his dad could still have him on the roster.

When they were both at H-O-R-S, Danny said, "Your dad know you're here, by the way?"

"He's out of town on bank business. My mom brought me."

"What would he do if he knew?"

"Yell."

Ty twirled the ball on the tip of his left index finger as effortlessly as Richie Walker did.

"He's not so bad, really, my dad. He just tries too hard."

"With sports?"

"With everything."

Danny said, "He doesn't seem to like me very much."

"I don't think it's you," he said. "It's the whole thing. You. The Warriors. Your dad. My dad likes to be the biggest guy in town. Like he waited his whole life to be the biggest guy in town. Now there's this bunch of little guys . . ."

His voice trailed off.

Danny shot and missed. Ty shot and missed. Down the hill, Danny could see Tess getting out of her mom's Volvo station wagon.

Danny dribbled to the spot where he'd missed against Hanesboro. Not that he was still fixed on that or anything. Then he shot the ball a little higher than usual, higher than he had yesterday, and hit nothing but net.

Sure.

Today he hits nothing but net.

Ty missed, then missed the extra shot you get at the end of the game.

"Good game," Ty said.

"That," Danny said, knowing he was getting off the kind of pun Tess usually did, "is a left-handed compliment."

Ty gave him a low five with his left hand as they heard Tess say, "Fancy meeting you boys here."

Tess: In a ponytail today. With some kind of long red sweater, one that went nearly to her knees, with the sleeves pushed up to her elbows. Tess in jeans and Timberland boots, the Timbys looking as new as Ty's LeBrons.

Carrying her camera.

She snapped one of Ty and Danny standing there next to each other.

"You two look like a team to me," she said.

"I wish," Danny said.

The three of them went down the hill, destination Candy Kitchen. Danny didn't even mind walking between them, looking like their little brother.

THEY DECIDED TO SPEND CHRISTMAS TOGETHER, LIKE A REAL FAMILY.

Or, Danny figured, as close to a real family as they were likely to get.

His dad said he probably wouldn't get up early enough for the opening of presents, telling Danny that the only part of him that was still a ballplayer—that still *worked*—was his body clock. But he said he would be there for Christmas dinner, the roast beef dinner with all the trimmings that Ali Walker had promised them, followed by strawberry shortcake for dessert, Danny's favorite.

According to his mom, dinner would be served at what she called a "soft two o'clock."

"What does 'soft' mean?" Danny asked.

"It means that showing up on time, for anything other than basketball, has always been real hard for your father."

Christmas was still Christmas when his dad wasn't around, when it was just him and his mom. But after all the waiting for it, all the anticipation, it sometimes seemed to be over for the two of them before Christmas Day was even over. They'd go over to have Christmas dinner with friends sometimes, families like Will's and Bren's that had four kids each in them, and there would be presents everywhere, under the tree and all over the house.

It was smaller with him and his mom.

Always came back to that.

Danny didn't know how much teachers made at St. Pat's, or anywhere else, for that matter. Even if his mom told him what her salary was, he wasn't sure he'd understand where it fit into the whole grand scheme of things. The one time it had come up, a couple of years ago, his mom had said, "I make more than a year's allowance for you, and somewhat less than Michael Jordan used to make." Then she laughed. She always went for a laugh when the subject was money, but Danny usually thought it was like the fake laughter you heard on television shows even when nothing funny was happening.

Her heart never seemed to be in that, the same way it never seemed to be in dating the guys who would come to the house to pick her up sometimes.

There were some subjects Danny tried to avoid at all costs, and one of them was this: Whether his mom would ever get married again.

"What?" she said when they talked about that one from time to time. "And give up our life on Easy Street?"

Then she would fake-laugh again.

Danny could never figure out, on Christmas Day or any other day of the year, why they *weren't* on Easy Street. His dad had made it to the NBA, even if his career hadn't lasted very long. *Those* salaries he did know something about, even if he didn't know squat about what teachers made. And he knew that if you were a first-round pick, even back when his dad was a first-round pick, you got a three-year contract, guaranteed.

So there had to have been some money in the family once, right after he was born, when his mom and dad were married and they were a real family more than one day a year.

Where had it all gone?

That was one he never asked either of his parents about, how it worked out that his dad didn't seem to have any money left and why he and his mom were living in the Flats, at 422 Easy Street. . . .

Tess had helped him shop for his mom. She had asked him exactly how much money he'd saved up from allowance and birthdays, and he told her.

Tess said, "I just need to establish our price range."

"I'll give you the money and you get her something," Danny said. "I hate to shop. You know I hate to shop."

"You'll love it," she said. "Shopping with me is like playing a round of golf with Tiger."

She took him to Wright's, the only jewelry store in Middletown, and helped him pick out a silver charm bracelet. Done, Danny said when they'd agreed on the one they both liked, thinking how quick and painless the process had been, jewelry shopping with a girl four days before Christmas.

Tess said they weren't quite done, and then somehow talked the woman behind the counter into throwing in a single silver charm—a basketball—for an extra five dollars.

The bracelet, with the tiny ball hanging from it, made his mom cry after he insisted she open her present first, really cry, as he helped her fasten it on her wrist, his mom telling him it was the most beautiful piece of jewelry anybody had ever given her, ever.

Then she hugged him and started crying all over again.

He was never going to understand girls of any age as long as he lived, he was sure of that. But he was going to run upstairs the first chance he got and IM Tess and tell her that they'd hit the stinking jackpot with the charm bracelet.

It was his turn to open then.

Real jackpot.

His mom had bought him a new laptop, the first brand-new laptop he'd ever had in his life, a Sony VAIO.

And even a dope about money knew it was way out of their price range.

Way, *way* out of their price range.

"Mom," he said, when he was able to get some words out, imagining how buggy his eyes must have looked to her as he stared at the inside of the box, afraid to even lift the unit out of there. "You can't . . . we can't . . ."

"Can," she said. "Did. Done deal. Merry Christmas."

"But—"

"But nothing," she said, helping him get the white Styrofoam out of the box so they could gently remove the computer. "Been doing a little extra tutoring on the side."

"You ask me, it must have been a whole *lot* of extra tutoring—"

"What*ever*," she said in her dippy mall-girl voice, as a way of ending the conversation.

Then, in her real voice, about as soft, Danny thought, as the snow starting to hit the ground outside the living-room window, the Christmas snow she seemed to have ordered, his mom said, "I knew that if I made enough money on the side I could buy myself the kind of Christmas-morning face I'm looking at right now."

She hugged him again and then had him open another box, the one that had the new LeBron James Nikes in it, the ones like Ty's he had described to her after he got home from McFeeley that day.

The sneaks were so cool, coming right on top of the laptop, that he managed to act excited while he opened the remaining boxes, the ones with the shirts and sweaters and new school khakis in them. Then the two of them went upstairs to his room and un-plugged and unhooked the old computer, somehow managed to follow the directions—the two of them giggling their way through the whole thing—until they had the Sony up and running with Microsoft Word and e-mail and IM and passwords and codes and all the rest of it.

When they were done with that, they attached his old speakers to it.

His mom kept telling him, Do *not* lose anything.

He said he was being careful.

She asked where he was going to put the box and the directions and the warranty. His closet, he said. "Oh no!" she said in *Freddy vs. Jason* fright. "Anywhere but there!"

She left him alone then, knowing he was twitchy to IM Tess and Will and the rest of the Danny Walker Network, telling them about his stuff and asking about theirs.

Then he could hear the Christmas music coming from down-stairs as she went to work in the kitchen; nobody liked Christmas music more than his mom, she started playing it in the house and in the car the day after Thanksgiving. Always telling him that if Christmas shopping had started, it was time for Elvis to start singing "Blue Christmas."

Even when the presents weren't as jackpot big as they were today, even when Christmas wasn't as big as it felt like today, his mom loved Christmas as much as he did.

New laptop on the desk. New LeBrons on his feet. Snow coming down. His dad coming over for Christmas dinner at a soft two in the afternoon.

The Warriors might still suck.

Today didn't.

His dad showed up early, saying the roads were getting bad as the snow came down harder, and he didn't want to take any chances.

"You were the one who always wanted a white Christmas," his dad said to his mom when he was inside, brushing the snow out of his hair. "This white enough for you?"

"There can never be enough snow on Christmas to suit me," she said, taking the old Syracuse letter jacket he was wearing, navy with orange trim, and leather sleeves.

"Enough to you always meant snowed in."

"I'll take that deal," she said.

He was carrying a big paper bag, set it down near the tree and just left it there. He didn't say anything about it, so neither did Danny.

His mom had a fire going in their small fireplace. She made popcorn for everybody, and said she'd whip up some eggnog while Danny took his dad up to show him his new computer. That didn't take long, his dad not being a computer guy, so Danny challenged him to a game of *NBA '05* instead. His dad said he was almost as bad at video games as he was with computers, where he was the absolute world's worst, but he'd give it a shot.

"I haven't even whipped your butt yet and you're already making excuses," Danny said.

He showed him how to work the controllers. They each got into a beanbag chair, even though Richie said that once he settled in it might take a forklift to get him out.

Richie Walker wasn't the world's worst at video ball, as it turned out.

"Ringer," Danny said.

"Is that what you kids call a guy trying to get the most out of his ability?"

"Ringer," Danny said.

He was either a ringer or the fastest learner Danny had ever met, because it was 112–112 with ten seconds to go.

Both of them clicking away like madmen.

"Don't let me win," Danny said.

"Wasn't planning to," Richie said.

McGrady, who was on Danny's team, made one over Vince Carter at the buzzer and Danny's team won, 114–112.

"Yes!" He jumped up and made one of those dance motions with his arms like he was stirring some huge pot.

"You cheated," his dad said, still clicking away even though the screen was frozen. "There was one second left!"

"Was not."

"Was so."

A much calmer voice from the doorway said, "Dinner, children."

They turned their heads at the same time and saw Ali Walker in her Santa apron, smiling at them, hands on hips.

"What's so funny?" Danny said.

"Oh, nothing."

Richie said, "There was one second left."

"Was not," Danny said.

The three of them went down to have Christmas dinner.

As soon as Danny picked up the bag, he knew it was another ball.

"You didn't need to get me a new ball," he said. "You got me a cool ball last Christmas."

"Not this ball. Open it."

The Spurs were playing the Nets on television. The fire was still going strong. The snow was coming down even harder, making it hard to see across Earl Avenue. Richie had just announced that he better be going soon.

It was an official Spalding NBA game ball.

Danny twirled it slowly in his hands, then ran his right hand over the surface of it.

"Leather," he said.

"Full grain," Richie said.

From the couch, Ali Walker said, "You say that like it's pure gold."

Danny looked at his dad and they both shook their heads sadly, that one person could be this ignorant about something as important as an official leather ball.

"Sorry," she said, and went back to reading *Vanity Fair*.

Richie said, "I think you ought to check it out a little more closely," and pointed to where "NBA" was.

There were autographs on either side, so neat and legible you could have thought the ball came with them.

Jason Kidd.

John Stockton.

"Your two poster guys," Richie said.

"The two you say were the best."

Richie corrected him. "The best *lately*."

"How did you get them both to sign it?"

"I just told them it was for a point guard they ought to be rooting for the way people always rooted for them."

Danny went over and hugged his dad. No man hug here. The real thing.

Richie hugged him back. "Merry Christmas, kiddo," he said.

They were both on the floor. When Danny pulled back, Richie pulled himself up on his second try.

"I sound like a pocketful of loose change," he said.

To Ali he said, "I didn't know what to get you."

"You got me all you needed to get, Rich."

To Danny he said, "First game back, we're going to use this ball as our gamer. I have a feeling it's going to change our luck. Then if it works, we'll save it for the next time we need our stinking luck changed."

Danny put out a closed fist. His dad touched it lightly with one of his own.

Richie said, "On account of, our luck is due to change."

They all stood near the front door while he put on his Syracuse jacket. Ali said that he should drive carefully. He smiled at her. "I always do," he said.

"Now, anyway," he said, with that shy duck of the head he gave you sometimes.

He opened the door, turned around.

"This was a good Christmas," he said to both of them. "Been a long time since I had a good Christmas."

"Drive carefully," Ali Walker said again.

"See you at practice," Richie said to Danny, and then walked slowly on the slippery walk toward his car, looking more like an old man than ever.

Danny and his mom went and stood on the porch in the snow, watched the car pull away from in front of the house, watched it until it made the turn on Cleveland Avenue and disappeared.

He had the basketball under his arm.

When they got back inside, she took it from him.

"Go ahead," she said.

"Huh?"

She grinned at him and dribbled the ball twice on the floor in the foyer. Not really dribbling it so much as slapping at it, as though trying to squash some bug sitting on top of it.

"Go ahead," she said, handing the ball back to him.

Danny tricky-dribbled around her and then past her down the hall and through the kitchen and into the dining room.

Dribbling through the house like he was a young Richie Walker.

20

HAVING THE NAMES OF STOCKTON AND KIDD ON THE BALL DIDN'T HELP.

"Stockton and Kidd *handling* the ball, now that would help," Bren Darcy was saying.

"We need *that* Kidd, not the kids we've got," Will Stoddard said.

"No *kidding,*" Danny said. "Get it?"

Will said, "Okay, we have to stop now."

They tried the new ball in the first game back, against Kirkland, and lost by six points. Tried it again the next day, played well for three quarters against Piping Rock, the best team in the Tri-Valley with a record of 8-0 coming in, but ended up losing by ten.

Colby missed a couple of shots in the last two minutes, and after the second one, Bren made a face. Danny called a time-out, and when they got to the huddle, Will told Bren that he could make faces when people missed as long as *he* never missed, and Bren said that Will should be worrying more about winning the game than sticking up for Colby. Before Danny knew it, they were nose-to-nose and Danny had to get between them.

"You guys have been buds as long as I've been buds *with* you guys," he said. "So cut it out."

Will said, "Tell him to stop making faces."

Bren said, "Tell *him* to mind his own freaking business."

"Hey!" Danny said. "Both of you. Zip it now. We're getting better, let's not blow it now."

162

They *were* getting better.

Matt Fitzgerald, in particular, was starting to look like a real center, the private work he'd been doing with Richie finally starting to pay off. Colby got better every game. Will was taking basketball seriously—or as seriously as Will could take anything—for the first time in his life.

No team, no matter how big, wanted Danny and Bren Darcy harassing them in the backcourt.

"It's like being chased by freaking *bees,*" one of the Kirkland guards had said the day before.

They just couldn't win a freaking game to save their lives.

It was the middle weekend in January now, about a month from the start of the play-offs, and their record was 0–9. They were kidding about Jason Kidd in the layup line, getting ready to play Seekonk at St. Pat's.

Colby showed up a little late, and the minute she walked through the door, everybody spotted her new kicks:

Old-school Converse high-tops, white, yellow toward the heel, some purple in there, too; even guys their age knew these were the ones Magic Johnson used to wear for the Lakers.

Danny had known from the start how cool Colby Danes was, not that he would have admitted that to his buddies. Now it was official.

A girl in Magic's Cons.

"Girlfriend is *stylin',*" Will Stoddard said.

Bren slapped him five on that, their fight at the end of the Piping Rock game already ancient history.

Oliver Towne, their only black kid, said, "Stoddard, you are, like, *pathetically* white."

"Oh," Will said, trying to act hurt, "like you have to rub my pasty face in it."

Colby, who was now one of the guys on the Warriors, because she was cool *and* could play, said, "You are all sooooooo jealous that a girl has cooler sneaks than you."

Will couldn't let her have the last word. Will would sooner leave town before he'd let somebody have the last word.

"Maybe I can borrow them someday," he said. "If I ever grow into them, of course. Like, when I'm in college."

But this time, Colby got him.

"You're right," she said. "This is, like, totally messed-up. Isn't it the boys who're supposed to have big feet and the girls who are supposed to have big hair?"

The rest of the guys whooped as she took her place in line, casually high-fiving Danny as she passed.

Danny looked around and thought: We act like a team, we have fun like a team.

When do we play all four quarters like a team?

It turned out to be against Seekonk.

The Seekonk Sailors—they were the next town up from Port Madison, on the Sound—were even smaller than the Warriors. And not nearly as well coached. They didn't have anybody who could get in front of either Danny or Bren, anybody who could stay with Colby, anybody who could keep Matt Fitzgerald off the boards.

When they tried going with a two-one-two zone, Will made five outside shots in a row, an all-time personal best.

The 0–9 Middletown Warriors were ahead 18–4 after the first quarter.

They were ahead 26–10 at halftime.

They were ahead twenty points by the fourth quarter, and Richie had them making ten passes before they were even allowed to look at the basket. By then, he had the O'Brien twins in the backcourt, Michael Harden playing center, Will and Oliver Towne at forward.

Richie had taken Danny out halfway through the third quarter.

"I think your work here is done," Richie said.

Danny took a seat next to him. "Somebody said these guys have won two games," he said. "I don't know how they did that, but they're not going to win another one the rest of the season."

"Don't worry about them," his dad said. "You were worried we weren't going to win a game the rest of the season."

"Excellent point."

"And when it's over? You make sure the rest of the guys—and girls—act like they've won before."

"Even though we haven't?"

"Especially because we haven't."

It ended up Middletown 42, Seekonk 22.

Final.

Richie Walker said for the players and parents to meet at Fierro's about five o'clock, the pizza was on him.

"Is your mom here?" Richie said to Danny.

Danny nodded to the row of folding chairs up on the stage. "She came late with Tess."

"See you all at Fierro's," his dad said.

They tapped clenched fists.

"We're on the board," his dad said.

They were on the board.

His dad still wasn't there at five-thirty.

"See?" his mom said. "The game's over. He thought it was a soft five."

The Warriors and their parents had taken up most of the front room at Fierro's, pushing four tables together. They finally decided to order, a bunch of plain pizzas and a couple of pepperonis, huge greasy paper plates covered with mountains of French fries, pitchers of Coke and Sprite. They were playing oldies on the old-fashioned Fierro's jukebox as usual, but nobody could hear them over the mega-amped-up noise of the place, and laughter, and excitement, as the kids on the team replayed just about every basket of the game.

In honor of the Warriors' first win, Al Fierro announced that the ice cream sundaes were on him today.

The waitresses, all of them from Middletown High, were starting to clear away the plates and pizza platters when the pay phone on the wall next to the front door rang.

Al Fierro answered it, called out "Ali," and motioned for her to come up there.

Danny watched his mom take the receiver.

Watched the smile leave her face.

Saw her free hand come to her mouth.

"Not again," he heard her say.

She nodded hard a couple of times, placed the receiver back in its cradle, walked over to where Danny was sitting between Will and Tess.

"It's your father," she said. "There's been an accident."

SHE CONVINCED HIM IN THE CAR THAT HIS DAD WASN'T GOING TO DIE.

"But he's broken up pretty badly," his mom said, her hands gripping the steering wheel like she was holding on for dear life.

Maybe she was.

"But they can put him back together, right?" Danny said.

"They did it before, they can do it again. It's his hip again, his shoulder. One of his lungs collapsed, but they said they fixed that when he got to the hospital. However they fix things like that."

"He must have stopped somewhere after the game," she said. "They say he lost control of his car, right before that big curve where 37 intersects with 118. You know where that is, right? Near the Burger King and the Home Depot?"

Danny said he knew it, but he didn't remember a big curve.

"At least he was wearing a seat belt this time," Ali Walker said, turning her head slightly to talk to him.

They were doing it by the book today, Danny sitting in the back where he belonged.

"Coming home from a game, just like last time," his mom said, not really talking to him now, more like she was talking to herself.

"You okay?" she said.

"I'm okay."

He wasn't going to cry, that was for sure. Somehow crying

to him meant that the whole thing was worse than he wanted it to be.

We're on the board, his dad had said.

Danny sat in the waiting room looking at the pictures in the front of *Sports Illustrated,* just so he had something to do while his mom talked to the doctors.

When they finally got into his dad's room, all he could see were tubes, coming out of Richie Walker's arm and stuck in his nose. There was a thick bandage covering his forehead.

"Did I miss a good party?" Richie said when he saw them at the end of his bed.

"We're not staying long," Ali said. "The doctors say you need your rest."

"Before they do their body and fender work on me in the morning."

"Well," Ali said, "it's not like the hip and shoulder they gave you last time around were top-of-the-line, anyway."

Richie said, "I asked them to try something besides used parts this time."

"Good one, Dad," Danny said.

He realized when he took his jacket off that he was still wearing his Warriors Number 3, the jersey hanging all the way down to the knees of the gray sweats he'd put on after the game.

His mom stood on one side of the bed now, he stood on the other. Richie reached out with his left hand, the one not in the sling, and took Danny's left hand.

Danny squeezed it hard.

"I wasn't drunk," Richie said, holding on to Danny but looking at Ali.

She said, "Rich, you don't have to—"

He said, "I know I don't. But I want to. I'm not going to lie to you, I thought about breaking the pledge, stopping for a cold one, just to toast our great victory. But I knew better this time."

"Don't talk," she said.

"Hey," Richie said to her. "Did you ever think you'd be telling me not to talk?"

She said, "This is like being in class. What part of 'don't talk' aren't you getting here, mister?" She tried to smile at the end of it, but then she got that lower lip going and made Danny afraid she was the one who was going to lose it.

But she didn't.

Danny had always known she was the toughest one of all of them.

"The doctors said they're going to fix up Dad as good as new, didn't they, Mom?" Danny said.

"Only if they're grading me against the curve, right, teach?"

"Close your eyes now," Ali Walker said.

He did, and a few minutes later, was sleeping.

They were scheduled to operate on his right hip and his right shoulder at nine the next morning. Danny didn't want to go to school, but his mom made him, saying he wasn't going to do his father or anybody else any good hanging around the hospital and staring at the clock.

"You'd rather have me sitting in class and staring at the clock?" he said.

"You're going to school," she said. "I'll wait it out at the hospital. The second he's out, I'll call."

Mrs. Stoddard picked him up. Right before first period, the

principal at St. Pat's, Mr. Dawes, an old guy who was retiring at what Will said was the age of dirt at the end of the school year, came over the intercom and said all students should keep Danny Walker's dad in their thoughts today, even though he was sure Mr. Walker was going to come through surgery that morning with flying colors.

They were in their English classroom by then.

Will leaned over and said, "Hem and Haw Dawes makes the operation sound like a pop quiz your dad is trying to pass."

Danny had already decided that he wasn't going anywhere today without either Will or Tess—or both—with him.

Danny said to Will, "You're my official spokesman today."

"Finally," Will Stoddard said. "Finally, my brother, you have seen the light."

They still hadn't heard anything at lunch, but Tess said that wasn't unusual for a hip operation.

"How do you know that?" Will said.

She stuck her nose up in the air. "I know things," she said.

"You, like, researched Mr. Walker's surgery?" Will said.

"Last night," she said. "Some people actually use Google to look up things besides somebody's lifetime batting average."

"Mom said the same thing," Danny said. "She said that if they were done by lunch, that would be fast."

Will and Danny had already finished eating the hamburgers they usually got in the cafeteria on Mondays. Tess cut off a small corner of hers, and chewed it carefully. As usual, she was working on her food as though it were some kind of tricky math problem.

"Can I ask a completely selfish question?" Will said.

Tess said, "We'd expect nothing more of you."

"Or less," Danny said.

"Who's gonna coach the team if your dad is laid up a while?" Will said.

"I knew it was going to be something incredibly messed-up lame," Tess said. "He's not even out of *surgery* yet."

"It's okay," Danny said, putting a hand on her arm. "I've been thinking about it, too. Just to have something to think about *besides* the surgery."

"You guys never cease to amaze," she said. "All guys never cease to amaze."

"No, really, Will's right," Danny said. "Mr. Harden's going to be out of town on a case for the next month, Michael was talking about that at the party. Oliver's only got his mom. Bren's dad is all jammed up coaching his brothers in hockey. Mr. O'Brien's got that Wall Street job that has him in London, England, half the time. Colby said that the only time Dr. Danes ever coached her was in soccer, that he gave up coaching anything after that because he's on call so much on the weekends."

So who *would* coach them, Danny wondered.

Fifteen minutes into Spanish, Mr. Dawes—who reminded Danny of Alfred, the butler from the Batman cartoons—appeared in the doorway, and motioned for Danny to come out in the hall.

For the first time since they'd all been at St. Pat's, Mr. Dawes was smiling.

"Your mother just called from the hospital," he said. "Your father made it through the surgery just fine. He's a little worse for wear, but there were no surprises, she said to tell you, and no complications. She wanted me to tell you that she'll pick you up here after school and drive you over there."

Danny thanked him, even shook his long, thin bony hand.

When he came back into class, he gave a thumbs-up to Will and Tess, sat down at his desk, and thought: His dad had been a little worse for wear for as long as Danny could remember things.

Ali Walker called off Warriors practice on Tuesday night. But after dinner that night, the whole team went to visit Richie at the hospital.

Colby brought the present they had all chipped in to buy him, ten bucks a kid:

An official Spalding NBA ball they'd all signed in Magic Marker.

"Now you've got a gamer of your own," Danny said to his dad.

Richie still had the IV-tube attached to his right arm. With his left, he placed the ball next to him on the bed.

"Just because I'm a little stiff," he said, "I'm going to let you knuckleheads off without making you learn a couple of new plays I've got cooked up against the man-to-man."

There were only two chairs in the room; the O'Brien twins grabbed those. The rest of them stood at the foot of the bed so Richie could see them without turning his head. Any time he tried to move at all, Danny saw, there was a look on his father's face like somebody had punched him. In addition to everything else that had happened at the intersection of 37 and 118, he'd broken two ribs.

He let the kids do most of the talking. Will made everybody laugh—Richie included—by asking him if he'd mind just sliding over on the bed a little and handing Will the remote for the television set that came down out of the ceiling.

Richie said, "The surgery didn't kill me. But you making me laugh with busted ribs might make me do myself in."

"It's a burden I have to bear, Coach," Will Stoddard said. "Some people are just too funny."

Richie promised them all he'd be back before they knew it. The room then filled with the sound of *Cool* and *That's right* and *Now you're talking, Coach.* Even though they all knew he was lying, just by the looks of him, by what their own eyes were telling them.

Finally the kids ran out of small talk and nobody knew what to say and it was at that moment, as if on cue, that the nurse stuck her head inside the door and said it was time for them to go, her patient needed his sleep.

Danny was the last one to say good-bye.

And now, after three days of holding everything in, even when he was alone in his room at night, thinking alone-in-his-room thoughts, he started to cry.

And, as he did, he blurted out something he'd been holding inside along with the tears:

"Why does this crap keep happening to you?"

In a voice that was about one level above a whisper, Richie said, "You mean why do I have to be the victim of the world?"

"Yeah, basically."

"I'm not a victim," his dad said. "Even though I've been playing one for a hell of a long time."

He told Danny to tell his mom he was going to be a few extra minutes, then to come back and pull up one of those chairs, it was time for him to set the record straight, once and for all.

"YOU HAVE MORE THAN JUST THE BEST HEAD FOR BASKETBALL I'VE EVER seen—and that includes me," his dad said. "You've got a great head, period. So I'm going to talk to you like you're older."

Danny didn't know what to say to that, so he didn't say anything. Just sat there thinking again how quiet hospitals were, especially at night, the only loud sound he could hear being the soft ding of the elevator down the hall.

"I didn't just come back for you," his dad said. "I came back for me."

"I didn't care why you came back," Danny said. "You were back, that's all that mattered to me."

"But I can't have you feeling sorry for me anymore," Richie said, trying to sit up a little, squeezing his eyes shut for a minute as he did. "I've been letting people feel sorry for me, you included, for as long as you've been alive."

He made a motion toward the glass of ice water on the table next to him, and the pain pill the nurse had left for him. Danny got up and handed both to him, waited while his dad swallowed the pill, then took the glass back. "Your mom's right about something. Something she's been telling me for a long time. That's no way to live, just a slow way to die."

Danny nodded, as if he understood.

His father smiled.

174

"I don't expect you to get all of this. But it's important that you get this: The accident that wrecked everything, for all of us, it was my fault."

"The roads were bad that night," Danny said. "I've read all about it a bunch of times. You lost control of the car."

"I lost control of the car because I was drunk."

Now the only sound in the room was the ticking of the clock above the bed.

"I never liked to let the sportswriters see me drinking after the game. Didn't want to screw up my image. But I'd always liked a few after the game, even at Syracuse. I had this equipment room down the hall where I'd go before I went out after the game. Even had a little cooler back there. That was one of the nights I drank a whole six-pack before I got in my Jeep."

"Why are you telling me this now?" Danny said. "Why do I have to know this now? I know you drink, okay? I heard you and Mom that night at the gym. I heard her call you a drunk. Okay? I don't need to know any more bad stuff right now."

He was shouting.

His dad didn't shout back, came at him with a voice so soft Danny imagined the words barely making it off the bed.

"It's time you knew," Richie said.

Danny heard the ding of another elevator, wishing it were the bell telling him it was time to go to the next class.

"The cop who found me in the ditch took me to the hospital, as busted up as I was. He told them afterward that he was afraid to even call an ambulance, he thought I was dying. They asked him why he wasn't afraid to move me, and the guy—Drew Nagelson was his name—said he was afraid not to. He could smell the beer on me. He had to know I was loaded. But I remember him telling me in the car that he was a big Warriors fan." Richie Walker smiled.

175

"They always want to tell you that. Anyway, he asked me if I could chew some gum. I said, 'What?' He said, 'We've got to get the beer stink out of you.' He threw my shirt away, put a blanket on me, took me to the hospital. The doctors worked on your old dad all night. By morning, it was too late for them to take a blood alcohol test."

"Huh?"

"It's a test they have to see how much alcohol you have in your blood system."

"Oh," Danny said.

"Sergeant Nagelson came by the next day, and I thanked him for saving my life. He said, 'And your rep.' I said, 'Yeah, and my rep.'" Richie reached out and ran his hand over his new basketball. "And from that night on, everybody has felt just awful about America's lovable little point guard getting a bad break like that. Having his career end that way. And I let them, kiddo. I let them."

"Does Mom—?"

"Yesterday," he said. "When I finished telling her, I told her it was the drugs talking. But it wasn't. It was the truth, the whole truth, nothing but. There was, like, a million times when I started to tell her. But I never did. And you want to know why? Because as mad as I knew she was at me for leaving the two of you, I wanted her to feel sorry for me, too." He looked at Danny with those sad eyes as he worked his mouth into a crooked-looking smile. "The rest of the time, when she was yelling at me how drinking had ruined my life and hers more than the accident had, I just didn't have the guts."

"No," Danny said, not wanting to believe it.

"Yes."

"All these years, you just let Mom think—?"

"That I was still the toughest guy going."

"But what you did," Danny said, "that was, like, the opposite of tough."

176

"But it kept up the myth of little Richie Walker," his dad said.

Richie said he was too tired to tell him all of it tonight, all about his drinking life. Another time, he said, when they had more time. When he had the strength to get it right.

"It's funny how things work out, though," his dad said. "The thing that started everything—drinking—is the thing I kept turning to after I felt like my life had turned to crap."

Danny told him about Teddy Moran saying one time that people knew the "real truth" about him, and Richie shook his head, no, saying that people suspected he was drunk that night, just because he drank as much as he did after the accident. But the only people who knew the "real truth," at least until now, were Richie Walker himself, and Sergeant Drew Nagelson, big Warriors fan.

"Why did you come back?" Danny said. "This time, I mean?"

"I didn't have a specific plan," his dad said. "I just knew you were my best part, and that I had to do something about that before you got too big."

Now Danny smiled. "Me? Too big? Not a problem."

"The only time I got drunk after coming back was that one night at Runyon's, when I started to think that starting this team was a big dumb mistake, that you guys getting your brains beat out every game was worse than if you didn't have any games at all."

"The yelling day."

"The yelling day," Richie said. "I let myself get messed-up 'cause of drinking one last time. Haven't touched a drop since, if you want to know."

"I don't, Dad," Danny said. "I don't care."

"I know," he said. "But I do."

The door opened. The nurse's head appeared again and she said in her perky nurse voice that it was getting late, and we needed our rest, didn't we, Mr. Walker?

"One minute," Richie said to her.

To Danny he said, "I wanted us to have this season."

"We still can."

"*You* still can," Richie said. "I was full of it with the other kids before, I'm going to be on the disabled list for a while."

Might as well ask him.

"Who's gonna coach us?" Danny said.

"Don't worry," Richie said. "I got a guy in mind who'd be perfect."

KELVIN NORRIS—THE GREAT COACH KEL FROM LAST YEAR'S TRAVEL TEAM, cool-guy hero to all his players and all their parents—was waiting for them in the gym when they showed up for Thursday's practice. With the exception of Danny, who knew Coach Kel was coming, the rest of the players were expecting Mr. Harden to run his last practice with the Warriors before leaving town the next day.

Except they walked into St. Pat's at six-thirty and there was Coach Kel, in baggy sweats almost as dark as his skin and a bright yellow T-shirt that read "B. Silly." The sight of him got an immediate whoop out of Bren and Will, the guys he'd coached before. And even from Matt Fitzgerald, who remembered him as being cool just from having tried out for the sixth-grade team.

"You couldn't tell me he was coming?" Will said to Danny. "Not even a stinking hint?"

Danny shrugged. "I wanted to surprise you."

Will said, "Once trust is gone in a relationship, what is there?"

From across the court, in a boom-box voice, Coach Kel said, "Stoddard, why don't you go run some laps instead of runnin' your mouth."

Will's mouth opened and closed and, for once, nothing came out.

Coach Kel grinned. "I'm just playin'," he said. "You know."

Bren said, "I can't believe you're here."

"When Richie Walker calls from his damn hospital bed and asks for a favor, you don't say no, I'm not in the mood, Richie Walker. Or, no, I'm too busy, Richie Walker."

Coach Kel went around and introduced himself to the other Warriors.

"Say hello to your substitute teacher," he said. "You ever hear of a movie called *To Sir, With Love*? Starring the great Sidney Poitier?"

He got blank looks from everybody, as if he'd started speaking Russian to them.

"In that case," he said, "go get in two lines and shoot some damn layups."

He told them Danny was going to be his assistant coach tonight, just so they could make things feel like normal, run practice the way they usually did when Coach Walker was there.

"Just want to see your basic stuff," he said.

You always got the feeling with Coach Kel that he wanted to use another s-word instead of *stuff*, but kept it inside him like he was a bottle with the cap still on it.

Once they got going, got into their stuff, Danny realized this was exactly like the picture of the court, the other players, he'd take sometimes when they were starting their offense; when he didn't even have to look at the left side of the court when he was over on the right side because he knew where everybody was. He knew what drills they were supposed to run, in what order, what plays his dad had them working on at their last practice, the new way he had them set up when they went to a zone press.

Coach Kel leaned over at one point and said, "Even when you were just eleven, I used to tell people I was just waitin' on that little body of yours to grow into that big basketball *brain*."

"You sound just like my dad," Danny said.

"Gonna take that there as a compliment," Coach Kel said.

He had shaved his head completely bald, and as soon as he started getting on the court and showing them how he thought they should be doing something, you could see the little raindrops of sweat start to form on top of his head. He was also wearing retro Air Jordans, the red-and-black ones.

Will once said that guys would notice what sneakers you were wearing before they noticed whether or not you were carrying a paint gun.

They scrimmaged hard for the last half hour, really hard, Coach Kel saying he was going to push them, that he really wanted them to show him what they all had. And they did. Maybe it was because of what had happened to Danny's dad, but it was serious ball with the Warriors tonight, even less messing around than when Coach Walker was in the gym and blowing the whistle and calling the shots.

Somehow—and not just because Coach Kel was a high-energy guy who always kept you fired up, about basketball and life—they all seemed to know what they were supposed to be doing tonight without being told.

Go figure.

When they were done, right before parents started showing up, Will said, "See you Saturday, Coach K."

Coach Kel looked at him. "Say what?"

"I said, we'll see you Saturday," Will said. "For the Kirkland game."

Coach Kel said, "Won't be here Saturday, big hair. I guess I should have told y'all from the jump. I'm coaching the JV at Christ the King this season. I just came tonight to get you *through* tonight. Like I was sayin', as a favor to Coach Richie."

"Then who's going to coach us against Kirkland?" Bren Darcy said.

"Don't know," Coach Kel said. "Danny's dad just said that him and the other parents were gonna come up with a Plan B by then."

Will said, "Excuse me, but we thought you were Plan B."

"Only for tonight."

On their way out of the gym, Will said to Danny, "You got any bright ideas, Mr. Point Guard?"

"I thought you were the idea man," Danny said to him.

"Not this time."

Danny said, "Then we better do what we always do when we have a crisis."

He looked at Will and at the same time they both said, "Call Tess."

It had been arranged with Ali Walker before practice that Coach Kel would drive him home.

"Keep your eye on the prize, little man," Coach Kel said when he got out of the car.

"I'm trying, Coach K," Danny said. "I'm trying."

When he got inside, his mom was walking around with the portable phone. She put her hand over the mouth part and said, "I'm talking to Mrs. Stoddard, we're trying to come up with a plan for Saturday's game, and the other games before the play-offs."

He went upstairs to work on some English homework he hadn't been able to finish in study hall, just because his mind kept going back to his dad's crazy plan. When he was done with homework, he opened his door a crack and gave a listen. His mom must have finished with Molly Stoddard, because right then he heard the chirp of the phone.

He had a feeling he knew who it was, and what was coming next.

Knew there was probably going to be some yelling in the house.

The first thing he heard: "No. Absolutely not. Out of the question."

Danny didn't cover his head with a pillow this time. He pulled on his new hooded Gap sweatshirt, part of his Christmas clothes, grabbed the Infusion ball out of the closet, went quietly down the stairs, slipped out the back door, put on the driveway floodlight and the light over the basket, went out on the part of the driveway near the basket he had shoveled himself, having managed to keep that area—his area—bone dry despite all the snow they'd been having lately.

He had forgotten to shut the back door. When he went over, he heard his mom say, ". . . a head injury the doctors must have missed. Because you can't do this, Richard. I won't let you."

"*Richard*" was never good, that had been Danny's experience.

He closed the door firmly this time, shot around for a couple of minutes, then stepped away from the basket and went right to the double crossover.

He went back and forth with the ball. Then again. Then again. Three times without missing, then four, never looking down at the ball once. His fingers felt like icicles in the night, but even that didn't matter, because for this night Danny felt as if he had the ball on a string.

As if he could do anything he wanted with it.

His mom was still on the phone when he came back inside. But now she had closed the door to the small study off the dining room that served as her office.

At least she wasn't yelling anymore.

He snuck over, put his ear to the door, heard: "I understand you can't quit now. That they can't quit now. It's why we're having the parents' meeting here tomorrow night. . . . No, *you* can explain it to them, Rich."

183

They had at least moved off "Richard."

Danny went to the kitchen, microwaved himself up some hot chocolate, took the mug up to his room.

Time to get Tess into the loop.

CROSSOVER2: Hey. Tall Girl. You there?

When in doubt, *always* talk to the tall girl.

CONTESSA44: On 24-hour call. Even when doing our dopey outline on *The Pearl*.
CROSSOVER2: You mean Earl the Pearl?
CONTESSA44: Don't tell me. Another legend of the hardwood.
CROSSOVER2: Hardwood?
CONTESSA44: You forget. My dad talks like he goes through life doing the six o'clock sports report.

Danny went to his door, poked his head out. No yelling from downstairs. No talking, period. Unless she'd worked herself all the way down to whispering.

Maybe she was actually listening.

He went back to his new Sony.

CONTESSA44: What's on your mind, cutie?
CROSSOVER2: ShutUP.

It was like they were waiting each other out. Or she knew he had something on his mind.

As if she could read his mind, too.

CROSSOVER2: We have to get a new coach. Or we're toast.

CONTESSA44: I heard.

CROSSOVER2: Coach Kel did tonight.

CONTESSA44: Will told me. But just tonight, he said.

CROSSOVER2: Yeah.

CONTESSA44: So we need a plan.

Downstairs, he thought he might have heard a laugh.

CROSSOVER2: My dad actually came up with a plan.

He could hear his mom coming up the stairs.

CONTESSA44: Who does he want to coach?

It didn't take long to type out his answer.
He could keep up with her when he kept it this simple.

When he'd replay the scene in his head later, another scene he thought would have to be in the movie, he remembered getting the answer he wanted from the two women in his life pretty much at the exact same moment.

His mom was in the doorway when he turned around, hands on her hips the way she had been on Christmas Day when she had watched him and his dad finish up their video game.

Basically smiling the same smile.

"Hey, Coach," she said.

He turned back to the screen when he heard the old doodlely-doo.

ConTessa44: Cool.

When he didn't respond right away, she did.

ConTessa44: Very VERY cool.

Before he got himself calmed down enough to think about going to sleep, he took the Kidd poster off the wall, carefully laid it out on the bed, made sure to smooth out any wrinkly places, took off his LeBrons, went over to the wall, placed the pen on top of his head.

Made his mark.

Turned around.

The new line was an inch higher than the line he'd made in October the last time he'd measured himself.

Fifty-six inches.

He took out the tape measure just to make sure.

Fifty-six on the button.

He'd grown an inch!

"WHAT FINALLY CONVINCED YOU?" DANNY SAID AT THE KITCHEN TABLE.

It was way past his bedtime, but his mom wanted to talk. And Danny knew by now that when she wanted to talk, the Walker house turned into the place where time stood still.

She had made them some real hot chocolate from scratch, boiling the milk in a pan on the stove, slowly stirring in the Hershey's chocolate from the can.

After she poured it into their mugs, she even threw a couple of marshmallows on top.

His mom thought microwaved hot chocolate was for sissies.

"What convinced me?" she said, pushing her marshmallows slowly around with a spoon. "I guess you'd have to say it was when your father hit me with, 'We're one-and-nine with me coaching, how could the kid do any worse?' I have to admit, that one got a good laugh out of me."

Danny said, "Not a lot of laughs around here lately."

"No," she said, "there haven't been."

She saw that his cup was almost empty, got up without asking him if he wanted more, poured the last of the hot chocolate from the pan. Usually she guarded against any kind of chocolate intake around bedtime. Like she was the Chocolate Police.

Not tonight.

Danny took a look at her as she made sure not to spill any. A

187

good look. His friends liked to needle him sometimes by telling him his mom was hot, knowing that would get a rise out of him. But he didn't need them to tell him that, he knew she was pretty, movie pretty, that was a given. You could count on that with her, the way you could count on her always wearing nice clothes, never really looking like a slob, even when it was just the two of them hanging around the house on what his mom would sometimes call slob weekends. And when he compared her to some of the other moms, it was no contest. Some of the other moms, it was like they'd packed it in, they didn't care how they looked anymore.

Ali Walker always cared.

But tonight he saw how tired she looked, noticed the bags under her eyes, what he thought of as worry bags.

She said, "I had been telling him—yelling at him—for most of the conversation about what a ridiculous idea this was."

"I heard."

"Figured," she said. "But I didn't care, I meant it. I told him it was way too much pressure on a twelve-year-old boy, even one with supernatural basketball powers, and that on top of that, I wasn't sure the other parents would go for it."

"What did Dad say to that?"

Ali Walker, elbow on the table, rested her cheek in her hand, as if keeping her head propped up. He could see it was going to be a fight to the finish now, her need to talk against her need to go to bed. "He did what he always used to do when I was yelling at him," she said. "Waited me out."

"Yeah, but when he finally said something, it must've been pretty good." He reached over and plucked the marshmallow out of her cup and swallowed it.

"Hey," she said.

"I could tell you didn't really want it."

"What would I do without you?" she said.

Danny said, "Dad always says that it was harder turning you around on stuff than it used to be playing UConn on the road."

"I know," she said, and sighed. "Anyway," she said, "he told me that this had been your team from the start, not his. That you knew it better than he did. That for all the normal screwing around the other kids did, they all took their lead from you, even through all the losing. That no matter how much they hung their heads, they didn't quit because you didn't quit."

"He said that?"

"He did. Then he hit me with this: Kids always make the best game."

"Wait a second," Danny said, "that's my line."

"He told me it was. And you know what? I knew he was right. Then he finished up by telling me that you might learn more about basketball doing this, even for a few games, than you've ever learned in your life. And then he said one last ultimate thing that sealed the deal for old Mom."

"What?"

"He said that even he never had the guts to coach one of his own teams."

She reached across the table now with both of her hands, with those long, pretty fingers, and made a motion with them for him to get his hands out there. He did.

His mom's hands were always warm.

"Truth or dare," she said.

Danny said, "Truth."

"You can do this?"

Danny made sure to look her in the eyes. "I can do this."

"You're sure?"

"If it's okay with the guys—"

"—and Miss Colby—"

"—and Colby. If it's okay with them and the parents say they're good with it, yeah, so am I."

"We're going to have a team meeting here, tomorrow night, seven-thirty," Ali Walker said. "We'll run the whole thing up the flagpole, bud, and see who salutes."

"You have some very weird expressions, Mom, have I ever mentioned that to you?"

She came around the table, pulled him up out of his chair, put her arms around him, leaned over as she did and put her face on top of his head.

"I grew an inch," he said.

"I thought there was something different about you," she said. "I just assumed it was the stature that comes with your new job."

"Funny."

"Go to bed," she said. "And no more IM."

Danny said, "Haven't you heard about how little sleep dedicated coaches get?"

"Not when they're in the seventh grade," she said.

Tess was waiting on the sidewalk in front of the school when Danny and his mom came around from the teachers' parking lot. As soon as Ali Walker was gone, Tess said, "We're good to go."

"Where?"

"Everybody on the team is completely fired up about you coaching," she said. "With the possible exception of the wimp-face O'Brien twins."

"What's their problem?"

"Not a problem, exactly. They just said what they say about practically everything."

"What?"

"You're close," Tess said. "Actually, it was what*ever.*"

"You already conducted a poll this morning?"

"Last night, right after you IM'd me."

Danny said, "Well aren't you a busy little bee?"

"*Queen* bee," she said, giving her hair a little shake.

The Warriors all sat together at lunch, at the big table by the window facing the soccer fields. Before they got around to talking about their team, Will and Bren informed the group that Colorado boy—Andy Mayne—had suffered a severe high ankle sprain, worst kind, the day before, playing touch football in the parking lot after school.

"Black ice," Will said. "Never saw it."

"Heard he was lucky he didn't break his ankle instead of just twisting it like a pretzel," Bren said.

"They've got him in some kind of soft-cast deal for now, so he doesn't make it any worse," Will said.

"Might be back for the play-offs, might not," Bren said.

"That means they'll only beat us by twenty points in the play-offs," Will said.

"'Stead of forty," Bren said.

"I don't want to talk about them," Tess said. "I want to talk about us."

Danny knew he probably had the goofy look on his face that he felt come over it when Tess Hewitt said or did something that really got to him, but he didn't care.

"*Us?*" he said.

"Yes," she said. "*Us.*" She looked at him and said, "What, you thought I was going to sit the big adventure out?"

Then she wanted to know if everybody had followed her on-line instructions, and kept their big fat stupid mouths shut around their parents about Danny coaching the team.

"Explain to me again why it has to be a surprise for all the mummies and mummified daddies," Will said.

"It's just better if Mrs. Walker tells, is all. So nothing gets lost in translation." She hit Will with her raised eyebrow and said, "Mrs. Walker," she said, "is, like, *good* with words."

"Go ahead," Will said, trying to act wounded. "Lash out at the ones you care the most about even on this happy day."

Bren said, "I'm asking the new coach for shorter practices."

"And no suicides, ever," Colby Danes said from across the table.

The Warriors applauded.

The O'Brien twins were dressed exactly the same today, so nobody had any idea which was which.

"Are we going to have to play more minutes?" one of them said.

The other one said, "This season feels too long already."

"Hey, Mary-Kate and Ashley," Will said to them. "Zip it."

Colby said she had a question.

"What if the league says you can't coach, that we need a grown-up?"

Danny said, "My mom thought about that already, she says she's got a backup plan."

"Oh, good," Will said. "Now we go from Plan B to Plan C."

Tess smiled now.

"No, Plan D," she said. "For Danny."

She held his hand under the table.

And he let her.

THE WALKERS' DOORBELL RANG AT SIX-THIRTY, EVEN THOUGH THE PARENTS' meeting wasn't scheduled to begin for another hour.

Ali Walker yelled down for Danny to get it, she was still getting dressed, and if it was somebody selling something, tell them it was too late to be coming around.

When he opened the front door, Mr. Ross was standing there.

"Hello, Danny," he said.

"Mr. Ross."

"Is your mom home? I saw the car."

Danny jerked a thumb over his shoulder. "She's upstairs."

"Would you mind if I come in? I've got something I want to say to both of you."

Danny called up to his mom and told her Mr. Ross was here. Then, trying to think what she'd want him to do, he asked if he could take Mr. Ross's black overcoat, which felt as soft as a baby blanket as Danny started to hang it on the coat rack.

"Would you mind using that little hook up by the collar?" Mr. Ross said.

They went into the living room to wait for his mom. Mr. Ross sat down on the couch.

"I hear your dad is feeling much better," he said.

Danny felt like saying, compared to *what*?

"I've been meaning to stop by the hospital and see him," Mr. Ross said.

Danny said, "I'm sure he'd appreciate that," only because he couldn't say what he really wanted to say, which was that his dad would appreciate that about as much as having his bones broken all over again.

Ali Walker came breezing into the room then, saying, "Well, isn't this a surprise."

Mr. Ross got up and looked like he was leaning over to kiss her on the cheek when his mom stopped him by putting her hand out for him to shake, stopping him the way a crossing guard would have.

"I was going to call first," Mr. Ross said. "But I had an errand to run and I was passing the house, and I just decided to drop by."

Even Danny knew that was bull.

"So," Ali said, "to what do we owe the honor?"

Danny was in one of the chairs on the other side of the coffee table from the couch, one of the two that they'd just had done over with new flowered covers that looked exactly like the old flowered covers to Danny. Ali Walker sat down in the other.

They both waited patiently for him to get to it.

"Well," he said, "I came with an apology, and what I think is a pretty neat idea."

Danny looked over at his mom, in her dark blue dress, hands folded in her lap. She smiled at Mr. Ross. Still waiting. Danny folded his hands in his lap and did the same.

Mr. Ross said, "First, I want to apologize to you, Danny. I don't know what my evaluators were thinking, but you should have been on the Vikings this season."

His mom still didn't say anything, and neither did he.

"Sometimes," he said, "adults don't know when to get out of

194

the way when it comes to youth sports. And sometimes they don't know when to get *in* the way."

Danny was staring, fascinated, at Mr. Ross's white shirt, whose collar looked as stiff as a board.

"What I'm saying," Mr. Ross said, "is that I should have done something. And we all should have seen the greatness in you."

Now Ali Walker spoke. "Tough to miss," she said.

"I realize that now, Ali. I was so hell-bent on maintaining the integrity of the process—"

"—right, the *process*," she said, nodding, as if trying to be helpful.

"—that I let a talented boy like the one sitting across from me not make a team he should have made."

He cleared his throat.

"Anyway," Mr. Ross said, "Richie said something to me that was absolutely correct, but I didn't want to hear. He said the best kids are supposed to make the team. And we all should have realized that Danny's always been one of the best kids in this town, despite—"

"—his size?" Ali Walker said.

Who was more helpful than her?

"—his size. Yes. But it seems this time his size worked against him for whatever reason—"

Holy *schnikeys*, Danny thought. A made-up Will word. *Whatever reason*? The reason, Mr. Rossface, was that you told them to make the team bigger.

"—and that's wrong."

There was another silence. Danny had been watching *SportsCenter* on the kitchen set when Mr. Ross arrived, and he could still hear somebody in there screaming about something.

Danny had sat in on his mom's class a few times, she said she wanted him to see her work, to have a better understanding about what she did, why she loved it so much, why she had gone back to college to give herself a chance to do it for a living. And every time he saw her teach, he saw how she'd go out of her way to help out any kid struggling to find the right word or the right answer. Sort of like she was throwing the kid a life preserver.

Now she seemed perfectly willing to let Mr. Ross go under before she'd make this any easier for him.

"Which brings me to the second reason for my visit," he said, "now that I understand there may be a problem with Danny's team."

"The Warriors," he said.

"Quite right, the Warriors. By problem, I mean insofar as your dad is going to be laid up for a while, and Ty says there may be a problem finding another parent willing to make the time commitment necessary to fill in for the rest of the season."

Danny looked over at his mom. He wasn't sure if Mr. Ross saw her give one shake to her head—basically telling him to shut up—or not.

Danny got her meaning, though.

"So I thought Danny could come play for the Vikings," Mr. Ross said. "Where he would have had the ball all along, if we hadn't dropped the ball."

He looked at his watch, as if he needed something to do with his hands after his big announcement.

"Even with the loss of Ty and young Mr. Mayne—"

"Andy Mayne was their point guard, Mom." Danny knew he was interrupting, which he was never supposed to do with grown-ups. But he wanted her to know. "He wrecked up his ankle yesterday. Might be out for the season."

"That must have hurt," Ali Walker said. "Both him and the Vikings, I mean."

"Knowing we'd be getting Ty back for the play-offs," Mr. Ross said, "I thought we had enough talent to make it out of the state and go all the way back to the nationals. And even without Andy, I think we still can, especially if I can convince Danny here to come aboard."

His mom leaned forward. "What about the rest of Danny's team?" she said, in a pleasant-sounding voice.

"Well," he said, "if they can find another coach, of course, they can go ahead and finish the season." He shrugged and made this gesture with his palms turned up. Like: Who cares? "And if they don't, well, they'd only be missing a handful of meaningless games. I'm sure that even Danny would admit that they haven't exactly been tearing up the league."

Ali Walker answered that one by turning to face Danny.

"My husband always said that it's not the team you start with that matters, it's the one you end up with," she said. "Isn't that right, sweetheart?"

He'd almost missed the question, all he heard after "my husband"—which she never ever said anymore—was blah blah blah.

"Dad says he wants to see who's out there and what they're doing the last two minutes of the game, not the first two."

"I didn't mean any disrespect by what I said about the other Warriors," Mr. Ross said. "Really, no offense, to either one of you."

"None taken," Ali Walker said.

"Danny's different from the others," Mr. Ross said.

"He was in October, too," she said, and stood up. "I've got some people coming over. I'll leave you and Danny alone, this is his decision, then I'll come back and see you out, Jeff."

She left them there.

"I finally figured out what you and Ty have known all along," Mr. Ross said. Giving him a weird grin that made him look like a jack-o'-lantern, as if the two of them were buds all of a sudden. "You two knotheads should be playing together."

Danny couldn't help it then.

He laughed.

"Did I say something funny, Danny?"

"Not really," he said. "It just kind of occurred to me that you're the biggest guy in our town, Mr. Ross. Seriously."

"Oh, I don't know about that."

"And here you are talking to me like *I'm* the biggest guy in town all of a sudden."

"I'm offering you a chance to play for a winning team."

"I'll take my chances with my team," Danny said. "Even *against* your team."

He stood up, came around the table, stuck his hand out, made eye contact the way his mom had taught him.

"But, sir?"

"Yes, Danny?"

"Thank you *so* much for stopping by."

Most of the kids on the team sat on the living-room floor. The parents sat on the couch, the two extra flowered chairs Ali Walker had brought in from the front hall, the four wooden chairs she brought in from the kitchen; the rest just stood around drinking coffee or wine or soft drinks. The Warriors were all drinking Gatorades out of plastic bottles. Tess Hewitt was with them, having come with Molly Stoddard and Will.

Danny's mom said she appreciated everybody taking time out to do this on a school night, and would do everything in her power to keep the proceedings brief.

Will Stoddard raised a hand. "Take as much time as you need, Mrs. Walker. I haven't done Spanish yet."

His mother smiled down at him like he was the most precious, wonderful boy in the whole world, then pinched his upper arm hard enough to make him yelp.

Danny leaned over and whispered to Tess, "You do not *ever* want to get the arm pinch from Mrs. Stoddard."

When Ali was convinced everybody had arrived, she laid out Richie's plan for them. She said that she knew that there were enough parents on the team with enough free time that they could probably find a way to share the responsibilities of coaching the Warriors. But that Richie frankly didn't think that was good enough, that the kids were starting to come together, turning into the team he'd hoped they could be all along, and that the coach had to be someone who not only knew them, strengths and weaknesses, but also knew basketball.

And that in his opinion the one who fit the bill best was Danny.

Will said, "Please hold your applause until the end."

Molly only faked the pinch, but Will spazzed away from her anyway.

Mrs. O'Brien, the twins' mom, who'd always reminded Danny of a hummingbird with short black hair, said, "A *child*? Coaching the other children? I just don't know how that would *look*, frankly."

One of the twins, Danny thought it was Steven, he did the most whining of the two, said, "But Mom, you said you didn't care if one of the lunch ladies coached the team as long as you got us out of the house on weekends."

Danny bit down on the knuckles of his right hand, but then all of the adults in the room were laughing, so he did, too.

Mrs. O'Brien gave Steven a death look and said, "Mommy was *joking,* honey. But we'll *discuss* all that in the *car* later."

It turned out that Mr. Harden was there, having flown back for the night from his case in Florida. He said, "I've been around this team more than anybody, with the exception of the players, of course. And from the start, Richie called Danny his coach on the floor. So I don't see his job description really changing all that much."

Molly Stoddard said, "I called over to the league office today. I didn't tell them why I was calling, just said that we might have some problems with logistics before the season was over, and was there an actual league rule about having an adult on the bench. And they said that there had to be at least one."

Ali Walker said, "That would be me."

Jerry Harden said, "*You're* going to be the bench coach?"

"Just filling in until you get back from West Palm," she said. "And if you don't make it back, I'll do it the rest of the way." She smiled. "I've learned from the best, after all," she said. "The former coach and his potential replacement."

Way to go, Mom.

She said, "I don't really care whether the other team thinks I'm coaching our team or not. If they think I've taken over, fine. But Danny will handle all the basketball stuff."

"There's no heavy lifting, I can testify to that," Jerry Harden said. "All you have to do, other than being a good cheerleader, is keep track of time-outs and fouls."

"I'm not even going to do that," Ali said.

"Who is?" Danny said.

Ali said, "Tess."

In a voice that seemed a little louder than she intended, Colby Danes said, "*Yes.* More girls."

Another laugh from the room. Mostly from the moms.

When it subsided, Molly Stoddard said to Danny in a serious voice, "You know we consider you a member of our family. But are you absolutely certain you want to do this?"

"My dad wants me to," he said.

He looked over at his mom. She winked.

"I appreciate that you want to do this for your dad," Molly said. "What I want to know—what I think we all want to know—is if you want to do this for yourself?"

Danny stood up, as if he had the floor now. As soon as he did, he could feel his hands shaking, the way they did when he'd have to get up and say something, or read something, in front of the class.

So he stuffed them into his pockets.

"I told my mom before everybody got here that if the guys on the team . . . and the girls," he said, giving a quick nod to Colby, "want me to do it, then I'm doing it."

Danny said, "I mean, they all said they were cool with it at school. But if anybody's changed their mind since we all talked about it at lunch, well, I'm cool with *that,* too. No harm, no foul."

He looked over at Will, who was sitting on the floor next to Tess now. Then at Bren. And Matt Fitzgerald.

For once, they were all looking *up* at him.

"My dad said that this started out as my team," Danny said, "and maybe it did. But now, like, it's all our team."

"Why don't we do it this way?" Ali Walker asked. "Why don't we ask the Warriors, and their new assistant coach, Tess, to vote."

Tess stood right up.

First in everything.

"I vote for Danny," she said.

Will got up. "Danny."

Bren walked over from Danny's right. "Dan the man," he said.

Then the rest of them got up, all of them looking a little self-conscious, knowing all the adults were watching them.

"Danny," they said, one by one.

Then Will Stoddard, clearly thinking everything was getting way too dramatic, turned the whole thing into a chant.

"DAN-ny! DAN-ny! DAN-ny!"

Even the parents joined in.

Danny put his hand about halfway into the air, the way you do when you think you may have the answer a teacher was looking for, but aren't really sure.

"Hey, guys," he said, "listen up. Okay?"

They had warmed up in two layup lines, the way they always did. Now it was time to actually start practice. His mom and Molly Stoddard were sitting up on the stage, not even paying attention to them, both of them with their yellow legal pads, making plans for the Valentine's Ball the parents had at St. Pat's every February.

So Danny was in charge.

Except he really wasn't, since no one was listening to him.

The O'Brien twins were doing what they always did when they thought there was a break in the action, which was sitting on the floor. Colby had walked away from the group and was shooting free throws at one of the side baskets. Will was trying to make outside shots over Matt Fitzgerald from the deep corner.

It reminded Danny of recess.

"Guys," he said, a little louder this time.

Nothing.

Tess was sitting in a folding chair at mid-court, watching him. She'd come with the Stoddards, explaining to Danny when she showed up, "If I'm going to be team manager, I want to see how things work."

"I thought your title was assistant coach?" Danny had said.

"I'm more of a management type."

Now Danny put his hands out to her, the way you did when you were pleading with somebody for help. Tess gave him a slow nod, as if she got the picture. But then, she always seemed to get the picture. Danny watched as she slowly got up out of her chair, cleared her throat as if she were about to sing some kind of solo at the spring chorale, then put two fingers into her mouth and issued one of the most ear-shattering whistles Danny had ever heard in his life, one that would have done a big-whistle NBA coach like Pat Riley proud.

The whistle got their attention.

"Thank you," Danny mouthed at her.

"My pleasure," Tess mouthed back, gave him a quick little curtsy, sat down, as if nothing had happened.

Danny motioned for the Warriors to get around him at mid-court.

"I know this must be a little weird for you guys, because it's a *lot* weird for me," he said. "But we need to get to work. We've only got the gym for an hour tonight, we're playing Kirkland tomorrow afternoon, and we gotta get after it."

"Coach?" Will said. "Would you mind slowing down, you're going a little too fast for me."

Colby said, "Shut*uppppppp*," in a singsongy voice.

Danny said, "We tried to go man-to-man against them last time, but nobody could handle their big guy."

"Bud Sheedy," Bren said.

"We couldn't handle him, we couldn't handle their press," Danny said. "So I figure we might as well go with a zone tomorrow. You guys okay with that?"

They nodded.

"But maybe not our normal zone," he said. "I thought we might try a one-three-one. Let me show you."

He went over to where he'd left his backpack, next to Tess's chair, reached into the side pocket, brought out the coach's board his mom had bought him, and the erasable laundry marker that came with it.

"Oooh," Will said, "he brought *toys*."

From her chair, Tess said, "Will Stoddard, if you don't zip it, I'm going to tell the whole team who you like."

Danny knew it was Colby. And he knew Tess knew. He couldn't believe she'd rat him out now in front of the team—in front of Colby herself—but sometimes he couldn't tell when Tess Hewitt was bluffing.

"What, now that he's the coach, this has turned into, like, a mirth-free zone?" Will said.

"Tonight it is," Tess said. "Are we clear?"

"As Clearasil," Will said, rather gloomily.

Danny drew up the zone he wanted them to play, then did some quick *X*-and-*O* work with their inbounds offense against the Kirkland press.

"See, Oliver, you're going to take it out instead of Matt," Danny said, trying to draw as fast as he was talking. "Matt, you're going to *get* the first pass instead of throw it. You flash to the near free throw line, with your arms up in the air, like you're a tight end getting ready to catch a pass."

He gave a quick look up. They were all really watching.

And all really listening.

Hot *dog*.

"Oliver, you make sure you give him the ball where he can handle it. Matt, as soon as you get it, you turn. Now you're a quarterback. Bren will be flying down the left side, like he's going for a bomb. I'll be at half-court, over on the right. But I'm just a decoy."

Colby Danes said, "I don't like this."

Danny ignored her. "If Bren's ahead of everybody, throw it to him. But *only* if he's wide open. If he's not, give it to Colby, who'll be a few feet away, on your left or your right, depending on where she is after the first pass. They won't be expecting her to bring it up. But she's going to."

"You and Bren are the ball-bringer-uppers," Colby said. "Don't make me bring it up." She brightened. "I'll pay you."

Danny said, "You can do this. You can handle the ball better than you think. Remember that dorky guy they had covering you in the first game? The one with the thingies in his hair?"

"Highlights," Colby said.

"Him," Danny said. "He couldn't cover you in the half-court, he's too slow. He's not gonna have a chance covering you full-court. When he sees you coming at him with the ball, and a head of steam, he'll start backing up like he just saw something in that *Blair Witch* movie we watched the other day in audio-visual."

"How do you know that?" Colby said, still sounding pretty skeptical.

"Can I say one thing?" Will said, looking over at Tess. "Without being threatened?"

"Okay, but just one," team manager Tess said.

Tess understood the situation, because everybody who knew and loved Will did:

He totally zipped it about as often as he saw Mars.

"He knows things," Will said. "I'm talking about basketball things. Don't ask him to fix a flat on his bike. Or burn a song."

"Don't even think about asking him to diagram a sentence," Tess called out.

206

"But if he tells you something is going to happen in basketball, it's probably going to happen," Will said. "Annoying, but true."

"This'll work great," Danny said to Colby. "Trust me."

"You want me to bring the ball up the *whole* game?" Colby said.

Just against the press, Danny assured her, and then said, c'mon, they could all walk through it.

They did. The only person playing defense was Michael Harden, guarding Colby after she got the ball from Matt. Danny had told him to back off a few feet, the way he was sure the highlighted dork from Kirkland would, not try to steal it from her. But after they'd half run, half walked through it a few times, Danny motioned for Michael to get up on her.

And when he did, the Warriors' girl, looking as if she was about to have the ball stolen from her, put the ball behind her back—a move none of them had ever seen from her—and just absolutely dusted Michael Harden.

Colby Danes did that to war whoops from the rest of them, with the exception of Michael, who was on the ground trying to get them to believe he'd twisted an ankle.

Danny went over to Colby, jumped up, gave her a high five.

"See," he said, "sometimes you can do stuff you didn't know you could do."

It was a short practice, but a good one, everybody rallying around Danny the way they had that night with Coach Kel.

At least until Danny yelled.

At Will.

They had all just decided—group decision—that next basket won in the scrimmage. They were going four-on-four by then: Danny, Bren, Oliver, and Colby against Steven O'Brien, Michael, Matt, Will.

Danny passed it to Colby, who missed. Michael got the rebound, fed Will, who was flying up the court. Matt had taken off down the court early, as soon as he saw nobody was going to contest Michael for the rebound. So it was Will and Matt in a two-on-one against Oliver Towne, the Round Mound of Towne, who was sucking wind big-time, the way he usually did by the end of practice.

Will on Oliver's left, Matt on his right.

Oliver was so tired, Will could not only have walked past him, but rubbed the top of his head for luck on the way by. Instead, maybe to show off for Colby, show that he could go behind his back, too, he threw this behind-the-back pass that Matt wasn't expecting, one that hit him on the side of the head, before bouncing harmlessly out of bounds.

"Hey, Will, cut the crap, okay?" Danny yelled, and just the way he did let everybody know he meant it.

His voice as loud in the gym as the air-raid siren they still used when they practiced evacuating school in case of an emergency.

Will looked at Danny as if he were the one who'd just gotten hit in the head by the ball, hurt and surprised at the same time.

Danny didn't know why he was as hot as he was. But he was. "What's the deal, it was too big a job for you to throw one simple pass so we could get our butts out of here?" he said. "Is that, like, some kind of *problem*?"

He looked around and saw the whole gym now the way he could see the court when he was coming up with the ball. Tess in her chair. His mom and Will's mom watching from the stage. The other players on the Warriors frozen in place as if somebody had hit the Pause button.

Will said, "You sound like a dad."

And, just like that, Danny knew his best friend was right.

He did sound like a dad. Like *his* dad had sounded that night when he was in a bad mood and his mom yelled at him about his drinking afterward.

At least Dad'd had an excuse, Danny thought now.

What's mine?

Sometimes he was a little slow out of the chutes figuring stuff out. Not now. Now he was the one who got the picture, just like that. He'd sounded like a schmuck and gotten busted for it. He looked bad in front of his friends, and knew he had to get out of it right now, even if it meant backing off and looking like some kind of wimp.

"I'm going to tell you something you already know," Danny said to Will. "Sometimes, I've got a pretty big mouth for a little guy."

He saw his mom watching from the stage, standing next to Will's mom. Ali Walker had always told him that there was no great skill to being right about something, anybody could carry that off. The trick, she said, was knowing how to be wrong.

Danny walked over to Will and put his hand out. No high five, no low five, no clenched fist, no secret handshake. He was just looking for a normal handshake. Strictly regulation.

"Sorry, dude," he said.

Will grinned. "You're the first coach ever to apologize for being too stinking loud."

"Nah, I was just another coach who forgot whose team it really is," Danny said.

Then he said, "We've been telling you to shut up all night. Anything you want to say to the team before we call it a night."

"Yes," Will said. "Kirkland sucks."

Words to live by.

He and his mom stopped off at the hospital before they went over to St. Pat's for the Kirkland game. When they got there, his mom said he ought to have a few minutes alone with his dad, she'd be upstairs in the cafeteria having a cup of coffee and actually being able to read the morning papers for a change.

"The nurse said he had kind of a rough night," Ali Walker said. "He had a pretty high fever, which sometimes happens after extensive surgery like he had, but they finally got it under control a few hours ago."

Danny said, "He's going to be all right, though. Right? I mean, like, *really* all right?"

"He is," she said. "Just not as fast as he wants. Or you want."

"I don't get this," Danny said. "Everybody said all the operation stuff they needed to do went the way it was supposed to."

They were standing near the nurses' station. She walked him a few feet away, put her hands on his shoulders, scrunched down a little so they were eye to eye. "Now pay attention," she said.

"What did I do?" Danny said.

"Nothing," his mom said. "You just have to understand something for today, and for however long it takes your dad to get better. Yes, the surgery went fine. Yes, he's *starting* to get better and *is* going to get better. Eventually, okay? But when he had the first accident, he was in the best shape of his life. Now it's ten years later, honey. And it's the second time the sky fell on him. And this time, he doesn't have any, well, *wellness* to fall back on the way he did when he was younger. So when I tell you it's going to take time, it's going to take time."

"But he's going to be able to walk okay."

"Yes."

"You promise?"

"Cross my heart."

"Do it," Danny said.

She stepped back, wrote a big *T* on the front of her sweater.

"Now you go let your father get you all ready for the big game," she said.

Richie Walker's eyes were closed, and for a minute Danny thought he might be sleeping, even though the nurse had said he was awake, he'd just had an early lunch. But when the door closed, Richie opened his eyes, saw who it was, and smiled, though pretty weakly.

Somehow, Danny thought, the cast on his dad's leg, going all the way to his hip, seemed even bigger than it had the last time he had visited him. And there seemed to be even more tubes than before. Even the bed seemed to have grown in the last couple of days.

All of it seeming to swallow up his dad.

Richie said, "Hey, Coach."

"Hey, Coach," Danny said.

"C'mon over closer, let me see you. Sometimes these pain pills give me such a jolt I feel like I've got the sun in my eyes all of a sudden."

Danny was wearing an old orange Syracuse sweatshirt his dad had given him a couple of years ago; Danny didn't like to wear it that often, mostly because he still hadn't grown into it.

But he figured he'd go with something from Syracuse today, the last place his dad still felt like the king of the world in basketball.

"Where's your mom?"

"She said she was going to have coffee. She's probably got one of the doctors against a wall, trying to get stuff out of him."

Richie said, "If I don't get out of here soon, they're going to make her chief of staff."

"She's pretty good at bossing people in that quiet way she has."

"Tell me about it," Richie said.

"We're on our way to the game," Danny said.

"You ready?"

Danny laughed, he couldn't help himself. "Heck no."

"You'll be fine."

"Easy for you to say," Danny said.

Richie moved his head from side to side on the pillow. "Nothing's easy for me to say these days. Not even, good morning."

Danny said, "I'm just worried that if I worry too much about coaching, I won't be worrying enough about playing. Which makes me worry that I won't be able to handle either job too well."

"That's way too much worrying over one travel basketball game," his dad said. "Just play. The rest of it will take care of itself."

"But what if I have the wrong guys out there? Or forget to get everybody enough time? You want another one? What if—"

"Daniel Walker?"

"What?" Danny had nearly what-if'd himself out of breath.

"Shut your piehole."

"I'm just saying—"

"Shut your piehole *now*."

He did.

Thinking: At least now you sound like my dad.

"Let me ask you something, bud: Who would you rather be today—you or me?"

Danny looked down and studied the toe of his left LeBron. "Me," he said, without looking up.

"Maybe I told you this before, maybe not, I can't remember anything anymore. But listen up now: There isn't an adult who'll be in the gym today who wouldn't change places with you in a freaking heartbeat. You, or Big Matt, or Miss Colby. Or Will. You got that?"

He studied his right toe now. "Got it."

"Do you really get it?"

"Yes," Danny said.

"Good. Because if you put all this dumb pressure on yourself, then it means your mom was right the first night, her precious little boy can't handle this, boo freaking hoo."

Really sounding like his old dad now, the one who could cut you in half with a single word.

"The other players? They *want* to follow you today. They'll be watching *you*. If you look like the whole thing makes you want to wet your pants, they're gonna want to do the same."

For some reason, Danny turned around, as if he could feel someone watching them. And there, in the window that faced out to the hall, the drapes just open enough for him to see her, was his mom. Not wanting to interrupt by walking in on them. But pointing at her watch, like they had to get going soon.

"It's your ball today," Richie said. "Your game. So don't worry about the rest of that . . . stuff."

Danny said, "You can say the s-word in front of me, Dad. Or any of the other biggies. It's not like I haven't heard them before. Or used them myself."

Then Richie smiled and used a whole bunch of biggies in one sentence, telling him what he should do with all his worries and what he wanted the Warriors to do to Kirkland.

Then he motioned for Danny to come close, like he wanted to whisper something, and kissed him on the cheek.

"Don't do it for anybody except yourself," he said. "Make yourself proud today."

Danny said, "I love you, Dad."

With his good hand, Richie gave him a little shove. "Beat it now," he said.

As Danny opened the door, he heard him say, "I love you, too, bud."

Danny turned back around then, smiling, trying to remember the last time he'd heard his dad say that.

"Remember the team rules," Richie said. "Play hard. Have fun. Shoot if you're open."

"If you're not," Danny said, "pass it to somebody who *is* open."

"And I want to add one more, just for today."

Danny waited.

"Beat Kirkland's ass," his dad said.

THE WARRIORS WERE THE ONES GETTING THEIR BUTTS HANDED TO THEM.

Total nightmare from the start.

Richie Walker had told Danny one time about what he said was the old coaches' nightmare. He said he'd heard it from a little guy who used to coach St. John's, one Richie called Coach Looie, at a dinner one time right before the Big East tournament.

"It's like a school nightmare you'll get someday, even when you're not in school anymore," Richie said. "It's one where you have to take a test, only you're scared out of your pants because you haven't been to class all semester. This is the basketball version. The coach wakes up with the heebie-jeebies in the middle of the night because his team is playing this game and, no matter what he tries, they can't make a single basket."

Danny was the twelve-year-old coach having the old coaches' nightmare now against Kirkland.

Only problem was, it was real.

The Warriors couldn't score a single basket.

The whole first quarter.

Kirkland 10, Warriors 0.

"I'm going to be the first coach to ever get shut out for a whole game," Danny said to Will with five seconds left in the quarter, while Kirkland's best player, Bud Sheedy, was making the first of two free throws.

Sheedy was a tall sandy-haired kid, taller than everybody else on his team, who was a lot like Ty, which meant he wasn't really a guard, or forward, or center.

He was another cool basketball kid whose real position was just basketball player.

"Well," Will said, "I *have* been telling people all week that you were going to make history."

Danny was playing tight; they *all* were. Will had missed at least three wide-open shots he would normally knock down. Colby fumbled the ball so much trying to bring it up against the press she reminded Danny of someone trying to play basketball wearing the kind of floppy oven mitts his mom would wear in the kitchen sometimes.

Every time there was a chance for the Warriors to get a rebound, Bud Sheedy was making Matt Fitzgerald look like he was the one who was fifty-six inches tall. Same with Michael Harden. Same with Oliver Towne.

Danny called his first time-out when it was 6–0, after they'd played just over four minutes.

"Everybody relax," he said in the huddle. "And when I say everybody, I'm talking to myself, too. Okay?"

"Roger that," Will said. "The way things are going, we figured it was only a matter of time before you started talking to yourself."

Danny heard some stifled laughs, as if they didn't know whether that was allowed or not.

"See, Will's starting to relax already," Danny said. "And listen, no lie, there's a long way to go."

Colby Danes said, "That's what I'm afraid of."

"We are gonna come back in this stupid game," Danny said. "For now, let's try to change the zone a little, make it more of the two-on-two my dad usually has us play. Maybe that will slow down these scumweasels."

On their way back out on the court, Will said, "Scum*weasels*?"

Danny said, "I didn't want to say scumwads in front of Colby."

The only thing keeping the Warriors in the game was that except for Bud Sheedy, no one was doing much scoring for Kirkland, either. But even after the time-out, the Warriors still couldn't make anything. When Matt picked up his third foul a couple of minutes into the second quarter, just to make matters worse than they were already, Kirkland had stretched out its lead to 14–0.

Danny called another time-out after Matt got his third, just to get him the heck out of there, afraid that if he left him in for even another minute, he might foul out by halftime.

They all gathered around him in the huddle—players, his mom with her clipboard, Tess with her scorebook—and waited for him to say something brilliant, or maybe inspirational.

Nothing came out of his mouth.

For one quick second, he felt so helpless—the way you do when some bigger kid gets you down on the playground and you can't move or even breathe—he thought he might cry.

He didn't, just because there was a part of him that knew it would go on his Permanent Record forever, worse than any black mark any teacher could put in there: How Danny Walker tried to coach the team and started crying.

The best he could do, finally, was: "Okay, listen up."

All he had.

He looked around at some of the faces, staring at him, waiting for the boy coach to start coaching. Only he still didn't have the words. Like he was the one with the whole game sitting on his chest.

Then, from behind him, he heard: "You guys are doing this all wrong."

Danny was on his knees in the middle of the huddle. He craned his neck around and saw Ty Ross standing there behind Oliver Towne and Michael Harden.

Ty said, "I played against Buddy Sheedy all summer in this camp league we have out at the beach."

They all turned to look at Ty now. Danny didn't even wonder about what he was doing here; he was just thrilled that someone seemed to know what he was talking about.

Ty said to Danny, "You've got to box-and-one him. That's what teams always do against me." He grinned. "It even works against me sometimes."

Danny had two thoughts, one right on top of another. One was that Ty was right about the box-and-one. The second was: How come *I* didn't think of that?

Box-and-one. One guy playing man-to-man against Bud Sheedy. Everybody else in a packed-in zone.

Ty said, "Put Will on him. Buddy's got the height. But Will can dog him all over the place." He gave Will a playful shove. "Maybe even talk to him a little bit."

Will said, "I think I can handle that."

The ref, Tony, their regular guy, poked his head past Ty and said to Ali Walker, "Fifteen seconds, ma'am."

Danny said, "Okay. Matt, I changed my mind, I'm keeping you in. Oliver, you play down low in the zone with Matt. Will, you've got Buddy, follow him to the bathroom if you have to. Colby, you sit for a minute. Bren, you're bringing it up with me."

They all put their hands in the middle and yelled "DEE-fense!"

As they broke the huddle Danny said to Ty, "You busy?"

Ty shook his head.

Colby was sitting on the folding chair next to Tess and Ali Walker. Danny motioned for her to move over one.

"Have a seat," Danny said. "I'm deputizing you."

Will didn't care where the ball was when Bud Sheedy didn't have it. He just went wherever Sheedy went, like he had blinders on. And whenever the two of them were anywhere near Danny, he could hear Will talking to Bud, as if they were sitting together on the bus.

After one play when the refs couldn't decide who'd knocked the ball out of bounds, Danny went over and stood next to the Warriors' bench area.

"Will's gotta be careful he doesn't go too far," Ty said, "trash-talking really isn't allowed in the Tri-Valley League."

"He's not really talking smack," Danny said. "He's just talking."

Ty said, "About what? I'm too far away to hear."

"When they went by me a minute ago, I heard him saying something about the Knicks' playoff chances," Danny said.

It was 14–8 by then. Will had finally shut up long enough to make two open shots. Danny had put Colby back in for Oliver. Colby scored. Danny had assisted on all three baskets. Then he broke away for a layup when his guy thought he was going to pass to Colby again.

When Kirkland called time-out, Danny said to Ty, "The defense is working."

"So far."

Ali Walker said, "Is it really called the boxcar-and-one?"

At the same time, Danny and Ty said, "*Box*-and-one."

"Well," Ali Walker said, "I think boxcar is more vivid."

"Mom," Danny said, "we're trying to work here."

Ty said, "If Will starts to get tired, go to the triangle-and-two, and you help out."

Bud Sheedy started to get frustrated now, even complaining to the ref one time about Will's relentless chatter. He finally threw up a long hook shot, more in frustration than anything else. He seemed as surprised as anybody in the gym when it went in. Now it was 16–8, Kirkland. But Danny took the inbounds pass and beat everybody down the court and fed Colby for the layup that made it 16–10. Then Matt Fitzgerald shocked everybody by making two straight free throws for the first time all year. 16–12.

Right before the horn sounded to end the half, the Warriors had a three-on-two break: Danny with the ball in the middle, Will on his left, Colby on his right. He passed to Will, who seemed to have a step on his guy. But the guy got in front of him. Will passed it back to Danny.

It was as if the ball barely touched Danny's hands.

He half passed it, half slapped it to Colby, who made another layup.

Kirkland 16, Warriors 14.

Whole half to go.

Game on.

Danny took them all out into the hallway at halftime. After his mom passed out the Gatorade bottles and the oranges she'd cut into perfect wedges, he said, "Anybody got anything to say?"

"I've got to save my voice for Buddy Boy," Will said. He ran a hand through his thick hair. Danny was surprised, as usual, that the hand could make it all the way through in one shot. "He still won't tell me whether he thinks Hilary Duff is hotter than Britney, by the way."

Ali Walker said, "Will honey? You could make prisoners of war talk."

Danny said, "Will, you just keep doing that mad thing you're doing to him. On account of, it's working. Matt, remember: No fouls. If you don't have a clear path to the rebound, forget it. None of that reaching-over crap." He gave a quick sideways look at his mom. "Sorry, Mom," he said.

"That's Coach Mom," she said. "I can take it."

Then he told Bren that the guy guarding him was backing off, and that Bren might get more shots in the second half than he'd gotten all season.

"Cool," Bren Darcy said.

Then Danny looked over at Ty. "You got anything?"

Ty said, "Just remember: The only other guy on the team besides Buddy who can hurt you is the kid up front who's almost as big as Buddy. I forget his name. He doesn't get to shoot much, but he can make an open shot. So Matt, you've got to keep an eye out for him down low."

Matt said, "He smells."

"But that doesn't mean he can't make an open shot," Danny said.

Matt said, "No, I mean he really *smells*."

Tess said, "Well, on *that* manly-man note."

They were all standing around Danny then. "I'm gonna tell you all the last thing my dad told me today when I went to see him," Danny said. "Beat Kirkland's—"

"Daniel," his mom said.

"—butts," Danny said.

Matt picked up his fourth foul halfway through the third quarter, doing exactly what Danny had told him *not* to do, going over the top trying to take a rebound away from the smelly kid.

Danny took him out and put Oliver Towne in the middle of the triangle, between Colby and Bren. Will was handling Bud Sheedy

221

most of the time, Danny coming over to help out when he could, which meant any time he wasn't afraid that he was leaving about three guys wide open.

Six minutes into the third quarter, the game was tied at 24.

All of a sudden Colby Danes—the one Richie Walker had called the basketball girl of Danny's dreams—couldn't miss. She made the first three shots she tried in the second half, two from the outside, one of them *way* outside, the other one over Bud Sheedy after she took a rebound away from him and got an easy put-back.

Every time she made a basket, she'd jump a little higher in the air and her smile would get a little bigger, and then she'd go bounding down the court like a colt, ponytail bobbing behind her.

It didn't take great powers of observation to notice that Bud Sheedy and the rest of the Kirkland Comets liked having a girl show them up—for the time being, anyway—about as much as they would have liked wearing her clothes.

Then, just like that, as if somebody had accidentally switched off the power, both teams seemed to stop scoring. It went on over the rest of the third quarter and into the fourth. It was either really good defense causing it, or really bad offense. Or maybe a combination of the two. By the time there were five minutes to go, the game was still tied, 28–28, and as excited as Danny was, as they *all* were, about having a chance to win, he was worried that Will was getting tired. So he replaced him on Bud Sheedy with Michael Harden.

But Michael couldn't stay with him. Sometimes Michael *and* Danny together couldn't stay with him. Bud got loose and made two straight shots for the first time since the start of the game. Danny knew he couldn't let him get hot, not coming down the stretch, when he could run them right out of the gym.

During a break in play, while the refs tried to untangle one of the nets, Danny said to Tess, "How many time-outs do I have left?"

"Three," she said.

"Are you sure?"

Tess gave him the raised eyebrow. "I'm going to forget I heard that," she said.

Danny called time, walked down to where Will was sitting with a towel on his head that he'd fashioned into some kind of turban.

"Uh, Mohammed?" he said.

Will said, "I was actually going for that do-rag look defensive backs go with when they take their helmets off."

"You actually remind me of one of my dad's nurses," Danny said. "I need you to go back in and stay in the rest of the way on Bud."

"I may have to talk a little less," Will said, taking the towel off his head and spiking it as he stood up.

Danny said, "I can live with that."

They walked down to where the rest of the team was waiting in the huddle. As soon as Danny got in there, a laugh jumped out of his throat like one of those magician's bunnies jumping out of a hat.

"How much fun is *this*?" he said.

It came down to the wire—Kirkland 32, Warriors 30, with twenty-five seconds left.

Danny called for the same clear-out play he'd tried at the end of the Hanesboro game, him and Colby over on the right.

Kirkland played it about the same way Hanesboro had.

Danny ended up with pretty much the same shot, just inside the free throw line.

This time it was Bud Sheedy running at him from his left.

One step too late.

Danny got his shot up in the air. Telling himself to shoot it higher this time. Give it a chance to come down softer.

Drained the sucker.

It was 32–all. Fifteen seconds left. Before Kirkland could inbound the ball, Danny called his last time-out.

Ty said, "They won't expect you to put the press back on."

Danny had taken the press off when he put Will back in the game, just as a way of saving Will's legs, which were wobbly even after Danny had given him his short rest.

"No," Danny said to Ty. "Yes, you're right, they won't be expecting it. But no, I don't want to take the chance that somebody gets beat, especially without Matt back there to play safety."

He had put Matt back into the game with four fouls at the same time he put Will back in, but the big guy—who'd been coughing and wheezing with a cold all day and seemed almost relieved to be able to sit down for good—had fouled out a minute later.

Danny said, "They're going to try to isolate Bud. Because whatever they might want us to think they're doing, nobody else besides Bud will have the stones to take the shot."

He looked up at his mom. She just made a motion with her hand, like, just keep doing whatever it is you're doing.

Danny said, "He'll get the ball behind that double screen they've been running. Then everybody'll get out of the way, and they'll let him try to dribble through all of us."

Danny looked at Ty, who nodded.

To the Warriors, Danny said, "Everybody just play the D straight up, the way we have been. Once they see the press is off, they'll probably have the point guard bring it up. Will? As soon as he crosses half-court, you leave Bud and run right at him."

"Ex*cuse* me?" Will said. "We're going to leave Buddy Boy without anybody on him?"

"Trust me," Danny said.

"And what will you be doing?"

"Trying to win us a ball game," Danny said.

They put their hands together, came out, set up their triangle-and-two one last time. The point guard brought it up quickly, the way Danny had figured he would. Will was over on the right, where the smelly kid and one of the Kirkland forwards were coming out to set their screen.

Will was still with Bud.

As soon as the point guard crossed half-court, about twelve seconds showing on the clock, Danny could see him looking for Bud Sheedy.

Will ran at the kid with the ball like a maniac.

As soon as he did, the kid got bug eyes, and you could see he couldn't wait to give the ball up to Bud Sheedy. Who popped out, away from his screen, the way he was supposed to, even took a couple of steps toward the ball, not away from it, the way they were taught all the way back in Biddy Basketball.

Bud just didn't move toward the ball as quickly as a streak of light named Danny Walker.

Who had been playing possum behind the double screen, arms at his side, like Bud Sheedy was somebody else's responsibility now.

The pass was in the air before the point guard, or Bud Sheedy, saw Danny making his move, cutting between them and grabbing the ball out of the air as if the pass had been intended for him all along.

He caught the ball and had the presence of mind to give one fast look at the clock over the basket at the other end—the *Warriors'* basket—as he did.

Four seconds left.

Will Stoddard had always said something about Danny that people used to say about his dad:

He was faster with the ball than everybody else was without it.

Will would tell him afterward that Bud Sheedy, no slouch himself when it came to running the court, was coming so hard he was sure he was going to catch Danny from behind.

"I knew nobody was going to catch Coach Walker," Bren said.

Everybody agreed on this: There was one second showing on the clock when Danny released his layup maybe one foot further away from the basket than he would have preferred.

He didn't know anything about where Bud Sheedy was, or how close he came to catching him, or the clock behind the basket. He was going by the clock inside his head, keeping his eyes on the prize:

That little square right above the basket.

He pushed off on his left leg, going up hard but laying the ball up there soft. He saw the ball hit the square as if there were a bull's-eye painted on it. The last thing he saw before he went flying toward the stage was the ball go through the net, right before the horn sounded.

He was sitting on the floor with his back against the stage when the Warriors came running for him.

Warriors 34, Kirkland 32.

Final.

When Danny managed to break loose from the Warriors, he saw Bud Sheedy and the rest of the Kirkland Comets still on the court, lined up and waiting to shake hands.

Danny said to his teammates, "Hey, we had enough practice losing. Now we gotta act like we know how to win."

Still coaching, to the end.

He was last in line. Bud Sheedy was last in their line. When it was just the two of them, Bud said to Danny, "We heard something about you coaching, but nobody really believed it."

"We sort of did it together," Danny said, and meant it. "Ty probably did more coaching today than I did."

"Nah, you did it to us and we know you did," Bud said. "You knew exactly what you were doing on defense with that last play." Bud smiled and shook his head. "That was, like, *sick,* dude."

The word always made Danny smile.

Somehow it had worked out that *sick* was right up there with the highest possible praise one guy could give another.

"Thanks," Danny said.

Some of the Warriors were sitting on the folding chairs that served as their bench, some were on the floor, and all of them were eating the Krispy Kremes that Tess had brought in the green-and-white boxes that made your mouth water just thinking about what was inside. Tess waved at him, telling him to come over and eat.

But Danny was looking for Ty, who he thought was the real hero of the day.

He knew the Vikings had a game here in about an hour, against Hanesboro, and had just assumed that Ty would hang around for that. Only Danny didn't see him anywhere in the gym, and when he checked the back hallway where they'd had their team meeting at halftime, he wasn't out there, either. Or in the boys' locker room, where the Kirkland kids were getting into their coats. Danny asked Bud Sheedy if he'd seen Ty once the game ended. Bud said, "His dad showed up to watch the last few minutes. Stood over there in the corner by himself. Then as soon as you made your shot, I saw him come get Ty and take him by the arm." Bud hooked a thumb in the general direction of the front door of St. Pat's. "They went that-away."

Danny went back through the gym, made a motion to Tess like, one sec, pushed through the double doors that took him into the foyer, where all the glass doors were like a giant window facing out toward the front steps, and the parking lot.

Danny ducked over by the machine that dispensed bottled water, so they wouldn't see him.

They meaning Ty and Mr. Ross.

The two of them were on the top step in the cold, Mr. Ross doing all the talking. You could see his breath in the air between him and Ty, coming out of him in bursts, like machine-gun fire.

His face looked like the kind of clenched fist you made when you were looking to throw a punch, not tap somebody five.

Danny could see that as clear as day. He also noticed for the first time—he'd been too wrapped up in the game before to look past the game—that Ty didn't have his cast on his wrist anymore, just had it wrapped in an Ace bandage the color of his skin.

Good hand and bad hand, both at his sides, Ty stood there helpless while his father talked to him. Talked *at* him. Danny couldn't hear what he was saying through the thick doors, but could feel Mr. Ross's voice even in here, the way you could sometimes feel the beat of loud rap music from the car next to you.

Occasionally Mr. Ross would poke Ty in the chest.

Finally Ty couldn't take any more of what Mr. Ross was dishing out and started to cry.

Danny wanted to look away, this was the last thing he wanted to see. But he couldn't.

For a moment, Mr. Ross didn't say anything. Danny could just see his chest rising and falling, as if he had tired himself out.

It was then that Danny saw Mrs. Ross standing at the bottom of the steps. Maybe she said something to them, because Ty turned and saw her, too.

When he tried to leave, took just one step in his mom's direction, Mr. Ross grabbed his arm, turned him back around.

Then a pretty amazing thing happened:

Ty Ross shook him off, like his dad was just another defender who couldn't guard him, and walked down the steps to where his mom was waiting for him.

She touched him on the shoulder, still glaring up at her husband, and then she turned away and walked with Ty across the lot to where her red station wagon was parked.

The beginning of the end, that's the way Danny would think of the scene later.

Tess, who loved to play with words, said it was actually the end of the beginning.

Her description, they both decided, was more accurate.

THEY WON AGAIN THE NEXT DAY AGAINST SEEKONK, THE TEAM THEY'D BEATEN for their first win, in a game that now seemed to have been played when they were all in the fifth grade.

They were ahead by so much at halftime that Danny went with both O'Brien twins—at the same time, a first—for the entire second half, even though both of them were complaining by the middle of the fourth quarter that they were more tired than they usually got after sleepovers.

Three wins now for the Warriors, who'd started out thinking they weren't going to beat anybody.

One game to go, a rematch with Hanesboro, before the play-offs.

Maybe, Danny had started to think, they had finally turned into what they were supposed to be, what Richie Walker had talked about the very first time they were all together, the team nobody wanted to play.

Then Matt Fitzgerald's bad cold somehow turned into full-blown pneumonia and he ended up in the hospital.

Will called with the news, saying he didn't want Danny to read all about it in an IM box.

"Who do we call about ordering up some size?" Will said.

Danny told him he'd been asking himself that question his whole life.

Danny had three IM boxes going on his screen as he talked to Will: Will's, Tess's, Colby's.

"I would like to make one other observation," Will said.

"What?"

"Turns out it's a small world after all," Will said.

"You can't help yourself, can you?" Danny said.

"Other people say I *need* help," Will said, and then said he was getting off, if any other brilliant thoughts popped into his head, he'd send them along by e-mail. But not before adding, "Don't worry, you'll think of something."

Danny took down Will's box and Colby's.

Just him and Tess now.

Just the way he liked it.

CROSSOVER2: Matt's got pneumonia and I'm the one who feels sick.

Her response didn't take long.

What did they used to say in the *Superman* cartoons? Tess Hewitt was faster than a speeding bullet.

CONTESSA44: You'll come up with a plan.
CROSSOVER2: You sound like Will.
CONTESSA44: That is a cruel and heartless thing to say.

He looked out the window and saw a wet snow starting to fall, the worst kind; if he didn't shovel it right away around the basket, it would be slippier than a hockey rink out there before he knew it.

CROSSOVER2: I need a secret weapon. When was the last time you played center?

CONTESSA44: We're not that desperate yet.

CROSSOVER 2: Getting there.

CONTESSA44: You don't need me.

Sometimes you had to let your guard down, put yourself out there, not try to be so much of a guy.

Which meant telling somebody the truth.

CROSSOVER2: I always need you.

CONTESSA44: I know. And back at you, by the way.

Before he could think of something clever that would lighten up the mood, not let things stay too serious, she was back at him.

CONTESSA44: YOU'RE our secret weapon. 'Nite.

He left the computer on while he washed his face and brushed his teeth, then went down to say good night to his mom, who had propped up a bunch of pillows and had a blanket over her and was reading in her favorite spot in front of the fire.

When he came back up to his room, he heard the old doodlely-doo from the computer.

Incoming. Tess?

He walked over and stared at the message on the screen.

What?

He sat down in his swivel chair, closed his eyes, opened them, stared at the screen again, just to make sure it wasn't some kind of weird figment of his imagination.

It wasn't.

Then Danny Walker, knowing his mom would think he was a crazy person if she walked in on him, sat there and laughed his head off.

Will Stoddard *was* insane.

But he sure wasn't alone.

The Warriors beat Hanesboro the next morning, even without Matt Fitzgerald, mostly because Colby Danes had the game of her life, scoring twenty points and, according to ace statistician Tess Hewitt, grabbing fourteen rebounds.

Tess also pointed out after the game that Danny'd had twelve assists.

"You don't know how to keep assists," he said.

"I'm going to forget I heard *that*," she said. "First you act like I can't keep track of time-outs, something my cat could do. Now this ugly charge."

"You really know what an assist is?"

"When it all gets too complicated for me," she said, "I find a big hunky boy and ask him to explain whether that was a pass I just saw, or some kind of unidentified flying object."

Danny said, "I should drop this now, right?"

"I would."

Danny and Tess stayed at St. Pat's doing homework after the Hanesboro game, eating the lunches their moms had packed for them. When they were done with lunch they walked back to the gym to watch the Vikings play Piping Rock in the game that would determine which one of them finished first in the league.

He also wanted to see the new kid on the Vikings Ty had told him about. David Rodriguez, his name was, a five-eight kid from the Bronx who had been born in San Juan and whose family had moved to Middletown three days before. According to Ty, the dad was a policeman and had gotten tired of working for the New York police, and had up and taken a job on the small Middletown force.

"I only watched him at the end of one practice, when I went over to try shooting around a little bit," Ty had said. "I think the Knicks could use this guy."

David Rodriguez was even taller than Matt Fitzgerald and, without Ty in the lineup, the fastest kid on the Vikings as soon as he took his warm-ups off. Mr. Ross didn't put him into the game until the start of the second quarter, but Danny only had to watch him for two minutes to know he was the best center in town now, better than Jack Harty, better than Matt.

Great, Danny thought, just what the Vikings needed:

More size.

They hadn't just added a player, they had added a *New York City* player.

"Why couldn't he go to St. Pat's?" Danny said. "Then I could have recruited him."

"He is pretty good," Tess said.

"Only if you like a tall guy who plays like a little guy," Danny said. "I hear they call him Da-Rod. As in A-Rod."

"Who's A-Rod?" Tess said.

"Only the best baseball player in the world."

"One sport at a time, pal," Tess said, "one sport at a time."

They were sitting at the very top of the bleachers the janitors rolled out when there was enough of a crowd; the old-fashioned wood bleachers stretched from foul line to foul line. And as good as the game between the Vikings and Piping Rock turned out to be, Danny found himself watching Mr. Ross as much as he did the players. Figuring that if he studied him he could finally come up with an answer about why twelve-year-old travel basketball— *winning* at twelve-year-old travel basketball—seemed to mean so much to him.

And the more Danny watched him, and watched the dad coaching Piping Rock, the more he kept coming back to the same question:

Why were they even doing this?

It wasn't that either one of them was a screamer once the game had started; neither one of them was shouting at the players very much, or the refs. Danny didn't see either one of them really lose his temper one single time, even though they made plenty of faces every time somebody on the court did something wrong.

It was just that neither one of them seemed to be having any fun.

They looked like they were *working.*

Without ever getting near each other, or really looking at each other, Danny still got the idea that they were competing against each other. It was like watching a college game on ESPN sometimes, at least until he couldn't take it anymore and had to turn the sound off. Even if it was a game he really, really wanted to see. Because the more he listened to the announcers, the more he started to get the idea that it was Coach Kryzyzewski of Duke competing against Coach Williams of North Carolina instead of the Blue Devils going against the Tar Heels.

He always came back to what his dad constantly drummed into his head:

It was a players' game.

It just didn't come across that way on television, at least not often enough.

It sure wasn't that way here.

The two dads were coaching so fiercely, they were *missing* a great game.

And it *was* great, back and forth the whole second half, guys on both teams making plays, some of the plays so good Danny couldn't believe his eyes sometimes. He couldn't remember a single time in the game when either team was ahead by more than four points. The game was so great Danny understood now what Ty had been going through all season, sitting there watching while everybody else got to play.

Even though Danny had been dragging at the end of the Hanesboro game, he wanted to get back out there all over again, mix it up with these guys.

A game like this always made you want to get your sneaks back on.

The Vikings should have been having a ball playing in a game this good, the level of play this high, the top seed in the tournament riding on it. But they weren't. Even when one of them, Jack Harty or Da-Rod or Daryll Mullins or the hated Moron Moran, would do something nice and get their team a basket, Mr. Ross would be up almost before the ball was through the net, like he'd been shot up out of a James Bond-type ejector seat, telling them where to go on defense, what to do next.

They all seemed like they were afraid to enjoy doing something right, because in the very next moment they might be doing something wrong.

The Vikings gave Piping Rock a run, all the way to when Jack

Harty's shot fell off the rim at the end of overtime and Piping Rock won, 49–48.

The Vikings, without Ty, without Andy Mayne still, had lost, but Danny knew they were the better team, especially with Da-Rod in the house now.

They just didn't seem to be having much fun.

How did Will put it?

The Vikings were a no-mirth zone.

"I don't want to be with them anymore," he said to Tess when the game was over. "The Vikings, I mean."

"I can see why," she said.

It had taken almost the entire season, but he finally knew he was with the right team, after all.

The setup for the first round of the tournament was pretty basic, the number-one seed playing number eight, number two playing number seven, and so on. The teams with the better records got to play home games. Seekonk, for example, which had finished in eighth place, had to go to Piping Rock. The Vikings, at number two, also got a home game, at St. Pat's, but home court didn't matter very much to them, because it was going to be Middletown versus Middletown. They were playing the number-seven Warriors, one o'clock, the following Saturday afternoon.

The Warriors' last practice before the play-offs, the Warriors minus Matt Fitzgerald, would be on Tuesday night. Their last full practice, anyway. Danny still planned to get the key guys together at his house the next night.

That included Colby Danes, who was officially one of the guys now, even if Will Stoddard certainly didn't think of her quite that way.

Colby liked Will as much as he liked her, at least according to Tess. It didn't change the fact that she was the only person Danny knew about who could cause Will's mouth to malfunction on a fairly regular basis.

The fact that he was able to concentrate on basketball when the two of them were playing basketball together was a minor miracle.

Tess would be at the meeting, too. Danny couldn't believe they had ever tried having a team without her.

And his mom, who had come up so big, the last few days, especially.

"Point Mom," is what she'd started calling herself.

"*Point* Mom?" Danny said.

"Don't worry," she said, "I've got the lingo down now."

This was on Tuesday, Ali Walker driving Danny over to St. Pat's before going over to the hospital to visit his dad. Mrs. Stoddard had volunteered to be the team mom for tonight while Danny ran practice.

"Truth or dare," he said to his mom from the backseat.

"Truth."

"Can we really do this?"

They were in front of the gym, the engine idling, the heat going full blast. Ali Walker turned to face him. "It's like I've been telling you your whole life," she said. "You can do just about anything you set your mind to."

"I set my mind on making the Vikings," Danny said. "How'd that work out for me?"

"I never said it was a one hundred percent foolproof plan," she said. "But it's still a darn good one. And you know it."

She faced front, but he could see her smiling, her reflection in the windshield lit by the dashboard lights.

Danny vaguely remembered some old song she liked to sing along to that had "dashboard light" in it. Another one of her oldies but goodies.

"As far as I'm concerned," she said, "this all worked out the way it was supposed to."

Then she told him to scoot, his team was waiting for him.

THE NEXT NIGHT. WEDNESDAY.

The small team meeting was over, the minipractice in the drive-way had ended, the ice cream sundaes had been consumed by the unlikely group of kids and moms in the Walker kitchen.

Tess was the last to leave. Her parents had gone to the movies, then called to ask if it was all right if she stayed there a little longer while they stopped and had a quick bite at Fierro's.

Tess and Danny sat on the two seats in the backyard swing set Ali Walker said she hadn't taken down because she was never tak-ing it down. It was cold out and getting colder by the minute, but neither one of them cared.

"Tonight, I finally figured out why you love it out here so much," she said. "I mean, on your own private court."

Danny said, "I'm just trying to get better, is all."

"It's more than that and you know it, Daniel Walker," Tess said. "This is your own little basketball world back here, and nobody can screw things up."

"My mom says it's my own private Madison Square Garden."

"More like a *magic* garden, if you ask me."

She reached over and took his hand out of the big front pocket of his hooded sweatshirt, and held it in her own hand. It made Danny feel as if he'd put a glove on.

They stayed that way for a minute and then, because neither

one of them seemed to know how long you were supposed to hold hands, she let him go.

They kept rocking.

"It's a *really* nice world back here," Tess said.

"You always know what to say," Danny said. "What would you call this? The quiet before the storm?"

"Works for me."

"Whatever happens, we're gonna give Middletown basketball a day it's never going to forget," Danny said.

"Like in your dad's day," she said.

"Not that big a day," Danny said. "Nothing will ever be that big around here ever again."

They went back to rocking in silence. Danny put his head back and stared at the stars. And suddenly, because Tess Hewitt was always full of surprises, because Danny knew in his heart, even at the age of twelve, that she would be full of surprises as long as the two of them knew each other—which he roughly hoped would be forever—she leaned over and kissed him on the cheek.

"Don't be so sure it won't be that big, little guy," she said.

It was all right for her, calling him little guy.

Because when he was with her like this, Danny felt like the biggest guy in town.

When he heard the Hewitts' car in front, he walked Tess up the driveway, told her he'd see her tomorrow at school, then went back inside.

His mom was holding the phone out for him as soon as he got through the front door.

"Your father," she said.

Danny put his hand over the mouthpiece. "Isn't it a little late for him to be up?"

"He has some trouble sleeping sometimes, at least until the pills kick in."

She pointed toward the phone. "Talk," she said. "My two big talkers."

Danny took the phone with him up the stairs, saying, "Yo."

Which he'd never say to his mom.

"Hey, bud."

He went into his room, turned on the light next to his bed, adjusted the shade so it shined up on John Stockton like a spotlight, lay down on his back staring up at it.

Waiting for his dad to say something now, on the other end of the phone.

Some parts of it between them, Danny knew, would never change. Even lately, with so much to talk about, they'd sit there in the hospital room with nothing but air between them.

Sometimes Danny compared the two of them starting a conversation to his mom trying to get her car engine to start up on one of these cold mornings.

"Well," his dad said.

"Well."

"Here you are."

He sounded a little groggy. Danny had been with him a few times when the sleeping pills started to work, and it was like somebody had hit his dad with a knockout punch.

"No," Danny said. "Here *we* are."

"Nice try, bud. But it's all you now."

"I wouldn't even have a game tomorrow if you hadn't come back when you did," Danny said. "And did what you did starting the team."

Another long pause.

"Yeah, yeah, yeah."

Which sounded more to Danny like: Lose the nerdy-weepy crap.

Danny didn't know what to say, so he didn't say anything until his dad said, "Anyway, I was just calling to wish you luck. I told your mom not to stop by tomorrow, they've got a bunch of tests they want to run. And they're going to put a smaller cast on my leg so I can get around a little better. Unless, of course, they decide they want to run me into the chop shop again."

"The Vikings are really good," Danny said, "even without Ty."

"Big . . . frigging deal. You guys are better than ever."

"I don't know."

"Well, guess what? You better damn well know by tomorrow."

Coming alive a little bit. Cracking the whip.

"Okay?" his dad said.

"Okay."

"Hey, bud?"

"Yeah?"

"Get after it tomorrow, every minute you're out there," he said. "On account of, you never know which day is gonna be the best day of your whole life."

The next thing Danny heard was a dial tone.

He shut off the phone, looked over at the clock next to his bed. Ten-fifteen.

Talking to his dad had made him want to play a little more before he went to bed.

He didn't have to change, because he still had his sweatshirt on. He figured that if it wasn't okay with his mom, going back out at this time of night, she'd come right outside and tell him once she heard the bounce of the ball.

He grabbed the Infusion ball from under his desk.

Slipped out the back door and switched the lights back on.

Warmed up by shooting a few from the outside.

Made a little tricky-dribble move and then put up the shot he'd missed against Hanesboro in the first game, made at the end of the Kirkland game.

Nothing but net.

Feeling jazzed now, as if the night were just beginning, with all his dreams, and schemes.

Andy Mayne's ankle was all better. He'd be playing tomorrow, at least according to Ty, which meant Danny would be going up against a point guard just as good as he was, and a lot bigger.

Nothing new with the part about bigger.

He thought to himself: Bring it on, Colorado boy.

He was ready to play the game right here, right now.

He stepped back until he was about twenty feet away from the basket, tried the double crossover a couple of times, back and forth, not putting the ball too low, just fooling around with it.

Then he was ready to try it for real, imagining he needed it to split Andy Mayne and another defender in the Vikings' press, get himself into the open court in the last minute of the game.

Or even the last ten seconds.

Left hand, right hand.

Then the same move again, just slower this time.

Ready to make his move, right out of the last dribble, his body nearly as low to the ground as the ball.

He made his move, between the imaginary defenders, exploding at the basket like a toy rocket taking off.

And slipped as he did.

Slipped on the patch of black ice he didn't know was there, his feet going straight out from under him like he'd slipped on a banana peel in a comic strip, flying backward through the air without even a dope like Teddy Moran around to break his fall.

31

HE DIDN'T TELL HIS MOM ABOUT HIS SHOULDER IN THE MORNING. HE WASN'T going to tell anybody about his shoulder, as sore as it was. He didn't like tennis too much, it wasn't his favorite, but sometimes when one of the big tournaments was on, he liked to listen to John McEnroe. And one time during the U.S. Open, he'd heard McEnroe talking about what some old Australian guy had told him about injuries when McEnroe was a junior player.

"If you're hurt," McEnroe said, "you don't play. If you play, you're not hurt."

He was playing, case closed.

Even though he did want to call his dad and ask him if they made junior pain pills, preferably chewable.

He took a longer shower than usual, letting the hot water beat on his shoulder as long as possible. When he came downstairs, his mom was in the living room.

There was a big box in the middle of the floor.

"Whatcha got?" he said.

"Take a look for yourself."

They were white basketball jerseys, packed in a zipped-up plastic bag. He unzipped the bag, and pulled one out.

"Middletown" was in blue letters on the back, above the numbers.

"From your father's team," she said.

"No *way!*"

"Way."

"Was this Dad's idea?"

"Nah," she said, "this one came from the old point mom."

The second jersey Danny pulled out of the plastic bag was Richie Walker's Number 3.

Danny tried it on, careful pulling it over his head, knowing that if his face showed any pain, his mom would pounce; he tried not to even think about the shoulder, worried about her mutant mind-reading powers.

His dad's Number 3 fit him as if he'd special-ordered it out of a little-guy catalogue. He didn't have to tuck half of it into the sweats he was wearing right now, didn't lose half of the "3" in the front.

Didn't feel like Stuart Little.

It fit him like a dream.

He looked at his mom. "How . . . ?"

"From Mrs. Hayes. After Mr. Hayes died."

There hadn't been a dad coaching Middletown travel when Richie Walker's team had won the national championship. Their coach had been a local basketball legend named Morgan Hayes, who'd coached basketball at Middletown High until being forced to retire at the age of seventy.

Danny said, "Dad always said Coach Hayes knew more about basketball than any coach he ever had after that."

"I think the only reason Coach Hayes ever agreed to come out of retirement," Ali Walker said, "I mean back then, was because he knew how special your father was, and he was a little sad he wasn't going to be able to coach him in high school."

His mom went on to say that after Mr. Hayes died three years ago, his wife found this box in their basement. In those days, his mom said, the kids didn't get to keep the uniforms when the season was over, they went back to Middletown Basketball. But they'd allowed Morgan Hayes to keep these uniforms because his Vikings had won the title.

"Of course your father had left . . . town by then," his mom said. "But somehow I couldn't bring myself to throw these uniforms away. There wasn't any Middletown Basketball Hall of Fame I could give them to. So I just kept them in the basement."

She looked at Danny. "I think you should wear them today," she said.

He went over and put out his fist. She put on a face that had some attitude in it, like she was saying *uh-huh*, and tapped it with her own.

"*Very* cool idea," he said to his mom. "You think they have any magic in them?"

"The Vikings won't know what these uniforms mean. But you guys will."

They took the rest of the uniforms out of the box and folded them neatly. Danny said they could pass them out when everybody was at St. Pat's. When they finished their folding, the two of them were still kneeling on the floor, facing each other. His mom took his hands.

Don't pull too hard, he thought. *Please.*

"What started out with the worst day of your whole life is going to end up with the best," she said.

"Promise?"

"Cross my heart."

"Everything's all right with the league?"

"We sent over the new and improved Daniel Walker Play-off Roster yesterday."

The doorbell rang then. Danny knew who it was.

More perfect timing between them.

Same as on the court.

He ran over and opened the front door for Ty and Mrs. Ross.

"Wait till you see what my mom has," Danny said, not even bothering with hello or good morning. "The uniforms my dad's team wore!" Danny caught himself. "And your dad's team, too."

Ty said, "Cool."

"Well," Ali Walker said from behind Danny. "Good morning to the newest member of the Warriors."

"'Morning, Mrs. Walker," Ty Ross said.

Lily Ross said to Ali, "He wanted to go to the game with Danny."

Ali said, "Things any better at home?"

Lily Ross shrugged. "I told my husband at breakfast what I've been telling him all week: It's just a basketball game. And it's a game that was never supposed to be about him in the first place." She pointed toward Danny and Ty, already moving into the living room, Danny asking Ty what number he wanted to wear. "It's about them."

Danny and Ty raced for the uniforms then, Ty telling him he wanted to see if Number 1 would fit him.

The whole thing had been Ty's idea.

He had IM'd Danny the night after Mr. Ross called him out in front of the gym after the Kirkland game. It was the last message Danny had gotten before he went to bed.

TyBreak1: I want to play with you guys.

Always a man of few words.

Like Richie Walker.

Danny remembered sitting there at his desk and laughing his head off, just at the craziness of it.

248

CROSSOVER2: You CANNOT be serious!

Another McEnroe line.

TYBREAK1: I wouldn't be quitting something. You can't quit
    something you never started.
CROSSOVER2: Can you? Play with us, I mean.
TYBREAK1: My mom says yes.

Moms rule, Danny thought.
Trying to slow down his brain from going a hundred miles an
hour.

CROSSOVER2: Don't tell anybody yet.
TYBREAK1: That include Tess?

Danny smiled to himself that night.
Everybody knew who the real boss was.

CROSSOVER2: First I want to talk to my mom. Then have her talk
    to your mom.
TYBREAK1: Deal.
CROSSOVER2: Dude?
TYBREAK1: Yeah?
CROSSOVER2: We are gonna rock their world.

He'd had to keep it a secret for more than a week, from Will and
Tess and everybody, the longest he'd ever kept a secret his whole
life. Because once the moms got involved—the conspiracy of
moms, is what Ali Walker called it—they wanted Danny and Ty to
take some time, think things through.

Danny knew that Ty and Mrs. Ross had finally told Mr. Ross the Tuesday night before the play-offs, while the Warriors were practicing at St. Pat's. Ty said on the phone that night that his dad had hit the roof, got as mad as he'd ever seen him, which pretty much meant as mad as anybody had ever gotten.

But then, he said, something awesome had happened:

Ty's mom had sat there across from him at the kitchen table when all the yelling stopped and then—Ty's words—totally dominated him.

Mrs. Ross hit Mr. Ross with what she called his "little recruiting trip," the one where he'd tried to get Danny to join the Vikings. She hit him with the scene between Mr. Ross and Ty after the Kirkland game.

Mr. Ross had finally looked at Ty and asked how he could turn his back on his own team?

"It was never my team, Dad," Ty had told him. "It was always your team. I didn't feel like I was part of anybody's team till I helped Danny coach."

And that, Ty said, was pretty much that.

Danny thinking to himself: Maybe *Mrs.* Ross was the biggest guy in Middletown now.

The next night, Danny couldn't have gotten their full squad, plus Ty, together even if he'd wanted to. Though he didn't mind very much that he couldn't. Michael Harden had tutoring, the O'Brien twins had to go watch their younger sister's ballet recital, and Oliver Towne had gone to a Knicks game with his neighbors, even though it was a school night. Danny had everybody else in his driveway, walking Ty through the Warriors' basic plays with Colby, Will, and Bren.

Tess even came over, pretending she was the center.

When they went inside for ice cream afterward, Mrs. Ross having shown up by then to pick up Ty, they all agreed to keep Ty joining the team a secret for a couple more days, until they made absolutely sure it was all right with the league, a kid switching teams this way, this late in the season. But both Danny's mom and Ty's mom were confident it was going to be all right, since Ty had never even played a league game for the Vikings.

Even if his dad coached the team.

That night in the kitchen Lily Ross said, "It's funny, I was never interested in being a team mom until it was somebody else's team."

Ali Walker said, "It's about time."

Lily Ross said, "I was watching them from the car before. Our sons should have been together all along."

It was agreed that Danny would tell the rest of the Warriors on Saturday morning. Telling a couple of blabberfaces like the O'Brien twins any sooner would have been like hiring one of those skywriters you saw flying over the beach in the summer.

Now it was Saturday morning.

Danny wearing Number 3 in white, Ty wearing Number 1.

They looked at each other in the living room, then both of them rolled their eyes.

Ty said, "This is nuts."

Like, *sick,* Danny told him.

They went upstairs to send out an instant-message to the rest of the Warriors, telling them that they'd added a pretty decent player for the big game.

Danny took them into his mom's classroom and passed out the uniforms there, once everybody was done high-fiving Ty and pounding him on the back as if he'd made his first three shots of the game.

The guys thought the old-school uniforms were even cooler than some of the old-school NBA uniforms their parents could order for them online. Tess was the only one frowning, saying she wasn't thrilled that the blue trim on the jerseys really didn't match up with the blue of the Warriors' shorts.

Danny looked at her as if she'd grown another perfect nose.

"I'm just making a fashion statement, is all," she said.

Danny said, "I'll take the hit on the blue thing."

Colby went outside to change into her Number 4. When she came back in, she twirled around and said, "How do I look?"

"Let's ask Will," Danny said, feeling good enough about the day to bust his best friend a little on Colby.

Will playfully gave him a slap on the back, catching Danny right where he'd landed on the ice. Danny couldn't help himself, he bent over as if Will had hit him from behind with an aluminum baseball bat.

They were off to the side from everybody else, so only Will noticed how much pain Danny was in.

"Dude," Will said, "what's *that* about?"

"I fell last night in the driveway," Danny whispered. "But don't say anything to anybody, okay?"

"I'd say I've got your back," Will said, "but that doesn't seem like such a hot idea." Now he managed a whisper. "Can you really play?"

"I never could go to my left, anyway."

Will said, "You go to your left better than any right-hander in town."

"What is this," Danny said, "a practice debate in Miss Kimmet's class?"

There was still a lot of loud, excited chatter in the room when Danny tried—in vain—to get their attention, the way he had at practice that first night. When he couldn't get anybody's attention, he caught Tess's eye, shook his head in resignation, and put two fingers to his lips.

She did her whistle thing, and the room quieted like it did when any teacher walked into any classroom. Even Mrs. Ross and Mrs. Stoddard stopped gabbing over in the corner.

Danny said, "They're gonna want to wipe the floor with us, you all know that, right?"

There were nods all around. "You got that right," somebody said.

"They would've wanted to do that even before Ty joined up with us, because they don't think we're even supposed to be *on* the same floor with them. But now it's gonna be like the Civil War of Middletown or something."

He saw Will take a step forward, start to say something, then stop when Tess and Mrs. Stoddard both threatened him with pinching motions at the same time.

Danny said, "You guys all know how much I hate making speeches. So I'm just gonna say this: Let's do what my dad told us we might be able to do back at the beginning."

They were all staring at him.

"Even though it's only the first round of the play-offs," he said, "let's see if we can win the championship of all guys like us who ever got told they weren't good enough."

They charged out of Mrs. Walker's classroom and down the hall, running as hard as you did on the last day of school, just running this time toward the first round of the play-offs.

Running, really, at the top of their lungs.

When the Vikings took the court, Danny was positive they'd grown somehow since last Saturday. Da-Rod Rodriguez in particular looked even taller on the court than he had from the top row of the bleachers.

Andy Mayne had his right ankle taped up so high you could see the white bandage above his high-top black Iversons, but that didn't catch Danny's eye as much as this:

He seemed to have grown more than the inch that Danny had grown since October.

The Warriors had come through the door next to the stage, so they didn't have to pass the Vikings to start warming up at the stage end of St. Pat's. That meant they didn't have to pass Mr. Ross, either; he was standing under the basket at the opposite end, arms folded, watching the Vikings shoot layups as if that was maybe the most fascinating thing that would ever happen to him.

When the Warriors got into their own layup line, Danny heard the loudest pregame cheer they'd ever gotten, and that's when he noticed how full the bleachers already were. Down at the corner of them, directly across from the Vikings' basket, was a television cameraman, and the guy who did the sports on Channel 14, the local all-news channel.

After all the *hey-little-guy* taunts in his life, he had to admit this was pretty big stuff.

Maybe that's why his heart was beating as fast as it was.

Tess was standing near the row of folding chairs that served as the Warriors' bench. She was staring straight at him, and when she started to bring her hand up, Danny was terrified she might blow him a kiss. But she did something even better, something that got him revved a little more.

She made a fist with her right hand and pumped it a couple of times.

He went right back at her with a fist-pump of his own.

Mr. Harden, Danny saw now, was right behind her. Michael said he'd been able to fly back from Florida because it was a weekend, but that he planned to sit in the stands and let Danny and Ali Walker and Tess Hewitt just keep doing what they were doing.

Danny got out of the layup line for a second to run over and shake his hand and thank him for coming.

"Just keep on keepin' on," Mr. Harden said to him.

"Huh?"

"Something people used to say—"

"—back in the day?" Danny said.

"One of those," Mr. Harden said.

Before he went back on the court, Danny asked if his mom was anywhere around and Mr. Harden said he hadn't seen her. Mrs. Ross had driven Danny and Will to the game, but Ali Walker had said she'd be right behind them.

"I'm sure she's here somewhere," Michael's dad said, before adding, "take it right to these guys from the jump."

Danny took the Warriors out of the layup line and started the "Carolina" drill they always did before practices and games, two lines under the basket, everybody seeming to move at once, passing, shooting, rebounding, all of them in a pretty neat formation.

When Danny noticed that the clock showed seven minutes and counting until the start of the game, he told the Warriors to get the rest of the balls and just start shooting around.

Will came out near half-court and stood next to him.

"This is, like, *ill*, dude," Will said.

Danny said, "I think I'm the one who's going to be sick."

"How's your shoulder?"

"Don't feel a thing," Danny lied.

A ball bounced away from Steven O'Brien and Danny went to

retrieve it. He reached down, stood up, and before he could pass it back to Steven found himself face-to-face with Teddy Moran.

"If it isn't Coach Mini-Me," Teddy said, his face looking, as always, like he'd just smelled some rotten milk.

"Teddy," Danny said. He whipped the ball toward Steven and started to walk away and Teddy grabbed his right hand, smiling as he did so. To anyone watching, this didn't look like anything more than a Viking wishing a Warrior luck.

"You didn't steal enough of our players to win the game," Teddy said.

"You have a good game, too," Danny said.

"Tell Ty Ross to watch himself today."

Danny smiled back at him now. "He's right there, tough guy. Why don't you go tell him yourself?"

"Yeah, right," Teddy said.

"You Morans," Danny said. "You sure do have a way with words."

He was walking with his back to the Vikings' basket when he heard the gym go quiet, except for the bounce of all the balls, as if somebody had found a way to turn down just the crowd noise.

He turned around and saw his mom just inside the middle door to the gym.

Next to her, one crutch under his right arm, the left one up in the air a little bit as he tried to balance on his new cast, was Richie Walker.

Danny knew that most of the people in this crowd knew who his dad was, and knew about the accident. Suddenly, they started to applaud.

Danny wanted to run to his dad, right through the Vikings, but caught himself, and started to walk toward him instead.

Richie Walker saw, shook his head, grinned. Then, looking

256

pretty nimble for a guy on crutches, he picked the left crutch all the way off the ground and pointed it at Danny.

Then he mouthed one word:

Play.

This time Danny understood him without any words at all.

"He's okay to do this?" Danny said when his mom came over.

They'd set his dad up with two folding chairs at the end of the bleachers, at the stage end. One for him to sit on, one to rest the cast on.

"Just don't go diving for any loose balls over there," his mom said.

"He'd said they were doing more stuff today."

"He lied, except for the part about the new cast, which they put on yesterday," she said. "If the doctors hadn't said okay, I would have had to bust him out."

"He can come over and coach, if he wants."

"He said you're the coach."

The horn had sounded, meaning they were about to start. Danny huddled his teammates up, knelt down in the middle of the circle, took a deep breath, and just started rattling stuff off. Who was going to start. That he was going to bring Ty off the bench sometime in the first quarter, depending on how the game was going. Will and Oliver, almost at the same time, said Ty could start in place of them. Danny started to say something but Ty cut him off, saying they'd decided he should come off the bench, fit in that way.

And, he said, he could be a bench coach when he was on the bench.

Danny said, "I'm all out of pregame speeches. Anybody got any bright ideas?"

Will Stoddard, looking serious for a change, as if he'd left the class clown back in Mrs. Walker's classroom, said, "I do."

He looked down at Danny. "You're the biggest kid here," he said. "I just thought somebody needed to say that."

The Warriors responded to that by jumping up and down and going *woof woof woof,* like somebody'd let the dogs out.

Danny remembered what his dad had said, and decided to steal the line for himself.

"You never know what day might turn out to be the best day of your whole life," he said.

He gave them all a no-biggie shrug.

He said, "How about we make it today?"

The Vikings started Da-Rod, Jack Harty, Teddy Moran, Andy Mayne, and Daryll Mullins. Danny went with himself, Colby, Bren, Will, and Oliver Towne. Right before they had broken the huddle, Ty had said to Danny, "When you make it a triangle-and-two against Da-Rod, tell them to pack the triangle in tight."

Danny smiled. "I was hoping they'd allow us to use a triangle-and-four."

It was 8–4, Vikings, after four minutes.

Danny had made the first basket of the game, sneaking behind Da-Rod Rodriguez and breaking away for a layup. Then Da-Rod, who was already giving Oliver Towne fits—Danny having Oliver try to shadow him—made three straight for the Vikings.

Colby came back with a bomb from the corner, right near where Richie Walker was sitting, that made him pound one of his crutches on the floor.

Daryll Mullins came right back for the Vikings, streaking down the lane and going up so high over Colby that Danny pictured him actually dunking the sucker for a second.

They got a whistle when the ball went skipping through a door that wasn't closed all the way. When they did, Danny motioned for Ty to go to the scorer's table and come in for Oliver.

"You take the big guy," Danny said.

Ty smiled, just because he was back in the game. "My pleasure," he said.

"You get tired, you tell me," Danny said.

Ty said, "I'm rested enough."

They tapped fists.

Ty went over and stood with Will now, while the refs reset the clock, which had kept running when the ball had disappeared through the door.

Danny couldn't help himself, he looked over at Mr. Ross, who was staring across the court to where Ty and Will were, Ty laughing now at something Will had just said.

Danny thought he'd look mad, but he didn't. There was something else on his face, not a smile, just this curious kind of look.

Tony the ref blew his whistle, meaning they were finally ready to go.

Mr. Ross stood up then and said, "Could you wait a second, Tony?"

His voice sounded loud in the gym.

He leaned down and whispered something to Daryll Mullins's dad, Daryll Senior, his assistant coach. Then he reached down next to his chair and handed Daryll Senior his clipboard.

Then he waved for the Vikings to come over real fast, and now he was the one kneeling in a circle of players, talking and pointing.

Now he was smiling. Tony the ref came over and Mr. Ross put a hand on his shoulder and leaned close to his ear.

Then Mr. Ross folded up his folding chair and walked diagonally across the court toward the bleachers. And then Ty's dad did something even more amazing than leaving the bench.

He went over to where Richie Walker was and reached down and shook his hand and unfolded his chair and got ready to watch the rest of the game from over there.

As great as Ty Ross was at basketball, as easy as he'd made it look from the time Danny first played with him in fifth-grade travel, he didn't have superhuman powers. So he looked rusty on offense from the start, missing his first three shots, even turning the ball over a couple of times. He was giving Da-Rod Rodriguez all he wanted at the other end of the court, though, even keeping him off the boards, outsmarting him time after time when the ball was in the air and beating him to the right spot under the basket.

But even if everybody else didn't know how much he was pressing on offense, Danny could see it as clear as day.

It wasn't until the last minute of the first quarter, a fast break, that Ty showed everybody in the gym just who it was they were watching, and reminded Danny—who really didn't need much reminding—why he'd wanted to hoop with Ty Ross in the first place.

Will came up with a long rebound, beating Teddy Moran to the ball because Teddy had stood there waiting for it to come to him. The Vikings, sure Teddy was going to come up with the ball and keep them on offense, relaxed for just a second. By then, Will had passed the ball to Danny.

Ty, who could always see a play happening about five seconds before it happened, took off for the other end of the court.

Jack Harty had gotten back on defense, maybe because he'd never expected Teddy Moran to hustle after a ball.

Danny came from his right with the ball, Ty from Jack's left.

Two-on-one.

Danny didn't want to be coming down the left side of the court. His left shoulder was aching constantly now, the way a toothache ached, and he was afraid that if Jack backed off to cover Ty, Danny might have to shoot a left-handed layup.

He wasn't sure at this point that he could even raise his arm high enough.

If he went with his right hand, he was begging Jack to try to block his shot, even if Jack had to get back on Danny in a flash to do it.

Danny was at full speed as he passed the free throw line. Jack backed off to cover Ty. Or so Danny thought.

Jack Harty had suckered him. He only head-faked toward Ty, waited until Danny went into the air, and then came at him with arms that looked as tall as trees and seemed to be everywhere at once.

Danny had already committed himself, was already in the air. But instead of putting up his shot anyway, instead of even trying to raise his left arm, he underhanded the ball—hard—underneath Jack Harty's arms and off the backboard.

It was a pass, not a shot.

It was a pass that caromed perfectly off the top of the backboard, came right to Ty on the other side of the basket, Ty catching it and shooting it in the same motion, not even using the backboard himself, putting up a soft shot that was nothing but net.

Like this was a move they'd spent their whole lives practicing.

Vikings 12, Warriors 10.

Nobody scored from there to the end of the quarter. When they ran off the court after the horn, Danny said to Ty, "Okay, dude, you're back."

"I still can't shoot."

"They'll start to fall."

"How do you know?"

"I know the way I know we're gonna win this game," Danny said.

He stopped Ty, turned him around so he was facing where Richie Walker and Mr. Ross were sitting, Richie pointing toward the Vikings' basket and talking a mile a minute, Mr. Ross nodding his head.

"If *that's* possible," Danny said, "*anything's* possible."

"Good point, point guard," Ty said.

The good news was that they were still only down a basket at half-time.

The bad news—double dose of it—was this:

1. Teddy (the Moron) Moran had accidentally figured out that Danny was hurting.

2. Ty, despite scoring ten points in the second quarter and looking like his old self, had picked up three fouls along the way.

He had three fouls and so did Bren.

So did Colby.

Danny was going to take Ty out of the game after his second foul, but Ty told him not to worry, he could make it to halftime without picking up his third, there being only ninety seconds left, if they went into a straight zone. But the next time the Warriors had the ball, Ty made a move to the basket against Da-Rod, and Teddy Moran came over to help out. Ty didn't see Teddy coming, and barely brushed him as he spun into his move against Da-Rod, but Teddy threw out his arms and flopped backward as if he'd been sideswiped by a truck.

Tony the ref gave him the call.

Offensive foul on Ty.

Third foul. Ten seconds left in the half.

The Vikings gave the ball right back when Andy Mayne got called for stepping over the line when he was trying to inbound the ball. So the Warriors would get the last shot of the half. The Vikings put a half-baked press on them, Teddy covering Danny. While they were waiting for Tony to hand the ball to Colby, Teddy slapped Danny on the back. Smiling again, like they were practically best buds.

But Teddy had caught him on the spot back there that hurt the most, the exact place where he'd landed last night. Danny couldn't help himself, he yelled out in pain, even getting the attention of Tony the ref, who turned around to see what the problem was.

Danny waved him off.

Like they were just kidding.

"What have we here?" Teddy Moran said quietly.

Then clipped Danny again for good measure, right before Danny broke away so Colby could pass him the ball.

They went out into the hall for halftime the way they had at the Kirkland game, Danny's first as coach. Richie Walker always said that when you had a good routine going, stay with it. So they all had Fruit Punch red Gatorade again. His mom brought the oranges.

There was even more excitement crackling around them now, one half in the books, than there had been before the game.

Because of this:

Because they'd showed they could play with the Vikings.

Danny hadn't dominated Andy Mayne when Andy had been guarding him, not by a long shot. But Andy, despite having the size on Danny, and the strength, had only scored one basket. Danny, on the other hand, had at least six assists, probably more than that.

It was right before halftime when Daryll Senior had decided to switch Teddy Moran over on Danny for a couple of minutes, which had to mean only one thing—he was worried that trying to stay in front of Danny was wearing Andy out.

In the hallway, Danny said, "Everybody on this team is a coach now. Anybody has anything to say, speak up now. On account of, now's the time."

Ty said, "I should sit at the start of the third."

Danny said, "Maybe the whole third, if we can just hang in there."

"Keep it close," Bren Darcy said, "and then bring the big dog back."

"*Bad* dog," Will said.

Then the guys started with *woof woof woof* all over again, so loud Danny knew the people inside the gym could hear them. Maybe the Vikings, too.

Tess looked at them, shaking her head, this disappointed look on her face. "Boys," she said.

Danny stood up.

"Here's the deal, okay? I saw the Vikings play Piping Rock. Piping Rock may have gotten the top seed, but they aren't better than these guys."

"Your point being?" Will said.

"If we beat these guys, we're going to win this tournament," Danny said. "No question."

Ty pointed to the front of his jersey.

"We're number one," he said.

After warm-ups, Ty took the chair closest to where Tess was sitting at the scorer's table. With Robert O'Brien in Ty's place, Danny moved Will to a forward position in the triangle, asking both him and Oliver Towne—asking them as nicely as possible—to somehow prevent Da-Rod from turning into Tim Duncan while Ty was out of the game.

There was another delay before the start of the quarter while the refs checked the clock again. Ali Walker came back from the ladies' room and waved Danny over when she saw which players were on the court.

"Question," she said.

"Shoot."

"We did all this to get Ty to play for us, and now he's not going to play for us?" she said. "Discuss."

"It's like this whole deal, Mom," Danny said. "Don't worry about how things are at the start. Just at the finish."

"Check," she said. "Now gimme five."

He did.

"Hey," Tess said from behind him.

For the first time since he'd known her, she looked nervous. Scared, almost. Looked extremely un-Tess-like.

"You okay?" he said.

"You didn't tell me sports were this hard," Tess said.

"Are you kidding?" he said. "We're just getting to the good parts."

Said the one-armed boy to the tall girl.

Halfway through the quarter, the Vikings had stretched their lead to ten points. Not good. Danny called his first time-out of the half at 28–18, thought hard about bringing Ty back right there, decided to stick to his guns. Telling himself that fourteen points was the cutoff point, if the lead got that big, Ty was coming back in.

He explained all that when they got to the huddle. When he finished, he looked over at Ty and said, "I'm right. Right?"

"Your call," Ty said.

Danny said, "When you come back in—for good—I want you to play full out. We just need somebody to get hot until then."

Will Stoddard and Colby Danes somehow got hot at the exact same time.

It's a terrible thing, Will had always said, for a guy to be hot and not know it. He meant, to not be getting any shots at all. Daryll Mullins had been shutting him down the whole day in the Vikings' man-to-man, but suddenly Will got open for two jumpers. Then another. The Vikings tried to double-team him a couple of times after that, and when they did, Will swung the ball to Danny like a champ, and he made two passes to Colby.

Great passes to Colby, if he did say so himself.

One was a bounce pass that went right through Teddy Moran's fat legs, because that was the only way to make it. The other one was a no-looker to her in the corner.

Both Andy Mayne and Teddy kept trying to overplay him, make him go left, because they'd figured out that was the side bothering him. But he made the passes to Colby after going to his left. Then Will and Colby were both hot, and all the Vikings started paying more attention to them, trying to shut them down until Ty came back.

Missing the point, the way people did all the time about basketball.

He'd always known that everything started with the pass, because that's how everything had started with his dad.

A good pass never cared how big you were.

Or how much your stinking shoulder hurt.

It came down to this:

Vikings 37, Warriors 33.

Three minutes left.

Ty had come back in at the start of the fourth quarter and as soon as he did, Danny set him up for three straight baskets. On the last one he drew Da-Rod over, floated the ball over him like he was putting a kite up in the air, knowing it probably looked like an air ball to everybody watching.

Danny didn't care. He knew that Ty knew it was a pass.

Ty had read Danny's eyes all the way, caught the ball when it came down over Da-Rod Rodriguez, faked Daryll Junior to the moon, put it up and in.

Now they had to find a way to make up those four points in three minutes.

The Warriors hadn't been in the lead since Danny's first basket had made it 2–0. Bren had fouled out by now, and so had Colby. Will was sucking so much wind Danny could hear him breathing every time there was a stop in play.

The whole game, Danny had been telling himself—and the Warriors—they'd find a way to win.

Now he wasn't so sure.

No matter what they did, they couldn't catch up.

Ty scored off a steal from Teddy Moran, who stood and cried to the ref he'd been fouled instead of chasing after Ty, who got a bunny layup.

They were only down a basket. But Jack Harty muscled his way in and scored for the Vikings. Will answered by throwing up a prayer from the corner after he got double-teamed, then acting as if he knew he had it all along.

He ran by Danny, still wheezing a little, and said, "I still got it."

Danny called his second-to-last time-out with a minute and thirty showing on the clock. He wasn't even trying to hide how much his arm hurt by then; when he came running over to the sideline he must have looked like he was carrying some kind of imaginary load on his left shoulder.

He was also tired enough to take a nap.

He told everybody to get a drink. Then they all stood around him. Nobody spoke. All he could hear now was everybody's breathing in what was suddenly a fairly quiet gym at St. Pat's.

Vikings 39, Warriors 37.

Tess handed Danny a Gatorade. Gave him a quick squeeze on his good shoulder. Smiled one of her best smiles at him, just because she seemed to have an endless supply of those.

Ali Walker said, "Just exactly how bad is that shoulder you failed to mention to your sainted mother before the game?"

"I just need to rub some dirt on it, is all."

Tess said, "Rub some dirt on it?"

"Baseball expression," he said. He was too tired to smile. "I know, I know, one sport at a time."

To the Warriors he said, "Just don't let them get another score." He pointed to the scoreboard and said, "Forty points wins the game."

Then he told them, no screwing around, what they were going to run.

When they broke the huddle, Danny passed by Teddy Moran, heard Teddy say, "You're going down, little man."

Danny stopped.

"Ask you a question, Teddy?" Danny said.

"What, squirt?"

"You ever, like, run out of saliva?"

The Vikings were still in a man-to-man, and Danny and Ty ran a perfect pick-and-roll. Or so it looked until Jack Harty came racing over and jumped in front of Ty, blocking his path to the basket.

Ty didn't hesitate, gave the ball right back to Danny.

Now he was the one with a clear path to the basket.

Until Teddy Moran grabbed him from behind with two arms before Danny could even bring the ball up, knocking Danny down like it was a football tackle, falling on top of him, planting Danny's left shoulder into the floor.

Ty got to him first as Danny rolled from side to side on the ground, Ty probably remembering the fall he'd taken in the scrimmage. Then he pulled Danny carefully up into a sitting position.

"Deep breaths," Ty said.

Danny finally managed to get his breathing under control, saw his mom start to run out on the court as he did, froze her where she was with a shake of the head, even though his shoulder now felt like Teddy Moran had set fire to it.

Tony the ref had already thrown Teddy out of the game for his flagrant foul. Danny could see Teddy's dad and Teddy yelling at Tony from behind the Vikings' bench. Tony turned and told them that the next thing he was going to do was throw them both out of the gym.

That finally shut up the whole Moran family.

A flagrant foul in their league meant two shots for Danny, and also meant the Warriors got to keep the ball. Tony asked if Danny could shoot his free throws. If not, Danny knew, there was this dumb rule that the Vikings were allowed to pick a shooter off the Warriors' bench. Which would mean one of the O'Brien twins.

NC.

No chance.

"I'm good to go," Danny said.

He stood up, got what he thought might be the loudest cheer he'd ever gotten, took the ball from Tony, went through his little four-bounce routine. Made the first free throw. Missed the second.

Vikings 39, Warriors 38.

Still Warriors' ball.

Jack Harty was waving his arms in front of Oliver Towne when he tried to inbound the ball to Ty. Oliver forgot you couldn't run the baseline after a made free throw the way you could after a made basket. As soon as he took two steps away from Jack, Tony the ref called him for traveling.

Vikings' ball.

They called their last time-out, came out of it, tried to run out the clock. But when they finally swung the ball to Da-Rod in the corner, Danny and Ty ran at him at the same time, trapping him. In desperation, he tried to bounce the ball off Danny's leg. Danny jumped out of the way. Da-Rod threw it out of bounds instead.

Warriors' ball.

One minute left.

Danny called *his* last time-out.

Instead of going back to his bench, he walked all the way across the court to where his dad was.

When he got there, he crouched down in front of him.

"Got a play for me, Coach?" he said.

Richie Walker looked at Mr. Ross, then back at Danny.

"Yeah," he said. "Mine."

His dad started to describe it to him. Danny cut him off, saying he didn't need anybody to draw him a picture on this one.

"I've known this play my whole life," he said.

"They'll be looking for you to pass," Richie said.

"Yeah," Danny said. "Won't they?"

Then he ran back across the court, feeling fresh all of a sudden, and told the Warriors he had a play he thought just might beat the Vikings.

Ty and Michael Harden were on opposite sidelines, just inside the mid-court line. Will and Oliver Towne went to the corners. Danny had the ball at mid-court.

He could hear Daryll Senior yelling at the Vikings to watch Ty.

"He's gonna give it to Ty," Daryll Senior said.

Danny kept it instead.

He dribbled toward the free throw line, straight down the middle of the court; when Andy Mayne and Daryll Junior double-teamed him, Danny wheeled around at top speed and dribbled right back outside.

Forty seconds left.

Now he dribbled to his left, toward Ty, just as Ty ran toward him. Da-Rod, still covering Ty, seemed sure Danny was about to pass it to him. Except Danny didn't pass, just put the ball through his legs, spun around again, came back to the middle.

Thirty.

He looked over at Michael Harden. Behind Michael, he could see his mom and Tess, standing there, holding hands, like statues. Danny wondered if his mom knew what she was watching: Watching him dribbling out the clock the way his dad had.

The only difference was, Richie Walker's team had been ahead by a point at the end of the big game, not one behind.

With ten seconds left, Will and Oliver ran out of the corners the way they were supposed to. Ty ran down to where Will had been, in the left corner. Daryll Senior yelled at Daryll Junior to stay where he was, forget his man, guard the basket like he was the back guy in a zone.

Danny made his move down the middle.

When he got inside the free throw line, Daryll Junior stepped up to double-team him along with Andy Mayne.

Danny Walker went left hand, right hand, then back again, the ball as low to the ground as dust, splitting the two of them with a perfect double crossover.

Like in the driveway.

He was wide open, but only for an instant.

On account of, here came Da-Rod.

Now Danny passed.

He passed with a left hand that suddenly didn't hurt one single bit, made a perfect bounce pass to Ty Ross without even looking, knowing exactly where Ty would be, just as if he were one of the folding chairs in the driveway. Then Danny turned his head to see Ty make the catch.

And the layup that beat the stinking Vikings.

Everything seemed to happen at fast-forward speed after that, like somebody in the crowd had a remote in his hands.

He saw his dad standing and pumping his arms over his head,

crutches forgotten on the floor next to him, looking as happy as Danny had ever seen him.

Then his mom was over there with his dad, an arm around his shoulder, his mom acting like his crutch.

Tess Hewitt came running for Danny then, started to put her arms around him, then pulled back, remembering his shoulder.

"Is a hug allowed?"

He said, yeah, it was allowed, and she ducked her head and leaned down and hugged him and he hugged her back.

When he pulled away from Tess, not sure where to go next, Ty Ross was standing in front of him, grinning this goofy-looking grin from ear to ear.

"Nice pass," he said.

"Nice shot," Danny said.

The two of them shook hands the regular way.

The old-school way.

Then Ty kept holding on to Danny's hand and somehow lifted him up in the air in the same motion. Then Will was there, and Bren, putting Danny up on their shoulders, carrying him around the court, the way the old Vikings had carried his dad once.

Danny looked down on the day and thought:

So this is what everything looks like from up here.